THE RISING OF THE MOON

THE RISING OF THE MOON

BY

William Martin

CROWN PUBLISHERS, INC.
NEW YORK

Published by Crown Publishers, Inc.
225 Park Avenue South, New York, New York 10003
and represented in Canada by the Canadian MANDA Group

CROWN is a trademark of Crown Publishers, Inc.

Library of Congress Cataloging-in-Publication Data
Martin, William, 1950–
    The rising of the moon.

    1. Ireland—History—Sinn Fein Rebellion, 1916–
Fiction.   I. Title.
PS3563.A7297R5   1987   813'.54   86-19642
ISBN 0-517-56315-0

10 9 8 7 6 5 4 3 2 1

First Edition

For my children

Boston

March 11, 1916

1

"Bless me, Father, for I have sinned."

"How long has it been since your last confesson?"

"Six weeks and three days."

"A long time," said the priest, then he listened for the response that he had been expecting, and fearing, for years.

"Not if you're an honest man."

Mother of God, thought the priest. "It's coming, then?"

"It's coming soon. That's why I'm here."

The priest turned his face to the screen beside him. In the gentle darkness of the confessional, he could make out reddish hair, a long face, a light, sallow complexion. Galway, he thought, or perhaps Kerry.

"How can I help you?"

"Guns, Father."

"Guns," whispered the priest. "Guns is it?"

"Guns . . . to arm the soldiers of Christ."

The priest sensed sarcasm. It was not something to which he was accustomed in his confessional. "Guns . . . indeed. If ever we're to jump on John Bull's back, this is the time."

"Well said, Father, but before the guns"—the penitent brought his lips close to the screen—"something more urgent."

The priest tried to focus his eyes on the face a few inches from his own. "Yes?"

"John Bull may be looking at the Kaiser, but he has eyes in the back of his head."

"And they're watching you?"

"No, Father. At the moment, they're watching the votive candles flicker on your altar."

The priest's hands closed tight around his breviary. "British soldiers in my church?"

"British agents is my guess. I'm not sure where they picked me up. I never noticed them on the ship."

3

"Them?" The priest swallowed down the fear that rose like bad meat at the back of his throat. "How many?"

"One at the altar rail, another outside."

The priest peered through the little window in the door of the confessional. He saw Mrs. Kelly in the closest pew, saying her beads and examining her conscience, troubled as it usually was with the sins of gossip and envy. Behind her slumped Jimmy Duggan, a choirboy with the voice of an angel and a weakness for the most common transgression of the fourteen-year-old male.

Others were scattered across the great, dark nave of the Holy Trinity Church. Some knelt with heads bowed, some sat and stared at the stained glass, some moved slowly along the outer aisles, following Christ's journey in the Stations of the Cross, some scurried to the altar rail, said their penance, and left renewed. Saturday afternoon, confessions three to five, and then, thought the priest, for most of them, it would be home to franks and beans and brown bread, the weekly bath, a few shots or a pint, poker or pinochle, perhaps a long wait with a rolling pin for a late-wandering spouse, and for Jimmy Duggan, the nightly struggle with his own hormones. From one parish to the next, the hopes and fears, the petty sins and prejudices of these people were always the same, and Father Sean O'Fearna knew them all.

But he did not know the man in the rumpled tweed suit who knelt at the rail on one knee, as though expecting a bolt of lightning to strike him for advancing too close to the Catholic tabernacle. A Protestant for sure, thought O'Fearna, and an agent of the Crown as well.

The priest turned back to the screen. He could see blue eyes and wide, black pupils, watching him in the same way that he watched his penitents when he thought they weren't telling him the truth. "I expected they'd send one of their best when the time came."

"They have, Father."

"How is it, then, that the one they sent didn't know the Brits were on his tail until he led them into my church?"

"Haven't you heard, Father? The best of Ireland's best left for America when the potatoes went bad. I'm the best that Ireland's got left. If you're going to help, you'll have to put up with my failings, which also include a weakness for women and strong drink."

The priest saw the smile curling on the other side of the

screen. He liked a man who could joke at his own blunder. It was a sign of cool courage . . . or the mark of a dangerous fool.

"Do you have a name?" asked the priest.

"Padraic Starr . . . but my passport says O'Mahoney."

"And do you have people in Boston, family who'll put you up, now that the house of God is no longer safe refuge?"

"Cousins, by the name Tracy."

The priest leaned close. "Tom Tracy, the mayor's boy?"

"I wouldn't know about that. All I know is that they live on a street called Gloucester Place."

"About three blocks away, in Cathedral Parish. Go there and I'll contact you tomorrow."

"That still don't solve the problem at hand, Father, unless this confessional has a trapdoor and you're after droppin' me into the cellar."

"The trapdoor in here leads to a much hotter place than the cellar, my son."

The penitent laughed softly.

Once more, Sean O'Fearna looked through the small window in the confessional door, and his eyes fell upon the choirboy. An idea began to form.

He turned back to Starr. "Would you like absolution?"

"Will it get me out of here?"

"No, but at least you'll be ready if the Brits catch you and hang you."

"That won't be happenin', Father."

The priest studied the eyes—steady and unblinking—that studied him through the little holes in the screen. Whoever this Padraic Starr was, he was one to be reckoned with. "I don't believe it will. Now, then, how much time do we have?"

"I've promised a ship, loaded with guns and ammunition, six weeks from now in the Bay of Dunslea."

"Holy Week?"

"That it is."

"We've not much time, then."

"Indeed not, Father, so let's not be wastin' any more of it in this tight spot. If you've got some ideas, I'd like to be hearin' them. Otherwise, I'll be about the business at hand."

"The business at hand," whispered the priest firmly, "is absolution. Even if you want none, I suggest you go to the altar rail and say a few Our Fathers and a few Hail Marys. It'll do you

5

good. Then cross the altar and leave by the sacristy door when you hear a boy singin'."

"Singin'?"

"Just do as I say, and don't forget to genuflect before the tabernacle."

Sean O'Fearna closed the wooden shutter and heard the rebel step from the confessional. Then the shadow slipped past his window, and he peered out. What he saw gave him some confidence, for a six-footer with brawny shoulders might joke about a blunder and be able to back up the joke.

Padraic Starr wore brown corduroy trousers, heavy hobnail boots, a white turtleneck sweater of Donegal wool, and for all his size, he moved with the loping grace of a Wexford thoroughbred. He carried in one hand a duffel bag and in the other a tweed scally cap of the sort that most Irishmen wore, whether they lived in Boston or Ballyshannon. But this rebel did not seem concerned about concealing his Irish identity. Instead, he went straight to the altar rail and knelt just a few feet from the man in the tweed suit.

A bold one, thought the priest, one worth helping.

Jimmy Duggan stepped into the booth. The priest pushed the slider and heard a nervous little cough.

"Bless me, Father, for I have sinned. It's been a week since my last confession, and I done the . . . the usual, Father. Six times."

"The spirit is willin' but the flesh is weak, Jimmy. Just try to get out there and start swingin' the baseball bat. With the weather warmin' up soon and the Red Sox in spring trainin', you've no reason at all to sit home in your room lettin' your hand and your mind wander where they shouldn't."

"Yes, Father."

"For your penance, an Our Father and a Hail Mary. Now, make a good Act of Contrition."

The boy recited the prayer as the priest spoke the words, *Ego te absolvo . . .* , that erased his adolescent sins. Then Jimmy Duggan blessed himself and started to leave.

"There's one more thing, Jimmy."

"Yes, Father?"

"I want you to sing."

"You want me to *sing* three Our Fathers and three Hail Marys?"

"No, no. But I need a little favor." The priest wiped a trickle

6

of perspiration from his forehead, "Do you know the song 'The Rising of the Moon'?"

"My father taught it to me."

"A noble song about bold men fighting for the redemption of Ireland."

"Yes, Father," muttered the boy.

"Now, then, push your curtain back just a bit and look up at the altar rail." O'Fearna heard the fabric rustle. "Do you see a sort of red-faced fellow in a rumpled tweed suit, kneeling in front of the votive candles? He looks a bit jittery, like he just went to confession, but he didn't tell all his sins?"

"Near the big guy in the white sweater?"

"That's him," whispered the priest. "For your extra penance, I want you to kneel down next to that fella, on his left, and sing 'The Rising of the Moon' in the loudest voice you've got . . . right in his ear."

"While he's saying his penance?"

"For him, hearin' that song is penance in itself. Now you just do as I ask, and don't let him get away from you till the song's done."

After a time, the boy said, "All right."

"And Jimmy . . ."

"Yeah?"

"Mind you, what's said in here's a secret."

While the boy scuffed up to the altar rail, Sean O'Fearna prayed. He prayed that his plan would work. He prayed that Padraic Starr would be worthy to the cause. He prayed that he would not offend God in the weeks ahead. Then he blessed himself.

At the altar rail, Padraic Starr kept his head bowed and his hands tightly folded. He was not accustomed to the position, but he would assume it for a few minutes, if it aided his escape.

He was certain now that the man in the tweed suit was an agent of the Crown. He saw the bulge in the jacket, where a pistol was holstered, and although he had never seen the face before, he had seen hundreds like it. Shapes and features might differ, but the eyes were always the same—suspicious, haughty, contemptuous—whether they were the eyes of the resident magistrate in the village where Starr was born, or the guard in the visitor's room at Kilmainham Jail, or the man now kneeling a few feet from his dangerous Irish quarry.

And Padraic Starr was very dangerous. In his boot he carried

7

a knife with a six-inch blade stropped to the fine sharpness of hammered gold. He could open an artery in an instant and disappear at high noon in the Dublin Markets or at midnight among the peat bogs. He did not fear the Englishman beside him. His only fear was that by his carelessness he had endangered the rising. And for that he was heartily sorry.

The young boy from O'Fearna's confessional came to the rail and knelt, carefully positioning himself between Starr and the man in the tweed suit.

Starr heard the boy clear his throat. He realized what was going to happen. He reached down and felt the outline of the knife handle beneath his trousers.

The boy blessed himself and stood.

Starr loosened the knife, so that he could snap it clear in an instant.

The boy licked his lips and took a deep breath. Starr rose to one knee. But the boy hesitated. The man in the tweed suit shifted slightly and looked up at him.

Then the priest came out of his confessional. He was bigger than Starr had expected, and he looked like a bull in his black cassock.

When the boy saw the priest marching angrily down the side aisle, he took another deep breath and turned himself toward the man in the tweed suit.

Now, thought Starr. Sing your lungs out, lad.

The voice was a high and piercing tenor. *"Oh, now tell me, Sean O'Farrell,/ Where the gath'ring is to be . . ."*

Starr leaped over the altar rail. The man in the tweed suit jumped up and shoved Jimmy aside, but the boy clutched at his elbow.

"In the old spot by the river,/ Right well known to you and me." Jimmy Duggan's high C was the most powerful instrument in the choir, and he played it right in the man's face. *"At the rising of the moon, the rising of the moon . . ."*

Padraic Starr did not stop to genuflect in front of the tabernacle. He flashed across the marble floor and disappeared through the sacristy door before the refrain was finished.

". . . With your pikes upon your shoulders, at the rising of the moon."

"Jimmy Duggan!" boomed the priest. "What do you think you're doin'?"

"Father, you said . . ."

The Englishman pulled out of the boy's grasp.

But O'Fearna came charging across the front aisle. "I'm terribly sorry, sir." He clapped a pair of huge hands on the man's shoulders. "I think the lad misunderstood his penance."

The man was tall and thin, with a nondescript face well-suited to his work. He growled something and tried to break free.

But the priest held tight. "What was it you said, sir?"

"I said let me go." The man could not disguise his Liverpool accent.

"And what parish did you say you were from?"

The man pushed O'Fearna away and jumped over the altar rail.

"Here, now!" cried the priest. "Get off my altar!" He opened the gate and ran after the Englishman, but when he reached the sacristy, the robing room beside the altar, he felt a cold draft. The outer door was swung open and the sun was reflecting off the snow outside. Starr and the Englishman were gone.

"Father . . ." Jimmy Duggan came in from the church. "I just did what you asked, Father. Why'd you yell at me?"

The priest patted him on the shoulder. "You did fine, Jimmy."

Father Hans Ritter, rotund, balding, benign, waddled into the room. He spoke in a thick German accent he had been trying to hide since the sinking of the *Lusitania*. "What is happening? Why singing and shouting when people is trying to tell me their sins?"

"A mistake, Father. Jimmy didn't understand the penance I gave him."

"And those two men?"

"One yelled at Jimmy, the other said, '*You* be quiet. It's a grand song.' I imagine they've gone off to discuss it."

Padraic Starr was racing down an alley at the rear of the church, along a run-down row of back alleys and loading docks. An old man was sitting on a fire escape, bundled in overcoats and blankets. Two women were poking through the pork trimmings in a trash barrel behind a butcher shop. A wagon and team were backed up to a dock where a worker was rolling beer kegs out of a small brewery. And the man in the tweed suit was racing after Padraic Starr.

Under different circumstances, Starr would have turned and killed him as soon as they were outside the church. Or he would have chosen not to run at all but to mislead him more subtly, over several days, into believing that he had come to America to visit relatives or see the sights. However, open violence was too dangerous, and there was no time for subtlety.

So he grabbed two trash barrels, spun them back, and ran.

The great oak doors at the rear of the church had been opened. Although the temperature was no better than forty degrees, the sun was high and bright, and even in the South End, the air smelled of promise.

"You never sung better, Jimmy," said the priest. "And if any of them old biddies in there go to gossipin' about this, you just tell your ma and pa to come to me and I'll set 'em straight."

O'Fearna watched the boy bound off the steps and disappear into the traffic on Shawmut Avenue, then he noticed a man leaning against the lamppost. The man's body was short and square, shrouded in a blue wool overcoat. He wore a black derby, had a black handlebar mustache, and chewed on a black briar pipe. Ordinarily, the priest would not have noticed him, but in the moment that they glanced at each other, the man seemed to study everything from the size of the priest's shoes to the cut of his cassock. Moreover, he had positioned himself so that he could see the front and side doors of the church at the same time.

This, the priest knew, was the second British agent, and the only door that he could not see was the door that Padraic Starr had taken.

The alley behind the church led Starr to Dover Street. Two blocks to the south, the elevated station rose above the traffic. Padraic Starr dodged a fish peddler's pushcart and ran for the train.

The cart stopped at the mouth of the alley. The Englishman bumped into the peddler, who lost his grip on the handle, sending the cart banging onto the sidewalk. Halibut and cod splattered everywhere. The peddler cursed in Italian and grabbed for the fish, then snatched at the tweed coattails, but the Englishman was already weaving through the crowd of shoppers, chasing the white wool sweater that was halfway to Washington Street.

By the time he reached the corner, Padraic Starr had taken a block lead on the man in the tweed suit. The elevated tracks above Washington Street cast a deep and perpetual shadow, fractured by little shafts of sunlight that slipped through the cracks like rays of hope in purgatory. The intersection was jammed with autocars, lorries, and wagons, all stopped because a draft horse had fallen and an ice wagon now blocked the intersection. Horns were squawking, the driver was whipping the horse, and two policemen were trying to unsnarl the traffic.

Police. No police, thought Starr, no matter what.

Then the clouds of exhaust beneath the tracks began to billow toward him, pushed along by a sudden wind. The sunlight disappeared. The darkness grew darker. A distant rumble rose in pitch and volume until it swallowed all the noise of the intersection. And the elevated train arrived at Dover Station.

Starr scrambled across the street, took the stairs two at a time, ducked under the turnstiles, elbowed up a second flight through the crowd coming down from the train and jumped onto the front car an instant before the doors slammed shut.

He had escaped.

Every seat was taken. People were hanging onto handstraps and gripping side rails. Their closeness made Starr feel secure. His nostrils were struck with the smells of damp wool, perspiration, and whiskey. He heard the familiar lilt of two Kerrymen, bricklayers, arguing about someone called Babe Ruth and whether he mattered more to the Red Sox—whoever they were— as a batter or a pitcher. He noticed a colored woman, wearing a maid's uniform beneath a threadbare topcoat. She was sharing a side rail with a man who looked like a rich merchant. Their hands were almost touching, but their heads were turned carefully in opposite directions. Starr hooked his wrist into one of the handstraps and waited for the train to start.

Instead, he heard the doors on the second car pop open and saw the Englishman jump onto the train. The chase was still on, the chase which had gone on for centuries, the English hound and the Irish fox.

Starr tried to peer into the second car through the rear windows of the first, but the bodies were packed so tightly that he saw only details: the top of a bald head, an ostrich feather in a hat, an upturned collar, a newsaper with the headline "French Push Germans Back at Verdun" . . . and the eyes of the man in the tweed suit.

The train kicked ahead. While Starr pushed toward the doors at the front, as far from the Englishman as possible, the train tilted forward. Bodies shifted against the slant, sunlight faded, and the subway tunnel suddenly concentrated the sound of the train, like a magnifying glass straightening a beam of light.

By the time Starr reached the front doors, they were sliding open at Essex Street, the first underground station. He stepped aside and let several passengers slip off. He wanted to spring for the stairwell himself, but it was blocked by turnstiles, and he knew that the Englishman would expect him to run at the first chance. He waited instead for the next station and planned a more subtle escape.

The doors banged open again. Starr peered out at the mosaic sign: Washington Street. He noticed the manikins in the underground department store window. *This way for Filene's Automatic Bargain Basement.* But he did not move. Not yet, he thought.

He glanced toward the second car. The tweed jacket was poised by the door, waiting for him to run. Not yet, he repeated to himself.

Three Sisters of St. Joseph stepped onto the train, followed by a drunk who could barely stand. The conductor between the cars leaned out to check the doors. *Now.*

Starr jumped off the train. The tweed suit leaped from the second car and came toward him. The doors began to slide, and at the last moment, Starr jumped back onto the train.

The doors slammed so close behind him that they nearly snipped the button from his back pocket. Now, he was certain, he had escaped. He craned his neck and looked out onto the platform. No Englishman. He glanced toward the rear of the car, and through the thicket of arms and handstraps, the eyes appeared again. The Englishman had not been deceived. Instead, he had slipped from the second car to the first.

He was a good one, Starr thought, too good for his own good.

Starr knelt in the little space around him and tightened one of his bootlaces. When he stood, the handle of his knife was in his hand, the blade was concealed in his sleeve, and the drunk was supporting himself against Starr's shoulder. Starr did not want to use the knife. But if he had to, he would try not to slice through the tweed, because he could not be certain of a lethal cut. Instead, he would slip his hand under the suit jacket, drive the blade through the maroon sweater, into the heart, and leave the Englishman dead on his feet, supported by the press of bodies around him.

The tweed suit was halfway down the car now, and Starr was trying to gauge the moment to strike when he felt the train slowing once more. The doors slid open: State Street.

He grabbed the drunk and threw him into the nuns. People went down like ninepins on a rich man's lawn. Starr leaped from the car and raced for the escalator, a treadmill of grooved wooden slats rising to the street. He stepped on and slipped. He grabbed the handrail and balanced himself against the strange move-ment, then he began to climb, pushing past a young couple, stumbling over a woman and knocking her bundles from her hands. Bright oranges and toilet paper went tumbling down the dirty brown escalator.

Padraic Starr came out at the head of State Street, where the tall buildings formed a corridor that stretched all the way to the harbor. He shouldered his duffel bag and began to run. He crossed over a wide circle of cobblestones in the middle of the street. *Site of the Boston Massacre*, said the center stone. He stopped and looked back. The subway station was in a Georgian brick building whose facade was still decorated with the Unicorn and the British Lion. A remnant of America's colonial days, thought Starr, and a bad omen, made worse by the British agent now emerging from below, ignoring the traffic, and coming straight at him.

State Street was a place for banks and brokerage houses, all four steps above the street and all but deserted on a Saturday afternoon. At the first corner he came to, Starr turned onto a narrow street called Merchants Row, which led to Market Square, where the Saturday life of the city spread before him.

Wagons and lorries swirled. Crowds of shoppers shuttled be-tween the red brick building on the left and the three soot-covered granite rows running away to the right. Peddlers were shouting. Beggers held out dirty fingers and drunks slept in doorways. Someone hurried past carrying a side of beef. A boy came out of the Fulton Fish Market and tossed a bucket of slop into the sewer. A Cadillac roadster blew its horn at Starr, then stopped at the building with the granite pillars, and the chauffeur climbed out with a grocery list in his hand.

It all reminded Starr of Covent Garden, but from his Boston guidebook, he recognized this as Faneuil Hall and the Quincy Market. If he could not lose himself here, he thought, he had no right to call himself a rebel.

An alley ran down the rear of the long market building to Starr's right. He saw a man roll a barrel across the alley, then disappear directly into the side of the building. From where Starr stood, he thought it was an illusion. He went down the alley and found a pedestrian tunnel cutting through the row. He ducked into the tunnel and performed the illusion himself.

The tunnel led him to South Market Street. Peddlers' stalls stretched back to the square and down toward Commercial Street. Wagons rattled along, squashing horse droppings into the cobblestones. Cabbage leaves and banana peels rotted in the gutters, giving the street the odor of a garbage dump. A rat scuttled around a puddle and stopped to nibble one of the leaves, and a scrawny cat burst from a fish stall to chase the rat.

But Starr's chase was over. The Englishman was gone. The illusion had worked.

Dodging wagons and turds and rolling barrels of beer, Starr loped across the street and into the central building, where he would lose himself a bit longer before chancing the subways.

In the magnificent rotunda of Quincy Market, Starr felt, for a moment, as though he had entered another church. The noise of the merchants rolled down the arcades and rose into the sky-blue dome like the singing of a secular choir. In a city that would pay such homage to commerce, thought Starr, a man could surely find anything for sale, including five hundred rifles and a million rounds of ammunition.

He went down the arcade that led back to Market Square. On either side were stalls, framed by handsome white pillars. H. A. Hovey—Butter, Eggs, and Cheese. Adams, Chapman, and Company. Carrol and Liley—Butchers Supplies—Saws, Cleavers, Cutlery, Grinding, Saw Filing.

Many of the stalls were closing, since it was after five o'clock, but the sellers of fresh produce and dairy were shouting lower prices to every shopper that trundled by, because by Monday morning most of the vegetables would be rotten and the milk turned sour. Starr stopped and bought a bunch of carnations for his Aunt Josephine Tracy, who had not seen him in sixteen years and was not likely to welcome him when he appeared at her door. Then he decided to head back to the South End.

He was a few stalls from the exit when he saw the tweed suit. The Englishman was at one of the granite pillars outside. He had finished scanning the square and was turning to come into the market.

Starr cursed. He was a head taller than most of the people around him, and he was carrying a bunch of red and white flowers. The Englishman was certain to see him.

A door opened to Starr's left. A butcher came out of a cold room. MacClean Beef Company, Stall 57. The butcher was cradling a leg of lamb that he carried to his block and dropped in front of a customer. The door closed with a loud *thunk*.

A moment later, Starr was hiding behind a side of beef.

The cold room had granite walls and a vaulted ceiling and was more damp than cold. There were three rows of meat hooks, three dozen hunks of meat, and the smell of beef tallow in the dark was like the smell of the grave.

Starr waited and listened and hoped that he would not have to use the knife. What he heard, above the hundreds of feet shuffling by the cold-room door, was the sound of a bottle dragging a short distance over the floor, sloshing toward a mouth, and pumping whiskey down a throat. It was a sound that Padraic Starr knew well. Someone was sitting in the dark, in the far corner, and too drunk to notice him.

Then the door popped open and the light came on. The drinker noticed *that*. He inhaled and held his breath. Starr could see the drinker's feet and his white butchers' apron. The door *thunked*. Starr peered between stiffened carcasses. He saw the tweed and cursed to himself. The footsteps came slowly toward him. Then he saw the barrel of a pistol. He twitched his fingers and snapped his knife into position.

"Step out of that corner," said the Englishman, "or I'll shoot through the meat."

"Holy Jesus!" cried the drunk in the other corner, "I'm just takin' a snort to warm up!"

The barrel of the pistol swung away from Starr and a side of beef swung at the Englishman, with Starr hurtling after it. The beef knocked the gun from the agent's grasp, and Starr drove in with the knife, cutting through tweed, through wool, skittering off bone, and into the chest.

The Englishman let out a cry and stumbled back, hitting another side of meat and sending it swinging into the one next to it. Then he lurched forward, grabbing for Starr's arm. But the knife slashed again. A line of red appeared just above the Englishman's collar. Arterial blood trickled onto the white, then poured out all at once.

The Englishman opened his mouth, as if to speak, but a side of beef hit him and knocked him to the floor at Starr's feet, where his blood mixed with sawdust and dried bloodstains.

"Holy Jesus!" came a voice from somewhere near the floor. "You killed him!" The drunken butcher's face appeared, horrified, looking up from under a dressed lamb.

The meat swung back, then forth, and Starr kicked hard into the butcher's face.

After that, he worked quickly and efficiently. He dragged the butcher back to the corner and poured another shot of whiskey into his mouth. Although it sickened him, he lifted the Englishman and slipped a meat hook through the tweed, taking care to keep the blood from his white wool sweater. He shoved the pistol into his duffel bag, then took the Englishman's wallet, to make it look like a robbery. He slid two sides of beef close to the body and spread sawdust over the fresh blood on the floor. For as long as the butcher remained unconscious, he hoped, no one would notice the Englishman hanging in the corner.

He picked up his duffel bag, then reached for the bunch of carnations, but the white flowers had been turned to red. He switched off the lights in the cold room and headed for the home of Josephine Tracy and her boys.

2

*F*our and four. That makes eight. The point's eight. Get your money down. Get your money down. Get your money down."

The dice rattled in a pair of dirty hands. Worn shoes and scuffed, snow-covered boots tightened around the semicircle of pavement. Half-pint bottles passed from glove to glove. The sweet smell of whiskey mixed with streams of breath billowing into the air. Dollar bills slapped down. And rough male voices rose like vapors in a distillery.

"The kid's lucky. I'll take five."

"You're covered."

"Gimme a buck."

"Two and a half."

"Rattle 'em, kid."

"Seven-eleven. Seven-eleven. Seven-eleven. Two bucks calls on seven-eleven."

"Eight's the point. I say the kid throws an eight."

"How much?"

"Two-fifty."

"Covered."

"Snake eyes, kid. Lookin' right at ya."

The dice flew against the brick wall and dropped into three and three.

"Roll 'em again, kid."

"This time he craps out."

"So let's see some green."

More bills slapped down. Boots and shoes stamped in the cold. The dice rattled again.

"Last bet." Another bill landed on the pile in front of the player.

"No bets!" A foot stamped down on the money and a hand grabbed the fist that held the dice. The shoe was the finest Vici leather, the glove was gray kid, buttoned at the wrist.

The player looked up. "What the—"

"Ma don't want you gamblin'." Tom Tracy ripped the dice from his brother's hands and pulled the boy to his feet.

"Hey, this punk's in the game." The man weighed over two hundred pounds. His face was stitched together by a spiderweb pattern of white scars that seemed to shine in the dim alley light, and when he breathed through his broken nose, he sounded like an old bulldog.

"The kid's goin' home." Tom Tracy jammed the dice into the man's breast pocket.

"Not until he craps out. Now get your ass out of the way, unless you want to make a bet."

"I wouldn't be talkin' like that," cautioned someone in the group, "This Tracy swings a lot of weight."

"Yeah? Who's he think he is? The mayor?"

Tracy smiled, but he did not move. He knew the man: Strong-arm Flaherty, union-buster, bagman, and small-time bookie who, since his parole, has been moving in on every street-corner crap game in the South End.

Standing beside him was Harry the Knuckle Horgan. And standing behind Tracy was Tris MacGillicuddy, who could swing a bat like Tris Speaker, except that he used his on kneecaps instead of baseballs.

"Now, step back, or you might get them fairy clothes of yours all dirtied up," said Flaherty.

Tom Tracy tugged at his red silk cravat and adjusted the stickpin. He was dressed in razor-crease blue trousers, camel's-hair chesterfield, a Gothic-style Arrow collar, and a new silk derby. Although he came from the same streets as the dozen or so men now clustered around him, Tom Tracy wore his wardrobe as though he'd been born to it. And if there were those in the South End who resented his dress and manner, they seldom spoke of it, at least to his face.

But Mr. Strongarm Flaherty had been a guest of the Commonwealth during the time that Tracy rose from railyard worker to secretary of the mayor's political club. And like most men of his calling, he had little respect for dandies. "Your brother's cleaned out half the guys here with his lucky sevens."

"That's what they get for lettin' a sixteen-year-old kid shoot craps with 'em."

"They let him play, it's okay with me. 'Sides, the kid gives me good business."

Tom Tracy looked at his brother. "What kind of business?"

"I gotta pay him ten percent to play," said Danny Tracy.

"Ten percent? For *this* game?"

Danny looked down at the cobblestoness.

"Most bums take five percent when they run a crap game on the corner . . . if they can find enough suckers."

"The boys want to play on my turf," said Strongarm, "they pay my price."

"Since when's this your turf? And tell that bum MacGillicuddy to back off." Tracy did not bother to turn around.

Strongarm winked at the man with the baseball bat.

"You know the business, Tommy," said Sticker McNulty, a familiar face in back-alley crap games and political meetings. "Strongarm runs a good game and he covers all the bets."

"Yeah . . . and he skins my little brother, too."

"I call it protection money," said Strongarm. "Now, we got a game goin' here and the kid's hot."

"So let me shoot some more, Tommy," said Danny.

"Yeah. Give him the dice," grumbled someone in the crowd.

"You're hurtin' my business, doll-face. I don't like that." Strongarm Flaherty fixed his eyes on Tom Tracy while he pulled the dice from his pocket and dropped them into Danny's hand. "I have friends who won't like that, either."

"Fuck your friends." Tom Tracy slapped the dice away.

Strongarm flipped a backhander that sent Tracy's derby flying into the crowd. Then he swung his open hand and hit Tracy a loud slap across the side of the face.

Tracy's head snapped and his ear began to ring. He had been expecting a punch, straight-on and hard. Instead, Strongarm Flaherty tried to humiliate him, then stepped back and folded his arms. Strongarm, it was clear, had been away too long.

Danny Tracy slid himself between his brother and Mac-Gillicuddy's baseball bat.

"Get your guard up, Strongarm my boy," muttered Sticker McNulty, "or you'll be wearin' your nose on the other side of your head."

Strongarm smiled, revealing three spaces and five yellow teeth.

Tom Tracy wiped away the small trickle of blood that appeared at the corner of his mouth, then he wiped the smile from Strongarm Flaherty's face with a short right hand that most of the men in the alley, Strongarm among them, never saw.

Strongarm hit the wall and dropped to the street like a pair of dice on their way to snake eyes.

"Bejesus, what a wallop," said someone in the crowd.

"Bring on Jess Willard!" Sticker McNulty clapped Tracy on the shoulder.

"Gimme my hat," grumbled Tracy, keeping his eyes on Harry the Knuckle.

"Nice work, Tommy. He's an asshole anyway." Danny Tracy crouched to pick up the wad of bills, and his brother's foot came down on his hand.

"Leave it."

"But I won it, fair and square!"

"You won nothin'. Leave it. All but what you came in with." Tracy put his weight down.

"You better give up, kid, before your big brother—"

"Shut up," snapped Tracy at Sticker McNulty.

"Sure thing, Tom."

The boy's face went through several contortions of thought, which turned to pain when his brother exerted more pressure. He took five dollars for himself and handed thirty-three more to Tom, who then told him to take the wad of bills from Strongarm's pocket.

Tris MacGillicuddy raised the bat. In the flash of a fist, he was stretched out beside Strongarm, the bat was in Tracy's hands, and Harry the Knuckle was backing away.

Tracy turned to Sticker McNulty. "How many men in the game?"

"Eleven bettin', Tom."

"And everyone bettin' about the same?"

Tracy looked around. Several men nodded. Tracy counted the money and shoved the bills into Sticker's hand. "Everyone gets eight dollars and thirty cents, and from now on, for Chrissakes, keep this game out of sight. Otherwise, I'll have the cops down here.

"Sure thing, Tom," said Sticker.

"Let's go." Tom Tracy smacked his brother on the back of the head, gave Harry the Knuckle a last look, and left the alley.

"That Tom Tracy's all right." Sticker McNulty handed out the money.

"As long's he's got the mayor on his side," said Harry the Knuckle. "But there's plenty around wouldn't mind takin' him down a peg or two."

Sticker looked at the figures stretched out on the ground. "And so far, they've all ended up like Strongarm here."

Strongarm Flaherty's eyes were closed, but his mouth was open and there were now four spaces and four teeth.

Danny Tracy plowed through slush and puddles like a convicted man on his way to sentencing. Tom skirted the ice and piles of snow while, in his head, he composed a note to the mayor about enforcing the city's ordinance on sidewalk snow removal.

To the casual observer, glancing from the window of his bowfront or peering through his lace curtains, Tom and Danny Tracy looked more like father and son than brothers. Danny made his money as a newsboy, spent it in the back alleys, and dressed in hand-me-down trousers and a leather jacket he'd won in a game of blackjack. Whatever part of his salary he did not give to his mother Tom Tracy spent on clothes. Had he been working in the railyards, his wardrobe would have been an extravagance. But as a young politician struggling for attention in a city full of young politicians, he considered his clothes an investment in his career.

Tom and his brother came from the tribal strain known as the Black Irish—black hair, heavy brows, and light northern complexions, a clash of tones that made them seem dour and threatening until they smiled. However, their mother always said that the Creator practiced on the round-jowled, auburn-haired Celtic cousin, then fashioned the refined features of the Black Irish face.

It was, in fact, Spanish blood, flowing in the fifteenth and sixteenth centuries, riding the Atlantic current with the remnants of the Armada and trading in the Catholic city of Galway, that accounted for the dark strain in the Irish breed stock. The dark strain in the Irish character had other derivations.

The Tracys walked down Washington Street, beneath the shadow of the elevated tracks that sliced through the South End like steel scissors through an old watercolor. Seventy years before, developers had created the South End out of landfill and meadow as the new home for the gentry of Boston, a place to escape the high prices of Beacon Hill and the immigrant hordes crowding the waterfront. Handsome bowfronts had risen, in the London style, around ovals of elm and oak, and brick rowhouses had lined long thoroughfares. But the gentry had stayed just long enough for the filling of the Back Bay. Then they had moved again, leaving the South End to the middle class, the immigrants, and, some would have said, to decay as well.

The South End was mostly Irish, but it had changed too quickly for a single group to gain control. Jews lived on one street, Greeks on another, Germans at their corner, Italians at theirs. And even Negroes lived around the edges. Wooden rowhouses grew up on side streets and dead ends. The mudflat slums near City Hospital were the worst in Boston. Kids with slingshots hunted rats in vacant lots. The el thundered past second-story windows every seven minutes. Muckrakers and social reformers from across America came to the South End to study poverty, social disease, and the feeble efforts of the settlement houses to provide hope. And yet, in its decay, the South End overflowed with life.

A dozen languages could be heard along Harrison Avenue, Yiddish theaters thrived near Washington Street, saloons thrived on every corner, the best vaudeville acts in America played at the Castle Square, and there were enough Irish Catholics to form four healthy parishes. The bowfronts were now cold-water flats and rooming houses, but the rents were low, and any immigrant could find a place to stop on his journey from the crowded ships to the quiet suburbs. In the South End, he would be treated no worse than anywhere else, and if he settled on the right street, he might decide to stay, even if he could eventually afford to leave.

Tom Tracy grabbed his brother by the collar and pushed him into the pedestrian tunnel that led under the Madison Hotel. It was damp, dark, occasionally dangerous, and always smelled of fresh urine. But it was a fine shortcut for people in a hurry, and even when he was not, Tom Tracy liked to seem that he was so that people would appreciate it when he stopped to chat and made them feel that he had taken time just for them.

At the end of the tunnel, Tom stopped. Danny climbed three steps, then turned. "What's wrong?"

"What's your name?"

"Hunh?"

"What's your name?"

"You know what my name is."

"Your name is *Tracy*." Tom jabbed a finger at his brother. His voice echoed down the tunnel. "And no Tracy lets a bum like Flaherty stiff him in a crap game. A Tracy's supposed to have too many brains to get in over his head and too much pride to let himself get stiffed."

Danny stuffed his hands into his pockets. "Does that mean it's okay to shoot craps with kids my own age, so long's I can lick 'em?"

"No. You don't gamble when your mother tells you not to. It's a sin."

"Ain't that why we got confession, to clean off the sins every few weeks?" Danny spat into the puddle by his feet.

Tom Tracy watched the ball of saliva push little circular waves across the puddle. Then he grabbed his brother by the collar. "Listen, you little snot, if it wasn't for me, we'd have nothin' comin' in but what you make sellin' papers. So do what I tell you and don't give me any cheap shit about confession."

Danny pulled away. "I can take care of myself."

"Maybe so . . . but in this family, we all take care of each other, and we all try to do what Ma wants. Now get the hell home and I won't tell her where you been this afternoon."

Danny grinned. "And I won't tell her where you're goin'."

"Where's that?"

"To see your Jewish girlfriend."

"I'm going to Tim O'Day's wake."

Danny looked up at the small patch of sky reflecting light into the tunnel. "It's after sunset. The Jews'll be comin' out any minute now."

"You've got a smart mouth, Dann-o." Tom Tracy shoved his brother up the stairs. "Go bundle your newspapers."

The South End was Tracy's turf, but any young man with his ambition was always looking at the world beyond his borders. And whenever Tom Tracy glanced at the front page, he was reminded once more that the world was coming apart.

At an insignificant fortress town called Verdun, half a million French and German soldiers clashed in frenzy, each side hoping to win the Great War by bleeding the other to death in a single battle. At a place called Gallipoli, the bodies of two hundred thousand Australian and Irish soldiers were testament to Turkish machine guns and British blunder. In Flanders fields, the frozen ground was slowly turning to mud, and the frozen British dead were beginning to thaw. At sea, German submarines were sinking merchant ships and drowning American passengers, while German diplomats exchanged polite notes with the United States government. And over the protests of Mexico's government, the United States Cavalry had crossed the Rio Grande to capture a rebel bandit named Pancho Villa.

As ancient monarchies and established governments hemorrhaged along trench-line incisions, new forces with new goals gathered far from the fronts. In Switzerland, a man named Lenin collected his Bolshevik followers and plotted his return to Russia. In the Arabian desert, an obscure British officer named T. E. Lawrence organized nomadic tribes into a guerrilla force that would fight the Turks and establish an Arab state on the edge of the Ottoman Empire. In Palestine, Zionists formed a unit to fight alongside the Allies, so that the British would help *them* to carve a homeland from the Turks as well. In Ireland, a quarter million men answered Britain's call to arms, while thousands more remained at home and waited because, as the ancient saying went, England's difficulty was Ireland's opportunity.

The United States, in spite of its foray into Mexico and the sinking of the *Lusitania*, had sought to remain neutral. But neutrality was not a simple course in a nation of European immigrants. While American politicians debated, spies, intelligence agents, saboteurs, and rebels operated up and down the East Coast. Some worked with the knowledge of the government; others were constantly watched by the Secret Service. Some performed in public forums; others functioned only under cover.

Except for the arrest of several German saboteurs, however, foreign operatives had attracted little attention in Boston, leaving the city to its own time-honored struggles—the Irish Catholic politicians against the Yankee Protestant businessmen, and the Irish Catholic politicians against each other.

Tom Tracy considered himself a front-line soldier in both struggles, an ally to the Irish mayor and an Irish iconoclast in a city of monuments.

There were monuments in Boston to white men who led Negro units in the Civil War, monuments to Nordic explorers whose longboats crossed the Atlantic long before an Italian discovered America, and monuments everywhere to the good Protestant rebels perspicacious enough to see that British rule through the tyranny of taxation was something sound men should not bear. Those rebels established a nation and a government and a rich merchant class that ruled Boston well for two hundred years. The graveyards were filled with headstones to their greatness, and the tapestry of the city was woven through with the red brick buildings where their revolt had begun to stir.

But the Irish of Boston had fought a rebellion of their own against the descendants of those good Protestant rebels. It had begun when the immigrants of the potato famine first organized themselves around ward bosses offering jobs, housing, and Christmas turkeys in exchange for votes. It had reached a turning point in 1888, when the son of an Irish farmer was elected mayor. But in 1916, it continued.

No longer could sign painters make steady income by lettering the words *No Irish Need Apply* on the windows of Boston businesses, because the men who held the city's political power were now Irish themselves. But the men who owned the banks and the property were still descended from those good Protestant rebels, and in their attitudes toward the Irish, it was not difficult to trace their heritage back to its British roots.

Boston's current mayor, and Tracy's boss, was the son of an Irish laborer who died winning a bet that he could lift a four-hundred-pound stone. James Michael Curley had been an alderman, a ward boss, and a congressman, and he had learned well the sources of power in his city. Shortly after his inauguration, he had announced his intention to pave Boston's streets, provide the poor with public baths and places of recreation, and, in the process, create more city jobs. He did not mention that more city jobs would mean more patronage, which would mean more votes for James Michael Curley. That was clear to every banker, ward boss, and unemployed laborer in Boston.

To finance his projects, Curley presented a bill to the Massachusetts Legislature requesting an increase in Boston's tax rate. In response, the descendants of those good Protestant rebels ordered their Republican representatives to stand once more against the tyranny of taxation. And whenever the mayor grabbed for more patronage, the Irish ward bosses stood against him as well.

In 1914, the three most powerful bosses, Martin Lomasney, Patrick J. Kennedy, and Smilin' Jim Donovan, had supported their own incumbent, John F. "Honey Fitz" Fitzgerald, for mayor. Curley took City Hall from Fitzgerald in a bitter campaign and announced that the era of the ward boss was coming to an end. Then he began to concentrate the powers of patronage in his own office so that by the end of his term, as one newspaper cried, there would be no boss but Curley.

Martin Lomasney was powerful enough and shrewd enough to reach a truce with Curley. Kennedy retreated to running his saloon and enjoying the grandchildren now issuing from his son and Fitzgerald's daughter. But in the South End, Smilin' Jim Donovan was still battling the mayor. And in the South End, Tom Tracy was the mayor's man.

In every ward, there was a character called *they*, the ubiquitous, anonymous voice that passed gossip and opinion from the saloons to the sweatshops to the parish halls and finally to the voting booths. In Ward Nine, *they* were saying that if Smilin' Jim Donovan could not get the grandson a city job or deliver a food basket to the sick aunt or set the city health inspector on the landlord, Tom Tracy could. And when the sick aunt finally died, *they* said Tom Tracy would always be there with a consoling smile.

Every morning, after he read the sports page, Tom Tracy would turn to what he called the Irish social calendar, also known as the death listing. He would circle the names that were familiar to him and try to go to as many wakes and funerals as he could. He might go because he knew the deceased or the loved ones or the priest who was saying the Rosary, but he always went because it was the duty of the ward politician to be seen comforting the bereaved, and those who did it well were well rewarded in November.

When Tom Tracy stepped through a door draped in black crepe, he went to work as surely as he did on Monday mornings. When he knelt at the casket to pray, he blessed himself as slowly and respectfully as possible, so that anyone watching could follow his hand through the Father, the Son, and the Holy Ghost, Amen. When he approached the loved ones seated by the casket, he made certain that he could put the right name with even the least familiar face. And when he stepped into the kitchen, where a bottle was sure to be open, he always remembered a story about the guest of honor, something to make everyone smile and give Tom Tracy a good line to leave with.

Tim O'Day's body had been found four days earlier on the beach at Plum Island. His ship, a lumber schooner running from Maine, had broken up in heavy seas, and the old captain had swum a mile and a half to shore. He froze to death before anyone found him, but the papers called his swim a heroic achievement. And his corpse was about to achieve what no one had managed since Curley took office: bring Tom Tracy together with Smilin' Jim Donovan and Jason Pratt, the son of Curley's most implacable Republican enemy and a direct descendant of those good Protestant rebels.

While Donovan was a fixture at most wakes, members of the Pratt family seldom ventured into South End neighborhoods, except to collect their rents. However, Tim O'Day's ship had been owned by Pratt Shipping and Mercantile, one of Boston's oldest trading houses, and Jason Pratt was paying for the funeral.

"He was a good one," said Tracy over Tim's body. "I'll miss him like he was my own uncle."

"After the cold water, the cold air was too much on him, Tommy." Tim's daughter Ursula pulled a handkerchief from the sleeve of her black dress and touched it to her nose.

The casket had been placed in the bay window, the drapes drawn behind it. A picture of Christ crowned with thorns lay on the coffin lid, and brown wooden rosary beads, which matched the color of Tim's suit, were wound through his fingers. Long white candles in tall brass sticks glimmered in the drafts on either side of the casket, but no shadows danced on the ceiling above the body, because Ursula O'Day had turned up the lamps, ignoring the cost of mantels and gas, so that her father's last guests would feel welcome in the parlor.

Two dozen people were jammed into a room that was hot enough, thought Tracy, to make the corpse sweat. The old widows were in their usual places on the sofa, where they could study everyone who came through the door and whisper comments to one another without seeming obvious. The younger people stood nervously in the doorways; the boys studied the girls and none glanced at the corpse. Tim's other daughters and their husbands sat on folding chairs at the head of the casket. One daughter was consoling an aunt, the other delicately mopping the perspiration from her neck and blowing her nose on the tissue. In the dining room, where the lights were lower, people ate cakes and drank coffee and chatted softly with Father Ryan, while from the kitchen, louder voices rumbled and occasionally rolled into laughter.

The Irish clung to life no less tenaciously than any other race, but they faced death with a strange mixture of acceptance and defiance that Tom Tracy could always hear in that muffled laughter. Perhaps it came from a faith that taught them death was a beginning as well as an end. Perhaps it came from a history of occupation that, for centuries, had demanded both acceptance and defiance in every Irish life. But the Irish knew how to bury their dead, thought Tracy, perhaps because they had had so much practice at it.

"It looks like he didn't suffer a bit." Tracy had first heard that remark by his father's coffin. He had not believed it then or now. Tim's face had settled grotesquely, and the makeup on his cheeks was so thick that this rough old seaman looked like a fading actor playing the corpse in a music-hall farce. The mortician's art had failed Tim O'Day, just as it had failed Tracy's father, who went to his grave with a blackened face and a hangman's bloody rope burn chafing against a respectable white collar.

Tom blessed himself, then stood and put his hand on Tim's. The flesh felt as cold as a lamppost.

"He liked you a lot, Tommy," Ursula O'Day placed her hand on Tracy's. She was the youngest daughter, and to her had fallen the responsibility of remaining at home and unmarried so that her father would have a warm meal whenever he returned from the sea. In her bearing, she showed the pride of one who had done her duty and stepped into the bright light of spinsterhood. She was not unattractive, however, and already, *they* had begun to speculate on her future.

"We'll miss him," answered Tracy.

"Before his last trip, he was sayin' what a fine thing it was for Tom Tracy to be bringin' that young woman to Christ."

Tracy slipped his hand from between father's and daughter's. "What young woman?"

"Miss Levka. She's here with her father. They even brought a Mass card." Ursula flipped through the stack of envelopes on the pedestal beside the casket and handed one to Tracy.

It promised that six Masses would be said for the repose of the soul of Timothy O'Day. At the bottom of the card it read, "Gift of the Levka Family."

Tracy put the card back into the envelope. "The Levkas are fine people."

"Like Sister Cunegunde always said, bringin' a convert to the faith guarantees a happy death."

He forced a smile. "Sister Cunegunde had a saying for everything."

"Rachel's in the dining room," Ursula whispered. "But Tommy, don't forget what Sister used to say about mixin' cults."

"Don't be worryin' your head with mixed cults, Ursula. Just get yourself over the next few days."

Tracy worked through the parlor, shaking hands, exchanging pleasantries, offering sympathies to the other O'Day daughters, and taking special care to move slowly, so that he seemed no more interested in Rachel Levka than in the corpse of Tim O'Day.

It was a sign of a man's generous spirit if his coffin was visited by members of other faiths. But when two people of different faiths began to see each other socially, *they* began to whisper. When the young man was a Catholic with political ambitions and the young woman the daughter of a prosperous Jewish baker, *they* could be heard gossiping from the Fort Point Channel to the Back Bay.

At the dining-room entrance, Tracy stopped and looked about for Rachel Levka.

"Did you get the word?" Denny Morrissey, the mayor's man in South Boston, came up behind Tracy. Denny had four chins and a belly that hung over his belt like a carpenter's nail pouch, and he could deliver his precinct in the middle of a blizzard.

"What word?"

"Curley's called some pain-in-the-ass meeting for tomorrow at noon."

"Tomorrow's Sunday."

"Must be important."

28

Through the mass of serge and wool and cake plates, Tracy saw her face. She was sitting in a dark corner, beside the china cabinet. She was talking with Mrs. Walsh, the Harrison Avenue Branch librarian. Her clothes were dark and simple, her black hair was piled primly on top of her head, and her hands were folded on her lap.

"Take this from a friend," whispered Denny, "she could be real trouble for you."

The kitchen door swung open and Avram Levka, a florid little man in a high starched collar, came into the dining room. He was carrying a large cake with purple frosting, purple the color of mourning.

"Real trouble." Denny licked his lips. "Even if her old man bakes the best pastries in Boston."

"The meeting, Denny. What's the meeting about?"

"Some Englishman got himself hung on a meat hook at Quincy Market this afternoon. The British consul's all pissed off."

"So what?"

"Beats me. Show up tomorrow and find out."

"Is Smiler in the kitchen?"

"Yeah, and there's a Pratt in there, too, and neither one of them means as much trouble for you as that Jewish dame . . . but she ain't bad to look at."

"I hardly know her."

"That ain't what they say." Denny Morrissey went to the table, piled a plate with cakes and pastries, and pushed his heavy way back to the kitchen.

Tom Tracy entered most rooms in the way that he had entered Strongarm Flaherty's crap game. But for a moment he hesitated. His good sense told him to follow Denny into the kitchen. That was where he might win a few votes, score a few points, make a few friends. And Denny was right. The girl could be trouble, especially when *they* were all watching and waiting to see what he would do. But Rachel had seen him and she was smiling. And from the day that she first smiled at him over the counter of the bakery, he had been drawn to her.

"A word to the wise, Tommy." Ursula O'Day whispered in his ear. "Father Ryan'll be startin' the Rosary in five minutes, and when it comes to contemplatin' the sorrowful mysteries, there's no one who takes more pleasure in it. If you'd like to leave, you've got the blessings and the thanks of all the O'Day sisters."

Tom patted Ursula's hand. "As they say, a word to the wise is sufficient."

Whenever the beads began to jangle, Tom Tracy headed for the door. And most people understood, because a politician who stayed through every Rosary would never visit more than a corpse or two in a night. Ursula was telling Tom that he had five minutes to work the crowd in the kitchen, otherwise he would have to kneel for half an hour while Father Ryan droned through the decades.

He looked again at Rachel. Her eyes were still on his face, but she was no longer smiling, perhaps because she sensed his hesitation, perhaps because her father was now sitting next to her. Tracy gave them a small wave, then went into the kitchen.

The haze of smoke stung his eyes. The heat brought the perspiration to his upper lip. And the rich, malty smell of whatever the men were drinking was far more potent than the smell of fifteen people crammed into a room with one window. His heart began to race, as it had when he walked into Strongarm's alley, as it always did when he approached a fight. He forgot Rachel and her father and surveyed the kitchen.

Near the icebox, a familiar figure was making a speech. "So an English guy gets hung on a meat hook. So what? It ain't just Boston that's comin' apart at the seams, it's the whole damn world. And no one's got any idea of how to put it back together again."

"That's because there aren't enough people prayin' the Rosary, Smilin' Jim."

The man stuffed a cigar into his mouth and squinted at Tom Tracy.

'But I have the solution." Tracy picked up a mug and dipped it into the beer bucket in the sink. "Give the cardinal a call and ask him to write a pastoral letter. Have it say, 'City Councillor Smilin' Jim Donovan wants us all to pray the Rosary for peace.' Then, when the war ends, you can take credit for the whole thing and get yourself elected mayor."

There were a few snickers, Denny Morrissey laughed out loud, spraying cake crumbs, and the gentleman leaning against the stove smiled politely.

Donovan ignored the remark and studied Tracy's face. "Who gave you the mouse?"

Tracy brought a hand to his cheek. It was bruised and tender from the fight. "One of your old constituents."

The Smiler smiled. "Yeah? Who?"

"Strongarm Flaherty. You must remember him. They say that back in the old days, you counted on five or six votes from him every election day."

Donovan puffed on his cigar. "You're a punk, Tommy, and everybody in the South End knows it, and one of these days, your little world's gonna land on your head, right when you're kissin' the mayor's ass."

"Pray that you're not standin' there pickin' his pocket when it happens." Tracy dipped another mug into the beer bucket and brought it over to Donovan. "Have a beer, Councillor."

"I'm not thirsty."

"That's rare." He offered the mug to the man leaning against the stove. "You're Mr. Pratt?"

"Jason Pratt of Pratt Shipping and Mercantile, master of the schooner *Abigail*." He took the mug. "You must be Tom Tracy of the Tammany Club."

"Tom Tracy, the mayor's errand boy," grunted Smilin' Jim.

Tracy raised the mug to Donovan. Although never one for admitting such things Tracy admired the ward boss, because Smilin' Jim Donovan was a true professional. He knew how to talk and how to dress, and no one in the city handed out better cigars. "Mr. Pratt stands corrected."

Then Tracy turned back to Pratt, who had the deep-set eyes, the hooked nose, and the downturned mouth that, in the mayor's words, made every Pratt look as though he had everything he ever wanted but never had enough. In spite of his handsome gray suit and silk tie, however, it was clear that this Pratt had not watched his thirty-odd years go by from the windows of the family boardroom. His face was windburned, his nose had been broken more than once, and beneath his eyes was a pattern of scars common to club fighters who cut at the touch of a glove.

Tracy toasted him. "To the gentleman who has eased the financial burden on the O'Days in a terrible time."

"Here, here." Denny Morrissey held up a piece of cake. Smilin' Jim toasted with his cigar, and the others who were listening raised their glasses and mugs.

"It's the least I can do for a faithful captain," answered Pratt. "My company stands by its people."

"Loyalty's a grand thing." Denny Morrissey shoved the cake into his mouth.

"Tim O'Day was loyal to the last," added Donovan.

"Indeed he was," said Pratt.

"A grand, loyal fellow, and a good friend," contributed Tracy to the litany.

"And while we're on the subject of loyalty," said Pratt, "perhaps one of you gentlemen can tell me why it is that a South End employer like myself, loyal to his people, can't get proper city services."

"You get the same services as everyone else," answered Donovan.

Tom Tracy looked down at his beer. He knew what was coming, but he was surprised that Pratt had come to it so publicly.

"I wrote to you three weeks ago, Councillor, asking that you repair the water main at the entrance to my wharf. The main leaks, the water freezes, and my trucks go sliding all over Albany Street."

"And I sent the request to Public Works," answered Donovan. "In my ward, Pratts who treat people fair get fair treatment themselves."

"Then why is it that the water main still leaks?"

Smilin' Jim Donovan's cheeks reddened. Then he turned to Tracy and slowly removed the cigar from his mouth. Over the years, he had refined this gesture until it was nearly as unsettling as slowly removing the nose from his face. "Why?"

Tom Tracy took a swallow of beer and licked the line of foam from his upper lip. "They're damned busy down at the Department of Public Works right now. This is the beginning of the pothole season, you know."

"You mean the beginning of the *ass*hole season, don't you, Tommy, when some smart asshole in the mayor's office puts out orders to ignore Smilin' Jim, so that Smilin' Jim looks like an asshole."

The other conversations in the kitchen had died away. *They* were listening. Tom Tracy told himself to be careful. He remembered the mayor's advice: When someone attacks you with the truth and you can't think of a response, smile politely and turn your attention to someone else. Tracy smiled and turned to Pratt, but what he said was more reckless than he had intended. "Sometimes the mayor's office can cut through the fat at DPW faster than anyone in the wards. I'll have a crew at your wharf on Monday morning."

At that, Denny Morrissey swallowed a whole piece of cake, and someone else gagged on his beer. Tom Tracy had buried the boss's request and was now challenging the boss's power in public. Smilin' Jim slipped his cigar back into his mouth and, for the moment, seemed too shocked to speak.

"Fine, fine." Jason Pratt adjusted his tie and said, with feigned innocence, "You must know that I spend most of my time at sea, gentlemen. I'm not well informed on the local infighting. When I want something done in the ward, which of you do I ask?"

The attack begun, Tracy saw little sense in backing away. If the son of the mayor's most powerful enemy had to come to Tracy for favors, the voters of the South End would begin to recognize the growing power of Tom Tracy. "Speaking to me, Mr. Pratt, is like speaking to the mayor."

"That, sir, will not endear you to my father." Pratt tipped his head back and downed his mug of beer in a single draft. "I, however, don't give a damn. I'll expect the water main to be fixed on Monday."

Tom Tracy dipped his mug into the beer bucket again. "Count on it."

"Count on nothin' in this ward," grunted Smilin' Jim Donovan, "until it happens."

Politics, Tracy knew, could be like streetfighting. He might knock out Strongarm Flaherty with one punch, but he was not yet skilled enough to knock Smilin' Jim Donovan over a water main.

Donovan slowly removed his cigar. "Count on nothin', unless I say so."

"I've given Mr. Pratt my word," said Tracy, "and he can count on that, just like anyone else in the ward."

"Then maybe he'll vote for you when you try to steal my seat."

"No one will steal your seat," said Tracy. "The voters'll take it away from you and give it to someone who deserves it."

"It won't be you." The Smiler smiled. "When they find out what *you're* doin' these days, they'll vote you right into the shithouse."

"What's he doin'?" asked one of Donovan's cronies.

Tom Tracy felt like a boxer who realizes he has punched himself out and can no longer hold up his arms. What had been whispered through the ward as rumor was about to become public truth. Demean the ward boss to his face, in front of his constituents, and expect no quarter.

Donovan looked around the kitchen. "Not only is Tommy Tracy usin' that smart mouth to kiss the mayor's ass every day.

He's also usin' it to kiss Avram Levka's Jewish daughter whenever he gets the chance."

Tom Tracy heard the surprise rush out around him like a small wind. He saw the slack jaws and the smile spreading across Pratt's face. He took a swallow of beer, then another, and he heard Denny Morrissey muttering, "Trouble . . . nothin' but trouble."

Smilin' Jim Donovan put his cigar in place with a triumphant little flourish. "And you just try gettin' elected in Ward Nine with a Jew-girl on your arm."

Tom Tracy's wit deserted him. If he responded with the anger that he felt, he would be admitting that Smilin' Jim Donovan had found his weakness, and in the long run, the girl might be no more than that, a seductive, and perhaps passing, fancy. If he denied he was seeing her, after so direct a challenge, he would not be able to take her in his arms or look her father in the eye again.

"I don't like your attitude, Jim," he said. An old Curley trick to buy time.

Tracy placed his mug of beer on the counter, then drew himself up like an orator approaching the podium. "When I take your seat, I plan to be councillor for everyone, not just the Irish Catholics."

He looked around, at Pratt and Smiler's cronies and the faces of *they* floating in the cigar smoke. "When the ward boss starts to pick and choose over religions, it won't be long before he's pickin' and choosin' over the street people live on, or the parish his Catholics belong to, or who gave him the most campaign money. Nobody's safe when the politicians start to play favorites."

Denny Morrissey was smiling. And Smilin' Jim was turning red.

Tracy knew that he had taken the right line of attack. "That's not how it's supposed to be in America . . . and it's not for me."

"Well said, Tom." Jason Pratt raised his empty mug, and two or three people applauded.

Tracy put up his hands. "This is a wake, gentlemen. Let's not get carried away."

"Yeah." Denny laughed. "At a wake, the only one who gets carried away is the corpse."

Smilin' Jim Donovan bit so hard on his cigar that the saliva trickled out of it and rolled down his chin.

"Now, if you'll all excuse me," said Tracy, "there's a young lady in the next room with her father. Since they were kind enough to attend this wake, I'd like to speak with them both. They won't be staying for the Rosary, mind you. But I will . . . and I expect that all of you will be doing the same."

"After that speech," said Jason Pratt, "even the Protestants will stay."

Tom Tracy was getting better at this all the time. He had taken the Smiler's worst punch and turned it against him. His only disappointment was that when he went into the dining room, the girl and her father were gone. Now he would have to apologize, if her father would let him past the front door. But on a day when he handled Strongarm Flaherty and Smilin' Jim Donovan, he had no fear at all of Avram Levka.

"Is your father at home?"

"Do you want to see him or me?"

"I missed you both at the wake."

"You looked right at us. Everyone else we knew came over and chatted."

"Can I come in?"

"You know what my father thinks of Irish suitors, especially Irish suitors who won't even acknowledge his daughter in public."

"Why should that bother him? He doesn't want her to be *seen* in public with them, anyway."

"That's what I like about you, Tommy." She smiled. "In a crazy world, you're always looking for the logic."

A light came on above a nearby entry. A door opened.

The Levkas lived in a bowfront on Union Park Street. Most Jews who could afford more than a flat moved to Blue Hill Avenue in Dorchester, but Avram Levka had chosen, when he grew prosperous, to remain in the South End, close to his business and to Temple Ohabei Beth Shalom, where he had first settled when he brought his family to America.

"The neighbors are getting nosy," Tracy said. "Can I come in?"

"After this evening, I should leave you out there to freeze, but if you'll help me rehearse my speech for tomorrow . . ."

"The one about your Zionist friends?"

She nodded.

He stepped back and tried to peer in the living-room windows, but the drapes were closed. "When your father makes a list of things he doesn't like, he puts the Irish suitor in the slot between rancid lard and Zionists. Is he going to let me sit in the living room while you practice your speech?"

"No."

Tracy looked up and down the street, like a burglar about to step into a house. "Am I correct in assuming that your father is out for the evening?"

She nodded and opened the door.

When he imagined her without clothes, which he had done often but never spoken of in confession, he saw a Rubens painting that hung in the Museum of Fine Arts, a fine, fleshy woman with rounded hips, full bust, and the broad shoulders of a farm girl. Rachel's complexion was much darker than any Rubens from northern Europe, however, because her mother's ancestors had migrated to Lithuania from the shores of the Caspian in the seventeenth century, bringing with them the black hair, brown eyes, and dark southern blood of Uzbekistan.

She was not beautiful in the delicate sense that the Gish sisters or Blanche Sweet were beautiful. She had heavy brows and a straight, severe nose, but when she spoke or smiled, her expressive lips gave life to her face.

She stood by the upright piano, a music stand for a podium, and read her speech. Tracy sat in a straight-backed chair, a cup of tea on his lap, and watched her lips form each word. While he tried to concentrate on her speech and her presentation, her lips were inspiring other ideas.

"We in Boston's Jewish community are honored today to welcome Rabbi Ben Zion Mossinsohn to America." Rachel looked at Tracy. "The rabbi will be sitting behind me. Should I turn and nod to him?"

"Don't turn away from your audience. They'll be more interested in looking at you, anyway."

She glanced at her speech again. "You all know the story of Rabbi Mossinsohn. The leader of the Hebrew Gymnasium at Jaffa, he was arrested by the Turks and condemned for conspiring—"

" 'Condemned for conspiring'—that's good. It sounds like us. Condemned for conspiring to mix the cults."

"Stop it." She frowned. "—condemned for conspiring with the British to overthrow Turkish rule in Palestine. But the American ambassador intervened and saved him from the gallows."

Tracy raised a hand, like a schoolboy. "The ambassador's name?"

"Henry Morgenthau."

"Then use it. People want names."

She gave him an annoyed look, then wrote something on her sheet of paper. "Now an exile from his Palestinian homeland—"

"Eye contact, Rachel."

"But I'm reading."

"Break the speech into stops, so you can look up periodically. Either that or memorize it." Tracy stood. "Now, make eye contact."

She stared at him. "Now an exile from his Palestinian homeland—"

"Your eyes are like dark pools of mystery."

"Stop it. They expect three thousand people at that meeting tomorrow. I've never been so nervous in my life."

"Then don't do it."

"I was the one who asked the Zionist rabbi to come. I *have* to introduce him."

"All right, then. Repeat the last sentence."

She cleared her throat. "Now an exile from his Palestinian homeland—"

Tracy stepped over to the settee. "Eye contact."

She looked at him. "—the rabbi is traveling across America—"

"Eye contact." Tracy went over to the Victrola. "Imagine that it's me looking up at you from every seat."

"—the rabbi is traveling across America speaking of the great goals of Zionism—"

Tracy stepped in front of the music stand. "Eye contact."

"—and the opportunities that the current cataclysm presents for those with dreams of a better world." She looked straight into his eyes. "We in the Boston chapter of Hadassah are proud to introduce Rabbi Ben Zion Mossinsohn."

"Dreams of a better world. That's the story wherever you go." Tracy leaned on the music stand. "You're beautiful when you're making a speech."

"Stop it. If somebody found out you were in my living room with no one else here, there'd be a big scandal."

"We're a scandal now." He kept his eyes on hers. "Why not a big one?"

"Because you're afraid of a *little* scandal. You won't even say hello to me at a wake because you're afraid of the gossips."

"I told you, I was there for business first."

"Business first. So sit." She pointed to the chair. "If my father comes home and finds you here, I want this to look like what it is. A speech lesson."

"Your father's playing cards. He'll be out all night."

"Sit. Business first."

He did as he was told, but before she began again, she came over to him. "Will you be there tomorrow?"

He brought the teacup to his lips.

"You know how much it will mean to me." She leaned forward and put her hands on the arms of his chair.

"If you want, I'll become an honorary member of the Zion Association of Greater Boston."

"You won't back out at the last minute, because you're afraid of the gossips?"

"Don't insult me, Rachel," he said seriously, although he *was* afraid of the gossips.

"The place will be packed with Jews and newspaper reporters," she warned.

"It's also open to the public." He was remembering his own speech to Smilin' Jim, and it made him feel courageous. "I'm a young politician who wants to broaden his horizons. I'll be there. I promise. You can introduce me to the rabbi and Louis Brandeis, too."

She threw her arms around his neck. "I was afraid you wouldn't come."

She smelled of perfumed soap, and her skin felt warm against his. He moved his face and kissed her cheek.

She quickly brushed his lips with hers, then straightened up. "Can we run through it again?"

"Business first?"

She went back to the podium, and for a moment she shuffled through her papers. "Thank you, Tommy."

She spoke Lithuanian, Yiddish, and English perfectly, but her accent was strictly Bostonian, with long, flat *r*'s that sounded like poor relations slipping out the back door while the other guests left by the front. Except for a few Irish phrases, Tracy sounded much the same.

Halfway through the speech, he put up his hand.

"What now?"

"You're not projecting."

"Because we're in my living room."

"Speak from the diaphragm. Even if you speak softly, the words will still reverberate."

She tried. "Now an exile—"

"Lower."

She dropped her voice an octave. "Now an exile—"

"You're still not speaking from the diaphragm. If you want to be a real Zionist, you have to learn how to project those radical ideas of yours."

"What's radical about wanting a homeland for my people?"

"You have a homeland right here. You're an American, just like me and my brothers, just like the Pratts, and *they've* been here for two hundred years."

"We're immigrants, Tommy. We should be doing something for the people still suffering."

"They suffer because they never had the courage to pack up and leave."

Her brows became a single, hard line across her forehead. "We've been through all this before."

"You can't say it too many times. Let Europe take care of itself. Put your energy into changes right here, where you have the chance to make them."

"Like what?"

"Women need to get the vote. Fight for that."

"I'm on the Boston Women's Suffrage Committee already. What else?"

"There's one bathtub for every twenty-five people in this city. Help the mayor to win his tax increase and we can build bathhouses for the poor. They deserve to be clean, too."

"I leave that one to you and the mayor. You leave me to the Zion Association."

"All right." He dropped into his chair. "Once more, and this time from the diaphragm."

"Now an exile from his Palestinian homeland—"

"Your diaphragm, Rachel." He went over to her and, without any of the hesitation that accompanied an embrace, placed his right hand beneath her breasts. "There it is."

"Thomas." She drew her breath sharply. "You shouldn't—"

"That's where the voice should be coming from." He lowered his own voice and tried to sound completely professional, like a doctor performing an examination.

"All right," she said. "Now sit down and listen."

Instead, he put his other hand on the small of her back. "Speak properly, and your whole body becomes a . . . a musical instrument."

For a moment, neither of them spoke or moved.

Then she whispered, "Tuba or piano?"

"A delicate harp." His fingers played along her spine to the strands of loose hair at the nape of her neck.

"Sit down, Tommy, or we won't get much further."

"I have to feel the sound."

She laughed. "That's not what you're trying to feel."

"It's the . . ." His voice caught somewhere between his own diaphragm and his throat. "It's the only way to know if you're speaking properly."

"Yes," she said, pretending to convince herself. "Yes, I suppose you're right." She lowered her voice. "How's that?"

"Not bad." He moved one hand slightly higher, and his index finger pressed against the soft roundness of her breast. With the other hand he touched the flesh of her neck. "Try again, this time with eye contact."

She looked into his eyes and lowered her voice to a whisper. "Now, an exile . . . would like a kiss."

Before she was finished, one hand was drawing her face to his, and the other was caressing her breast. He touched his lips to hers. She sighed and opened her mouth against his. For six months, they had been kissing in cold shadows, always wrapped in heavy wool overcoats, always frustrated by the knowledge that some passerby might discover them in an embrace, and always uncertain of the distance they intended to travel together.

But this evening, in the warmth and quiet of her home, they had nothing to control them and found that they could not control themselves.

His lips left hers, and she tried to protest. But his mouth traveled across her cheek to her earlobe, and her protest died. When he touched her there, he felt her body stiffen and press against his. Then he moved his lips along the soft sensitive flesh of her throat, kissing and nibbling toward the top button of her blouse.

"Tommy, we shouldn't," she whispered.

He groaned his agreement and continued to kiss her while his fingers teased the points of her breasts through the layers of fabric.

"We shouldn't," she repeated, and she began to unbutton her blouse.

"It wouldn't be right," he said, and he kissed the palms of her hands, then pushed them away and lifted her and carried her to the settee.

"Oh, God, Tommy," she whispered as she stretched out, "are we going too far?"

"Yes," he said, and he placed his hand against the middle of her skirt.

She gasped and spread her legs, and he pressed harder. At the same time she twitched her undergarments around and freed one of her breasts for him. The nipple was stiff with excitement and the flesh around it pulled taut by the jumble of clothes.

"You're beautiful," he whispered.

She grabbed a handful of black hair and pulled him to her breast.

And that was how Avram Levka found them. He had just lost fifty dollars playing a straight against four aces. He was in no mood for Zionist speeches, Irish suitors, or passion in his parlor. When his daughter had put her clothes back together and his voice had quieted from a shriek to a shout, he said that he was going to carry a gun, and next time he would shoot the Irisher in the head or, worse yet, in the bulge between his legs.

3

*I*t was snowing again. It had been the snowiest winter in memory, but Tom Tracy liked the snow. It covered the mansions of the Back Bay and the slums of the South End in the same soft mantle of white, and this evening, its gentle falling softened his frustration. But nothing could soften the sound of Avram Levka's voice still threatening in his head, or cover the differences that mattered, even in America.

He hurried down Harrison Avenue and turned onto Gloucester Place, a dead end of wooden rowhouses around an unpaved mud rut. It was not one of the better addresses in the South End, but the neighbors were friendly, and Josephine Tracy and her brother owned the building, which counted for something.

In the back stairwell, Tracy smelled his mother's bread, and it made him feel a bit better.

Then he heard the sound of a strange voice. He stood and listened in the darkness, and the voice became familiar. Suddenly, all of the passion, frustration, and embarrassment of the previous hour, all the small victories and defeats of his Saturday evening, were forgotten. Tom Tracy was recalling the burn of his first cigarette, the sting of his first swallow of whiskey, and the taste of his own blood the first time he lost a fight.

"If it's Tommy Tracy on the other side of that door, he'd better be showin' himself."

"If it's Paddy Starr I see at my mother's table, he'd better be watchin' his language, because he's sittin' between my two little brothers."

Danny, eighteen-year-old John, and Uncle Martin Mahoney clustered around Starr like children around a storyteller. Starr shoved a last piece of brown bread into his mouth and stood. He was bigger than Tracy remembered, as big as Tracy himself.

"You've grown up, Tommy."

"You've done the same." Tracy offered his hand.

"A pleasure to see you, a pleasure indeed." Starr wiped his palms on his trousers and took Tracy's hand. "From your grip and the cut of your fine suit, it looks like you're a man who works at a desk."

"He runs the Tammany Club for the mayor," said Uncle Martin, "and he makes a damn fine livin' at it, too."

"That he does," said Josephine Tracy. "Now, the both of you's sit and eat. I didn't bring out another whole meal to watch it go cold as the stones of Dublin Castle."

Tom Tracy dropped into a chair and smiled across the table at his cousin. He remembered the high, freckled forehead, the rust-red hair, the honey-sweet voice that had charmed old women and farm girls from the time that Starr was fourteen, and he remembered the smile. His mother had once called it the grin of the old Celtic sin-eater, friendly and comforting and faintly blasphemous in the bargain.

She was at the stove, heaping another plate with food. In the years since she brought her three sons to America, she had created for them a ritual of routines that were, like the rituals of the early church, the mortar that bound her community together. Saturday night was set firmly upon a meal of home-baked brown bread, beans, and knockwursts (which the butchers had taken to calling liberty sausage since the sinking of the *Lusitania*), the bundling of newspapers for Danny's Sunday route, baths for everyone, and a quiet game of cribbage with her brother Martin, who lived in the downstairs flat.

During her sixteen years in America, Josephine Tracy had welcomed dozens of immigrant relatives, from her husband's sister Mazie to the most forlorn and unfamiliar cousin from County Antrim. Tom Tracy knew, however, that she had not welcomed the sight of Padraic Starr, and she had never welcomed it, not even in Connemara.

She slapped a plate in front of Tommy and, without a word, took Starr's plate and filled it again.

Tracy picked up his knife and fork. "It's grand to see you, Padr'ic."

"Grand, indeed." Martin Mahoney took a plug of chewing tobacco from his pocket and bit off a chunk. "A voice from the old country's like a warm wind in December, I always say. How's Connemara, Padr'ic?"

"As green as ever."

"A grand country, it is, God's country. That's what I call it, and one of these days"—Martin worked the chaw around in his mouth and broke it down—"I'm bookin' two first-class cabins for me and the baby sister."

"Wait till the war's over." Josephine dropped another full plate in front of Starr. "Then book second."

"If it's second you want, second it'll be." Martin Mahoney belonged to that special class of Irishman known as the bachelor brother. When his mother died he transferred all of his affections to his sister because he could never quite find the right woman to marry. And if he *had* found her, he would never have quite found the courage to ask her.

Because he was so placid as to seem mysterious, it was whispered about the blacksmith shop that he concealed some dark secret beneath his scally cap. A few suggested that he had killed a man with a single punch, for his hands were huge and his forearms like piano legs. But the only secret he had ever divulged was his dream: to shoe the horses that pulled the trolleys that brought progress to the great and growing cities of America. Because his dream was simple, he had been able to fulfill it, at least until progress had overtaken the horses and electricity had taken over the trolleys.

"Well, the war'll soon be over," said Martin, "with men like Paddy Starr making heroes of themselves."

"Hero?" Tom Tracy cut into one of the knockwursts. The juice squirted halfway across the table. "My cousin Padr'ic?"

"He killed a whole squadron of Germans," said Danny proudly.

Starr smiled at the boy. "I only killed a few . . . to cover our retreat."

"But he won this. The king of England give him this." Danny slid a jewelry box across the table.

Tracy opened it. On a bed of velvet was a bronze cross, suspended from a crimson ribbon. At the center of the cross, the British lion stood atop a coronet, and beneath him the words *For Valour*.

"That's the Victoria Cross," said John.

The medal looked authentic, and Tom Tracy's first thought was that Starr had stolen it. "I'm impressed."

"Impressed ain't the word." Martin took a tin can from under his seat and spat a gob of brown saliva. "I'm honored to be sittin' at the same damn table."

"How did my cousin from County Galway get himself into the British army to begin with?" asked Tom.

Starr smiled. "A long story."

"And do all winners of the Cross get discharges?" Tracy stuffed knockwurst into his mouth.

"Another long story." Starr scooped up a spoonful of beans.

"But a fair question," said John. He had just come up from his bath. A drop of water slipped from his slicked wet hair, trickled down his neck, and soaked into the collar of his robe.

Josephine put a plate of bread on the table. "Padr'ic's a guest in our house, John, and even if it's a fair question, he don't have to answer it if he don't want to."

Tom Tracy picked up the pitcher of beer and filled Starr's glass. Then he filled his own and his uncle's. "We're glad to see you, Padr'ic, however you got here."

"No question about it," added Martin.

Starr touched his glass to Tom's, then to Martin's. "To a fine American welcome." They all drank, and Starr turned his glass to John. "To a fine young priest in trainin'."

John pulled the robe around his neck. "How did you know that?"

"It's in the eyes," said Starr. "Any good priest shows it."

Martin looked at his sister. "Did you hear that? I think our Padr'ic's got the magic in him."

Starr poured himself another glass of beer. "They say the eyes are the window on the soul, Uncle Martin. I just gaze in."

"It's the magic just the same," answered Martin. "Don't you think so, John?"

"The church teaches us not to believe in magic," said John.

"Ah," Martin raised his hand, "there's things that happen, even the church can't explain."

"I can also see by the eyes around this table that a few of you are wonderin' if I'm a deserter or a man with a fair reason to be free of the war."

"Now, Padr'ic," said Josephine, "if you mean to be spendin' your time here lookin' into everyone's eyes and tellin' them what they're thinkin', I don't think you'll be welcome here for too long."

"You can't look into somebody's eyes unless they want you to," said Tom. "And if you want a clue that John's studying for the priesthood, all you need to do is see the breviary on top of the icebox."

Starr winked at Tracy and finished a knockwurst.

"I never thought you were a deserter," said John. "And if you were, there's some in this city might say a prayer for you."

"I'm no deserter, but I'll take the prayer," answered Starr.

Tom Tracy cleaned the molasses and mustard from his place with a slice of bread. "Are you looking for work?"

"I'm here to see the sights of the grand and glorious country I've heard so much about."

Josephine picked up the two empty plates. "Anything else?"

"I'm done," said Starr.

"So soon?" she answered. "You only et five plates."

"And every bite more delicious than the last."

"A man with the magic and a kisser of the blarney stone, too." Martin nudged Tom in the ribs. "And not bad with the fork, either."

Tom picked up the pitcher and topped off the glasses. "I can't match him with the fork, but from here on in I'll match him beer for beer."

Martin slapped his hand down on the table. "There you go, Paddy, a challenge."

"We'll have no drinkin' contests in my kitchen, thank you," said Josephine.

"It's no contest," said Tom. "Just a friendly exhibition between a student and his teacher." Tom held up his mug. "To the cousin who introduced me to the evils of drink."

Starr responded, "To the cousin who came through the worst and prospered in America."

They touched glasses and both drank straight to the bottom, but Starr finished first and planked his mug on the table.

"It may be that you've learned how to drink, but I can still do it faster, Tommy."

Tracy finished his beer and refilled both glasses. "You can do it faster, but how long can you last?"

They raised their mugs once more.

"To the cousin who taught me that slow and steady was better than a flash in the pan," said Tracy.

"To the cousin who knew that slow and steady was the only way to make it through the bad times."

Josephine swept the beer pitcher off the table. "The bar's closed. And we had it no worse than anyone else who come to this country."

"That's right, Ma." Tom reached out and put his arms around his mother's waist. "Because we've always had someone to hold on to."

In her youth, she had been known as a healthy girl, with wide hips for bearing children, broad shoulders for hard work, and full breasts that were a sign of plenty in a rock-hard land. Her eyes were set too close together and her jaw was too wide for her mouth, but the men of Galway had considered Josephine Tracy a prize. At fifty, her body now settled like a solid old house, her eyes sunk deep, her smile less bright and less frequent, she had become the simple force of gravity that held her family together.

"There's no one who came to this country in a worse way than you," Starr said. "A week after watchin' your husband walk the gallows."

Tom Tracy felt his mother stiffen. He took his arm from around her waist and leaned across the table. "I thought you'd be smart enough not to bring that up."

Starr sat back and looked around at the kitchen, the new cook-stove, the modern icebox, the fresh coat of red enamel on the floors. "I'm just complimentin' you on all that you've made for yourselves here."

"Thanks for the kind words, but don't be bringin' up the boys' father again." Josephine put the beer pitcher in the icebox, then

46

began taking the plates and mugs from the table, scraping out the heavy pots and pans.

Starr looked at Tracy. "I'm sorry. I thought you'd talk more about your father."

Josephine dropped the black iron skillet on the stove, and the shock made the beer splash in Tracy's mug.

"His memory is honored in this house every day of the year," said Tom evenly.

"And we pray for him every evening," added John.

"I just wish I'd got to meet him," said Danny.

Josephine turned to her youngest son. "You know all there is to know of him, Danny, right down to the night before he died, when he touched my belly and said, 'If it's a boy, name him Daniel, after your father.' "

Martin Mahoney laughed nervously. "Don't start talking about our da, sis, or *I'll* start tellin' stories and I'll be here all night."

"You'll be talkin' to the icebox, then, 'cause the rest of us is goin' to bed. Padr'ic can sleep in the attic. It's cold, but the blankets is warm."

"Anything's better than steerage," Starr said.

Josephine ushered everyone off, leaving Starr and Tom Tracy alone at the table.

Tom went to the icebox and took out the pitcher of beer. He filled each mug until the beer foamed over and spilled onto the oilcloth.

Starr picked up his mug and took a long swallow. "Do you think God created beer right after he got finished with woman? Or was it the other way 'round?"

"That depends on whether you're askin' a man in a bed or a man in a bar." Tracy lifted his mug, but before he drank, he said, "I'm going to ask you this just once, Padr'ic, and I'll expect a straight answer."

Starr put down his mug.

"What are you doing in America?"

"I'm here to see what America has to give Ireland after all we've given to her."

"That's no answer."

Starr picked up his mug, tilted his head back, and drank the beer to the bottom. "Not countin' what I had before you got home, I'm two pints ahead of you now. Drink up, Tommy."

"You didn't answer me."

"I'll not answer a man who's tryin' to stay sober when I'm on my way to a good drunk. Now, drink before your mother comes down and throws all this beautiful beer into the sink."

Tracy took a swallow.

"C'mon, Tommy, the whole pint, or I'll start thinkin' them soft hands of yours ain't the only soft thing about you."

Tracy lowered the mug briefly, then threw his head back and drank. And drank. Halfway through the pint, he wanted to stop. His stomach was full of beer and knockwurst and fresh bread that felt like it was starting to rise again inside him. He tilted back farther and tried to breathe through his nose. The beer spilled out both sides of the glass and trickled down his chin, but the last of it poured down his gullet. He slammed the mug down on the table and dragged a sleeve across his mouth. Then a fat bubble of gas slithered back from his stomach. It stopped for a moment to rearrange itself in his throat, and popped out with a triumphant little belch. "Now answer my goddam question."

"Your eyes are waterin', Tommy."

Tracy did not blink. A belch was acceptable between two men emptying a pitcher. Watery eyes were not. He picked up the pitcher and poured the last two pints.

Starr watched the beer foam to the top of Tracy's glass. "You never was one to back down on a dare."

"We have a good life here, Padr'ic, and you're welcome to anything we have. But I want no trouble. And I smelled trouble the minute I stepped into the back hall."

"What you smelled down there was your mother's bread. But you have my word. There'll be no trouble. I won't even mention your da again, except to toast his memory." Starr raised his mug. "To Jack Tracy, a fine Irish patriot."

Tracy did not respond.

"I'm drinkin' to your da, Tommy. You must have room in your stomach for a little more beer if I'm drinkin' to your da."

Josephine's footsteps came creaking down the back stairs.

Tom Tracy sat up straight, touched his mug to Starr's, and said, "To the memory of the man who told me to come to America and make my way. . . ."

———————— 1 9 0 0 ————————

"Your da wants to see you alone, Tommy." Josephine knelt down beside her ten-year-old son. She tightened his necktie and

*straightened the strands of hair that fell across his forehead.
"Stand up tall and look him in the eye and give him the best
handshake you can. Make him proud."*

*The boy rose, took his hat in his hand, and went to the steel
door.*

*"Excuse me now, son, but you'll have to be puttin' your
arms up and leanin' yourself against the wall for a bit." The
guard was enormous, his breath smelled sweetly of porter, and
there were small crumbs of bread hanging in his mustache.*

*The boy did as he was told. The guard ran his hands down
one arm, then the other, stopping momentarily at the armpits
and the crotch.*

"All right, then. Stand easy."

*The door swung open, and Tom Tracy, with a glance back at
his mother, stepped into the Kilmainham Jail visiting room.
The door clanged shut behind him, the sound echoing like a
gunshot across the hills. The boy felt his lunch of apples and
cheese rise to his throat, then slip back to his stomach.*

*The guard outside locked the door. Another guard, inside the
room, stood against another steel door and slapped a nightstick
against the palm of his hand. The only window, too high for
anyone to look from, was barred, so that the feeble shaft of sunlight slanting through it was broken into smaller shafts that
spread little light and less warmth.*

"Over here, Tommy."

*The boy's eyes were drawn to the shadow in the corner. His
father was sitting on a bench at a long table. The voice, once as
clear and certain as the bell in the Clifden Cathedral, sounded
like the hoarse whisper of an old man.*

"Come on over, boy, and see your old da."

*The boy remembered that when his grandfather had died a
few years before, he had been afraid to approach the body laid
out in the wooden box. He had been afraid to look death in the
face, afraid to see what it had done to his grandfather, afraid
that it would somehow reach out from his grandfather's body
and grab him by the throat. But his father had offered a hand
and called gently. The boy had moved closer, and with his father, he had knelt to pray. Then he had looked into the old,
bloated face and touched the flesh as cold and lifeless as the
skin of a plucked chicken. And his fears had faded. "He's gone
to sleep now," his father had said softly. "He'll sleep until the
Resurrection, and then you'll see himself the way I knew him*

49

when I was your age, when he was as young and strong as a stallion."

Tommy Tracy felt the old fears now, except that the father who was urging him to cross the room would become, by the following day, the body laid out in the wooden box.

Then Tommy remembered his mother's words. He pulled himself up as straight as he could and went over to his father.

"Hello, Da." He took his father's hand and forced himself to look into his father's eyes.

"No touching," warned the guard.

"Let me feel your hand."

People said that Tommy Tracy was the image of his father, but Jack Tracy had grown old in four months. His powerful body had shrunk. His clear eyes had clouded. And his complexion had gone as gray as his prison shirt.

"You look fine, boy. You've grown." He stood and threw his arms roughly around his son.

"No touching," repeated the guard.

"He's my son. I'll hold him if I want," answered Jack Tracy, "and if you come a step closer, I'll take that stick away from you and play 'Lillibulero' with it on your skull."

Jack Tracy winked at his son and told him to sit. For a moment, the boy's fears disappeared. He felt his father's strength, and once more, he found it easy to be strong.

They talked of life at home, of little Johnny and his first efforts at speech, of salmon fishing and turf-cutting, and then Tommy said that he had been making a novena at St. Brendan's.

"What for?"

"For you." The boy felt his chin weakening. He bit his lip and looked into his father's eyes.

"For the repose of my soul?"

Tommy nodded.

"Well, son, don't be too worried about that. Father Breen'll be here this afternoon to hear my confession, and I don't guess I'll be sinnin' any tonight." Jack Tracy brought a finger to his eye and wiped at the corner, trying to slip away the tear as though it were nothing but a cinder of peat.

"I've been praying that you'd be comfortable here too, Da."

Jack Tracy managed to laugh as he looked around at the brown walls and peeling paint and gave himself a few more moments to blink back the tears. "This place is like home to me,

Tommy. After the Fenian rising of '67, I got to spend ten lovely years here."

Tommy Tracy looked down at his hands, and with his right thumbnail, he began to dig dirt from under the fingernails of his left hand.

"Kilmainham Jail is where most old Fenians end up, son," said Jack, "and once a Fenian, always a Fenian."

His cousin Padr'ic had taught Tommy to take three deep breaths when he was about to cry after a lost fight or a fall from a horse. Tommy concentrated very hard on his breathing, then looked at his father. "Logan O'Leary's been sayin' some terrible things about you, Da. And so's his boy Donal."

"And that bruise on your cheek comes from a fight with Donal?"

Tommy brought his hand to his face.

"Did you win, son?"

"I never lose, Da . . . 'cept with cousin Padr'ic."

"Have you seen him lately?"

"Nobody's seen him much since the trial."

Jack Tracy ran his hand back and forth across his chin. "Don't be fightin' with Padr'ic. And don't be keepin' company with him, either."

Tommy shrugged. "What about Donal O'Leary?"

"Oh, I suppose you'll have to fight him sometimes, but remember. What he says about me is true." Jack Tracy put his hands on his son's shoulders. "I killed Donal's Uncle Liam and Jamie Hamilton, too, just like they say."

Tommy looked his father in the eye. "Were you an informer? Donal called you an informer and that's why I fought him."

"Do you believe that about your father?"

Tommy shook his head.

Jack drew the boy as close as the table would allow. "Liam O'Leary and Jamie Hamilton were on their way to do the stupidest deed that's ever been done in Ireland, Tommy . . . kill the queen herself. I did it to stop them."

"But Donal says his uncle was fightin' for Ireland and he went to you because you were a Fenian and fought yourself."

"The days of the Fenians are comin' to an end, Tommy. If we use our brains, we can win with politics. Parnell proved that. If you want to help Ireland, run for MP. Don't go killin' the most popular little woman in history, because you'll destroy the future right along with her."

Tommy looked at his hands and dug at his fingernails and took three more deep breaths. "Then why do you want us to go to America?"

"Tommy," said Jack Tracy evenly, "you know the truth about me. But if you stay in Dunslea, you'll have a bitter time of it. The Protestants, like our friend the magistrate, they'll hate you because they convicted your old da of conspirin' to kill the queen. And your own kind, they'll be hatin' you because they think your da was an informer."

"But I love Dunslea."

"In Ireland, Tommy, we don't ever bury the past and let the grass grow over the plot. We've the terrible habit of leavin' it out in the sun, where it rots till it's nothin' but a bleached skeleton, remindin' us every day of things we'd do better to forget. You might try to bury me, son, but there's others who'll keep diggin' at the bones."

Tommy Tracy worked one thumbnail under the other. He scraped away the dirt that his mother had missed that morning. He dug into the quick. He brought the blood oozing to the surface and watched it spread under the nail. "Don't let them hang you, Da, please."

Jack Tracy stood and swept his son into his arms. The guard took a step toward them but stopped when Jack Tracy glared. Then the father sat back in his corner and turned his son toward the wall so the guard would not see the tears, and he let the boy cry out all of his pain.

"It'll be all right, son," he whispered, and his huge, rough hands stroked the boy's cheek. "Go to America, to Uncle Martin's. Go and start fresh."

"I don't want to go to America." Tommy was crying uncontrollably now, trying in vain to take steady, deep breaths, succeeding only in swallowing more fuel for his tears.

"Before too long, all the Irish who've gone there and gone into politics, they'll make it the best country in the world, and then the Brits'll have to listen, by Jesus, when a smart young American born in Dunslea stands up in Congress and says it's high time the Irish had a chance to make their own mistakes for themselves, high time they had Home Rule."

"Don't make me go."

"It's . . ." Jack Tracy wiped a sleeve across his eyes, then spoke as though he were telling his son to milk the cows. "It's my last request."

52

Jack Tracy pulled his son's face to his, and the boy cried until there were no tears left and the salt had dried on his lips. Then for long past the fifteen minutes, Jack Tracy stroked his son's soft face and Tommy Tracy for the last time breathed the familiar, comforting smell of his father's body.

4

"Remember, Man, that thou art dust and unto dust thou shalt return." Father Sean O'Fearna placed his fingertips on the open pages of the gospel, as though balancing his weight on the book. "With these words, we began last Wednesday the most solemn and holy time on the church calendar. The blessed palms from last year's Holy Week, the green, fresh garlands that welcomed Christ to the city of his death and the scene of his resurrection, were burned down to black ash . . ."

He spoke without notes. His homily for the first Sunday of Lent was one of his simplest and most pointed, perhaps because the application of the ashes was among the simplest and most pointed of the church's symbols, far easier to understand or explain than the mystery of the Eucharist.

" . . . to remind us that all is fleeting save faith and what flows from it."

He was saying the seven o'clock Mass this Sunday morning, and even during the sermon, the stragglers were still slipping in at the rear of the church, sliding into the back benches, and blessing themselves hastily. Once he would have stopped his sermon to berate them for their disrespect, or he would have stared until all the righteous souls in the rest of the church turned to stare as well. But if, in his priesthood, Sean O'Fearna had learned little more about God than he knew on his first day in the seminary, he had learned much about the frailties of the preacher and his people. And while he still considered the latecomer an affront to God and to his own eloquence, he had learned that tolerance could salve the faithful more surely than zeal, and a welcoming smile during the sermon could say more than the eloquence of Aquinas.

"When the priest makes the Sign of the Cross on your forehead, you should be reminded, whether your faith is strong or weak, of what your body will one day become. It is at that moment that the weak among you have the best chance to embrace Christ's promise, because the alternative is etched on your face for all to see. And it is at that moment that the faithful among you know that these six weeks of sacrifice will be six weeks well spent."

And Sean O'Fearna was finished: simple, brief, eloquent.

"In the name of the Father, and of the Son, and of the Holy Ghost . . ." His hand stopped. A wave of heat rose from his alb to the crown of his head. He had tried somehow to put the previous day out of his mind. He had prayed that Starr and the Brits would go away and leave him in peace. But he could not mistake the black mustache, the square body, and the steady gaze. The Brit was sitting on the left side of the church, a row behind the Ryan sisters.

In the eighteen hours since the Irishman first appeared, Sean O'Fearna had lied several times, misled a young boy, and aided someone who, according to the newspaper reports, might have committed murder a short time later. Now that a rebel had stared through his confessional window, the priest's courage had faded, along with his confidence in rebellion. If British agents were tracking rebels in Boston, what hope could the rebels of Ireland have?

He made the Sign of the Cross and tried to get on with the Mass.

The British agent named Hugh Dawson pulled out a half-dollar for the collection. He could not be certain that the priest or the little boy knew Padraic Starr. But for the moment, they were his only link to what had happened inside the church the day before.

Dawson was now alone in Boston. He had lost his partner and his quarry, and was sitting like a shadow on a priest's conscience, because he could think of nothing better. Although he was a Belfast Presbyterian, he dropped his coin in the Catholic collection basket and prayed that Padraic Starr would show himself soon.

Dawson had cabled a report to the office of British Naval Attaché Guy Gaunt, the chief British intelligence operative in the United States. It was forwarded to Room 40 of the Admiralty Building in London, nerve center of the British Secret Service. From there, it had been relayed to the office of Major General L. B. Friend, Competent Military Authority for Ireland, at Dublin

Castle. The cable now sat on the desk of Friend's secretary, Lieutenant Ian Lambert-Jones.

On a Sunday morning in March, with the streets of Dublin deserted, with the mist covering the low buildings along Wellington Quay like a film of tears, with the River Liffey flowing as slow and gray as sadness itself, Ian Lambert-Jones often wondered why Henry II had ever crossed the Irish Sea in the first place.

Up ahead, a ragged band of men was marching. The leader was calling out cadences, like a drill sergeant, while the others tried vainly to keep step. They wore rough tweeds and woolens, scally caps and fedoras, a few wore the belted raincoats favored by officers in trenches, and a few more paraded in the green tunics, bush hats, and white belts of the Irish Citizen Army. They carried .22 caliber bird guns, German Mauser rifles run ashore at Howth in 1914, and pieces of wood whittled into the shape of weapons.

They were the Irish Volunteers, and according to the estimates of Crimes Branch Special, there were thirteen thousand of them, forming a civilian army within the southern twenty-six counties, ostensibly a militia to protect Ireland from German invasion, but in reality a rebel force ready to fight king, country, and the Ulster Volunteers of the north, should the issue of Home Rule be settled by the partitioning of Ireland. And they, as much as the mist and gloom, caused Ian Lambert-Jones to curse this island and his latest assignment.

"Avoid any incident," the undersecretary's directive had said. "By allowing the Volunteers to drill in the open, without interference, we lessen their importance, making of them a minor nuisance, something that must be tolerated, rather than a group of brave revolutionaries waiting to seize the moment and the nation itself."

Foolishness. These slackers mocked their Irish brothers and cousins, who died bravely each day on the Western Front. And Ian Lambert-Jones had resolved to stop them. That was why he was hurrying to his office on a Sunday morning.

Dublin Castle was the great stone heart of England's rule in Ireland, a twelfth-century battlement built by Henry II to defend against Irish kings, and by 1916, the seat of the viceregal government. A collection of Georgian brick buildings and quadrangles had risen around the original walls, and the castle now resembled nothing so much as a venerable old public school somewhere in the Midlands.

The guard at the gate was a member of the Royal Irish Constabulary, grown too old to do anything but check passes and turn keys. Lambert-Jones saluted him and limped across the upper yard, through the south crossblock, to the Gunner's Tower, the oldest part of the castle.

The cable was stamped URGENT. Lambert-Jones read it twice before taking off his coat.

11 MARCH 1916

DUNDEE IS DEAD STOP KILLED WHILE IN PURSUIT OF STARR STOP STARR IS AT LARGE COMMA AWARE OF SURVEILLANCE COMMA IN CONTACT WITH AMERICAN ASSISTANCE STOP WILL ATTEMPT TO REESTABLISH CONTACT COMMA DETERMINE AMERICAN SOURCES COMMA AND LEARN OBJECTIVES STOP DO NOT SUSPECT CLAN NA GAEL COMMA HIBERNIANS OR UNITED IRISH LEAGUE STOP STARR SEEMS TO BE INDEPENDENT STOP

Lambert-Jones cursed to himself, then picked up Starr's intelligence dossier, which had been on his desk for several days. He had requested the surveillance on Starr, and because he wrote his requests over General Friend's signature, they received attention.

He opened the dossier. Starr's photograph was affixed to the top sheet, which contained statistics and biographical sketch:

NAME: Padraic Liam Starr

DATE OF BIRTH: 15 December 1884

PLACE OF BIRTH: Dunslea, County Galway

HEIGHT: 6'0" WEIGHT: 14 stone

HAIR: Red EYES: Blue

ADDRESS: None

FATHER'S NAME: Sean Liam Starr (19 June 1865–13 January 1890)

MOTHER'S MAIDEN NAME: Maureen Tracy Mahoney (2 April 1868–12 March 1904)

BIOGRAPHICAL INFORMATION: Grew up in County Galway, in town of Dunslea. No siblings. Father a fisherman lost at sea. After mother's death, left Dunslea, drifted eventually to Belfast, returned each summer to work Dunslea fishing fleet. By age of eighteen, linked to rebel organizations. Known to have been engaged in 1914 to young Belfast woman (name not available) who died in munitions-factory accident, Belfast, 1915. Woman was believed to be Protestant.

30 September 1914: Enlisted in Connaught Rangers.

22 March 1915: Fought valiantly during action near Neuve-Chapelle . . .

And Ian Lambert-Jones remembered. The day was sunny and clear and surprisingly warm for March, and it had been obvious since early morning that the attack had failed. The British spirit had been broken by the German artillery, their line shattered by the German counterattack. In Lambert-Jones's section, five mixed companies of Connaught Rangers and Royal Dublin Fusiliers had fought and fallen back, first through the woods on the north, then across the bridge and through the village that the spring rains had turned to mud.

Lambert-Jones and a company of volunteers had stayed behind to hold the bridge for the rearguard. The bridge was made of wood, no wider than two donkey carts. It spanned a stream that in spring was swift and deep, and Lambert-Jones thought it would be a good place to make a stand.

He dug his men in on the north side, so that the bank would protect them when the rearguard broke from the woods. He planned to pour covering fire from fifty rifles, then pull his men back and blow up the bridge.

However, the young lieutenant, fresh from Sandhurst, blundered that day. He believed that the village behind him was deserted, and he did not secure the buildings along the south bank. He was turning to his sergeant to give an order when his sergeant's head blew off.

Lambert-Jones dropped to his stomach. And the north bank was slashed by bullets. He wiped blood and brain matter from his eyes and saw the men of his command disintegrating before him. Two German machine guns had slipped into position in buildings along the quay and now commanded the bridge and the woods and everything in between.

Lambert-Jones and the two dozen men still alive scrambled for cover under the bridge. He ordered four men to fire, and all four were shredded. He ordered his marksmen to try to fire from under the bridge, but they could not see the targets. His men were trapped, and the guns were beginning to tear methodically at the pilings and planks of the bridge.

Ian Lambert-Jones looked at the frightened faces of men who had endured rolling barrages and blind charges across fields of barbed wire. He could think of nothing. Then he heard the sound of the rearguard engaging the German infantry. In a few minutes, brave men would be crushed between the hammer and the anvil, all because of his blunder.

He called for volunteers and led a five-man charge at the guns. For four, it was courageous suicide. But the shot that smashed into Lambert-Jones's leg lifted him into the air and threw him over the bridge railing. For a moment, he thought that his life had ended, and in the cool peace of the river, he did not despair. Then he burst to the surface and gasped. The guns tore at him, but the current caught him and pulled him under the bridge. He reached for one of the pilings, but he had no strength. He snatched for the hand of one of his soldiers, but he could not stretch far enough. He was swept from under the bridge, and the guns began to clatter again. Then a pair of powerful hands grabbed him by the collar and pulled him back.

He screamed that his leg was shattered.

"Better your leg than your head." A big red-headed private tied a belt around the leg to slow the bleeding. Then he said, in a quiet voice, "Enough of this," and stripped off his tunic.

He commanded the corporal crouched beside him to fill a knapsack with Miller bombs, then he waded into the water, with the bridge above him for cover and one hand in the air to keep the sack of bombs dry. In the middle of the stream, the current caught him and pulled him out from under the bridge. The water began to dance with shellburst splashes, and he was hit once, a grazing shot in the scalp. His forehead turned red with the blood, but he kept the knapsack above his head and screamed for covering fire.

At the sound of his voice, men who had cowered under the bridge forever broke into the sunshine and fired. Half of them fell, but the Irishman reached the south bank with his body intact and his bombs dry. For a time, he lay in a place where the guns could not depress to take aim on him. He wiped the blood from his eyes. He took several long breaths. Then he took out one of the bombs, pulled the pin, and raised his head above the river-bank.

The ground around him came to life, as though machine-gun

bullets were seeds of dust blossoming the instant they were sown. But by some miracle, the Irishman was not struck.

Someone beneath the bridge muttered, "It ain't his time, Lieutenant. Ain't his time."

He flung the bomb. It exploded in a window on the second story as he smashed through a window on the first. Then there was another explosion, muffled and distant. Dust blew out of the windows and roof joists, and for a moment, both guns were silent. Smoke drifted on the breeze. Shadows danced across the bridge and dissolved in the spring sky. Then the rearguard broke from the woods and the second gun began to clatter again, this time pouring its fire five hundred yards beyond the bridge. A soldier dropped at the edge of the woods, then another.

Then, abruptly, the second gun stopped. No one saw the Irishman run from one building to the next. No one knew if he had even survived the explosion of his own bombs. But two German bodies dropped from the window, and Padraic Starr appeared, holding a bloody knife for all to see.

"Take your positions and hold them," he shouted, and the men on the north bank cheered.

Lambert-Jones received a citation for valor in a London hospital shortly after, but he had never seen such bravery as the Irishman displayed that day.

30 April: Starr receives the Victoria Cross for conspicuous valor. Promoted to corporal.

10 May: Joins review of Irish VC winners in Dublin.

11 June: Boards steamer in Dublin to return to Front, and disappears.

19 September: Unconfirmed report places him in Munich, in company of Sir Roger Casement, traitor who is attempting to organize captured Irish soldiers to fight alongside Germans. Throughout autumn, further reports, unconfirmed, of Starr in Belfast, Dublin, County Kerry. Rumor also places him, for a time, in secret residence at St. Edna's, private school where Padraic Pearse, poet and rebel agitator, is master.

10 February 1916:   Plainclothesman from Crimes Branch Special sees Starr on night train to Clifden, County Galway. RIC is alerted, but Starr eludes them and is not seen again.

5 *March:* Purser of Cunard liner *Carpathia* recognizes Starr in steerage.

8 *March:* Agents H. Dawson and J. Dundee alerted to Starr's arrival in Boston, under assumed name, on or about 11 March. Agents are ordered to trail Starr and attempt to discern his reasons for American trip, his possible American contacts, before requesting arrest by American authorities.

Lambert-Jones took out a pencil and added another entry: "11 March: J. Dundee killed while in pursuit of Padraic Starr."

Then he looked at the photograph, into the eyes of the man who saved his life: Padraic Starr, in corporal's uniform, Connaught Rangers, the Victoria Cross around his neck. If not for that medal and all that it represented, Starr would have been forgotten the day that he disappeared from the front. But his conduct in the action near Neuve-Chapelle had made him a hero, while the reports of his dalliance with rebel agitators and his appearance in Munich (which Lambert-Jones doubted) had made him a traitor. And no man was more dangerous than the hero who turned against the flag.

Starr was smiling in the photograph; his eyes were clear and his gaze was steady. Lambert-Jones had seen photographs of the other rebel leaders—MacNeill, Pearse, and the rest—and they all resembled ancient Irish monks crusading for freedom in 1916, rising against the Cromwell who had raped their monasteries, taken their land, and outlawed their faith. None frightened him as Starr did, however, because even in a photograph, Starr had something that the others lacked.

He did not need a political position or the anger of a Catholic God to rouse support. He simply had to call for cover, as he had done that day at the bridge, and strangers would risk their lives.

Lambert-Jones wrote out a cable to Room 40, requesting the rotation of another agent to Boston, then he wrote to the inspector general of the Royal Irish Constabulary, requesting information on Starr relatives who had migrated from Dunslea to the city of Boston. Such information might be impossible to come by and useless if available, but Ian Lambert-Jones believed that Ireland was about to explode, and somehow, Starr was one of the fuses.

5

*T*om Tracy arrived at City Hall a few minutes before noon. Four inches of fresh snow covered the six inches already on the lawn, and the statue of Ben Franklin wore a new white cap and mantle.

James Michael Curley, the mayor of Boston, was standing by one of the windows. His hands were clasped behind his back, his eyes fixed on Franklin's head. His lower lip, which could pout or pick a fight without speaking a syllable, seemed to be at rest, as though his face were trying to keep the sabbath holy while the rest of him seethed.

"Good morning, Tommy." The mayor did not turn around.

"Good morning, your honor." Tracy quietly took a seat on the sofa.

Surrounding him were the bosses from the Irish wards, along with Curley's captains from the South End, South Boston, and Roxbury. Half of the men in the room were staunch Curley supporters, one was neutral, and the rest were sworn enemies, which was about the average in any room where politicians gathered around the mayor.

"Your honor," said Standish Willcox, "I think that gives us a quorum." Willcox was the mayor's personal secretary, a man of impeccable manners and patrician demeanor, who knew more about the social graces, boasted Curley, than all the Pratts in Boston.

"My deepest apologies, gentlemen, for dragging you in here on a Sunday when you should be at home with your families." James Michael Curley spoke in a resonant voice that he had managed to lower by nearly an octave since first entering public life. And his accent, over the years, had become a careful mixture of all Boston's accents, from the broad *a* and rolling rhythm of the Harvard Brahmin to the brogue of the latest immigrant. No one in Boston sounded quite like James Michael Curley, but it was his genius, thought Tracy, that most people thought they could hear their own kind when Curley spoke.

"I know there may be a few roast beefs drying up in a few ovens around town, and for that I apologize as well."

"Can we get on with this?" Smilin' Jim Donovan stood in a

corner. "We're so damned worried about Sunday dinner, I'd like to go home and eat mine."

"Don't you mean *drink* it?" said Sticker McNulty.

"Gentlemen, please," said Standish Willcox. "Save the insults for political rallies."

Tom Tracy had learned a great deal since graduating from Boston College, and most of his education had come in this office, with its mahogany paneling, high windows, and history of high ideals. Once, it had been the province of old-family Protestant Republicans. Now, whenever the Irish mayor met here with the Irish bosses, Tom Tracy was reminded of an old maxim: If the Irish had no one else to fight, they fought with each other.

The mayor said, "I assume you've all read the newspapers this morning."

"And he don't mean Mutt 'n' Jeff, either," said Sticker Mc-Nulty, a former firefighter on disability pension, although no one knew what his disability was, outside of a weakness for craps and New York chorus girls.

"What I mean," said the mayor, smiling indulgently at Sticker, "is the story you'll find on page one or two of every Sunday edition. It concerns the murder and apparent robbery of an Englishman at Quincy Market yesterday."

"So what?" said Donovan.

"The killer may be hiding in one of your wards," answered Curley. "He has to be found."

"I believe we have a police force for these things," said the man who sat in the corner, his hands folded across his huge paunch, his bald head shining in the glare of the snow-reflected sun. He was Martin Lomasney, the ward boss from the West End, also known, for both his looks and influence, as the Mahatma.

"The police are on it," said Curley evenly. "But I want to know what they're saying on the street about armed Englishmen getting hung on meat hooks in Boston."

"The papers didn't say he was armed." Donovan puffed on his cigar.

"We're trying to keep it away from the press," said Willcox. "He was a British trade representative, licensed to carry a side-arm because he occasionally carried large sums of cash. He was found with an empty holster."

"We think he's a British agent," added Curley.

"So what?" said Donovan. "We got German agents all over town. The Krauts set up an office right on Milk Street, used it as home base to blow up half of Canada, and Boston's finest still needed a bunch of federal agents to figure out what in the hell was goin' on down there."

"Can the palaver, Jim." The tone of Curley's voice did not change, but his lower lip fluttered like a small-craft warning. "Because we've *all* got a problem here."

"So what is it?" demanded Donovan.

"According to the one eyewitness we have," explained Willcox, "the Englishman was chasing an Irish lad."

The mayor glanced at Tracy and Tracy nodded, the usual exchange whenever the mayor mentioned the Irish in Tracy's presence. Because he had been born in Ireland, Tracy's polite little nod expressed unspoken wisdom in matters Irish. There were times, however, and this Sunday morning was one of them, when Tom Tracy did not know why he was nodding and felt more like the mayor's trained horse than his trusted lieutenant.

"At the moment," said Standish Willcox, "we're trying to keep his nationality quiet as well. The only eyewitness was an old butcher born in Kilkenny. He said he didn't get much of a look at the guy, then he described where every bit of his clothing came from . . . white Donegal wool sweater, scally cap of County Clare tweed, rust-red hair, and the hobnail boots of a Galway potato farmer."

Curley glanced at Tracy again, but Tracy did not notice the mayor or nod. He sat as still as a rock fence. He already recalled that Starr's hat was tweed, his hair was rust-red, his boots from Galway. He was trying now to remember the color of his sweater.

"Did this butcher talk to the killer?" asked Denny Morrissey.

"No," answered Willcox. "The Englishman cornered him and said a few things, then the killer slashed his throat and stuck him in the chest for good measure."

Curley sat back on the edge of the desk and looked at Tom Tracy. His lower lip drew the rest of his face into a smile. "What'll the Irish voters say if we arrest a Galway man for killing an Englishman?"

Tracy did not look away. He had learned from the mayor himself to meet a man's gaze, even when the eyes were the mayor's own—calm, inquisitive, demanding—small eyes, set so far apart that some people believed Curley could see around corners.

"First off, your honor . . ." Tracy raised his voice and sat up straighter and tried to seem calm in spite of his panic. "First off, half the guys in Boston dress like they're from County Galway, and almost as many sound that way."

This time, it was Curley who nodded.

Tracy raised his voice a bit more. "Beyond that, half the Irish in Boston think of the English as villains, no matter what they do."

Curley nodded again.

Tracy did not know where his thoughts were taking him, but he was trying to frame them like one of the syllogisms that the Jesuits had taught him in high school. Say something that sounds logical, even if it isn't, and you'll seem to know what you're talking about. "And when an Irishman kills an Englishman," he continued, "there'll always be people who see it as part of the ancient struggle, even if the Irishman's nothing but a pickpocket." Tracy sat back and folded his arms so his hands would not shake.

The radiators began to bang as steam rose from the boilers below. Smilin' Jim Donovan coughed and spat into an urn. Denny Morrissey shifted his weight on the cushion beside Tracy. The mayor warned him against passing wind, and Sticker McNulty laughed like a stable mule.

Then the mayor turned to Tracy once more. "And?"

Tracy could think of nothing else.

"Tommy's right," said Denny Morrissey. "String up an Irishman over somethin' like this, there'll be hell to pay with the voters."

"If he's an Irish rebel and he got away," announced Donovan, "'I say good for him and let's all go home."

"No." Curley slammed a hand on his desk. "We have to go after him. It's the law. Plain and simple."

"A noble position, your honor," said Martin Lomasney.

"Yeah, and if he's innocent," said Sticker McNulty, "he might even get off."

"If he's got the right friends," said Martin Lomasney, "he'll get off even if he's not innocent."

Curley hooked his fingers into his vest pockets. "When we catch him, I want to find out who his friends are."

Tracy heard the steam hissing from the radiator valves and felt his face beginning to burn.

"If he's a rebel," said Curley, "he can be sure to have friends in the Clan na Gael or the Hibernians—"

"I know the Hibernians inside out," offered Denny Morrissey.

"—and if he's from Galway, he'll probably know people in the Friendly Galway Society, too."

64

"And we'd all be carryin' hods if it wasn't for them groups gettin' out the vote," said Smilin' Jim Donovan.

"Absolutely," added Martin Lomasney.

"So what do we do if we find one of them hidin' a rebel?" asked Donovan.

Standish Willcox stopped writing. "We see that he's arrested before the federal agents find him."

"The death of foreign nationals is their business," said Curley. "We should be hearing from the feds in the morning. I'd prefer our own police to catch him and get the credit, then we do whatever we can to make this look like the fault of British agents on American soil."

"The Brits'll deny it from here to Victoria Station," said Denny Morrissey.

"I'm not worried about the Brits. I simply want our constituents to know that we're all pro-Irish. We belong to their groups and we support the cause. Then we remind them"—Curley made a fist with his right hand and slammed it into his left palm, as he always did when he reached the climax of his speech—"that we're Americans first and Irishmen second. We have laws, and we don't like to be caught with our pants down, which is where something like this puts us."

Smilin' Jim Donovan took several puffs of his cigar. "The mayor's worried about his tax bill, gentlemen. That's what this is all about."

Curley turned to Donovan and worked his lower lip back and forth, the way some men spit on their hands before a fight.

"If we catch this guy and he hangs, the voters hang us in November," said Donovan. "If we don't put on a big show of upholding the law, the Yankee Protestants hang us in the press. A nice smelly scandal and the Republicans vote down the tax increase."

Curley folded his arms. "They're likely to vote it down anyway."

Tom Tracy tried to laugh. "You've never been too worried about the Yankee Protestants before, Mr. Mayor."

"I always worry about them, Tommy," said Curley. "Just like I worry about the Italians and the Jews and the Lithuanians. I worry *more* about them because they were here first. We may try to break their balls when we get the chance, but we still have to do business with them. That's politics, and that's what we practice in this city, politics"—Curley slapped his hand on his desk—"not rebellion."

"Then let's play politics." Smilin' Jim Donovan dropped his cigar into the urn. "What's in it for the City Council if we get the word out on this guy and still manage to keep down the tempers in the wards?"

With a perfectly straight face, Standish Willcox said, "The gratitude of the people of Boston."

Smilin' Jim Donovan smiled. It was not sunniness of personality that earned him his nickname, but rather his talent for using a smile to play whatever tune he needed, to make it leer or laugh, to turn it sympathetic or twist it as scornfully as he did now.

James Michael Curley jammed his thumbs into his vest pockets once more and rocked back and forth on his heels, his favorite stance when lecturing the voters. "If you do us a favor, Jimmy, you know for sure we won't forget it."

Tracy saw the look that passed between the mayor and his adversary. A promise, of some sort, was made.

Donovan's smile changed in tone if not in width. "I know I can take the mayor at his word."

"And the mayor can rely on us." Sticker McNulty jumped up and pumped Curley's hand as though the God of Patronage himself had given Sticker a lifelong contract to do whatever he had been doing since he fell from the fire wagon. "We'll let them know that we're all Americans here and we don't want to get our things caught in our zipper."

With those words of wisdom, the mayor adjourned the meeting.

Although he wanted to go home and grab his cousin and demand a few answers, Tom Tracy remained to chat with the mayor, as he always did after meetings, while Standish Willcox finished his notes and Smilin' Jim Donovan lingered to light a cigar.

The wrapper came off, a match flared, and Donovan looked at Curley. "Did you hear about the new hunting license? The one they're giving out at the start of the asshole season?"

Tracy smiled. "You're just jealous, Jim, because no one needs a license to hunt ward bosses."

Cigar smoke billowed around Donovan. "You said, your honor, that you're always worried about the Italians and the Jews and the Yankee Protestants."

"I also cover my back around certain Irishmen."

"Well, your boy here ought to be one of them."

Tracy brushed a piece of lint off his sleeve and pulled on his cuffs.

"Last night, he was kissin' the ass of one of the Pratts."

Curley's stare fell upon Tom Tracy. "Why?"

"I was following your orders," answered Tracy, "taking care of a constituent before anyone else got the chance. You've said yourself you'd love to have a Pratt or a Cabot on your side in this tax fight."

Curley nodded. "So I did. You're a good student."

"When you're done congratulatin' him over that, ask him if he really loves this girl he's been seein', or if he's just tryin' to line up the Jewish vote."

Curley looked at Tracy. "Jewish vote?"

"Avram Levka's girl." Donovan started to leave, then stopped, like the seasoned actor he was. "If you think the voters'll set fire to your pants when we hang an Irish rebel, wait'll you see what they do when the secretary of the Tammany Club marries a Jew."

Curley's lower lip worked itself back and forth several times.

"In any case," Donovan said, "you don't have to worry about the Jews or the Pratts anymore. Tommy's doin' it for you."

"Get out," snapped Curley, but Donovan was already on his way down the stairs.

Curley pivoted to Tracy. "Why didn't I know about this?"

"It may not be any of your business," said Standish Willcox. "After all, you're not his father."

"I'm close enough. And if he's giving Donovan ammunition to shoot at me, I want to know about it so I can duck." Curley turned back to Tracy, and in the way that he could change his mood in a moment, he said, "Is she pretty?"

Tracy nodded.

"Are you in love with her?"

Tracy shrugged, then shook his head.

"What's the matter with the nice Irish girls?"

Tracy shrugged again.

Curley looked at Willcox. "My man in South End, and all he can do is hunch his shoulders like Quasimodo. No wonder Donovan's got control down there."

"He may be trying to tell you that the nice Irish girls are *too* nice," said Willcox.

"I just like her," said Tracy.

"Well, don't marry her." The mayor jabbed his finger at Tracy. "The Jews and the Irish are on the same side in a lot of things around here, Tommy. We mix in business and we mix in politics, but we don't mix in romance."

"I'm not planning to marry her, your honor."

"Then what are your intentions?"

"Now you're starting to sound like the *girl's* father," said Willcox.

"Nothing wrong with that. Levka's a good man. I'm proud to break bread with him." Curley went over to Tracy and stood above him. "He'll be a fine ally if you're running against some Protestant Republican in a statewide election, but he'll do you no good at all as a father-in-law in an Irish ward."

"We've all known good marriages between Irish and Jews," said Willcox.

"And who was the last Irishman to get himself elected with a Jewish wife?" The mayor turned back to Tracy. "The only kid in your generation who's got half your chance to make it in politics is Pat Kennedy's boy. Fortunately for you, he's more interested in running banks than running for office. But take a lesson from him, Tommy. When it comes time to take a wife, get yourself the best-born Irish girl you can find."

"Yes, your honor," said Tracy.

"But if you find that you love this Jewish girl, forget what I've just said." Curley's expression softened. "With a Jewish father-in-law, you ought to do damn well in business."

"But it's not business I'm interested in. It's politics."

In the midday sunshine, the snow had begun to melt, trickling into downspouts, dripping over the edges of copper gutters, and rolling down Ben Franklin's face like a film of perspiration, or, thought Tom Tracy, a veil of tears. In ancient Rome, it was believed that when the gods were displeased, their statues would cry or bleed. Perhaps Franklin was displeased with the meeting just ended and with James Michael Curley's display of pragmatism. But pragmatism was simply good politics, and no one had been better at it than the man cast in bronze on the City Hall lawn.

Perhaps Franklin was displeased, thought Tracy, because a young student of the pragmatic art now faced two very difficult problems. One was of his own making: his attraction for Rachel Levka. The other had been created by a cousin acting in the ancient faith that blood was stronger than political ties or legal rope. Both problems sprang from a single root: the importance of the tribe. You did not offend the tribe by looking outside the circle for a mate. You risked the tribe's wrath by betraying one of its heroes.

And if you misled the tribal chieftain, you would be destroyed. In this case, the chieftain had befriended the Tracy family when he was a South End ward boss, had written letters to Boston College on behalf of Tom Tracy, had hired the young B.C. graduate to silence hecklers at his rallies, and had rewarded him after the mayoral election by making him secretary of the Tammany Club.

When Tom Tracy asked what he could give in return for such a favor, he knew the answer before Curley spoke it. *Loyalty.* Until now, Tom Tracy had always been able to deliver.

The house was empty for two hours while the family was at Mass. From the foyer, Tracy called Starr's name. No answer. He went straight to the attic. The bed was in a corner. Beside it were a washstand and chamberpot.

Tracy pulled Starr's duffel bag from under the bed and opened it. The white wool sweater was stuffed into the mouth of the bag, on top of the box containing the Victoria Cross. Tracy examined the medal again. Perfectly authentic. Beneath it were three shirts of rough cotton, one of flannel, a pair of corduroy trousers and a pair of tweed, a half-dozen brown socks rolled into balls, and a passport, issued by the British government in Dublin, 8 January 1916.

Starr's height, weight, and eye color had been recorded, but the name was Seamus O'Mahoney. There was a single entry stamp: "U.S. Customs Bureau, Boston, Massachusetts, March 11, 1916."

Tracy slipped the passport back into the bag and sank slowly onto the bed. He wiped his hands on the wool blankets to dry the sweat, then pulled out a pair of wire-rimmed glasses. He held them to his eyes. The lenses were made of clear glass, good only for disguise.

His hand struck a small, neatly tied bundle, an oily cloth wrapped around something the weight and shape of a pistol. He untied the strings, and taking care to point the barrel toward the wall, he removed the wrapping.

Some men experience an intense feeling of revulsion the first time that they hold a pistol. But the general reaction, even in the most civilized drawing rooms of the Back Bay or Merrion Square, is one of almost irresistible attraction. When a man picks up a pistol, he cannot help but grasp it, as Tracy did now, by the handle, and aim it at some imaginary target. If the weapon is well made, like this Colt revolver, he will notice how neatly the grip fits his hand. He will feel the seductive balance. He will turn his hand over and back, admiring the way the weapon looks, and he will sense the energy compacted there, as surely as a bricklayer does when he holds a good trowel.

Perhaps then he will catch a reflection of himself in a mirror or a window or his own mind's eye. He may return the gun to its box or the back of the drawer where it has been hidden. Or, like Tom Tracy, he will deny that a spirit has passed through his hands, that he has held power as neatly as he would a pint. He will hold the gun again in his palms and examine its design and markings. And he will remember that history has been changed more than once by a pistol.

The mere presence of three pistols in the back of a wagon had been Jack Tracy's undoing. And on a summer afternoon a year and a half before, in a place called Sarajevo, a man with a pistol had begun the great European madness.

Padraic Starr had seen the madness. He had been part of it. Tracy stared at his pistol and wondered if Starr had come to Boston to escape . . . or bring the madness with him.

Suddenly, something very cold and very sharp was pricking in his ear.

"Don't move."

"I didn't hear you come up."

"Maybe you'd like me to be cleanin' out the wax, then." Padraic Starr held his knife so that the tip poked at the flesh.

"You haven't been straight with me, Padr'ic."

"Straight begins at home, Tommy, where we don't go pickin' through the guest's goods when the guest's off seein' the sights."

Tracy slipped the pistol from his lap and pointed it at Starr's boot. "Take the knife out of my ear, Padr'ic, or I'll blow your toes off."

"Standoff ended." Starr twisted his fingers and the knife disappeared.

Tracy threw the gun on the bed and turned. "An Irishman who looked a lot like you killed some Brit yesterday at the Quincy Market."

70

Starr leaned against a roof support.

"You carry a forged passport, phony glasses, a loaded gun—"

"A sharp knife." Starr took out a handkerchief.

Tracy felt the blood running down his earlobe. He snatched the handkerchief and daubed at his ear. "You're no tourist."

Starr shook his head.

"Then you're a deserter."

"Deserter in one army, soldier in another."

"What army?"

"The Irish Republican Brotherhood."

"Never heard of them."

"You will, Tommy, but when you do, I'll be a long way from Boston. I promise you."

In their boyhood together, Tracy had seen much to admire in Padraic Starr: his physical courage, his speed with his fists, his willingness to try any temptation at least once, and his ability to draw girls as poteen draws drunks. But on the wide beaches and rocky hillsides of Connemara, or the choirloft at St. Brendan's, he had never once found reason to admire Starr's sense of the truth. He saw no reason now to accept Starr's promise.

"Last night, you gave me your word that you brought no trouble for me or my family."

"That I did."

"Then why the pistol?"

"I can see a bit of trouble for myself, Tommy, if I make a wrong move. But like I told you, there'll be none for you or your family, not unless you're thinkin' it's worth it."

"I'm thinkin' about turnin' you in, unless you give me good reason not to."

Starr simply stared, his eyes wide and blank, intelligent and innocent. The goat's-eye stare, he used to call it, employed to good effect on nuns, gullible priests, aunts and uncles, and the Royal Irish Constabulary.

"If you killed a man, Padr'ic, you could become quite an embarrassment for me."

"If you turn in your own cousin, you'll become an embarrassment for yourself, Tommy. They'll say what they used to say of your old da, only this time, it'll be true."

In the uncomfortable silence that followed, both men heard the echoing sound of someone pounding on the door below.

A drop of blood slipped from Tracy's earlobe and a small red stain spread on his shirt. "Did you kill him?"

Starr took the handkerchief out of Tracy's hand and pressed it against the ear. "Hold it until it stops."

Tracy wiped the blood away and stuffed the handkerchief into his pocket. "I won't ask you again."

Starr put his foot on the bed, then dropped the knife from his sleeve into the top of his boot. "I'm going back to Dunslea, Tommy. I need guns and a ship and a few good men. We're gettin' ready to settle some old accounts, and if I remember right, there's one in Dunslea that should matter to you."

For a time, Tom Tracy could not speak. The pounding echoed through the door, across the foyer, and up the stairwell to the attic. The past had crossed the Atlantic, broken through the wall of time, and stuck a knife in his ear.

"The resident magistrate, William Clarke. You remember him."

"I remember."

"The man who did in your own da."

The pounding grew heavier.

"Whoever's down there, Tommy, it sounds like they're after breakin' in the door."

Tracy opened the window and looked down. "Who is it?"

A boy stepped back into the street and looked up. "Mr. Tracy? It's Jimmy Duggan."

"Hello, Jimmy. What can I do for you?"

"I got a message for someone named Starr. He with you?"

In the moment it took Tracy to say no, Starr crossed the attic and jumped down the stairs. When Tracy reached the foyer, Starr was reading the message and Jimmy Duggan was waiting with his hat in his hand.

"Give the young lad a tip, will you, Tommy?"

Tracy handed the boy a nickel. "Say hello to your dad, Jimmy, and be off with you." He slammed the door and turned on Starr. "I want you out of here. I don't want to know what you're doing. I don't care where you go. Just go." He ran up the stairs and came down a moment later wearing his coat and derby.

Starr was still studying the note. "It's from Father O'Fearna at Holy Trinity. He's my contact."

"The ward boss will make a novena to Our Lady of the Blessed Accessory if he finds me harboring a killer, even an Irish rebel. Now beat it, and don't give me the goat's eyes."

Starr blinked. "You remember the goat's eyes? That must mean you remember your da, too."

Tracy opened the door and the cold air rushed in.

"It's his work that I'm doin' here."

Tracy went down the stairs to the sidewalk. "It's my word to him that I'm keepin' here. Be gone when I get back."

"Are you off to see your Jewish gal?" Starr leaned against the doorjamb like the master of the house. "Danny told me all about her. She sounds fine, no matter what anybody else says."

Tracy started down the street. "I don't want to see you again, Padr'ic."

"Have you told your gal about the village of Dunslea? What about William Clarke? And the bridge where we used to fish?"

"Goodbye, Padr'ic," Tracy shouted over his shoulder.

"I'm plannin' to stand on that bridge at Easter. Listen to the sound of the gentle-runnin' river, as your da used to say. I'd be proud if you stood with me."

"So long, cousin." Then Tracy heard whistling. He recognized "The Rising of the Moon," the old rebel song. With his thumbnail, he scraped away the blood now dried on his ear. He thought of Connemara and the bridge at Dunslea.

6

onnemara. The word seemed to whisper: of streams running rich with salmon, of green hills rolling into soft gray mist, of valleys lined with fuchsias and firs, of turf piles drying in the warm summer sun, of thatched-roof cottages, of sly little men sipping poteen from their own secret stills, of rugged ponies bred for loyalty and strength, of strong, loyal people living close to the land and closer to God.

Connemara. A poetic word that did not speak of the endless rocks and the ceaseless winds, the thick fogs and icy drizzles that settled for days like a shroud upon the land, the mud-walled cabins where the thatched roofs leaked and turned the floors of the cabins to mud as well, or the barren fields where potatoes once grew in little round hills that looked now like the burial mounds of a generation.

Connemara. Where the people were strong because they needed their strength and loyal because they needed each other, where the old men made poteen because it filled the belly when there was nothing to eat and warmed the spirit when the faith could not.

The Dunslea River was born in the Connemara mountains known as the Twelve Bens, a dozen rocky peaks that rose from the landscape like the apostles of some harsh but majestic faith. The river wound west through the lonely valleys between the bens, across the upland bogs, down a rocky gorge to the sea. It traveled twenty miles, was never wider than fifteen feet, never deeper than three or four.

Whenever he crossed the bridge, Seamus Kilkeirnan stopped his bicycle and had a smoke and listened to the sound of the gentle-runnin' river. It did not matter that this afternoon he was carrying a telegram from Dublin Castle itself, addressed to the district inspector of the Royal Irish Constabulary. Seamus was seventy-one years old, and he held his own habits in the highest esteem.

The bridge stood at the juncture of Dunslea Point and the Ballinakill Peninsula, two fingers of land that stretched into the Atlantic, with hills as high as six hundred feet and as green, according to Seamus, as the robes of St. Patrick himself. At the place where the river met the sea, the bay was a mere fifty feet across. Four miles away, between the tips of the fingers, was more than a mile of blue water.

The town was named after the eleventh-century fortress that stood on the tip of Dunslea Point. The Connemara chieftain known as Bloody Sean Slea had constructed the tower and the attached chapel (even then, much violence could be justified if the name of God was invoked) to withstand attacks from other Irish tribes and marauding Northmen. It had stood through nine centuries of bloodshed, warfare, and Atlantic weather. Most of the outer buildings had fallen now to rubble, but the circular central tower, called the keep, was as solid as the day that the Northmen first rowed up the bay.

The town was built in two neat little rows that ran north and south from the bridge. The men did their business on the first floor, their families lived on the second, and turf smoke curled from every chimney. The straight square rowhouses, white-washed or pastel-painted, seemed like someone's small effort to bring order to the wildness of Connemara, while the only free-standing structures in town seemed devoted to taming the wild-ness of the inhabitants themselves. The Catholic church, St.

Brendan's, rose over the small square just south of the bridge. And on the north side of town stood the barracks house of the Royal Irish Constabulary.

Beyond the town, the cottages of fishermen and farmers leaned with the wind, and the steeper the hillsides became, the more numerous the sheep and the longer the rock fences that divided the fields.

A hundred and fifty Catholics and forty Protestants lived around Dunslea. Most of the Protestants worshiped at the New Church of Ireland in Clifden and lived in the larger homes on the north side of the bay. Most of the Catholics lived in the cottages on the south.

Seamus Kilkeirnan said there was a logic to this. "It's as simple as a peg in a hole," he would expound after a few pints in Finnerty's. "The Protestants don't want us to have nothin' we don't pay for, so they settle on Ballinakill and their houses face south to catch the winter sun, while out on the point the Catholics spend six months shiverin' in the shadows with the north wind blowin' through the front door. I'm not complainin', mind you. It's just the way things is."

He said it was a fine town nevertheless, and with a few notable exceptions, everyone got along. "After all," he was fond of saying, "if you live your life in Connemara, you've a bond with your neighbor that's as good as the Holy Chrism, even if his grandfather rode with Cromwell."

Seamus Kilkeirnan's smoke was finished. He tapped his pipe against the bridge railing, and the ashes fell into the river. He watched them swirl with the current, then he was off to deliver the telegram and tell at least three other men what it said:

> DUBLIN CASTLE
> 12 MARCH 1916
>
> INSPECTOR HAYES
>
> PLS INQUIRE AS TO IDENTITY OF ANY DUNSLEA RESIDENTS COMMA ESPECIALLY RELATIVES AND FRIENDS OF PADRIAC STARR COMMA WHO MIGHT NOW BE LIVING IN THE AMERICAN CITY OF BOSTON STOP PLS RELAY ANY INFORMATION PROMPTLY STOP
>
> NEVILLE CHAMBERLAIN
> INSPECTOR GENERAL RIC

* * *

In a shed behind a cottage on Dunslea Point, a woman named Deirdre Hamilton started a small gas generator. She did not like to use the generator, because its noise might attract the attention of a curious neighbor or a passing patrol of Royal Irish Constabulary. However, there was no electricity on the point, and lately, she needed power.

She could be found during the week at the Dunslea schoolhouse, where she was the only teacher. On Saturday mornings, she tended her sheep. On Sundays, she had what Magistrate Clarke considered the honor of riding with his family to services in Clifden. And on weekend afternoons, after she started the generator, she went into her kitchen closet, slid back the trapdoor in the ceiling, climbed the ladder into the small loft, and took the sailcloth from off the wireless. She positioned herself by the tiny window, so that no one coming from town would arrive unnoticed, and for the rest of the afternoon, she listened.

She did not attempt to create sentences from the swirl of dots and dashes, for she knew that the Royal Navy and the German U-boats laid their own sophisticated codes over the International alphabet. She was instead preparing herself to lift a single word from all the noises dancing between ship and shore and send a single word in response.

Some time in April, a ship would draw near the Bay of Dunslea, and Padraic Starr would transmit the word *Cuchulain* on a clear frequency. When she heard the name of the ancient Irish king, Deirdre Hamilton was to respond with the word *Tara* if all was clear, *Cromwell* if, for some reason, the Dunslea fishing boats could not meet the ship.

Since she was not a trained radio operator, she had been familiarizing herself with the sounds, so that she would be ready when the moment arrived. She held the headphones tight to her ears, closed her eyes, and tried to catch each letter as it was tapped out in the radio room of some British ship or German submarine.

When they discussed Deirdre Hamilton in Finnerty's Pub—and everyone was discussed in Finnerty's—Seamus Kilkeirnan would offer his opinion on her spinsterhood: "She's a fine-lookin' woman, if you like a good horse. Eyes as blue as the bay and good wide hips for carryin' the child, but when she looks at you, you first get the terrible feelin' that she's about to ask you for a lump of sugar, then you realize that she knows more than you, whether you're talkin' about the poets or the right way to cut peat. A woman like that's usually two things: so damn smart she's frightenin', and single for a long, long time."

In a country where a good horse was well appreciated, her long, thin face and prominent jaw were not entirely a drawback. However, her intelligence was forbidding enough that she had reached the age of thirty-two without a husband. Then she had shocked everyone by accepting the marriage proposal of Donal O'Leary, a Catholic fisherman four years her junior.

Donal was known for his skill with a seine net and his strong opinions about Irish freedom. But he was not the sort to study Yeats or Lady Gregory or expound on the fine writing from the young playwrights of the Gaelic Revival.

However, Seamus pointed out that she did not accept O'Leary's proposal until six months after Padraic Starr disappeared and was presumed dead. He said there was a logic to this because, from the time they were thirteen, Deirdre had loved Starr. Seamus knew the story because he made it his business to know about most things in Dunslea.

He was one of the few people who knew that shortly after Deirdre accepted Donal's proposal, Padraic Starr appeared at her door. Rebellion was on Starr's mind, however, and not romance. He revealed his plans for the rising to Deirdre, to Donal O'Leary, who led the Irish Republican Brotherhood in Dunslea, and to Seamus himself, whose love of gossip was renowned, but whose access to the Dunslea/Dublin cable traffic was invaluable.

Deirdre Hamilton was deep in concentration when she saw a shadow appear on the eaves above the trapdoor. Someone was in the broom closet. She removed the headset and reached for the revolver she carried in her skirt. The weak rung creaked on the ladder and someone started to climb.

"Who is it?"

"Don't shoot." The top of a scally cap appeared.

It was Donal's voice. She lowered the gun, and his broad, freckled face appeared in the shaft of light. At the same time, the faint aroma of fish floated across the attic.

"You'll be the death of me yet, sneakin' up on me like that."

"I was only testin' you." He boosted himself up and sat on the edge of the trap, so that his legs hung down into the kitchen. "And you passed with your colors run up, if not exactly flyin'."

"Now, what's that supposed to mean?" She turned off the transmitter and threw the sailcloth over it.

"Well, Deirdre, my darlin', I managed to come up the road,

into the kitchen, and halfway up the loft before you knew I was here."

"And if you were a constable, you'd've had your head blown off."

"But that's not what we're wantin' right now, is it? At least not until Easter."

She came over and stood above him. "I'm the strongest link in the chain, Donal. I've made no mistakes and I'll make none. I need none of your damn tests."

He reached out and wrapped a hand around her ankle. She was wearing gray woolen stockings. "No more will be given, my dear." He slid his hand along her calf and up under her skirt. "Without you, there'd be no risin' at all . . . anywhere."

"Don't be givin' me your dirty meanings, Donal O'Leary." She slapped his hand away. "Just because I'll be your wife, it doesn't mean I have to listen to your filthy talk." She went back to the little window by the transmitter. In the glass, she could see her own reflection, the little gray hairs beginning to sprout at her temples, the wrinkles around the eyes. She turned and said more gently, "I was not expecting you till the dinner hour."

"Seamus stopped at the boat a while back and told me about a cable from Dublin Castle." Donal climbed out of the trap and came over to her. "The Brits are on to Padr'ic. They want the names of all the Dunslea people who've moved to Boston in the last twenty years."

"Oh, dear." She brought her hand to her mouth and her body sagged against the window frame. "Can we warn him?"

"We don't exactly know where he is." Donal paused, and the edge of jealousy cut into his voice like a fillet knife through a salmon's belly. "Or do we?"

She lowered her hand. "We know he's in Boston. And that's *all* we know."

"Good." He put his arm around her. He was a burly man with broad shoulders, a solid big belly, and a scraggly blond beard that gave him the look of an early Norse invader. He smiled, revealing a missing canine, then he tried to kiss her.

She pulled her face away. "Stop it."

"What's wrong with a man gettin' a little kiss from his wife-to-be? A little proof of her love?"

She broke out of his embrace. "You don't need any proof, Donal, and you'll get no more than a kiss until we marry." She went over to the window on the other side of the loft. The tower of Dun Slea rose just beyond the next hill. "Now what do we do about saving Padr'ic?"

"Nothing," he said coldly.

"To start with, we name the families who've moved to Boston." She counted them off on her fingers. "The Tiernans, the Malloys, Kevin O'Hara. And of course . . . Josephine Tracy and her boys."

"He'll never stay with *them*, if he knows what's good for him."

"Jack Tracy was Starr's godfather."

"Jack Tracy was a fuckin' informer."

"Don't use that language."

Donal crossed the loft, ducking his head to avoid the roof-beams. "Jack Tracy killed my uncle and your brother. He'd inform on us if he knew what we were up to. So would his damn family."

She turned to him. "We can send cables to all those people in Boston and hope that one of them knows where he is."

"He didn't tell us where he'd be, so it's his own damn fault." Donal put his arms around her again and pulled her body against him.

She realized that there really *had* been a reason why she had accepted his proposal. He was handsome, in a rough way, he was strong, and yet he was more vulnerable than people knew.

"I want you to marry me this month. Then I won't worry about Padr'ic anymore."

"You have nothing to worry about."

"Then what's his picture doin' out on the kitchen table? All glossy and smilin', like Mickey Dazzler himself, with the Victoria Cross around his neck?"

In response, she pressed her lips to his. She did not tell him that when she was feeling lonely, she took out the photograph and an envelope of clippings about Starr and sat with them in her kitchen.

"Marry me this month," he said.

"Not before the rising."

"After the rising, my darlin' we may all be dead, shot down on Dunslea Bridge or hung by the neck in Dublin."

She had seen him like this before. For all his size and bravado, Donal O'Leary was as frightened as any man, and the surest way to restore his courage was to challenge his manhood.

"If you're afraid, drop out. Let Tim Cooney cut the cable to the RIC barracks whenever they repair it."

"I'm twenty-eight years old, Deirdre, and all I'm afraid of is goin' to me grave without havin' you." He brought his mouth down on hers again.

At first, she did not resist. She had kissed him often. Sometimes, she had enjoyed it, and usually it was enough to satisfy him. But when she tried to pull away, he would not let go.

"I want you to marry me next week."

"Let go, Donal."

While he held her with one hand, he raised her skirt and pulled down her cotton knickers with the other.

"No, Donal."

"If we can't marry before the risin', at least we can know what it's like to be man and wife."

His calloused hand scraped across her belly. She tried to close her legs together, but the hand pushed them apart and plunged down through her hair, pulling and snagging as it went.

"Stop!" She kicked at him.

"Do you love me?"

"Yes."

"More than Starr."

"Yes."

"Then show me."

"Stop it, Donal. I'll not marry an animal."

She pushed him away. His head banged against the straw thatching.

She had long prepared herself for her first sex with Donal. It would be necessary if she was to have the child she wanted. She knew that he could be rough and brutish, but for as long as she had known him, she had always been able to control him. When she was sure that he was shocked by his own behavior, she turned toward the wall and clumsily pulled up her knickers, careful not to lift her skirt and expose her thighs again.

"I'm . . . I'm sorry."

"Get out," she said with her face to the wall.

"It's just that, a young man like me, tryin' to be virtuous and all . . . it's not easy."

Still she would not look at him. "Get out."

He went back to the trapdoor. "What I did was natural, Dee. Up here, in the hot attic, alone with you. It was only natural."

"Natural for the barnyard, maybe. Not for my house." Her hand was at her mouth and her words came as a whisper.

"Deirdre . . ."

80

Finally, she looked at him.

"I'm sorry, Deirdre. I just don't want to be losin' you. If anyone tries to take you away from me, before we're married, or after, I'll kill him."

Deirdre stood for a long time in the dusty heat of the loft, she stared out at the battlement atop the ancient tower, and she thought of Padraic Starr.

She had surrendered to him there, one warm summer's night, on the stones of Dun Slea. She had loved him once. But when she thought he was dead, she had embraced her fisherman and looked to the future. Then he had come back, reviving her dreams of love and her brother's dreams of rebellion.

On the stones of Dun Slea, her brother and Liam O'Leary, a Protestant and a Catholic, had conspired to kill Victoria. In 1900, when the fires of Irish rebellion burned low, they had believed that the death of the queen would bring down British wrath like oil on embers. For help, they had gone to Jack Tracy, a Fenian, a Land Leaguer, a man who had used the gun for Irish freedom. Tracy had informed the authorities of the foolish plot, then stopped the assassins with a shotgun as they rode to the train.

Now, the fires of rebellion flamed, and Starr had come to feed them. She damned him, because she knew that the love he promised would never be fulfilled, and the rebellion might martyr them all. And she damned herself for still believing that this time, it all might work.

7

When he came out of the Scollay Square subway station, Padraic Starr was wearing wire-rimmed glasses, a brown fedora with a yellow feather in the band, and a camel's-hair chesterfield. Beneath that, he wore a gray flannel suit, blue polka-dot tie, and butterfly collar with a pearl stickpin. In a house where it was acceptable to go through a guest's duffel bag, he decided, it was perfectly all right to rifle the host's closet, especially when a change in wardrobe might confuse the police.

Following the priest's note, he went down Court Street to

Howard. He passed saloons, palmists, tattoo emporiums, and burlesque houses, but on Sunday afternoons, Scollay Square was closed, except for the alleys and doorways where men bought and women sold.

Halfway down Howard Street, Starr came to a building that looked like a grand Gothic dowager in a line of chorus girls. Starr would have tipped his hat or made a small cross on his forehead, but this was no church, in spite of the arched windows and handsome cupola. Strung across the front, a white banner proclaimed:

BURLESQUE

Always Something Going On

At street level was a marquee, in the same classical shape as the windows. It read, in permanent gilt letters, "Howard Atheneum," and beneath, on a fresh four-sheet, the announcement:

Now Playing
The Ladies of the Carnival Big Show
Starring
Top Banana Louie "the Lip" Lee
And the Most Gorgeous Gals
With the Most Gorgeous Gams
Since They Lit the First Footlights
Of Old Broadway!

A pair of sailors were reading the marquee. A bum was asleep on the steps, a bottle of wine beside him. The Old Howard, as it was known, was one of the most famous burlesque houses in America.

Starr went down an alley to a side door and stepped into the darkness. Onstage, a dozen women in tights were kicking in time, and their heels striking the stage sounded like rain hitting an empty barrel. At the piano, a little man wearing derby and vest was pounding out "Alexander's Ragtime Band," while a man in striped trousers and spats kept cadence with a cane.

"Hey, bub, we're closed," growled the bouncer, who looked like nothing more than scar tissue and knuckle in the dim light.

"Have I come to the right place for the priest?"

The bouncer pointed to the balcony.

Starr went up the side aisle to the rear of the theater and glanced back at the stage. The girls kicked, pivoted, bent over, and shook their bottoms at the empty seats.

"No! No! No!" screamed the man in the spats, driving his cane into the stage with every word.

The dancers straightened up with sudden self-consciousness, like little girls chastised for raising their dresses in front of company.

"When you wiggle your bums, wiggle to the beat. You look like cows on the way to the barn, wiggling every which way so that no one knows which way to look."

An apt description, thought Starr, of the impending rebellion. If enough rebels were moving to their own rhythms, in their own little corners of Ireland, the British wouldn't know which way to look, and at least some of them would strike through to the British vitals.

"I'm glad you could make it." Father O'Fearna was wearing a black wool overcoat and a black fedora with the brim pulled down. In the darkness of the balcony, he was almost invisible, except for the white Roman collar that caught the stagelight.

"I came to watch the girls," said Starr.

"I admit it's a strange place to be meeting a priest of a Sunday afternoon."

The balcony smelled like the stall where Starr slept for three nights after deserting the British army. And the women dancing within the box of light below looked as distant and intangible as the women he had dreamed of during those nights, the women he still dreamed about. There were two of them, both Protestants. One he had planned to marry, but a munitions-factory accident took her life. The other had hoped to marry him, and now she waited by her wireless.

"These are strange times, Father."

Onstage, the girls turned again to the empty theater and wiggled their bottoms like a dozen metronomes keeping time with the piano.

"A special ministry of mine," explained the priest. "I come here because I can't resist lost causes, like spreading virtue in a vaudeville house—"

"Or helping Ireland break free from the Brits?"

The man in the spats complimented the girls and called an

end to the rehearsal. Then the piano player announced that his friend Father O'Fearna was in the balcony if any of the girls needed a spiritual chat.

"Spiritual chat?" muttered Starr. "Is that what they're callin' it these days?"

"Spiritual, and only that." The priest drew his rosary from his left pocket and let the beads pour into his right hand.

"Why are we meeting in a burlesque house, Father?"

"Because the British agent who appeared at the seven-o'clock Mass would not think to look for us here." The priest paused. "Now, then, was it you killed the Englishman, the one in all the papers?"

Starr looked down at the dancers and injected his voice with the false lilt of the stage Irish. "D'ye think ye could be arrangin' a little . . . spiritual chat . . . between me and that third colleen from the left?"

"Killing a man is a mortal sin," said the priest gravely.

Padraic Starr gently turned the priest's hand over and took the rosary. "I killed him on the battlefield, Father. I did him a favor, because if you die on the battlefield you go to heaven, and if you kill on the battlefield, it's no sin, just line of duty. At least, that's what they told us in the trenches, before they sent us over the top."

"Why have you come to me? Why not the Clan na Gael or the Hibernians?"

"Those groups raise money and write angry letters and tell their politicians that America should help Ireland get Home Rule, and that's grand. But on Saturday nights, they're social clubs, places for big talkers who drink watery Guinness and sing sad songs and get all teary-eyed about a place they wouldn't move back to for all the jewels in the Tara brooch." Starr studied the small crucifix in the palm of his hand. "A single priest raisin' money for the cause will keep a better secret."

"Who told you I raise money for a cause?"

"A priest in Dublin. He told me to say 'six weeks and three days' in Sean O'Fearna's confessional and coffers would open."

"My coffer, as you call it, is a small charity, blessed by the cardinal, called Shoes for Ireland."

"I hear that the people of Boston have dug deep to save Irish soles . . . and to buy German rifles before the war. But then, you know all about that."

"No, I don't." The priest snatched his rosary and jammed it into his pocket. "If you want help, go see the Clan na Gael in New York."

"Well, your eminence"—Starr rolled his eyes—"the Clan's a bit busy right now, what with sendin' messages from our people in Ireland to the German embassy in Washington."

The priest took out a flask and unscrewed the cap, which he then filled with whiskey. "The Germans are helping you?"

"We've asked them for officers and a few good troops. All they've offered are weapons."

The priest handed the flask to Starr. "Ireland's got a quarter million boys fighting Germans."

Starr sipped from the flask. "Jameson's. The taste of the bogs, it is."

"It sounds to me like you're stabbin' those lads in the back."

"The lads in the trenches should turn themselves around and fight on the other side," said Starr, "and there's some think that after Easter they will."

O'Fearna drank down the two ounces of whiskey and held out the cup.

Starr filled it to the top, because every man needed a point for focus when the world began to spin around him. "Sometime before Easter, a ship will leave Germany under neutral flag, loaded with guns. It will arrive in the Bay of Tralee on Holy Thursday. Trawlers will bring the guns ashore and pass them out among the men of the west counties."

The priest drank down the whiskey.

"On Easter Sunday, during regular maneuvers, detachments of the Irish Volunteers and Irish Republican Brotherhood will take over Dublin, declare independence, then hold on while the west rises."

The lights came up again. Two men in baggy pants and the chorus girl third from the left walked onstage. One man was wearing a sandwich board that read "Rubber Balloons, 5¢." The other was holding the pages of a script, and from the elongated shape of his mouth, Starr guessed that he was Louie the Lip Lee.

"This is the best bit I ever come up with." Louie the Lip handed the woman several pages, then told the other man, "When you get your cue, walk on and say, 'Rubber balloons, rubber balloons.' "

The scene started, and for a time, the two men in the balcony watched silently. The young woman put her hand to her forehead and said, "Oh, I feel faint. It must be this hot day." And she removed her sweater, revealing a black corset.

"You surely have come to a land of plenty," whispered Starr.

"Why do you need my money?"

"I don't believe the Germans can sneak past the Royal Navy. I want to run guns to Galway at the same time."

"Oh, my," shouted the girl on the stage, "I'm still so hot. What am I to do?" She pretended to think for a moment, then pulled off her corset, revealing a well-filled camisole.

The priest took a deep breath and muttered, "Mother of God."

"She ain't that, but she'll do."

"Oh, I'm so hot." The woman performed an amateur swoon and lowered herself to the stage.

"What about Home Rule?" the priest asked. "The Brits have promised Home Rule when the war ends. Ireland gets the same kind of power the states have here. The Irish are all for it."

"It was a liberal government passed Home Rule. Now the Conservatives are in a coalition and there's Ulstermen in the cabinet and they've dreamed up somethin' called an Amendin' Bill."

"What's that?"

"It says the northern six counties won't have to join the Dublin government. They want to take Ulster away from us, and with it all our industry and all the smart Protestant civil servants who've been runnin' the damn country for six centuries. So," said Starr very softly, "to hell with Home Rule and grab for independence."

The man in the baggy pants came onto the stage and knelt next to the girl. "She's fainted. What am I to do?"

The priest took his rosary from his right pocket, dropped it into his left hand, then back to his right. "What am *I* to do?"

"I'll make it easy for you. I'll whisper a name." Starr leaned close to the priest's ear. "Charles Stewart Parnell."

Padraic Starr let the name of the Irish patriot echo through the priest's memory. "They tell me there was no greater Parnellite than yourself twenty-five years ago."

The priest fixed his eyes on the stage. "He was the greatest leader since O'Connell, and a Protestant to boot. I greatly admired him."

"But when you found that he was dallyin' with a married Catholic lady, you and all the clergy screamed bloody murder and hounded him into his grave."

"He betrayed our trust. We had to speak out."

"And it's been hauntin' you ever since."

Onstage, the man in the baggy pants announced that the only

way to save the beautiful woman was to give her "mouth-to-mouth restitution."

Sean O'Fearna removed his hat, adjusted the crease, and put it back on. "I'm a priest. Nothing haunts me."

"Then why raise money to carry on Parnell's work, if not to pay him back for wrongin' him? And why sit here looking at all the boobs and bums, unless you know you've got the same desires he had, and you're tryin' to keep yourself strong to fight them, so you don't end up like Parnell?" Starr drank from the flask. "Or is it that you've already given in and you know now what a sin it was to hound Parnell?"

The priest took the flask out of Starr's hand and replaced the cap. "Get out of my sight, mister. Go back to Ireland."

As Louie the Lip knelt beside the girl, she opened her eyes and put a hand on his lips. "This is rehearsal, Louie. Keep your hands to yourself."

"Listen, doll." Louie's rubbery face squashed itself into a frown. "If you want to get yourself out of the chorus line, you play the game *my* way. Otherwise, we'll let you dance till your tits start to flop, then boot you."

The girl scowled but closed her eyes and put her head back on the stage.

"You've got yourself a wonderful ministry here," whispered Starr.

The priest was watching the stage the way that he watched most of life, from a safe distance, insulated by the collar, the confessional, and his own Irish eloquence, safe to observe, offer help, and then to let people work through their troubles for themselves. O'Fearna knew that much of the money he had collected in the Shoes for Ireland baskets had been spent for weapons, but he believed that his job was to give the help; it was for others to use it wisely.

Louie's lips stretched toward the girl's face, touched her mouth, and drew it obscenely into his. Then, when the imaginary laughter had subsided, he announced that "restitution" hadn't worked. "What'll I do now? Maybe I should roll her over and rub her back."

The second banana walked onto the stage wearing the sandwich board and carrying three balloons on a stick. "Rubber balloons!" he shouted. "Rubber balloons!"

"Rub her balloons?" Louie the Lip smacked his forehead with his palm. "And *I* was gonna rub her back."

87

"Rubber balloons." Starr pulled on Tracy's leather gloves. "You certainly have some funny fellers in America. I'd like to stick around. But I think I know where this is goin', and I've work to be doin'. Like you said yesterday, when I thought you were a bit more of a man but no less of a priest, if we're ever to jump on John Bull's back, this is the time."

Louie attacked the girl's breasts like a baker at two rolls of dough. He rubbed them up and down, back and forth, spread them apart, pushed them back together, and all the while the second banana chanted "Rubber balloons" in rhythm to the movements.

"The poor girl," the priest muttered.

"Don't worry about her, Father. They're *payin'* her to take advantage of her . . . not like the Brits and the Irish.

And the young woman screamed, "Enough!"

"Good girl," whispered Starr.

"Enough, you lousy slob. If you want your ashes hauled, pay me ten bucks and I'll think about it, but don't be handlin' the merchandise and callin' it art." With every word, she slapped Louie's hands, then jumped up and stalked offstage.

Louie the Lip pulled out a flask. "Broads."

After the stagelights had gone down, the priest looked at Starr, "I guess I have to help you."

Starr smiled, and Sean O'Fearna felt a strange chill.

"How much money do you have, Father?"

The priest hesitated. He had never before divulged the accounts of Shoes for Ireland. "Eight hundred and fifty-five dollars."

"How much?"

The priest repeated the figure.

Starr snatched the flask and threw down two quick gulps. "Eight hundred and fifty-five dollars?"

"How many guns will that buy you?"

"The priest in Dublin said you had fifteen thousand, maybe more. Enough to buy five hundred rifles and hire a ship."

Father O'Fearna reached into his pockets and pulled out a bill and a handful of change. "Eight hundred fifty-six dollars and thirty-seven cents."

It was nearly five-thirty. Twilight glimmered in the white snow of the Common and the red brick of Tremont Street and, for a time, made Boston seem like a place of magic. Perhaps this was the reason so many had come here, thought Starr, for that moment at the beginning and the end of the day when the city itself seemed to shimmer with the promise that anything was possible . . . even for a rebel with *eight hundred fifty-six dollars and thirty-seven cents.*

Starr spat into the snow. The sky above the most miserable Connemara cottage could shine with the same glow, and for most of the men of his age, red sky had come to mean merely that the killing was at an end . . . or about to begin again.

And he recalled the dawn of his first attack, after a night spent crouched in the mud of the trench, cursing the English and the Germans and the God he did not believe in, crapping like a dog in the corner where his trenchmates had crapped before him, praying to the God he did not believe in, the God who had created the English and the Germans and allowed them to create this horror, and finally, after the artillery barrage had crested, propelling himself over the top, toward the blood-red sunrise he was certain would be his last. That evening, he crouched in another trench, a thousand yards farther east, beneath another blood-red sky, and wiped the blood from his bayonet and his boots and the forehead of his best friend. The attack, they said, had been a success.

Padraic Starr had deserted, crossed the Atlantic, killed a man, and revealed the plans of the rising, all for *eight hundred fifty-six dollars and thirty-seven cents.* And yet, he needed only to think of that dawn, and he was thankful to be here, fighting for something he understood.

He had enlisted because the Presbyterian girl he loved had said that Catholics and Protestants should fight together, to save Western civilization, to guarantee Home Rule, and to convince her father that a certain Catholic could be loyal to his daughter. Her father was not convinced, Home Rule was postponed, then amended, and while the girl was doing her best for Western civilization, she died packing gunpowder into shells. Starr spat again. So much for the father, Home Rule, and Western damn civilization. So much for infatuations.

The priest had said he knew two people who might help to get guns. One was the piano player at the Old Howard. The other was a member of Holy Trinity Parish, which was commonly known as the German Church, for it had been established when the population was heavily German. "A German parishioner," the priest had said, then he had touched the side of his nose and winked, *"most* active."

Starr understood. If a German agent offered help, Starr would take it. But he would not rely on the Irish social clubs, and he could no longer rely on the priest. He would need Tom Tracy, and he could not wait. He pulled out his Boston guidebook and looked up the address of Gordon's Olympia. That was where Danny Tracy had said Tom would be found on Sunday evening.

8

*T*hree thousand people. They filled the orchestra and the balcony and jammed the aisles of Gordon's Olympia. *Three thousand*, among them the most famous Jew in America, Supreme Court nominee Louis D. Brandeis, and in a few moments, they would all be listening to her. Rachel Levka tried to imagine Tom Tracy's face looking up from every row. But she did not see it anywhere, not even in the aisle seat she had reserved for him.

If she hadn't been so nervous, she would have been furious. She pulled her speech from the pocket of her skirt and read it once more. She had memorized it, so that she could make the eye contact that Tracy said was so important. But where was he?

"Shall we go up, ladies and gentlemen?" said Jacob de Haas, founder of Boston's *Jewish Advocate*.

Rachel mounted the stage first, followed by Brandeis, who was honorary president of the Zion Association of Greater Boston, Ruth Korff of Hadassah, Rabbi Benjamin Wise of New York, de Haas, and Rabbi Ben Zion Mossinsohn of Palestine.

Three thousand people. Now they were standing and applauding. They were not all Zionists, she knew. There were ninety thousand Jews in Boston, but most of them believed in assimiliaton. They wanted to be Americans before anything else. That was why they had come to this country, to escape the past, to forget the horrors. Even her own father would not come to hear her speech.

When Avram Levka arrived in America, he threw off the ways of his village and embraced American Reform Judaism, which had taken root a block from their house, at Temple Ohabei Beth Shalom. He said he had found his homeland. He did not need Zionists calling for a new one. Her father believed in the same

American melting pot that Tom Tracy did. But even in America there were limits. That's what Avram Levka had said when he found them making love in his parlor. Apparently, Tom Tracy agreed. Otherwise he would be here now.

After Rabbi Wise and Brandeis had spoken, Jacob de Haas introduced Miss Levka, the young Hadassah woman who had invited Mossinsohn to Boston. Many Hadassah members had disapproved of the invitation, but Rachel had convinced them that in America, every Jew should hear every Jewish point of view, and every American should know about Zionism.

She looked over the three thousand faces and tried to make eye contact before she spoke. She saw the long earlocks and black beards that she expected, the notepads of the reporters, the work clothes and the expensive suits, the threadbare cloth coats and the mink stoles, the intense faces of her Zionist friends, and the Irish faces and the Yankee faces mixed among the Jews. In the city that Irish mayors and Harvard presidents alike called the Athens of America, people of every background turned out to hear men and women of ideas. They had come to hear the good Protestant rebels of the eighteenth century and the Abolitionists of the nineteenth, and they came now to hear a Zionist witness of the twentieth-century cataclysm.

Then, on the aisle to the right, Rachel saw the familiar camel's-hair chesterfield and brown felt fedora. *He had come . . .* no. He looked like Tracy, in a strange way, but he had reddish hair and wore wire-rimmed glasses. She glanced down at Tracy's seat and saw an old lady removing the "Reserved" sign. The moment of hope made the disappointment sink deeper in her stomach.

For the six months that they had been seeing each other, she had tried to understand Tom Tracy's hesitance to be seen with her in public. It came with his work. It came with their life in an immigrant city. It came with the rituals of courtship that equated public appearance to public announcement. But after this, it was coming to an end.

The applause settled. It was time for her to speak. Her knees felt like dough, the inside of her mouth like a floured pan.

Then she saw him. He was standing at the back of the house, wearing his tweed chesterfield and his black derby. When she looked at him, he patted his stomach, just above the middle button. She smiled out at him and spoke from the diaphragm.

When she was done, Tom led the applause. He cupped his

hands and pounded them together as hard as he could, because he was proud of her, and because he was glad for any release from the tension tightening down his spine since morning.

Rabbi Ben Zion Mossinsohn stepped to the podium. He did not look to Tracy like a man who had recently escaped a Turkish sentence of death. With his long black beard and black suit, he seemed like a walking shadow, someone who knew the feel of the knot and fully expected to feel it again.

But he was a strong orator. In a few bold strokes, he described the Turks' tottering Ottoman Empire and the opportunities that the Great War had brought to the Middle East. "We Zionists are prepared to fight alongside Great Britain, because victory over the Turk is our best hope for a homeland. The Turk is stubborn, as we have seen at Gallipoli, but force of arms and right will prevail."

Tracy noticed Harold Forsythe, the British consul, nodding gravely. Forsythe tied his pince-nez to his boutonniere with a strand of velvet and wore his dignity, in Curley's words, "the way a cheap shirt wears starch." As the political and business representative of the British Empire in Boston, he gave receptions, attended meetings, and officially greased the wheels that kept the goods flowing from the New England to the old.

The rabbi continued, his voice rising. "While the war is fought, you in America, who can see so clearly from these peaceful shores, must raise your Jewish voices through a Jewish convention. Help us to speak out for equal rights in all lands where Jews dwell. Help us to reoccupy and resettle Palestine. Help us to make it the moral and spiritual center of the Jewish life and soul."

Tom Tracy joined the applause, but the rabbi's words sent his mind spinning back to the center of the Irish soul and Irish life, and he thought of the strange mirror in which Jews and Irish could see each other reflected. The Jews longed for a homeland where they could escape oppression. The Irish had left their homeland to escape seven centuries of it. The Jews were going to rely on the British, the Irish on anyone but. And yet, for both, America had become the sanctuary.

"Before we can build our dream," said the rabbi, "the war must be won by the brave forces of democracy."

Mossinsohn clutched the pulpit and leaned forward, thrusting his black beard at the audience like a sword of truth. "The Zionist must rely on no one but himself, for no other man has his interest so much at heart, but I urge you to speak for the British cause.

In spite of her alliance with the czar's Russia, a pact made to win a terrible war, Great Britain has proved in Belgium that she is a friend of democracy, a friend of the small nation. I stand with any country that stands against the Ottoman Empire. I am proud to stand with the British lion. May the one God to whom we pray bless our efforts."

The rabbi stepped back and the applause rose again around him. He shook hands with the people on the stage, then he came down to the front row and the British consul. Someone sitting in the second row reached over the consul's shoulder and took the rabbi's hand. Then an old couple scurried up the aisle and pressed a check into his palm. Then someone from the other side asked for an autograph. And the reporters closed in.

For a few moments, Tracy remained at the back of the theater while a sea of wool overcoats began to rise and shift between him and the stage. He watched Rachel shaking hands and making conversation with Mrs. Korff, with Jacob de Haas, and, however nervously, with Louis Brandeis. Then she brought a hand to her forehead and looked out across the crowd.

Tracy knew that she was looking for him. He knew that *they* would gossip, but if he did not go to her now, she would be hurt and angry. Besides, how much could *they* gossip when Louis D. Brandeis had delivered the first speech?

He gave Rachel a small wave and forced a shoulder into the crowd.

She jumped off the stage and pushed up to the aisle to meet him. "Mr. Tracy—"

"You did a wonderful job, Miss Levka."

"I'm glad you could take time from your busy schedule to come." She spoke in the formal tone she always used when they met in public.

"It's an honor to be here." He gave her a little bow.

"Come and meet the rabbi." She took him by the arm, and they edged closer.

Tracy caught splatters of conversation around him. His eyes searched for friendly faces and for the faces of *they,* for people who would remember in the voting booth that they had seen him here, broadening his horizons, and for people who would hold it against him.

Just then the British consul pushed past Tracy and Rachel. "A fine speech, Tom. Although I daresay Mayor Curley mightn't appreciate it."

"The mayor's always been a friend of the Jews," answered Tracy. "In Congress, he fought to cancel our Russian treaties because of the pogroms. The Jews have always remembered him for that, even if the British haven't."

"I'm referring to the pro-British remarks, Tom. Not the pro-Jewish."

"When the British are defending democracy," said Tracy, "I'm all for them. So is the mayor."

"Spoken like a diplomat." Forsythe offered his hand.

Tracy liked Forsythe. He liked his parties, his clothes, and the pleasure he took in gently annoying Boston's Irish politicians.

"What does the mayor intend to do about the unfortunate incident at Quincy Market yesterday?"

"Nothing," said Tracy with studied calm. "It's a police matter."

"But there are political implications. An Irishman murders a British trade representative. Rather suspicious."

"Nobody said he was Irish, but I'll personally guarantee his capture"—Tracy looked Forsythe up and down—"if you give me the name of your tailor."

Forsythe laughed. He was turning to the young woman at Tracy's side when someone in the crowd began to shout.

"Rabbi, Rabbi! You say you'd be proud to fight beside Britain because they're the friend of democracy."

Tracy recognized the voice, then the face behind the wire-rimmed glasses. And the coat and hat were *his*.

Mossinsohn turned and thrust his beard at the Irishman like a sword of self-defense. "I stand by my words."

"Have you ever been to Ireland, then, Rabbi?"

What was he doing here? Tom Tracy felt the panic pounding in his chest.

One of the reporters began, "Rabbi, Henry Morgenthau said—"

But Starr shouted louder. "The British have been in Ireland for seven hundred years, and we've got no democracy at all."

"Not true," shouted someone. "You've got seventy members of Parliament."

"An *English* Parliament. We want one in Dublin."

Mossinsohn answered, "You want your parliament in Dublin. We want ours in Israel. We have the same dream."

"Another diplomat," said Forsythe. "The place is crawling with them."

Tracy gave Forsythe a professional smile that suggested nothing. Like many of his small gestures, it was one he had learned from the mayor.

"Rabbi, we might have the same dream," Starr was shouting, "but we sleep in different beds."

"My God, I should hope so," muttered Forsythe.

Tracy's eyes were fixed on Starr's long, sallow face; Rachel's eyes were on Tracy's face.

"All men strive for freedom," Mossinsohn said in his deepest voice. "The desire for freedom makes us all brothers."

That brought applause and bobbing pencils as the reporters scrawled the words.

"If that makes us all brothers," Starr responded, "why is it some of us brothers try to get free by sidin' with the Brits and stickin' the Germans, and some of us do it the other way 'round?"

"That's simple, my friend," said Brandeis, who was standing on the stage, his hands folded behind his back, his shock of graying hair dropped down over his left eye. "The world is a complicated place. There are no easy answers."

"The wisdom of the ages," said Mossinsohn.

"Of the ages indeed," answered Starr. He reached over someone's shoulder and shook the rabbi's hand. Then he gave Brandeis a jaunty wave and disappeared into the crowd. "The wisdom of the ages."

"Thomas," whispered Rachel, "you're perspiring."

He gave her one of his professional smiles, then he looked toward the rabbi. The crowd had once more closed around him with questions and money and proffered hands.

"Well, old boy." Forsythe tightened his silk scarf and buttoned his cashmere overcoat. "I must be off. You wouldn't happen to know the blighter who just raised such a fuss?"

Tracy shook his head.

"He sounds like the sort the Germans would love to have working for them at the docks, planting cigar bombs on our transports and whatnot."

"It only seems that Thomas knows every Irishman in Boston, sir." Rachel smiled at Forsythe.

"Fortunately for his sanity, he does not, dear lady." The consul shook Rachel's hand. "A pleasure to meet you. And, Thomas, tell the mayor that King George will be forever grateful if your police capture that murderer, whoever he is."

"Maybe the guy who just shot off his mouth is the same one who hooked your trade representative."

"You're pulling my leg, Tom. Cheerio."

Sometimes the truth could be the best deceit, and Tracy was learning how to twist it. If Padraic Starr continued to appear unannounced at gatherings like this, Tracy would have to become an expert very quickly.

The six-ten from New York arrived at South Station eight minutes late. Hugh Dawson folded a newspaper under his left arm to identify himself.

That afternoon, a telegram had come to him:

PLS MEET TWO NEW REPRESENTATIVES STEWART AND HUD-
DLESTON STOP ARRIVING FROM NEW YORK ON EVENING
TRAIN TO HELP WITH DETAILS STOP CONTINUE PURCHASES
STOP

The telegram was sent from the Lyman Import/Export Firm in Eastcheap, Dawson's official employer, and also an excellent cover for his other activities.

American neutrality laws did not permit American companies to ship directly to foreign governments, but they did allow representatives to purchase whatever the European carnage required, from condensed milk to mortar rounds, pay for it and take possession of it in the United States, then contract for shipping.

American businessmen had no scruples in the matter. Neutrality did not permit scruples. They would sell as willingly to German agents as to British, French, or Russian, but the British navy had strangled German-American commerce. In every American port, German liners and freighters had lain at berths since the beginning of the war, because British ships, as the German diplomats said, sat three miles and one foot off the American coast, with their guns ready.

The Germans had responded by dropping a noose of U-boats around England. However, since the sinking of the *Lusitania,* the U-boats had operated with a length of rope that the Imperial High Command adjusted by the month, depending upon the tone of the latest notes between Washington and Berlin.

On land, it seemed unlikely that the Germans could be defeated. At Verdun, they were learning the folly of the offensive, but across the rest of the front, from the Alps to the North Sea, they waited by their machine guns while the Allies launched the attacks and died by the thousands.

But to win the war, the Germans faced a difficult task—stopping American supplies from reaching England while at the same time placating the forces of American neutrality. Because unrestricted U-boat warfare would bring a million American troops into the fight, the Germans had resorted to other methods for keeping American goods out of Allied hands.

While Allied purchasing agents placed orders, filled warehouses, and loaded ships, German agents went about the business of sabotage. They employed German-Americans, German merchant mariners, and Irish dockworkers to plant bombs on transports, set fires in warehouses, and create labor troubles and production confusion in American factories.

The British countered with their own agents. Scotland Yard detectives, brought in to guard the New York docks, worked in concert with the American Secret Service. A ring of Czech and Slovak Americans, led by Emanuel Victor Voska, worked undercover in Austrian and German embassies, restaurants, hotels, and anywhere else that they might pick up information. Then there were men like Hugh Dawson and the two now walking toward him through the steam of the South Station platform.

The primary British intelligence efforts in America were directed by Captain Reginald Hall from Room 40 of the Admiralty Building and by Captain Guy Gaunt, British naval attaché in Washington. Their objective, after protecting British shipping, was to uncover information that would bring America into the war on the side of Allies. Their agents were instructed to avoid any incident that would antagonize the American authorities or the American public, and when they discovered important material, it was to be passed, through proper channels, to the American Secret Service. But, like the Germans, the British had people in American cities who, for pay or patriotism, could be called upon to perform services that were occasionally dangerous, usually thankless, and sometimes finely balanced on the edge of the law.

"Hugh?"

Dawson extended his hand to a pair of men he had never met. "Wonderful to see you both again."

"Yes," said the taller of the two. "Terrible thing about old Jim, isn't it?"

"I lost a fine friend." Dawson took the taller man by the elbow. "Have you much baggage, then?"

"No, no. We'll be here just a day or two to help you clean things up."

All of this went on in voices loud enough that anyone who was listening might be misled.

The wide sidewalk in front of the station was crowded with travelers and trunks, and every taxi was already taking on passengers. Dawson said, "I live in a flat on Charles Street. We can walk."

"I'm Stewart," said the taller man, who spoke with the accent of a well-bred Oxford man. "This is Huddleston."

The smaller man's face was long and thin, his eyes sunk deep in purplish bags, and his last dozen strands of hair carefully combed over the top of his head. It looked to Dawson as though Huddleston had eaten something disagreeable on the train.

"You should be wearing a hat in this cold Boston weather."

"Hats keep in the poisons," muttered Huddleston.

"Edward's feeling moody," said Stewart. "He's been trailing a German named Von Igel, who represents himself as a Wall Street broker. We think he's behind the explosions that have been disabling the steering mechanisms on our transports."

"Nailing him seems to be a far higher calling than tracking down another Irish ruffian in another American city filled with Irish ruffians," added Huddleston.

Stewart wore a belted raincoat and a black fedora with the brim turned down. From the width of his shoulders and narrow cinch of his belt, he was built like a music-hall strongman. Dawson wondered briefly what flaw of personality left him here, operating undercover, when he looked young and fit enough to be leading an infantry company on the Front.

"Some lieutenant in Dublin Castle seems to think this Starr could stir up as much trouble as all the German agents in lower Manhattan," offered Dawson.

"Then let's find him and finish him," said Stewart.

"Find him, certainly, but not finish him until we've learned his American contacts and his objectives. Otherwise, we could have the American authorities arrest him for a deserter and be done with it legally."

"His objectives are the same as always," muttered Huddleston. "Causing trouble. As for his contacts, he's got aunties who'll put him up while he does his dirt, he's got friends to suck up to in the Clan na Gael, he knows the local German scum, and he's got the sympathy of every brass-farthing politician in the city."

"Most of the German scum were rounded up a month ago,"

answered Dawson. "The American Secret Service pinned the bombing of the Canadian Parliament on them."

"Admirable job, that. Wiped out quite a nasty little cell," said Stewart.

They were several blocks from the station now, walking down the middle of Summer Street because the sidewalks were still covered with snow. Dawson could hear the distant shouts and scraping shovels of a snow gang clearing a street.

"What do we have to go on?" asked Stewart.

"A priest and a young boy, but nothing concrete. I've been trying to work on the priest's conscience."

"I'm afraid appeals to the conscience are a bit esoteric in this line of work." Huddleston shifted his briefcase from one hand to the other and glanced over his shoulder. "While we wait for further information from Ireland, I suggest we find the boy."

"Look for the soft spot," said Stewart.

Dawson laughed. "I've been here long enough to know that these Irish lads don't have any soft spots at all."

"You find the boy. We'll find the soft spots." Stewart smiled.

Hugh Dawson did not like his new partners.

"You knew that man, Tommy, the one who raised such a fuss." Rachel and Tom Tracy walked together down Stuart Street, through the cold, deserted shadows of a Sunday evening.

"I said I didn't."

"You came late to the speech. You barely smiled all afternoon, except when you thought you could see a vote drifting past. You were hardly civil to Brandeis and the rabbi. What's bothering you?"

He grabbed her by the elbow to hurry her along. "Nothing's bothering me."

She pulled her elbow away. "Who is he?"

"My cousin."

Rachel stopped in the middle of Tremont Street. "Cousin? And you let him say all those things to the rabbi, in front of Louis Brandeis?"

A horn blasted at them, and they scurried to the other side of the street. For several blocks, they walked in silence. They were taking the long way home, as they always did on Sunday evenings. They turned at Arlington Street, where the First Corps Armory stood like a medieval nightmare. Built of granite in the

Gothic style, decorated with turrets and a parapet wall around the roof, it covered most of the block, and after twenty-five years, the soot of the city had turned the granite black.

"Why didn't you tell me that he was your cousin?" demanded Rachel.

Tracy put his hands on her shoulders. A gaslamp illuminated her face. The tip of her nose was red from the cold. He realized that she was the only person he could trust. "Because he's an Irish rebel, and he's gotten himself into some trouble."

"What kind of trouble?"

"Just trouble, that's all."

Rachel looked down at the ground, her eyes moving back and forth as though she had lost something in the snow. "If he's in trouble, what was the point of that display back there?"

Tracy shook his head. "I don't know. He has to be crazy, although"—and Tracy surprised himself—"what he said to the rabbi . . . it made sense."

"About fighting Great Britain?" Rachel's expression hardened, the black eyebrows pulling toward each other. "Only if you're Irish . . . or German."

"He's doing exactly what the rabbi's doing. He's raising money and support for the cause."

"Get rid of him, Thomas. When he started yelling at the rabbi, he frightened me. He frightens you, too."

"I thought you'd approve of him. After all, he's out to overthrow the old order in Europe. Next to hard rolls and Beethoven, that's been your favorite subject since they shot the archduke."

A mantle flared in a nearby gaslamp. The light on her face brightened, then faded, in the same way that her anger went past. "Before anything else, I'm a baker's daughter, and I'm more concerned about you than I am about the old order of Europe."

"I'm sure the Kaiser will be very disappointed."

"King George, too."

He wrapped his arms around her waist and pulled her close to him.

A sleigh jangled by, filled with revelers singing and shouting and flashing silver flasks. The steel runners went sparking over the bare patches in the street, while a few of the riders noticed the couple embracing in the shadows and began to applaud.

Tom pivoted Rachel into a small niche created by a granite pediment. The sleigh went on, its noise and sparks receding, and in the darkness, Rachel's mouth found Tom's. The dry, hard cold became the setting for the warmth of their kiss, and when their lips parted, the steam from their breath mingled in the air.

For several moments, they said nothing. Her hands were around his neck, his encircled her waist, and through the layers of heavy wool, they could feel each other responding.

"Thank you for being there," she whispered, "even if you arrived late."

He brought his mouth down on hers again, and from the shadows came a loud, smacking sound, followed by several low, taunting whistles.

"What's that?" whispered Rachel.

"Shitheads."

Tracy leaned around the pediment and looked back toward Stuart Street, but he saw nothing.

Then a voice came from the darkened doorway of an insurance agency on the opposite side of the street. "Yeah, I guess you heard right in O'Day's kitchen. He really *does* kiss her on the mouth."

Tracy tried to put a face with the voice.

"Do you think he fucks her, too?" That voice came from their own side of the street.

Tracy recognized it. He took several steps down the sidewalk.

Rachel grabbed him by the elbow. "Let's go, Tommy. My father's expecting me at six-thirty."

Tracy ignored her. "Show yourself, Harry Horgan."

The response came in low whistles and smacking lips.

The whites of Rachel's eyes reflected the glow of the gaslamp. "I think I hear four, Tommy. Let's go."

A Model T clattered over Arlington Street from the South End, went past them, and skidded around the corner onto Stuart Street. Then all was silent.

"Please, Tommy."

Tracy did not move. "Nobody says what Harry the Knuckle just said and gets away with it."

"You hear that, Harry?" It was the fourth voice. It came from their side of the street. It was Strongarm Flaherty. "I think the Jew-kisser's mad at you, Harry."

"Don't take on four of them." Rachel grabbed Tracy by the elbow and turned him up toward the bridge.

More jeers and whistles, and now the four voices took shape in the shadows, two on each side of the street.

Tracy decided that Rachel was right. Four was too many. He could find them when they were alone. He took her arm and they started up Arlington Street.

"Who are they, Tommy?" she whispered.

"Donovan cronies, with a few things against me already. They're out to get some dirt on the two of us."

"Is that what you call it? Dirt?"

"That's what the Smiler calls it."

She glanced back at them. Two were crossing the street, so that all of them were on the same side, twenty feet behind.

"Keep walking," said Tracy.

The Arlington Street Bridge spanned the sunken railyards that separated the Back Bay from the South End, the rich from the poor, like a train-filled moat. The wind snapped cold and hard along the roofs of the boxcars and blew swirling clouds of snow onto the bridge. Tracy turned up his collar and put an arm around Rachel.

"What's a Russian Jew doin' in the South End anyway?" said one of the shadows.

"Yeah, they belong in the West End, where Lomasney takes care of them. Or over in Chelsea."

"You know what the German Jews call these Russians?" said another voice. "Kikes. They're the ones who came up with that."

"It takes one to know one," said Strongarm Flaherty, and they all laughed.

Tracy stopped.

Rachel pulled at his cuff. "There're too many for us to fight."

"I don't expect you to fight."

"*Kike,*" someone snickered. "That's as bad as nigger."

"Ignore them." She tugged at his arm.

"You heard what he called you."

She hooked her elbow into his and led him along. "I've spent the afternoon with some of the most prominent men in America. I don't care what a few thugs call me. Besides, they don't know their history."

"These bums don't even know the alphabet."

"It was the immigration officers gave us the name. When an illiterate Russian Jew makes his mark, he won't make an X because it's a devil sign. He makes a circle instead. The Yiddish word for circle is *kikel.*"

"Learn something new every day," muttered Tracy, and for a short distance more, they all walked in silence.

When they reached the middle of the bridge, several hundred feet from the buildings on either side of the moat, a shadow said, "Imagine, an Irish guy diddlin' one of them."

"Makes you sick, don't it, Charlie."

"Naw . . . not if we find out where she lives. Then we can all get a little piece of kike tail."

That was enough. Tom Tracy stopped and turned. He knew that they had been sent to taunt him, to draw him into a fight, and leave him with bruises earned in defense of his Jewish girl-friend, so that the rumors would spread further into the ward. It didn't matter. Let the rumors spread.

He had been outnumbered before. He was fast enough that he might handle two of them with quick punches. Then the fight would be fair.

"Hey, boys," said Strongarm, "the Jew-kisser's mad."

"Tommy—"

"Keep going, Rachel. I'll be along in a minute."

Two of the shadows moved into the street and swung around to Tracy's right. They would come at him from the side and the front, and jam him against the bridge railing.

"Tell your Jew-girl to get goin', Tracy. She don't want to see this," said Flaherty.

To Tracy's right, brass knuckles caught the light of a gas-lamp. A sock loaded with BB shot appeared from a pocket.

"Get goin', Rachel," said Tracy.

"No, Tommy." She reached up and pulled a long hatpin from her hair.

"She got a sticker," said someone.

"Watch your eyes, fellas."

Tracy glanced over his shoulder. She was as stubborn as he was, he thought, and she knew that her presence would make him fight all the harder, and he loved her for it.

"Leave us alone," said Rachel. "We're not bothering you." The wind blew again, and her hat tumbled into the street. One of the shadows stopped it with his foot and stepped on it.

"You're dirtyin' up the streets, honey," said Strongarm. "*That* bothers me."

"If you touch her," growled Tracy, "I'll kill you."

Strongarm laughed. "C'mon, Tracy. Beatin' up on kikes and Jew-kissers, that's as American as baseball."

A whistle screamed, and the headlamp of an outbound engine probed through the rows of rolling stock below them.

Tracy glanced toward the light, then he said, "You bums better be ready to kill me. Otherwise, I'll come after every one of you. And no matter what happens, Strongarm, I'm comin' straight at *you*."

"Then come on. The boys'll lay off, and this time, there won't be no sucker-punchin'." Strongarm's shadow extended its arms and clenched its fists, inviting the fight.

The train whistle screamed again, like a woman attacked in an alley of boxcars. The engine was half a minute away from the bridge. Tom Tracy took a step back. He knew that Strongarm was lying. But if he could keep talking another thirty seconds, he could take them all.

"Would you like your hat back, miss?" Harry the Knuckle took the hat from beneath his shoe.

"Stay away from her," said Tracy, and he angled his body. The bridge was beginning to vibrate. Tracy could tell that it was a big engine, a four-six-four at the very least, and the bigger the better.

"Harry's bein' polite, Tracy. And you ain't." Strongarm made a small move. "Nothin' worse than a Jew-kisser with bad manners."

Tracy moved back a bit more and bumped against Rachel. The semicircle was tightening. "Stay back, Strongarm, 'cause I'm takin' you down first."

"I'm waitin', doll-face."

The bridge was shaking. The engine had reached them.

Strongarm shouted, "Show me your stuff!"

Steam and cast iron pounded under their feet. A gout of black smoke blew up around them. Shadow and light disappeared. And Tom Tracy struck in two directions at once.

His boot caught Flaherty near the groin while he drove a left hook in the direction of the brass knuckles. His fist sank into the soft cartilage of Harry Horgan's nose, but his foot missed Flaherty's vitals. He spun toward Strongarm, and through the smoke he saw the fist.

Light exploded in front of him, then a vicious pain spread out across his nose. He shot out with the right but hit nothing.

Then, above the sound of the engine, he heard Strongarm scream, "Bitch!" The hatpin had found a target.

Tracy aimed another punch toward the sound of Strongarm's voice, and the BB sock caught him behind the ear. He staggered back and nearly fell. The sock whistled again, this time catching him on the forehead. He was stunned, but his instincts threw him at the body that held the sock, and like a wobbled boxer, he took hold and drove a fist at the kidneys.

At the same time, Rachel Levka felt a hand grab at her hair. She poked through the smoke. The hatpin hit a leather sleeve and bent in half. The hand twisted her hair, and she screamed. Then an open palm smashed into her cheek.

The hand was pulling back to smash her again when another shadow appeared through the smoke, big and square, shrouded in a long coat. She saw the hand yanked back. In the blackness, she saw four teeth flash with surprise. A fist came from somewhere in the smoke and smashed into the side of Strongarm Flaherty's face. He crumpled into the snow.

The engine was pounding and bellowing and belching smoke all around them, and another set of hands was still grabbing at Rachel. She coughed and screamed at the same time, and in the swirling, soot-choked blackness, she saw the new shadow swooping to his left. His arm came back, and a long thin blade sliced through the smoke. The hands released her and the thug shrieked, "Jesus Christ! My ass! My ass! What stuck me?"

"This!" came the answer. The blade flashed, and the man shrieked again.

"Now you've got two new holes. Get goin' or I'll widen the old one."

As the thug went running off, a hand cupped around each buttock, two bodies slammed past Rachel and crashed into the bridge railing. Tom Tracy was wrapped around another shadow, still driving his fists into its back.

"Send him for a ride, Tommy!" shouted the shadow with the knife.

The sock smashed down on Tracy's head, but he did not let go.

"A skull like a rock, that's my Tommy!" The sock spun into the air again. A hand grabbed at the wrist. "Over the top with him!" Tom Tracy and Padraic Starr lifted the last thug into the air.

"A pleasant voyage to you!"

Rachel saw the man tumble into the smoke. She heard a frightened shout, then a dull, empty thud.

"He'll be in Pennsyltucky or some such place before mornin', Tommy."

Through the smoke, Rachel could see the thug, spread out on top of a moving boxcar, looking like a little boy waking from a nap in a strange place. She turned to the man beside her, and he smiled. She recognized him now. He was Tracy's cousin. She brought her hand to the top of her head and felt for her hat. She realized that her hand was shaking.

A final cloud of black smoke blew back on them. Rachel retched, and Tom Tracy's body shook with coughing. But the cousin continued to smile, oblivious to ash and soot. He picked up Rachel's hat and handed it to her. Then he pounded Tracy on the back several times to help his coughing.

"It was a fine plan, Tommy, waitin' for that smokescreen and all. And you had a fine soldier on your side." He glanced again at Rachel. "But you was outgunned."

The smoke blew off at last. The pounding of the engine receded down the line of boxcars.

Tom Tracy picked up his derby and put it on, but only long enough to wince with the pain of three lumps rising out of the side of his head.

"A terrible thing, to be outgunned."

"Rachel," said Tracy, "meet Padraic Starr."

It took the four blocks between the bridge and Rachel's street before she stopped trembling. But as her nerves settled and the pain in her scalp receded, her body seemed to fill with energy. Her arms and legs felt light and pleasantly wobbly. She was almost giddy. If this was why the Irish had gained a reputation as streetfighters, she could understand it.

Union Park Street, where Rachel lived, still retained some of the elegance of 1860. The oval at night seemed like a dark, quiet secret in the middle of the city. Snow covered the trash in the small park. Gaslamps threw heavy shadows onto the faces of the buildings. And the elevated train traveling two blocks away sounded like nothing more than the rumbling of an impolite stomach.

Although she was a half-hour late, and she knew she would anger her father, Rachel was still too excited to say good night. She led Tracy and his cousin into the park. Between a pair of tall winter-stripped oaks, she stopped and turned to them.

A small wind forced its way into the oval, and the trees shivered. Rachel felt the cold slip under the hem of her coat, but it was not the cold that made *her* shiver. To her left, she felt the calm, assuring presence of Tom Tracy, who always thought carefully before he made a decision and seldom did anything that he or anyone around him could not anticipate. To her right, she sensed something dangerous and, in its way, exciting. Padraic Starr looked like a less refined version of his cousin, with coarser features, a longer nose, a more prominent jaw, and the red hair curling at the back of his neck because he did not visit a barber every week.

Like the tree and the wind, Rachel would have thought, but her mind seldom worked in a poetic way. She trusted instead in reality. Padraic Starr intrigued her, but as yet he was nothing more than a voice shouting across Gordon's Olympia and a shadow rising through the smoke of the Arlington Street Bridge.

"Thank you both for what you did back there," she said.

Starr glanced at Tracy. "Our pleasure."

Rachel saw the angry look that passed from Tom Tracy to his cousin. She slipped an arm into the crook of Tracy's elbow. He had seemed quiet on the walk home, at first a bit groggy, then strangely sullen in his cousin's presence. "I'm proud of my Tommy."

"You show a fair amount of spirit yourself," said Starr. "No wonder Tommy'd fight for you."

"She showed plenty of spirit at the podium this afternoon," said Tracy, "but somebody dressed like me spoiled it for her when he started shooting off his mouth."

Starr swept off his fedora and executed a small bow. "My apologies, Miss Levka, for speaking my mind to the rabbi."

"Why were you there, Padr'ic?" demanded Tracy.

"To keep you guessin', Tommy." Starr looked at Rachel. "My cousin turned me out of his house this afternoon. I wanted to let him know he can't get rid of me that easy. I also wanted to meet the young woman I've been hearin' so much about."

"Don't be givin' her the blarney, Padr'ic. She knows you're some kind of rebel. She said I should get away from you."

"I said he *frightened* me," corrected Rachel. She was staring at Padraic Starr with open fascination.

Starr pulled the hat down around his ears. "As one rebel to another, Miss Levka, you must know that keepin' folks a little frightened is part of the work."

Rachel smiled. No one had ever before included her in a brotherhood of rebels. But then she took a step back, as if to put a bit more of Tom Tracy between herself and Starr. She felt like a child studying a strange dog, interested yet cautious, attracted and yet instinctively aware of the danger. "If you're not going to be easy to get rid of, what will it take?"

"The right question." Starr looked at Tracy. "Are you sure you want your young lady to know the answer?"

"I know plenty about you already," she said.

Starr smiled at Rachel and took a long deep breath. The steam from his mouth smelled like a mist of Irish whiskey. "If you hear what I'm about to say, it commits you."

"It commits her to nothing," said Tracy.

"It commits her to secrecy," answered Starr. "You're committed to the blood."

Tracy grabbed Starr by the lapels. "I'm committed to my family and my own life in America, not to some village in the west of Ireland and the memory of a hatred that's as old as the ages."

Padraic Starr did not struggle against Tracy's grasp. Instead, he lowered his voice to a whisper and shifted his eyes to Rachel. "Not too long from now, some friends and me are plannin' to do for the Irish what your Zionist rabbi's hopin' to do for the Jews. I've asked Tommy here to help me over on this side . . . do a bit of service to the place and the race that bore him."

Rachel looked at Tracy and waited for him to speak, but he simply removed his hands from Starr's coat. In all the time that she had known him, Rachel had never before seen Tom Tracy without something to say. She could not tell if he was silent for anger, for confusion, or because Padraic Starr's words had somehow struck his conscience.

"Will this rebellion be against the British?" she asked. "The British who are helping the Zionists in Palestine?"

"Like your friend Brandeis said, this world's a mighty complicated place." Starr smiled. "But then, an Irish boy and a Jewish girl sneakin' kisses in the shadows of Boston, they know all about that."

Rachel felt her cheeks reddening. Then, somewhere in the west side of the row, a door swung open. The electric porch light came on in front of the Levka house and Rachel's father, shawl over his shoulders, peered out.

"I have to go," she whispered, and she was glad for the reason to leave. She did not know what she was confronting here. She needed time to think about this Padraic Starr.

"Rachel!" called her father. "Is it you out there in the shadows?"

"I'm coming, Father." Rachel hurried across the street and into the house. As the door slammed, Avram Levka began to shout at his daughter. "I see him out there in the park. . . . I asked you not to. . . . Damned Irishers . . . damned Zionists. . . ."

For several minutes, Tracy and Starr stood in silence while the muffled shouts continued within. Then Rachel rushed up the stairs. The light came on in the bedroom overlooking the park. Rachel pulled the drapes.

Starr said, "You let this go on all the time?"

Tracy started to walk away.

Starr grabbed him by the elbow. "Let's stay, Tommy. Your young gal's a real looker. Let's watch her shadow undress."

Tracy pulled away and headed toward Washington Street.

"Considerin' what just went on, I don't guess you've seen that sight yet, have you?"

"What sight?"

"The young lady in the altogether. No, no, not a good Catholic boy and a nice Jewish girl, not before marriage . . . if there's ever to be a marriage." They walked a short distance in silence, then Starr said, "How old are you, anyway?"

"Twenty-six."

"Twenty-six and never been laid yet?"

"What are you after, Padr'ic?"

"I guess a gay blade like you, he's had a few hoors, at least. Otherwise he's missed the best screwin' years of his life."

"What are you planning to do with the guns?" Tracy kept his head down and continued to walk.

"I'm going to take the bridge at Dunslea, cut off the RIC barracks on the north side, then spread guns south and west to all the volunteers in Connemara. We'll hit the barracks in Clifden and Westport, if we have the strength, pin them all down until the rebels take Dublin. Guerrilla war, Tommy. Hit and run. We'll make it so hard on the Brits, they'll throw up their hands and leave." Starr smiled.

The grin of the old Celtic sin-eater, thought Tracy. "You've come on a fool's errand, Padr'ic, and you bollixed it yesterday at Quincy Market. The men who could help you will have to arrest you if they find you."

"Your old da would have been with me, Tommy. I expect you will, too."

"He wouldn't, and I won't."

"Whatever he told you in that cell, he still would have been with me on this."

"He told me that guns won't do it. They never have. They never will. That's what he wanted me to remember."

"And would he want you to forget your hospitality?"

Tracy turned up his collar and kept walking.

"Like you saw at the Gordon's Olympia, Tommy, if I'm runnin' around this city with nowheres to stay, I may pop up in some damn embarrassin' places."

Tracy stopped. "You could stay in jail. That's where you belong."

"Keep me out of jail, Tommy, for one week, and I promise you I'll keep out of trouble."

Tracy looked at his own wardrobe on Starr. "Just keep out of my damn closet."

9

It was said in Dunslea that Father John Breen rode his donkey with the same proud bearing that other men displayed on the backs of fine thoroughbreds. Each Monday morning, he mounted Old Flavius and rode out Dunslea Point to visit the sick and bring the host.

He had learned, after thirty-five years in the priesthood, that if he did not sit exactly in the center of the animal's back, one or the other of his feet scraped along the ground and wore out his shoes. Although Old Flavius could travel miles farther than Father Breen could walk, he moved no more quickly. And the priest's cassock, which he unbuttoned when he rode, flowed down over the donkey's haunches, making the priest look from the rear like an enormously fat woman with a tail and a very uncertain gait.

But John Breen never complained and never asked the parish to supply him with a horse. A saddle, given by the parishioners on his sixtieth birthday, had been his only concession to comfort.

"If an ass was good enough for the Lord," he would say, "it's good enough for a simple priest like me." And off he would ride, as dignified as the bishop of Dublin.

When he returned from his visitations this Monday morning, he had a visitor of his own at the rectory door. He was not surprised. He had been expecting the young man since the previous afternoon.

"Good morning, Father." Brian Hayes stood stiffly in the bottle-green uniform of the Royal Irish Constabulary. His thumbs were hooked into his belt, and he wore on his face an expression of almost idiotic good humor. He had been smiling for six months, since he first arrived from Galway to take command of the district barracks. Some thought he smiled because he was only thirty years old and hoped to cajole loyalty from the men in the barracks and the people in the town. Seamus Kilkeirnan said he smiled because he was too young to know better.

"How are we this morning, Father?"

"We're fine, but I'm afraid poor Mrs. McTiernan's bound for a funeral before Friday."

"A pity, most surely."

"Not when you're eighty-nine and in the state of grace."

The rectory was in the first of the rowhouses along the south side of town. Father Breen invited Hayes into the front room. "Would you care for some tea, Inspector?"

"I don't mind if I do."

The priest stood three peat bricks on the ashes in the grate, and the fire jumped. Then he hung an old black kettle in the flue and gestured for Hayes to sit in the hard-backed chair by the fire.

Hayes's ceremonial saber slipped between his legs when he sat and nearly tripped him. He took a moment and straightened his tunic. "As I say, Father, I'm sorry to bother you—"

"You didn't."

"Excuse me?"

"You didn't say you were sorry to bother me . . . until just now." The priest smiled. He still had all his front teeth, yellowed though they were.

Hayes's smile widened in response, but his eyes remained as small and gray as two nailheads. He took a telegram from inside his tunic and handed it to the priest.

Father Breen put on his spectacles and read quickly. It was the message about Padraic Starr and emigrants to Boston. He already knew what it said, because Seamus Kilkeirnan had recited it for him the previous afternoon.

"Any ideas, Father?"

The priest looked over his spectacles. "Why do you need this information?"

"Padraic Starr is a rather famous deserter. They think he may have found his way to America."

"Are you askin' me to inform on him?"

"We're askin' you to help us uphold the law. After all, most Irish families have men at the front. They deserve justice."

"Indeed they do. Indeed." The kettle had begun to hiss. The priest lifted it from its hanger and filled the teapot with water. "We'll have good strong tea in a few minutes, Inspector."

"Excellent. While we wait, perhaps you can go through your records and find a few names that I can send back to Dublin Castle." He crossed his legs, and the saber scraped on the floor.

The priest laughed softly. He had not seen a ceremonial saber on an RIC inspector in years. "I'm beginning to understand how you've risen so fast through the ranks, Inspector, bein' a Catholic and all."

Hayes responded by cocking his head slightly and changing the width of his smile.

"In your own quiet way, you're as aggressive as a chicken hawk."

Father Breen sat down at his desk and leaned on his elbows. To do that, he had to push aside foot-high piles of papers, pamphlets, and books, and the dust rose around him in a small gray cloud. "What you're seein', Inspector, is what you might call my . . . *records*. And if I kept up with all the names and addresses of all the people who've left this parish and moved to America the last thirty years, I'd need a desktop the size of the bar at Finnerty's."

"You're sayin' you can't be of help?"

"Sure, I'm not sayin' that at all, Inspector. I'm sayin' that I'll need a bit of time. In the meanwhile, perhaps you should talk with the resident magistrate. He has a fine memory and a fine instinct for the criminals among us."

Inspector Hayes stood and straightened his tunic and adjusted his saber. "I'm afraid the magistrate is off in Dublin at a horse show. He's not due back until Thursday."

"Are you not stayin' for tea, then?"

"I must be off, Father. While you search your memory, I'll search the rest of the district." Hayes's salute was as crisp and neatly trimmed as the young man himself.

The priest said, "It's not often you get a cable from Dublin Castle . . ."

"This seems a very important matter, Father."

"I'll promise you nothin', but I'll see what I can do. We want to keep the Castle hacks happy, don't we, now?"

After Hayes left, the old priest threw on another peat brick and watched the flames eat into it. The damp earth itself could be dried and burned to warm an old priest's bones. A young man named Starr could grow up steeped in rebellion, earn honors defending the realm he detested, then condemn himself through desertion. God's world, he thought, was filled with paradoxes.

He tried to remember the names of the people who had left the parish for Boston in the last thirty years . . . the Donahues in '97, the Malloys, the Tiernans in '08, Denny O'Hara, who most surely had ended up in an American jail, if his boyhood confessions were any prophecy, the Tracys . . . Jack Tracy, one of the finest men John Breen had ever known, and godfather to Padraic Starr.

The old priest stared at the flames and recalled the night of the shooting, when Jack Tracy was brought in. . . .

———————— 1 9 0 0 ————————

The lanterns of the RIC barracks were like smudges of light on the dark mist. As he rushed up the hill from the church, Father Breen looked at his watch: one-thirty in the morning. Liam O'Leary and James Hamilton had been murdered on the Clifden road, and Jack Tracy had been taken with the murder weapon in his hands.

John Breen could not believe it.

Tracy was stretched out on the table in the barracks kitchen. His trousers and shirt had been cut away. Blood was seeping from the dozens of small wounds in his left leg, making him look like an old ram dressed for mutton.

"Jack, what happened?"

"I tried to stop somethin' stupid. Got shot full of birdshot doin' it."

Breen examined the wounds in Tracy's leg. "I think you should be sendin' for the doctor instead of the priest."

"He'll be along, Father. I'd like you to hear a confession, since I'd hate to be lyin' here with a couple of killin's on my soul, even if they was an accident."

Father Breen pulled out his purple stole, the symbol of his sacramental office, and put it around his neck. "In nomine patri et filii et spiritu sancti." He made the Sign of the Cross with a bony hand. He was only forty-four, but his hair had already begun to gray, his windburned face retained none of the contour of youth, and his body had grown as hard and gaunt as the landscape in which he lived.

"Now what is it you'd like to tell me, Jack?"

Tracy began to make the Sign of the Cross, but a wave of pain pushed through him. He grabbed for the wooden spoon at his side and bit down hard on the handle.

"Why isn't this man in a cell?" The door swung open and William Clarke stepped into the room.

Instinctively, John Breen put himself between the resident magistrate and Jack Tracy's body. Clarke was the tallest man in Dunslea, well over six feet, and easily the most imperious.

"The resident magistrate's out late of a Friday night," said Tracy.

"We're about to have a confession," said Father Breen. He stared into Clarke's calm eyes and drew himself up to his full five-feet-nine. As one of the more educated men in the town, he appeared often before Clarke in defense of some ignorant fisherman or farmer charged with a petty offense. As the religious leader of most of the townsfolk, he always felt tension in the presence of the man who kept the secular order. "I want privacy when I hear confession."

"Someone conspires to kill the queen, shoots two foolish farmboys, and all he needs to say is he's sorry and you send him to heaven." Clarke stepped around the priest and looked at Tracy. "I'm afraid 'sorry' will not be good enough for the Crown."

"Those two lads were on their way to kill the queen," growled Tracy. "I stopped them."

Clarke looked down at the blood on the table. "Do you suppose the Queen's Court will believe the testimony of a man who spent ten years in jail after the Fenian uprising and then led the Land League cell responsible for the murder of three landlords in Connemara twenty years later?"

Tracy looked at Breen. "The RM's pullin' off the old scabs,

again. His sire, Black George Clarke, was known as the mean-est landlord in the district."

"That is a lie, Father," said Clarke softly. "The truth that should matter to you is that three men killed him one night in '88. Only two were captured. The third, whoever he was, was too intelligent." Clarke used his riding crop to lift the flap of Tracy's trousers and inspect his wounds. "It seems, however, that intelligence wanes with age."

"I had no part in your father's death." A piece of birdshot had torn a jagged hole in Tracy's cheek so that when he spoke, bloody spittle formed at the corners of his mouth.

John Breen knew the story of Black George Clarke's murder, and everyone in Dunslea knew the stories of the myste-rious third gunman. Breen watched the riding crop begin to tap against Clarke's boot. At petty sessions, Clarke used the crop instead of a gavel when he wanted order, or when he wished to show annoyance with testimony he had just heard.

"Three men killed my father. Only two were caught." The crop continued to tap. "But whatever I think of you will have no bearing on the conduct of this case. There is enough evi-dence now to hand up a recommendation for first-degree murder."

"Or self-defense," offered John Breen. He knew none of the facts but felt compelled to protect a man he admired.

"Give me a piece of paper," Tracy commanded the priest. He closed his bloody right hand around a pencil and scrawled the words: Victoria is to be assassinated when she visits Muckross House this Saturday. The perpetrators are unknown, but their plans are made. For the good of all, save the queen. *Then he handed the note to Clarke.*

The riding crop tapped steadily against the boot.

"Would it be that the handwriting and the message are fa-miliar to you, Resident Magistrate?" Tracy asked.

The riding crop stopped moving.

"You received those words, written by my hand, yesterday morning. The writer was anonymous, the delivery a secret."

Clarke handed the note to Father Breen. "He admits to being an informer as well as a killer. That should set well with the people of Dunslea."

"I informed on no one." The blood spattered from Jack Tra-cy's lips.

"I wired this note to Killarney immediately. Had your young accomplices been captured, it would have been upon your head."

"They weren't my accomplices."

"They weren't smart enough to plan an assassination. It was your doing, but then you lost your nerve. You realized the enormity of the deed, you tried to back out, they wouldn't let you, so you killed them to conceal your part in the crime." Clarke pointed the riding crop at Tracy. "Within that little story there are several permutations of murder, conspiracy and other felonies I'll think of by morning."

"And you can't prove any part of it." Jack Tracy spat a mouthful of blood into the spittoon on the floor, then blessed himself and looked at Father Breen. "I'm ready."

Clarke slipped his riding crop under Tracy's chin and turned Tracy's face. "I can prove that you have been a Fenian and a Land Leaguer and believe in the violent overthrow of Parliamentary Rule in Ireland."

"The days of the Fenians are dead. Parnell proved we can win with words," whispered Jack Tracy, and then, for a moment, he lay silent, his eyes on Clarke, the riding crop against his chin. "We no longer need our guns . . . and you no longer need these." He tore the crop from William Clarke. He whipped it viciously across Clarke's face, opening a four-inch gash.

"Bloody bastard!" Clarke dove at Tracy.

The priest threw his body in front of the resident magistrate and dug his fingernails into Clarke's tweed riding jacket. "Restrain yourself, sir!"

Just then, the door swung open. Clarke pulled the priest's fingers from his lapels and turned.

Constable Ryan, a big, cheerful Galway man with mutton-chop whiskers, carried in a small wooden box. "I have evidence, your honor. Wherever them two lads was goin' in their donkey cart . . ."

"They were going to meet the night train in Clifden," said Tracy, "to make connections in Galway and be in Killarney tomorrow noon."

"Well, they weren't plannin' on goin' alone, I don't think." Ryan opened the box and held it under Tracy's nose. Inside it were three railroad tickets and three pistols.

Father Breen said a silent prayer, because he could tell that Jack Tracy was shocked by what he saw in the box.

"*The train tickets were in Liam O'Leary's pocket, and the three pistols were in the box in the back of the cart,*" *said the constable.*

Clarke took the box and studied its contents. "*Railroad tickets and weapons enough for three men to get to Muckross House and assassinate the queen. One loses his nerve, kills two in the hope of saving himself, but is done in by the evidence in this box.*"

"*Highly circumstantial evidence,*" *said the priest.* "*The third ticket and the third gun . . . they weren't for you, were they, Jack?*"

Tracy shook his head and closed his eyes. The blood loss and the exertion, and perhaps this evidence, thought Breen, had exhausted him.

Clarke raised his chin, so that the blood from the gash trickled across his cheek. "*The evidence indicates that this Fenian is guilty of conspiracy to kill the queen and murder on the Clifden road. I shall recommend that the court in Dublin take all possible measures against him.*"

"*I've know him the five years I've been here,*" *said Constable Ryan,* "*and never's the word I've heard from him in favor of Fenianism.*"

The blood reached Clarke's jawbone and trickled back toward his ear. "*Inspector, once a Fenian, always a Fenian.*"

After they went out, the priest leaned close to Jack Tracy. He smelled the faint leathery odor of a man who had spent much of the night in a saddle and the sweet odor of blood. "*The third gun and railroad ticket, they'll be strong evidence against you, Jack. They might even convict you.*"

Tracy closed his eyes and nodded.

"*Were they yours?*"

Tracy opened his eyes but did not answer.

"*Are you protectin' someone in this?*"

Tracy wiped a sleeve across his bloody lips. "*The railroad ticket was not mine . . . nor the gun.*"

10

uns. The word cut through the outer layers of sleep and he stirred. He had promised them *guns*. The word worked down to the center of his brain, and he opened his eyes. For a moment, he did not know where he was, but he knew he had promised them *guns*. He stretched. His feet fell off the end of the lumpy cot in Tracy's attic. He had promised them *guns*. And they were waiting. He had a week, perhaps two, but no more than that, because in early spring, the Atlantic might be as calm as a millpond or an icy gray hell where wind and salt spume were the devil's fire and smoke. The crossing could take three weeks or it could take six . . . if he had a ship.

A *ship*. Starr stretched and rubbed his eyes.

Guns and a ship with *eight hundred fifty-six dollars and thirty-seven cents*. Before he thought of anything else depressing, he got up and put on Tracy's blue trousers.

The German. The priest had promised a German. Starr did not trust the Germans who had promised aid from Berlin. That was why he was here and not waiting in Kerry for German gunrunners. The men in Dublin trusted the Germans because there was no one else to trust, but *they* were ready to rebel with nothing more than their own pistols and poems and revolutionary pamphlets. They saw the rising differently than Starr. They were fools.

And that was what he had said to Padraic Pearse in October, on the night he stayed at St. Edna's. Pearse was the leader of the secret Military Council of the Irish Republican Brotherhood and one of the architects of the rising.

"It is time," Pearse had said, "for the blood sacrifice . . . to wash away Ireland's sins."

Starr had laughed. "I'm a soldier. I believe in the blood sacrifice if it's the other feller's blood."

Pearse had raised his head, thrusting out the weak chin that people said was the only weak part of him. "I'm a soldier too, Starr, for Ireland and her ancient glory."

"A fine sentiment, but what about tactics?"

"We'll seize the General Post Office and Dublin Castle and

declare our government. In the west, our people will use German guns to take the RIC barracks in every village."

"Those aren't tactics. They're just nice-soundin' plans. And what if the Germans fail to land their guns?"

"There are plenty of weapons in Ireland," Pearse had said without hesitation, "and plenty of spirit."

"Spirit won't beat the Third Cavalry Brigade."

"Whether we win or lose, whether we hold our objectives or not, it is time for sacrifice, Mr. Starr. Christ spilled his blood and gave birth to the faith. We shall spill ours and give birth to Ireland."

That night Padraic Starr had begun to form his plan. He would break away, become his own secret committee of one within the Military Council. Let others rely on German diplomats and Irish-American intermediaries. Let others be driven by mystical visions of Christian sacrifice. Starr would organize his district and bring in the guns himself.

He knew that armed and dedicated rebels, striking suddenly from the Connemara mist, could tie down a British division for a month. And if the Irish could cause that much trouble, the Germans would come to view them as allies, not simply supplicants. Then they would send real help. The Germans were like anyone else. Their respect had to be earned. Then they could be trusted.

Starr smelled coffee and went down to the kitchen. Josephine had left a note on the table:

Padraic,

Still the slug-a-bed, I see. You must get up earlier if you expect to make your way in America. I've gone marketing. Coffee is hot and eggs are in icebox.

Aunt J.

Starr knew that she distrusted him, but still she mothered him. He wondered if she knew the part he had played in her husband's tragedy. Or did she simply believe that he was, as she had once told his mother, "a mischievous little divil who brings down all the boys around him"?

That made Starr think of his own mother, widowed six years after he was born, wedded to poteen a few months after that, dead now for over a decade.

"Mama, why do you drink?" he would ask her when he was feeling courageous.

"It's the Brits," she would respond. "The Brits, who've robbed us of our birthright and kept us down for seven hundred years."

If she'd had enough to drink, she would say the "fuckin' Brits," but if she had only drunk a little, she would still try to speak like a lady. "The Brits, who cut down Ireland's trees to build warships and left us to live in houses made of mud and straw. The Brits, who burned down our monasteries and tried to force their damned Protestant religion on us, and when they couldn't do that, didn't they take away our rights and our land and leave us beggars in our own country? The Brits, who watched us starve by the millions when the potatoes went bad and sat back and said 'We can't give 'em food, for they'll get lazy, and expect it all the damn time.' And while we were starvin', weren't the Protestant landlords takin' our sheep and our barley for rent, and exportin' food as fast as the graves was bein' dug? Thanks to the Brits, Paddy, there's poor folk like us, livin' in hovels all over Ireland. And sure, if them's not good reasons for a woman to take a drink now and then, I can't think of a one."

As he grew older, Padraic Starr came to understand that if it had not been the Brits, it would have been the Connemara weather or the little people or the fall of Parnell that made his mother drink. The Brits were merely a convenient excuse, and far less painful than the truth: She drank because she was a widow and her son was fatherless.

But when he thought about the man who became like a father to him, Padraic Starr recalled two things: the sound of the gentle-runnin' river, where Jack Tracy taught him to fish, and the litany of British transgressions in Ireland, which Jack Tracy could recite as readily as Starr's mother. But Tracy would always add that the Brits were simply tending their own interests first and the Irish second, and all that the Irish wanted was a chance to make their own mistakes for themselves.

Starr poured a cup of coffee and made toast on the stove. The Tracys lived well in America, he thought. Their roots were here now, where any man could make his own mistakes for himself. But Tom Tracy still owed a debt to the father who saw what America promised, to the truth for which his father died, a truth that Starr understood. And without Tom Tracy beside him, Starr would never be able to repay his own debt.

He put on Tracy's camel's-hair chesterfield and fedora and followed his nose to the Fort Point Channel. From the Northern Avenue Bridge to the City Hospital, the channel was lined with wharves, warehouses, and pipes that drained the waste of Boston's factories and toilet bowls faster than the tides could take it. Like the business it served, the channel was slowly dying.

The days of the wind ships were nearing an end, but because of the Great War, there were not enough steamers to carry the world's commerce, and the tough old schooners of the Atlantic coasting fleet had been granted a few extra years of hauling. Starr looked at the masts rising over the wharves and decided to deal with *eight hundred fifty-six dollars and thirty-seven cents.* He stopped at a dozen shipping offices, and discovered that most schooner captains had no interest in chancing icebergs and U-boats for less than top price.

After an hour of failures, he headed for the Brass Rail Saloon. He crossed the street, stopped in front of a gunsmith where he might try to buy a few pistols if everything else failed, then smelled chocolate. Up ahead was a small candy factory. As he crossed the alley beside the building, he heard shouting. A group of boys were huddled around a trash can, and he recognized one of them.

Danny Tracy pulled a handful of chocolates from the trash can and stuffed them in his mouth. "I don't see why they throw 'em away. They're still good. Everybody fill their face, then we get to the craps."

The five other boys pulled bags of chocolate shavings and trimmings from the trash can, then they went around a corner into another alley. There were blank brick walls on two sides, a loading dock at the end.

"It's my game," Danny announced. "Everybody who plays pays me a buck."

He collected chocolate-smeared bills, then shouted, "Get your money down, get your money down, get your money down."

A Chinese boy flung the dice against the wall.

"Snake eyes. Dead already, sap!" shouted Danny. "Who's next?"

"Me."

"Who are you?" said one of the boys.

Starr took the dice from Danny's hand. "The guy who's throwin' next. If I win, you all go back to school. If I lose, you still go back to school."

"Ah, fuck you," said the tallest boy, who was dressed in filthy overalls and had a scrawny growth of hair on his upper lip.

"Yeah," said another, better dressed than any of the others, in crisp clean clothes and shined shoes. He grabbed the dice from Starr. "Go back to the old country, you fuckin' Irish turkey."

"This is business, Padr'ic," said Danny.

"Say, Danny," demanded a scrawny kid who was dressed in black and had two earlocks stuffed up under a scally cap, "who's this asshole think he is?"

Starr's eyes shifted, and the Jewish boy stepped behind one of the others.

"He's a war hero," said Danny, "and he carries a knife, so lay off."

"A war hero, and a bloody deserter, boys."

The Belfast accent felt like the barrel of a gun on the back of Starr's neck.

Hugh Dawson thought: *We have him.*

Dawson had sent Huddleston to shadow the priest while he and Stewart hunted for the choirboy. That morning, they had waited outside the Abraham Lincoln School on Fayette Street and the Andrews School on Oswego. Then they had visited street corners where boys hawked papers, and after that they had sifted the side streets and back alleys between the el and the channel, listening for the shouts of a truant's crap game. They had found not the choirboy but Padraic Starr himself.

"That's right," said Stewart, "this gentleman's a coward who ran away from his country's fight. Stand aside, so that we can relieve him of his knife and turn him over to the proper authorities."

"You a cop?" said the boy with the earlocks.

"We're special constables come to arrest a deserter," said Hugh Dawson before Stewart pulled out his gun. "We're working with the Boston police."

"And unless you boys hand over the dice and move off, I shall take your names and report you." Stewart kept one hand inside his coat and extended the other to the boy in front of Starr.

"Don't give him the dice, Richie," said Danny Tracy. "This guy won a big medal fightin' Germans. They can't touch him."

Be quiet, Starr was thinking. Don't tell them anything.

"You seem to know a great deal about this gentleman," said Stewart. "What's your name?"

"Yeah, Danny," said the boy named Richie. "Tell 'em so we can get out of here."

"My name's none of their fuckin' business." Danny pushed to the front. "And I don't rat on my friends."

"Yeah," the Jewish boy said to Richie, "and neither do you if you want to shoot craps with us."

Stewart said, "Give us the dice, Richie, and then all of you may leave."

"Don't give him shit," said Danny.

Starr's mind was spinning around the close-ended alley like the fox trapped with the hound at his heels. In a moment they would draw their guns and end this little jig. The bravado of Danny Tracy and his friends would evaporate quickly when the barrel of a revolver was pressed against someone's nose.

Starr decided that the best path would be to the rear, onto the loading dock and through the door. And he would have to drag Danny along. One of them might be shot before they reached the door. If the door was locked, they might be shot while they pulled at the handle. But Starr knew that the Brits wanted information as much as they wanted him. Otherwise he would have been shot on Saturday, or arrested by American feds.

"Hand over the dice, now, Richie, like a fine fellow," said Stewart.

Richie dropped the dice into Stewart's hands.

"There's a good lad," Stewart said.

Then Starr heard noises in the outer alley. A big man carrying a nightstick swung around the corner, followed by two others. The smaller one held a baseball bat, the larger wore a pair of brass knuckles and a bandage across his nose.

"We got assholes running a game on my turf, eh?" The man had four teeth and four spaces in the front of his mouth.

"Cheese it, the Strongarm!" shouted Danny Tracy, and a half-dozen hookjacks scattered.

Trash barrels tipped. Chocolate shavings spilled across the alley mouth. The barrels banged and rolled, and Danny Tracy bolted. Hugh Dawson grabbed Danny, but MacGillicuddy's bat hit Dawson across the back and knocked him to the ground.

"Get that little shit Danny!" shouted Strongarm.

Danny leaped over a barrel, kicked it back at MacGillicuddy, and disappeared around the corner.

The Jewish boy ran at Harry the Knuckle. He dodged right, he dodged left, then right, and ran. Starr tried to follow the boy, but Harry managed to grab Starr's sleeve. The knuckles flashed. Starr ducked, then came up hard with both fists and lifted Harry the Knuckle off his feet.

Then Strongarm turned on Stewart and swung the nightstick. "This is my fuckin' turf."

Stewart staggered back, and the boy named Richie ran around him.

"Grab that kid, Harry!"

"Yeah." Harry tried to stand, and Starr kicked him in the stomach.

Hugh Dawson rolled to his knees and gulped air back into his lungs. Strongarm swung the nightstick, and Dawson landed facedown in a puddle. At the same time Padraic Starr started down the alley.

"Hey, you!" shouted Strongarm Flaherty. "Come back here!"

"I'm late." It was clear to Starr that Strongarm did not recognize him from the night before.

"I ain't finished with your friends, and I ain't finished with you, either."

"Another time," answered Starr, "and thanks."

Nigel Stewart scrambled to his feet. "Don't let him get away!"

"Fuck him and take your licks like a man." Strongarm swung the nightstick.

Stewart raised his hands. "Stop it, you fool, stop it!" But the nightstick knocked him to the ground again.

Strongarm crouched for another whack, and the barrel of Dawson's revolver pressed against the back of his head.

"Drop the stick, you horse's ass."

The sound of wood bouncing off cobblestone echoed in the alley. "Yes, sir."

Dawson looked down the outer alley toward Albany Street, then up toward Harrison Avenue. "Gone."

"Bloody hell." Stewart got up and rubbed the side of his face. "Did you see which way he went?"

"No. Nor the urchins."

"Bloody hell."

"Hey, Harry," said Strongarm.

"Yeah?"

"We got Brits and Harps cuttin' in on our turf."

"Quiet, fool." Stewart pulled out his revolver and jammed the barrel into the space between Strongarm's two top teeth.

Strongarm mumbled something that sounded like "Yes, sir."

Stewart brought his face as close as he could without smelling Strongarm's breath. "Now, listen to me, you trash. I want the last name of the kid you called Danny."

Strongarm mumbled and shrugged.

"Don't lie to me. You know who he is. What's his name?"

Strongarm gestured to the gun.

Stewart removed it. "Tell me his name, or the next time I'll pull the trigger."

"Sheehy."

"Where does he live?"

"I don't know where the hell—" The gun went into his mouth again. "Someplace over in Southie . . . C Street maybe."

Stewart put up his gun. "You can keep your bloody crap game, but if we don't find this Danny Sheehy, we'll be back."

Dawson and Stewart stepped out into the service alley. Stewart headed toward Albany Street, Dawson toward Harrison Avenue.

"You was pretty smart, Strongarm," said Harry the Knuckle.

"It don't take no brains to play ball when somebody's got a gun in your mouth, but a smart guy makes the most of a bum setup."

"Yeah?"

"I think we just got somethin' on Tom Tracy."

The business of politics went on, even when Irish rebels were loose on city streets. Tom Tracy, in a way, was thankful, for while he made his Monday rounds, he could put Padraic Starr out of his mind.

At the Pratt Wharf on Albany Street, a city crew had torn up the cobblestones and two men were repairing the water main. The power of the mayor's representative, thought Tracy, was plain to anyone passing by. He waved to the workers and went down the wharf, to the offices of Pratt Shipping and Mercantile. Before going inside, he stopped to admire the schooner named *Abigail*.

Tracy knew nothing about ships. But whenever he visited the wharves and heard the shouts of the longshoremen and smelled the pungent soup of tar and salt water and saw the sails flapping in the breeze, he dreamed of getting himself to sea. He had never gone yet. His good sense always overwhelmed his instinct, and his feet always took him back to the Tammany Club. This morning, however, he was thinking that a sea voyage might be just the thing . . . for Padraic Starr.

"There she is. My best old girl." Jason Pratt came up behind Tracy. "Two hundred feet from her taffrail to the shark's fin at the tip of her jib, a double hull of tough Georgia pine, three eighty-foot masts from the tallest trees in Maine, and the most modern appointments, including a wireless. As tight as a jug and as brave as a Spartan."

Her hull was painted green with white, her masts and deck-houses were white trimmed with tan and red. The tide was rising and her deck was well above the wharf, making her seem enormous.

"A lumber schooner, built for hauling through the Delaware Canal and up the Potomac. She's got a shallow draft, a square hull, and damn little speed. But she's steady and she's afloat, which is more than I can say for forty percent of my fleet."

Pratt was wearing a captain's cap and blue peacoat that seemed well suited to the scars on his face and the cold gray day.

"A pity to lose the O'Day schooner a few weeks after another loss," said Tracy. O'Day's schooner had been lost to the weather, the bark *Annie B.* to a German mine in the English Channel. Tracy had heard rumors that both ships were underinsured and Pratt was now in financial difficulty. He was hoping this morning to find out the truth.

"These are dangerous times for wooden ships and iron men," said Pratt. "I'm the only Pratt left who cares for the wind-ship trade. That's why I'm so concerned about the access to my wharf."

"On Saturday you made it my concern as well."

Pratt glanced back toward the crew digging around the water main and snarling traffic on the street. "You've done a fine job."

"Does that mean you'll deliver the Back Bay vote in the next election?" Tracy smiled.

Pratt laughed. "My father warned me not to ask a Curley man for a favor. And the Back Bay vote is not easily delivered anywhere, least of all to an administration that Back Bay voters consider corrupt, simply because it's Irish and Democratic."

"I trust you feel differently."

Pratt put a hand on Tracy's shoulder and led him up the gangplank. "The corruption of the Boston Irish politician is the work of the rank amateur when you read the history of some of our fine Brahmin families. My great-great-grandfather dealt opium to China and thought the triangle trade was the greatest idea since the astrolabe. There's even a legend that he had a Revere tea set stolen from the White House to keep the company afloat during the War of 1812."

They both laughed, and Pratt invited Tracy to lunch. Tracy

was surprised by the beauty of the main cabin. It was paneled in mahogany, had a small coal stove, and a skylight made it seem as bright as outdoors. A black man named Henry Huntoon waited on them with the kind of quiet dignity that hired men often master in middle age.

As they ate Huntoon's fish chowder, Tracy asked a few subtle questions and learned what he wanted to know, because knowledge, as the mayor said so often, was power. Pratt had indeed been underinsured. In addition to the *Abigail,* he owned a four-master hauling tires to Liverpool and a Maine lime schooner, and he might be forced to sell one of them to offset his recent losses.

Worse yet, the *Abigail* was scheduled to take on a load of medical supplies, raised by a Boston charity, and deliver them to the Red Cross in England, for free.

"I offered to do it in a moment of drunken lust," Pratt explained. "I have a fondness for the young maids of Boston charity, especially those who ply me with kisses and their father's brandy before asking me to do outrageous and unprofitable things."

"Back out."

"No, no, I gave my word," Pratt responded. "I'll simply have to find a small cargo to pay my expenses and not take up too much room."

That was the right answer. Tracy was beginning to like Jason Pratt. He sensed that Pratt was the family rogue, but a man of honor. He wondered how much space a few hundred rifles and a troublesome Irishman would take.

After the table was cleared, Pratt filled two snifters, sat back, and studied Tracy.

If a stranger treats you well with no reason, the mayor always said, you'll learn the reason when the waiter brings the check. Tom Tracy sensed that they were about to come to the point. Pratt's hand went into his coat and drew an envelope halfway out.

Then the shadow of a seagull seemed to land on the table.

Pratt snatched a spoon and flung it at the skylight. The bird above them leaped into the air and fluttered away. After a moment, Pratt laughed. "If I didn't do that, I'd have a birdshit roof instead of a skylight."

The hand did not return to the pocket. Pratt leaned back, and for half an hour they talked about the business of shipping and the big heavyweight fight between Moran and Willard. And Tracy liked Pratt a bit more.

"I can see by your face that you've done a bit of boxing yourself," Tracy said.

"Over the objections of my father." Pratt smiled.

"We should go down to Shaughnessy's and put on the gloves sometime."

Pratt said he would like that.

When they returned to the quarterdeck, three Red Cross trucks had maneuvered onto the wharf and a gang of longshoremen were gathering by the *Abigail*.

"Tom, I admire the way you've taken care of the wharf. My instincts tell me that you're going to defeat Smilin' Jim Donovan in 1918, and probably go a lot further than that."

Tracy's ambition was common knowledge in the South End. He was surprised and secretly pleased that it was discussed in the drawing rooms of the Back Bay. "*My* instincts tell me the same thing, but one office at a time."

"Well, then." Pratt took the envelope from his pocket and slapped it into Tracy's hand. "I'd like you to consider this as a campaign contribution."

There was a point to this, after all. Tom Tracy had long expected that someone would try to make a premature investment in him, and he knew exactly how to respond. He handed the envelope right back. "When I announce my intentions, I'll open a campaign bank account and call you with the number. Until then, you keep the money."

"An honest Irish politician," muttered Pratt.

Beneath the good fellowship, thought Tracy, Pratt was no different from his father, who often said that while the bastard Curley ran City Hall, Pratt money ran the city. "When we fight, maybe we should go bare-knuckled."

"I think you're taking this wrong," said Pratt. "A hundred-dollar contribution—"

Tracy laughed. "A hundred? I've always heard you Yankees were cheap. Next time, don't try to buy someone for less than a thousand, and don't do it in public." Tracy strode down the deck, past the longshoremen, and off the ship.

Padraic Starr hurried along Harrison Avenue. He was looking for Danny Tracy and the other boys. At the corner of Rochester

Street, he noticed the Jewish boy in a doorway beside the Levka bakery.

The boy looked around furtively, then took off his scally cap. His earlocks dropped down along the sides of his face. He shoved his cap into his book bag and took out a black hat with a round brim. After setting the hat carefully on his head, he went into the bakery.

A moment later, the agent with the Belfast accent came down Rochester Street and stopped at the corner. He took out a cigarette, lit it, and leaned against the wall.

Starr knew that when the boy left the bakery, the agent would appear beside him, threatening him and demanding names. Starr could not let that happen.

"Good morning, Rachel." The little bell above the door jangled as Simon came into the bake shop. He was the only customer.

"Why aren't you in school, Simon?"

"Ah . . . they let us out for lunch today. The . . . ah . . . school cafeteria didn't get a food delivery because of the snow. That was it."

Rachel smiled. She liked Simon and felt sorry that his father, unlike her own, had not embraced American Reform Judaism. In a *shtetl*, it might have been easy for a little boy to grow up Orthodox, but not in a mixed neighborhood like the South End.

"What can I give you, Simon?"

"A bulkie roll, perhaps, and a fig square." He pressed his finger against the case. "That one."

Rachel took a piece of waxed paper in her hand and reached into the case. "This one?" she joked. "The little one?"

But through the glass, she saw Simon's eyes widen. A look of fright crossed his face, and he turned quickly to leave.

"Simon!" She stood. "Where are you going?"

"Stop him!"

Rachel turned, and then she screamed. Padraic Starr had materialized behind her.

"Stop him! He's in trouble."

Simon was twisting the door handle.

"Come back here, Simon, or I'll tell your father you hooked."

The boy looked back at Rachel. "But . . . but it's the cafeteria."

"I don't believe that. Now come here," she commanded.

The boy dragged his book bag across the floor.

Rachel spun back to Starr. "What are you doing here? How did you get in here?"

"Your bakers take an early lunch. They're all gone." Starr raised the hinged countertop and told the boy to step around.

"Didn't my father see you?" She sounded panic-stricken. "He's right in his office."

Starr shook his head. "He must be off with the bakers at the local pub."

"He doesn't drink."

Starr shrugged and knelt down beside Simon. "I want you to promise not to say anything to anyone about what happened back in that alley."

Rachel knelt and whispered, "What happened? What are you talking about?"

"Simon knows, don't you, boy?"

Simon nodded, slack-jawed with fear.

"It wouldn't be too good if anyone knew you were shootin' craps this mornin', would it?"

The boy shook his head, and one of the strands of his earlock caught on his lip. He blew it aside and said, "No, sir."

"Shooting craps? Simon, that's terrible."

"For the next week, I'll be wantin' you on your best behavior," said Starr like a stern schoolmaster.

The boy nodded.

"Go to school in the mornin' and go straight home in the afternoon, and don't be stoppin' to pass the time of day with anyone. If you see either of those two characters, you run like you just seen the divil himself . . . because if they catch you, they'll tell your father what you were doin'."

The boy nodded again.

"And if you see any of your friends, tell them what I've said. I was doin' you lads a favor."

Rachel glanced nervously through the curtain that led into the rear of the bakery, where there were three banks of ovens, mixing tables, iceboxes, and bags of flour. In the office just beyond the curtain, her father was taking off his coat and sitting down to his ledgers.

"Mr. Starr, I'd like you to finish whatever you're doing and get out of here before I'm forced to explain you to my father."

Then the Belfast man appeared in the window.

"Stand up," Starr said to Rachel, and the urgency in his voice forced her to respond. Then he pushed the boy through the curtain into the back.

Avram Levka looked up. "Who are you?"

Starr brought a finger to his lips. "Shhh."

"Don't shush me!" Levka got up and came around his desk.

On the other side of the curtain, the bell rang and the door opened.

"Tell him the boy left by the back way," Starr whispered against the fabric. "And convince him you don't know the boy's name."

"What is going—"

Starr clamped a hand over Avram Levka's mouth and pushed him back into his office. Avram tried to call for his daughter.

Starr squeezed. "Please, Mr. Levka. I'll explain in just a moment." As he heard the man say "Good afternoon," Avram Levka kicked him.

"Can I help you?" asked Rachel.

"Yes, you can, I think," said Hugh Dawson, and he allowed his Irish accent to thicken. "I'd be lookin' for a little Jewish lad who came in here just a moment ago."

"He knows I'm Jewish," whispered Simon.

The boy was standing directly behind the curtain, and his feet could be seen from the shopfront. With a snap of his head, Starr gestured for the boy to come into the office, but the boy did not move.

"Many Jewish boys come in here," Rachel was saying. "This is a Jewish bakery."

"The one a few moments ago. The little Orthodox lad."

"Yes," said Rachel, swallowing her nerves. "What is it you want with him?"

"Well, it's a bit of a personal matter between me and the lad."

Starr whispered, "Will you be quiet if I remove my hand?"

Avram Levka kicked him again.

Starr looked over his shoulder at the boy and snapped his head once more, but the boy seemed frozen in panic.

"Well, he's not here," Rachel was saying.

Dawson looked around her at the curtain. "Is he in there?"

Unconsciously, Rachel took a step back. "He bought his fig square and bulkie roll and went out the back just before you came in."

"Would you mind tellin' me why would he go out the back when he came in the front?"

Avram Levka sank his teeth into Starr's hand. Starr muffled a cry, and Avram kicked him again. Starr managed to reach his shoe and pull out the knife. He held it in front of Avram's face. "Be still. Now."

Avram Levka stopped struggling.

The little boy looked up at Starr. "He knows I'm here."

Starr pressed the blade against Avram's throat and said, "Don't make a sound." Then he took his hand from Avram's mouth, snatched the boy by the collar, and pulled him into the office.

"We always let the little boys cut through," said Rachel. "It's a fast way to get to the kosher butcher on the next alley. They take their rolls and cut them open and buy three slices of salami for a penny."

Excellent, thought Starr. Now get rid of him.

"May I take the shortcut too?" Dawson started to raise the hinged gate.

Rachel stepped in front of him. "We let *little* boys use the shortcut. You'll have to go around the block." Then she smiled and added, "Unless you're in a hurry and have to get back to Hebrew school for the afternoon session."

"Good girl," Starr whispered at the bulging eyes of Avram Levka. Then he heard the bell above the door.

"Thank you for your help," Dawson said. "You don't happen to know the name of the boy, do you?"

She shook her head.

Starr heard the door slam. The knife disappeared.

For a moment, the Levka shop was silent: the bakers were at lunch, Rachel was trembling, the little boy was panic-stricken, and Avram Levka was speechless with fear and rage.

"I'm sorry, Mr. Levka," said Starr gently. "It's just that we wanted to protect the boy from any trouble with that gentleman. He's the new truant officer."

"So you put a knife to my throat? Is that how you help my cousin's boy?"

"Please don't tell, Uncle Avram," whimpered Simon.

"Rachel! Rachel!" Avram Levka pushed back the curtain and went into the front. "What is it happening? What have I done that you cause me such grief? You draw these Irishers like flies to the fishwharf. One I find with his hand in your blouse, one comes here and asks you all questions to which you must lie, and that one in there puts a knife to . . . and hello, Mrs. Kreplow." The little bell was ringing and an old woman was coming into the shop. Avram attached a smile to his face. Rachel went into the office.

The boy was sitting on a stool by the wood stove, and Starr was talking softly to him.

Rachel poured a glass of tea. She did not look at Starr or the boy until she had drunk half of it.

"Thanks," said Starr gently.

"Why did you have to frighten me and my father and this little boy?" She looked down at Simon, who was tugging nervously at his earlocks.

"I thought you'd understand. You of all people," said Starr. "If that guy started askin' questions, he'd be learnin' things we don't want him to know. Isn't that right, Simon?"

The boy nodded. Starr had terrified him sufficiently that he would say nothing, about any of this, to anyone.

Rachel drank down the rest of her tea and poured another glass.

Starr stepped closer to her. "You done yourself a fine job, just like last night."

She tried to ignore the Irishman, who took up most of the space in the tiny office, and she tried to swallow the strange pride she felt when he complimented her. She asked the boy if he would like some tea.

Simon nodded.

"I could use a bit myself," Starr said.

"You must leave."

"I'd like to be makin' an apology to your father. I don't think he understands what just happened here." Starr smiled.

Rachel looked down at the floor and brushed several strands of hair away from her face. His smile frightened her. She could not measure its meaning, any more than she had been able to measure the man himself or her reaction to him.

"Do you think he loves you?"

She poured Simon a glass of tea.

"My cousin, has he never told you he loves you?"

She handed the glass to the boy. "Drink it slowly, Simon. It's very hot."

"He probably hasn't said it because of somethin' stupid, like religion."

"I asked you to leave." She looked at him at last, and she felt a strange chill.

"If he's not told you he loves you, it's sure that he should, for you're quite beautiful, and you handle yourself like a vet'ran."

She put on the expression she saved for mashers who made rude comments in the street. "I helped you because of Simon, and because I . . . I believe people should fight for their homelands."

Starr placed his hands on her shoulders. She wanted to pull away, but his touch was firm and comforting, and it stilled the trembling.

"Has Tommy told you about *his* homeland, the village with the bridge and the gentle-runnin' river and the magistrate named William Clarke?"

"Yes . . . enough."

"Then you know a bit of the reason why I'm here, and why I need Tommy's help. You'll understand if he gives it."

She looked into the calm blue eyes. He soothed and frightened her at the same time. "Of course."

That made him smile again. "And before I go, I'll see that he tells you his mind."

"You'd better go right now," she said, but she did not attempt to move away from him.

He slipped his hands from her shoulders to her arms and kneaded the muscles. "From what I can see, he's a damn fool if he ain't spoke his mind to you yet."

"Take your hands off my daughter." Avram Levka stood in the doorway to his office.

Starr turned and tipped his hat. "All my apologies, your honor. I was just tryin' to help the boy, and I guess I'm a bit too quick with the knife."

"Get out, before I call the police."

"Please don't do that." Starr thanked Rachel again and disappeared.

"Another Irish suitor?" Avram shouted at his daughter.

She looked down and shook her head.

"Then who?"

"He's . . . Tom's cousin."

"Irishers! More damned Irishers I cannot stand. You should have gone to Hebrew school like Simon. It might have taught you that while you are American, you are also Jewish, and you have a duty to birth Jewish children."

Rachel bit her lip and looked away from her father.

The bakers were returning from lunch, and Frau Hoffman, the chief mixer, was calling for Mr. Levka.

"You have a duty to love your father and your father's faith, just as your father loves you." Avram turned and went out.

Rachel looked down at Simon, who shifted his eyes to the tea leaves in the bottom of his glass. "You have a duty to your father, too. Stay here for the next hour and do your sums, and say nothing of this to anyone."

She tucked her hair under the net that she wore in the shop, then she went back to the front and peered through the windows. Padraic Starr was gone. She wrapped her arms around herself and kneaded the muscles as he had done. Where Tracy's touch, for all his confidence, was tentative and delicate, Starr's hands had a power in them that seemed to summon her own strength. Whatever had happened in the shop, she was glad she had helped him.

11

Rachel Levka left the bakery at six o'clock. She told her father that she was going to a meeting of her Hadassah chapter, and then she walked the three blocks to Gloucester Place, where she stepped into a doorway and waited. The night was cold, and after a few minutes in the shadows, she began to shiver, but in Boston a young woman did not appear unannounced at the home of her gentleman friend, especially when she had not yet met the gentleman's mother.

In Josephine's kitchen, the Tracys gathered for the Monday-night supper of chicken and dumplings. An extra place had been set for a houseguest who had not come home, and his absence was nearly as upsetting as his presence.

Josephine held the meal until ten after six. "That's as long as I'll wait for one of my own boys. I'll wait no longer for Padraic Starr."

Thomas blessed himself and led the family in reciting grace. Then Danny grabbed for the dumplings.

"Padr'ic was still asleep at half-nine this morning," said Josephine. "He'll never get what he's after in America goin' about it like that."

"Ah, sure, he's a fine lad," offered Martin. "But a bit strange in his ways, if you ask me."

"How's that?" said Tom, without looking up from his peas.

"I seen him walk by the barn this mornin'. I run out and called after him, but he kept on walkin', like he didn't hear me. Then he ducked into Duggan's shipping office on the next wharf. And here I was, hopin' to show the boys a real war hero."

Tom cut into a dumpling. "I think it would be a good idea if we stopped telling the world that he's here."

Josephine dropped her knife and fork and leaned across the table to Tom. "He's here to cause trouble, ain't he?"

"I've not said that."

"If you know something you're not telling us," said John, "I think you should be out with it."

"What's he doin' here, Tommy?" demanded Josephine.

"He's here for a week, then he'll be gone. That's all you need to know."

Josephine stood and took the plate from in front of him. "You may be the man of the house, but I'm the woman who brought you all into the world, with the blessed help of Jack Tracy—"

"God rest him," added Martin.

"—and I say that the family's got the right to know what you ain't tellin' us."

"It won't matter if you know, Ma, so . . ."

She put his dinner plate in the icebox and slammed the door. "You'll get no supper till you're out with it. Is your uncle makin' a damn fool of himself for wantin' to show his nephew around? Are we gettin' ourselves into some kind of trouble?"

Tracy decided that if they knew, they might be more careful. He popped a dumpling into his mouth. "He's a rebel."

"Is *that* all?" said Martin.

"Here in the greatest secrecy," continued Tom, "to get guns for the rising that's planned for Easter."

"Rising?" said John. "They're actually going to do it?"

Josephine shook her head. "Like a bad wind, he is."

"It would be best not to tell anyone about him because the Brits are on to him. They have agents looking for him."

"Mother of Jesus," whispered Josephine.

Danny stood and excused himself and tried to slip out of the kitchen.

Tom grabbed him by a belt loop. "Word's on the street that Strongarm rousted a crap game and beat the snot out of a couple of guys who turned out to be an Irishman and a Brit. What do you know about that?"

"Nothin'."

"I gave a call to the truant officer—"

"Ah, Jesus," said Danny.

"Watch your language," said Josephine.

"—and I found out that you weren't in school."

"Mother of Jesus," said Josephine. "Cuttin' school to shoot craps? Martin, take off your belt and hand it here."

"Now, Josie, just hold on."

"Take off your belt, Martin," she commanded, "and Daniel Tracy, you bend over the sink."

"Like hell. I'm sixteen, and Padr'ic told me I stood up to them agents like a man this mornin'. I've bent over a sink for the last time."

"You stood up to them?" Tom felt the dumplings turning solid in his stomach. "How did you do that?"

Danny described the crap game and the lecture Starr had given him later in the day. "He says the Brits'll be lookin' for me and my friends now, so we gotta be careful." The boy grinned. "I told him we know how to disappear like smoke when there's trouble."

"Holy Mother of Jesus Christ Almighty," Josephine Tracy blessed herself. "I thought we left this behind."

"Padr'ic says that you never leave it behind," answered Danny.

"He's wrong," said Tom. "We're all Americans, and you more than any of us. You were born here."

Josephine went into the hall and came back in her hat and coat. "I'm goin' to the police."

"No, Ma," said Tom. "You can't."

"I certainly can and I will. I'll turn the bastard in, and them agents, too."

Martin Mahoney's forearm slammed against the table. "You'll do nothin' of the sort. You'll listen to your oldest son. He knows what Padr'ic's doin', and he's decided it's right. I can see it in his face."

"I see nothin' in his face but confusion."

"That's because you lack the magic, Josie. You're a fine woman, but you don't have the magic."

Josephine buttoned her coat and went to the back door. "There's no such damn thing as magic."

Martin snatched her purse from her hands and sat on it. "I'll not see my sister become an informer."

"They called Jack Tracy an informer," said Josephine, "and he was the finest man we ever knew."

"That's for sure, God rest him," said Martin, "but—"

"*I* never knew him," said Danny angrily, "because after he informed, the Brits hung him anyway."

"It's not as simple as that," said Tom.

"Indeed it's not," added Martin.

Josephine looked around. "If none of you's got anything else to say, I'll be goin' down to Station Four."

Tom Tracy turned to John, because in matters of morality, in family questions of faith, Josephine listened only to the quiet middle son, bound the next fall for the seminary. "Tell her about the Protestants and their guns."

John looked at his mother. "When Home Rule was passed, the men of Ulster said they'd never go into a government in Dublin. They ran guns into Belfast, five thousand, just before the war started. The Catholics in the south did the same thing, but they could only afford fifteen hundred. The Brits looked the other way when the Protestants did it. They fired into the crowd when the Catholics tried."

"And none of that should matter a damn to me and me family." Josephine buttoned her coat and started for the door.

"Home Rule was Da's dream," said Tom.

"Yeah," said Danny. "Uncle Padr'ic said that in Ireland, we got what we wanted by talkin'. We played by the rules that our da died for and won—"

"And right away, the Protestants started lookin' for ways to change the rules on us." Tom realized that it was the first time in many years that he had referred to the Irish of Ireland as *us*, and the first time in memory that his youngest brother had shown interest in the world beyond the South End.

Josephine went to the door. "Jack Tracy believed in politics, not gunrunnin'."

"I don't remember him too well," said John, "but I believe he had great charity in him, Ma. He'd tell you to protect Padr'ic, if you could."

"And protect the Tracy name," added Danny. "Padr'ic says if we turn him in, we could kill the whole risin'. They'd call us informers. I ain't gonna face my pals with that around my neck. No way."

"And I'd hate to face the voters in November after betrayin' my cousin," said Tom softly. "Da would tell you to sleep on this."

Josephine Tracy looked around the kitchen, at the faces of the people she loved and trusted most. And slowly, she unbuttoned her coat.

"That's our girl." Martin Mahoney patted his sister's arm.

Tom looked at Danny, who was stuffing another dumpling into his mouth. He had shaved that morning, but he had missed patches of hair along the underside of his jaw. He was trying to grow up, thought Tom, but he was still a boy. And to the boy becoming a man, nothing was more attractive than rebellion. Danny was reason enough to get Padraic Starr away from them.

Outside, the night grew colder. Rachel waited for Tom to come down Gloucester Place, past the doorway where she shivered. But there were no wakes in the ward, and Tom never went out on Monday nights for any other reason. Rachel waited until the cold made her toes feel like small pieces of lead in her shoes. Then she went down to the Tammany Club, wrote Tom a note, and left it under the door.

"I want Tom Tracy's ass."

James Michael Curley stopped chewing and put down his fork. "I *told* Willcox that dinner with you was a waste of time. I was right."

Smilin' Jim Donovan smiled and sliced into his steak. They were sitting at a secluded table at the Parker House. For generations, the politicians of Boston had been gathering there, in the rich, stained-oak darkness, amid the civilized clatter of crystal, china, and solid heavy silver.

Curley took a roll and tore it in half. "Tom Tracy wants *your* ass, and in 1918, I'm planning to let him go after it."

"In '18, you'll be fightin' for yourself, and I'll be doin' my damnedest to tear your head off."

Curley picked up the bread basket. "Have a world-famous roll from the Parker House."

"When I'm fightin' you, I don't want some young ward heeler tryin' to shoot my seat out from under me."

Curley buttered his roll. "If this is about the Jewish girlfriend again, I don't give two damns about her."

Donovan soaked his roll in the juices seeping from the steak. "This afternoon, one of my . . . let's call him a constituent . . . broke up a crap game."

"So what?"

"Interfering with my constituent, as he tried to do his civic duty—"

"Save the speeches."

"—were a pair of well-dressed strangers, one Irish, the other English, and a third Irishman who seemed more interested in getting away from the other two." Donovan put the roll in his mouth, chewed and swallowed.

Curley sat back and wetted his lower lip. "So what?"

"When the scrape was over, the gentlemen, whom I suspect to be British agents, wanted the last name of the kid they called Danny. My constituent refused to tell them, although he knew."

Curley bit into his roll.

"Do you want to know?"

Curley chewed and studied his next bite. "No."

"Tracy."

Curley tore another section from the roll.

"Beyond that," continued Donovan, "my constituent claims that the one they were after wore a hat and a camel's-hair coat just like the ones that Tom Tracy struts around in."

"And you want Tom Tracy's ass for that? You're crazier than King Lear's fool."

"I don't want to ruin the boy, just get him out of my ward."

"You have no evidence of anything."

"I think Tommy knows this Irish rebel. He may even be hiding him. And if I place a call to some Curley-hating reporter over at the *Transcript,* you watch what happens."

· "You're afraid of him, aren't you?"

"You're damn right. You ought to be, too." Donovan chewed another piece of steak. "He's playin' games with the Jews, whether you want to hear it or not. He does business with the Pratts. Now he's keepin' you in the dark about this Irish business. And it's put your pet project in big trouble."

Curley stopped eating and leaned back in his chair.

"Like we said Sunday, if the Republicans smell a scandal that keeps Curley and his corrupt bunch of Irish bums from getting their tax increase, you won't be able to bring this city into the twentieth century." Donovan sawed off another piece of steak. "Which means you'll be out on your ass next election."

"And you won't have to lift a finger."

"I want to beat you myself, James. And keep you beat." Donovan spit a piece of gristle onto his fork.

"You're supposed to cover your face with a napkin when you do that."

Smilin' Jim Donovan swirled his mashed potatoes around on his plate, then raised his fork and held it in front of his mouth. "We're potato skinners, Jim. You and me, Kennedy and Lomasney and Honey Fitz . . . the lot of us. We owe everything to the Irish voters. That's why I'm not usin' this thing to pull your head out through your asshole right now."

Curley pursed his lips and squinted at Donovan. "You're not using it because you don't have a thing. You're just blowing smoke."

"If there's an Irish rebel runnin' around this city, you can bet there's somethin' up in Dublin, and I don't want to be the guy that queers it." Donovan stuffed the potato into his mouth. "But if I have a good piece of dirt about one of your boys, I'll be dipped in shit before I keep the lid on it and don't get somethin' in return."

The waiter came with the check.

Donovan picked it up. "Give me Tom Tracy's head by St. Patrick's Day, or I'll forget I'm a good Irishman and throw the lot of you to the *Transcript*."

"James Michael Curley is loyal to his people."

"You are, but what about Tom Tracy?"

Curley stood and took a long cigar out of his breast pocket. "Here. Smoke a good one for a change."

That evening, in a tiny backstage room at the old Howard, Padraic Starr met one of the men the priest had promised would help.

"James McHale's the moniker, but everybody calls me Jimmy the Butcher."

"A formidable nickname." Starr offered him a swallow from the priest's flask.

"Nope, nope, never touch the stuff." The little man in the derby dropped onto a stool. "If I could handle the hootch I'd be out on the circuit, second banana, maybe top in some little show somewheres. But them days is gone. Yep. Them days is over. Now I'm glad to tickle the ivories at rehearsal and play the candy butcher at intermission."

"Candy butcher?"

"The candy butcher is not a butcher and doesn't sell candy," explained the priest, who leaned against a pile of boxes in the corner.

"Yep." Jimmy's left eye was permanently squinted above the burning tip of his cigarette. "I sell whatever the travelin' boys bring 'round, everything from French envelopes to dirty pictures to cheap watches so's you'll know what time to get off the old lady and put on your pants and go to work."

The tiny room was filled with the junk that Jimmy sold at intermission. A pile of rubber chickens lay on a shelf. An ashtray in the shape of a hand extended its middle digit. And anywhere that there was not a shelf or a pile of boxes, there was a picture of a naked woman.

Starr gave the priest a look that was both puzzled and annoyed, as if to ask why they were wasting their time with a broken-down burlesque bum.

"Jimmy is one of my closest friends," said the priest. "He helped to establish my ministry here. He knows all there is to know about human frailty—"

"Firsthand frailty," added Jimmy.

"—and he knows where to buy and sell anything and everything for sale in New England, including guns."

"Guns!" Jimmy gave a little half jump from the stool and rattled his derby on the top of his head.

"Guns," said Starr softly.

Jimmy dropped back onto the stool and smiled a crooked comic's grin. "You like that move with the derby? I learned it from the little guy with the mustache, the one in the picture shows."

"Charlie Chaplin," said the priest.

"Yep. The little tramp."

Starr leaned close to Jimmy. "Guns. In complete secrecy."

"No blabberin' from me, no sir, but no guns, neither."

Starr's body sagged. "How do you know?"

"I asked around, strictly on the QT, y'understand. And I didn't have much luck, nope, not much at all. A few here, a few there, but damn, rifles is hard to come by on the sly. The Allies are takin' them all on the up-and-up. Top dollar, too. Thirty bucks apiece. And you ain't got that kind of dough. No, sir."

Starr looked at Father O'Fearna. "What about the German?"

"His name is Klaus Bremer. He's a member of the Prinz Henrys, one of the local German bunds—"

"And a horny bunch of bastards, if you can believe the girls," added Jimmy McHale.

"Father Ritter is the bund chaplain. He thinks highly of Bremer, calls him a loyal son of the *Vaterland*."

"All hail the Kaiser!" Jimmy rattled his derby on the top of his head and swept his finger around the room like a machine gun.

Starr gave Jimmy a look, then downed another swallow of whiskey.

"I told Bremer as much as I thought necessary," said the priest. "He would like to meet you, tomorrow night. In the balcony."

"Better a German agent than some bigmouthed Hibernian." Starr glanced at Jimmy. "I don't like bigmouths."

"Me neither, no siree." Jimmy rattled his derby. "Give me a tight-lipped Kraut every time."

"A tight-lipped candy butcher, too." Starr turned to the priest and sucked on the flask again. "I want to meet this Bremer alone."

The priest nodded. "Look for reddish hair and a billed cap with a *B* on the front."

"Fine. And I don't want you anywhere near this theater." Starr took a final swallow and handed the flask back to the priest. "If someone's on your tail, let's leave him sittin' right outside the rectory."

"I will go to my room and pray that the German takes you out of our lives forever."

Starr smiled. "I won't be leavin' *your* life, Father."

"Why not?"

"Because I'm expectin' you to be my chaplain."

The orchestra was playing an off-key version of "Swanee." But in the tiny room, there was silence. Jimmy lit a fresh cigarette and puffed the air full of smoke.

The priest coughed. "I'll do nothing of the sort, Starr. My ministry is here."

"This ministry is your small penance to Parnell. I'm givin' you the chance to pay him back with style."

There was a knock on the door. Starr dropped into his crouch and the knife appeared in his hand.

"Jesus Christ!" Jimmy jumped back.

Starr stood quickly and slipped the knife into his sleeve. He was still thinking too much about the men he had met in the alley that morning.

"Hey, Father," said Jimmy, "you got your holy oils with you?"

"Why?"

"He does that knife trick again, I'll be ready for the last annointin'."

There was another knock.

Starr looked at Jimmy and whispered, "Who is it?"

Jimmy grinned. "I may not be much in the guns department, nope. But the father tells me you took a shine to one of the girls. So, as a son of Ireland, accept this as a gift from the son of a son of Ireland." Jimmy turned the handle. "Miss Rubber Balloons herself."

The door opened, and Padraic Starr's opinion of Jimmy the Butcher went up. The tiny space filled with the aroma of lilac-scented body talc and fresh female perspiration.

"Let me introduce Miss Jenny Malloy."

She was wearing pink tights and a dove-gray corset with matching gray mules. Beneath the rouge and red lip salve, her face had a hard and bony pallor, but Starr did not notice, because he was admiring the breasts that spilled out over her corset.

She folded her hands behind her back and leaned against the door. Her eyes moved from Starr to O'Fearna. "You a real priest?"

"Indeed he is," said Jimmy, "so you've got no worries."

She smiled a bit. "He's human, ain't he?"

"Only too true, my dear," answered the priest.

She looked at Starr. "And what about him?"

Jimmy introduced, "Mr. Padraic Starr, a real Irish war hero."

"The Irish in a war?" She spoke with a hard, flat accent that Starr did not recognize.

"We certainly are," Starr said. "We're calling it the Great War."

"Oh. I heard about that one. How come you ain't still fightin' in it?"

"A long story, one I'd be glad to relate after the show."

She looked Starr up and down, inspecting the finely tailored suit and studying the face the way a woman in a grocery studies the melons. "Where we goin'?"

Starr glanced around. "Where should I take this beautiful young woman for dinner?"

"Jake Wirth's," said the priest.

"You comin' too?" she asked.

O'Fearna shook his head.

She pursed her lips like a disappointed little girl. "Too bad." Then she looked at Starr. "You look like you got some dough and you might be a gentleman, which is what I'm after. I'll have dinner, but no funny stuff." She opened the door and gave her bottom a twitch toward the priest. "You can come too, if you want. You're kinda cute."

After she went out, O'Fearna smiled. "A young temptress."

"I usually charge five bucks for this service. But for you, Paddy"—Jimmy rattled the derby—"it's on the house."

Miss Rubber Balloons was all that Starr had expected. When they left the theater, he noticed that she was still wearing her pink tights, and all during their late dinner, his mind was filled with the image of the corset and the milky white breasts above it.

But Padraic Starr played the gentleman. While she ate her Wiener schnitzel, he described his experiences in the trenches and his work as an Irish businessman. While she drank her beer, he told her what a wonderful performer she was. When he stopped at the door of her room in the Crawford House Hotel, he did not enter until she invited him.

There was a double bed with a carved oak headboard, a washstand, a hard-backed chair, and a threadbare rug. The gas lamp threw a dim, greasy light. The room seemed to smell of a thousand empty nights and a thousand lonely lives.

"Do you share this place with someone?" he asked.

"Yeah, but I told her to bunk with one of the other gals."

She lowered the gas and went over to the windows, which looked out onto Scollay Square. She folded her arms around her waist but did not move. Not did Starr, who stood in the shadows and studied her magnificent silhouette. A coal truck clattered by. Starr heard two drunks singing "Sweet Adeline" somewhere in the street. And Jenny Malloy took off her dress. After a moment, she turned toward him. She was wearing the corset and the tights and nothing else.

Her white breasts were like moonlight, thought Starr, and he like a dreamer awake in the night.

She came to him and put her mouth on his, and the dream found life. He ran his fingertips across her shoulders. He loosened the top hooks on her corset. Her breasts slipped free. He buried his face in their softness, and the dreamer entered the dream. They fell back onto the coverlet. Her red lip salve tasted like clay. And the dream spun downward, from the softness of moonlight to the firmness of earth. He tore at the tights and split them at the crotch. She ripped his fly and pulled him through the tear.

It was over quickly. He had been away from women for too long. But Jenny Malloy was a revelation, even to a man as worldly as Padraic Starr. She took off her clothes, then his, and she mounted him. She rode him, he thought, as a lonely rich woman rode her horse. Then he rolled her over and took her as if she were his mare, and when they were done, she thanked him.

"I was a very depressed man a bit ago."

"Another body makes you forget," she said in the darkness, "at least for a while."

"A different one in every town?"

"We play a big circuit. I'll be here all week, and back again in June, if you're still around."

"I'll be gone by then." He swung his legs out of bed and found his trousers in the jumble of clothes on the floor. "Can I see you tomorrow night?"

She said yes, and she added that she did not always invite her lovers back.

"I'm flattered." He buckled his belt and buttoned his fly. "And I'm curious."

"About what?"

"Why did you taunt the priest?"

"It was a priest who told my mother I was a trollop, when my belly swelled 'cause I couldn't count to twenty-eight."

"Priests are human. Some are better than others. I think O'Fearna's a good one." Starr knotted his tie.

She sat up in bed. "They tell you that what we just did is wrong. And I like it. Next to the gals in the line, it's all I got."

"There's more, darlin', or so I've been told."

"Well, I ain't found it."

"Me, neither." Starr pulled on his chesterfield. "Did the church help you find a home for your baby?"

In the darkness, she nodded. "The nuns were good to me."

"Some folks are better than others. That's the way it is everywhere. . . . Tomorrow night, then." When he closed the door, he could hear her crying softly.

He took off his boots before he went upstairs. The two younger boys were snoring in their room. Josephine's door was closed, but Tom's was open. The tip of his cigarette glowed and flickered.

"Out late, Padr'ic."

"I been seekin' a little comfort."

"Guns?"

"Not with eight hundred fifty-six dollars and thirty-seven cents."

"If you can get the guns without paying," Tracy whispered, "eight hundred might get you a ship."

Starr stepped into the room. "You've decided to help?"

"There's only one reason—to get you to hell away from my family."

"Get me a ship, and I promise you, one of us will put a bullet in William Clarke's brain on Easter Sunday."

Tracy drew on his cigarette again, and in the darkness, the tip flared like the muzzle of a pistol. "Get the guns. Then we'll see about the ship. And I'll be staying in Boston."

Starr patted Tracy on the leg, like a father having a late-night talk with his boy. "You'll just have to follow your conscience."

Rachel Levka lay awake. When she opened her eyes, she saw the strange smile of Padraic Starr, floating in the square of light that the streetlamp threw on the ceiling. When she closed her eyes, she saw the face of someone who terrified her even more. He came to her only at times like this, when she was confused or frightened. And when he appeared, all other emotions were driven away like clouds before the wind, and she was filled with terror and rage. . . .

She was four years old on the morning that they came. She was sitting on the front step of the cottage, talking to the little knot of rags and mop strands that her father had fashioned into a doll, and the ground began to rumble. The noise grew louder and the earth trembled, and the little girl thought that the dybbuk had risen from the underworld.

Then a great cloud blew past her and the rumbling suddenly

stopped. She looked up and saw the dybbuk and all his legions, mounted on horses as tall as her house.

The sight of him left her too terrified to call or cry out. She clutched her doll to her chest and stared at evil. He wore a tall fur cap, tilted to one side, and a tunic of gray and red. His black mustache drooped over the corners of his mouth, and there was a long red saber scar on the side of his face. But his eyes did not glow with fire, as she expected. Instead, they were black, like the earth he had risen from.

"Where is your papa, little girl?" he said in a gentle voice.

"He is not here, Cossack Captain." Rachel's mother stepped out of the cottage and swept her little girl into her arms.

So this, thought Rachel, was not the dybbuk after all, but what they called a cossack, always with the sound of fear in their voices.

He swung a leg over the haunch of his horse. His spurs dragged like chains on the ground. His body blocked out the sun. And he smelled of an onion field in August. "You are lying, Jewish mother."

Rachel buried her face in her mother's bosom and felt the heart pounding beneath it.

"I do not lie," said Sophie Levka. "My husband is not here."

"He is not at his bakery. And my men, they need a cook."

"My husband is a baker, not a cook. He cooks like . . . like a cossack's horse, if a cossack's horse could cook."

The cossack laughed softly, as though he liked a small joke at his own expense. "He cooks bread, little mother. He is known as the best baker in Lithuania."

At these words, Rachel raised her eyes to his face.

He reached out and stroked her straight black hair. "You are very pretty, little girl. And so is your dolly."

Rachel held her doll as tightly as her mother held her.

"If my husband is not in the bakery, I do not know where he is. Can't one of your men cook?"

The captain looked over his shoulder at the others. "None of my men want to cook, little mother, because if the cook cooks bad, someone wants to kill him. Our last cook made a stew of pigs' feet and turnips, and they drowned him in it. It is very dangerous work."

The cossack gently removed the doll from Rachel's hands and turned it over, examining the sinews of thread and string. "Not half so dangerous, though, as lying to a hungry cossack."

148

"My husband is not here. Search the house if you want."

The Levkas lived at the edge of town. They kept chickens and a small vegetable patch and were among the most prosperous Jews in the *shtetl*. On the other side of the road, a small river wound toward a larger river that flowed to the Baltic. Behind the cottage, the land rose to a low hill of trees which now caught the attention of the cossack.

"Is he up there, little mother?"

Sophie shook her head. Rachel, taking courage from her mother, shook her head, as well.

"The little girl says what the mother says." The cossack brought his huge face close to Rachel's. The smell of onions made her eyes water. "If I send a man up there to find your papa, I will have to tell him to shoot your papa, which will make me angry, because bullets cost money. But if you tell me the truth, we will let your papa bake our bread."

"Do not frighten my little girl." Sophie Levka grabbed the doll from the cossack's hands and shoved it between her own body and her daughter's. "Now do what you have come for, or leave us alone."

Rachel heard the sound of steel sliding across steel. The saber flashed from its scabbard. She closed her eyes and squeezed her doll. Her mother screamed. The doll dropped, and the sight of it froze in Rachel's mind forever. As the doll fell into the dirt, Rachel was torn from her mother's arms and lifted into the air by the collar of her blouse.

Sophie grabbed for Rachel.

The cossack whacked her across the face with the flat of the saber, knocking her to the ground. "Where is your husband?" The cossack held the tip of the saber against Rachel's stomach.

"I do not know," screamed Sophie Levka. "He went to his bakery this morning. If he is not there, I do not know where he is."

Rachel's tears and spittle were hanging in long streams from her face. She flailed her limbs like a frightened kitten.

"Your husband," demanded the cossack.

"I do not know," whispered Sophie Levka. "Give me my child."

Later Rachel remembered spinning toward the ground like a maple seed. Then her mother's body was on top of hers and her mouth was filled with dust.

Rachel spit and licked her lips and peered out from under her mother's arms like an animal from its burrow. She saw the tops of the boots and the sharp silver spurs. "Burn the barn!" And the boots turned away.

Rachel felt her mother's body stiffen with rage. She heard the words "Cossack pig!"

Later, Rachel thanked God that her face was pressed against the ground and she did not see what happened.

Steel slid against steel. Something whistled through the air. There was a strange thumping, the sound that a knife makes when it cuts into a squash. And the dybbuk and his legions rode away.

Only then did Rachel open her eyes. She smiled, because her mother was looking at her . . . but something was wrong. Her mother was not smiling. And if her body was on top of Rachel, how could she be looking into Rachel's eyes? How could she bend her neck that far, and twist it so that her head was upside down?

That was how Avram found them later. First he saw Sophie's body, then the pool of blood, then the head, upside down, staring back at the body and the little girl paralyzed beneath it. He had gone that day to the provisioner in the next village.

The cossacks did not come back. They found another cook. But Avram Levka decided to leave. In that place he would never be able to erase the terrible sight. His little daughter, now speechless, would never be the same. And they would never overcome the hatred rising in Russia as the century began.

One spring night, Avram Levka loaded his daughter and his sister and a few belongings onto a wagon and left the village where they were born. He had saved enough money that the family was able to travel in a private cabin, far below the waterline, on an old steamer. Rust bubbled through the paint on the bulkheads. The decks smelled of vomit of a thousand seasick peasants. But Rachel spent her days at the rail, feeling the rhythm of the sea, watching the horizon rise and fall, and finding in the motion of the ship the gentle rocking of a mother's arms, soothing her back from her terror.

When they reached America, she had begun once more to speak. As they came into New York Harbor, her family crowded onto the deck to see the great statue that welcomed every ship. And when she asked who the statue was, Avram Levka said that it was Columbus, holding up a loaf of bread. . . .

She was safe now, and the cossack, she was sure, was dead.

She closed her eyes and imagined him once more, galloping across the field at Tannenberg, into the German machine guns. The thought soothed her and she slept.

12

*H*err Doktor."

"*Ja?*"

"Mine arm hurts vhen I do zis." Mr. Feldstein flapped his arm up and down.

"So don't do zat."

Klaus Bremer slipped into a seat in the balcony of the Old Howard. The floor was sticky, and the stuffing had been torn out of the seat next to him. He chose the spot because no one was sitting within ten feet in any direction.

Onstage, an actor who called himself Herr Doktor was performing an examination on a character named Feldstein. Herr Doktor wore a white coat, a stethoscope, and an eyepiece. Mr. Feldstein wore a long black coat and a Vandyke plastered to his chin.

Bremer disliked what passed for humor among Americans. A nation of immigrants themselves, they were always looking for immigrants to laugh at. In this scene, it was the Germans and the Jews. Later, it would be the stage Irish, with clay pipes and Kelly-green derbies, or the Italians grinding their organs, or the shuffling blackfaces rolling their eyes.

"Vhat else is bozzering you?"

"Zis pain I have, it goes down, zen up, zen down again, from my sroat to my belly, zen back again it goes. Vhat is it, ziss pain?"

Herr Doktor studied Feldstein's face, walked around him, studied his behind, then said, "You haff ze dizeez called 'fartitis.' "

"Oh, no."

"*Ja.* Your face looks so much like your ass zat ze gass don't know vich vay to go."

The college boys four rows from Bremer snickered and giggled and passed a silver flask. Three sailors in the front row booed, and one of them shouted, "Bring on the girls!" A man at the end of Bremer's row was awakened by the noise. He looked about in panic, rose halfway out of his seat, then dropped down and went back to sleep.

"Fartitis." Padraic Starr sat down next to Bremer. "The British say it's Germany's national affliction."

"We eat steel and fart shrapnel." Bremer was wearing a peaked white cap with the letter *B* on the front, and he was dressed in the rough clothes of a day laborer.

Starr offered his hand. The German had reddish hair and a friendly smile, and was without the usual Kaiser-style mustache. Starr guessed Bavaria rather than Prussia.

"Father O'Fearna told you about me?" Starr said.

The German nodded. "And no one I've spoken with, in Boston or New York, seems to know who you are. That is even better."

"Well, then. How are you going to help the Irish rebellion?"

"I personally do not give a damn about your Irish rebellion. I do, however, need *your* help."

"And in return?"

"Guns . . . if you're man enough."

Jimmy McHale looked up from the sports page as Father O'Fearna stepped into his stockroom.

"Where's Starr?"

"In the balcony, but Father—"

O'Fearna pivoted back into the hallway.

"—he asked you not to come tonight." Jimmy heard the house door swing open. He threw down his paper. "Ah, Jeez."

Onstage, Herr Doktor was examining a man in blackface. "I'm afraid ve vill haff to amputate your organ."

"What-u-tate my who?"

"Cut off your pecker. Ve call it an organ." Herr Doktor disappeared behind a screen, leaving the blackface alone.

"Organ, hunh?" The blackface looked down at his crotch. "Well, if you-all is an organ, you done played your last tune."

Herr Doktor reappeared holding a crosscut saw. The audience roared and the lights went out.

In the sudden darkness, the British agent named Edward Huddleston lost the priest. He had paid his fifteen-cent admission and had come in at the back of the house when he saw the bulky black figure of Sean O'Fearna storming up the side aisle.

He waited for the stagelights. The band began to play "Ballin' the Jack," and the chorus girls danced out onto the apron. But the priest had disappeared. Huddleston cursed. For the second night he had lost his quarry.

"On Sunday night," Bremer whispered, "a train will leave the Winchester Weapons Factory in Connecticut, bound for Boston. It will carry twenty thousand Enfield pattern 1914 rifles and five million rounds of .303 Mark VII pointed-bullet cartridge."

Bremer paused. Onstage, the girls pivoted to the audience and swung their behinds in perfect rhythm. The college students and the sailors cheered. The sleeping man at the end of the aisle awoke, and Bremer watched him until he had settled back again.

"He's just some bum," Starr said.

"I like to be careful. Federal agents arrested most of my associates last month, after the explosion at the Parliament building in Ottawa."

"Your people did that?"

Bremer nodded. "And the bombing of the munitions plant in the town of Woburn last summer. We've also tried to destroy several railroad bridges on the Canadian side of the Maine border."

"How is it you're still on the loose?"

"Caution . . . and luck." Bremer tugged on the brim of his baseball cap. "But I have decided to forget the caution and use up the last of the luck."

Onstage, the girls tried a pirouette. One of them stumbled, a few did it well, and the rest looked as clumsy as dancing dogs.

"I am going to blow up that train."

Sean O'Fearna stopped outside the balcony door. He took out his flask and drank down a long swallow of Jameson's, which did nothing to calm the mixture of anger and fear boiling in his stomach and sending steams of panic through his whole system.

At the stand in the lobby, Edward Huddleston bought a bag of popcorn and watched the men coming into the theater. He had etched in his mind the image of Padraic Starr wearing a Victoria Cross, and he was certain that within a few minutes the image would come to life.

Then he noticed a man wearing a derby and green armbands watching him from one of the staircases. A few moments earlier, the man had been watching him from the back of the theater as he searched in the darkness for the white Roman collar. Huddleston casually tossed three or four pieces of popcorn into his mouth and strolled toward the opposite staircase.

Jimmy the Butcher was starting up to the balcony when the commanding voice of Dr. G. E. Lothrop boomed his name.

Jimmy looked over his shoulder. "Hiya, Doc."

"Come here, Jim." Lothrop was the owner of the Howard.

Jimmy went down the stairs. "What can I do for ya?"

"Go backstage and get ready to butcher. The lights are coming up after this act."

"We got 'Rubber Balloons' before intermission." Jimmy saw the man with the popcorn going up the stairs on the other side of the lobby.

"Louie the Lip's drunk," said Lothrop.

"Can't you run the second banana?"

"He's drunker than Louie. Get back and get ready."

"In a jiff." Jimmy tipped his hat and turned to the balcony stairs.

"Jimmy!" said Lothrop. "Not in a jiff. *Now.*"

"Yes, sir." Jimmy wanted to help Starr, but Dr. G. E. Lothrop was not a man he could ignore.

"With the assistance of a German-American in the railroad routing office, the train will be sent over the Northern Avenue Bridge instead of the Channel Bridge, on its way to South Boston." Bremer spoke just loudly enough to be heard above the music. "You and I and a German explosives expert will be waiting."

"How many men will you need?"

"Four, maybe five."

"There must be an easier way to get a few rifles."

"None that you can afford, Herr Irish. You have no money to buy weapons. You have no support from the Clan na Gael in New York—"

"I never asked for any."

"—so you must steal the weapons. The explosion will destroy the evidence of theft, and the blame will be laid to German saboteurs. Ambassador von Bernstorff has ordered that railroad sabotage is to end. He fears American opinion. But this target I cannot resist." Bremer smiled in the half-light. "And since we have the dynamite . . ."

"The damn shame of this war's that we have too many stupid

men makin' our decisions for us." Starr offered the German his hand. "I like someone who'll act on his own when he sees the chance."

Bremer's eyes shifted to the end of the row. A man in a black coat was coming toward them. Bremer's hand went to the pistol in his jacket. "He was told not to come."

Sean O'Fearna dropped into the seat on Starr's right and took out his flask.

"That's a darlin' Roman collar 'round your neck." Starr snatched the flask from his hand and drank. "Next time, wear a green cummerbund with the words *Erin go Bragh* printed in gold. That'll attract more attention."

The priest ignored the sarcasm. "Two strange men cornered Jimmy Duggan in an alley this afternoon."

"The choirboy?" Starr lowered the flask.

"Did he talk?" asked Bremer.

"They beat him, but he told nothing. He believes he's bound by the seal of confession."

"Does he have bruises?" asked Starr.

"He told his father they came from a streetfight." The priest's eyes filled with tears. "I've endangered him needlessly. . . . I can't be helpin' you any longer."

The girls finished their act, and the curtain came down as they danced offstage. The college students and the sailors cheered and whistled and stamped their feet. And Edward Huddleston sat down two rows behind the priest.

"Where's my pig bladder?" Louie the Lip Lee was lurching across the backstage.

"You ain't ready yet, Louie. We're takin' an intermission so you can sober up," said the stage manager.

Louie saw Jimmy the Butcher wearing his baggy pants and coat. "It ain't time for him. Get my pig bladder."

Jenny Malloy came up behind Louie. She had put on two layers of underwear and a pink dress for the sketch. In the red backstage lights, she looked like the daughter of innocence lured to the cathouse. "Louie, there ain't no pig bladder in 'Rubber Balloons.' Have another coffee."

Louie leered. "You let me kiss you good out there?"

"Sure, just don't go on drunk."

The audience was stamping and whistling and shouting, and the band was playing "Alexander's Ragtime Band."

"Awright," said Louie, "but you give me some tongue when we do the bit."

"You're on, Jimmy." The stage manager steered Louie back to the coffee pot.

The house lights came up and the audience began to jeer. They wanted Louie the Lip, not intermission.

Jimmy looked at Jenny Malloy. "Do me a favor, honey."

"Why should I?"

"I got you a nice meal and a nice fella last night."

"He was okay."

"The best-lookin' guy you ever had, and he's in a scrape with some bill collector in the balcony right now."

"What's it to me?"

"I ain't sure, but when you go on, get this place shoutin' and screamin' so nobody's watchin' what's goin' on around them. Then he can slip away."

"How do I do that?"

"You're in a sketch where you take off your dress, for Chrissakes. Use your imagination."

Then Jimmy went out. The crowd stopped jeering. The regulars who had seen him work before began to applaud.

"Howdy, boys. It's your old buddy Jimmy the Butcher, here to sell you what's hot and tell you what's not."

Some sailor shouted, "Cut the bullshit."

"Make your own sandwiches." Jimmy knew all the best lines.

Three men laughed.

"Where's Louie?" shouted somebody else. "In jail?"

"He's warmin' up them famous lips of his. He'll be out in a jiff, with the best-lookin' *soubrette* on the circuit."

"Hey, if you can talk French," hollered a fat man in the front row, "you must be sellin' some French ticklers."

"I got French ticklers, French perfume, French doors, French toast, and"—Jimmy jumped off the apron into the center aisle—"I can even promise you a French kiss if you'll buy this packet of French postcards." He reached into his pocket and whipped out a stack of cards. "Just one dollar for ten of the finest views in all of gay Paree, and when you're finished with 'em, you'll know why the Eiffel Tower was—ahem—*erected* in France."

He offered the postcards to the fat man, who shook his head and threw up his hands.

"He ain't interested." Jimmy gave him a squint, then rattled the derby on top of his head. "All right, seein' as how we got such a large crowd here tonight, I guess I can make a little discount. I'll offer these ten fine views of the natural wonders of Paree at eighty-five cents a pack, and just to show you what a good sport I am, I'll give you all a free sample. Yes, sirree." He slit the package open with his thumbnail and looked at the first card. "That's Yvette the wet, my little pet." He spun the card across the audience and a dozen men grabbed for it.

He took out the next card. "Here's Noelle, the kind of gal you'd follow to hell." He flung her to the other side of the theater. "And here's . . ."

He made a face and pretended to study the next card, as though it puzzled him. "Why, this is an English dame."

A few men whistled and hooted.

"How in the hell did someone from England get in here?" He scaled the heavy postcard up to the sailors in the balcony. One of them leaned out to grab it and almost fell into the orchestra. "I guess we'll call her Millicent and put her up in the balcony."

The knife appeared in Starr's hand. He turned on the priest. "Someone followed you."

"I came in the stage door. Nobody gets in the stage door unless they're known."

"Perhaps so," whispered Bremer, "but I believe the candy butcher is warning us about the man eating popcorn in the last row."

"Do you know him?" Starr did not turn around.

"I know the face. I've seen him in New York. Now that he has seen us together, we cannot let him leave."

"A man's life as simple as that?" said Sean O'Fearna. "I will not allow it." He tried to stand.

Starr grabbed him by the elbow and with a sharp tug pulled him back into his seat.

Edward Huddleston stuffed dry popcorn into his dry mouth and tried to swallow. The popcorn caught in his throat. The priest had led him to the center of the plot, and he had arrived alone. Stewart was having dinner with the British consul; Dawson was walking South End streets looking for young crapshots.

Huddleston shifted in his seat, rearranging his shoulder holster so that he could grab his pistol without fumbling. They were on to him. He stuffed more popcorn into his mouth. He tried to decide if he should run with what he knew or try to discover more.

With the lights up, Jimmy could see him, a few rows behind Starr, eating popcorn and waiting for the girls like any burley hound.

He held up a pair of black silk knickers. "Now who's buyin' this very hot stuff for their lady friend?" Jimmy looked around, but no one held up a bill. He made a disgusted face. "Who'll buy it for the wife?"

The band was coming into the pit for the second act.

"All right. If you's change your mind, I'll be out at the end of the show. If you don't buy nothin', you'll send me home drier than a popcorn fart, and my old lady'll need a pound of butter to get me greased."

Starr watched Jimmy waddle off and whispered to Bremer. "We lure Mr. Popcorn outside, into an alley."

"No," said Bremer. "His friends may be watching the exits. We do it inside. Make it look like a robbery."

The priest drank from his flask, but he did not offer it to the others.

Jenny Malloy was perspiring, and in the backstage draft she had begun to shiver.

"Remember, babe," said Jimmy the Butcher, "a little diversion so our friend can get away."

"I don't know why I should do nothin'."

"You like the guy, and he's in trouble."

"And remember what I said, sweetie." Louie the Lip came up behind her. He was known as the most professional drinker on the circuit, because he could turn sober in a five-minute intermission. He was sucking on a piece of candy. "When I give you the kiss of life . . ."

She stuck her tongue out at him.

"See that?" Louie said. "She knows her line by heart."

The band had reached the last bars of "Who Put the Overalls in Mrs. Murphy's Chowder?" Louie slapped Jenny on the bottom. "You're on."

A flat dropped from the flies and the curtain came up. The scene was a city neighborhood, a row of bright red brick buildings, gray streets, and pastel-blue skies. Jenny glanced at Jimmy, then at Louie, who licked his lips. She opened the parasol and strolled onto the stage.

After the applause subsided, she peered out from under the parasol at the imaginary sun. "Ooh, I'm so hot," she said in her nasal voice, "and this parasol is doing no good at all. What should I do?"

"Take off your dress," shouted a drunk.

"What should I do?"

"Your dress. Take it off."

The sailors and college boys hooted when Jenny Malloy pulled her arms from her dress. It slipped from her body and blossomed on the floor around her feet. Then she wondered aloud if she was cool enough.

"No!" shouted a sailor.

"What should I do? What *should* I do?"

"Take off your corset," shouted one of the college boys in front of Starr, and his friends began to hoot.

Jenny looked up toward the balcony. "I guess I'm still pretty hot." She dropped her voice half an octave and untied a ribbon on her corset.

The priest was saying, "I won't let you kill a man."

"For five years, your money's bought guns and ammunition," Starr responded. "On Easter, them guns'll kill Brits and RIC, and your hands'll be as dirty as if you pulled the triggers yourself."

Sean O'Fearna had come here to tell Starr that he would no longer help, that he would not endanger innocent lives. Now he was being asked to sit quietly while a man was murdered. He twined his fingers around the rosary beads in his pocket and tried to listen to the clear voice of his conscience.

But Padraic Starr was beside him, whispering in his ear. "I see them fingers workin', Father. Don't be botherin' God for an answer on this. He's been tellin' you the same thing for five years. *That* should tell you what has to be done now."

The priest stopped working the rosary and looked down at the stage.

Jenny untied the last ribbon on her corset. She looked up at the balcony, she smiled, and she let the corset slip slowly to the floor. The Old Howard seemed to deflate as three hundred men gasped. Jenny Malloy wore nothing but black silk knickers and a black camisole, held up by the slenderest of shoulder straps. Quickly she crossed her hands in front of her so that the men would not see the outline of her nipples.

And the theater nearly burst with the rush of noise.

Dr. Lothrop came in at the back of the house. The stagehands were stopping their work to watch. Louie was licking his lips. "All she got to do now is faint, and boy oh boy, we'll have a ball."

Huddleston slipped his hand into his jacket and wrapped it around the grip of his gun. He had made the decision to stay on Starr's trail and use the gun if he had to. It was possible that they were not on to him after all, and the chorine onstage had inspired such a riot that a .22 caliber pistol shot would not be heard above the noise.

Jenny Malloy had gone as far as she or anyone else ever had on the circuit. She looked into the wings, and Jimmy Mc-Hale nodded encouragement. "I'm still awful, awful hot," she said tentatively, and the men roared with a single voice that she found both frightening and exhilarating. She looked up toward the darkness in the balcony and said, "What should I do?"

The drunkest of the college boys jumped up and screamed, "Take off the rest."

Jenny did not know if she had heard Starr's voice above the others, but she no longer cared.

She looked down at the band members in the pit and the men in the first few rows. They were leaning forward, their faces red, their eyes wide, and those who weren't shouting for more seemed to be sitting in an open-mouthed trance. For the first time in her life, she was stealing the show.

She smiled out at them and slowly unfolded her hands. She let her fingers play across her breasts and her shoulders, and she raised her arms high above her head, so that the whiteness spilled out around the sides of the camisole.

"You can't kill him," the priest said. "He's a human being."

"Get up and go back to your church and pray," said Starr. "Either that or stick around and see somethin' you been wonderin' about since you started comin' here."

"What are you talkin' about?"

"Tits."

Jenny was out on the apron now, parading back and forth with a queenly stride to which the drummer was adding a steady beat. At one side of the apron, she stopped and looked up into the boxes. "I'm *still* too hot." She ripped the left strap off the camisole. The drum beat and the men roared.

"This is a very daring young woman," said Bremer. He was speaking in his normal voice now, because the noise was so loud a whisper would not be heard.

"She's doin' a fine job," Starr answered, "and we'd better do ours before she finishes and the house lights come up."

Dr. Lothrop pushed his way through the mob of stagehands in the wings. "What does she think she's doing?"

"The bitch is stealin' my scene," said Louie the Lip.

"But the boys sure are enjoyin' it," said Jimmy.

"If she takes off any more," said Lothrop, "she could shut us down. Get her in here."

Jenny marched with the drums to the other side of the apron. "I'm *still* too hot." She ripped off the right strap. The drum beat and the men roared.

Bremer whispered, "If he follows me, I'll lead him to the men's room. We will leave him in a stall. Otherwise you will have to kill him here, with the knife." Bremer stood. "Be fast."

Huddleston's hand once more went into his coat and wrapped around the revolver.

Sean O'Fearna's fingers were on the rosary and his eyes were on Jenny Malloy. If he acted now, he could save the Englishman, but he would destroy the rising.

Padraic Starr slipped the knife from his sleeve and watched Bremer step over the sleeping man at the end of the aisle.

"I'm *still* too hot." Jenny stood in the middle of the apron, her hands holding up the camisole. The men were standing, screaming, cheering.

Lothrop went over to the electric board and grabbed the main stagelight switch.

Bremer stopped at the exit on the side of the balcony. The Englishman was not moving.

"Maybe if I . . ." Jenny lowered her hands, revealing the tops of her breasts. "Mmm, that's cooler."

Sean O'Fearna stood and turned and opened his mouth to speak.

Huddleston looked at the priest, then saw Bremer coming at him from the other side. He drew his pistol.

"Maybe I should . . ." Jenny threw her arms into the air. Her camisole dropped to her waist and her breasts swung free.

For an instant, there was silence. Then the shout of three hundred men, as loud as an artillery volley. Lothrop threw the switch. The Old Howard went black.

A muzzle flashed in the back row, but no one heard the shot, not even the man who pulled the trigger.

In the darkness, Huddleston swung his pistol toward Starr. The image of the naked woman on the bright stage was still imprinted on the backs of his eyes, and the black shadow of Padraic Starr seemed to be jumping through it. As Huddleston fired a second time, Starr's knife slashed into the left side of his throat and severed the carotid. The bullet went through the seat in front of him and through the one beyond that and spent itself in the folds of Sean O'Fearna's overcoat.

Starr's hand went over Huddleston's mouth. The Englishman put the gun to Starr's belly and tried to fire again, but the blood had already drained from the left side of his brain. His right arm went limp. The gun fell from his hand. Starr drove the knife into his heart.

When the stagelights came up a few moments later, the band began to play "Maple Leaf Rag." But the men wanted more of what they had just seen. They were shouting and clapping and the college boys were chanting "Bring back the boobs!" And when the chorus danced onto the apron, they jeered.

Padraic Starr climbed off Huddleston and dropped into the seat beside him. O'Fearna was still standing two rows away, with his mouth open. The words of warning had never come out. "Sit down," Starr growled, and O'Fearna obeyed.

Starr looked at Bremer, who was sitting two seats away. "Are you all right?"

Bremer nodded, and then his body shuddered.

Jenny Malloy was beaming. "How did I do?"

"You want to get us shut down?" demanded Lothrop.

She glanced at Jimmy, who shook his head.

"I just wanted to liven things up a bit."

"Well, you'll never work the Howard again," said Lothrop.

"And if you can't work the Howard," said Louie the Lip, "there ain't no room for you in our show. So pack your bags and beat it. Showin' your tits like that. Fuckin' disgrace."

Jenny looked out into the house. The audience was still roaring. "They liked it."

"They don't give out the licenses," answered Louie. He turned away from her and shouted, "Where's my pig bladder?"

Jimmy McHale threw an arm around her. "I'll make it up to you, babe."

She pulled away. "You bastard."

Bremer's hands were clutching his chest, and the blood was seeping through his fingers.

"Can you stand?"

He shook his head. *"Kronprinzessin Cecille,* Pier D, East Boston. Lieutenant Kuntz. He has the dynamite. He will help you. Now, give me your knife."

Starr slipped the blade into Bremer's hand.

"And your hat."

Starr put his scally cap on Bremer's head and took the baseball cap.

"A British agent and a German agent have killed each other in a burlesque house. Casualties of war," Bremer said with most of the strength he had left.

The audience was beginning to settle down. The cooch dancer had come onstage, and her creativity with her waves of fat was winning them over.

O'Fearna knelt beside the German. "You are Catholic. Make a confession."

Bremer was looking at Starr. "I have done you a great favor. In return, you must blow up that train."

"Are you sorry for your sins?" the priest said.

Bremer turned his eyes to the priest. "In wartime, all is sin, but there are no sinners."

"Are you sorry?"

Bremer merely smiled. His right hand rose to his forehead, as though beginning the Sign of the Cross, then dropped to his lap. In his eyes the reflection of the cooch dancer wiggled and spun.

The door on the far side of the balcony swung open, and three sailors began looking about in the darkness for seats.

"He's dead," Starr said. "Let's go."

"I'll absolve him," answered the priest, and he began to speak in Latin.

Starr grabbed him by the collar and dragged him to his feet. "He's sorry. And we'll be even sorrier if we're caught."

Sean O'Fearna made the Sign of the Cross over Bremer's body and left with Starr.

It was nine-thirty when Tom Tracy came up the stairs to the Tammany Club. The hall was already arranged for the St. Patrick's Eve banquet, with fifty round tables, five hundred chairs, and on the wall behind the head table, an American flag the size of a railroad car. Tracy did not turn on the lights, because whenever the neighborhood ladies saw lights in the hall, they marched in expecting a rally and acted insulted if the mayor was not there to greet them personally.

Tracy barked his shin on a folding chair while picking his way to the office door. Halfway across the hall, he stopped. Someone was sitting at the head table, completely in shadow.

"Hello?" said Tracy.

The shadow did not respond.

"Rachel?"

"He came to the shop yesterday, Thomas." Her voice echoed off the tabletops and hardwood floors. "He pulled a knife on my father. He got my cousin Simon in trouble. And I had to lie to a British agent to get them out of it."

Tracy looked up at the white stars and stripes that stood out in the darkness behind her, but he said nothing.

"My father told me I can't see any more Irishers . . . and this time he's serious." She paused. "Tonight he thinks I'm at Hadassah."

Tracy dropped into a folding chair. "Like a bad wind."

Her shadow rose and the chair legs screeched on the bare floor. She came toward him, moving among the empty tables, he thought, like the bride at a spoiled wedding feast. It was cold in the hall, and she was wearing her brown overcoat. "The last thing your cousin wanted to know was if you'd ever said you loved me."

"Strange question for a rebel."

She knelt down in front of him and took his hands in hers. "He looked at me as if he knew what I was thinking, as if he knew what you're thinking. What is he after, Tommy?"

"Guns, a boat, two or three souls."

After a moment, she said, "Have you offered yours?"

He reached out and raised her chin, so that he could see her face, because the tone of her voice told him nothing. Her dark brows and sober expression told him little more. "He's brought back the past, Rachel. The past always has a hold on us, even when we think we've escaped."

"Then it's true," she said, and in the darkness, he saw her smile. "You're helping him."

Tracy had found her note under his office door that morning. *We must talk. Here, 9 P.M.* He had wondered all day what she wanted. He had suspected that Starr was the cause. He had not expected this. "Rachel, my cousin is a dangerous man."

"I know," she answered. "And you've made a difficult decision. If you're standing up for him, I'm glad."

"I'm making a compromise. I'm much better at compromise than decision."

Her smile faded.

"I'm compromising him out of my family's life with the least damage to *his* plans or *my* reputation."

She stood and stepped back. "That's not what I hoped you'd say, Tommy."

"The first time you met him, you said he frightened you."

"He does. But Rabbi Mossinsohn frightens me, too. Men who challenge you always frighten you. But I was willing to stand up for the rabbi, and I was willing to do what Starr asked me yesterday."

She turned toward the head table.

"Rabbi Mossinsohn didn't leave an Englishman hanging on a meat hook at Quincy Market the other day."

Rachel stopped, as though she had stepped into a wall in the dark.

Tracy had not intended to tell her about the murder, because the closer he held the secret, the easier it would be to control. But for the second night, he felt Starr coming at him through someone else, someone who found Starr's dreams of rebellion and revenge even more attractive than his brother did.

"I'm harboring a killer." He went over to her and gently put his hands on her shoulders. She seemed to shrink from him. "That's why I haven't seemed too cheerful lately."

Outside, the el rumbled down Washington Street and screeched into Dudley Station.

"Tommy, a hundred thousand men are dying every day to see what strain of imperialists rules the world next. If Starr had to kill one man to bring some freedom to one corner of the world . . ." She paused, as though feeling her way uncertainly toward a conclusion. "I . . . I don't think you should simply call it murder."

"If he does it in Quincy Market, it's murder."

"Then why don't you turn him in?" she asked, almost as a challenge.

"The American part of me says that I should. It's the law, plain and simple. But I'm still Irish, too. I still remember." He smiled. "And I know what happens when you inform."

That made her spin around and look him hard in the eye. "The Irish voters turn against you."

He tried to respond, but she kept talking.

"This cousin of yours is forcing us to decide what's important, Tommy. Is it my father and his fear of a gentile for a son-in-law? Is it the voters, who don't give a damn what the politicians steal, as long as they don't kiss the wrong lips? Or is it each other?"

Then she twisted away and went over to the dais. She rested her elbows on the head table and her head on her hands.

In the dark, he thought, the green crepe decorations looked black. He came over to her and touched the skin at the back of her neck, as he had done on Saturday night. "It isn't that simple for us, Rachel. You've known that from the start."

"I thought if your cousin could help you to face the past, you might be able to face our future, too."

"I face it every day." He put his hands on her shoulders and turned her toward him. "I could marry some Irish girl, we'd have ten kids and take them to the most crowded Mass every Sunday, and when I took a shot at City Hall, they'd be my greatest asset. If I was the calculating bastard I sometimes seem like, I'd be courting Ursula O'Day right now."

"Then maybe you should. She's Irish. She's available. And she's a decent person."

"She certainly is." He wrapped his arms around her waist and pulled her against him. "But every morning for the last six months, you've been my first thought." He kissed her. She did not resist, but she did not join the enterprise. "Does that answer Starr's question about whether I love you?"

"It's easy to answer it in the dark, Tommy. I want to step into the light."

"So do I."

"When I saw you fight those four thugs the other night, I decided I'd never leave you. And I won't, dark or light. Just give me some reason to defy my father."

"If I get Starr a boat to take him away, will that be enough?"

"You called it a compromise, Tommy. I want you to *help* him. Get him the guns if he asks you. Go back to Ireland if he needs you." The words came out in a rush, as though she had been trying to hold them in. "But do it, and don't be afraid."

He spoke calmly, to counter her sudden intensity. "If I go back to Ireland, I'll never return."

She brought her hands to his face. "I'll go with you, Tommy. We'll start that fight, then, somehow, we'll get ourselves to Palestine and join the Zionists. I'll fight for your people and you can fight for mine."

He wrapped his arms around her and whispered her name. He was frightened by what she was saying, because she seemed to believe it. Until now, her good sense had always been equal to her passion, whether she was talking about life in the ward or world politics. But in a single Sunday afternoon, she had met a Zionist rabbi, an Irish rebel, and four homegrown American bigots, and she had begun to change. She wanted him to change with her, and he sensed that if he did not, she would no longer accept their world as it was.

"We belong right here, in Boston," he said.

"I hate Boston." She pulled his face to hers and kissed him, pressing her lips hard against his, pressing until the kiss became painful. "But I love you. And if you're ready to stand up, I am too."

"I'll stand up in Boston, Rachel, but I'm not going back to Ireland. If I do, I'll kill the man who killed my father, and my father told me it would do no good."

"If I could kill the man who killed my mother, Tommy, I'd do it with my bare hands." She stepped back suddenly, as though her own memories terrified her. "I . . . I'd better make an appearance at Hadassah." She turned and walked across the hall.

As she approached the door, he called her name. She stopped and turned. The light from the street below cast her in silhouette. He told her he loved her. He saw her hand rise to her face, perhaps to brush away a tear.

"We can't help who we fall in love with," she said.

"That's a good thing," he answered.

And she left.

Tracy looked around at the darkened hall and saw it as it would be two nights later, filled with Irish revelers, politicians, representatives of every ethnic group, and the band playing "Tipperary." He wanted to invite Rachel to the banquet, introduce her to the mayor, stand beside her in public, but he knew that he could not. It would be like announcing their engagement, and it would probably end his career. Someday, perhaps, he would be able to do it, but until he had rid himself of Padraic Starr and the voice softly goading him to revenge, he could face nothing else.

He stared at the bold, confident stripes and the rows of stars standing out in the darkness. From the first day that he had seen them fluttering in front of the Boston Custom House, he had seen order, freedom, and the promise of the future. But now, stars and stripes began to flicker against the dark background, like shadows and light on a moviehouse screen, and onto the rectangular cloth his mind played another image: Ballinakill House, ancestral home of the Clarkes, its lights glimmering across the bay to the darkened cottage where the little boy wept for his father.

13

Donal O'Leary stepped out the door of the old Tracy cottage, pulled up his suspenders, and rubbed his eyes with the heels of his hands. The moon was full but well past the apex. He guessed the time to be about three hours after midnight. On the bay, little chips of silver light danced with the waves, and the night was bright enough that he could see the houses and cottages on the shadowed mass of Ballinakill Peninsula.

Lanterns were burning at Ballinakill House, in spite of the hour, and a pair of headlamps was bouncing west along the road. That would be William Clarke's car. He had taken the night train from Dublin to oversee the search for Starr's relatives. Donal knew of this because Seamus Kilkeirnan had been reading official cables passed through his office. But the RIC direct wire, cut a week earlier, had been repaired Tuesday afternoon. That was the reason Donal had risen in the middle of the night.

He went into the cottage and took an ancient revolver from his dresser. He slipped it into his belt and put on a thick black wool sweater. He was fully awake now, and the fear had sunk into him like a foul hook in a salmon's flank. Black clothes would made him harder to see, and the black hat would cover his blond hair. He even considered shaving off his beard and covering his skin with lampblack, but a smooth-faced O'Leary would attract the suspicion of every constable in the district.

In the shed behind the cottage, he got a pair of wirecutters with wooden handles, which would not conduct the electricity. He wheeled his bicycle into the moonlight and started silently down the road.

Just outside the village, he stopped at the cottage of Tim Cooney. Before Donal knocked, Cooney was out the door. He nodded to Donal, pulled his scally cap over his eyes, and strapped his Mauser to his shoulder. No one in the town had ever seen Tim Cooney show fear, anger, or any of the other emotions that rose in most people like foam on a mug of porter. And few, outside of his wife and two small sons, had ever seen him laugh. He climbed onto his bike and kicked off without a word.

They slipped past the quay and the quiet row of buildings on the south side of town, then headed toward the bridge. A nighthawk screeched in the hills. A gentle wind pushed down the river and tapped the clapper against the bell in St. Brendan's tower.

The sound frightened Donal for a moment, but Cooney pedaled on, oblivious to the bell or the bright lights at the barracks gate. Before crossing the bridge, they turned inland and took the road along the south side of the river. Soon the light from the barracks faded, and the branches of the riverbank trees scattered the moonlight. Donal O'Leary felt the hook of fear working loose.

When they reached the Clifden road, they stopped.

"Where do we cut?" asked Cooney.

"Same place as last time. They won't be expectin' us there again."

Cooney nodded and pedaled on.

The wire had last been cut at the place where the Clifden road met the cart path to Cleggen. It was a treeless spot, blanketed by peat bogs, scraped over by rocky hills. Most nights, it was silent and deserted. On this night, in the low run of hills beside the road, the Royal Irish Constabulary waited.

Chief Inspector Hayes counted two dozen telegraph poles within his view, and the moon was bright enough that each one cast a clear shadow. Hayes was certain that they would return here to make their next cut. If not tonight, then one night soon, and when they did, he would take them.

On the night that Home Rule passed, Brian Hayes stood at a bonfire and celebrated with the rest of Ireland. When the war started, and Home Rule was postponed, he believed the Irish members of Parliament, who said that by fighting bravely on the front, the Catholics of Ireland could guarantee Home Rule and prove to the Ulster Protestants that a Home Rule Ireland would be Britain's best ally.

His brothers had answered the call, while Hayes had dedicated himself to maintaining order in a district where malcontents were as common as turf piles. He had resolved that he would not allow rebels their way in Connemara while Irish boys were dying on the front, because it was the soldiers who were fighting for Irish freedom, not the night riders of the IRB.

"Something just swung 'round the bend, sir," said Deputy Moore.

Hayes squinted into the darkness. "Two bicycles." He turned to the back of the lorry. "Carbines, gentlemen." Then he climbed out and wrapped his hand around the grip of the floodlamp attached to his door.

The bikes rolled into the intersection. Before Donal had stopped, Tim Cooney was off, searching the darkness with his Mauser at his hip. To the east, the road disappeared around a bend. To the west, lights flickered in the village of Cleggen. And to the south was the run of hills, almost all in shadow. "Clear," said Cooney.

Donal O'Leary rubbed his sweater against his flanks to soak up the sweat, then leaned his bike against the pole. He stepped onto the seat, and from there swung his foot onto the first steel rung. When he reached the top, he wrapped an arm around the pole, and the fear hooked into him again. On the pole, he was open to RIC fire, and if he was careless, he might electrocute himself. He raised the wirecutters above his head.

"Stop in the name of the king!" Three powerful lights burst from the hillside.

"Jesus Christ!" shouted Donal.

"Cut the wire," Cooney commanded, then he dropped to his stomach and took aim.

"I repeat. Stop in the name of the king, or we'll open fire."

A bullet exploded into Hayes's floodlamp, and he screamed, "Fire!"

Three carbines began to flash from the black shadow of the hill. Bullets tore up the dirt around Cooney, and two shots slammed into the pole that Donal clung to.

"Jesus Christ!" cried Donal, and began to clamber down.

"Cut the wire!" Cooney fired a quick shot that took out the lorry's right headlamp.

"I'm hit!" screamed O'Leary.

"Cut the wire!' Cooney shouted.

"I'm hit!"

"Cut the wire or I'll shoot *you!*"

Donal O'Leary was terrified. He had awakened in the middle of the night and stepped into the nightmare that had taunted him from the time Starr came back to Dunslea: He was caught in the open while bullets splattered around him. His hand trembled. His cutter sank into the wire. The spark jumped, and the wire snapped with the sound of a giant fiddle string. Then three more bullets smashed into the pole.

And Donal O'Leary lost his handhold. But a man could fall faster than he could lower himself. In an instant, Donal slipped down the splintered wood, stumbled over his own bicycle, and slammed to the ground.

"I'm hit."

"In the ass you're hit."

"Hit is hit." Donal scuttled to his feet and, ignoring the pain, swung a leg over his bicycle. "Come on, Cooney."

"Two shakes, Donal." As cool as a rock, Tim Cooney stitched a line of bullets across the grille of the lorry and knocked out the left headlamp. Glass shattered and steam hissed from the radiator like smoke from the cracks of a cheap kettle.

"Now we can leave." Cooney leaped onto his bicycle, and the two night riders sped away from the RIC muzzle flashes.

"Shot in the ass, is it?" Logan O'Leary stood over his son's bed.

Donal took the pillow from off his head. It was not the voice but the strong smell of sheep and clothes worn too long that woke him. "Nicked in the left buttock."

"Well, you better be showin' yourself 'fore the day's out, for whatever damn-fool thing you done last night, Seamus says the RIC is askin' questions all over."

"Then I'll not be goin' into town at all . . . till I'm free of my limp." Donal dragged himself to the edge of the bed and sat up, carefully putting all his weight on his right side. It was almost noon. He had gone to bed at six that morning.

He yawned and stretched, and his father pulled the blankets out from under him. Donal landed on the floor. He clenched his teeth against the pain. Then his anger rose, and he jumped up.

"Lay a finger on your father, and you'll never sleep another night in this house." Logan O'Leary was fifty-six years old and one of the few men in Dunslea larger than his son. Like Donal, he wore a thick, full beard. His was lined with stripes of gray, and while it covered most of the pockmarks on his cheeks, it did not conceal the nose that looked like a single throbbing vein. Logan O'Leary kept sheep and pigs, and farmed a plot behind his cottage, and one night at Finnerty's he'd thrown a stranger through the window for sitting on his favorite stool. "Now put on your pants and come say hello to Seamus."

The bottle of poteen was open on the table, a full glass in front of Seamus and another at Logan's place. Kathleen O'Leary, near as big as her husband, was making tea.

"It's a fine jar of a drink you make, Logan." Seamus sipped his poteen and looked at Kathleen. "And the O'Leary cottage is a place where a man's always welcome."

The main room was half again as large as most, with a wide hearth and a cast-iron oven. The floors were polished stone. In Jack Tracy's time, they had been covered with colorful rugs woven on the best Irish looms. Now they were covered with straw, because on cold nights Logan let in the lambs. The walls, darkened by turf smoke and cooking grease, had once been whitewashed. A rough crucifix hung by the door. And above the fireplace were two framed pictures: a faded rotogravure of the Sacred Heart of Jesus and a photograph of the O'Learys' younger son, Joseph, in the uniform of the Connaught Rangers.

Donal came out of his bedroom, walking like a barefoot man on a rocky beach. "Hello, Seamus."

"A rough night, was it?"

Donal grunted and sat carefully at the table. His mother put a cup of tea in front of him.

Logan sat down on the other side. "What the hell was he up to, Seamus? And what're you doin' here of a Wednesday afternoon?"

"Sociable, ain't we?" said Seamus.

"Oh, my yes," said Kathleen. "It's grand to have a visitor of a Wednesday noon." After thirty years of marriage, Kathleen Mary O'Toole O'Leary had learned to carry on no matter her husband's mood.

Logan took a drink of the poteen and kept his eyes on Seamus. "Me boy's in this Irish Republican Brotherhood, and he's out at night after cuttin' telegraph wires, ain't that so?"

Seamus was a small man with narrow shouders and a huge head. When he shrugged, he looked as if he might tip over. "The RIC wire's been cut more than once, and it happened again last night."

"Do you know, was there gunfire?"

"I wasn't there."

Logan looked across the table at Donal. "Do you take me for a fool?"

"He's your son," said Kathleen. "He loves you. Now drink your drink."

Logan ignored his wife. "Do you remember what happened to your uncle?"

"Jack Tracy shot him dead," Donal answered.

"Because he had some damn-fool notion of killin' the queen. And the only good that come of it was that we got to buy this house on the cheap."

"It was the notion of a brave man, braver than most I've known." Donal insulted his father, and he was sorry for it, because it meant another fight.

Logan O'Leary stood slowly and glared down at his son.

Seamus tipped back his glass and emptied it. "It's a fine still you've got workin' behind your shed there, Logan."

"Will you be stayin' for lunch, Seamus?" Kathleen began to busy herself about the stove.

"You've a brother fightin' Germans at the front," Logan said to his son. "You've a nice house in a peaceful town, a fine, smart Protestant woman to take to your bed in a month, your own fishin' boat with charts drawn up by the Royal Navy, and Home Rule when this war ends. You've no more reason to cause trouble than your damn-fool uncle had."

"Me uncle was a hero and Home Rule smells as bad as sheepshit in the corners on a cold morning."

"Well," Seamus picked up the poteen bottle, "that remains to be seen. Kathleen, bring us two more jars, and we'll all drink to Home Rule. Then we'll drink to sheepshit."

Logan leaned across the table and brought his face close to his son's. "I want no damn-fool rebels in me house. Y'understand me, you ignorant spalpeen?"

Donal's face reddened. His fists clenched around his tea.

Seamus looked from father to son and quickly raised his jar. "To Private Joseph O'Leary, a good brother to Donal and a fine son to Logan."

Neither Donal nor Logan could ignore that toast. They raised their drinks, then they heard the motorcycle. Forgetting the pain to his pride and his backside, Donal jumped up and ran out. The hillsides were fresh early-spring green, the ocean a hard blue.

The motorcycle seemed like a small whirlwind blowing up the road.

Donal pulled an envelope from his back pocket. Then, as the cycle drew closer, he noticed that the clover had already begun to blossom. He picked a small flower and shoved it into the envelope. He hoped that Deirdre would take it. Then, at least, she could *read* his apology, since she had refused to speak to him for three days. He held out his arm like a mail hook. He felt the air rushing ahead of the bike.

A huge pair of goggles covered most of her face, and the wind had flattened the rest against her jaw and cheekbones. Her hair was snapping out behind her like a pennant. She snatched at the blur of white held out to her and sped on, leaving Donal standing in the dust.

"A strange courtship." Seamus was standing at the window. "Strange indeed. Indeed."

"Any courtship between a Catholic and a Protestant is strange." Logan poured himself another jar. "And you ain't yet told me why you're here."

"Oh, yes. Father Breen asked me to invite you down to the rectory for tea tomorrow night."

"Tea? After sundown?"

"He might give you a glass of water, then," said Kathleen, and she asked Seamus what the priest wanted.

"Well," Seamus cleared his throat nervously, because Logan O'Leary was not an easy man to predict. "The father's got a few questions about the old Tracy family."

"And what should *we* know about them?" boomed Logan.

"Not a thing that I know of." Seamus stepped toward the door. "But the father figures you might answer a question or two. Old Clarke across the bay, he's prob'ly thinkin' the same thing."

"I see they shot up your face. Did you nail the bastards?"

"Beggin' your pardon, but I'm afraid not." Hayes's right cheek was bandaged, he had changed into a clean uniform and had once again affixed a smile to his face.

"Damn." William Clarke was sitting on the back of Fire, the champion show horse he had raised from a colt. The horse was retired now, too old to take the jumps with grace, but each afternoon Clarke and Fire rode the groomed trails that ringed the estate, took a few stone walls, and stopped on the western promontory of Ballinakill Peninsula to watch the waves crash against the rocks. Although the family had a front pew at the Church of Ireland in Clifden, Clarke said that he never felt closer to God than on his daily ride with Fire.

He swung his leg over the horse and dropped to the ground. He was six feet three, or, as he was fond of saying, nearly nineteen hands high. He wore jodhpurs and riding boots and this morning a brown tweed jacket over a turtleneck. At fifty-eight, his life as Connemara horseman and resident magistrate had suited him well. His hair was the dark brown of fresh-cut peat, and his face had the limestone hardness of the landscape itself.

He snapped the riding crop against his boot and looked across the bay. "A damned nuisance, and getting worse."

"Yes, sir." Although he was officially subject to the County Galway district inspector, Hayes worked closely with the resident magistrate, who passed judgment on crimes of property, examined evidence, and handed on recommendations in cases of more grievous nature. It was not necessary for a resident magistrate to have any legal training, and the position was often given to a retiring colonel in His Majesty's Army or the richest squire in the district. But William Clarke had been a barrister at the Law Courts in Dublin, he had controlled his district for twenty-five years, and he had commanded the respect, loyalty, and obedience of every inspector ever to work in Dunslea.

"Now, then." Clarke tethered his horse at the fence. "When your wire arrived, I was a few quid away from purchasing what may be the finest show horse since Fire. That should suggest to you the importance of this Padraic Starr business."

"Indeed, sir." Hayes's smile widened, although Clarke's back was turned to him. "We can't afford to have deserters sabotaging the recruitment effort. I agree with that entirely."

"I don't give a friar's fart for deserters." Clarke spoke like a schoolmaster disappointed with a student's answer. The sharp angles of his brow and jaw became sharper. "If the military are foolish enough to enlist a ne'er-do-well like Starr, it's their own problem. My concern is more immediate. It has also to do with your face."

Hayes brought his hand to his cheek and touched the bandage. "The trouble last night?"

"People don't challenge the RIC on the Clifden road without some reason, and Dublin Castle does not inquire after long-ago emigrants to America unless they somehow affect us."

"Do you think that Starr is working in concert with people in Dunslea?"

"If not, they are probably working toward the same end," said Clarke.

"Which is?"

"Some sort of armed rebellion, of course. It happens every two or three decades, and inevitably when we're embroiled in international crisis." He snapped the riding crop against the side of his boot again.

Clarke's groom came around from the stable. "May I take Fire for you, your honor?"

Clarke handed him the reins and watched the horse lope away with a fondness that most men reserved for their children. "Do you know why horses have such a hold on the Irish mind and spirit, Inspector?"

"Why, sir?"

"Because they are so unlike the Irish people. Once you've figured them out, you can always trust them. Break a mean horse, and he may stay mean, but you know you'll be able to climb on his back. Live in a country for two hundred and fifty years, become part of the landscape, love the place as my family have, and still you will never know when some night rider is going to try to put a bullet in your brain, simply because you are more intelligent, better educated, and hence better off than he." Clarke stared off across the fields for a few moments and gently tapped the riding crop against the side of is boot.

"Father Breen was little help," Hayes said, his smile shortening almost to neutral.

"What names have you so far?" Clarke's eyes were still fixed on a point in the distance.

"Tiernan, Malloy, O'Hara . . . Denny O'Hara had a history of minor crimes here, but somehow managed to get into America. He would seem like the best suspect."

"Has the name Tracy been mentioned?"

"Not as yet, sir."

The riding crop continued to snap against the boot, now with greater force. "Mrs. Tracy was first cousin to Starr's mother. Mr. Tracy was a rebel and a murderer, although his memory in this town is somewhat different."

"Considered a hero?"

Clarke's eyes were focused on the stone gate a half mile across the fields. "An informer."

"And they're in Boston?"

"The family moved to someplace in America after the father's deeds finally brought him to the gallows."

In his mind, William Clarke heard the gunshot that had waked him thirty years before. He remembered reaching for his pistol, hearing a second shot, then a third, then feeling his wife, heavy with child, rolling toward him. *What had happened? Were they attacking the house? Had his father come home from Finnerty's or was he still on the road?* He jumped to the window. In the waning moonlight, he saw three riders galloping away. Then he heard his mother's terror shrieking down the hallways of the great house. He grabbed a lantern and ran out, across the fields, down the road, through the gate, and when he drew close enough, he stopped.

His father's head was resting on a boulder, as though he had lain down for a nap. Two bullets had pierced his chest, a third his left temple. In the glow of the lantern, the flowing blood glistened like wine at a candlelit table.

William Clarke knelt down and closed his father's eyes. Then he smelled the sickening sweet stink of vomit. One of the murderers had no stomach for what he had done or for the chunks of chewing tobacco that lay in the puddle and gave a strange earthy smell to the curdling stink.

Even now, when he walked through that gate and glanced at the rock and the place where the puddle had been, William Clarke could feel his stomach turn at the stench of vomit and tobacco, and the hatred would rise in his throat once more.

It had taken him a dozen years, but he had brought all three killers to justice . . . including Jack Tracy.

He snapped the riding crop against his boot so sharply that it frightened a flock of grackles into the air. "Send O'Hara's name to Dublin Castle today. We shan't send the Tracy name until we're certain they're in Boston."

14

*T*he headline in Hearst's *American* read: "Great War Comes to the Howard." Beneath that was the subhead: "British Businessman, German Agent Fight to Death in Back Row." The story became the topic of conversation in the saloons of South Boston, the breakfast rooms of the Back Bay, and the office of the mayor.

For James Michael Curley, the news meant that a crisis with the voters and another with Tom Tracy had been averted. The Englishman had been killed in precisely the same fashion as the Quincy Market victim four days before—a slash cut across the left carotid and a puncture wound into the heart. The German wore a Donegal tweed cap, he had red hair, and the knife carried traces of the blood types of both Englishmen. John Sullivan, the butcher who had witnessed the murder through the swinging side of meat, signed an affidavit stating that the man he saw on the slab Wednesday morning was the same man who had kicked him on Saturday afternoon.

Smilin' Jim Donovan saw the headline when he came into his office. Before he finished reading the story, the phone was ringing.

"Tom Tracy stays," said James Michael Curley. "And he beats the pants off you in the next election."

"If you've got the right man down in the morgue and he's a Kraut on top of that, congratulations." Donovan had lost the skirmish, but a longshoreman had given him new ammunition. "I'd still watch out for Tracy, though."

"Is there a cigar in your mouth?"

"Yeah. Why?"

"You're blowing smoke again."

"Monday your boy was on a Pratt ship down at the channel."

"We've been through all this, Smiler."

"He took an envelope from Jason Pratt."

"I don't believe it."

"Suit yourself." Smilin' Jim sat back and put his feet up on his desk. "But when the mayor's fightin' the Pratt Republicans on Beacon Hill, why is the mayor's boy playin' ball with them on the wharves, unless he's playin' both ends against the middle?"

"Tommy's a good boy, Smiler. Lay off."

"Tom Tracy in bed with the Pratts. That might not be as good as Tom Tracy hidin' a killer, but I like the sound of it." Donovan paused, then said, "I want his head, by St. Patty's, or the papers hear about the Pratt envelope."

When Sean O'Fearna looked at the newspaper, it reminded him that the nightmare had not been a dream. He said the six-thirty Mass, waited until Father Ritter had said the eight-o'clock, and then asked the old German to hear his confession.

In the dark box at the side of the church, he said, "I have failed as a priest . . . and a man."

"How is this so?"

O'Fearna fixed his eyes on the crucifix above the little window and spoke of everything he had done in the last few days. "I did not have the courage to save the Englishman while Bremer and the Irishman planned his death. I did not have the courage to remain and absolve Bremer properly. I did not even have the willpower to turn away when the young woman took off her clothes."

Father Ritter looked through the screen and cleared his throat. He was not O'Fearna's regular confessor, but O'Fearna knew that his little cough was a way of asking for more information.

O'Fearna rubbed his eyes. They were irritated and bloodshot because he had not slept at all. "I raise money that I know will buy guns for Ireland. I endanger the life of a young boy. I protect the identity of a murderer. And I have created a ministry at the burlesque house, partly because I have the church's hope to offer to lonely women, but partly because I am lonely myself."

He had admitted his sins at last, but the relief he had hoped for did not flow over him, as it had when he was a boy. A mere Act of Contrition could not erase the decisions he had made or obsessions that haunted him, or anything he had done in the last four days, but the gentle voice of a good friend could help.

"Have you touched any of these women?"

"The temptation is strong, but no." He laughed a bit. "They told us that if we could get through our twenties, the hardest part would be over."

"We are men, after all. Just get yourself away." Ritter paused a moment. "Now, about this other matter . . . they tell us our first responsibility is to God, then to our bishop, and finally to our conscience."

"And they usually leave the bishop to do God's interpreting," said O'Fearna.

"If I were in France, I would not do as the French bishop told me, because I believe the French are wrong. But your bishop is William Cardinal O'Connell, and he has preached of Irish freedom and the greatness of your race at hundreds of Hibernian Communion breakfasts. Therefore, if your friend is a true rebel, your conscience is clear."

Sean O'Fearna wanted to believe Ritter's words, but in the confining darkness of the confessional, his shoulders hunched against the wall, his belly pressed against the rail, he could not look away from the truth. The fathers of the church understood the power of darkness as well as its comfort. "Do you know the meaning of the word *sophistry*?"

"Does it have something to do with the Jesuits?"

O'Fearna laughed softly. In a way, he was conducting his own confession, and he was beginning to understand why the gentle old German was such a popular confessor with the parish youth. "It's the game of words we're playing here now . . . the same one I play when I finger my rosary and watch the chorus line."

"Of course. You are right. We must obey the law, and for true penance, we must make public restitution."

And now came the part that Sean O'Fearna dreaded. "That is the church law."

"Although he loves the Irish, the cardinal would tell us to turn the rebel in for his crimes."

O'Fearna clasped his big hands together and squeezed. "I do not think I can do that, Father."

"But you must," said the German.

"If I must, I do not know what I will do." In the darkness, Sean O'Fearna felt himself reaching a decision that terrified him and yet, at times, seemed like his only choice. "In the last few days, I have considered leaving the priesthood."

Ritter drew a sharp, angry breath. "That is a sin for which I will not offer comfort, especially to a man with your gifts for the vocation."

"My gifts have become a burden."

"Then make a good Act of Contrition and pray for God to help you carry your burden."

* * *

Jenny Malloy stretched and reached for Starr, but he was gone, and someone was knocking at the door. She threw on her dressing gown and let Jimmy the Butcher into her room.

"Is he here?"

She shook her head. "The story of my life."

Jimmy handed her the newspaper. "Did he tell you anything about this last night?"

She read the headline and sank onto the edge of the bed. "Did Patrick do this?"

Jimmy nodded. "He ain't no businessman, babe."

"Am I in some kind of trouble?"

"Not if you don't panic."

"Why should I panic?" Her eyes widened, and her black eye liner made the whites stand out.

Jimmy took the paper from her, opened to the third page, and read: " 'The gunshot was not heard because, while the two men were fighting in the balcony, a young chorine named Jenny Malloy was performing a dramatic "dance" that culminated when she removed an article of underclothing that revealed the upper portions of her anatomy, causing a near-riot.' "

"You bastard, Jimmy! You told me this guy was clean and classy, you bastard!" She swung a fist and knocked his derby across the room. "I did him a favor 'cause you told me. I showed my tits to half the jerks in Boston, and what did I get for it?" She caught Jimmy on the chin with a right hand that knocked him onto his behind. "Shit! That's what I got."

Then she dropped into a pile on the floor beside him, a tangle of scattered blond hair, flannel, white legs, and kneecaps. After a moment she said, "You got a glass chin or somethin'?"

"Naw. I just dropped so you'd stop hittin' me."

"The company's leavin' after tonight's show, Jimmy," she said softly. "All the family I got, and I can't go with 'em."

"You got money, doll?"

"After last night, I got nothin'."

Jimmy threw his arm around her and drew her close to him. He tried to see himself as an uncle to his girls, but there were times when he wanted to be more. "You got me."

"All you get me is into jams, whenever I come to this crummy town."

"I get you out of them, too."

"What if some cop asks me what I was doin' with my tits hangin' out?"

Jimmy looked down at the tops of her breasts, which showed above the flannel. "Tell 'em you're an artist and you was breakin' new ground in burley."

"What on earth was he doing in a burlesque house?" asked Hugh Dawson.

"Following the priest." Stewart was methodically cleaning each chamber of his revolver.

"And what was the priest doing?"

"What anyone does in a burlesque house—watching the tits and bums and laughing at the bad jokes."

Dawson looked down at the cars on Charles Street. The day was cold and gray. A layer of frost covered the glass.

Stewart put the cylinder in the clamp. He snapped the revolver shut, spun the barrel to test it, then broke the pistol and jammed a bullet into the first chamber. "The priest led him to Starr, and Starr killed him."

"The German?"

Stewart loaded another bullet. "Irish scum and German scum float together."

"Did Consul Forsythe identify the body?"

For a moment, Stewart could not speak. He concentrated his eyes on the barrel of the gun.

Dawson understood. He had been through it when Starr killed *his* partner. Instead of cleaning his gun, he had spent two hours walking the streets and two more in bed with a pint of Duffy's pure malt whiskey. For men like Stewart and Dawson, operating away from the machine guns and the rolling barrages, there was time for grief when a comrade was killed.

Stewart loaded another round. "The consul has also been contacted by federal agents."

"Our position in this is quite delicate." Dawson scratched idly at the frost. "And we've already overstepped our bounds. The Crown will give us little support if we're caught in illegal activity."

Stewart spun the cylinder of his pistol. It made a threatening metallic sound.

"I carry no gun, Stewart." Dawson held his coat open. "It can lead me into places where I might have to use it."

"What about Huddleston and Dundee? If they'd used theirs, they'd still be with us, wouldn't they?"

"If they'd used theirs, they would not have been fulfilling orders. Find Starr's plan, determine his American contacts, and at the proper moment, hand the information to American authorities, so that Starr can be arrested and extradited."

"We are *not* going to extradite him." Stewart snapped the pistol shut and spun the cylinder. "We are going to capture him and question him. Then we are going to kill him."

"Do you see this?" Avram Levka came into the bake shop and threw the paper on the counter in front of his daughter. "This is why you should be not getting mixed up in all these politics. Because murder is what happens."

Rachel picked up the paper and read the headline. "This has nothing to do with Zionism or with Rabbi Mossinsohn."

"With Mossinsohn it has to do, with the British and the Zionists and the Germans and the Turks. Even it has to do with the Russians who killed your mother."

"You're getting excited, Papa. Go mix some batter." Rachel scanned the newspaper.

"Listen to me, Rachel. The British who fight in Palestine against the Turk do it for themselves, not the Jew. They do it because the Turk is the friend of Germany. They help the Zionist because the Zionist is the enemy of the Turk, and the enemy of the Turk is the enemy of Germany, and so must be the friend of the British. But the Russian who makes the pogrom against the Jew, he is the friend of the British, because he fights the German in his backside." Avram Levka stopped for breath.

Rachel realized that it had to do with the Irish as well. From what she read, Padraic Starr had struck again.

She took off her apron and went into the back. She had to see Tom Tracy.

". . . and the Irish," Avram was saying. "They will fight with anyone who stabs the British, even if it means the Germans. This world is all craziness, craziness. The only place sane is America."

She came back through the shop in her coat and hat.

"And what we want to be is Americans. . . . Rachel, where are you going?"

She stopped at the door. She was not sure. Even if Starr had committed this murder, she thought, it did not change her opinion of him. He was a rebel, taking advantage of the same cataclysm that the Zionists hoped to use. And this murder, she told herself, changed nothing that she had said to Tom Tracy the night before.

"Where are you going?" repeated her father.

"Nowhere. For now."

"For now? What for now? Where are you going ever?"

She walked over to him and looked down at his hands. The rough skin of his knuckles was whitened by flour where he punched and pounded the dough. She put her hands on his. "I've told you before, Father. Someday I may go to Palestine."

"Germans and English bring the craziness here, and if not them, Irishers and Zionists talk about going back." He turned his hands over and took her palms in his. "Forget those thoughts, Rachel. Because murder is what happens."

Murder had happened. And she knew the murderer. Deep inside her, it terrified her, because in the eyes of the law, her mere knowledge made her a criminal. But this was different. This was war.

She felt in the strength of her father's grip the fear of an old man whose only child was following a dangerous path. In his eyes, she saw tears beginning to well. She tried to soothe him. "I won't be going anywhere soon, Father. Maybe never."

"Hate is everywhere, Rachel. And most people have only God to protect them from it. But here, God has given us this Constitution that I memorize to be American. The Jew and the Jew-hater, the Catholic and the Protestant, the black and the white, this Constitution protects all. And someday it will make America more powerful than King George and the Kaiser and the Czar himself, God spit on him."

She smiled and said playfully. "Does this Constitution say that a Catholic man and a Jewish woman—"

He pulled his hands from hers. "Enough. If you want the craziness, go to Palestine. If you want gentile children—"

"Father—"

"God has given us this place to practice our faith in freedom. If you do not, God will be too angry."

"Is God angry that we go to the Reform Temple on Sundays, and listen to organ music?"

"I do not know God's mind." Avram Levka wiped a pile of crumbs from the countertop. "But I know that this is our promised land."

"And everyone else's."

"And everyone should thank God in the faith of their father."
There were enough crumbs that Avram Levka popped them into
his mouth. "And stay away from trouble."

Danny Tracy's first paper-route stop was the bathroom beneath the stairs. Uncle Martin read the newspaper before he
went out at seven. An hour later, Tom came down, flushed away
the urine that Martin always left in the bowl, and read while he
prepared himself.

He was lathering his face when he heard Starr come home.
He looked down the hallway. "Out with the hoors, Padr'ic?"

"Givin' thanks to a young woman who did me a bit of a favor."
Starr stepped into the bathroom and noticed the newspaper,
which was folded and propped on the shelf beneath the mirror.
The *Boston Post* had given the killings the bottom right quarter
of the page, beneath a story on the hunt for Pancho Villa: "Two
Found Dead in Howard; One Suspected German Agent."

"Slashed in the carotid, stabbed in the heart." Tracy took the
leather strop that hung by the sink and slapped the straightedge
against the hide half a dozen times. "That's two you've killed. Or
is it three, counting the German?"

"Two. And the police blame the German for everything."

Tracy put the razor to his face and scraped away a line of
lather. He snapped the razor against the side of the sink. "Should
I be relieved?"

Starr raised the toilet seat. "I am, and I'm about to be as
well."

"I'm not." Tracy kicked the bathroom door shut. "I told you I
couldn't help you if you got into any more trouble."

"I got in, I got out, and I got myself in the clear." Starr unbuttoned his fly. "Did you get me my ship?"

"Not yet."

"Well, you'd better hurry, because my late German friend told
me about a train bringing rifles and ammunition from the Winchester plant in Connecticut." Starr spoke over the sound of his
urine hitting the bowl. "On Sunday night, it's routed over the
Northern Avenue Bridge to Pier 1." Starr finished and buttoned
his fly. "That's where I'll be gettin' my guns, if I can get the help
of a few good men."

Tracy studied his cousin, looking for a smile or suggestion of
a joke. Then he began once more to shave, methodically scraping

his face, snapping the lather into the sink, rinsing the blade under hot water, and scraping again.

"It's time you took some action, Tommy." Starr's face appeared in reflection behind Tracy. "And I don't just mean the ship. You're in love with a girl, and you're afraid to tell her because you might lose some votes. You've got a hatred for the man who trumped up your da's case, and you can't raise the courage to go and kill him and finish what your da spent forty years fightin' for."

"Sometimes, the courage is in not killin'." Tracy realized that Rachel and Martin Mahoney were right. Starr knew what people were thinking. He had the magic. "There's no future in killin'."

"For you, maybe not. But if you help me stop that train, Ireland's got a future, and that's what your da wanted most."

Tracy toweled off his face and splashed himself with a bit of bay rum. Then he combed his hair and studied his reflection, as he always did in the morning. He had learned from the mayor that people liked their leaders well dressed, well spoken, and, if possible, as handsome as autocar ads. He had also learned that to get out the vote, to win an issue on the streets, to beat the Protestant Republicans, the politician appealed to the conscience of every voter. "Your one ballot may make the difference to the future of this city," he had heard Curley say. And one person could make a difference to the future of Ireland.

In the mirror, Starr adjusted the angle of the scally cap he had bought that morning from a street peddler. It was not Donegal tweed, but it was the same dark green as the hat now worn by the late Klaus Bremer. "Remember what your da used to say, Tommy. It's high time that Ireland had the chance to make her own mistakes herself."

Tracy remembered. Ireland deserved the chance, but this was not the way. "Stopping a train is craziness, Padr'ic. You'll never get away with it. You'll be caught and the rising will be ruined."

Starr picked up the razor and tested its sharpness on his thumb. "I've little time and less money. I'm stoppin' the train. Sunday night, I'll be on the Northern Avenue Bridge, and I'll be needin' some help."

Tracy gently took the razor from Starr's hands. "I'll have you arrested."

"Sunday night." Starr saluted and opened the bathroom door. Danny Tracy jumped back from the keyhole.

"Top of the mornin' to you," said Starr.

"I been listenin'." Danny shoved his hands into his front pockets, then into his back pockets, then pulled them out and planted them on his hips. "I been listenin', Padr'ic, and I'll be with you on Sunday night."

Starr turned to Tom Tracy and raised an index finger. "There's one good man. I need four more."

Tracy ordered his brother upstairs, then slammed the door and pointed the razor at Starr. "You can't drag him into this."

"I'd rather not." Starr glanced down at the razor. "But if he's with me on Sunday, you won't be blowin' the whistle on Monday."

Tom Tracy grabbed Starr's chin in his left hand and brought the razor to Starr's neck. "You said you loved my father, but still you come bringin' the trouble he sent us here to get away from. Why?"

"It's your da that sent me."

Tracy pressed the razor hard against Starr's throat. "If you're jokin' on him, I'll slit your throat right now."

"Do you remember the last time you saw him?" said Starr through Tracy's clenched fingers.

Tracy nodded. "Like yesterday. And I remember what he said to me."

"I saw him a few hours later, and I remember what he said to me, too."

Tracy took the razor from Starr's throat. . . .

—————— 1 9 0 0 ——————

"Your name ain't down in the book," said the guard with the handlebar mustache.

"But I come all the way from Galway," said the tall, lanky boy. "He's my uncle. I gotta see him."

The man ground his teeth and tugged at the mustache, and after a moment, he rapped on the door behind him. "Bring up Tracy."

For a long time, young Paddy Starr waited at the table in the visitor's room. He looked around at the peeling paint and the rodent droppings in the corners, but he did not look at the guard, who tapped his nightstick against his hand and studied Paddy Starr with eyes suspicious and hateful. The boy had seen those eyes in too many places, on too many men.

Then the inner door swung open and the gray, hunched ghost of Jack Tracy, in leg irons and manacles, rattled into the room.

"Uncle Jack!" The boy jumped up and ran over to Tracy.

"Paddy!"

The guard raised his club. "Sit down."

"I've come to save you," blurted the boy.

"What?" said the guard.

"Nothin'," said Jack Tracy. "He's just a boy."

"Well, you'll be stayin' in your manacles, in case this kid's got some plan to be gettin' himself killed." The guard shoved Jack Tracy over to the table, and Padraic followed him.

"I've come to help you, Uncle Jack," whispered the boy. "I'm ready to do whatever I can to get you off."

Jack Tracy brought his finger to his lips, and his eyes shifted toward the guard. "If there was anything you could do, right up to swingin' in my place, I'd let you. But I'm doomed, son." He raised his voice, so the guard would hear him. "I killed them two boys as certain as spit."

"But you did it to save the queen. Don't that count for somethin'?"

"They've been wantin' my hide since '67," he said bitterly. "That's what counts."

Padraic Starr looked down at the tabletop and blinked the tears from his eyes. "I'm sorry, Uncle Jack."

Jack Tracy reached out and grabbed the boy's face and turned it toward him.

"No touchin'," said the guard.

"Go to hell," answered Jack Tracy. Then he said to Starr, "Don't be sorry for nothin', son. I don't give two damns about the pasty-faced little dwarf in Buckingham Palace. And I cared a lot for them two boys." Jack Tracy shook his head and bit his lip to hold back the anger and hatred. "But I couldn't let them do what they planned."

Starr ran his hands through his hair and looked his uncle in the eye. "I ain't much at prayin', Uncle Jack, but I'll pray hard for you. I promise."

"Leave that to the priests. I want you to promise me somethin' else."

"Anything, Uncle Jack."

"I've got one boy on his way to America, to learn politickin'

and to organize the Irish in a place where they have some real power. I want to know I've got a boy in Ireland, too."

"I'll never leave," said Starr, "if that's what you want."

"I want Tommy to remember Jack Tracy the politician, who worked for Parnell and ran for MP. I want you to remember Jack Tracy, the Fenian who fought at Ballyhurst."

"Yes, Uncle Jack."

"Tommy's the sort for smart talkin', but we both know that you're the sort for gunplay."

Starr looked down at the top of the table.

"Look at me!" Tracy snapped his hands so that the chains clanked like a weapon being loaded.

His uncle's anger terrified the boy and burned the next words into him.

"If the day ever comes when the politickin' fails, and it's a fact as plain as Christ on Christmas, then I want you to ask yourself what Jack Tracy the Fenian would do."

"I will."

"It's all you owe me, son. And I'll pray you don't end up like me." Jack Tracy covered his face in his hands.

The door swung open. "Time, son," said the guard. "The father's here for confession."

Paddy Starr reached out and touched Tracy's hands. "I love you, Uncle Jack."

After a moment, Jack Tracy looked up with the old Tracy grin and said, "Live a good life, son."

15

The St. Patrick's Eve banquet at the Tammany Club was three hours away. In the hall, the band leader was complaining because the caterers were clattering china and silver while the band tried to practice. The caterer said it was too damn bad because a banquet without music was still a banquet, but a banquet without food was just an all-night drunk.

Tracy tried to settle the dispute, then went back to his office, where the telephone had been ringing all day. Sticker McNulty and Ursula O'Day, secretary of the ladies' auxiliary, were answering the calls. Tracy picked up the latest pile of messages.

Honey Fitz called. His daughter Rose and son-in-law Joe Kennedy are coming, and he wants them to be seated with Kennedy's father at table number one. "That's already been taken care of."

"I never thought I'd see the day when Curley would have Honey Fitz at the head table," said Sticker. "Or back him for senator. He ain't got a chance."

"That's why Curley's backin' him," said Ursula.

John L. Sullivan wants to buy a table for the Irish Temperance Union. Tracy handed the note to Ursula. "Give the champ table fifteen."

"Yes, Tom."

Captain Pratt has considered your proposal and says it is not enough. Tracy crumpled the note and stuffed it into his pocket. He had spoken with Pratt about delivering machine parts to the impoverished village where he had been born. He said he was hoping to modernize the production of Irish wools and linens, put money back into his old village, and make a profit as well. But Pratt was bargaining for more than Tracy could deliver.

Sticker McNulty hung up the phone and handed Tracy the latest message. "Here's a good one."

Artemus Pratt and wife accept the mayor's "gracious invitation"; they will be accompanied by Mr. James Dolliver, Republican State Representative from the Back Bay, and wife. They wish to speak in private with the mayor. "Them and everybody else."

"The old son of a b. never accepted an invitation before," said Sticker. "He figures he's on the ropes in this tax-rate fight, so he's comin' to play some ball."

"Give him the last slot, ten minutes to eight."

Put in Denny Morrissey, and be there yourself. Signed by the mayor. The tea in Tracy's stomach turned acid. Tracy had called Denny Morrissey, the treasurer of the Hibernians, to solicit contributions for the new Irish charity that no one, not even the mayor, was to hear about. He had not specified that it would be a weapons fund.

By approaching Jason Pratt and Denny Morrissey, Tracy had taken the first steps in helping Starr. He believed the story of Starr's last meeting with Jack Tracy. He knew the path of his father's life, from the political violence of his youth to the Parnellite politics of his final years, and it did not surprise him that Jack Tracy had asked his son to study politics while leaving Starr as the seed of violence. But Jack Tracy could not have foreseen the threat that Starr would become to the Tracy family, especially if he tried to steal fifty crates of rifles from a moving train.

Tracy considered the slot where the mayor would be the most distracted, where Tracy might be able to talk himself and his secret fund out of trouble. "Give Denny the ten minutes in front of the Pratts." He looked down into the street. The caterers were carrying in great vats of Irish stew and potatoes Colcannon, but Tracy's appetite was gone.

Then a call came in from Rachel Levka. Tracy reached for the phone, then shook his head.

Ursula made an excuse to Rachel.

That morning, Tracy had called the bakery and left a message for Rachel. In beginning to help Starr, he had decided that he might also begin the delicate task of introducing Rachel Levka to the public. If it was rumored about the ward that he was seeing a Jewish girl in the shadows, perhaps he would do better to court her in the bright light of the St. Patrick's dinner. But after reading his messages, Tracy's confidence had begun to fade.

"The train will cross the bridge between one and two in the morning," said Heinrich Kuntz.

"How good is your intelligence?" asked Padraic Starr.

"Excellent." Kuntz wore the dress blues and white hat of a bosun in the German merchant marine, and he had the icily supercilious manner to accompany the uniform.

Kuntz had left his ship in East Boston and gone to the eighteenth floor of the Custom House, where he had conducted some insignificant naval business. Then, instead of returning to the lobby and the federal agent who usually followed him, he walked the last seven flights to the observation deck. There Padraic Starr was peering out at Boston like a tourist. On a bitterly cold March afternoon, however, there were no other tourists in the Custom House tower.

"You're sure of the time?"

"Our man in the routing office is sure. He says the train will be sent down Atlantic Avenue instead of through the south yards at one A.M. Americans do not like to see munitions trains traveling their streets, so they condemn them to the night."

"What will they do if a train is destroyed?"

"Some will scream. Many others will say that America should not do any munitions business, because it will bring her into the war."

Below him, Starr could see the whole waterfront, alive with wartime commerce. He scanned over the masts of the Atlantic Avenue fishing fleet and the Fort Point Channel schooners, and across the Northern Avenue Bridge to the British freighter loading at Pier 1. Then he watched the ferries crossing the harbor to East Boston, where the *Kronprinzessin Cecille* and the other German liners had lain since August 1914. And he could understand why an officer of the German Naval Reserve, blockaded into Boston for a year and a half, would commit himself to destroy British commerce.

Despite the German's coldness, Starr could feel his frustration and resolved to use it. "Bremer called it a damnable war, when a good man couldn't be fightin' for his country."

"*Ja*," said Kuntz harshly. "Since we cannot reach Europe, we will fight Britain where her supply lines begin."

"Bremer knew that the Irish were ready to help." Starr extended his hand. "Now you know it."

Without removing his glove, Kuntz took Starr's hand. "I will provide dynamite, blasting caps, and my knowledge of demolitions. You will deliver four men to neutralize the bridge keeper, uncouple the boxcars, and take your guns."

"Agreed. But what about guards?"

"The British have hired Pinkertons to protect some of their trains. And they were allowed to bring Scotland Yard into New York to protect the docks when we were planting cigar bombs. So much for American neutrality." Kuntz smiled for the first time. "Guards will probably ride the engine. But at the Northern Avenue Bridge, we will be able to separate the engine and strand it completely."

Starr looked down at the bridge. Traffic had stopped on the approaches because a schooner was moving down the channel, and the bridge was turning on its axis to let a ship pass. "Sunday night, then. Sullivan's barn, Albany Street."

The bar opened at six-thirty, and the music started at seven. "Hot Time in the Old Town Tonight," Stephen Foster favorites, "Tammany," "Tipperary," three renditions of "When Irish Eyes Are Smiling." The beer was spring bock in barrels tapped for the occasion, the whiskey was Jameson's, brewed in Dublin since 1705, and for the ladies, an amiable fruit punch laced with Kelly-green limes.

The spinsters and widows of the club arrived first, like plump mourning doves, fluttering up the stairs in small groups, chattering and laughing and pecking about the punchbowl for gossip, while filling the air with a cloud of rosewater perfume. Tom Tracy, in a new tuxedo with black satin lapels and black studs, greeted them all by name and shook their hands and inquired after their families like a faithful nephew, then went to the bar for a quick Jameson's.

Soon the young married couples began to arrive. The men wore suits, crisp tweeds and shiny serge, and almost all of them had clean fingernails. The women were powdered and dressed in their best, and even those who had already lost a few teeth looked radiant. They filled the hall with the conversation and laughter of young parents freed for the evening from their children, and Tom Tracy knew that by their votes, they controlled the future of Boston. He took great care to greet them all.

When his mother arrived with the rest of the family, Tom escorted her to her table and proudly pinned a corsage of green-dyed carnations onto her green dress. Everyone applauded, and Tom made a little bow while the band slid smoothly into "Mother MacRee."

For Josephine, this was the grandest night of the year, and not even Padraic Starr could dim her happiness.

As always seemed to happen, the mayor swept in just after Josephine, with his wife on his arm and his children in tow. The band played "Tammany" while Curley waved and shook hands and kissed old women. Then he paraded to the Tracy table, bowed to Josephine Tracy, and complimented her on the family she had raised, in spite of all her hardships. "You're the symbol of every wonderful mother here."

After the mayor went into the private office, Tracy sent the first of a long stream of supplicants to see him, then went to the bar and ordered another Jameson's.

The band played Sousa marches and Irish songs, and by seven-thirty, Tom Tracy had spoken with almost all of the five hundred people now filling the hall.

John L. Sullivan, a great walrus of a man, nearly broke Tracy's hand with the force of his grip. Rose Kennedy greeted him warmly, as she did most everyone she met, but her husband, Joe, offered barely a handshake. Ambitious young Irishmen could always smell ambition as great as their own, and it made them wary. Tom Tracy thought that his own ambition was beginning to smell a bit rancid, but he did not mention that to Kennedy.

Father Hans Ritter arrived with the twelve-man choir from the Prinz Henry bund, all dressed in blue jackets with the Prinz Henry standard on the breast pocket. Within a few minutes, he had to stand on a chair and request that everyone stop buying drinks for the Germans, because if they drank too much, they would not be able to sing. A few of the Germans jeered in a good-natured way, then Sticker McNulty shouted, "Three Cheers for the Kaiser! Hip Hip . . ."

"Hooray!'

Tracy noticed that the Pratts did not join in the cheer, but otherwise, they were surprisingly cordial. Tracy had purposely sat them at a table with their weekend chauffeur, one of their upstairs maids, and the ex-con who delivered their groceries. Artemus Pratt, a tall man with an elongated face, managed to wear a pained smile with his green necktie, and he even bought a round of drinks.

At seven-forty, Tracy went into the office for his own meeting. The mayor was shaking hands with John F. "Honey Fitz" Fitzgerald. In 1914, when Mayor Fitzgerald refused to hand over City Hall gracefully, Curley had attacked him in a campaign that showed how rough—and entertaining—he could be. He announced that he was going to give a series of lectures relating ancient history to the Fitzgerald administration. The first speech was entitled "Graft and Corruption Under Nero and Honey," the second "Great Orators, Big Talkers," and the last "Great Lovers, from Cleopatra to Toodles." Toodles was a waitress at Fitzgerald's favorite roadhouse on the Newburyport Turnpike. Honey Fitz retreated from the race before Curley delivered the last lecture. And now the former enemies were allies. *Friend,* Tracy knew, was too strong a word.

"You've got wonderful color, your honor," Tracy said to Fitzgerald.

"That's what a month in Florida does for you," answered the banty little man. "Better be getting all my Florida time in now, because after the next senatorial race, I won't have much time for winter vacations."

"Truer words were never spoken," said Curley.

As Fitzgerald left, Curley sat down behind his desk. "I suppose I'll have to ask him to sing 'Sweet Adeline.' "

"He'll sing it whether you ask him or not."

"Where's Morrissey?"

"Not here yet."

Curley rubbed his right fist with his left hand. On the wall behind him was a painting of the signing of the Declaration of Independence, showing golden rays of God-sent light streaming from the clouds above the Founding Fathers. It was Curley's favorite painting, and he had lectured Tracy often on all that it celebrated.

Tracy sat on the edge of his own desk and swung his leg, as casual as a man resting on a rock fence.

"Morrissey says you went to him for money."

Tracy cocked his head. "What do you mean?"

Curley came over to him. "Don't play cute, Tommy. You're not good enough yet. Two days ago, Smilin' Jim Donovan said that you knew all about this so-called Irish rebel we thought was on the loose. I decided right then that if you were hiding something, you were out."

The band was playing "The Irish Washerwoman." Tracy could hear the sounds of laughter and talk rising above the music like water spilling out of a cistern.

"I would have had you on the carpet at ten o'clock yesterday, but a dead German in the Old Howard saved you." Curley slipped his thumbs into the pockets of his black satin vest and strode across the room. "I was thrilled beyond the power of eloquence to have you in the clear. I called Donovan and told him to go to hell."

"That's a good place for him."

Curley pivoted and pointed his finger at Tracy. "And you'll be the one to send him there, if you keep your nose clean and cover your reputation."

"I try, your honor." Tracy reminded himself to keep swinging his leg, as though he had nothing to hide.

"So why did Morrissey call me this afternoon about the secret fund you're collecting for? What's this big secret? And stop swinging that leg."

If Tracy told the truth, he would destroy Starr, perhaps the rebellion, and brand himself an informer for life. If he lied and it was discovered, the mayor, for all his Irish fervor, would destroy Tom Tracy.

"I haven't hidden anything from you." As he lied, Tracy felt himself stepping into the dark, cold bog he had escaped sixteen years before. "I have a friend in Ireland, he wants to start a newspaper and stir things up, because the British are getting ready to conscript Irish boys."

Curley's lower lip worked back and forth like a stimulant to his brain. "An Irishman who believes the pen is mightier than the sword?"

"He wants to print before the Brits get wind of him."

The office door swung open, and the sound of laughter and music flowed in ahead of Standish Willcox. "The Pratts are waiting to see you, sir."

"Two minutes." He waved Willcox out and fixed that calm, inquisitive stare on Tracy. "I'll ask you once: Does Donovan have anything on this Irish business that can hurt us?"

Tom Tracy looked the mayor in the eye and said no.

"Then tell Denny Morrissey I approve your secret fund."

Tracy smiled and thanked the mayor and tried to conceal his relief by swinging his leg once more.

The mayor pulled his watch from his pocket and glanced at it. "Now, what about the Pratt outside the door? Do we have to worry about him?"

The thoughts leaped in Tracy's head like muzzle flashes. What else did the mayor know? Had someone told Curley about the negotiations with Jason Pratt? And he surrounded another lie with two truths: He had seen to the repairs on the Pratt wharf, but he had never done any other business with them, and he had never met Artemus Pratt in his life.

The lip began to work again, wetting itself and ruminating. What was he thinking? Tracy wondered. What did he think he knew?

Curley was about to speak when the door swung open, bringing the scent of fresh adversaries. The mayor winked at Tracy. "Now we'll have a lesson in treating with the wily Brahmin." Then he extended his hand to Artemus Pratt and James Dolliver. "Welcome to the Tammany Club, gentlemen."

"It's a rare pleasure," said Pratt, "to sit with my servants and celebrate the birth of their saint."

Curley glanced at Tracy. "You gave our guests a good table, then?"

Tracy nodded. "The best, sir."

Curley invited them to sit. Mr. Dolliver, who had the squashed face, squat physique, and nasty temperament of a Boston terrier, sat in the leather chair beside Curley's desk. Artemus Pratt went over to the window and leaned against the sill.

Curley had once told Tracy that the Pratts always chose the seat by the window because, during the day, it made everyone else look into the glare. At night, however, all it did was expose Pratt backsides to the draft.

Tracy saw the resemblance between Pratt and his son. The deep-set eyes, slightly hooked nose, and downcurved mouth were almost the same. But where the son's face was windburned, the father's was white and soft, highlighted by a thin mustache that followed the droop of his mouth, and his slender hands were certainly more familiar with the stock tape than the tiller.

"And so," Curley said, leaning back in his chair and slipping his thumbs into his vest pockets, "the leaders of the Brahmin community have never before graced this gathering. Could it be that they are about to lose a nasty fight on Beacon Hill, and they're here to make peace?"

Pratt's voice came out high and thin. "We're here to see the faces of all the smiling Irish who'll find their rents raised if the mayor wins a tax increase."

"And," said Dolliver, "we've come with a proposal. As tomorrow is a holiday and your bill comes before the House on Monday, this seems the best opportunity to present it."

"You mean," said Standish Willcox, "when the mayor is in a magnanimous mood?"

"No," answered Pratt. "When his constituents are so close that he can smell their sweat, which will smell much stronger when I raise the rent ten percent in all my properties to pay for this ridiculous tax increase."

Curley took the green carnation from his lapel and passed it beneath his nose. "You try that, and the people of this city will string you up by the testicles."

"The Pratts have fathered seven generations in Boston," said Pratt. "We always pass on our tax increases, and no one yet has laid hands on the family jewels."

"Mr. Pratt's business tenants are by no means numerous enough to offset the tax increase." James Dolliver took off his spectacles and polished them. "It must come from the residentials."

"You're going to have inspectors crawling up your nose while the assessors come down your pants," said Curley calmly.

"Ten percent, and my buildings always pass inspection."

"Your tenants will move out and leave you with empty buildings." said Curley.

"Where will they go? When Jew landlords see us raising rents, they'll do the same thing."

Tracy watched Curley's lip working back and forth. The wily Brahmin had taken the best of the exchange, but Tracy knew that Curley was not yet finished.

It seemed, however, that Artemus Pratt was. He straightened up from the windowsill and took a green carnation from the vase on Curley's desk. "So there you are, your honor. Withdraw the bill before it comes before the House, or face the consequences." He slipped the carnation into his lapel. "Erin go Bragh."

Dolliver stood and tugged at the corners of his vest. "We've got two reports ready to hand to the *Transcript*. One says that Republican legislators and the mayor hammered out a compromise this evening. The other says that because of your improvidence in demanding a property-tax increase, Irish families face huge rent raises in April."

Curley jammed his thumbs into his vest. His eyes shifted from Pratt to Dolliver, and Tracy waited for his harangue about "champagne-hoisting, homburg-wearing Brahmin Republicans" who owned the city and laughed at the poor, his own sainted mother among them. But James Michael Curley allowed anger and sentiment to surface only when they might have some effect. The Pratts understood stronger language, and Curley could speak it fluently.

He looked at Tracy and asked for the city assessor's maps.

Tracy placed the map book on his desk, opened it, and waited for Curley's next move. Curley invited Pratt to look over his shoulder, the long, lean Brahmin with the white whiskers beside the robust, potato-faced Irish mayor.

Curley pointed to the map. "What's this property?"

"The Boston National Bank on Federal Street."

"I believe you're a major stockholder."

Pratt nodded. "On the board of directors as well, and I guarantee you that if that rate increase passes, I will make it very difficult for you to float a bond with any Boston bank."

Curley rocked back on his heels, and Tracy knew that he was about to deliver an Irish cross to the locked Brahmin jaw. "If that tax bill doesn't pass, I intend to make it impossible for your bank to do business with *anyone*."

"Don't threaten us," said Dolliver.

Curley ignored him and pointed again to the map. "You see the blue line, Mr. Pratt?"

Pratt said nothing.

"That's a water main. And you see that?" Curley moved his finger again. "That's a main shutoff valve, directly beside your vault. If I lose on Beacon Hill, or if I see ridiculous rent increases two months from now, there could be a blowout at that valve, and if, God forbid, it happens on a weekend, your vault will flood and ruin all that money and all those safety-deposit boxes." Curley took the carnation from Pratt's lapel and sniffed. "Erin go Bragh."

Tom Tracy suppressed his grin. Standish Willcox looked down at the floor and covered his face with his hand.

Dolliver shook his head. "You grow more outrageous all the time."

Curley looked hard at Dolliver. "I mean what I say, and if you go to the *Transcript,* I'll go to the *Post.*"

"I believe you, Mr. Curley," said Pratt. "You are a difficult man. You had better be, because you face a difficult fight. Fortunately, the generation that succeeds you seems more reasonable." Pratt looked directly at Tracy, and his eyes seemed to warm, as if an idea had filled him with great joy.

He took another carnation from the vase, then offered his hand to Curley. "Good evening, Mr. Mayor, and congratulations on the birth of your saint."

"Be sure to tell me when you decide John Calvin's birthday is worth celebrating," answered Curley.

"Perhaps we'll march on July fifteenth, like our Ulster coreligionists." Pratt raised a finger to Dolliver, then headed for the door.

Tom Tracy was watching Pratt's eyes, and as Pratt came toward him, Tracy sensed that he was about to become a casualty in the ancient struggle.

Without stopping, Pratt clapped Tracy on the shoulder, as familiar as an old friend. "When you hear something, Tommy, let us know."

The door opened. The German choir was singing "Tipperary," and the powerful male voices seemed to vibrate through Tracy's head. Then the door closed behind Pratt. The singing was muffled, but for Tom Tracy the vibration grew worse.

He turned slowly and looked at Standish Willcox, who looked

down at the rug. Then his eyes met the mayor's. The song ended. The vibration stopped, but under Curley's gaze, Tom Tracy felt like a piece of peat impaled on fork.

"Yesterday," said Curley softly, "the Smiler told me you were seen on board a Pratt ship, taking an envelope from that bastard's son. I didn't believe it until now."

Tracy stretched his neck to loosen his collar. "Did he say that I also gave the envelope back?"

Curley's eyes were small and angry. "What's going on?"

"They tried to make a campaign contribution. I told them to save it until I ran."

"And you told me that Smiler had nothin' on you!" Curley turned to Willcox. "He's as good as on the take."

"Don't ever accuse me of that," shouted Tracy, and for once he forgot his caution around the mayor.

Willcox cleared his throat. "If Tommy was on the take, do you think Pratt would have let us know about it like that? He's simply trying to sow distrust in the enemy camp."

"Thank you, Standish." Tracy could feel the vibration once more. They were singing again.

Curley studied Tracy, and his lower lip worked back and forth. Then he raised a finger under Tracy's nose. "Don't take their money, Tommy. Ever. Don't promise to take it. Don't even act interested. Because money's all that matters to those people. If they dangle it and you dance, they think they own you. And if they *think* they own you—" Something in the hall distracted Curley. He cocked his head for a moment and listened. It was the singing.

"*Am Rhein, am Rhein, am Deutschen Rhein, wer will des Vaters Huter Sein.*"

"What the hell is that?"

"The Prinz Henrys," said Willcox. "The social committee asked them to sing a German song."

Curley listened, his face reddening.

"*Lieb Vaterland mach Ruhig sein. Lieb Vaterland mach Ruhig sein.*"

Tracy said, "Your honor—"

Curley raised a hand for silence.

"*Fest Steht und Treu die Wacht, die Wacht am Rhein!*" And the Tammany Club exploded in wild cheering for the Germans.

Tracy clenched his fists in his pockets. His reputation was in tatters, and the mayor was more concerned about the way it would look when the papers reported that a choir sang German patriotic songs. "Your honor—"

Curley looked at Willcox. "People in the audience were singing along."

"The ladies wanted to show our support of Germany's cause."

"We do *not* support Germany's cause," said Curley angrily. "We don't support England's, either."

The applause subsided. Then the band began to play "Tammany" again.

"There's your cue, your honor," said Willcox.

The marching beat improved Curley's mood as soon as he heard it. "Tammany" was his song, played at rallies and parties like an anthem or a call to war. Curley paced around and took several deep breaths, and his barrel chest expanded.

"Your honor," said Tracy.

Curley did not seem to hear him. "Let's go out and greet the people. And give them a little civics lesson."

As he started for the door, Tracy grabbed his elbow. Except to shake hands, it was the first time Tracy had ever touched him. Curley's eyes dropped to Tracy's hand, and Tracy removed it.

"Do you believe me, your honor?"

Curley studied Tracy for a moment. The anger was now gone from his gaze, but Tracy sensed a new distance, as if Curley were looking at him for the first time, studying him as he would a Republican recently elected to city office. "If you tell me it's the truth, Tommy, I believe you. You've had a bad week. You've been deceitful, you've been stupid, and you've got Smilin' Jim Donovan hunting your head. That's two dumb mistakes and a good reason to stand behind you." He pointed a finger at Tracy again. "But don't ever take money from the Pratts or start secret Irish funds again without telling me."

"Time, your honor," said Willcox.

Curley's eyes bored into Tracy. "James Michael Curley is loyal to his people. He expects nothing less in return."

The mayor's door swung open, and the applause began like raindrops before a downpour. Curley smoothed his black hair and tugged at his vest, then he stepped through the doorway, and the crowd thundered.

They loved him, thought Tracy, with good reason. Curley had won power in a city still owned by the Pratt at table ten, a man who judged the Irish when he read of them in letters from his

English cousins, when he saw them pouring out of steerage and onto Boston docks just ahead of the rats, when he collected their rents in the tenements of Roxbury or the North End, when he saw them swarming from the subways to search for work in the city his ancestors had built. Curley had achieved in America what the Irish, after seven centuries, had failed to gain in their own country.

The ovation flooded the hall and spilled down the stairs to Dudley Street. Tom Tracy's anger at Curley and his rage at the Pratts were washed away with it. But it could not uproot the thought that Pratt had planted: Tom Tracy had followed the rules; he had refused the money; he had acted honestly. But the Protestant landowners had still tried to use him. Thirty-five hundred miles away, the Irish Catholics had followed the rules; they had fought honestly and won in Parliament. But the Protestants and English conservatives had still tried to use Irish goodwill, under the specter of the Great War, to win the fight against Home Rule.

As he listened to the ovation thundering over "Tammany," the idea blossomed and spread, like an Irish vine breaking through the cobblestone streets of Boston: The struggle was the same on both sides of the Atlantic. In Boston, it was fought with subtlety, deceit, and threats of flooded bank vaults. But in Ireland, politics had failed; the struggle needed men like Starr, who would cut to the heart, without fearing the voters, the tax rate, or the Boston press.

Curley raised his hands and drew his body close to the podium. He needed no microphone, for his powerful voice filled the hall. "Ladies and gentlemen, many thanks to you all for that stirring welcome. Whenever I need strength to carry on against the demons of this city, I need only feel the warm embrace of my Tammany friends." And the members of the Tammany Club began to applaud once more, as though they truly believed James Michael Curley needed their inspiration.

Tracy went to the bar at the back and ordered a warm embrace of a different kind. He brought his third Jameson's to his lips and looked out across the hall. The Pratts had left, unable to keep up their end of the witty chatter at table ten. Uncle Martin and brother John were listening to Curley; Danny was studying the young girl at the next table; and Josephine Tracy was looking at her eldest son in the same way that she would watch the horizon if he sailed off to war. He raised his glass to her in a small gesture of assurance.

Curley, surrounded by representatives of every Boston ethnic group and religion, looked down the head table to Father Ritter. "I would like to thank the members of the Prinz Henry choir for the wonderful serenade." He called for a round of applause, and cut it off as soon as it seemed polite.

Tracy sipped his drink and watched a master at work.

"But I would like to point out to you all that while some of us may enjoy singing 'Tipperary' and others 'Watch on the Rhine,' the song that should be nearest and dearest to all of us is the one that honors the noble cloth behind me." Curley swept an arm back toward the flag.

There was only scattered applause. Curley was chiding his audience like a stern but wise father.

"I am an American of Irish blood. I am not pro-English, I am not pro-Ally, I am not pro-German. I am pro-American."

The applause grew louder. Tracy leaned an elbow on the edge of the bar and admired the mayor's skill in guiding an audience through their own emotions to his conclusion.

"We owe nothing but our business as Irishmen to the British Empire. Four and a quarter million of us have been decimated there by famine, torture, exile, and execution. We owe nothing to the Teuton, either. But we owe everything to the United States of America." Curley paused. His eyes sought out the Tracy table, then searched over the crowd until they found Tom at the bar. "Our life, our liberty, and our *loyalty!*"

The applause began again, quickly becoming steady and confident, as if to affirm the beliefs of everyone in the hall. Curley raised his hands, and the audience grew quiet. He leaned forward and lowered his voice.

"We may have to fight with the winner at the end of this European war, and when we do, we'll do it as *Americans*, because this is the country that welcomed us. We owe it to America to be loyal to her flag first"—Curley's arm swept behind him again—"and all others after. . . . Now, let's all of us, Irish-Americans and German-Americans and all our guests, join the band to sing 'The Star-Spangled Banner.' "

In Ireland, politics had failed. In Boston, Tom Tracy had failed at the politics he had studied for sixteen years. Like a drunk, balancing himself on the brass rail at the bar, hoping that someone might throw him a quarter, he had conducted his life with too much care, he had sacrificed too much to ambition, and when he stumbled, he had shaken the confidence of the man he admired like a father.

James Michael Curley was as demanding, as possessive, and as loyal as a father, but Tom Tracy's real father lay in a grave in the Dunslea cemetery, a martyr to Ireland's bloody past and his dreams for Ireland's political future.

I want Tommy to remember Jack Tracy the politician. . . . But if the day ever comes when the politickin' fails, and it's a fact as plain as Christ on Christmas, then I want you to ask yourself what Jack Tracy the Fenian would do.

When the singing ended, Josephine Tracy glanced toward the bar. Her son was gone.

16

Avram Levka opened the door and looked out. He was wearing his yarmulke and his prayer shawl. In his hand he held a small copy of the Torah.

"I want to speak with Rachel."

"She is not home."

"Her light's on."

Avram put the book down on a table, then carefully took off the yarmulke and the prayer shawl. "You are not to see my daughter again. I do not care if the Mayor Curley wipes your bottom and changes your diapers. My daughter sees no more Irishers."

"I don't want to go against your wishes, Mr. Levka, but I'm going to see her."

"The Jews and the Irishers, they don't mix. My girl will see her own kind."

"She'll see me," said Tracy.

"And will she see the other one, your cousin, who protects the little children?" Levka clenched a fist and held it against Tracy's neck. "A knife! To my throat your cousin put a knife, and he said he was protecting the children. We come here to get away from knives and guns and fear, and you Irishers, you bring it anyway. Get out."

"Thomas . . ." Rachel was standing on the stairs. She was wearing a light green skirt, a white blouse, and a Kelly-green velvet bow at her collar.

Tracy realized that she had dressed for the banquet, hoping that he would invite her. He went to the bottom of the stairs and looked up. Her eyes were red. She had been crying, but now she held her chin high.

"Come to the parade with me tomorrow," Tracy said.

"No," said Avram softly.

Rachel glanced at her father, then back at Tom. "Why should I?"

"Because we have to talk."

"I was ready to talk tonight. I was ready to go to the banquet."

"I'm sorry. Tomorrow?"

She looked again at her father, then gave Tracy a nod. "At noon."

Tracy offered Levka his hand.

"Get out."

The cold air rushed in, and the glass in the door rattled when Tracy slammed it.

Avram looked up at his daughter. "Does your religion mean anything to you? Your God?"

"If there is a God, Father, He cannot smile too well upon our religion, considering all the ways He has tortured us for four thousand years."

"He afflicts us because He tests us. We are His chosen ones."

"That's what they teach the Catholics, too."

"See him tomorrow," said Avram firmly, "and leave my house the day after."

Without a word, Rachel went back up the stairs. For a time, Avram Levka stood alone in the foyer, an old man who had failed once more to build a wall between the world and the women of his family. He returned to the rocking chair by the coal stove. He put on the yarmulke, he wrapped the shawl around his shoulders, and he began softly to cry.

Padraic Starr celebrated St. Patrick's Eve between the legs of

Jenny Malloy. Then he thanked her for what she had done and promised that he would send her money from Ireland. She said that after all she had done, she expected to sail with him. He kissed her on the forehead and left.

Then he went to the Old Howard, where Jimmy the Butcher promised he would care for Jenny as long as she needed him. He said it was the least he could do for the Irish rebellion. Starr said that the rebellion would also expect to see him Sunday midnight at Sullivan's Barn on Albany Street.

"Nothin' dangerous?"

Starr shook his head. "We just need a hand with some heavy liftin'."

Jimmy rattled his derby.

A short time later, pebbles rattled against Rachel Levka's window. She climbed from her bed and looked out.

The broad-shouldered silhouette stood beneath a streetlamp. Rachel was half asleep and uncertain if it was Tracy or Starr. When the shadow waved for her to come down, she went.

"What do you want?"

"I need the help of someone as intelligent and observant as yourself," whispered Padraic Starr.

She cocked her head and heard the faint but steady rumble of her father's snoring. She knew he would not stir until four in the morning. "How long will it take?"

"A few hours, maybe. All very safe. Please."

She hesitated only a moment. She had said that she would help him if she could, and she meant it.

They hurried to Dover Street and caught the last train on the Atlantic Avenue line. They got off at the foot of State Street and walked back, under the elevated structure, to the Northern Avenue Bridge.

The streets were deserted and the night was cold. This was a district of warehouses and shipping offices and wharves that fanned out from Atlantic Avenue like the feathers of a dirty, tarred pheasant. The wharves had been connected, first by cobblestone, then by freight lines running down the middle of the avenue, and finally by elevated tracks that ran above it.

Rachel and Starr stopped at a warehouse with bricked-in windows and looked out at the bridge. It was a flat span across the Fort Point Channel, two lanes for street traffic and two for the rail lines running to the South Boston piers. A few hundred yards beyond its steel framework, Rachel could see the lights of the British freighters loading munitions and food around the clock.

The world had gone crazy. And she wondered for a moment what she was doing here at the edge of the craziness.

"A weapons train crosses that bridge on Sunday night."

"Your guns?"

"Write down everything you see for the next hour. How many ships come down the channel, how long it takes the bridge to open and close, and how often—"

"I get the idea," she said.

"I knew I could count on you," he whispered, "from the moment I saw you stand at that podium.

She swallowed nervously. "One rebel to another."

He brought a hand to her face and stroked her cheek. "One rebel . . . to another."

She felt the warmth of his hand. For a moment, she closed her eyes. She wanted to help him, but she had resolved, after he came to the bakery, that she would resist his touch when it came again. Then she felt the cold air on her cheek. She opened her eyes and saw that he was already loping across Atlantic Avenue, as though he knew how close to come to her before stepping away.

She watched him follow the tracks that curved out from under the el. He stopped at the keeper's shed beside the bridge. Through the window, she could see the keeper's head. When the keeper looked up, Starr pulled out a flask and offered him a drink. He was playing the friendly drunk to get information. She wondered if he sometimes played the lover to get help.

Then a coal wagon came over the bridge from the South Boston side. Rachel wrote down the time and put her suspicions out of her mind. Starr was a rebel, she told herself, doing what he had to.

After that, she recorded everything she saw. At one-twenty, the bridge opened for a tugboat pushing a barge up the channel. It took two minutes to open, two minutes to close. At one fifty-seven, it opened for a lumber schooner. At two-sixteen, a switcher engine chugged over the bridge from the South Boston docks. And at two thirty-four, a pair of policemen came along Atlantic Avenue, checking windows and doors. Rachel ducked down an alley and hid behind a row of trash cans. After the police had gone on, she put her head back for a moment and closed her eyes.

"Fine, fine job." Starr was flipping through her notes. "Even if you did fall asleep."

Rachel sat up. "What . . . what time is it?"

"Three-fifteen."

"Oh, God . . . my father." She got up and straightened herself. "You said we'd be back in time. He'll expect his breakfast in an hour." She began to run.

He caught up to her and put an arm around her. "Don't worry, darlin'. We'll be back in twenty minutes, even if I have to throw you over my shoulder and run all the way."

She was angry that he had used her without concern for what she would face when she got home. "Why did you ask me to help you?"

"Because I've no one else to trust."

"What about Tommy?"

"Tommy wants me to stay clear of trains, but I need to make plans, and secret's the way to do it. Don't even tell *him*."

"One rebel to another?" she said sarcastically.

"He's takin' you to the parade tomorrow?"

"How did you know?"

"It's what I was hopin'. It means we've made him see the value of takin' hold of things, of runnin' things instead of lettin' *them* run *him*."

"That makes you happy?"

"If I can help a few folks to somethin' better along the way, I'm happy." He slipped his arms around her waist.

Her body stiffened. "Please don't do that."

His hands did not move. "Me and your Rabbi Mossinsohn, we're the ones who show the way for the rest. When we're finished, there's those that hate us for what we've done durin' the fight and those that love us because we've brought them some freedom . . . from somethin'."

Her body relaxed. His touch was reassuring in the alien darkness of the waterfront alley, and his soft words soothed her anger. She placed her hands on his arms. "I understand what you have to do, Padr'ic. I do."

"Just promise you won't hate me."

She shook her head. "If I hated you, would I be helping you tonight?"

"I still need your help," he said.

"If you need me on Sunday, I'll be here."

"Something more than that."

"If you want me to go to Ireland with you—"

He shook his head. "Something less."

"What?"

"I've given you to Tommy. Now you have to give him to me."

She drew her hands from his arms, as though she felt some dangerous current surge through them. "Why?"

"He has to come back with me, Rachel."

"To kill the magistrate?"

"We'll probably kill more than one before it's finished. So will your friends in Palestine." And before she could respond, he brought his lips to hers. She turned her head. He did not force himself on her but kept his face close to hers, the warmth of one cheek against another. "We'll kill corrupt magistrates . . . and cossacks, too."

"How did you know about the—"

He turned his face quickly and kissed her once more. This time she did not push him away. She let his lips linger against hers, and when they parted, she responded. It was a way to confront her fear of him and satisfy the attraction she had not admitted until now. *But how did he know about the cossack?* Had Tommy told him? Or was it what they called "the magic"?

"Tommy *has* to come," he whispered, "for his own good, for you, and for the place that gave him life."

"Let me come," she said, and her own words surprised her. "If I come, he'll follow me."

"Just do what I ask, Rachel, and what you learn from me you can teach to the Zionists, because we're all fightin' for the same thing." He kissed her again, gently caressing her lower lip between his, drawing it into his mouth as though drawing her soul into his rising.

There was an energy about him that she had never before felt, and she pressed herself against it. He took her arms, slipped them under his coat, and wrapped them around his waist.

If she and Tom Tracy had buried the same hatreds, she and this rebel had dreamed the same dreams.

"I'll send Tommy back to you more of a man, I promise."

She felt his hands at the lower buttons of her overcoat, then they were inside the coat, then at the waistband of her skirt. A button snapped at her hip.

"If he doesn't come back to you, I will." His hand slipped into her skirt, then under the waist of her cotton slip. "Damn few women understand what this is all about."

She felt his fingertips against the warm flesh of her stomach. She gasped, and their mouths met. His tongue touched hers. His hand went farther, slipping her bloomers aside.

"Bacon for breakfast? On a Friday?" said Martin Mahoney.

"If you read anything but the sports page, you'd know that the Pope himself said we could eat meat on St. Patrick's Day." Josephine poured coffee for Martin, then poked at the bacon in the black skillet.

Danny came in stamping snow from his feet and sniffing the air while the aroma of bacon and coffee wafted up the stairs and woke the rest of the family. John appeared first, in robe and slippers.

"A great day for the Irish, Johnny," said Martin.

"Bacon?" he grunted.

Starr walked in. "Has this household gone Protestant?"

"It's called dispensation." Tom staggered in and dropped to his seat. "From the Pope himself. And if we were all such good Catholics in the things that mattered, we'd be on our way to heaven this very instant."

"It all matters," said John haughtily, "as long as the Pope says so."

Josephine put the bacon on a plate, then dumped a bowl of scrambled eggs on top of the sizzling fat in the skillet. "If we was all so observant of our manners, Tommy, the mayor wouldn't have been askin' where in God's name you disappeared to last night."

"Yeah," added Danny. "Where was you?"

"Where *were* you?" said John.

Tom told them that he'd taken sick.

"But better this mornin'?" said Starr.

"I think so." He held out his cup to his mother.

As she poured, Josephine gave him her angriest look. She had learned from the nuns a way of grinding her teeth and squinting down her left eye that could make the most recalcitrant little boy quiver. Tom watched the coffee fill his cup instead.

"You'll be going to the parade, then?" asked Martin.

Tracy nodded.

"With the family?" said Josephine.

"With Rachel."

"Glory be to God, you're not!" Josephine spilled the coffee over the rim of the cup.

Tom jumped back so the coffee wouldn't burn his lap.

"Are you pickin' her up at her house?" asked Martin.

"Union Park Street." He drained a bit of coffee into his saucer.

"Glory be to God." Josephine blessed herself. "A Jewess for a daughter-in-law."

"Is that the custom?" asked Starr. "A man takes a woman to the St. Patty's parade, and he has to marry her?"

"Not at all, at all." Martin dropped a fourth spoonful of sugar into his coffee.

"And a good thing," Danny snickered. "Otherwise Johnny would've married Fiona Muldoon when he was twelve years old, and he wouldn't be joinin' the Jesuits."

Everyone laughed except Josephine, who went back to the stove and scooped around the edges of the eggs in the skillet.

"It says somethin' to the world," John said, lowering his voice to sound more priestly, "when a young man takes a woman on his arm to a public function. We don't have professional chaperons and marriage brokers, as in Ireland."

Josephine spun about. "It's what it says to the voters that worries me. A fine Irish-Catholic boy, with everythin' goin' for him, and he can't find a gal of his own kind to be sharin' it with?"

"I've got no plans to be marrying anyone," said Tom Tracy. "But I'm twenty-six, and I won't be hiding myself either. Now, I'll hear no more talk about it."

"You'll get none from me." Josephine left the kitchen.

Soon enough, Starr and Tom Tracy were alone at the table, watching the bacon fat congeal into white paste on the uncleared plates.

Starr poured Tracy a second cup of coffee. "What prompts your brave decision?"

"It's not brave."

"As brave as Cuchulain, it is, steppin' out of the shadows with your beautiful girl, facin' the wrath of all the righteous voters. As your da would say, if you don't arch your back, there'll be none to respect you."

Tracy ran his finger through a drop of marmalade on the edge of his plate. "You don't need to use his name again, Padr'ic."

"Does that mean you've heard his message?"

"It means that when you go, you'll have rifles and ammunition, because I'm going to get them."

"You're helpin' me take the train, then?"

"No." Tracy slammed his hand on the table, and the silverware rattled. "The train is craziness."

"It's there for the takin', Tommy. I can see by your eyes that you believe that yourself."

"I won't do it, and I won't let my brother."

"He's a good lad, with a head of his own," said Starr, his voice quietly threatening. "And we'll have Uncle Martin besides."

Tracy laughed and licked the marmalade from his finger. "Martin's got muscle, and he can get us a wagon, Tommy."

"And he'll keep it secret till the next tide."

Starr tapped a finger to his temple. "I've a feelin' that our old uncle's seen more than he lets on."

"You're countin' too much on the magic, Padr'ic. Count on money."

"Eight hundred and fifty-seven dollars and fifty-six cents?"

"I'll need every nickel of it. And I'll get more."

"Where?"

"I've told a few good lies already, and I'll tell a few more when I have to. There's no need for the train."

Starr leaned over his plate. "Why this change in my careful cousin?"

"Let's say that in the last few days, I've learned a bit about the way the world works."

"Like your da always said, there's a time for talkin' and a time for fightin'. You get the guns and I'll start the fight, and together we'll set things straight in Dunslea."

To that, Tom Tracy was silent. He looked down at the crumbs scattered over the oilcloth, at the little sparkles of sugar where Martin missed his cup, at the front page of the newspaper and the headlines screaming that the world was blowing apart. He picked up his cup and sipped his coffee. He knew that in law, silence implied consent.

"Curley didn't fire him," grunted Smilin' Jim Donovan.

Strongarm Flaherty took a peppermint candy from the jar on Donovan's desk and put it into his mouth. "Curley must've said *somethin'* to him. He disappeared durin' the anthem and never showed up again."

Donovan looked out his window in the City Hall annex. Across the alley was the New England Merchants Bank. The lights were off because March 17, conveniently, was a Boston holiday, commemorating the day in 1776 when the British sailed away. In the non-Irish wards, it was known as Evacuation Day.

"Whatever he said, it wasn't enough." Donovan pointed his cigar at Strongarm. "I want somebody to follow that kid night and day. I got a hunch that if we do it right, we can finish his career before it ever gets started."

"There's two or three guys can help, but it'll cost—"

"Listen to me, you big bum. If it wasn't for my contacts on the parole board, you'd still be crackin' rocks. And if it wasn't for my pals on the police force, that floatin' crap game of yours would've floated out of town on the last high tide. Now get on his ass."

Tom Tracy dressed in a gray suit that did not clash with his Kelly-green tie and left his house before Strongarm Flaherty found him.

Two inches of snow had flurried down before dawn, then the wind had swung around to the north, scrubbing the sky blue and dropping the temperature toward the teens. It would be the coldest St. Patrick's Day in memory. Tracy put a hand on his derby so it would not blow off and went to the German Church.

His first impression was that Father Sean O'Fearna had once been a dockhand, broad-shouldered and brawny. But for all his size, the priest seemed strangely deflated. Most priests were confident enough about the next life that they could afford to be certain about this one. But Sean O'Fearna did not once look Tracy in the eye.

Tracy mentioned six weeks and three days.

O'Fearna smiled weakly. "I know who you are, Mr. Tracy." He pulled out an envelope and handed it over. "Eight hundred and fifty-seven dollars. And tell Starr I'm accepting his chaplaincy. He'll understand."

With the cash in his pocket, Tom Tracy headed for the Pratt wharf, where he intended to do both business and browbeating. He went up the gangplank to the *Abigail* and was met by Henry Huntoon.

"Where's the captain?"

"Ain't here." Huntoon spread his legs across the top of the gangplank.

Tracy folded his arms and leaned against the rail. "I'll wait."

"Till Monday? In this cold?"

A man appeared from the stern companionway. He wore a

black turtleneck and black watch cap, and in his hand he carried a length of braided leather that matched the color of his skin. "Mr. Huntoon, what's the disturbance?"

"Nothin', sir."

The man took several steps down the quarterdeck. His black clothes made him seem even smaller than he was, but his voice carried sharply over the snapping north wind. "It looks like a big *Irish* nothin'."

"I want to see the captain," said Tracy.

"We need no sailors, and no dandified Irish." The man gave the leather quirt a snap. "Get rid of him, Huntoon."

"Yes, sir."

"Who's that?" asked Tracy after the man went below.

"The mate. Mason Deems."

"Doesn't like Irishmen?"

"Nor Jews, nor Nigras neither. He don't like much of anybody. Least he's fair."

Tracy glanced back toward the quarterdeck, hoping for another look at Deems. "Do you have to be a bastard to be a mate?"

"Helps. Cap'n met Deems in some Bowery clip-joint toilet. Cap'n was lookin' for a place to piss. Deems was gettin' hung by three crewmen." Huntoon smiled and stroked the curls of gray and black at his chin. "They had the pullchain swung over a pipe, and they was tyin' it 'round the mate's neck. Cap'n laid out all three, then he said a mate who got fellers that mad had to be a good one. Deems moved his chest and his Bible aboard, and ever since he been the bastard of the *Abigail*."

"Mr. Huntoon!" Mason Deems smashed his quirt on the roof of the after house.

Tracy looked to the stern once more. "I need to see the captain, about a business matter."

"Monday."

Tracy gently shoved Huntoon aside and stepped onto the deck. "Today."

"Get rid of him, Mr. Huntoon, or you'll be on your way back to the cotton fields before lunch." Deems disappeared a second time, as though the challenge weren't worth his energy.

Tracy looked into the black man's eyes and saw neither anger nor offense. Instead he saw the neutral gaze of a man who had learned to ignore what he could not change.

"You better be shovin' off, Mr. Tracy."

"Where's the captain, Henry?"

Huntoon threw another glance toward the stern. "Show up tomorrow night at the Pratt house on the North Shore."

"I need to see him today, and Pratts don't mix with the Irish on Saturday nights."

"He's shacked up today, and you mix plenty tomorrow night. Just bring bettin' money."

"Bettin' money?"

"Cockfight."

"Cockfights are illegal," said Tracy.

"Better than usin' men. 'Sides, I get to cook the losers."

She waited in the window, not expecting him to come to her door in daylight. After all, it was St. Patrick's Day. The park was busy with parade-goers and neighbors and sober gentlemen already drunk. At quarter past twelve, she began to fidget with the buttons on her blouse. If he did not come, she would be disappointed. If he came, she would have to do what Starr had asked her to do the night before. And somehow, she feared, Tom Tracy would know.

In a waterfront alley, Padraic Starr had seduced her with word and touch. He had brought her to the edge of complete commitment, and he had left her there, while he slowly withdrew his hand and whispered, "Give me Tommy."

"Take *me*," she had responded. "Take me with you."

Instead, he had taken her home.

She still tasted her response, like the faint whiskey flavor of Starr's kisses, and she believed that she would repeat it when the moment came.

Then Tom Tracy appeared at the far corner of the oval, a bouquet of green carnations in his hand. She straightened her hair and put on her coat and tried to forget the night before.

"Erin go Bragh," she said at the door. He slipped a Kelly-green carnation into one of her buttonholes, slipped her arm into his, and led her boldly up Union Park Street, across Dover, along the edge of his own neighborhood, and over the Broadway Bridge to South Boston. Up Broadway they went, past taverns and businesses and horse barns, all hung with red-white-and-blue bunting and pennants of Kelly green. In the street, city crews were spreading coal ash on top of the rolled snow, so that the marchers would have sure footing. Along the curbs, children sat holding little green flags emblazoned with the golden Harp of Erin. On the sidewalks, men and women stood six deep, waiting for the parade that was still somewhere on the far side of the Heights but already rumbling in the vibration of distant bass drums.

The Irish day had arrived. And nowhere, not even in Dublin, was it celebrated with more energy than here.

South Boston was the first Irish suburb in America. Doctors and lawyers and professional men, whose parents had fled the Great Famine, lived now in spacious homes at City Point. Middle-class families lived in airy three-deckers clinging to the Heights where a hundred and sixty years before, Washington had sited the cannon that drove the British from Boston. And even the lower classes near the railyards had more room than their counterparts across the Fort Point Channel.

In South Boston, then, it was a day to celebrate Irish-American achievement. In the singing that could be heard on every street corner, it was a day to renew the Irish capacity for joy, especially when it meant a reprieve from Lent. In the flasks and bottles passing from stranger to stranger, it was a day of devotion to the belief that God had given the Irish whiskey to keep them from ruling the world. In the fistfights and brawls spilling from the taverns, it was a day to remember the pugnaciousness that seemed the soul of even the quietest Irishman. And it was a day to joke about Irish prejudice, for on St. Patrick's Day, as the saying went, there were only two kinds of people—the Irish and those who wished they were.

Tom Tracy usually found it all a bit more than he could stand. By the end of the day, more drunks and more fights could be found along the parade route than anywhere else in the Irish-speaking world. And the Irish of Ireland were always a trifle amused by the fanatic pride that their American cousins took in this day. But then, the Irish of Ireland had not come to a strange place and prospered. In the old Yankee city, this was a day to celebrate the power of the Irish voter, and up ahead, in front of the Courthouse, the most powerful Irishman of all was alighting from his open-topped limousine.

Tom and Rachel had said little to each other on their walk from the South End. Rachel knew that his presence beside her, on this day, on Broadway, was more eloquent than any words, and she felt his confidence whenever he tipped his hat to a voter and pulled her closer at the same time. A week before, she thought, this would have been the happiest moment of her life.

At the corner of the reviewing stand, they stopped. A little girl was presenting the mayor with a bouquet of roses, and the crowd was applauding. Tom Tracy turned to Rachel and kissed her.

"Tommy, what are you doing?" She laughed nervously.

"It's St. Patrick's," he said.

The mayor held the flowers for the crowd to see, then, with a grand bow, placed them across his arm and offered them back to the little girl. "For the fairest young beauty in Boston," he cried, and the crowd roared.

"To St. Patrick's"—Tom Tracy kissed Rachel Levka again—"the only day an Irishman can show public affection to a woman without some old lady callin' in the clerics."

"Or the cops." A round fat face pushed its way into their embrace. The small eyes were red, and the breath smelled like an empty keg. A bottle of beer came up under Tracy's nose.

"Denny, my boy," said Tracy, "I figured I'd find you around here." Tracy introduced Rachel to Denny Morrissey, a Curley captain and treasurer of the Hibernians.

"Erin go Bragh," said Denny. He grinned at Rachel. "She'll be trouble, Tommy, but up close, she looks like a hoodoo chaser for fair."

"Is that good?" whispered Rachel.

"The tops." Denny offered her the lip of his beer bottle.

She shook her head and gently pushed it away.

Tracy said, "You're on my shit list, Denny."

Denny offered Tracy the beer. "Have a drink, Tommy, and an apology. The mayor says your secret fund's in the clear."

Tracy took the beer bottle and tipped it back, keeping his best angry eye on Denny. "I trusted you, Denny, but you went rattin' to the mayor the minute I left the office."

Denny drank the rest of the beer. "C'mon, Tommy. In honor of the day, you get a grand from the Hibernian till."

The Boston College band started up Broadway, playing "Stars and Stripes Forever." The sound of the brass seemed to shatter the frigid air, like a hammer smashed against a pane of glass.

"Not enough," shouted Tracy over the music. "After what you did, I want three thousand dollars."

Denny glanced at Rachel. "Her heritage is rubbin' off on you, Tommy. You're turnin' into a real bargainer."

"More cracks like that, I'll want four."

"Fifteen hundred."

"Call it remembrance money." Tracy set his jaw. "Give me three, and I'll remember what a good Irish patriot you are, instead of what a rat you can be."

"You wise-ass . . ." Denny Morrissey smashed his beer bottle onto the sidewalk. Glass flew, and Rachel jumped back.

"Denny," came a deep voice from above. "A contribution of three thousand is in order."

James Michael Curley was standing, in top hat and morning suit, at the reviewing-stand rail.

"Sure, your honor," answered Denny. "Anything you say. I'll bring the cash to the Tammany Club on Monday."

Tracy whispered, "Gun money," to Rachel, and she smiled, because she knew now that he had made a decision.

The wind gusted, causing the bunting on the reviewing stand to billow up like a sail. Curley told Tracy to bring his lady friend up and get warm.

"You wanted me to stand beside you in public," whispered Tracy. "This is as public as you can get."

"Does it mean you're going back to Ireland?"

"It means I'm getting Starr his guns and his boat, and I won't give a damn who sees us ever again."

She pulled him toward her. "And Ireland?"

He looked at her for a long time, while the crowds swirled around them and "Stars and Stripes Forever" faded down Broadway. Then he said, "I'm joining the fight."

Rachel Levka felt the tears of pride and relief. She pulled a handkerchief from his breast pocket and wiped her eyes. "If you ask me, I'll go with you."

"Wait for me in Boston."

In front of the policeman guarding the reviewing-stand steps, she pulled him to her and kissed his cheek and said teasingly, "I'm sure it's something we can discuss later."

Then Tracy ushered Rachel Levka onto the stand, where five rows of familiar faces stared down. Tracy saw the fire chief, the police commissioner, Honey Fitz and his wife, Judge William Day, members of the School Committee, and several of the ward bosses.

Smilin' Jim Donovan was near the back, by one of the kerosene heaters. When he saw Tracy, he slowly removed his cigar. Tracy tipped his derby and pushed Rachel toward the row of chairs at the front of the stand.

Rachel did not know what she was expecting when she met

James Michael Curley. She had heard him described as everything from the Mayor of the Poor to the Jews' best friend to the worst political hooligan since Boss Tweed. He seemed, however, the perfect gentleman.

He stood and tipped his tall silk hat. "Miss Levka, you're as lovely as they've said."

She had hoped to say something witty, even sarcastic, but his smile and courtly manner drained her of wit. "Thank you, your honor."

"It would be *my* honor to have you sit beside me." He led her to the seat on his left and gestured Tracy into the seat beyond. "The best spot in the house, my dear, with the kerosene heater right by your toes."

She thanked him again. "It's certainly cold."

"Colder than the heart of Lady Macbeth."

She ran quickly through her memory and found a familiar quote. " 'Screw your courage to the sticking place and we'll not fail.' "

"Brave words, even in the mouth of that harridan."

"Tommy tells me you're fond of the classics."

"Also fond of the St. Vincent de Paul harmonica band," Curley chuckled and rubbed his hands above the heater. "Unfortunately, this cold froze the spit in all their mouth organs, and they had to drop out at L Street."

Rachel Levka brought her hand to her mouth and laughed.

Curley gently tugged at her forearm. "Now, now, don't be covering that dazzling smile."

Tom Tracy watched the mayor charm Rachel while she charmed him right back. He had never expected it to happen otherwise, but until the arrival of Padraic Starr, he had never imagined that he would bring them together so publicly. Tracy had finally chosen Rachel over the opinions of the people staring at him. He had finally freed himself. All that remained would be to buy the guns with Hibernian money, force Pratt into a shipping contract, and give Curley the letter he had composed the night before. In it, he resigned, blaming himself for "boring a hole into the hull of the Curley ship and allowing the suspicion of disloyalty to leak in." He added that he would be leaving Boston for several months to tour the rest of this "grand and glorious country," and he hoped that the mayor would understand.

Members of the Knights of Columbus Post 21 were marching by in their capes and feathered headgear, and most of them looked as though they might take off in the strong wind. Curley was waving to them while engaging Rachel in conversation about Rabbi Solomon Schindler, a founder of the Jewish Reform movement.

"He was before my time," said Rachel.

"Well, my dear, I had the pleasure. A fine man who did more for interfaith understanding in this city than anyone since John Boyle O'Reilly."

Rachel was impressed that Curley knew about Schindler. "The congregation at Ohabei Beth Shalom removed him as rabbi in 1893, when he began to condone marriage between Christians and Jews."

"Is that something on your mind these days, young lady?" Curley worked his lower lip back and forth, trying to control a smile, and his eyes danced toward Tracy.

Rachel answered, "In a neighborhood like the South End, we see it all the time . . . in spite of the problems."

Curley laughed. "Your young lady's a politician, Thomas. She teases the mayor, feints, then, with a few well-chosen words, slips smoothly away."

Tracy laughed nervously, "She's a natural."

"Then she'll understand if we discuss a bit of political business." Curley leaned across Rachel's lap and put his hand on the arm of Tracy's chair. "I don't want you to go to your office at the Tammany Club on Monday."

Tracy sat back as though the mayor had hit him in the jaw. He had seen Curley fire more than one man with a smile, and his first thought was that Curley had learned the truth about the Pratts or the secret fund.

But Curley was not finished. "Go to the State House. See Charlie Finnegan. Tell him I want you working the cloakrooms before the vote. You know enough of the legislators, and you're one of the best talkers I have."

Tracy's hand had reached for the letter in his pocket, but Curley was not firing him after all. He was making him a lobbyist and sending him into the biggest battle the administration had faced.

"There's nothing better than a good talker in the back rooms." Curley glanced at Rachel. "A man who does it well can do what he pleases with the rest of his life and never give a damn about the voters."

"Yes . . . yes, your honor," Tracy fumbled.

But Curley was an expert at finishing a conversation. "So there you go. A new job, and for your first task, you can nail those codfish aristocrats who tried to nail *you* last night."

It was several blocks before Rachel said how much she liked the mayor after all.

"He trusts me, Rachel." The confusion tormenting Tracy for days had returned. Curley was giving him the chance to stay in Boston, take his fight to the State House . . . and nail the Pratts.

"You've made the right decision." Rachel knew him well enough that she could feel, from the way he held her arm, what was going on in his head.

"He wants me to do his talking on Beacon Hill."

"Tommy, there are plenty of people who could do it. But damn few have a chance to change history."

He gave her a look.

"The Pratts will be here when you get back. Go to Ireland, and I'll go with you, beside you."

"And if I go to Beacon Hill?"

She stopped. They were at the door to a tavern. Three drunks were singing "The Wild Colonial Boy."

She swallowed and said, "I'll still go to Ireland, with Starr."

17

There were tears in the eyes of Seamus Kilkeirnan when he climbed off his bicycle in front of the O'Leary cottage. The telegram he carried held the sorriest news a mother could hear.

DUBLIN CASTLE
16 MARCH 1916

MR AND MRS OLEARY COMMA THE CROWN REGRETS TO IN-
FORM YOU THAT YOUR SON PVT JOSEPH T OLEARY DIED
WHILE DEFENDING HIS POSITION ON THE YPRES SALIENT
COMMA 12 3 16 STOP THE VICEROY AND UNDERSECRETARY
CONVEY THEIR DEEPEST CONDOLENCES AND ALL THE EM-

WILLIAM MARTIN

PIRE OFFERS ITS HUMBLE THANKS STOP YOU WILL BE IN-
FORMED OF THE FINAL DISPOSITION OF THE BODY WITHIN
THE WEEK STOP

LT GENERAL L B FRIEND

COMPETENT MILITARY AUTHORITY FOR IRELAND

Finnerty's turf fire burned bright and hot on the night of St. Patrick's. The people from the village and the surrounding hill-sides came by horseback and bicycle, carriage and cart, to hear the harsh, rich music, to drink the thick stout, to toast the patron saint, and to discuss the news, which this day was more tragic than on most.

A few came by motorcar, among them Resident Magistrate William Clarke and his wife in their twelve-cylinder Rolls-Royce roadster. The car was yellow, with a white roof that folded down, and when the RM drove past, the children of Dunslea stopped to look, for they had never seen anything so beautiful. There were some in the town who tipped their hats or pulled at their forelocks when the car went by. Others refused even a glance at the gleaming symbol of Clarke's riches and British rule.

According to St. Patrick's Day custom, Clarke bought a round of drinks for everyone in the pub, then raised his glass and said, "May the man who drove the snakes from Ireland teach us all to live in harmony."

The toast was answered by a scattering of polite hear-hears and a bit of applause. William Clarke was respected, though few in the village could be said to love him.

Then Seamus brought his fiddle to his chin, Digger O'Hara raised the tin whistle, Tim Cooney blew into the Uilleann pipes, someone else rattled the bones, the bodhran and the concertina started up, and Finnerty's filled once more with the harsh yet strangely melodic music of the west, music that carried with it the wail of the wind across the hilltops, the rumble of the ponies galloping along the strand, and the laughter of the people who came each night to the pub. The players knew the tunes as they knew the landscape where they lived, but when they played, each instrument sounded out as distinct as a single man crossing a field by the sea, and that was the beauty of the music. Later there would be jigs and reels and dancing so lively that the ring of kerosene lamps hanging from the ceiling would begin to vibrate, throwing strange shadows all about. But for now, the musicians played slow airs, quiet tunes that, according to Seamus, made it easier to grab a swalley between notes.

Clarke stood at the bar beside Father Breen. "It sounds like they're playing 'Bean an Fhir Rua.' "

"It must be then," muttered the priest.

"Your concertina's silent, Father. A rare thing on S'nt Patrick's." Although Clarke could speak the Gaelic that was the predominant language of the district and spoke English with a distinct brogue, he alway chose to sound British in the subtleties of his speech.

"Well, it's not a happy *Saint* Patrick's at all, is it, what with the news from the front?"

"The resident magistrate's office will be requesting a spiritual bouquet for the O'Leary boy."

"That's grand." The priest sipped his Guinness.

"And speaking of the O'Learys, Inspector Hayes tells me that Logan was no good at all on the matter of the Tracys. We haven't been able to provide much information for the Castle, you know."

"It ain't quite the time for that, is it? It's a day to celebrate the saint and a day to weep for one of our own. Save your detective work for tomorrow."

The doors of the pub swung open. Kathleen Mary O'Toole O'Leary and her husband, Logan, stood in the doorway, arms linked, like two tall pines grown so close that their branches formed a single tree. Seamus stopped playing his fiddle and put up his hand to the others. When the music ceased suddenly, the people in the pub looked first at Seamus and then at the door.

Logan O'Leary managed to smile and utter the greeting he spoke each time he stepped into Finnerty's. "God bless all here."

Until this night, no one had ever heard him say it as though he meant it.

"And God be with the both of you," Seamus whispered.

Kathleen's eyes were red from the crying, and her tiny voice cracked when she spoke. "Play us a song, Seamus."

Seamus turned to the half-dozen other musicians and whispered a title. The music began again, and as the O'Learys started to walk toward Father Breen, the people in the pub silently made way. Until the O'Learys had spoken with the priest, there was no other word of condolence that would matter.

Clarke looked at Des Finnerty and whispered, "Draw two. They'll both be in need of a drink, won't they?"

Clarke remained outside the conversation while Father Breen

clasped Kathleen O'Leary's hands and consoled the bereaved parents. But after the heads had settled on the Guinness, Clarke took the mugs and placed them in the hands of both O'Learys.

"Thanks, your honor," said Logan. He took a long draft which left a rim of brown fuzz on his mustache.

"How is your son Donal taking the news?" asked Clarke gently.

"Worse than us, your honor. He took to his boat an hour after we got the telegram. He's been out overnight."

"He's givin' us another worry," added Kathleen.

"I can understand, what with the new limp he's been carrying about." Clarke smiled as though making the most innocent conversation.

Kathleen looked into her mug. Logan scratched nervously at his beard.

And Father Breen turned to Clarke. "It's a dangerous, slippery life on a fishing trawler."

"Indeed," answered Clarke.

"And a bad way for a man to get a limp." Logan tipped back the pint and drained it in a single gulp.

Clarke put his arm around O'Leary's shoulder and led him to the bar. He ordered another Guinness for O'Leary then said, "Your son died a noble death, Logan. He's in God's arms this very night."

Logan watched the head settle on his second pint.

"He's gone to God," continued Clarke, "and a bloody deserter named Padraic Starr's gone to America."

Clarke knew that he would have only a few moments with O'Leary before the others in the pub raised the courage to come over and console him. Logan had refused to tell Father Breen anything about the Tracys, claiming he was no informer. But William Clarke suspected that Logan and the priest both knew where the Tracys lived, and at this moment, O'Leary was susceptible to persuasion.

"We believe," Clarke continued, "that Starr's staying with the family from whom you bought your house."

O'Leary sipped his Guinness.

"While your son fought and died for the Crown, Starr deserted and went off to stir up rebellion."

Father Breen took Kathleen to the snug, where the women of the village could comfort her, then he pushed his way back toward Clarke.

"I don't believe in rebellion," muttered Logan O'Leary.

"Neither did Joseph. But this Starr believes in it, and he has the power to infect others."

Logan nodded and picked at his beard. "I've seen that myself, your honor, but I'm not a man who believes in informin', if that's what you're tryin' to get me to do."

"I'm trying to protect this village and the young men who might throw away their lives."

Logan looked Clarke in the eye. "I wouldn't know nothin' about them."

"If Starr makes it back, we'll see more than a few wounded buttocks, Logan. If he doesn't, we might be able to protect the young men who've been led astray." William Clarke whispered, as if he could make his threat sound like a friendly plea.

"Logan, how are you bearing up?" Father Breen leaned against the bar.

"I'll be all right, Father. Like you say, it's God's will."

"Indeed, indeed," answered the priest. "And we can't do a blessed thing about it."

These Catholics could sound like Calvinists, thought Clarke, but he was not in the habit of accepting predestination. "We must try, however, to control events, if we can," he said softly.

Father Breen's gaunt, bony hand appeared on Logan's shoulder, as if to give strength.

"Don't you agree with that, Father?" asked Clarke.

"It's a fine theory, but not one the Brits have ever let us practice."

Logan looked at the priest, then turned to Clarke. "I'm no informer, but I'll tell you that the Tracys live in Boston."

18

Tom Tracy had heard stories of the North Shore cockfights. They were held usually on springtome Saturdays in the stables of the big homes, before the summer migration of sailors and polo players had begun. Bookies would be imported from Boston, the local police would be paid off, and gentlemen whose lives had seldom been touched by real violence would cluster about the pit and watch birds wearing steel spurs tear one another to pieces. The organizers dignified the cockfights by calling them evenings of Heels and Steel, and only those from the best families were invited.

The Pratt cockfights always started the season, as close to the first spring Saturday as possible. Although heavy snow was predicted overnight, Tracy had heard that the fights were still on.

He took the four-o'clock train to Marblehead, the old seafaring town that was now one of the yachting centers of America. Then he took the only taxi out along the coast road, past homes with broad, snow-covered lawns, to Searidge, the Pratt summer house. It was huge and white, and against the darkening sky it looked to Tom Tracy like a great ship under sail.

He went up the curving driveway, which had been shoveled and sanded, past long Cadillacs and Oldsmobiles, sleds piled with fur lapcoats, and handsome horses tethered and blanketed. Then he saw the chopping block, covered in gore, surrounded by rooster heads and yellow feet.

"Bring your money?" Henry Huntoon came up behind him.

Tracy swallowed back his stomach. "Makin' chicken stew?"

"Coq au vin." The black man smiled. "Simmerin' in the kitchen."

"Where's Pratt?"

Henry led Tracy into the tack room at the side of the barn.

"Good evening, Mr. Tracy!" Jason Pratt was holding a rooster and gently stroking its comb while a gentleman in a tweed hunting suit tied leather straps to the bird's legs.

"If I'd known you were a cock fancier, I would have sent a personal invitation."

Tracy looked at the rooster, a big Rhode Island Red. Its comb quivered as its tiny head twitched about in a mindless imitation of intelligence. "Watching God's stupidest birds hack at one another is only slightly less interesting than watching politicians try to do the same thing."

The handler gave Tracy a smile, then slid the leather sheaths from the gaffs, revealing razor-sharp steel hooks at the bird's heels. "Stupid but exceedingly nasty."

"We need to talk," said Tracy to Pratt.

"Afterward. Roger Williams is the meanest cock in Essex County." Pratt handed the bird to the other man. "I've bet a hundred on him, Tommy, and these days, that's a lot of money."

Pratt pushed past Tracy and went into the main barn. As soon as Roger Williams appeared, there was a roar of excitement from the two dozen men surrounding the chicken-wire circle. The barn was black around the edges, brilliantly lit at the center, and filled with familiar smells strangely mixed—kerosene smoke from lamps and heaters, dry straw, bourbon and Scotch from silver flasks, expensive pipe tobacco, and chickenshit from cages piled near the heaters.

Two birds were carried into the ring and held high. The men cried out their bets and the bookies around the circle wrote them down or passed them off, but no bills changed hands, because in this group, credit was good. Some of the sportsmen were wearing tweed jackets with leather elbow patches, a few were in riding clothes, and one or two wore raccoon coats, as though they'd come to a football game.

"A hundred dollars," Jason Pratt whispered to Tracy. "I may have overextended, especially since my profit for holding the game here is only two hundred. You wouldn't care to pick up a piece of my action, would you, Tom?"

"Your father tried to screw me the other night. He used me to shake Curley's confidence, to make it look like one of the mayor's closest aides was on the take."

"My father will do anything to win."

"And you learned the ropes from him?"

"Bill your birds!" shouted the referee.

The men began to shout.

"I don't operate like my father."

"You don't?" Tracy laughed. "Slippin' me an envelope in front of a bunch of longshoremen? Tell me that wasn't a setup."

The two handlers stood toe to toe and shoved their birds at each other. The angered roosters began to squawk and peck, and the shouting became more frenzied.

"It's no secret that I'm in financial trouble, Tom."

"The son of one of the richest families in America?"

"I've lost two ships. My father disapproves of preserving obsolete vessels and of me in general, but he wanted someone on the inside, near Curley, so he offered me a thousand dollars if I could deliver you. When I couldn't, he tried to use you anyway. It's an old family tradition."

"Prepare to pit your birds!" shouted the referee. The men around the circle were screaming in anticipation. The handlers crouched. Both birds were so angry that they could barely be held.

227

Tom Tracy was not surprised that the father would bribe the son into bribing someone else. He had expected it of the Pratts, and he had carefully prepared his next remark. "You'd take a thousand dollars to ruin me, but you wouldn't take eight hundred and fifty to carry an honest cargo to Galway?"

"An honest cargo of machine parts, you called them?"

"Ten or twenty big crates, maybe, fifty or a hundred small ones."

"Rifles in the big crates, ammunition in the small ones." Pratt smiled, then pushed closer to the fight.

Tom Tracy was shocked.

"Pit your birds!"

The roosters went down. The handlers released. The birds launched themselves into the air, necks extended, feathers erect, wings spread. And they crashed in an explosion of squabbling and slashing feet.

Roger Williams struck first, hooking his gaff into the other bird's breast. Men cheered and others groaned as though the pain were their own. The bird twisted on the gaff and sank its beak into Roger Williams's comb.

"Handle, please!" cried the referee. The birds were untangled, taken back to their lines, and released again, to the same result. The clashing and bleeding went on for nearly ten minutes, and when it was done, Roger Williams strutted about the body of the other bird, his head still twitching, as though he understood the wild cheers of the men around him. And these were the people, thought Tracy, who stood against Curley in his tax fight.

Pratt came back through the crowd, smiling broadly. "A hundred richer, Tom."

Tracy had regained his composure. "I take it you've handled contraband cargo before?"

Pratt led Tracy back to the privacy of the tack room. "I may not be any good at this political palm-crossing business, Tom, but I know a nervous smuggler when I see one."

"Then help me. After the other night, you owe me."

"Too dangerous, and I owe you nothing."

"I thought you liked to . . . take the measure of yourself every so often. Otherwise you could be down on State Street watching a stock ticker."

"I take my measure as I choose."

"Yes," whispered Tracy. "I can see it in your face. In the broken nose, in the little scars. You take your measure like a man.

And I think that what your father had you do to me has left you feeling a bit dirty. Take this cargo, and we'll be square."

Pratt shook his head. "Challenging you to a few rounds in Shaughnessy's gym is not the same as challenging the Royal Navy in the approaches to Galway Bay."

"I'll take one challenge if you'll take the other." Tracy pulled the envelope from his pocket and threw it on the table. "Let's give your friends something *real* to bet on. You and me, here instead of Shaughnessy's gym, gloves or bare knuckles. If I lose, you win eight hundred and fifty dollars. If I win, you still get the money, but you make a stop on the Connemara coast."

Jason Pratt studied the envelope, then smiled. "You know how to challenge me. Include three crew members and it's a deal."

Tracy counted Starr and the priest and, if necessary, himself. "Deal."

Leather gloves were Jason Pratt's choice, three-minute rounds until somebody dropped or threw in the towel.

Tom Tracy sat stripped to the waist on a small stool at the edge of the circle. He could see the faces now, familiar faces, New England faces, trust-fund faces. He did not see Artemus Pratt, but he saw others who looked like Pratts, plus society writer Lucius Beebe, a few prominent horsemen, the senior partners from several Yankee law firms, and Representative Dolliver of the Back Bay.

Dolliver called to one of the bookies and placed a bet. Then he clasped his hands in a small gesture of triumph and smiled at Tracy.

Tracy brought one of the gloves to his forehead and gave Dolliver a little salute.

"You sure a brave man." Henry Huntoon worked his powerful hands into Tracy's shoulder muscles. He had been appointed Tracy's second. "Jason Pratt was Harvard champ, and from what I seen, he ain't got no weaknesses."

"Has he done any streetfightin'?"

The black man simply laughed. "Keep your guard tight, elbows close to the ribs." Huntoon shoved a leather mouthpiece between Tracy's teeth. "And don't fight stupid."

Tracy looked across the ring at Jason Pratt, who lounged on his stool while two gentlemen in Edwardian suits massaged his shoulders. Their eyes met, and Pratt smiled. Tom Tracy filled his mind with the fury he had felt two nights before, when Pratt eyes brightened a moment before trying to ruin his reputation. He flexed the muscles of his shoulders and biceps and pumped them with his fury.

The timekeeper rang a cowbell.

Tracy sprang to the center of the ring.

Don't fight stupid. Don't lose the money or the boat or the chance to pay back the Pratts by using *them* to free Ireland.

From Pratt he expected footwork, feinting, technique, a few flicking jabs to find the weakness. Instead, Jason Pratt came straight at him and unloaded a right that caught Tom Tracy square on the jaw.

He staggered back four or five steps, but he did not go down. He never went down. Then he saw the shock on Pratt's face. He had taken Pratt's best punch and was still standing. He knew then that he would win, even if it took half the night.

And it did. Tom Tracy and Jason Pratt pounded each other for eleven rounds. Sometimes they boxed, sometimes they stood and smashed. Tracy spent three rounds hanging on for exhaustion and three more chasing Pratt around after Pratt was too punished to close with him again.

At the end of the fifth round, they detested each other. At the end of the ninth, they respected each other. At the end of the tenth, a left hook broke Tom Tracy's nose, starting a bleed that poured down his face and across his chest and soaked into his blue wool trousers. At the sight of the blood, the men who had bet on Pratt began to bellow, and Pratt pressed the attack.

But Tom Tracy did not go down. He never went down. And the sound of those Brahmin voices, cultivated, accented, and moneyed, screaming for his blood, would keep him fighting all night if need be.

"You bleedin' like one of the cocks," said Henry after the round.

"I can't breathe."

Huntoon laid his thumbs on either side of Tracy's nose and popped the cartilage back into place. After the beating he had taken, Tracy barely felt it.

"Any better?"

Tracy inhaled. Air came through one nostril, blood through the other. He spat red into the dust, then rinsed his mouth.

Henry rolled a piece of cotton between his thick black fingers, dipped it into the water bottle, then slipped it into Tracy's nose. "That'll stop the blood, but it'll stop the air too. You sure you don't want to quit?"

Tracy shook his head. "He'll go down before I do."

"Man, what you fightin' for? Ain't nothin' worth this beatin'."

"He'll go down," panted Tracy.

Henry began to fan Tracy with a towel. "That captain's the best man I ever met, fair to me every day of my life, and he get a fair day's work for it. But I never seen no one fight him like you."

Tracy spat another mouthful of blood. The cowbell rang, and Tracy got up.

"Before he throw that right, he always drop the left. You just keep your eye on that left. When it come at you, get out the way. When it drop, there's your chance."

The fighters closed. Tracy covered up, protected his nose, and Jason Pratt attacked.

A left jab. Tracy ducked. Another jab, and another. Tracy covered and watched Pratt's left. It dropped, and a right clobbered him. Too slow.

He staggered back and covered, and Pratt came at him again. Three more lefts. Then Pratt reached back. The left dropped, and Tom Tracy released his right. It traveled no more than ten inches and moved so quickly that most of the men in the barn, Jason Pratt among them, never saw it.

Henry Huntoon let out a holler. James Dolliver and the few who had bet on Tracy leaped up and cheered. Tracy spat another gob of blood. They were not cheering for him, he thought, but for the money they had won.

While Pratt's handlers broke a capsule of smelling salts beneath his nose, Tracy looked around defiantly at the circle of New England faces, and he was stunned when, one by one and then by groups, they stood and began to applaud. A few even cried "Bravo!" Then they stepped into the ring to clap Tracy on the back, congratulate him, and offer him a swallow from a flask or a drive back to Boston.

They admired courage and skill as much as any Irishman, thought Tracy, and they would remember him. On Monday, they would talk of him in their boardrooms and counting houses, and some day, if he chose to run, they might even vote for him. In Boston, that would be the greatest victory of all.

After a meal of *coq au vin*, Tom Tracy rode back to Boston

with Jason Pratt, James Dolliver, and Henry Huntoon. Because of the snow that had begun just as they were leaving, the drive took nearly three hours.

When Pratt pulled into the alley behind the family home at Commonwealth and Clarendon, Dolliver thanked them all for a magnificent evening. Then he admitted to Pratt that he had bet on Tracy.

Pratt smiled with the side of his face that was not bruised. "A wise choice."

"No offense, Jace."

"None taken, Mr. Representative."

"You see, gentlemen, betting is very much like politicsh." James Dolliver was very drunk. "You try to make the right decision and hope that you will offend the fewesht people in the process."

"That's what the mayor says, too," offered Tracy from the backseat.

"I hope that he adds an important proviso." Dolliver raised his finger like a schoolteacher. The finger waved unsteadily in the air. "When it comes to the differensh between the right choice and the opinion of the masses, it is the right . . . right choice that must always win, because the man doing the choosing must live with the choice."

"Always."

Dolliver drained the last of the whiskey from his flask. "Those of ush on my shide of the aisle wish we could believe Curley thought the same way. It would make everyone's job easier."

"A bit of trust is needed, then."

"Trust, yes." Dolliver thrust his hand into the backseat. "It's an imperfect system. But, after watching you boys tonight, it's better than the alter . . . alterna . . . the other choice. I'll see you on Monday in the cloakroom." Then the little man staggered off into the snow.

"*In vino veritas.*" said Tracy to Pratt. "Word travels fast."

"Will he be seeing you on Monday, or have you chosen the alternative?"

"In some places, politics has failed, and the time for the cloakrooms is over."

"That doesn't answer my question."

Tracy looked out at the snow. "At the moment, it's the best I can give. I'll tell you more after I find someone who sells guns."

Henry Huntoon smiled at Tracy. "Now I know why you take such a beatin' and don't give up."

"New weapons are impossible to come by," said Pratt.

Tracy nodded. "I know."

Pratt wrote a name on a piece of paper. "This man sells used guns, obsoletes, factory seconds that the Allies have rejected because they might backfire. He hasn't had much for a while, but when he's selling, he's cheap. Tell him I sent you and I'll get a commission."

"Mr. Deems ain't gonna like gunrunnin' for the Irish," warned Huntoon.

"I'll take care of him," answered Pratt. "We ran guns for Pancho Villa. We'll do it for Tom Tracy."

Tracy laughed softly. "Cockfights, gunrunning—"

"I'll do anything to keep my ships afloat, just like Horace Taylor Pratt. He did it because he loved money. I do it because I love the ships."

The snowflakes danced around the gas lamps like swarms of summer moths. The snow was ankle-deep, and Tracy's feet were freezing. But his instincts about Pratt had been true. It was the first time in days that he had been right about anything. In spite of his throbbing nose and aching fists, he was feeling better. He made a snowball and pressed it gently against his nose.

That night, he had fought for the rising. He had gotten the ship and a line on the guns. Now he had to make the decision he thought he had made the day before: Would he fight the ancient fight with the guns he bought, or take the mayor's new trust and fight on Beacon Hill?

An imperfect system, but better than the alternative. Didn't America's rebels, Pratt's own ancestors, fight when they decided that Britain's system was too imperfect for them? The old Republican representative was right about one thing: Whatever decision Tom Tracy made, he would have to live with it, whether Rachel approved or not.

And he did not want to lose her. He supposed that he would mind it less if they split because she chose rebellion and he chose politics. Between lovers, disagreements of principle could lead to reconciliation. But if he lost her to Starr himself . . .

Damn Starr and his magic, thought Tracy. And damn Curley, another Irishman who had the magic and knew how to use it.

233

And damn the father who said one thing to Tom Tracy and another to Padraic Starr.

As he went past the British consul's residence on Commonwealth Avenue, he noticed that the lights were still burning.

"When was your last communication?" Harold Forsythe stood in front of his fireplace.

"Two days ago," answered Nigel Stewart. "They sent us the name Kevin O'Hara. We found him living in a flophouse. Alcoholic. Makes his whiskey money shoveling snow on city work gangs. Hardly knew his *own* name, never mind Starr's."

"And where is Dawson?"

"Shadowing the priest. I'll be replacing him later. This afternoon Dawson went to confession."

"A Belfast Presbyterian in a Catholic confessional?" Forsythe laughed.

"Dawson threatened to go to his bishop. That seemed to frighten the priest." Stewart sipped Courvoisier.

"You know, the federals would certainly help us to capture a deserter." Forsythe brushed an ash from his satin smoking jacket. "If we asked."

"We're after a rebel agent and his American contacts," said Stewart firmly. "We have much to learn yet. Let's leave the federals out of it for as long as possible."

Forsythe threw another log onto the fire. "You want Starr all for yourself, don't you?"

"He killed my partner."

By the time Tom Tracy reached Gloucester Place, an inch of snow had piled on the brim of his derby, and it was blowing down so hard that he could barely see the blue light on the police box at the corner of Oswego Street.

He trudged toward the dead end, thinking of nothing but warm pajamas and a sip of Jameson's. Then, at the stoop, he saw the footprints. He had noticed them back at the corner and had wondered idly where three men could be going in the middle of a blizzard. Now he knew where they had come from, and who they were.

He shook the snow from his derby and forgot the Jameson's. The footprints were filling rapidly, but they remained as small dents in the blanket that covered Gloucester Place, Harrison Avenue, and Dover Street, down to the door of Sullivan's barn on Albany Street.

There, the footprints were met by three more sets, two male and one small enough to be a woman's. From the patterns in the snow, Tracy knew that in the last hour, the doors had been swung open and two pungs, sleighs used for heavy hauling, had left the barn.

"Fools!" he cried, and he slammed his fist into the barn door. Then he turned and followed the tracks. They led him down Albany Street and over the Atlantic Avenue Bridge, which spanned the complex of freight yards leading to South Station. The streets of Boston were deserted, but the freight yards never slept. The growling of the locomotives and switchers, the distant, feral screech of steel wheels against steel rails, the pounding of one line of cars into another, all muffled now by the snow and the wind, were the sounds of the city's engine, the steady hum to which it worked and slept, as soothing to the immigrants in their South End tenements as to the rich of the Back Bay, because the trains brought work to the poor, profits to the rich, and the future to Boston. And the trains brought guns.

"Fools!" he cried in the middle of the blizzard, and he ran.

Rachel Levka looked out at the Northern Avenue Bridge from the same narrow alley where she had offered herself to Starr the night before. Her hands were wrapped around the reins, and her teeth were clenched tight. She had promised to help him, and she would not be afraid.

In the sled behind her, Martin Mahoney calmly chewed his tobacco while the little burlesque comic sucked on his flask. He claimed that the only time he drank was when he was cold or frightened, and tonight, she knew, he was both. At the corner of the alley, Starr and the German gave Danny Tracy their final instructions. She watched Danny's hands slip into his jacket pockets, then his trouser pockets, then perch on his hips.

Everything was covered in white—the horses, the men, the girders of the elevated structure, the street, and the bridge a hundred yards away. So beautiful, she thought, and she tried not to admit her fear.

The German took a pistol from his pocket and handed it to Danny. "If you're caught at the coupling, you'll have to use it. Just fire into the air, like a madman."

"That's right." Starr clapped the boy on the shoulder. "Me and the Kaiser, we'll come runnin' like Billy Bejesus."

Danny dropped the gun into his pocket.

"Now you know what you're supposed to do when the train stops?" said Starr.

Danny nodded. A string of fluid had collected at the tip of his nose. He dragged a sleeve across his face.

"Good lad."

"Be brave, Danny," called Rachel from the sled.

"I ain't no chicken."

"Fools!" A man covered in white came out of the shadows.

"Tommy!" cried Starr, as though meeting him in a saloon. "I thought you were at the cockfights."

"What the hell are you doing?"

"The German information was good on everything but the night," said Starr. "Saturday instead of Sunday. Sorry, bucko."

Tracy looked around, at the faces of people he loved, faces transformed by cold and fear and hard resolve. "Rachel?"

"I told you I was ready to help him, Tommy," she said, "and you should . . . Tommy, what happened to your face?" She reached out to him.

Tracy turned back to Starr. "Whatever you're plannin', leave this kid out of it."

"No!" Danny wiped his nose again.

Tracy kicked his brother in the seat of his pants. "Get the hell home."

"No!"

The German pulled a pistol and pointed it at Tracy's head. "We do not have the time for cheap theatrics."

Tracy ignored him and looked at Starr. "I have the name of a gun seller."

Starr shook his head. "The Kaiser's friend in the railroad office says there's a bonus on this train, Tommy. Machine guns, all the way from Colt in New Jersey, just to go out on that ship." Starr pointed across the channel to the lights at Pier 1. "With machine guns, we'll win."

Tracy glanced at Rachel, then pulled the bloody cotton from his nostril and threw it in the snow.

"Tommy . . ."

Tracy looked at the second pung, at his uncle. "Martin, this is craziness."

"If it helps the cause, I'm for doin' it."

"The cause?" Tracy bent over his uncle. "Martin, men with guns protect these trains."

The wind gusted down the alley, blowing up swirls of snow. Tracy thought he heard Starr laugh. He turned, but Starr was looking out at the bridge.

Martin Mahoney chewed his tobacco until the gust went past. Then he spat. "Men with guns."

"You could die. Danny too."

"It won't be the first time I risked my neck. I did it plenty in the Land League days, when I rode with your da."

"You?"

Martin leaned down, put a huge hand around the back of Tracy's neck and drew him close. "When I was young Dan's age, many's the night I spent behind rock fences, shootin' at greedy landlords. It was men like me what give Parnell the muscle he needed in Parliament."

"I don't believe it," said Tracy, but in this alley, he did.

"No one ever knew, Tommy. Everyone says, there goes old, quiet Martin Mahoney." He straightened up and spat again. "It ain't always been so."

One of the horses began to paw nervously at the snow.

Then they heard it, growing louder with each piston-driven growl, pushing against the sound of the wind like a single deep voice in a choir of women.

"We've no more time to argue," shouted Starr. "Stay around and help if you like, but get in our way and I'll kill you."

"Help us, Tommy," pleaded Rachel.

Starr took a hammer and chisel from the boot of the first pung and handed them to Danny. "You've two minutes after the train stops, lad."

"To do what?" demanded Tracy.

"Uncouple," snapped Heinrich Kuntz.

"He's never done that in his life. They'll shoot him before he gets near the lift rod."

"I'm crawlin' under the carriage. They'll never see me," shouted Danny. "I ain't afraid."

"Remember, Tommy, I'll kill you." Starr and the German turned and ran across Atlantic Avenue, under the el, and out toward the bridge.

The keeper awoke when the felt something cold against his back.

"Do not turn," whispered Heinrich Kuntz.

"Yeah. Sure, mister. Anything you say."

"When I order, open the bridge, or I will kill you."

Padraic Starr ran onto the bridge itself. He climbed down a ladder on the side and pulled the three-foot handle that released a bridge lock. He did the same at the other three corners, then dropped down to the wharf beneath the bridge. At the end of the wharf was the compressor house. Starr pulled a blackjack from his pocket and went inside.

"Either stay and help or get the hell home, Tommy." Martin Mahoney spoke with more authority than Tracy had ever heard from him. "Don't stand there turnin' white on us."

"We don't have to do this. I can buy the guns."

"We're committed, Tommy," said Rachel. "We want the machine guns on that train."

"They won't help the Jews, Rachel."

"They'll help someone, and that's enough." One of her horses reared its head. She pulled down hard on the reins and called the horse by name. She had grown up driving her father's bakery wagon, and she knew how to handle a team.

Tracy put a hand on her leg. "Do you love him?"

"I want to love you, but you don't make it easy."

The pounding of the engine grew louder.

Tom Tracy felt it in his gut, churning his insides, pushing them up toward his mouth. The windows of the surrounding buildings began to rattle. The ground began to shake. And a shaft of light lanced through the snowflakes. Tracy watched it pivoting toward him, flashing over the elevated girders, skittering across the fronts of the channelside buildings, creating strange, frightening shapes and shadows, returning them to darkness an instant later.

"A train! They're jumpin' a train!"

Strongarm Flaherty and Harry the Knuckle Horgan crouched behind a row of trash cans farther down the alley. They had lost Tom Tracy earlier in the day, and so had been watching the Tracy house when three men came out at midnight. Strongarm and Harry had been a few hundred feet behind them ever since.

"What the fuck are they doin' with a train?"

"I don't know." Strongarm smiled so that his four teeth showed. "But it looks like they're after somethin' worth a few bucks. Maybe we do better to get a piece of it than go squealin' to Donovan.''

Harry tapped his temple. "Nice thinkin'."

Strongarm pulled his sawed-off shotgun from under his coat. "Even nicer when you got this to do the talkin'."

The train looked like an enormous animal trying to escape from the steel cage of the elevated structure. Within seconds, it was pounding past the alley, blowing great clouds of coal smoke and snow against the buildings, frightening the horses and terrifying the people in the alley.

Tracy looked at his brother. The boy was chewing on his lower lip.

Martin Mahoney came up behind Tracy and said something, but Tracy could not hear him, because the noise of the train seemed like solid matter.

Just beyond the alley, the animal found its escape: The track curved out from under the el for the hundred-foot run to the bridge. The five boxcars groaned and lowed like heifers hurrying after a great black bull.

In the keeper's shed, the German was crouched out of sight. The keeper was pleading for his life, telling Kuntz of a wife, a child, and a Victrola bought on installment. Kuntz was not listening. His eyes were fixed on the elevated structure and his hand was between the keeper's legs, holding his knife against the man's scrotum. He saw the engine turning toward the bridge. He commanded, "Open! Now!"

"But the engine'll go into the channel!"

Kuntz pressed the knife. "Open!"

"I can't," said the keeper. "You have to release the bridge locks."

In a stroke, Kuntz tore through the man's trousers and took a nick out of his scrotum. The keeper put a foot on one of the pedals and threw a lever.

In the compressor house, a bell rang, and Padraic Starr pulled a switch that started the compressors. Hundreds of tons of air rushed through a pipe to the giant donkey engine beneath the bridge. When the air pressure reached its level, another bell rang in the keeper's shed. The keeper threw another lever, and with a great grinding of gears, the Northern Avenue Bridge began to pivot. Starr stepped over the body of the compressor man and ran out.

*   *   *

"Guards! In the engine!" shouted Martin Mahoney.

"Don't worry about me!" shouted Danny. "I ain't afraid."

Tom Tracy was hypnotized by the blowing snow, the crushing noise, and the bridge swinging away from the street as slowly and ponderously as a ship leaving dock.

Danny pulled the hammer and chisel from his pocket and knocked them together nervously, trying to give himself the courage of his words.

"When the train stops, you have two minutes," shouted Rachel. "Somebody go!"

The sound of her voice snapped Tracy from his trance just as Danny started to run.

"No!" shouted Tom. He grabbed his brother by the collar and pulled him back.

"Let him go, Tommy!" Rachel jumped down.

Tracy wrestled his brother back into the alley.

"Let me go!" Danny swung his hammer.

"No!" Tom smashed his brother across the face and knocked him to the ground.

"It's now or never, Tommy," growled Martin. "Padr'ic's waitin' on us."

The engine wheels screeched and spun madly in reverse. The train slowed toward the channel edge.

"You've worked the railyards, Tommy." Rachel pulled the pistol from Danny's pocket and slipped it into Tracy's hand. "You know how to do it."

Tracy looked at the gun, then at his brother, who was struggling to stand and run once more.

"Keep him here," said Tracy to his uncle.

"I ain't afraid! Padr'ic said it's time to fight, and I ain't afraid!"

Martin Mahoney put a foot on the boy's chest. "Stay still."

Tom Tracy pulled off his chesterfield and handed it to Rachel. Then he grabbed the hammer and chisel and ran into the cloud of snow boiling after the last boxcar.

Two rifles appeared from the windows of the engine, but the detectives were looking forward, at the bridge. Tracy was in the open. The elevated tracks no longer kept him in shadow, and the snow, eight inches deeper, slowed him to a walk. But he knew that if he kept close to the boxcars, the men in the engine would not be able to see him because of the curve of the tracks.

The train stopped at last and exhaled a great cloud of steam ten feet from the edge of the channel.

Tom Tracy dropped into the snow and rolled under the lead boxcar. The run from the alley had taken him fifteen seconds. He now had less than two minutes to crawl to the front of the car and uncouple it from the engine. He had no time to be frightened.

"Hey," shouted the engineer to the bridge keeper, "What in the hell's going on? I nearly went in the drink."

"We, unh . . . we been havin' some trouble," shouted the keeper. "I'm fixin' it now."

"Got any Heinies hidin' around here?" shouted one of the detectives, and the other one laughed.

Kuntz twisted the knife.

Steam vented from the pistons, and Tom Tracy forced himself to move.

Padraic Starr had climbed onto the bridge, which had now pivoted into the middle of the channel. He was counting the seconds. The German would give the order to close in another minute. Any longer and the engineer or the guards were certain to become suspicious.

Tom Tracy dragged himself through a spatter of oil on the snow. He crawled a few feet more and reached the wheel carriage. The greasy couplings were just ahead of him. One connected to the boxcar, the other protruded from the back of the switcher engine. He slipped forward, then heard the sound of footsteps on the cab ladder. Quickly he dragged himself back under the wheel carriage.

One of the Pinkertons climbed down from the engine. His carbine was at the ready, and he was craning his neck so that he could see down the line of boxcars.

"Aw, shit," said Danny Tracy, and he wiped his hand back and forth across his nose.

Jimmy the Butcher was now standing with the others. He offered the boy his flask. "Say a quick prayer and have a quick drink."

"Give me a gun and I'll shoot the fucker," growled Danny.

In the shed, the German continued the count. Another thirty seconds and he would order the bridge to close.

Padraic Starr felt helpless. From where he stood, he could not see the coupling or the alley, and he could do nothing until the bridge moved again. The whole rising now hinged on whether a Tracy could pull the pin in time.

But Tom Tracy was frozen beneath the wheel carriage. He felt the pistol in his pocket and the snow slipping up under his vest. And he saw the pair of boots.

"You've got to do it, boy," whispered Martin Mahoney. "You've got to use the gun. Now."

"Starr said this wasn't dangerous." Jimmy the Butcher took another drink.

"Shut up and get into your pungs," ordered Martin Mahoney. Then he took out a pistol and ran through the snow to one of the elevated girders. From there he had a clear shot at the guard if he needed it.

Tom Tracy could see only the boots. Ten tons of boxcar blocked the view of the man and his gun. The boots stepped cautiously into the space between the engine and the boxcar.

Something had caught the detective's attention. Tracy saw the oil stain smeared across the snow. He had picked it up on his vest and left it after him like a slug leaving a trail of slime.

Tracy took out the pistol. Would he be able to shoot? Thou shalt not kill, said the faith. But this was war, and Tom Tracy had finally become a soldier.

The guard crouched. The tops of his knees and the barrel of his carbine came into view.

In the keeper's shed, the German twisted his blade. "Close it. Now." The bridge swung back toward the street.

The other detective poked his head out the engine window and shouted, "Let's go!"

Tracy held his breath.

The boots did not move. "Engineer, you leak oil?"

"Too much."

The knees disappeared. Then the carbine. After another hesitation, the boots pivoted toward the ladder.

Martin Mahoney slipped back to the alley, put away his pistol, and bit off a fresh chaw. Jimmy the Butcher took a drink. Danny Tracy pressed his thumb against a nostril and blew his nose into the snow. Rachel climbed back onto her pung and wrapped her hands around the reins. Strongarm Flaherty and Harry the Knuckle slipped down the alley.

Uncoupling was ordinarily a safe and simple matter of standing at the side of the car and raising the lift rod that pulled out the pin . . . but not with armed detectives riding in the cab six feet above the coupling.

The engine vented another shot of steam. Tom Tracy took a

deep breath and slid forward again. Then he reached up carefully and tried to pull out the pin. It did not move. He took the hammer from his pocket and tried to tap it loose, but snow and condensed steam had frozen onto the coupling like rime ice.

Tracy glanced at the bridge. He could see Starr riding it back toward the street. In thirty seconds, it would be closed and ready. Then the train would be gone, and with it the machine guns that might turn the tide in Connemara.

He had to take the risk. He rolled out from under the coupling and pulled himself close to the side of the boxcar. Then he peered up at the cab. There was a coal pannier at the rear, and four men —engineer, fireman, and two detectives—were toward the front, keeping themselves warm by the boiler.

Tracy wrapped his hands around the lift rod and pushed. *Still frozen.* He pushed harder, but nothing happened.

Ten seconds, Tommy, thought Rachel. Ten seconds.

Tracy pulled out the hammer and stepped between the engine and the boxcar. The coal pannier protected him from view of the cab, and if he waited until the engine started, he could swing the hammer without being heard.

The bridge slammed shut. The ground around Northern Avenue shook.

Starr ran to each corner of the bridge and pretended to secure the four locks, as he had seen it done two nights before. Then he waved the lantern to the engineer.

The train blew off another shot of steam, then slowly began to chug toward the bridge. Tracy counted three piston strokes, and on the fourth, he slammed the hammer against the coupling. Pieces of ice flew up around him, but the pin did not budge.

He tried to walk along with the coupling, slamming the hammer against it with each chug, but the train was gathering speed. In seconds, it would be up on the bridge and the guns lost. Tracy lifted himself up onto the couplers. He slipped on the ice and the grease but managed to balance himself, clinging with one hand to the lift rod while with the other he hooked the claw of the hammer into the coupling pin and pulled.

"Stop!" a detective appeared on the coal pannier above him.

Tracy saw the silver badge flash through the steam. The carbine was raised and aimed at his head. The train was moving. The snow was swirling. But Tracy's every instinct was focused, every sense sharpened. He felt no fear, no hesitation. He pulled harder at the pin.

243

"Stop!"

The pin held tight. Tracy heard the shot, but he felt no pain. The intensity of the moment protected him even from that. Then the carbine was falling, the man was dropping off the side of the cab. Someone had shot him.

Tracy glimpsed Starr racing across the snow, firing wildly into the air to take the attention from Tracy. The shots popped above the roar of the engine, and snow exploded around Starr's feet as the other detective fired back. But Starr kept running, and Tracy kept pulling at the pin.

Finally it slipped free. The engine immediately pulled away from the boxcars, so that Tom Tracy was straddling the space between them. He swung his body back onto the boxcar as it slowed, then dove into the snow.

In the keeper's shed, the German ordered the bridge to open again.

There was no argument. The gears groaned, the air rushed down the tubes, and the bridge began to swing.

The engine was being trapped on the pivot bridge in the middle of the channel, so that it could not back up to the boxcars or go forward for help. It slowed and stopped a few feet from the edge.

"Swim?" said Kuntz to the keeper.

"Hunh?"

Kuntz kicked open the door to the shed. There was a little catwalk, and beyond, the water. He grabbed the man by the collar and pulled him out of the shed.

"If not, learn."

The keeper flew over the rail and splashed into the Fort Point Channel.

At the same moment, Martin Mahoney ran down the line of boxcars and shot the locks off each one. Rachel screamed at her team and flailed the reins and drove the nervous horses to the middle boxcar, where they would be out of range of gunfire from the stranded engine. Danny Tracy slapped the reins and shouted at the second team. The pung lurched, and Jimmy the Butcher tipped backward.

On the other side of the train, Padraic Starr picked up the carbine.

Tom Tracy was looking down at the blood spattered on the snow, and the body of the detective.

"You did good, Tommy. You've got balls."

"Whatever we're doin', it better be worth it."

The words were stenciled on the sides of the crates: WINCHES-
TER WEAPONS FACTORY, NEW HAVEN, CONNECTICUT. 25 ENFIELD
PATTERN 1914 RIFLES or .303 MARK VII POINTED BULLET 1000
ROUNDS.

"Look for the machine guns," shouted Starr to the others,
"and work fast!"

The air was shattered by the mechanical shriek of the steam
whistle on the engine. Three short bursts were blown, then three
long, then three more short.

"SOS," said Kuntz. "The international call for help. A smart
one."

Three short puffs of steam, three long, and then three short
blew into the air.

"He'll have the cops down here in five minutes," said Tracy.

Starr raised the carbine and squeezed off four shots. The last
hit the whistle in the middle of a long blast. A silent plume of
steam shot into the air.

For the next few minutes, the remaining Pinkerton detective
fired from the engine at anything that moved, but his targets
were working on the other side of the boxcars, and neither he nor
the train crew could see what was happening.

Heinrich Kuntz planted the explosives and wired them to a
single four-minute fuse, while the others worked harder than
they ever had in their lives, all except Jimmy the Butcher, who
dropped down into the snow beneath the second pung and trembled like the horses with every gunshot.

Danny Tracy and Rachel Levka unloaded fifty-pound ammunition boxes from the rear car. Tom Tracy and Martin Mahoney
dragged out rifle crates and packed them onto the first pung.
Starr sifted through the fourth boxcar until he found the section
where the machine guns were stored. VICKERS PATTERN .30 CAL-
IBER WATER-COOL MODEL 1915. COLT FIREARMS, PATERSON, N.J.
Starr had loaded six of them onto the second pung and was going
back for a seventh when he heard Heinrich Kuntz shouting.

"Time is up!" Get in your pungs! I am finished." The German
brought the fuse to his mouth and bit into it, cracking the wax
coating.

"We can load another ten crates." Starr jumped down and ran
over to him.

"Time is up," repeated Kuntz. "Wait around for the police if
you like, but this train explodes in four minutes."

Starr grabbed the fuse from the German's hands. "We're not done."

As a motive to inspire daring, rebellion was only slightly more potent than greed. And only a man like Strongarm Flaherty, who lived by street smarts, gall, and the certain belief that he was entitled to a piece of whatever he could grab, would attempt to hijack a group of hijackers.

While Starr and the German argued and the others continued to load the guns, Strongarm and Harry slipped from their hiding place and ran toward the train.

Jimmy the Butcher saw them first, but before he could cry out, a shotgun barrel slammed down on his derby. His head thumped like a ripe melon and he dropped over in the snow beneath the pung. Then Strongarm leaped onto the back of the second pung and grabbed Rachel by the hair. She screamed as Strongarm jammed the shotgun against her chin. Harry the Knuckle threw an arm around Danny Tracy's throat and shoved a pistol into his ribs.

When Starr reached for his pistol, the Strongarm pointed the two barrels of buckshot at his chest.

"No nightstick this evenin'?"

"That's just for little stuff." Strongarm shouted over the blowing snow. "We got somethin' big goin' here, so I brung my cannon."

In the middle of the channel, the detective fired four or five shots that ricocheted off the boxcars and couplings.

Strongarm glanced between two of the cars at the stranded engine.

"They can't hit you," said Starr. "They don't have the angle."

Strongarm nodded. "You done a nice job. A damn shame if it all goes to waste."

Tom Tracy jumped down from the first pung.

"These things don't throw far, Tracy, but they sure throw wide," said Strongarm. "If I pull this trigger, I'll nail the three of you's where you stand. Then I'll take whatever I want, and the blacksmith and the bayso candy butcher from the Old Howard won't do a thing to stop me."

"Let go of the both of them, now."

"That's a subject for negotiatin'."

"No negotiatin'."

Strongarm adjusted the angle of the gun to keep Starr, Tracy, and the German within range. "We're talkin' about your little brother's life here, Tracy, and the girl's. And we ain't got a lot of time.''

"Then let them go. Otherwise, you're both dead meat."

Starr took several steps to his left, widening the angle. "What's your proposal?"

"No negotiatin'," repeated Tracy at the top of his lungs. "Let them go, and you might get out of here with your nuts."

"The deal," said Strongarm to Starr, "is that we keep the kid until you deliver half of this stuff to a warehouse in Charlestown."

"Tell him to go and fuck himself," shouted Danny Tracy.

Tom realized that the boy's expression mirrored his own. He was proud of the boy's defiance. The Tracys were standing together, and there would be no negotiating. "You aren't goin' anywhere, kid. Don't worry."

The wind gusted and the snow danced around them. It was coming down so heavily that footprints and sled tracks were starting to fill.

"Where can you sell a load of guns?" asked Starr.

"You ever heard of Mexico?"

"And will you charter a railroad car to deliver them?" sneered the German.

"We got friends who'll run 'em by boat, just like you boys."

A scattering of shots rang out from the engine. The wind gusted again.

"I'd say we ain't got much time, boys. Now, do I fire both fuckin' barrels and take it all, or do I give you half and keep half for myself?"

Tom Tracy saw no fear in Flaherty's face and little in Harry the Knuckle's. Some men were too stupid to be frightened, others too certain of themselves. But some men were too smart to be frightened. In another place, a few hours removed, Tom Tracy would have been terrified for his brother's life and infuriated that Rachel's now turned on the whim of the grinning hoodlum above him.

But as a boy, Tom Tracy had been forced to adapt often. In this nether world of black iron, swirling white clouds, and frozen people, he was adapting again. He pressed his arm against the outline of the pistol in his pocket.

Beneath the pung, the little figure of Jimmy the Butcher began to stir in the snow. Tracy noticed, and he was certain that Starr did as well.

Suddenly, Starr threw up his arms in defeat and dropped them against his sides, and Tracy saw the handle of a knife slip into the palm of his hand.

"Well, do we go along with him, boys?" shouted Starr.

Strongarm grinned. "Half of somethin' is better than none of nothin', that's what I always say."

Tracy knew that Starr did not intend to give up anything, but there was no time to discuss strategy. Tom Tracy began to walk toward Strongarm as casually as a man crossing a saloon.

Strongarm turned the barrel at Tracy. "I'll blast you, you sucker-punchin' bastard, and I won't bat an eye."

Slowly, without any attempt to hide the gesture, Tom Tracy reached into his pocket and pulled out the pistol.

"Are you fuckin' nuts?" Flaherty was shocked, more by the manner than the action itself.

Tracy raised the gun and aimed it at Flaherty's groin. "Let go of her and get the hell off that sled, or I'll kill you where you stand."

"You ain't got the balls," said Strongarm.

"No more talk. We're out of talk. You've got five seconds to let her go. Then we're both dead."

Jimmy the Butcher wobbled to his feet. "Somebody . . . somebody . . ."

Strongarm turned for an instant. Rachel twisted away. Tracy's hand came up under the shotgun. Starr's knife flew. And instinctively, Harry the Knuckle turned his gun on Tracy and fired.

The sound of a shot, at close range, is a terrifying thing. It snaps through the system like an electric shock. The body jumps, not in anticipation of the bullet, but because the sound scorches the nerves, the muscles spasm, and the spinal cord whips itself back and forth to be rid of the noise.

At the same time, the sound freezes the moment and leaves it suspended. Time stops until the bullet has finished its flight. The instant becomes eternity.

Harry's slug missed Tom Tracy's nose by inches, then tore into the snow and ricocheted off the cobblestones.

The horses jumped forward, and the pung lurched. Harry the Knuckle and Danny Tracy fell together.

In the confusion, there were two or three more shots. No one knew how many.

Strongarm Flaherty's shotgun sent a vicious spray of buckshot into the side of one of the boxcars. The horses jumped again. He released Rachel and fell into a sitting position on a gun crate.

Danny Tracy rolled and tried to knock the pistol out of Harry the Knuckle's hand, but Harry did not move. There was a small hole in the middle of his forehead, and Martin Mahoney held a smoking pistol.

Strongarm Flaherty raised the shotgun at Tracy, pulled back one of the hammers, and pulled a trigger. Rachel knocked the gun aside, but both barrels were empty. Strongarm looked down at the knife buried in his chest, then thumped into the snow.

"Now, we have no time." Starr turned to Kuntz and nearly tripped over the body of the German. "Damn." He dropped down and felt the pulse.

"Dead?" said Tracy.

Starr nodded. "Must've been Harry's shot."

In the dark, no one saw the small hole in Starr's pocket, where the bullet had come from. He had killed the German himself. It was all part of his plan, but he knew that the others would not understand.

He pulled his knife out of Strongarm's chest, then flipped the box of matches to Danny. "Light the fuse, lad, and we'll get out of here."

Tom Tracy was still staring at the body of the German.

"It's rebellion, Tommy. In rebellion, men die. The old makin' way for the new." Starr looked at Rachel. "You know that, honey, don't you?"

She buttoned up her coat and climbed onto the seat of the pung. "Let's get away from here."

The fuse began to hiss.

Starr climbed into the first pung, beside Martin Mahoney, and looked down at Tom Tracy. "Ride with your gal. After what you done tonight, she's liable to give you a big kiss."

"Get goin', Padr'ic," said Tracy.

Martin Mahoney called to his team, then pulled up suddenly at the reins. His hands went to his stomach. His body heaved. He spit out a mouthful of tobacco and vomited up his supper.

For a few moments, Strongarm Flaherty regained consciousness. He looked around him, at the elevated structure and the boxcars, and he saw a strange flame that seemed to be moving slowly through the air. He thought it might be the glowing tip of a good cigar, or a twenty-dollar gold piece reflecting the gaslight, or perhaps the Angel Gabriel. He dragged himself toward it, leaving a wide stain of red in the snow.

Then he realized what it was: a flame traveling along a slow fuse. He saw the point where the fuse split into five separate lines, and he knew that once the flame reached it, he was a dead man. He tried to move faster through the snow. If he could catch the flame, he would live, and he would fix those bastards for good . . . and then he'd run the best crap game and the best whores . . .

He lunged for the flame, but he fell short. The flame reached the knot, and like an old hatred, it became five flames hissing along five quick fuses.

19

*I*n war, thought Lieutenant Ian Lambert-Jones, some men were luckier than others. And even in death, there were degrees of luck. The man who died instantly was the luckiest, charging across no-man's-land, the shells exploding around him, the bodies and bowels of his comrades blowing through the air, the terror coursing through him, and suddenly . . . at peace. If one could not die so quickly, it was best to pass away in an English hospital, of a single neat wound in the chest, after a peaceful goodbye to sweetheart and mother, with a final rest in the family plot. The alternative was the field hospital, amid the cries of amputees and the stench of gangrene, with nothing awaiting but a mass grave in a foreign place.

On Sunday morning, these thoughts traveled with the Irish landscape as it sped past the window of Lambert-Jones's railroad car. He was returning from the funeral of a cousin who had died in a Belfast hospital, of a clean German chest wound, and who now slept in a graveyard with seven generations of ancestors.

Luck, rather than courage, determined life on the Western Front. Individual heroism had its place, more as symbol than weapon. But the massed infantry charge and the rolling barrage left little room for heroism. Hundreds of thousands of men and millions of bullets screamed across the same stretch of blasted land, and thousands died, not because of courage or cowardice, but because of the simple physics of luck.

There were some who considered Lambert-Jones to be among the luckiest of all—wounded badly enough to come home, but still wearing his regimentals with pride, and safely deposited at a desk in Dublin Castle. Lambert-Jones did not see it in quite that way. Had he not blundered at the bridge, he might still be standing with his comrades at the front. Had he not been wounded, he might by now have atoned for the blunder. But in Dublin, at least, there was room for individual intelligence, and he might yet atone from behind the desk.

He went straight from the station to Dublin Castle. A telegram awaited him. He read it and cursed. His cousin's death might have been lucky, but the funeral was ill-timed. While Lambert-Jones spent Saturday in Belfast, this information, which should have been forwarded through London to the men in the field, had been sitting useless on his desk.

RIC BARRACKS DUNSLEA
18 MARCH 1916

SIR ANOTHER NAME HAS COME TO MY ATTENTION STOP IN BOSTON A FAMILY NAMED TRACY ARE RELATED TO STARR STOP MOTHER NAME JOSEPHINE ELDEST SON THOMAS STOP REBEL ACTIVITY IS ON INCREASE IN OUR DISTRICT AND SUSPICION IS THAT STARR JOURNEY TO AMERICA MAY BE RELATED STOP

WILLIAM CLARKE RM

Lambert-Jones scrawled a dispatch for the intelligence offices, requesting that the Boston agents investigate anyone named Tracy. He signed the name of General Friend and quieted his anger. He should have been informed of this dispatch in Belfast, but chances were that no one with any influence had even seen it. It had arrived, after all, on Saturday morning.

But as the crisis threatened, it was becoming apparent to Ian Lambert-Jones that in matters of intelligence and national security, it was much the better course to rely on military men like himself than the career politicians who ran the Castle so casually.

At least the resident magistrate of Dunslea was one civilian who sensed what was happening. Not only was he among the most famous horsemen in Ireland, thought Lambert-Jones, but an excellent judge of character, as well.

Thirteen inches of fresh snow blanketed Boston by morning. The storm had ended, the clouds were flying off to the northeast, and Tom Tracy was ushering the eight-o'clock Mass at the Cathedral. Every second Sunday of the month, he led old women and young families to their seats and carried the collection box down the aisles at the offertory. He had been raised to believe that every layman had a duty to serve the church, and he knew that devout voters admired the politician who practiced the faith at the early Mass. He also knew that until the *Abigail* pushed her way down the Fort Point Channel, he and the others had to follow their regular routines and arouse no suspicion.

He stood at the back throughout the Mass, but heard little of the English readings or the soothing Latin poetry. He did not enjoy sacrificing sleep to make his early appearance on Sundays, and he should have been happy that another swatch of hypocrisy had been torn from his life. But in the last twenty-four hours, he had torn his life itself from its moorings.

When the priest came to the rail to dispense Communion, Tracy walked down the aisle, hoping that the host might fill him, as it had when he was a boy, with a sense of his own goodness and the certainty of things. The nuns had taught that Christ loved his people enough to make Himself a meal, to let His people consume Him, not simply symbolically, but as though a slice of His own flesh had been dried and dropped into the ciborium. When the host entered one's mouth, Jesus leaped out of it and into one's heart. The idea was too profound, too frightening, and too soaringly abstract for a young boy to comprehend. It was enough, on Saturday afternoon, for young Tom Tracy to search his dark soul in the darkness of the confessional, to cleanse his sins, and then, on Sunday, to receive God's love and the promise of eternal happiness. But as the week went on, his soul would always darken again, and the following Saturday, he would be back in the darkness of the confessional.

When I was a child, I thought as a child, but when I became a man . . . life became more complicated, and so did one's beliefs. Halfway to the altar, Tom Tracy hesitated. He had contributed to the deaths of four men. He had committed sins that condemned him to hell until confession had erased them. Or had he? He had committed himself, the night before, to rebellion, to an ancient war which was, at its withered root, a fight for the faith. He was sinner and saint together. He said an Act of Contrition and went to the rail. If God disapproved, they could discuss it later.

"Did you see the story in the paper this morning?" Smilin' Jim Donovan came up behind Tracy as he walked home.

Tracy had resolved to avoid Donovan after Mass, but Donovan had followed him.

"You mean the story about the Yankees tryin' to trade for Tris Speaker?" said Tracy calmly.

"Yeah." Smilin' Jim laughed. "Today they want Speaker, tomorrow Babe Ruth."

Tracy grunted. "Not a chance."

"The Indians want Speaker, too," said Smilin' Jim.

Tracy sidestepped a snowbank.

Smilin' Jim kept pace. "But it ain't baseball I'm interested in, Tommy."

He knew. The thought snapped through Tracy like a lightning bolt striking a sinner. God was already punishing him for receiving Communion.

"So what's on your mind?" Tracy said, squinting in the sudden glare as the sun burst from behind a cloud and reflected off the snow.

"That big story on page one of every late-morning edition in the city. About the munitions train."

"I haven't seen the papers." Tracy had read them all, and they agreed: German agents, working in concert with a group of Irish street hoodlums, had performed the most daring and aggressive act of sabotage since the attempt on the Welland Canal. They had stopped and destroyed a munitions train (no mention was made of theft) a quarter of a mile from its goal. They had killed a detective, and three of their number had died. The surviving detective, whose carbine had taken down the German ringleader, was already becoming a hero, except in papers sympathetic to the German and Irish causes. In those, the late-edition editorials were already decrying all munitions production as a threat to American neutrality.

"I don't really know the facts yet," Tracy added.

"Well, Tommy . . ." Smilin' Jim stopped. "I do."

An elevated train rumbled along the tracks above them, raining a shower of sparks and snow down on their hats.

"From the pieces they've scraped together, they think that

Strongarm Flaherty was one of the guys that got blown all over Atlantic Avenue."

"So he had his dick in the wrong bunghole. Guys like him draw trouble like hydrants draw dogs."

Smilin' Jim smiled. "I put Flaherty on your tail Friday morning. He was following you last night."

"He wasn't in my bed, and that's where I was." Tracy started to walk again, as if he could escape Donovan's knowledge by escaping his presence.

"What's up in Dublin, Tommy?"

Tracy stopped and turned. Another train went by. Tracy and Donovan passed from glaring sunlight into shadow, then back again.

"Level with me, Tommy, and we'll make a deal. Otherwise, the cops get your name." Donovan paused. The smile had disappeared, and without it his face looked almost pallid, as though he were preparing a deathbed promise. "I'm in the Clan, Tommy, and if you're hidin' a rebel, I'm on your side."

Tracy recalled Donovan's performance in the mayor's office a week before, when he had suggested letting the Irish murderer disappear into the alleys of the Irish city. But Tracy did not trust Donovan to help him. He could trust no one whose job he intended to take in the next election.

"What's your deal?"

A city work crew arrived at the corner of Dover and Washington. Men with shovels jumped off the wagon to clear the intersection while three-horse teams began dragging giant wooden rollers down the street to flatten the snow.

Donovan grabbed Tracy by the elbow and steered him into a pawnshop doorway. In the window behind him was a Victrola, a jewelry box, a bust of George Washington, and a brace of old dueling pistols. A small tag was attached to each item; everything had its price.

"Did you take guns off that train?" Donovan asked.

"Is that what you know?"

"That's what I guess. There's not enough left of the boxcars to know for sure."

Tracy said nothing.

"All right, then. What's up in Dublin? What are the guns for?"

"You said you had some kind of deal."

"Are you running guns to Ireland?"

The Smiler was a good guesser, thought Tracy. He would keep

guessing until he had figured it all out, or figured it wrong. And that could be more dangerous.

Tracy brought his face close to Donovan's and slipped a gloved hand under Donovan's lapel. "Do you know what happens to informers?"

"Don't threaten me, Tommy, or I'll have your ass on a flagpole in front of Curley's house by dinnertime."

They were close enough that Tracy smelled the coffee on Donovan's breath and saw a small crust of egg at the corner of his mouth. It seemed that Donovan had eaten breakfast, then ostentatiously received Communion at the eight-o'clock Mass. That, according to the church, was a mortal sin, as damning as anything that Tom Tracy had done since the arrival of Padraic Starr.

"What's your deal?" said Tracy.

"I know you're runnin' guns." Donovan smiled. "So here's the deal: Go do it. Stick the Brits a good one, and I'll do what I can to keep you in the clear."

Tom Tracy hid his surprise behind a pair of goat's eyes. "What about Strongarm?"

"Maybe it's not him." Smilin' Jim shrugged. "I been to the morgue, and I couldn't tell."

"In return for all this generosity?"

"You never run for political office."

"No." Tracy had not yet accepted that his future as a Boston politician might be over. He turned and started to leave. Always refuse the first offer in any negotiation. Curley had taught him that.

"Hey, kid." Donovan grabbed him. "You got no cards, so don't call my bluff."

"Why don't you just go to the cops?"

"Because cops are cops. We all hate cops." Donovan looked hard at Tracy. It was the stare of a streetfighter, of someone who had lived for sixty years by throwing his weight around when he could and by making deals when his weight was not enough. "Besides, my parents came here durin' the famine. If I can't fight for Ireland, I'll see that you and your friends get the chance."

Tracy realized he could do business with the Smiler, even if it would cost him another small piece of his soul. "Here's *my* deal: I do what I have to in Ireland, and when I come back, I never run against you or anyone you support. And anytime there's a fight, I fight on your side or stay out."

Donovan extended his hand and Tracy took it.

"You're smart, Tommy." The Smiler smiled. "If you weren't doin' this for Ireland, I'd nail you to the wall."

"If Curley knew I was dealing with you, he'd hold the hammer."

"That's because he's different from us. He's a politician first and an Irishman second."

Tom Tracy had sealed another pact. If there had been any hesitancy about the trip, it was gone. He was going to Ireland, not simply as the son of a gallows-walking patriot, but now as a representative of every second-generation English-hating Irishman in America. It was a role he did not relish. Americans sat safely in their cities and towns and worked at their jobs and went about their business. They shouted "Up the Irish" when the voice filled them and filled the coffers when called for help. But they were here, safe from the blood and the gunfire, from the cycles of repression and rebellion, of uprising and reaction, of murder and revenge. They would be happy for a rising, as long as they were safe in Boston. On the street, they had an expression that came to Tracy's mind when he heard Irish-Americans crying for rebellion: "Let's you and him fight."

At least Donovan was risking *something,* and for that, Tom Tracy had to respect him.

Jenny Malloy had not been in a church in six years, but she had nowhere else to turn. Jimmy the Butcher was drunk, drunker than she had ever seen him, and he was bragging about things that could get them all arrested and put Starr on the gallows.

She led Jimmy into the German Church and blessed herself with holy water. Then she dropped Jimmy's hand into the font, held it by the wrist, and used it to splash water over his face.

"Jesus Christ," he said, "what the hell—"

"That ain't what you say when you bless yourself, Jimmy."

The water roused Jimmy for a moment, and he said, "Father, Son, and Holy Ghost, Amen."

"Good boy, Jimmy." And she felt the eyes on her, all around her, the good Christian eyes condemning the drunk and pitying the poor wife.

On a burley stage, they judged her body. Here, she felt, they were judging her character as she stuffed her drunk into the rear pew and sat down beside him. By the sermon, Jimmy was in a stupor. By Communion, he was snoring.

"*Corpus Domine Nostri Jesu Christi, custodiat animam tuam, in vitam eternam.*" Father O'Fearna held the host. The communicant tipped back her head and extended her tongue. He placed the host on the tip, then moved with the altar boy to the next communicant. It was one of the beauties of Catholic theology, thought O'Fearna, that a sinful priest could bestow the sacraments and cleanse others in spite of his sin.

"*Corpus Domine . . .*"

"You gotta help us, Father." Jenny had waited until the very last to come to the rail, so that there would be no one on either side of her. "Jimmy told me all about last night . . . how scared he was . . . how drunk he got. He's on a bender, and he could blow everything."

Sean O'Fearna repeated the Latin words, as if to drive away the vision. He held the host in front of her. She shook her head.

"See me in the sacristy." He returned to the altar, his mind struck by the enormity of her sacrifices. She had exposed her body to save Starr in the burlesque house. Now she had exposed herself to the power of the host. As he polished the communion plate, he wished that at some time in his life, a woman had been prepared to sacrifice herself for him. Because sacrifice was love.

Hugh Dawson decoded the telegram while Stewart attended Episcopal services at St. James Church in the Back Bay. Then he took out the thick city directory he had bought when he first arrived in Boston. He looked for the name Tracy. He ran his finger down the row to *Tracy, Josephine, housewife . . . 13 Gloucester Place*. A few names farther down was *Tracy, Thomas, city employee,* at the same address.

The door swung open. Stewart threw the Sunday edition of the *Transcript* onto the table. "They have their guns."

Dawson threw him the telegram. "And we have them."

When he walked into the apartment, Tracy smelled the familiar perfumed soap and saw the suitcase by the door.

Rachel Levka was sitting in the living room, her hands folded primly on her lap, her hat and coat beside her on the settee.

"I knew there would be no one home, so I let myself in."

"The captain doesn't want women on the boat. Besides, you've done enough."

"I did as well as any man last night." She sounded bitter, for the men she had helped were leaving her.

He took his coat off and threw it on the chair. Then he knelt in front of her. "You're very brave, Rachel."

"So are you." She reached out and touched his face. "I'm glad you're going."

"After last night, I have no choice."

"You never had a choice." She took his face in her hands and looked into his eyes. "It's the right thing to be doing."

"Martin agrees with you, and we can't hold Danny back, either."

"Good. Strike the blow. Kill the magistrate," she said with sudden ferocity. "Ireland can be the start."

"Wait for me, Rachel."

Her hands slipped from his face.

He straightened up. "Has Padr'ic asked you the same?"

Rachel shook her head. Starr had toyed with her emotions, he had used her, but he had not taken her when she offered herself. In his way, she thought, he was an honorable man. "Padr'ic reached through me to you, Tommy. He has you now. That's all he cares about."

"Then wait for me." Tracy laughed. "I'm on my knees to you."

Rachel played with the buttons on her overcoat and pretended to miss the meaning of what he had just said. "This morning, when I went to the boat, Padr'ic reminded me that I'm a Jew, with my own fight. I've done my favor for the Irish."

"It's that kind of thinking you and I have been up against since we met." He took her hands in his. "You told me you'd stand beside me if I gave you a reason."

"I'm going to New York. My father thinks I'm going to see my aunts, but I'll catch up with Mossinsohn before he goes back to England. They say that as soon as the war is over, he's going to Palestine and establish a settlement."

Their world was blowing apart, thought Tracy, and they might never be able to put it together again. They might never *be* together again. "I wish we could turn things back a week and start over."

"The things I've learned the last week are things I plan to use, Tommy. Do what you have to do, and I'll do what I have to do, and maybe we'll meet in Palestine when the war ends."

"The Jews have had problems for three thousand years. You won't solve them in the four or five months that I'm away."

"The Irish have had problems for seven hundred."

Tracy laughed. "And I won't solve *them* either. So stay and wait."

She looked at him for a time, then slowly unbuttoned her overcoat.

Their silence seemed to draw in all the small sounds around them . . . the dripping of melted ice into the catch basin beneath the icebox, the creaking of the wood floors as the humidity dropped and the north wind gusted in, the rattle of the potatoes simmering on the stove.

She let the coat slip from her shoulders, then she brought her hands to his neck and pulled his face to hers. He wrapped his arms around her. They kissed with the passion and knowledge of old lovers long apart. They pressed their bodies together, like old lovers prolonging a moment of reunion. And, as gracefully as old lovers, they lowered themselves onto the sofa. The frame creaked, but they did not notice.

She drew her face back from him a bit and whispered "I'll wait, if you promise to come back alive."

"I promise."

She sat up. Her skirt billowed out around their bodies like a blue flower.

"Even if you promise, Tommy, this might be our only chance."

"It's for sure we'll have no chance between now and Easter."

Rachel unbuttoned her blouse and threw it on the floor. A strand of hair came loose and dropped down over her left eye. She blew it aside. Then she crossed her arms in front of her and lifted her chemisette by the hem. She tilted her neck and pulled the garment gracefully over her head.

Her breasts were not high and round, like those of the Rubens nudes. They were heavier, larger, more elongated, as if they had been caressed into shape by a sculptor who had made them his embodiment of woman's nurturing soul. As the artist's afterthought, there was a small mole just above one of her aureoles, a blemish to heighten the beauty.

Then Rachel leaned back. Her breasts rose and drew upward. A line of perspiration appeared from the small patch of hair at her underarm and trickled down her side. She shivered. Her dark nipples stiffened and stood out in the chilly room.

He placed his hands delicately on her waist, and she shuddered.

Then she lifted his face to her breasts. "If you know what's waiting, Tommy, you'll *have* to come back. You might even decide it's too good to leave behind."

His mouth found a nipple. A sound rose from deep inside him, an animal groan that was neither pleasure nor pain, but a rush of air, an inflating of his whole being.

She knew it was the right thing, even if she never saw him again. She moaned softly and lost herself in sensation.

After a time, they rolled together onto the floor. She lifted her hips and helped him to slip off her knickers and petticoat, then he peeled her stockings down to her calfs so that he could caress the cool flesh of her thighs. He ran his fingertips upward from her knees, then back, then again toward the center of her. Each time he drew closer, she spread her legs wider, until at last he touched her there and she gasped. "Tommy, we haven't much time."

He stripped off his clothes and stood naked above her. In a gesture as innocent as that of a milkmaid hiking her skirt to sit at the stool, she pulled hers around her waist. He dropped to his knees and took a cushion from the sofa and placed it under her hips.

There was no hesitation, no questioning of the past or future. He entered her, then lay still and felt her warmth envelop him. When he began to move, she moved with him. And after a time, she raised her legs so that he could touch her deep inside, touch her soul if he could. In that moment, he knew he would never leave her.

He thrust himself steadily and confidently and did not feel the fear that he had known with prostitutes, that he would finish after the first motion. He closed his eyes and glided through her sea with a calm, even-tempered passion, steadied by her moans, her whimpers, her cries of pleasure, and then . . . a scream.

Now, he thought, now he could take his own . . . But then, another scream. *Someone was in the room.*

She screamed again, and Tracy tried to roll away. A man's voice growled, "Don't move," and a pistol pressed against the side of Tracy's face. He dropped back and covered Rachel's body with his own, bringing his arms up to surround her.

"Sorry to interrupt you in the middle of your morning rut, old boy."

Tracy turned his head slightly, so that he saw the handsome face and the mustache and the downturned brim of the fedora.

"Frightfully sorry, indeed. Nothing like a pistol at the jaw to take the spring out of the old stinger."

Tracy felt himself shrinking, slipping out of Rachel's body, his testicles pulling up into his own in fear.

"However, I have a few questions."

Rachel stared out from under Tracy's arm. "Who is he, Tommy?"

"*Tommy.* . . . Then you *are* Tom Tracy?"

Tracy closed his arms more tightly around her, as if to protect her, and he said, "If you want money, it's in my pants."

"Give the money to your whore."

"Who is he, Tommy?"

"Never mind that," said the man. "Where are the guns?"

"I don't know what you're talking about."

The man cocked the pistol. "Where are the guns? Where is Starr? What is he planning?"

"Get out of my house." Tracy felt the frightened sweat running down his sides and spilling onto Rachel's breasts.

She said his name again, this time with a fear as old as her people. It was happening again. The nightmare had been reborn in the most passionate moment of her life. It was another body on top of her, another man invading her happiness, another weapon, but it was all the same.

"It's all right," Tracy repeated. "He's got the wrong guy."

"It is not all right. And *you* have the wrong guy."

Rachel peered from beneath his arms like an animal gazing from its burrow.

The man forced the gun against Tracy's back, pushing him down in a strange pantomime of their lovemaking.

"Tommy, answer his questions," she whispered.

"Where are the guns?"

"Here in this house," said Tracy. "In the cellar."

"My partner's in the cellar. We'll know in a few moments if you're lying."

Hugh Dawson had found nothing. He lit a match and looked through the coal bin. He lit another and stepped into the storage room. The match burned down to his fingers. He blew it out. As he fumbled for another, a fist smashed into his face and he collapsed on the floor.

When he awoke, he thought he was suffocating. He tried to

breathe and gagged on the oily rag that had been stuffed into his mouth. He was in darkness, on a dirt floor, and his hands were tied to his ankles so that he could not move.

Martin Mahoney came up the back stairs from the cellar and stopped at the kitchen door. He heard voices.

"You are not cooperating," said a man with an English accent.

Martin heard Tracy try to muffle a sound that was half whimper and half grunt.

"Make him stop, Tommy. Make him go away."

It was a girl's voice, the Jewish girl.

Martin stepped quietly across the kitchen, so that he could peer through the dining room and into the front parlor. Nothing in his life had prepared him for the sight of the two lovers and the man crouched beside them, holding the gun.

After he gagged back his tobacco, he looked at the clock. His sister would be home from Mass in ten minutes. If the man with the gun did not kill her, the sight of her son and the girl would.

"Starr is on a ship," said Rachel.

"What's he doing on a ship if the guns are here?"

"Don't tell him anything," said Tracy.

Martin Mahoney stomped across the floor and shouted, "Hello, Tommy? Your ma boiled me a vat of potatoes. I'll be takin' them down now."

With potholders, he lifted the vat from the stove and went into the dining room. He called cheerfully after Tommy several times, enough to get himself into the living room, and only then did he pretend to notice.

"Stop," said the Englishman, "or this pair will be all over the rug, won't they?"

At the sound of the accent, Martin felt an old, long-buried rage rising in this throat.

Rachel moaned. She was beyond humiliation, beyond terror. She was lost now in the depths of her memory. Her voice sounded distant and spectral, like the wind when it turns and blows toward the land. "Oh, God, please let me up."

"What are you doin' to those poor kids?" demanded Martin Mahoney.

"Torture," grunted Tracy. His perspiration was icy, his genitals shriveled, and there was no escape, no way to release his rage, because to move meant death.

262

"Interrogation," said the Englishman. "Tell me the name of the ship and Starr's plan."

"Heligoland," moaned Rachel. It was the name of the ship that had brought her to America.

"Darlin', say no more," muttered Martin.

"Keep talking," said the Englishman, "and this will all be over very quickly."

The gun pressed against Tracy's back. Tracy ground his teeth and tightened his body into a coil of muscle.

"Now, young lady, what is Starr planning in Ireland? Names, dates, objectives. Because a single bullet will go through both of you."

"Tell him, Thomas. Please tell him."

"No," said Martin. "Don't give him a thing."

Beneath him, Tom Tracy sensed a change. He felt Rachel's softness hardening in anger and fear.

"Tell him!" she screamed. "Tell him!"

"No!"

"Tell him! Tell him!" and she began to push against his body, trying to push him off.

"Stay still!" cried the Englishman.

She pushed harder against Tracy's chest and stomach and began to swing her legs. She did not care if the gun went off and killed both of them. It would be better than reliving the terror another second.

"Tell him!"

"No!"

"Get off! Get off!" Rachel Levka kicked the Englishman's arm. Her strength became that of a cossack . . . or the dybbuk. She flailed her legs madly, and the gun flew out of Stewart's hand.

Tracy rolled to his left and threw his body against the Englishman, knocking him off balance. But the Englishman smashed an elbow into the side of Tracy's face. Rachel rolled out from under Tracy, jumped to her feet, and covered her breasts with her chemisette.

Martin threw the vat of potatoes. Scalding water splashed the Englishman in the hands and face. He screamed and brought his hands to his eyes.

The water missed Rachel but splattered on Tracy's leg and left buttock, and the pain pulled him back to the beginnings of consciousness.

The Englishman wiped away the boiling water, and a layer of skin came away with it. Martin Mahoney kicked him in the face. He tumbled backward onto Tracy's legs. Martin kicked him again.

But the Englishman did not go out. He was big and powerful, and the second kick seemed to distract him from the pain of the scalding water. As Martin Mahoney came at him, he snatched the coal shovel by the stove and swung.

Martin Mahoney had once lasted three rounds with John L. Sullivan, but the shovel clipped him on the chin and he collapsed like a gunshot horse.

The Englishman turned and glanced down at Tracy's white, motionless figure. Then he looked at Rachel, who was huddling in the corner of the living room, behind the coal stove.

"Oh, God," she said. His flesh had been burned and bloodied, and his left eye oozed clear fluid.

"The rising? When? Where?"

"I . . . I . . ."

Tom Tracy felt an intense pain at the back of his head. He rolled over. The blistered flesh of his left buttock touched the floor. His cry brought the coal shovel whistling at his face. He spun away. The shovel smashed into the rug, then whistled again. Tracy rolled to his feet and flew at the Englishman.

The two bodies smashed together and broke apart and smashed together again, shattering pieces of furniture and knocking *The Last Supper* from the wall. Beside the Englishman, in his heavy trench coat, Tracy seemed small and vulnerable, his genitals swinging back and forth like a piece of porcelain jewelry.

The second time they hit, the man got his arms around Tracy and tried to crush his ribs. Tracy pounded his fist into the burned eye and remnants of flesh on the face.

Rachel heard the cracking of the small sinus bones. She saw the blood splatter each time he connected. And nausea mixed with her terror.

But the Englishman held tight, and as each blow struck, he shouted, "The rising? The rising?"

Tracy planted his feet and tried to spin free, and the two bodies lurched out into the hallway. Wood splintered and flew, and Tracy grabbed his genitals to protect them as the two bodies tumbled into the stairwell.

They stopped halfway down, Tracy's head pointing toward the

foyer, the Englishman straddling and slamming his head against the edge of a step.

Rachel screamed for them to stop.

Tracy's eyes rolled back in his head, and he felt his tongue slipping down his throat.

"The rising?" screamed the Englishman. "When? Where?"

"I'll tell you!" shouted Rachel, pulling on her chemisette.

"No!" Tracy forced the words out through the crushing fingers. "Get his gun."

The Englishman's eye widened. *The gun!* Tracy felt him weighing the dangers. Let her get the gun? Kill Tracy and let his partner take care of the woman? But where *was* his partner? In the moment's hesitation, Tracy grabbed the Englishman by the lapel and pulled. Together they tumbled down the stairs like lovers too frantic to wait until they were both naked.

Tracy hit the floor first, got up, and tried to run, but the Englishman grabbed him under the arms, so that Tracy's head was against his chest, his arms splayed out and useless. The Englishman slammed Tracy against one wall, then the other, and screamed, "The rising? When? Where?"

Each slam raised another dark bruise on Tracy's hips, and he thought that his ribs were breaking. He knew he was no physical match. His enemy was trained for this, had done it before. Without the gun, Tracy would die.

Rachel was reaching under the sofa, but she could not feel the gun. She heard a crash and the sound of porcelain shattering. She imagined Tracy's fragile nakedness. She ran into the kitchen.

On the floor of the foyer, a statue of the Blessed Virgin lay in pieces. The shards were cutting into Tracy's feet. But he had only one thought: *a weapon.* Where was Rachel? Where was the gun?

They struggled to the end of the hallway. The bathroom. The *razor.* He let the Englishman force him through the door. But before he could grab for the razor, his shins were slammed against the toilet. His legs were kicked out, and he dropped.

"Now, you bloody bastard, you'll talk."

Tracy's face was forced into the toilet bowl. He kicked and elbowed, but the Englishman was powerful and enraged and near enough to death that he surrendered nothing.

He pulled Tracy's face out of the water. "Tell me everything you know."

"I have," gasped Tracy, and his head was forced down again.

He thrashed and kicked and tried to grab for the razor on the shelf above the sink, but the Englishman held fast.

"Death struggle. That's what we're in now, with the Hun. We don't need our own subjects trying to stab us in the back while *we're* defending democracy, do we?"

Tracy fought the impulse to breathe.

"Talk or I'll drown you."

Tracy's head came out of the water. He gasped for air and got down one good gulp. "I—"

The Englishman slammed his face down again, smashing his nose against the bottom of the bowl.

Rachel came down from the second floor and followed the terrible sounds to the bathroom. At her hip she held an eight-inch carving knife. She stopped in the doorway, afraid to approach.

The Englishman looked as though he had mounted Tracy's naked body in the way that one animal mounts another. He was kneeling on the backs of Tracy's legs, with one hand on Tracy's head and the other twisting his arm behind his back. Tracy's left hand was flailing about, and the Englishman was saying things about the death struggles.

And now, Tracy's hands were not moving as much. The fingers were waving weakly. The body was bucking. He was going to die.

"I'll tell you," she cried.

The Englishman did not look up.

"I'll tell you everything, just let him live."

The Englishman did not respond.

And Rachel did it. She took three quick steps into the bathroom. She closed her eyes. She tried to imagine the cossack. And she drove the knife into the Englishman's back.

His head snapped, so that for a moment the awful mask of blood and pain looked straight into her eyes. Then he let go of Tracy, and from his mouth poured a long, silent wail of shock and surprise.

Rachel stumbled back.

The Englishman's hands reached blindly for the knife. One of them closed around the handle and pulled. His wail took sound, a strange, high-pitched cry of pain, but he kept pulling until the eight inches of blood-covered steel had been drawn from his back. Then he turned and stood. He was gasping now. One of his lungs had been punctured, and as it collapsed, it filled with blood. He spat red onto the floor.

Rachel backed into the hallway. She could see Tracy sucking down air and spitting back water. She told herself that she had saved his life.

Blood appeared at the Englishman's lips. With his last strength, he grabbed the doorjamb and tried to launch himself at Rachel. At the same time, Tracy came from behind with the razor, grabbed him, and bent his neck to the blade. But the Englishman collapsed before Tracy cut.

He turned to Rachel. She had sunk into a sitting position in the hallway, her arms wrapped tight around herself.

The Englishman twisted about on the floor, struggling for breath, gasping for every last second of life.

"You bloody bastard," growled Tracy.

The Englishman's good eye turned toward him. "Blood . . . brings . . . blood."

He was dead when Josephine Tracy returned from Mass.

20

It was the week of the vernal equinox. The sun had passed the equator. In the crowded streets and alleys of Boston, where buildings blocked the light and red brick absorbed it, the lengthening of the days still seemed less certain than cold and snow. But at sea, the sun rose from a flat blue horizon, and each dawn it moved a bit farther north of east, like the schooner now pushing toward Ireland.

The *Abigail* set a course that would take her across the Gulf of Maine, along the coast of Nova Scotia, and on to Cape Race, Newfoundland, a distance of nearly a thousand miles. From there she would face another twenty-three hundred miles of the most treacherous, storm-rolled seas on earth. The journey, in a vessel making ten knots, might last a month. Aboard the *Abigail*, it might take much longer.

For two days, she beat against a cold northeasterly breeze, while her crew of lubbers learned the rudiments of schooner rig and the fine art of tacking ship. A few of them were also forced to learn the finer art of vomiting breakfast, lunch, and green bile over the side without it blowing back in their faces, and they had learned none of it very well. The *Abigail* had spent as much of the first two days with her sails luffing as she had turning tack, and by Wednesday morning, she had made no more than a hundred and forty miles.

"Could've done better with oars," said Mason Deems.

"We've had worse crews, Mr. Deems."

"But never such a sinful cargo."

After their first voyage, Pratt had described Deems in his log: "A Nova Scotia man raised in love for the sea and the simple faith of the Scots Presbyterian, a man for storms and dead-calm seas, mutinous crews and stone-faced customs agents, the finest sailor and most loyal mate ever to sail the *Abigail*. And an impatient pain in the ass." After five years, the description had not been altered.

Pratt checked the heading and studied the trim of the sails. The breeze had swung around to the northwest, which improved shipboard spirits, because the fastest schooner moved like a barge on the tack, but even a lugger like the *Abigail* ran smoothly before the wind. And the thermometer tacked to the spankermast showed twenty-nine degrees, downright balmy for March in the Gulf of Maine.

Pratt ordered Deems to ring the ship's bell and summon the crew. Most captains addressed the crew on the first day. Pratt had learned from a Down East martinet named Able Speet to wait until the mate had broken them down, and once they had decided that no one could be more damnable than the mate, let them meet the man who gave the mate his orders.

Pratt stepped to the rail across the quarterdeck, and four Irish faces looked up at him. Tom Tracy had not taken food in a day and a half. Martin Mahoney was the color of seawater above a sand bar. But Padraic Starr and Tracy's brother had escaped the seasickness; they'd performed their duties well and downed Huntoon's cooking like old seamen.

The captain ordered Deems to ring the bell again and summon the others.

Not only had Tracy brought the crew he promised. He had also added a cleric who came aboard carrying the remnants of his priesthood in a duffel bag and calling himself the new chaplain, to the mate's disgust; a burlesque comic too drunk and too talkative to be left behind; a young chorine who had no home, no friends, no money, and threatened to sell what she knew if they

268

did not take her with them as well; and a wordless young woman with eyes as blank as the northern horizon.

When the bell stopped clanging, Sean O'Fearna lurched from the forecastle and hurried forward.

"Moves more like a horse than a seaman," muttered Mason Deems. "Good for ballast."

On Monday morning, the crew had been sworn under false names before a representative of the United States Shipping Office. And in addition to the guns and the medical supplies, Pratt had taken on a cargo of machine parts that he would deliver to Galway city after running the guns to Dunslea. The guns and ammunition had been placed in new crates, then covered over by layers of nuts, bolts, and metal machine pieces. The cargo manifest signed in Boston showed the proper number of boxes and crates, so that if the *Abigail* was boarded by the Royal Navy, her papers would be in order. Later, an expert bit of Pratt forgery would bring her into Galway city with a clean manifest.

Pratt clasped his hands behind his back. "Some smart landlubber once said that with a good captain, a good mate, and a good cook, a crew of one-armed blind men could sail a schooner 'round the world." Pratt took the pause he built into this speech the second time he ever delivered it. "From what I see below me, I thank God we're only crossing the Atlantic, and I wish to God we were just sailing down to Gloucester." Pratt leaned forward and looked at each man individually, letting his gaze fall finally on Tom Tracy. "Forget everything that went on in Boston, obey every order, and you will make it across the Atlantic. Question the mate or the captain at any time, and you'll be wearing irons when we raise the Irish coast. Is that clear?"

The men murmured and nodded.

"Is that clear?" demanded the captain in a loud, piercing voice.

"Yes, sir!" shouted Starr.

"I do not give a damn about your revolution or your guns or the three sad souls unable to grace us this morning. My concerns are for the safety of my ship and the payment contracted for. I have no objections to hauling your contraband. But I will know what it is, down to the last firing pin. Otherwise, false papers will not be able to conceal the truth.,"

Pratt looked at Tracy. "Two extra crates came aboard on Sunday night. Bring them up."

Starr tugged at his forelock, in the manner of a good merchant seaman. "Beggin' your pardon, sir, but I don't think we want to be doin' that just now. A few days from here, maybe, but . . ."

"I've just given you an order, Mr. Starr."

"Aye, aye, Cap'n."

The crates were dropped amidships. The five crewmen had been joined now by Henry Huntoon and Jimmy the Butcher, who had staggered on deck to see about another drink.

Captain Pratt pushed Danny and the priest aside and stood over the crate that was leaking water. He held a pinch bar out to Starr. "Open it."

Starr did not move. "I think the best thing, Cap'n, is to throw this crate straight over the side and say no more."

Jason Pratt tapped the pinch bar against his left hand. The breeze stiffened. The deadeyes creaked. The shrouds stretched and the *Abigail* heeled slightly in the wind. "Open the crate, mister, or you'll go over the side *with* it."

Tom Tracy slipped his hand into his pocket and wrapped it around the handle of his gun.

Starr, playing the obedient crewman, saluted and knelt by the crate. The nails squeaked out of the wood, then Starr slowly raised the lid.

"Holy Mother . . ." Sean O'Fearna saw the contents first. He blessed himself and looked away.

Danny Tracy's jaw dropped. Martin Mahoney gagged himself to the side once more.

"Dead man," whispered Henry Huntoon.

The snow in the crate had melted, revealing the bloody, boiled, half-frozen face of Nigel Stewart. His mouth was open, and the neck of a beer bottle lay against his eye, as though he had died of thirst for not finding his mouth. Where his flesh was not reddened, it looked blue.

Bloody bastard, thought Tom Tracy, and he felt the barrel of Stewart's gun against his neck once more.

"I'll take them beers if nobody wants them," muttered Jimmy McHale.

"Shut up." Pratt's mouth was screwed up in disgust. "This is not the contraband we contracted for, Mr. Tracy."

"Beggin' your pardon, Captain," said Starr, "but we used beer bottles in case the customs inspector opened the crate. He'd be thinkin' the snow was keepin' the beer cold."

"I don't mind the ladies, Cap'n," said Henry Huntoon. "I sort of like 'em. But if we carryin' dead men, I'm for turnin' back."

The captain stared at Tom Tracy. His eyes had been blackened in the fight Saturday night, and they had now begun to yellow.

"He was going over the side tonight," said Tracy.

"We had to bring him, Captain," said Starr. "You was never to know about it."

Pratt's eyes remained on Tracy. "I thought you were a man I could trust."

Starr slipped himself between Pratt and Tom Tracy. "It's me, Captain, I'm the one you can't trust. But then, when you make a deal with gunrunners, you know you ain't lyin' down among sleepin' babes, now, don't you?"

"The thing in that box was an animal," growled Tom Tracy.

"Maybe not that so much as a casualty of war," said Starr.

Every captain knew that men admired certainty, and captains who did not display it were not captains for long. Jason Pratt looked at the priest. "You're some kind of unfrocked cleric, are you not?"

The priest said nothing. The captain's words carried a sharp sting for a man so recently turned from his calling.

"Read the appropriate words, and let the body be buried at sea."

"We ain't turnin' back?" asked Henry Huntoon.

"We have a contract."

"With the devil!" Mason Deems had secured the helm and was coming forward. "These men are about the business of stabbing Nova Scotia sailors and Canadian soldiers in the back. This proves it."

Jimmy the Butcher grabbed for one of the bottles of beer. Pratt dropped the lid, and Jimmy yelped.

"They even blaspheme the dead with beer bottles!" Deem's eyes looked like two small rivets in a piece of leather. "Run them back with their guns and turn them in."

"You'll face smuggling charges right along with us," said Tom Tracy. "I guarantee that, Mr. Mate."

"We'll tell customs that we believed what was written on the bill of lading, and when we found out the truth, we turned back." Deems pointed his quirt southwest.

"These aren't the first guns we've run," Pratt said evenly to Deems.

271

"First dead man, though," muttered Huntoon.

"There's a man on board who knows what you're doing." Tracy went a step closer to Deems, to intimidate him. "If we go back to Boston, his word on the guns will be better than anyone's."

"One of you has a better word than a Pratt?" Deems looked around the deck and laughed in the contemptuous way that a sober man does when a drunk challenges him to a fight.

Tracy told Starr to open the second crate.

Starr stepped over Stewart's coffin, knelt, and jammed the pinch bar under the lid. He had opened the crate several times in the last few days, so the nails slipped out easily. As the lid came off, the stink rose out of the crate. It was not the smell of decay, but a living stink of ammonia and perspiration and feces.

"Another one!" cried Deems.

"But this one's movin'," shouted Henry Huntoon. "That make me feel a lot better."

Starr was leaning into the box, speaking softly to a lump of filthy clothes, trussed limbs, and ugly bruises that resembled Hugh Dawson, agent of the Crown.

"Keep your eyes closed," Starr was saying. "Give 'em time to get used to the light." He pulled out his knife and cut the ropes that bound Dawson's legs to his arms, then he pulled the gag out of his mouth.

Dawson whispered through cracked lips, "Thank you, you bloody bastard."

"Don't lose your spirit, bucko."

"Murderers and kidnappers," said Deems to the captain.

"He knows that the *Abigail*'s a gunrunner," announced Tracy.

Deems looked down at the mess in the crate. "He's half dead. He knows nothing."

"Well, dammit, the Christian thing's to help the poor man to his feet." Sean O'Fearna stepped forward and put a hand under Dawson's arm. Starr took him from the other side, and together they lifted.

Hugh Dawson rose like a living corpse. His face had gone white, except for the black circles under his eyes and the three-day beard. His hair was greasy, and urine stains covered his pants. He trembled as he stood, but his gaze was steady, filled with defiance, and he fixed it, in turn, on each member of the ship's company.

Tracy knew that the Brit had rehearsed this moment a dozen

times. He screwed his eyes shut and looked away, not because of Dawson's gaze, but because his mind was filling once more with the images and sensations of that brutal Sunday morning. Each was more painful than the one before, and none more painful than the image of his mother, rousing herself from her shock in the dark, blood-spattered foyer, giving her son her topcoat to cover his nakedness, giving Rachel her sweater, brewing tea to bring Martin about, and sending John to the junkman to buy two large crates.

Hugh Dawson's demonstration of British character could not overcome three days in one position, however. When he tried to pull himself erect, his legs cramped. He cried out and dropped to the deck, grabbing at his calves as though they had been pierced by knives.

Every man on deck, even Tracy, took pity upon him. None could ever have seen a more pitiful man. But when Starr and the priest knelt and tried to help him stand, again he seemed to fill with rage. He pushed them away, and with a great shuddering, he grabbed the side of his box and lifted himself up once more, in spite of the pain and the steady motion of the deck. He pulled his topcoat around himself and buttoned it. Then he looked at the captain.

"What is your name?" asked Pratt.

Dawson moved his lips several times before any sound came out. "Hugh Dawson. I was captured by rebels during the performance of my duties."

The *Abigail* heeled a bit more in response to the wind. Dawson spread his legs and leaned into the pitch.

"If we turn about," asked Mr. Deems, "are you ready to stand behind us in Boston?"

Hugh Dawson did not know how long he had spent in his living grave. Time had turned in upon itself. And his thoughts had turned as well, plunging through the surface of duty and politics, down to the depths of self-doubt: He was going to die soon, and he no longer knew why. During his ordeal, the only face he had seen was the face he had hunted for weeks, the only kindness he had received came from the man who had killed his partners. It was Starr who fed him biscuits, brought him clean rags, soaked in fresh water, and replaced the gags that dried in his mouth. He hated Starr for putting him into the box, but in the long hours of darkness, Starr had become his hope. With each visit, Starr had spoken softly to him, telling him not to worry, that he would not be killed, then suggesting that he think hard about Ireland's future and the cause of the rebels. In the process, Starr had filled Hugh Dawson with questions.

"I will . . ." Dawson had no voice. He swallowed several times, and Mr. Huntoon gave him a ladle of water. "I will stand behind anyone who stops this gunrunning. Give it up, and I'll say nothing against any of you." He looked at Starr. "*Any* of you."

Starr smiled. "You're so happy to be out of that box, I don't think you know what you're sayin'."

"He's givin' you another chance," growled Deems, "and that's more than *I'd* give you."

"That's why we're goin' on," said Tracy. "Because there's not enough who'll give us a chance. It's high time we took it ourselves."

Starr patted Tracy on the shoulder. "I'd heed strong words from my cousin. He's quite a fighter."

Jason Pratt slipped a belaying pin from the rail and tapped it against the palm of his hand. "Tell me, Mr. Starr, were you planning to dump Dawson's crate over the side along with the corpse?"

Starr shook his head.

"Then exactly what are you going to do with him?"

"Well, Captain, if we've thirty-four hundred miles of ocean to cross, I think I can convince my Belfast friend he's fightin' on the wrong side."

Hugh Dawson said nothing. His mind was not yet clear enough for him to protest, and after the last few days, he thought that Starr might be able to do what he proposed.

"On the other hand"—Starr looked at Dawson, glanced around at the men he had brought with him, then took a single threatening step toward the captain—"if I feel this scow comin' about, I'll shoot Mr. Dawson and take command myself, beggin' your pardon or not, Captain."

Mr. Deems and Mr. Huntoon both let out strange gasps, as though they were witnessing a man fall from the crosstree. Tom Tracy once again slipped his hand into the pocket of his peacoat and wrapped it around the grip of his pistol.

For a time, the only sounds were the wind flowing over the canvas and the water rushing along the hull. Jason Pratt studied Starr, eyes impassive, quiet in their fury. Then, with a gesture as sudden as it was practiced, he snapped the belaying pin into Starr's jaw, knocking him out.

Pratt quickly stepped over Starr's body and raised the pin at Tracy. "You make a statement like that, and I'll have your brains all over the deck."

The critical moment in the voyage had arrived after only two days at sea. Mutiny had politely been threatened. The leader lay unconscious on the deck. The British agent, almost on instinct, had stumbled to the rail and lifted a belaying pin. Mr. Huntoon had reached into the galley and pulled out a meat cleaver. Mr. Deems was swinging his quirt from side to side, like a leather metronome.

Tracy glanced at his uncle, who gave him a small nod, as if to say he was ready for whatever came next. Danny and the priest each carried a long seaman's knife, but the priest was looking down at the dead body and Danny was standing too close to Huntoon's cleaver. If it came to a fight, neither would be any help. And Jimmy the Butcher was squatting on the cargo hatch, his eyes shifting from Tracy to Pratt to the bottles of beer around the dead body.

Pratt ordered Mr. Deems to disarm Starr. Deems crouched down and pulled Starr's knife from his boot, then pulled the Colt revolver from Starr's pocket.

"A pistol, Captain." Deems handed the gun to Pratt.

"No guns are allowed in the fo'c'sle," Pratt said to the others. "If anyone else is carrying a pistol, hand it over now."

"There are no guns in the fo'c'sle," said Tracy, and his hand closed more tightly around the wooden grip in his pocket.

"If I order a search, I'll expect you to submit."

Tracy knew that refusal would be as good as admission. He stepped close to Pratt and said, as softly as possible, "We're at a dangerous pass, Captain. Honor your contract and sail on, or come about, if you think you must, and take your chances with the truth in Boston. But let us not quibble about searches." The tone of Tracy's voice told Pratt that if he turned, the ship's company would fight.

Pratt tapped the belaying pin against the palm of his hand several times. "Take Starr forward and chain him to his bunk until the midnight watch."

A hand pushed through legs around the crates and grabbed for a bottle of beer. Pratt snapped the belaying pin again and cracked Jimmy the Butcher over the head. "Chain *him* to the bunk beside Starr's, and don't release him until his shakes are gone. When they are, all liquor rations for the rest of the crew will be halted. I'll tolerate no drunks."

Then Pratt took the belaying pin from Hugh Dawson's hands. "You'll have no need of this. I give you my word you'll be safe aboard the *Abigail*. And you'll have the run of the ship."

"Shall I bring her about, Captain?" asked Deems.

"Hold her steady." Pratt dropped the pins into the rail. "We have a contract."

Tom Tracy took his hand from the gun and saluted, almost in relief. "We will honor it and obey your orders, Captain."

Mason Deems closed his hands around his quirt and snapped it like the neck of one of the ship chickens.

Henry Huntoon whispered into Danny Tracy's ear, "Lucky thing for you, boy, we got a cap'n keeps his word. 'Cause I'm awful good with this here chopper."

"Yeah?" Danny pulled his knife from his boot. "I'm even better with this."

Huntoon grabbed Danny by the ear. "Then come with me. You can use it on the 'taters."

Jason Pratt climbed the quarterdeck and went down the after-house companionway, toward the skylit cabin at the end. There were smaller cabins on either side of the passage, the captain's and mate's on the starboard, two guest cabins to port. He stopped and looked in on the girl.

"Good morning," he whispered.

She looked up. She had risen at dawn on both mornings to empty her chamberpot, but she had returned to her berth without speaking to anyone. Her small space did not have the rancid smell of seasickness, and her color was good, but her eyes were as blank as the eyes of the shipwreck that Pratt had once picked up off the Azores, a man who had been adrift in the Atlantic, staring at nothing, for over a month.

"Has the cossack come back?" she asked.

"No. We've thrown him overboard," said Pratt.

21

Three nights and three days Deirdre Hamilton had watched and waited. Although it was dark, she knew by the running lights that it was Donal's trawler, the *O'Toole*, pushing back up the bay at last.

At the sight of her standing by his slip, he smiled for the first time since seeing the telegram. He threw her the bow rope. She tied up the *O'Toole*, then jumped into his arms.

For three days, she had worried about *two* men rather than one. Starr remained somewhere beyond the horizon, endangered by the British and by the information that Donal's father had given to the resident magistrate. But Donal was here, his arms around her, his scent an earthy and familiar mixture of pipe tobacco, sweat, and fish, his presence more comforting than she could have imagined.

"I missed you, Deirdre. For the last three days, and for the whole last week," he said.

"Don't ever be goin' off to mourn without me again." She kissed him, then she told him the news: His father had passed the Tracy name to the resident magistrate.

Kathleen Mary O'Toole O'Leary was reading the Bible. Logan was staring into the turf fire. Black crepe was hung above the door. Logan heard the motorcycle beating against the distant silence. He looked up and said, "Deirdre."

"Perhaps she'll think to visit. I'll put on the kettle."

The motorcycle roared to a stop in front of the cottage.

The door swung open. "God bless all here."

"Donal!" said Logan.

Kathleen ran to her son and threw her arms around him.

"I'm sorry I run off," he said to her.

"You always was one to nurse a hurt by yourself." Logan came over and shook his son's hand.

They sat at the table and drank tea and ate the cakes that Mrs. Cooney had sent two hours after the town heard the bad news. They talked of Joseph's death, the memorial service that Father Breen was planning, and Donal's three days alone on the boat.

"Did it learn you anything?" his father asked.

277

Deirdre heard the anger cut into Logan's voice like a sudden shift in the wind.

"I watched the sun rise and set. I fished. I thought about me brother."

"I did that, too," said Logan, "but I was here to give your mother a bit of comfort in her pain."

"We been gettin' along." Kathleen pulled a handkerchief from her apron pocket and squeezed her nose several times, "We're glad you're back."

"It was damn selfish, what you did," said Logan, ignoring his wife.

Donal took a bite of cake. "If I knew what you was plannin' to hand to the RM at Finnerty's on Friday night, it's right here I'd have been the whole time."

Logan looked at Deirdre. His complexion reddened, and his red nose grew purple. "Who told you?"

"Seamus. He heard it from the priest."

"Some would say that what you did was"—Donal brought the teacup to his mouth and, as if he could take the edge from the word, he spoke it into his cup—"informin'."

"Now, Donal." Kathleen poured more tea. "Let's not be usin' them words at the table."

"What Jack Tracy did to your uncle was informin'," said Logan, with a calmness that surprised Deirdre. "What *I* did was give a bit of information."

"I've got no love for the Tracy name," answered Donal softly, "but I'd not be telling the RM the time of day."

"I don't give a care for the Tracys, or the RM, or that trouble-maker Paddy Starr. I care about me only son."

"Only son," muttered Kathleen. "That's the first time we've spoken them words since before Joe was born." She brought handkerchief to her nose once more.

Deirdre touched her hand.

"I'll not see me only son throw away his life in another damn-fool rebellion."

Donal O'Leary slowly put down his cup and looked at his father. "Out there on the boat, I thought hard about losin' Joey and about the chance that I might get killed myself."

Kathleen took Deirdre's hand and Donal's and brought them together in the middle of the table. "You got a good woman to marry you, Donal. You'll have fine strong children and fish these

278

coasts till you're as ancient as the mariner himself. Your brother died to give you that, so don't you be thinkin' on death."

Donal patted his mother's hand and looked again at his father. "I decided that if somethin' comes, I'll be as scared as a man can be."

"There's somethin' comin'," Logan interrupted. "You know about it, and if I ain't gettin' stupid in me old age, you're one of the fellas is plannin' it."

"And if it had come sooner, you might still have two sons."

In the silence that followed, Deirdre thought she could hear the tide sluicing softly into the bay and the blood pounding into the veins at Logan O'Leary's temples.

"It's a fine son I have. He leaves us alone with our sadness for three days, then comes home and spits on the memory of the brother he won't come up to if he waits till the second comin'."

Deirdre Hamilton was not quite certain what happened next, except that when it was over, Donal was riding home with her on the back of her motorcycle. Donal had muttered something that sounded like "ignorant bastard." His father had responded with the same subtle backhander he had used since the boys were first old enough to talk back. And Donal, for the first time in his life, had struck his father. He had knocked men down and knocked them out with his closed fist, but this open-handed slap had carried more power than the hardest punch he ever threw.

Kathleen had jumped between father and son and tried to make them apologize, but they were of the same mold, stubborn beyond time. After a moment of shock, during which the imprint of Donal's hand had appeared on Logan's face like a shadow, Logan had said, "Get out." And that was *all* he had been able to say, again and again, his voice growing in volume until Kathleen had pushed Deirdre and her son out the door for fear that the two men would kill each other.

After the motorcycle had left, Kathleen had come back into the cottage and found Logan O'Leary holding the picture of his son Joseph and crying like a child.

"You can sleep in the shed tonight," Deirdre said when they reached her cottage.

"I'd rather sleep by the fire."

Deirdre studied him a moment. "All right, then. Come in and get warm and have a cup, but if you try what you did last Sunday,

279

I'll shoot you in the belly." She pulled her .22 from her coat pocket, then dropped it back and patted his stomach. "You lost some pounds the last three days."

Impulsively, he threw his arms around her and drew her close to him. "I don't want to fight. I want to fish. And make little ones. But if it's a fight that's comin', I can't run away, even if it's Paddy Starr that's bringin' it, and the Tracys that's helpin' him."

He reminded her of a great hurt child, angry at the world because his parents had chided him. "Don't worry about Starr, Donal, at least not on my account."

"If he's with the Tracys, I worry that he'll never get back. And if he gets back, I worry that he'll try to take you from me."

They went in and had tea, and Deirdre said that she loved him for his bravery. "I'll tell Padr'ic the same when he gets here."

"*If* he gets here." Donal scratched through his beard. "You can't trust the Tracys. Just the mentionin' of the name can turn a good man like me da into an informer."

Eight weeks before the *Abigail* sailed for Ireland, a message traveled twice across the Atlantic on its way to Berlin. It came from the Military Council of the Irish Republican Brotherhood. A courier traveling as an Irish seaman delivered it to John Devoy of the Clan na Gael in New York. Devoy then passed it to the German embassy in Washington. The ambassador, Count von Bernstorff, attached it to a telegram regarding the *Lusitania* and sent it by wireless to Berlin, using diplomatic code number 13040, which the Germans believed to be ironclad.

Listening posts on the English coast intercepted the message, as they did hundreds each day, and it was delivered to Room 40 of the Admiralty Building in London. There, a team of cryptographers had broken code 13040, and they deciphered the message:

WASHINGTON DC
17 FEBRUARY 1916

HERR ZIMMERMAN

THE IRISH LEADER JOHN DEVOY INFORMS ME THAT A RISING IS TO BEGIN IN IRELAND ON EASTER SUNDAY STOP PLEASE SEND ARMS TO ARRIVE AT LIMERICK WEST COAST OF IRELAND BETWEEN GOOD FRIDAY AND EASTER SUNDAY STOP TO

PUT IT OFF LONGER IS IMPOSSIBLE STOP LET ME KNOW IF
HELP MAY BE EXPECTED FROM GERMANY STOP

VON BERNSTORFF

For reasons known only to the military, reports concerning this message and the German response did not reach Dublin Castle until March 23, the day that Hugh Dawson was released from his box. It was late afternoon when a courier from London delivered the intelligence pouch to the office of General L. B. Friend, Competent Military Authority for Ireland.

A half hour later, General Friend called Lambert-Jones into his office and told him to sit, then threw him the report.

Friend was a large mass of misused energy, frustrated by Home command while the rest of the Empire fought the bloodiest struggle in history. From the three broken pencils on the blotter, Lambert-Jones knew that this report had caused the general's usual bad mood to blossom like a rash.

The cover note, from Field Marshal Lord French, Commander in Chief of the Home Forces, urged that the information be held in the strictest secrecy and used "with the utmost discretion."

While Friend toyed with another pencil, Lambert-Jones studied the report. It told of an "absolutely reliable source" who had learned of a rising on Easter Sunday, supported by German weapons landed at Limerick. It was signed by General G.M.W. MacDonagh, head of Military Intelligence. A footnote added that a similar report had been issued to Admiral Sir Lewis Bayly, Commander of the Home Fleet in Ireland.

There had been few moments of satisfaction for Ian Lambert-Jones since the day near Neuve-Chapelle, but this telegram brought one of them. It told him that his senses had been sharp —the rising was not simply inevitable; it was imminent. He now believed more firmly than ever that the pursuit of Starr would be of value to the Empire. He looked up. His eyes were the hard gray of gunmetal.

"You're a smart lad, Ian. Why the secrecy over something like this? Who's the 'absolutely reliable source'?"

"There are two possibilities." Lambert-Jones spoke with the accent of a well-bred career military man, voice carefully modulated, words clipped neatly. "The source may not be at all reliable. Or . . ."

The general wrapped two fingers around the pencil in his hand. "Or what?"

"Room 40 have broken the German codes and they're not telling us."

The pencil snapped sharply. "Why in the hell not?"

"Because it would be crass stupidity to tell our politicians that we're reading every dispatch between Berlin and America."

"Ian . . ." The general leaned forward, so that his beefy face was inches from Lambert-Jones. "I am charged with keeping the peace and protecting the borders of Ireland. I most assuredly am *not* a politician."

"I'm sure they're aware of that in London, sir." Lambert-Jones brought his hands to his mouth and placed the tips of his fingers together, a gesture that gave him a judicious appearance and also shielded his nostrils from the tobacco-and-bacon-fat odor of the general's breath. "However, because of our task here, we must be in daily contact with the politicians, since they are charged with keeping the peace as well."

"I've no use for any of them. Put a good military government on this blasted island and you wouldn't see rebels marching through the streets, masquerading as a local defense force."

"We must decide, then, how much of this we tell the undersecretary."

"Nothing. It's the same sort of thing we hear all the time. A rising is planned for this date or that date. We wait, and nothing happens, because the moon's not right or the Kaiser has hemorrhoids or the little people have counseled against it."

"But, sir, what if we *have* broken the code?"

The general picked up another pencil and drummed it on his desk. "If the people in intelligence barely trust *us*, they can't trust the politicians at all. We tell them nothing outright. We simply lead them in the right direction, and when they make the proper assumptions, we nod."

"Indeed, sir."

"Besides, it's Admiral Bayly who's got the primary responsibility, isn't it? If he stops the Hun from landing his arms in the west, this thing falls through like a Fenian on the gallows."

In the castle yard, the cavalry detachment was returning from its daily parade down O'Connell Street. The clatter of the hooves echoed on the pavement, and Lambert-Jones went to the window. Their red coats and glittering lance tips were the symbol of order throughout the Empire, yet there were many in Dublin who cursed them as an insult to Ireland, and sometimes he could not understand why. After a half a century of reform, most of the Irish accepted their role in the Empire and were proud that Home Rule would soon become a reality, even if it did not include the six northern counties. As proof, they had sent their sons to fight and die with the rest of the Empire.

But there remained, like pockets of termites in a wooden post, groups of Irishmen who saw only the differences between the Irish and the other British races—Ireland's separation from the main island, its Gaelic language, its religion—and they waited for that change in the climate that would enable them to spread through the rest of the wood.

Lambert-Jones had been born to a well-placed family of the Protestant Ascendancy in County Wicklow. He had lived in Ireland the first ten years of his life, before going to public school in England, then Sandhurst. He was proud of his Irish heritage, and he could not understand the Irish desire for rebellion in the least.

The general fitted the pieces of one of the broken pencils back together, like a puzzle. "Intelligence reports indicate that the people of the west have neither the arms, the inclination, nor the leadership to fight on their own."

Lambert-Jones still watched out the window. The cavalry troop was disappearing into the stable, but a young lieutenant was exercising his mare. There was beauty in this land, he thought, beauty and mystery worth clinging to. The mare jumped, and her black coat flashed in the fading light. "They will have all three in Dunslea."

"Dunslea?" The general went over to the map and squinted at the small black speck between the two peninsulas. "Dunslea in Connemara? Why Dunslea?"

"Starr."

"He's in America with agents on his tail."

"We haven't heard from them in four days. He's either eluded them or killed them."

"Ian, I am quite sick of having you sign my name to cables requesting agents, only to learn later that Starr has killed them. He's a deserter. If he were some sort of rebel, he'd be in New York. That's where the money is."

Lambert-Jones picked up the report once more. "If this source is reliable, Starr will be in Dunslea on Easter Sunday."

"Doing what?"

283

"Delivering arms, perhaps. Leading the fight at least, and that's danger enough."

The general picked up a handful of pencil stubs, lined them neatly on his blotter, and studied them as though he were choosing a weapon. He picked up the longest and began to write. "I'll have Crimes Branch Special send an agent to Dunslea."

"I would not want to interfere with the RM in Dunslea. He's probably the best agent we could have there."

The general put down the pencil. "All right. Since you know Starr, I leave him in your hands. Now that we've heard this uprising rumor, only one thing matters"—he aimed a finger at Lambert-Jones—"that when the rising comes, whether it's on Easter or Guy Fawkes Day, the fighting is concentrated around Dublin, where we can control it and finish it."

"Very good, sir."

22

For ten days, Rachel Levka stared through the portlight. She watched the horizon rise and fall, steady and slow, like the chest of a great sleeping beast. She watched the waves boil out from the hull when the old schooner heeled to port. She watched the sky fill the small circle of glass when the *Abigail* leaned to starboard. She watched and dreamed and waited for her strength to return.

There were days when the ocean was a crisp and vigorous blue, days when it seemed as depressing and gray as an undertaker's gloves. But she knew, as she gazed, that no other feature would intrude upon her view. Nothing would surprise or frighten her. And when the ocean became too huge and empty to contemplate, she could turn her head and stare at the bulkhead beside her.

If she listened, she could hear the voices of the ship. The timbers of the *Abigail* groaning in the wind, the discussions between captain and mate, the retching of seasick Irishmen at the side, the sharp crack of the rifles during target practice, the clucking of the shipboard chickens, and, for three days, Jimmy McHale's cries for drink. But in that first week, Rachel did not wish to hear the voices. When they intruded, she listened instead to the sound of the water hissing along the hull, and she fixed her eyes on the small circle of light. And like an animal that hides when hurt, she tried to close her wounds alone.

Each day, Tom Tracy came to her with two mugs of tea. He would sit on the edge of her berth, they would sip their tea, and they would try to talk. But in the first days, Rachel could barely speak, and Tom Tracy had nothing to say. That Sunday morning, it seemed, had left Rachel without emotions and Tom Tracy with none but hate.

The intimacy that they had found for a few moments had been shattered by a horror that now made them strangers. They had seen too deeply into each other's souls. They had seen more than they wanted revealed. They had done more than they thought themselves capable of doing. As the days went by, they began to speak in scattered patterns about simple things, but they could not talk about the death of the Englishman and the shattering of their lives.

On Thursday, he told her about the threats of mutiny. He touched her hand and said not to worry.

On Sunday, she smiled and told him that she would soon be strong enough to come on deck.

On the second Tuesday, she asked him what he was planning to do when the ship reached Ireland. He told her that he was going ashore with Starr, start the rising, and kill the magistrate, just as she had told him he should on that terrible Sunday morning.

And she realized that it was not what she wanted from Tom Tracy.

Starr came to her as often as Tracy during her ten days of isolation. At first, he did not speak to her unless she spoke. He simply sat on the small stool beneath the portlight. Then he began to talk, first about the weather, the food, the life aboard ship, and finally, late in the week, about the slow progress of the *Abigail* and the need to reach Ireland before Easter.

He had brought them all to this terrible place, she thought, and the ease with which he spoke of terrible things angered her, but whenever he came, he could make her smile. He had settled his accounts with himself, and Tom Tracy was still struggling. Late in the week, she admitted to herself that Starr's confidence and conversation were helping to restore her more surely than long silences with Tom Tracy.

On Thursday, she asked Starr about the mutiny. He laughed and showed her the bruise on his chin and said there would be no need for mutiny, because the captain was a man of his word.

On Sunday, she asked him why they had brought her after all. Starr said he had seen shell shock in the trenches, he had seen the stare of the dead in living eyes, and he knew, when he saw her crumpled in the foyer of the Tracy home, that she could not be left behind. To send her back to her father would have been cruelty; to allow her to go to New York alone would have been murder. They had brought her, he said, to protect her.

On the second Tuesday, she asked him if Tracy was going ashore when they reached Ireland. Starr's smile faded. He said that no one but Tom Tracy could avenge his father's death. She said that when she was strong enough, she was going to try to stop him.

"I don't think you'll be able to," he said.

"Why?"

"The two of you were hit by a terrible wave that day, darlin'. You been ridin' it ever since, and now it's throwin' you onto the beach. Tommy tried to swim against it, and now he's part of it."

After ten days at sea, Jenny Malloy had overcome her seasickness and lost her stagelight pallor. The sun and the wind had reddened her complexion, and in spite of the black roots now showing at her forehead, she looked as healthy as a farm girl. When Mr. Huntoon heard that Jenny could sew—a task that most chorus girls learned to survive—he named her the ship seamstress. For eight hours a day, she sat on the deck, working with heavy needle and thread, a leather thimble strapped to the palm of her hand. She repaired torn oilskins and weak patches in the reserve sails, she reinforced buntline holes, and she even mended the captain's tablecloths. From old sailcloth, she fashioned several pairs of trousers, so that she could move about the deck with greater ease. Her only other task, since she could not cook, was to deliver the meals from the galley to the forecastle and the afterhouse.

However, the priest was always willing to help her with the food. Starr was right about the priest, she thought. He had a good soul, as tormented as anyone's. He worked constantly, scrubbing decks or helping in the galley or cleaning the forecastle. And when he was not working, he read from his Bible. But when he looked at her, his eyes were the eyes of the Old Howard. He wanted what every man wanted, and now that he had thrown off the cloth, she knew that he was simply raising the courage to reach for it.

But Jenny Malloy was aboard the *Abigail* to do some reaching of her own. She had learned in burlesque that when she fought for a spot in the line or struggled to take over as the new *soubrette,* she should always let her competition know who she was. Steal a scene or a joke if she could, give a little sideways kick to throw another dancer off balance, anything for a leg up. But in a business where talent was less important than looks, and looks less than toughness, it was always an advantage to intimidate the girls around her. She thought that love might be the same way.

At dusk, on the second Wednesday, she carried a tray to the afterhouse. The captain was ordering the sails lowered, and the *Abigail* was slowing to a stop in the middle of the sea.

Jenny knocked at Rachel's door, then pushed it open without waiting for an answer. A chicken had been sacrificed for stew that also contained carrots and potatoes, the only tubers that Mr. Huntoon had loaded, since he hated turnips.

Rachel was standing at the portlight. "Is that the reason we're stopping?"

About four miles to the north, an iceberg rose from the water like a spirit. The colors of twilight played across its face, giving it life and shape before the gathering darkness, while tiny whitecaps grabbed at its base.

"Iceberg? Yeah. Captain picked up on a wireless, they've seen dozens ahead. He says he won't sail through icebergs at night."

"So we're just going to sit?" Rachel asked.

Jenny nodded. "All night."

"What did Mr. Starr say to that?"

"How the hell should I know?" Jenny dropped the tray on the stool so that the stew slopped out of the bowl and soaked into the ship's biscuit. "And why do you care so damn much what he says?"

Rachel began to speak, then she looked down at the buttons on her blouse. Jenny's tone frightened her, and she still lacked the strength to fight back.

Jenny came closer. She stood a head taller and weighed twenty pounds more, and her sailcloth trousers made her seem even more threatening. "Whatever you give up for Paddy Starr, I give up more. And I don't like all the damn time he spends sittin' in here with you."

Rachel chewed on the inside of her cheek. "Then tell him."

"He got other stuff to worry about. But I get first crack at him. Y'understand?" Jenny grabbed Rachel by the collar. "He's the best thing I ever met. I give up everything to save his bacon, and I ain't losin' him to you." She banged Rachel's head against the bulkhead.

And like an amnesiac, Rachel found an emotion, her anger. She reached first for the stew, then grabbed a stale ship's biscuit and flung it in Jenny's face.

"From now on, honey, get your own meals."

"Get out."

At four bells, Mr. Huntoon shut down the donkey engine. For ten nights, the *Abigail* had plowed through the dark, because the wind never slept. Now she was motionless and silent. And like city dwellers who could not sleep in the country, her crew could not sleep on a calm sea.

Martin Mahoney, Mr. Huntoon, and Danny Tracy played poker in the forecastle. They had been playing every day, for matches, which Martin dutifully collected after each game, promising to settle accounts, at penny a match, when they landed.

Hugh Dawson and Padraic Starr sat on the afterhouse roof, as they did each night, and tested each other with words. Starr tried to convert Dawson to the cause, while Dawson puffed his pipe and tried to learn the plans of the rising. It was assumed that before the voyage ended, one of them would have to kill the other, but like enemy soldiers between wars, their distrust had become respect and grew toward friendship.

Mr. Deems was walking the deck, bow to stern and back again. The others were aware of his presence, but he was nearly invisible in his black turtleneck and moved as silently through the shadows as a fish through the waters around them.

Jimmy McHale, dry for a week, was puffing on a cigarette, trying desperately to ignore his thirst and the fear that left him only when the thirst was satisfied. Earlier in the evening, Mr. Huntoon had gone into the hold and had failed to secure the hatch afterward. Now Jimmy was wondering if the medical supplies included cough syrup.

Jenny Malloy was strolling the decks in an endless circle, up the port side and down the starboard. Whenever she went past

Starr, she slowed and tried to make conversation. Whenever she passed Sean O'Fearna, who stood alone on the port side, she looked down at the deck and hurried along.

And Tom Tracy watched it all from the mainmast crosstree. He had been climbing the mast each night and remaining in the cold wind for the four hours of his watch. He liked the separation from the life below him, and by toughening himself to the elements, he thought he was preparing for whatever lay ahead.

He stared out at the closest iceberg. It had been drifting south all day, but the *Abigail* was riding the same current. Another ship, a freighter, was stopped a few miles beyond, its captain as cautious as Jason Pratt.

Four years earlier, on another calm, cold spring night, the captain of the *Titanic* had ignored ice warnings, and a drifting white mountain had destroyed the most beautiful and advanced vessel on earth. Art and science were still subject to the irrational power of nature, especially when nature was abetted by human arrogance and error.

In the years since the sinking, thought Tracy, the world had been trying to prove that the iceberg was omen and not merely accident. The irrational had become the rule. Science served war, art served propaganda, and politicians served generals. In such a world, the irrationality of a politician running guns became perfectly logical.

At the Northern Avenue Bridge, Tom Tracy had found freedom from fear. When the detective aimed his carbine through the steam, Tracy had continued to pull at the coupling, because, at last, he had committed himself to something simple and concrete. And the next day, hatred had come to temper his commitment. When he landed in Ireland, he would not vacillate for fear of offending the voters, he would not make deals, he would not do favors to guarantee that the job was done. He would join with Padraic Starr in an action that would be as pure as it was violent.

He saw the match flare near the forward cargo hatch, and Jimmy the Butcher lit another cigarette. He saw Dawson stroll forward, toward the shadow of Mason Deems.

Then he heard the priest say something to Jenny as she went past. She stopped, and Tracy leaned closer. Watching the deck from this height was like looking down on a shadow play. Words were muffled, expressions indistinct; body movement and pantomime told the story.

WILLIAM MARTIN

It was, he supposed, the way God watched the world, interested but uninvolved in the small affairs of men and the grand
movements of history.

"Life at sea seems to agree with you, my dear."
Jenny smiled. "Two women and ten men, it's a pipe. You gotta
love it."
"A pipe?"
She laughed. "You spent time in burley houses and didn't pick
up the lingo? A lead-pipe cinch . . . as easy as pie."
"Ah," the priest nodded. "And with that pair of dancing blink-
ers, it's a pipe that young Jenny Malloy plays havoc with all the
johns."
She fluttered her eyelids. "A doll in a class by herself, eh,
Father?"
"You are very beautiful, Jenny." He wiped his hands on the
front of his peacoat.
"On a ship with ten men and another woman who don't seem
quite right in the head, how can I complain?"
O'Fearna looked toward the afterhouse roof. Starr's cigarette
flared in the darkness. "You can complain if the man who at-
tracts you does not love you."
"Him and me, we've had some good nights at the fo'c'sle
head, under the stars." She giggled at her joke and looked up at
the sky. "He'll be mine 'fore we're done."
"Impossible for any woman."
She fluttered her eyelids again. "Sayin' *that* ain't the way to
get my attention, Father."
"I've asked you for nothing."
"You've looked."
"I've looked, I've counseled." He touched her arm, the beginning of his clumsy effort at seduction. "When the captain refused
to take you aboard, I spoke on your behalf."
"If they didn't take me, I would have spilled the beans about
this whole show." She pulled her arm away.
"Starr will not allow a woman or an emotion to endanger his
rebellion."
"That night at the Howard was the night of my life, even if I
got fired. Whatever Starr wants, I'll do. I don't need no priests
tellin' me to watch out."
"I've left the priesthood." He brought a hand to her face. "And
I would not ask you to die for me."

290

Jenny laughed nervously. "Who's askin' me to do that?"

Sean O'Fearna had never touched a woman like this before. He felt none of the excitement he had imagined. He had preached of the weakness of the flesh, he had absolved it in confession, it was one of the reasons he had come aboard the *Abigail*. But in the moment when he came to break the vow, he found that his training would not permit it. He had been taught to look ahead, to the end of things, to their cost. That was what he spoke of instead of seduction.

He dropped his hand. "We are all being asked to sacrifice ourselves for Ireland. Whatever pleasure he gives you on the f'c'sle head, whatever any of us learns about himself on this voyage, we must remember what he will ask in return."

"Father, it's worth what it takes."

Tracy thought that the priest had made a pass at Jenny, because she turned away. Then she stopped. Tracy did not know why. The shadow play could not convey complex emotions. She seemed rooted to the deck, her body grown rigid. Tracy followed her gaze beyond the place where Starr sat to the aft companionway. Another shadow had emerged. Tracy could not see the face but knew the figure.

Rachel.

Starr saw her and stood. He flicked his cigarette, and a stream of burning ash spun from his hand to the water. They met at the starboard rail, halfway down the quarterdeck. Starr put his hands on her shoulders, and they spoke, the sounds murmuring up toward Tracy and filling him with jealousy.

Then the voice of Henry Huntoon bellowed, "Fire! Fire on the ship!"

Tracy saw smoke curling from the forward hatch.

"All hands on deck!" screamed Henry Huntoon.

"Ring the ship's bell!" shouted Tracy. He leaped to the ratlines, forgetting the scene at the quarterdeck.

"You get the bell," Starr ordered Rachel, then he jumped off the quarterdeck and ran toward the smoke.

"Ring the bell!" Tracy was shouting as he dropped himself down the rigging.

Starr stopped amidships and screamed at Rachel, "Ring it!"

The bell hanging from the spankermast began to clang. The alarm woke the captain and brought the men running from the forecastle. The noise rolled across the black waters and echoed off the icebergs. But Rachel Levka was standing where Starr had left her. She could not move. It was Jenny Malloy who seized the bellrope.

"Git the buckets!" shouted Mr. Huntoon. "Start the pumps!"

"No pumps!" screamed Starr.

"Them's bullets and guns down there, mister."

The smoke was pouring out of the cargo hatch and rolling up toward the masthead like a thundercloud. Starr slid back the hatch to get in, but the fresh air fed the flames and the fire sprang out.

"You givin' 'er juice! Shut the hatch!"

The flames jumped again. Huntoon grabbed the top of the hatch and pulled with Starr. But the flames exploded again, this time reaching high enough to singe the beard sprouting on Starr's chin.

Tracy dropped to the deck. His brother and uncle were watching the flames when they should have been following the ship fire drill. He screamed, "Sand! Martin, you fill the buckets, Danny, you bring 'em."

"Sand won't do!" The captain careened down the quarterdeck, nearly knocking Rachel over the side. "Start the pumps!" He looked at O'Fearna. "The intake hose, connect it to the pumps—"

"Wh . . . where do I find it?"

"We drilled on this. You're supposed to *know!*" He waved O'Fearna away in disgust. "Mr. Deems!"

The bell was still clanging.

"Mr. Deems!" the captain shouted over the noise of the bell. "Mr. Deems . . . Stop that damn bell, woman!"

Jenny Malloy could not hear. She was holding to her position, pounding on the bell, as though she planned to go down with the ship.

"Are the hoses up front?" asked O'Fearna.

"In the *forward* compartment, by the donkey engine."

"No hoses!" screamed Starr. "We use sand, like Tommy said."

The captain reached the forward hatch as another fist of flame burst upward, pushing waves of heat into the cold dark. "I called for hoses. Now!"

"Fire's just gettin' started, Cap," said Henry Huntoon. "Smell like burnin' cotton, prob'ly fired by the alcohol. Somebody been down there, Cap."

"*You* had the key!" cried Pratt.

"I been on this ship longer 'n' you, Cap, and I ain't started no fires in the hold yet!"

"Can you smell the munition crates?" asked Starr.

"Nope. It ain't gone out of control . . . yet."

Tom Tracy and Danny Tracy arrived from the stern with buckets of sand.

"Stop talkin' and start dumpin'," shouted Tom Tracy. He was the only man on board who was following the drill.

Starr took a bucket from Tracy and dropped it into the opening. The flames faded, then leaped again. Tracy and his brother ran back down the deck to the firebox.

As he went, Tracy looked toward the quarterdeck and saw Rachel, backing slowly toward the aft companionway. He wanted to hold her and protect her from the fear he saw closing around her once more, but he could not. He had to keep calm and follow the drill, or the *Abigail* would go down.

"Keep sandin' her till we get the pumps!" shouted the captain.

"No pumps!" screamed Starr. "It'll ruin the ammunition!"

Jason Pratt pulled a belaying pin from the rail. "Countermand my orders again, mister, and you're going over the side."

From the quarterdeck came the sputtering sound of the Domestic sideshaft engine. It blew out a gout of smoke, then the pump sucked air.

It was the job of Hugh Dawson to start the pumps. In a few moments, water would be pouring down through the medical supplies to the munitions stored below. If the British agent had his way with the hose, five hundred rifles and six machine guns would be left with nothing to fire.

Henry Huntoon burst from the galley and flung another bucket of sand into the hold. Tom Tracy and his brother came galloping forward, each carrying a brace of buckets.

Starr continued to plead with the captain. "The sand's smotherin' it. Give us a few more minutes . . . please."

Jason Pratt gave Starr no more than a glance or a thought. He turned to the stern and shouted, "Mr. Deems! Mr. Deems! Hurry up with that hose! . . . Where the hell is Deems?"

"He's below, Captain!" Dawson was dropping the intake hose over the side while Sean O'Fearna fumbled to connect the onboard hose to the pump.

"Below? What the hell is he doing below?" He strode angrily toward the quarterdeck.

Padraic Starr went after him, but Huntoon grabbed Starr and

shoved him toward the forward deckhouse. "They's more sand in the galley, for grease fires. If you want to keep them bullets from poppin' off, he'p me git it."

Rachel Levka had reached the aft companionway, and she was thinking of disappearing again into her cabin. There was nowhere safe on the wide ocean or the tiny ship, nowhere to escape from danger. But she could not run away now. She had to help. She watched the smoke and flames jumping from the hold, and she tried to make herself move forward. But the sense of helpless fear that had paralyzed her for ten days had descended again.

Mr. Deems burst from the afterhouse, knocking her into the helm as he came. He was carrying a canvas sack and, in his teeth, a box of matches. He glanced toward the bow, at the smoke still boiling up the mast. Half the crew were running about with sand buckets and half stumbling over the hoses and pump. And the ship's bell was ringing above the confusion like a bugle.

Deems took a long metal tube from the sack and set it up on the port side. Then he put what looked like a Fourth of July rocket into the tube and lit the fuse. Sparks flew around the wheel housing and splattered onto Rachel's skirt. The rocket shot into the air and burst above the ship, casting a strange green light. Then from across the smooth waters came the wail of the freighter's whistle, answering the signal of distress. Another rocket shot up in a shower of sparks.

Rachel Levka tried to get away, but her skirt caught on a wheel spoke. She screamed and began to beat at the tiny flames that leaped within the folds of wool.

Tom Tracy did not hear her cry, but Starr did. He dropped his bucket and ran halfway to the stern, then another ball of flame leaped behind him. He caught Jenny's eye and waved her toward Rachel.

Jenny stopped clanging the bell and pointed to herself. *Me?*

Starr shouted, "Help her! Help her!"

Jenny's hands dropped. She looked at Rachel, who was slapping madly and shaking at her skirt. She looked again at Starr, but he was racing back to the forward hatch. Another rocket streaked from the launching tube, and the sparks flew around Rachel's feet.

Jenny Malloy jumped onto the afterhouse roof and scrambled to the stern. When she reached her, Rachel was in panic.

Jenny grabbed Rachel's skirt by the waist and tore it off.

"When in doubt, strip, honey." She shook the skirt, and another rocket went rushing into the blackness, splattering sparks over both women.

Rachel screamed again, and Jenny slapped at her bottom to put out the embers smoldering in the slip.

Rachel's anger came back to her once more, this time releasing her from her paralysis and her fear. She screamed at the mate, "I could have burned to death, you idiot!"

"Now you know why we don't like skirts on shipboard." Deems stomped over the few embers still glowing on the deck.

Jenny wrapped the skirt around Rachel again.

"Thank you," said Rachel.

"I did it 'cause I was asked," answered Jenny.

"Into the yawlboat, ladies." Mr. Deems put his hands under Rachel's armpits and tried to lift her into the boat above the transom.

She kicked his shin. "I'm not going anywhere."

"Yeah, you little shit," added Jenny, and she called the captain.

Pratt was helping O'Fearna attach the pump hose. He adjusted the diaphragm, and the hose spit seawater onto the deck.

"Captain!" Deems cried. "I say we abandon ship."

The smoke was still pouring from the hold, but the flames were no longer leaping.

Pratt ordered Dawson and Martin Mahoney to take the hose forward. Then he hurried to the stern. "Why aren't you organizing the crews?" he demanded of Deems.

"I'm organizing the distress call. We should abandon."

"Abandon? In the middle of the Atlantic? There's no reason."

Deems pointed across the water to the freighter, which was starting to make steam. "We're not alone, Captain. The Lord would not visit this upon us unless he gave us a savior. But if we stay on a burning munitions ship—"

"Never mind that. How did the fire start?"

"Ask the drunk."

"Not Jimmy. He ain't on fire down there, is he?" cried Jenny.

"Where is he?" asked the captain.

"For what he did to my ship, burning in hell, I hope."

"Oh, shit." Jenny slumped against the wheel.

"A bad choice of words, Mr. Deems." The captain pivoted toward the forward hatch. "Now get down there and direct the crew."

Deems did not move. "You don't know how far that fire's gone or where it'll explode again. I say we abandon."

A light breeze pushed the smoke along the length of the ship.

Pratt stepped close to Deems, and the scars beneath his eyes seemed to whiten in anger. "I have had enough insubordination for one night."

Then, from the confusion of the forward hatch, came the cries of Henry Huntoon. "Captain! I think she's out."

Pratt pushed Jenny and Rachel aside and strode forward. "Mr. Dawson, lay on with the water."

"We don't need the hose!" Tracy was shouting at Dawson.

"The fire's out. *Out!*" added Starr.

"Captain's orders." Hugh Dawson was trying to aim the hose into the hold, but Tracy was wrestling him away.

"Water'll ruin the ammunition!" cried Tracy, and he shot a fist at Dawson's face, but Dawson ducked and came up hard with the heavy brass nozzle. It caught Tracy on the chin and knocked him onto the deck. Then Dawson aimed the hose. Icy seawater hit Starr in the chest with such force that it knocked him backward. He fell through the hatch into the smoking hold. Dawson turned the hose onto Danny Tracy, who was flying at him from the other side of the hold. Danny was spun off balance and landed on the deck.

Martin Mahoney had seen enough. He knew why Dawson was so intent on soaking the hold, even after the fire was out. He pulled a belaying pin from the rail and cracked the Belfast man across the back of the head. As Dawson went down, the stream from the hose shot into the air and sprinkled down through the open hatch like rain.

White steam hissed up from below, followed by the face of Padraic Starr. "It's out, Captain."

"Is Jimmy down there?" screamed Jenny.

"No, honey."

"Are you all right?"

Starr boosted himself out. "A damn sight better than I was before Tommy Tracy put out the fire."

"So where's Jimmy?"

"A fair question." Sean O'Fearna called Jimmy's name and went toward the forecastle with Jenny close behind.

"We should still soak the cargo," said Deems. "There's no telling when the fire will flare again."

"There's no need," said Starr.

Deems turned to Martin Mahoney.

"The man says there's no need," said Martin.

Deems tried to pull the hose out of his hands. Martin Mahoney whipped his arms once and threw the mate to the deck.

"This man belongs in irons, Captain." Deems snapped back to his feet as quick as the tip of his quirt.

"There's no one who'll be puttin' me in irons." Martin Mahoney's big round face showed no anger. It never did. He looked from mate to captain as calmly as a barkeep drawing porter on a slow afternoon.

"Soak the hold," said the captain.

In response, Martin dropped the hose so that the nozzle clattered down the side and splashed into the water.

"That's the quality of this crew, Captain," said Deems. "Mutinous! I say we let that freighter take them off and sail straight for England."

Tom Tracy was on his feet again, and he had put his body between the hold and the hose. "Soak the cargo and you won't have reason to go to England, Captain. You'll have to report to your . . . benefactors . . . that your mission of mercy was a failure."

"This is no mission of mercy," said Deems. "You're nothing but Irish thugs stabbing Britain in the back."

A cry of encouragement blew from the whistle of the freighter that was now steaming toward them.

Tracy did not respond to the whistle or to the mate. He wiped the sweat and soot from his face and looked at Jason Pratt. "Return to Boston with a water-soaked hold and you'll be the laughingstock of your club. Press on, and I guarantee you that we can all work together. We've just proved it."

Rachel Levka almost smiled. The previous few minutes had been like a comedy scene in a picture show, with confused people running crazily about, spilling water, throwing punches, and stumbling into open holds. Now Tracy was turning it into an efficient act of firefighting. He had not forgotten his skills after all.

The freighter fired another blast. It rolled past the *Abigail* and echoed back off an iceberg.

Jason Pratt blew out a long stream of breath and looked at Mr. Huntoon. "Get out the lantern. Signal 'all clear and thanks' to that freighter."

Deems's quirt snapped against his leg.

Henry Huntoon gave a jerk of the head to Danny Tracy. "Come on, son. I'll teach you the light signals."

Hugh Dawson rolled over and rubbed the back of his head.

Martin Mahoney helped him to his feet. "Sorry for the noggin, my friend."

"Is the fire out?"

"The captain seems to think that it is," said Deems. "I think that the captain is wrong."

"Then maybe the captain should see for himself," Starr reached into the galley and took out a lantern. "Come below, and if you ain't satisfied, we'll run a hose."

"Mr. Deems!" the captain said sharply. "Find out who started this, because he's going to be punished."

"I think I know."

At that, Starr let out a laugh. Then he dropped into the hold with the captain close behind.

Tom Tracy watched Dawson and Deems and waited for their eyes to meet. One of them had started the fire, and both deserved to go over the side. No mate abandoned ship until the situation was hopeless . . . unless he wanted to see her sink and knew for certain that he could summon rescue. And Dawson had nearly broken Tracy's jaw with the brass nozzle.

But no look passed between Dawson and Deems. Tracy decided *that* was more damning than winks across the deck. Deems went forward, drawn toward the sound of Jimmy McHale's retching. Dawson crouched down and picked a cigarette butt off the deck. He glanced at Tracy. "Jimmy the Butcher was smoking." He dropped the butt over the side and went off.

For a few moments, Tom Tracy and Rachel Levka were alone on the deck.

"What happened to your skirt?"

"Fire." She had tucked the remnants into her slip. She pulled the torn section together so that no white showed.

"Are you all right?"

She nodded. "Are you?"

He rubbed his chin where the nozzle had hit him.

She gave a little laugh. "Some greeting I get the first night I come on deck." She had not made a joke in a long time.

"I'm glad you've come out. If you have something to do, you'll have less time to think about things."

"I think about things all the time . . . what's happened . . . what's going to happen."

He put his hands on her shoulders, and she pulled away, as though they burned. "What's—"

She raised her hands. "Not yet, Tommy."

"I'm . . . I'm sorry we had to bring you with us."

"I wanted to come, remember?"

"Not the way it happened." He went to the rail.

"You had no choice. You couldn't leave me. That would have been worse."

He shivered. The icy water from the hose had soaked through his peacoat. "It was Starr's idea. He said we couldn't trust you."

She looked at him for a long time while he looked out at the icebergs. "Do you believe that?"

"I'd rather have you waiting for me safe in Boston."

"In Boston, I'd be powerless."

"To do what?"

Rachel pulled her shawl more tightly around her shoulders. She took a deep breath. "To stop you from throwing your life away."

Tracy's head snapped around. "When did you decide I'm doing that?"

"Someplace between your foyer and the iceberg fields."

He grabbed her by the shoulders again.

She tried to pull away. "Tommy, please don't touch me, not yet."

He ignored her. "What happened in Boston made me understand this fight. The man who stuck that pistol in my ear came from the same mold as the man who hung my father. It's a mold to be broken."

She pushed his hands away. "Do you remember what he said? Blood brings blood? The last ten days, it's all I've heard."

He stepped back from her. "Blood brings blood, and the weakest end up the bloodiest. Your Zionist friends would tell you that. So pick up a gun and join the target practice, and when we're finished in Ireland, we'll fight for the Jews."

"Captain! Captain!" Mason Deems came aft, holding the neck of an alcohol bottle.

Jason Pratt poked his head from below.

"The drunk needed a drink, so he went into the hold, and set it on fire."

"Where is he?"

"Passed out on the fo'c'sle head."

"Put him in irons."

"Captain!" Sean O'Fearna strode down the forecastle head. "I don't believe Jimmy McHale started that fire."

Deems waved the bottle beneath the priest's nose. "Then where did he get this?"

Suddenly, a terrified shriek tightened every line on the old schooner. Jenny Malloy burst into view, staggering and spinning back from the bow.

For a moment, no one knew what was happening. Then they saw the flames expanding in the folds of her trousers, flames from the sparks of the distress rockets. The fire touched a patch of tar in the sailcloth and exploded along her left thigh, across her buttocks, up her back, and ignited in her bleached hair. She staggered down the narrow strip of deck beside the forecastle, screaming in terror.

Rachel moved first, ignoring the fear that grabbed at her again. She ripped off her skirt and rushed toward Jenny, with the priest, Tom, and the others close behind.

The heat from the burning body singed Rachel's eyebrows and the hairs on her arms, and she fell back for a moment, then Jenny spun toward her, screaming, reaching out, her eyes bulging in horror and then disappearing in a sheet of flame as her hair swung across her face.

Rachel Levka leaped forward and smothered the flames with her skirt.

In the distance, the mountains of ice gazed impassively at the tiny ship.

23

*I*t was true, thought Josephine Tracy. When things were the worst, we cried the loudest to God. When things went well, we forgot Him. Josephine had been to church every day in the two weeks since the *Abigail* had left. She had prayed for her children, she had wept quietly in her loneliness, and she had not been so faithful to the Mass since Jack Tracy faced trial.

She had never wondered what the verdict of that trial had told her about the strength of her devotion. As Josephine always said when things went wrong, God worked in strange ways. A prayer denied did not mean the prayer had failed. It meant simply that God had a higher purpose, and the serenity that prayer brought was fulfillment in itself.

On the first Monday in April, she prayed that God would give to her and her son John the power to lie. She believed firmly that God would understand the request and answer the prayer. If she thought otherwise, she would not have been able to go to the mayor's office that day.

"I don't approve of this. Neither does Father Flynn at school."

"Mother of God, Johnny, you didn't tell him?"

"Only in the hypothetical. He says it's wrong to lie to government officials."

"You've got your story, John. Stick to it. Otherwise your brothers'll hang from a British gallows."

The mayor greeted them like an old friend at a funeral, warm and comforting, but as somber as the occasion. He was a grand actor, thought Josephine. He could fit his emotion to the moment, or give a performance that would change the mood of everyone in the room.

Standish Willcox brought tea, and they sat on the sofa by the fireplace. While Willcox chatted about the magnolias coming into bloom along Commonwealth Avenue, Curley sipped his tea and studied Josephine Tracy.

"You know," Curley began gently, "I've been visited by federal agents lately."

Josephine pulled a lace handkerchief from her sleeve and crumpled it against the palms of her hands.

"They've asked questions about Tommy, and about you. They've agreed to leave you alone, but I must provide answers."

Josephine looked at her son, and he forced a smile. "My mother is always thankful for the help of your honor."

"And she'll always have it, especially if British agents come bothering her."

"British?" said Josephine.

Curley gave Willcox a nod, and the secretary said, "From what we can gather, two British trade representatives—"

"Agents operating without permission," grunted Curley. "That's why the feds haven't pushed us all harder. They're annoyed about this."

"Yes," continued Willcox, "they were on the trail of a deserter and suspected rebel named Starr."

"A distant relative of yours, I believe?" said Curley.

Josephine picked at the lace trim on the handkerchief and felt Curley's calm eyes studying her. "A . . . a troubled lad."

"Because of your relationship," continued Willcox, "these two Brits were allegedly dispatched to your house, on Sunday the nineteenth."

"On a Sunday." Curley looked at John and shook his head. "Absolute sacrilege."

"Since that Sunday, Mrs. Tracy, they haven't heard from either agent."

"Well . . . they never came to my home, that I know of." Josephine looked at her son, who was sitting as stiffly as the mummified man she had once seen at the Marshfield Fair. The mummy skin had been brown and wrinkled, however. John's was turning so white that it was transparent, and she could see blue veins throbbing at his temples. "They never came that you knew of, did they, John?"

After a moment, the young man shook his head. "No, Mother."

"Good, then." Curley slapped his hands on the arms of his leather chair. "We'll take the word of a young man bound for the seminary."

The mayor stood as though satisfied, then turned and squinted at Josephine. "And this rebel relative of yours, he never showed up either, did he?"

"Mother of God, no." Josephine sensed John shifting in his seat. She had invoked the Blessed Mother in the midst of her lie. And Curley had pointed to John's life's ambition as proof of his honesty. She squeezed the handkerchief tightly and hoped that John could remain quiet.

"Good. And if the feds ask us, we'll back your story up with these." Curley picked up a sheaf of papers. "Minutes from a secret meeting in this office the day after the first trade representative got himself killed. They were trying to stick that one on the Irish when it was a German all along. I looked Tommy right in the eye and asked him what he knew about Irish troublemakers in Boston, and he said nothing. Nothing!"

"Mrs. Tracy, I must admit that I have always found that a bit difficult to accept." Standish Willcox smoothed his mustache. "Considering Jack Tracy's rather . . . colorful . . . past."

302

"Don't speak of my husband unless you knew him," muttered Josephine, and her voice suddenly sounded like the growl of an angry cat. "He was a hero who saved Victoria herself, and got himself hung for doin' it."

"We're all friends here, Mrs. Tracy." The mayor came around her chair and put a hand on her shoulder. Then he gave Willcox a subtle nod.

"Where are they?" demanded Willcox of John Tracy.

John's teacup clattered nervously onto the saucer.

Josephine glanced at John, then frowned at Willcox. "Is that a way to be talkin' to a young priest-to-be?"

"Be a bit gentler, Standish." Curley knelt beside Josephine, playing the friend protecting her from Willcox's questions. "Now, where is your son, dear?"

"Cal . . . California," said John nervously.

Curley took Josephine's hand in his. "If I am going to stand behind you, I want to know that I'm in the right. Is California where Tommy is?"

She nodded. "Yes, and his little brother Danny took off after him two days later. I . . . I got a wire from them about ten days ago." She pulled a telegram from her purse. The yellow paper had been folded and unfolded so many times that there was a hole in the crease at the corner. Tom had suggested the ruse: Send a telegram to a cousin in Baltimore and ask her to send the same message in his name back to Boston. She handed the telegram to Curley.

After a moment, the mayor's lower lip pulled his face into a relieved smile. "May I keep this, dear, to show if the feds come back?"

"Of course, your honor. Only . . ." She touched his arm. "Promise that you won't let them bother me."

Curley gently patted her hand. "A lady as lovely as yourself does not need such intrusions."

John Tracy had gone white again. He looked as though he might get sick.

After they left, Willcox said, "Do you believe her?"

"She's too simple to look me in the eye and lie that well," answered Curley. "And even if I didn't believe her, I'd want to."

The walk down Washington Street to the South End was passed in silence. When mother and son reached the pedestrian tunnel at the Madison Hotel, John said that he was going on to the Cathedral.

"To pray for your brothers?" asked Josephine.

"For myself."

"I never thought I'd say this, Johnny, but you're too damn pious."

John rolled his eyes like any adolescent enduring a mother's scolding.

"You just walked down Washington Street, past the Old South Meetin' House where they started the Boston Tea Party, past the buildin' on the corner of Essex Street where the Liberty Tree is carved right into the brick because that's where the tree grew." Josephine's face flushed with anger. "And if it wasn't for the men who met in that meetin' house and nailed their speeches to that tree and kicked the Brits out of Boston a hundred and fifty years ago, you'd have none of what you've got in America today."

An elevated train rumbled over them. The pigeons nesting beneath the tracks fluttered and scurried and sent a splatter of droppings down to the sidewalk.

Josephine ignored the white stains that spread near her feet. "You wouldn't have no rights. You couldn't walk to the Cathedral, for they wouldn't let you be Catholic. And you'd have no justice."

"The saints preserve us from unholy delusions." John blessed himself melodramatically and slipped a hand into the crook of his mother's arm. "Let me make sure you're home safe and sound."

She pulled away from him. "Don't be mockin' me, John Tracy. It might be hurtin' to you to lie like that, but think of me, lyin' awake nights, prayin', and cryin', and seein' what I saw that Sunday mornin'. I said right then, God sent this upon us because He needs Tommy, and this is His way. He wants Tommy to finish his father's work."

"A mother's knowledge of God's plan is a grand asset when her sons have gone astray."

"Sarcasm, is it?"

John reached out his hand and led his mother into the pedestrian tunnel. She brought her handkerchief to her nostrils to hold back the stink of the urine.

"It's a beautiful country, America," said John.

She pulled her arm out of his. "At least there's justice. Your own father told us that. When he couldn't get justice in Ireland, he told us to come here."

"Then why are my brothers going back?"

"You don't remember your only visit to Ballinakill House, do you, Johnny?"

"Ballinakill House?"

"You were with me the day I went there seekin' justice with nothin' but words. . . ."

———————— 1 9 0 0 ————————

It was a Sunday afternoon and the stone gates of the great estate were closed. Seamus Kilkeirnan jumped down from his jaunting car and pushed them open with the familiarity of a man who was known, if not entirely welcome, at every door in Dunslea.

As he climbed back into the car, he pointed to a large boulder by the gate. It was the same gray color as the rest of the rock of Connemara, except for one side that seemed almost brown in the afternoon light. "That's the rock where Clarke's father bled to death after he was shot down in the Land League days."

" '87," answered Josephine Tracy.

"You've a good memory." Seamus snapped the reins.

"It was not but a few months before my brother left for America."

"I'd not be pointin' it out"—Seamus sucked a bit on his pipe—"except the RM blames your own Jack for what was done that night. It's a thing you should know."

Josephine looked back at the rock. Such a meaningless lump, she thought, to have such terrible meaning for her family.

Her Tommy was looking down at it as well, and she wondered what he could be thinking. He was only eleven, but already he was dark and handsome, Black Irish like his father. The red necktie and white shirt made him look even older, with wisdom beyond his years. He was trying in vain to entertain little Johnny, who bounced about the cart and kept trying to climb out. She had thought to leave them at home, but she believed that the sight of two forlorn young ones and her own rounding belly would have some decent effect on the RM. She had also thought to dress them in their poorest clothes to make their sadness more obvious, but the boys were Jack Tracy's greatest pride, and she would present them with pride at the magistrate's door.

As they approached, Seamus explained that the great house

had been built in something called the Gothic style. "That means it can't make up its mind to be a castle or a church, so it ends up a little of both."

There were turrets at the four corners and fake battlements running along the roof. The main windows were arched and leaded. Griffin heads decorated the downspouts, the roof corners, and the portico. A pious, frightening place, she thought, a little like a rich convent.

"Why, Seamus," said the maid, Mrs. Burke, "you're supposed to deliver telegrams and such to the back." Then Mrs. Burke saw the jaunting car, the children, and the somber face of Josephine Tracy.

"Get the master," whispered Seamus.

Mrs. Burke had been in the service of the Clarkes for a quarter century. She was forty years old, dressed in a lacy white cap and apron, and too young, as Seamus said, to be called an old crone. "The master's at tea and don't like to be disturbed."

Seamus tapped his pipe against the stone framework of the door and threw the ash into the bushes. "This is important, darlin'."

"Don't darlin' *me, Seamus Kilkeirnan. I told you, he ain't to be disturbed."*

From inside the house a woman's voice called, "Who is it, Brigid?"

"Seamus Kilkeirnan, ma'am."

Adelle Clarke had been out for a ride. Her cheeks were flushed and she was still wearing her tweeds. As she came to the door, she was letting down her blond hair and shaking it out.

So beautiful, thought Josephine, and such a lovely smile. But when Mrs. Clarke spied Josephine with Seamus, the smile faded.

"What can we do for you, Seamus?"

"This is Mrs. Tracy, ma'am," said Seamus, casually packing his pipe.

"I know." She sent the maid back to her chores, then folded her hands in front of her skirt.

"I've come to speak with your husband, ma'am," said Josephine.

"If this is about a legal matter, I suggest that you bring it up at petty sessions. They're held every second Thursday at the courthouse in Clifden, promptly at half-one."

"Well, ma'am," said Seamus, "I think you know what this is about, and petty sessions ain't quite what the lady wants."

Josephine felt the aristocratic blue eyes examine her. There was a gentleness in them that gave Josephine some small cause for hope. Then the eyes shifted. Tommy had come up behind Josephine after harnessing little John to the cart. His hands were stuffed into the pockets of his shorts and he was looking up from under his dark brows like a sober young barrister. His gaze seemed to unsettle Mrs. Clarke. She told them to wait, then closed the door in their faces.

"I guess they'll not be invitin' us fer a taste of poteen." Seamus winked at Tommy.

"I told you to stay in the cart, Tommy," Josephine scolded.

"I have to pee."

"It's relieve yourself, *and not here. Go back to the cart.*"

"Hello, Seamus." William Clarke appeared in the doorway. He was perspiring from his afternoon ride. On his cheek was a wide bandage with a small spot of dried blood showing at the center.

"Good afternoon, your honor," blurted Josephine.

Josephine heard children's laughter coming from somewhere in the house. Then she saw two girls around Tommy's age, tumbling down the hallway. Behind them came Mrs. Burke and the teacart. When the girls noticed the people at the door, they stopped and peered out.

"Hurry up, ladies," sniffed Mrs. Burke, "or you'll get no cakes with your tea."

One of the girls snatched a cake off the cart and scampered away. Mrs. Burke scurried after her. The other girl, who had her mother's coloring and smile, remained in the foyer, staring out at the little boy, and said. "Shan't we invite them in for tea, Father?"

Her mother hurried her along.

"Lovely children," said Josephine. "Like my own."

"If you're here simply to spy into my foyer," said Clarke, "come 'round when there's no one home and the maid will give you a tour."

"That ain't why we're here at all, your honor." Josephine's mouth was as dry as thatch. "I've come—"

"About your husband."

She stepped around Seamus and put her body full in front

of Clarke, so that he could see her pregnant belly. "You know damn right well that Jack Tracy ain't no murderer."

Clarke simply looked at her, his eyes as blank as the rocks in the field.

When she realized he would not respond, she continued, "Them lads come to my Jack a week ago, askin' for help. But my Jack said no. After they left, he come to me and said, 'By God, we better stop them, or there'll be hell to pay.' "

Clarke slowly began to tap his riding crop against his boot.

"I seen him write the very note that he sent to your honor, warnin' what might happen."

The riding crop tapped more quickly.

"That's what he said," she continued, "and that's what he meant. You've got to believe that, your honor."

"Perhaps the court at Dublin will believe it."

"Dublin? You're sendin' him up?"

"Cases of such seriousness are always heard in Dublin, madam. He was judged well enough to travel and remanded to custody this morning, with the evidence and my recommendations for indictment."

Seamus took the pipe from his mouth. "You sent him on a Sunday?"

"We sent him when the court provided a constable."

Josephine felt her lower lip quivering. She clenched her teeth and tightened her small mouth into a thin, hard line. "My Jack's got two young ones, and a third on the way. Never's the minute in his life he's thought about killin' the queen, and if he shot them boys, it was an accident for certain."

Clarke simply stared.

Seamus whispered into Josephine's ear, "It's the magistrate's gaze he's givin' to you now, darlin', to tell you that he ain't convinced."

"Indeed not," muttered Clarke.

Josephine stepped closer to the resident magistrate. "My husband's guilty of nothin'."

"You may present your evidence in Dublin, madam . . . after I present mine."

A wave of weakness flowed through her. She put a hand on Seamus Kilkeirnan's arm. Then she felt her son at her side, a small but suddenly reassuring presence.

Tommy looked up defiantly at the resident magistrate. "My father's a good man, and nothin' you say can change it."

For a long time, William Clarke stared down at Tommy Tracy, his face calm, expressionless, perhaps slightly amused. Then he said, "That, young man, is for the court to decide." And he slammed the door in their faces.

"No!" Josephine threw herself against it and began to pound.

From inside came the sound of the dead bolts snapping into place.

"You can't convict Jack Tracy! We demand justice!" She had promised herself she would not cry, but she had made no promise about pounding. She punched the door. She kicked it. She shouted again for justice. But no response came from inside.

Seamus tried to throw his arms around her, and she pushed him away. He grabbed again and succeeded in pinning her arms.

"No!" she screamed.

"You've had your audience," whispered Seamus in her ear. "Now leave it in the hands of God, woman."

"No!"

"God," repeated Seamus. "Trust in God. . . . Besides, young Johnny's cryin'." He spun Josephine toward the cart and led her back to the little boy, who was calling for his mother with arms outstretched.

Josephine climbed into the cart and took her little boy and held him tight. Then she looked back at Tommy. "Come along, Tommy . . . Tommy!"

He was standing with his back to the cart. His two hands were in front of him, and a wide, wet stain was spreading on the carved oak door of Ballinakill House.

"Tommy!" she called again.

"Ah, leave the lad alone," muttered Seamus. "Many's the night an old man like me wishes he could make it flow that fast. It's a grand gift."

"You shouldn't ever have done that, Thomas Tracy," said Josephine, although she was secretly glad that he had.

"I told you, Mum," Tommy finished buttoning his fly, "I had to relieve myself."

As the cart pulled away from the great house, Josephine looked back. One of Clarke's setters came snuffling to the front door, stopped to study the stain, then lifted his leg and widened it.

24

Jenny Malloy lingered three days. With Rachel's help, the priest delicately dressed her orange, oozing burns. And each hour he gave her morphine, so that her moans became merely another rhythm aboard the *Abigail,* rather than the sound of agony.

But Starr could not listen. He could not imagine her disfigured beauty or let the others contemplate her suffering. On the third night, he went softly to her cabin and injected her with a triple dose of morphine. No one had seen him kill the German at the bridge, and none saw this. One was an act of war, the other of pity, and in the terrible poetry of his life, both brought death.

Jenny was buried at sea the following morning. Sean O'-Fearna read the Twenty-third Psalm, then said to the company, "She gave of herself, and in some way, saved us all. Some she saved for Ireland, some for love, and all of us she reminded of the hope and the pain in every life."

That night, the priest prayed for guidance in a rising that would be born in hope, promise pain, but offer no sure redemption for Ireland. And he prayed forgiveness for the words he had spoken from a Dublin pulpit a quarter-century before. *Parnell is an adulterer. His Catholic paramour is an adulteress. Turn your face from them, for they do not deserve the succor of decent Irish men and women.* Jenny had helped him to see Parnell's weakness in himself. If the church had forgiven Parnell, as God most surely had, there might now be no need for gunrunning.

Jimmy the Butcher saw no such grand meaning in Jenny's death. He loved her like an uncle, and he sobbed alone.

Padraic Starr thought of their nights of lovemaking at the forecastle head. And he hoped that her terrible death would not destroy the resolve of the crew.

Tom Tracy wondered if it was Deems or Dawson who had set the fire, and which of them he would kill to avenge Jenny.

Rachel Levka thought of the scorched skin, the first blood brought from the blood of the Tracy foyer, and she considered the terrible irony of Jenny's death. Jenny had not sacrificed herself for a political idea. When she took off her clothes in the burlesque house, when she demanded to be taken aboard the night they left, and during the fire, when she saved Rachel, she had been hoping simply to win Starr's love. Her dream, thought Rachel, had been more human and more promising than all the dreams of purging violence and political revenge that drove the others.

In the following week, the great springtime rotation of the equatorial winds began in Africa, sweeping westward to the New World, north along the American coast, then back across the Atlantic, driving the *Abigail* through bright blue days and clear black nights. But nothing could loosen the lines of tension that stretched over the old schooner like a second rigging.

Mr. Deems went armed about the ship, came on deck only for his watch, then returned to his cabin and his Bible. When Starr told the captain that he suspected Deems of starting the fire, Pratt threatened irons for any man who disobeyed his mate. But Deems no longer ate at the captain's table, for the captain, he said, had made a pact with scum. And so, the captain dined with members of the crew, often inviting Dawson and Starr so that he could listen to their debates.

Although Starr obeyed the captain's every order, he gave Deems no reason to feel secure. Each day, he assembled his tiny army for practice in field stripping and firing the Enfield Pattern 1914 rifle and the Vickers Pattern 1915 .30 caliber water-cooled machine gun. Tom Tracy and Martin Mahoney were Starr's soldiers. Danny Tracy was the recruit, although his brother insisted he would remain a sailor and return to Boston.

The popping of the rifles and the rattle of the machine guns became fierce counterpoint to the gentle music of wind and water aboard the *Abigail*.

Jimmy the Butcher ran from the sound and hid his head beneath the covers. Sean O'Fearna forced himself to listen, for he knew he would have to hear the sound often—or try to stop it—in the weeks ahead. Hugh Dawson always ignored the firing until it was finished, then carefully swept the shell casings from the deck and, with an ironic smile, handed them to Starr.

Rachel Levka watched it all from the cargo hatch, where she sat with leather thimble strapped to her palm and mended sailcloth, as Jenny had done before her. She knew that they had to learn to use the guns, but after Jenny's horrible death, she knew more certainly than ever that blood brought blood.

The men realized how far Rachel had come from the horrors of the Tracy foyer, and they did not press her to come further. Starr said that, in time, she would regain her resolve and join the weapons training, because she was a true rebel after all. A week after Jenny died, a day when sea, sky, and white icebergs seemed to glitter in the high April sun, Tracy offered her a rifle.

She ran her hands over the wood stock and the barrel and said, "I don't want to learn."

"This is a way to welcome you to the fight," said Starr, "just like Erskine Childers's American wife Molly, sailin' with her husband from Hamburg to Howth in a little yacht loaded with rifles, or Mary Spring Rice—"

"Or Cathleen ni Houlihan herself." Tracy gently took her arms and placed them in the proper position on the weapon, then he raised it to her face and gently pressed her head against the stock. "Just look down the sight, aim at that chunk of ice, two o'clock, and squeeze, don't pull."

She lowered the rifle. "You know how I feel, Tommy."

"It's what you wanted from me in Boston," he said softly. "It's what I want from you now."

She gave him a defiant look, then fired five wild shots. Her shoulder bucked and her head snapped with the recoil. Four splashes leaped on the waves, but the fifth shot hit the target and chunks of ice flew.

"They'll write your name large." Starr grinned. "The American Jewess who fought for the Irish when she couldn't fight for her own."

Rachel shoved the gunstock into Tracy's stomach and went below.

All of their names would be writ large, thought Tracy, if they simply kept their resolve. To gain strength, he climbed each night to the crosstrees and prayed—not the Our Fathers and Hail Marys that the priest was always muttering, but the wordless communication that began as he stared at the black, the blue-black, the shimmering silver of sky and sea, and wondered at his own insignificance. Such contemplation did not bring serenity, for a man who has left his home to join rebellion finds no serenity in thoughts of his own insignificance. Nor did it bring the certainty of God's approval, because too much that lay ahead was uncertain, and in the long run, God's plan—if there was one—could never be understood.

But there was something intoxicating about that lonely place and the steady rolling rhythm of the ship, something that let his mind wander with the wind. Beneath the endless sky, for all his insignificance, he was unique. He and the others had been given the chance to change history.

Filled with heroic thoughts, he came down from the crosstrees the night after Rachel's lesson. When he had brought the rifle to her face, he had put his arms around her for the first time since that awful Sunday, and her simple aroma had had all the effect of a rich perfume. They had grown apart, but now he wanted her.

Starr was at the helm as he came aft. "Seekin' a bit of comfort?"

"Mind your own business, Padr'ic."

"I been thinkin' about her myself."

Tracy put his hands on the spokes of the helm and held it against Starr's strength. The ship heeled slightly in response. "If you touch her, there'll be no rising."

"This close to Ireland, there's not a thing I'd do to make you mad at me."

Tracy went down the aft companionway. The captain was snoring in his cabin on the starboard side. Rachel's cabin was opposite.

Through the slats in the door, Tracy could see her naked back. She was sitting on a stool, washing her underarms. He swallowed his excitement and knocked.

"Who is it?"

He said his name.

"What do you want?"

"To kiss you."

She put on her blouse and opened her door. "What?"

For a time, he simply stared into the wide, dark eyes. The haunted, fear-gripped expression of the first days was gone from her face. Although she had lost weight, she did not look gaunt or worn, but toughened. Like Tracy himself, she had been growing scar tissue over her terrors, hardening herself for the future.

He wondered what she saw. He was no longer the polished South End ward lieutenant. His face was covered in black hair. His peacoat was splattered with stains from eating and drinking on a pitching deck. Where Pratt had broken his nose, it had thickened, so that he looked like a boxer. Their Sunday-afternoon walks, their conversations about Zionism and Boston politics, their kisses in the shadows, seemed now like part of another life.

"I said I want to kiss you."

She pulled her blouse more tightly around her. "No . . . not yet, Tommy."

Somewhere, a timber creaked. The captain stirred.

"After what happened . . . the love and the blood and the violence all mixed up." She looked down at the deck. "It's hard for me to think about loving you like that, or even kissing you."

"Rachel, the next two weeks on this ship may be all the peace we ever know." He put his hands on her shoulders. "I'd like to enjoy it."

'I would, too, but I keep thinking of what's happened. And what's ahead."

"I'm doing what you wanted to do for the Jews. I made the decision you wanted me to make."

She searched his face for some trace of the careful thought she had come to expect in Boston, some reflection of the calm that steadied her passion. But it seemed that their roles were becoming reversed. His beard had turned his face into nothing more than light and shadow.

"Maybe it was the wrong one." She closed her door.

The *Abigail* moved another night closer to Ireland. And like a god who had forgotten his wrath, the Atlantic continued its kindness toward the old schooner. The winds were light. The mercury showed forty degrees. When the watch changed, people lingered on the deck to enjoy the evening, except for Mr. Deems and Tom Tracy. Deems returned to his cabin and slammed the door. Tracy wrapped a hand around a starboard shroud and prepared to climb to his solitude, but he stopped when he heard Starr begin to clap his hands.

Starr and Dawson and Sean O'Fearna were at the port rail. Starr had been complaining that for a ship filled with Irishmen, the *Abigail* was too damned sedate. As Jimmy the Butcher shuffled out of the forecastle, Starr cried, "It's time for some entertainment, folks!"

"Somebody breakin' out the hootch?" grunted Jimmy.

Starr went down the deck, put his arm around Jimmy, and ushered him forward.

"We been at sea for three weeks, and in all that time, we've not had a song or a joke from one of America's grandest entertainers, Jimmy the Butcher McHale." Starr reached up and rattled the derby on Jimmy's head. "A joke to take our minds off all our troubles."

"I got troubles of my own."

"Then it'll be a favor to yourself as well." Padraic Starr clapped his hands again.

The priest and Dawson joined in, then Danny Tracy from the helm. Martin and Henry Huntoon strolled aft from the galley, each with a mug of coffee. And the captain came down the quarterdeck, drawn by the noise.

In the shadows, Rachel appeared next to Tracy and brought her hands together softly. "Clap, Tom. We could all use a joke."

Finally, Jimmy threw his hands into the air. "All right. A joke. A Pat and Mike joke." He jumped onto the cargo hatch.

"Jimmy, you're lookin' better already," cried Starr.

He had the magic, thought Rachel. For the first time since the fire, Jimmy the Butcher seemed to come to life.

"Pat and Mike, the two Micks, have themselves a terrible fight. Name-callin' . . . fists . . . a real corker. Pat stomps out of the bar, sayin' he'll never speak to Mike again. On his way home, he finds a lantern layin' in the gutter. Yep, a gen-u-ine *magic* lantern."

Jimmy bent down and pretended to pick it up, study it, and rub it. "He give that thing a little diddle, and out pops a genie the size of a Model T. Yep. And this genie, he says for Pat to make a wish. Well, Pat starts to thinkin' about money and barrels of beer and the new *soubrette* at the Howard, and while he's thinkin', the genie says, 'Just one catch. Whatever you ask for, your buddy Mike gets double.' "

Jimmy took off his derby and scratched his head. " 'You mean that if I wish for a million bucks, Mike gets two, and if I ask for a night with Blanche Sweet, Mike gets a weekend?' And the genie said, 'Yep. One for you, two for him.'

"So Pat thinks about the fight, then he says, 'If it's all the same to you . . . I'll take me a glass eye.' "

Jimmy rattled his derby on top of his head and jumped off the cargo hatch. The laughter and applause rolled into the blackness and were lost above the sound of the waves.

Tom Tracy was the last to stop laughing, but Rachel sensed more bitterness than mirth beside her.

Starr looked toward the shadows where they stood. "You like that one, Tommy?"

"It sounds like the history of Ireland."

"But, Mr. Tracy," said Dawson, "is it the Catholics or the Protestants askin' for the glass eye?"

Jimmy the Butcher threw up his hands. "Ah, cripes. I tell a joke, it starts talk about the troubles. Stupid is what it is."

"Perhaps, Jimmy." Hugh Dawson lit a match and drew the flame into his pipe. "A stupid thing to be fightin' the battles of the Reformation in 1916. But you Americans ought to understand. You've got the strongest civil constitution in the world—"

"That's because we have democracy," said Tracy angrily. "Why won't the Brits and the Protestants of Ulster let Ireland have democracy?"

"You elect members of Parliament," answered Dawson calmly. "And you'll have Home Rule when the war ends."

"And while the war goes on," said the captain from the quarterdeck, "the Protestants worm Ulster away from the south. That's not the kind of democracy my great grandfather fought for, is it?"

"Well, the answer is simple." Dawson pointed his pipe at Father O'Fearna. "It's somethin' he knows better than any of us."

The priest brought his hand to his throat, as if to cover his collar. But he had not worn the collar since the *Abigail* left Boston.

"Once the priests start whisperin' into the ears of all the Catholic legislators in a Home Rule government, the Protestants'll lose the right to divorce, the right to free speech . . . we'll lose everything because we're the minority."

"You're the minority now," cracked Tracy, "and you *have* everything."

Dawson laughed and snapped the pipe into his mouth. "That's the part I can't dispute."

Rachel had always liked it when Tommy turned a small joke during a political argument. In this strange place, in this strange debate, it made her feel that there was still cause for hope. She reached out and squeezed his arm.

He looked at her and winked, but she did not see the smile that usually came with his joke. She saw only hatred, and it frightened her.

"Don't they call the Catholics the niggers of Ireland?" said Henry Huntoon.

"In Ulster, they do," answered Starr.

"Then this Black Baptist's for freein' the slaves."

"You've got the wrong race," said Dawson. "We're like the Americans when they conquered the Indians. We came with Cromwell, we tamed the wilds, and we stayed. After three centuries, we're as Irish as you are."

"But the whites killed off the Indians," said Martin Mahoney, with sudden, surprising anger. "There were too many of us to kill off, even with the famine."

Sean O'Fearna raised his hands. "Now, gentlemen. Let's calm ourselves. We seek a meeting of the minds, not more hatred."

"You're right, Father." Martin spat a gob of tobacco over the side. "Just tell us one thing, Hugh. If you're as Irish as us, why is the flag you fly the Union Jack?"

"The insoluble question," said Dawson. "What do we do to answer it?"

"Well"—Starr rubbed his hand across the red beard—"if it's all the same to you . . . I'll take me a glass eye."

This time, the laughter was more nervous and no one applauded the punch line.

In the shadows, Tracy looked at Rachel and whispered, "If it's all the same to Hugh, we'll do it with this"—he reached down and pulled a knife from his boot—"and we'll start with him."

"No, Tommy." Rachel's eyes filled with tears. She realized she no longer knew him.

25

On the second weekend of April, William Clarke and his wife attended a wedding in Dublin. The daughter of a prominent Ascendancy family, one that boasted some of the finest horsemen in the kingdom, was marrying a lieutenant in the Royal Dublin Fusiliers.

It was a sedate affair, in spite of the gay splashes of color on the military tunics of the young men, because the groom's unit was bound for the front the following week. However, while festivity might have been wanting, there was a sure sense of history in the church where Cromwell stabled his horses, where Dean Swift preached his rage, and where the moldering battle flags from three centuries of British warfare hung proud and dust covered, fitting witnesses to the wedding of a soldier.

A well-placed Fenian bomb, thought William Clarke, would have destroyed most of the viceregal government of Ireland, including Undersecretary Matthew Nathan and the viceroy himself. But even in the blackest days of the Land League, no Fenian had ever dared bomb a church. And, at least according to the leading politicians, these were cooperative times in Ireland.

Ian Lambert-Jones, one of the groom's guests, recognized Clarke immediately. The resident magistrate's bearing, his finely cut wardrobe, the scar on his cheek, and his handsome wife were well known in horse circles. After the ceremony, Lambert-Jones approached them.

Mrs. Clarke was chatting with the viceroy's wife. The resident magistrate was reading a plaque on the wall near the main entrance.

Lambert-Jones said, "We've corresponded so often, it's a pleasure to meet you, sir."

Clarke turned and spoke as though he had known Lambert-Jones for years. "Have you ever heard the expression 'To chance one's arm,' Lieutenant?"

"No, sir, I haven't."

"It was born right here, in 1492. The Earl of Kildare and the Earl of Ormond had some sort of argument, and Kildare was besieged in the chapterhouse. Ormond had the upper hand, but he wanted to make peace. He went to the door of the chapterhouse and promised safe conduct to Kildare and his followers, but Kildare would hear none of it. He trusted Ormond not a bit. So Ormond cut a hole in the door and, in a supreme gesture of trust, thrust his arm into the chapterhouse."

"Was the arm cut off?"

Clarke laughed. "That was the fear. But those were more chivalrous times, Lieutenant. The siege ended and the two earls became friends again. . . . Things are somewhat more complicated today."

"I leave the complexities to the politicians, your honor." Lambert-Jones gave a half bow and clicked his heels. Whenever he wore dress reds, white gloves, ceremonial saber, and the decorations from Neuve-Chapelle, such gestures seemed appropriate.

"Spoken like a soldier. 'Theirs not to reason why . . .' "

" 'Theirs but to do and die.' "

"Excellent." Clarke smiled. He liked the young lieutenant already. "Give me Tennyson any day over Yeats and the young rabble-rousers of the Gaelic revival."

Lambert-Jones introduced the young lady at his side, Jane Carruthers, and invited the Clarkes to ride in his carriage to the reception at Dublin Castle. The journey down St. Patrick's Street took only a few minutes, and with the ladies present, the gentlemen had neither the time nor the inclination to discuss anything other than the dank spring weather and Irish horsemanship.

"Ian has told me all about your champion, Fire," said Miss Carruthers. "From what I've heard, he sounds more like an animal god than a mere equine."

The scar on Clarke's cheek brightened. "The lieutenant has excellent taste in horses, and, may I say, dear lady, in the fairer sex, as well."

Jane Carruthers answered with a decorous little nod, as though accustomed to such compliments. Her yellow dress contrasted perfectly with the red of Lambert-Jones's tunic, and her air of complacency, not unusual in a young lady of her breeding, seemed somehow heightened, perhaps because she, unlike the bride, had chosen a beau who would never again face fire on the Western Front.

Clarke's wife leaned forward and patted the girl's knee. "Never mind, dear. They'll stop calling you the 'fair sex' when you prove that you can ride their horses as well as they can."

Jane slipped an arm into her escort's. "I've proved that already."

"Then it's settled." Clarke looked at his wife. "They're coming to Ballinakill House on the earliest possible weekend. They can ride to their heart's content."

In his mind, Ian Lambert-Jones looked for an excuse. He felt less affection for Jane than she for him, and like her, he understood the significance of his shattered knee: He was a living hero in a land where eligible males grew scarcer all the time. Jane Carruthers was only one of several young women who enjoyed his company.

"Do you think my parents would object, Ian?"

"Nonsense," said Clarke. "We're the best chaperons in the west of Ireland. What about Easter?"

"They have family," said his wife, "and our Rebecca will be out to Ballinakill with her children."

WILLIAM MARTIN

"Easter would not be a good idea." Lambert-Jones ran a finger around the collar of his tunic.

"You can't take leave?" asked Clarke.

"Unlikely, sir."

Clarke turned again to the girl and took her hands. "Well, then, young lady, you come. We always have plenty of lamb on Easter, and perhaps the lieutenant will find it in his heart to follow you."

The carriage clattered through the arch on the north side of the castle and stopped at the entrance to the state apartments. Liveried attendants opened the door and helped the ladies down.

Then the gentlemen climbed out, and Lambert-Jones said, "Your district's been quiet since the wire-cutting?"

"As quiet as the grave."

"Any information on the perpetrators?"

"Dear boy." Clarke removed his homburg. "I *know* who did it."

"Why on earth haven't you arrested him?"

"Because his father seeks to protect him by passing me information about others in the district. What's more, if I give him enough rope . . ."

Lambert-Jones smiled and gave the resident magistrate a small salute. But before they could discuss the matter of Padraic Starr, Mrs. Clarke and Miss Carruthers were ushering them upstairs to the reception.

It was a grand source of irony, thought Lambert-Jones, that so much in Ireland was named to honor St. Patrick and so little of it honored the Catholicism that he brought to the island. St. Patrick's Cathedral had once been Catholic, of course. In 1320, the Pope had even founded a Catholic University there, but Henry VIII had changed all that. And St. Patrick's Hall, the center of Dublin Castle, had seldom, in the memory of Ian Lambert-Jones, hosted a Catholic wedding reception.

It was the most splendid room in all of Dublin, eighty feet long, forty feet wide, with arching windows and high ceilings and massive crystal chandeliers. There were Louis Quatorze chairs and settees covered in blue and red velvet, enormous and intricately patterned carpets, and enough gold in the gilded ceiling medallions to support everyone in a town like Dunslea for a year.

The wedding party stood in front of the fireplace and received guests, while champagne flowed discreetly and a string quartet played pieces by Bach and Mozart. Lambert-Jones was too polite to mention that if Bach and Mozart had been alive in 1916, their patrons would have been the Kaiser and Emperor Franz Josef.

Lambert-Jones and Miss Carruthers went through the line, visited with friends, and nibbled on canapés brought by polite Irish maids, and eventually the lieutenant found his way to the corner where William Clarke was in conversation with Undersecretary Matthew Nathan.

The undersecretary was a short, compact man of fifty-two. He had shiny black hair, a neat black mustache, a great store of nervous energy, and he had dedicated himself so completely to the service of the royal government that he had never married. His dedication had been rewarded with the thankless task of administering Ireland. Lambert-Jones thought he performed diligently and sometimes intelligently, and in a land where Catholics and Protestants had spent much of the last seven centuries trying to rip one another to pieces, Lambert-Jones appreciated Nathan's Jewish perspective.

"Ah, here's the man who may best answer you, William." Nathan's mustache twitched when he smiled.

"At your service, gentlemen," said Lambert-Jones.

"Resident Magistrate Clarke was asking me about the business with that deserter, the one you've taken such interest in . . ."

"Padraic Starr, yes. It seems that he has disappeared. We've even requested the assistance of the American Secret Service, and they've turned up nothing."

Clarke snatched a glass of champagne as it went by and placed his empty glass on the tray. "Not surprising, that. You should send in more of our own people."

"Those we've sent are either dead or disappeared." Lambert-Jones wrapped his hand around the hilt of his saber. "Frankly, I don't believe that Starr is still in Boston."

Nathan's black eyebrows rose. "Indeed?"

"He's on his way back to Ireland, sir."

"Now, why on earth should a deserter safe in America come back?"

"As far as we can tell, he's a member of the Irish Republican Brotherhood."

Nathan nodded. "Another group of troublemakers best ignored."

"They may not allow us to ignore them for much longer." Lambert-Jones raised his sword a few inches in the scabbard and allowed it to slip back, a small sound of punctuation.

"My sentiments as well." Clarke snatched another glass of champagne.

Nathan gave him a frown, more for the fourth glass of champagne than the sentiments.

Clarke smiled at Nathan. "If I were in Dublin, I should not allow rabble to march in the streets, calling themselves a local defense force."

Nathan raised his chin and clasped his hands behind his back. "Castle policy on the matter is firm, Resident Magistrate. In spite of the activities of these rebel groups, and the weekly rumors we hear of a rising, we believe they're powerless as long as they do not have the majority of the Irish people behind them."

Clarke laughed. "That was what an earlier King George said about a group of rabble-rousing Americans."

A young maid came by with a tray of toast slices, lemon slices, and caviar. Clarke spooned a piece of toast with fish eggs and gave the maid a little grin. Even if Clarke had not been a horseman, Lambert-Jones decided that by now he would have liked him anyway, because the RM held his liquor, had an eye for the ladies, and displayed no fear of his superiors at the Castle.

"Our mistake in 1775," said Nathan, in his schoolmaster's voice, "was that we gave them credence by responding so harshly to their agitation."

"Ah, yes, I'd forgotten." Clarke looked at Lambert-Jones. "Had we given them their heads, we might be holding this conversation in the U.K. dominion of New York or Massachusetts."

Lambert-Jones wanted to agree, but a young lieutenant working at the Castle should not incur the anger of the undersecretary.

"*I'd* have given them their heads," continued Clarke, "on the ends of my pikes."

Nathan brought a hand to his face and smoothed his mustache. "The Irish have given troops to the Crown, because the Crown has promised Home Rule when the war ends. We intend to do nothing to jeopardize that kind of support."

"We already *have* jeopardized it," answered Clarke. The champagne sloshed over the top of his glass. He slammed it down on a nearby table, then came back at Nathan.

"I am a Unionist, Sir Undersecretary. When the vote for Home Rule came in Parliament, I led a delegation to London to convince our MP to cast against it."

322

"And did he?" asked Nathan mildly.

"Of course not. He's a Catholic from Connemara. We lost in Parliament. I was prepared to accept the loss and uphold the new law, but now Home Rule is facing amendment and the trust of the Catholic majority has been violated."

Clarke's voice had risen enough that heads were turning, and Mrs. Clarke was pushing her way to her husband's side. However, the string quartet continued to play and delicately washed away any embarrassment.

Clarke picked up his glass and drained it. Then he said softly, "I hope the policies of Dublin Castle are worthy."

"We all pray to the same God." Nathan bowed and excused himself.

After Clarke waved his wife away, Lambert-Jones said, "On the one hand, you want rebel heads, and on the other, you curse the Ulstermen. I would not have expected that."

"I've been a barrister for twenty years, Lieutenant, a magistrate for twenty more. I believe in the rule of law."

"So do I."

"If the lawbreaking Mr. Starr is coming back, what was he after in America?"

"Money or guns, most likely." Lambert-Jones toyed with the hilt of his saber.

"Have guest and crew lists been checked on American ships bound for Ireland?"

"It's unlikely he's traveling under his real name."

Clarke nodded. "Has the navy been informed to watch for neutral vessels approaching the Connemara coast, gunrunners from America, perhaps?"

"Your mind works like my own. I've requested the cargo manifests of every vessel that's left Boston in the last month."

"And?"

"The wheels of the American Customs Bureau turn slowly."

"They'll never get through the Royal Navy."

Lambert-Jones shrugged. "The Royal Navy is spread thin watching for Germans. They may, however, have a bit of help."

"According to wireless reports, the mid-Atlantic is facing a storm with eighty-knot winds."

The resident magistrate thought this over, studied Lambert-Jones's sword, his medals, his red uniform, then stepped closer to him and whispered, "Is it Easter?"

Lambert-Jones brought a white glove to his eye and rubbed at an imaginary eyelash. "I beg pardon, sir?"

"Something's coming, Lieutenant. It would be just like these Gaelic poets, with their love of symbolism, to do it at Easter."

"It would seem that way, wouldn't it?"

Clarke nodded. He understood. "We shall be vigilant in Holy Week, then. And look forward to your visit."

"I'm afraid duty may call in Dublin."

"It may also call in Dunslea."

A maid came by with another tray of glasses. Clarke and Lambert-Jones each lifted one.

"To the rule of law," said Clarke.

"To the power of the mid-Atlantic storm."

26

*I*t was upon them.

The sky at noon was nearly black. The rain slashed down in squalls so sharp that the captain could not see the tops of the masts. The ocean became a desert of fearsome black dunes that rose and shifted and fell and nearly buried the *Abigail* every time she rolled. And the wind screamed, steady and unceasing, straight and hard from the north-north-west.

The schooner's topsails were reefed, her lowers swung loose to leeward, and she was running like a frightened child in a nightmare.

In twelve hours she had traveled over a hundred miles, more distance than she had made in any half-day since the start of the voyage. But now she was scudding south-southwest, ninety degrees away from her goal. If the gale roared for long enough, she would eventually fetch up somewhere on the coast of Spain.

There were those aboard her, however, who doubted that they would ever see land again, and those who feared that they would never see another day. In the forecastle, everything was soaked through, the clothes, the bedding, the duffel bags, the men. Decks and bulkheads were covered with water. Heavy seas pounding over the port side had smashed the door and broken the portlights and even put out the oil lamp.

The priest prayed. Jimmy the Butcher shivered in the wet cold and tried to make up a song to accompany his own chattering teeth. Danny Tracy said, "Wake me when there's sail to change," then dropped onto his soaking berth and pulled the covers over his head. Martin Mahoney sat at the table with a pot in front of him and filled the forecastle with the stench of his vomit.

After he secured the galley, Henry Huntoon stomped into the forecastle. His black face shone under the film of water, and salt crystals had formed in the tight curls of his beard. "Prayin', pukin', sleepin', and shakin'. If somebody in here shittin' his drawers, that's the five things a man's like to do in his first bad blow."

"We ain't goin' down, are we, Henry?" asked Jimmy between shakes.

"I been in worse than this, Butcher Man, and I ain't ever sunk yet. A coaster like the old *Abbie* here sails the roughest seas there is, 'tween Hatt'ras and the Maritimes. She'll do fine."

As if in response, the *Abigail* rose suddenly, tottered like a drunk at the top of a wave, then plummeted down into the trough, slamming everyone against the inboard bulkhead. Henry cursed, rosary beads flew, a pot of vomit spilled across the table. An instant later, the sea burst through the forecastle door.

At the stern, Tom Tracy jammed his knees into the spokes of the wheel. With the wind and sea pounding after the *Abigail,* there was no other way to keep her on course, and as it was, that last wave had nearly spun him over.

The captain stood beside him, his hand wrapped around a safety line, his sou'wester glistening in the gray light. Every member of the crew had rested a few hours since midnight, but Jason Pratt had not moved from the quarterdeck. He had made a decision that the mate called suicidal, and he planned to see it through.

From midnight to dawn, the *Abigail* had been able to ride with the winds, making up to ten knots while holding her course. Then, around dawn, the seas rose, the gale turned vicious, and Jason Pratt had decided to surrender.

"Run out the sails and raise the centerboard," he had ordered.

"In this sea?" Deems had said.

Pratt had repeated the order.

Deems had obeyed, then followed the captain below. In the privacy of the cabin, with their rain slickers dripping onto the Oriental carpet, Mason Deems had picked up the Bible. "All the power of this book will not help you, Captain, if you run before this wind."

"We've handled gales like this, before, Mr. Deems, from St. John all the way to Savannah."

"Not like this, Captain. You scud in this, you'll catch a followin' sea as sure as perdition, and that'll be the end of us. And while the Almighty may think that's a good idea, considerin' the cargo and the crew, there's a few aboard worth savin'."

"You try me, Mason Deems."

"And you, Captain, you're a man who knows all the answers, but he ain't yet figured out the right questions. Bring her into the wind, lower the centerboard, drop everything but the jib, and try to hold your position with a sea anchor."

"No. If we fight this sea with the centerboard down, we'll break her apart."

A shallow-draft schooner like the *Abigail* lacked the stability of a square-rigger and needed a centerboard to counterbalance the force of the wind. But a schooner that ran in a heavy blow with the centerboard extended faced enormous stress above the water and below.

Deems had shouted, "Without the centerboard, we're no better than a cork with canvas. We'll pitchpole in a flash."

"We've too much ballast to pitchpole. I'll risk that before I'll see us break up."

"She won't break up if you lower your sails and centerboard, and you won't catch a followin' sea."

"We can't lower them now," Pratt had admitted. "If we try, we'll tear them apart and lose crew as well."

"You'll tear them apart anyway. And lose your rigging. And take yourself down to bare pole before the day is out."

"We're committed." Pratt had turned.

"Captain! You are a coward." Deems had held up the Bible. "And this book offers no hope for cowards. You run before the wind as you've run all your life, from your heritage and your faith and the responsibilities of a man from your class, and now you run guns with Papists and Jews and burlesque whores." Deems had slammed the Bible down on the table, as loud as a gunshot. "God help us all."

326

"Indeed, Mr. Deems."

In the five hours since, Mason Deems had remained below, reading his Bible, while Jason Pratt faced the storm and proved to himself the quality of his judgment and courage.

"Step lively, Mr. Starr," the captain shouted through the speaking trumpet. "We need another hand at the helm."

Padraic Starr clutched a safety line and slid aft along the pitching, wave-washed deck. He reached the steps on the port side, waited for the ship to steady, then came up to the quarter-deck.

Hugh Dawson was crouched at the afterhouse, close by the pumps. The *Abigail* was taking on water, and the sideshaft engine was pumping furiously, pouring it out of the two bell-shaped collars that looked like small fountains in a rainstorm.

"Don't let that engine break down, or we'll be at the bottom inside of an hour," Starr shouted.

"I been givin' it some thought." He smiled from under his black sou'wester. Long icicles drooped from the ends of his mustache. "It's a quick way to soak your munitions."

"Don't do it, Hugh."

"We're closin' on Ireland, Starr. We can't chit-chat much longer."

The *Abigail* pitched to starboard, and Starr slipped toward the small, knee-high engine that sat exposed on the deck. Dawson grabbed him before he landed amid the gears and shafts and spinning belts.

For a strange moment, the men were in each other's arms.

"Is it true what they say about these schooners, Hugh?"

"What's that?"

"That they'll scare you to death before they'll ever kill you?"

"I'll pray that it is."

Starr grabbed the binnacle, levered himself to his feet, and glanced down at the compass. "Unless we heave to and hold our position, I may get another whole week to turn you into a rebel."

"You keep talking, Padr'ic, and so will I."

"Mr. Starr!" bellowed the captain. "I'll mind the binnacle. Your job is at the helm!"

"Aye! Aye!" shouted Starr. As he turned, his stomach seemed to drop out of him, and for the first time in his life, his bladder emptied itself.

A wave the size of Croagh Patrick was rising over the stern.

327

The top of it was frothed with blowing, spit-like spume. The body was slimy, shimmering gray, the color of a slug.

Starr screamed, "Hold tight!" and felt his own warm urine run down his leg.

Then, in an instant, the sea surrounded him, blocked out the light, sucked away the air, and swallowed the quarterdeck.

The water smashed through the companionway hatch and exploded into the main cabin, soaking Pratt's rug and knocking his favorite leather chair into the little fireplace. Chunks of glowing coal hit the water and hissed madly, filling the cabin with steam.

Rachel was sitting on her berth. She saw the puddle of water push under the door of her tiny cabin. She pulled open her door, and the water flowed in around her feet. *They were sinking!* She jumped to the ladder and fought furiously against the cataract rushing down the companionway.

Mr. Deems grabbed her and pulled her backward. She splashed into the water now a foot deep in the companionway. Deems stepped over her and swung a leg onto the ladder. Rachel grabbed at his foot and tried to pull him off the ladder.

"Let me out!" she screamed. "We're sinking!"

"Put on your weather gear and stand by for orders."

"Are we sinking?"

The force of the water was subsiding. The wash in the companionway was already running down the bilges. The wave had not taken her after all.

"We won't sink if Papists and Jews can pray to Christ and pull the halyards when I tell them."

On deck the water was rushing off through the scuppers. The wave had nearly broken Tom Tracy's back, but he was still at the helm, soaked through, gasping, and now, alone.

He called the captain's name, but there was no answer. He held tight to the helm. He would not let the *Abigail* go over.

For the thirty seconds that the wave was upon them, Padraic Starr thought that he was going to die. He did not pray, however. He lay on his belly and opened his mouth and screamed his fury against whatever fate had brought the wave, and he screamed until the water washed over him and he could breathe again.

Now, his hand was wrapped around a port rail baluster, and something was pressing against his shoulder. He pushed at it, and Jason Pratt screamed, "My leg!"

Pratt had been knocked down the narrow aisle between the port rail and the afterhouse. His right leg had caught on the afterhouse corner and was snapped below the knee, bent away at a grotesque angle, so that the bone was pressing against the fabric of his trousers.

Hugh Dawson leaned over Starr's shoulder. "Compound . . . bad."

"Let's get him below."

"No!" screamed Pratt, and he tried to get up. "I'll stand the deck till this ends."

"You've shattered your leg, man," answered Dawson. "You'll stand nowhere."

Mason Deems pounded on the ship's bell, and five men turned out of the forecastle.

"Hurry it up! Hurry it up!" Deems needed no speaking trumpet. His harsh voice cut across the wind and the rain, and now that he had taken command, it carried confidence with its anger.

"The Lord helps those who help themselves, Mr. Huntoon. He even helps Papists. We're turnin' her into the wind."

Starr came down the quarterdeck. "The captain sent up an order: Let her run."

Deems smashed his quirt into the puddle on the roof of the afterhouse. "I'm in command now, Mr. Starr. And somewhere out there is a wave worse than that last one. If you don't want it to take you stern first, you'll take my orders, or by the Lord Christ, I'll shoot you dead and make no repent."

Deems pulled a revolver from his pocket.

Starr looked down at the gray metal of the pistol glinting in the gray light. "I didn't know the mate went armed."

"On this ship he does. And it will take very little to make him shoot."

Jason Pratt was in his bunk, his face ashen, his fists clenched tight on the coverlet. Hugh Dawson had given him a long drink of whiskey, and it was beginning to dull his pain.

"I'm needed above," said Dawson. He was as tough as any man aboard, but he knew that he would be sickened by the sight of the leg.

"Send down the priest," said Rachel. "He knows about these things." Then she held her breath and carefully cut away the leg of the captain's trousers.

"Oh . . ." Rachel brought her hand to her mouth and nearly vomited. White bone had broken through the flesh, and blood was oozing out around it.

"Is it bad?" whispered Pratt.

"You'll be all right." Rachel's voice quavered. "We'll fix you good."

Sean O'Fearna stepped into the captain's room, saw the leg, and muttered, "Mother of God."

The ship pitched, and the captain screamed.

"More whiskey," said the priest. "We'll have to splint it."

"What's that sound?" Pratt's eyes opened wide, and for a moment the color rushed back to his face.

From somewhere within the ship came a deep, grinding rumble. Like a stone, thought O'Fearna, rolling across the mouth of a tomb.

"They're lowering the centerboard," said O'Fearna. "Mr. Deems is bringin' her about."

"That's against my order . . ." Pratt grabbed the side of the berth and tried to raise himself, just enough to put pressure on the leg, scream again, and pass out.

"Good. I never done this myself. I don't need him squirmin' like a worm on a hook." The priest touched the flesh around the white bone and gently twisted the leg. The captain did not stir.

"Do you know a prayer for this, Father?" asked Rachel.

"I don't think my prayers have much strength right now, Miss Levka. Besides, the Lord helps those who help themselves."

He put both hands on the leg and moved it about.

"Where did you learn this?"

"An Irish priest learns a little bit of everything. Doctors can be few and far between, but there's a church in every village."

The oil lamp swung back and forth above their heads, and their shadows swung on the walls.

"We couldn't help Jenny Malloy, but with your help, we'll save this man's leg." He took a deep breath, then wrapped his hands around the calf. "We file down the end of the bone some, tuck it back inside the flesh, then lay the filed end against whatever's inside and splint it."

"Thank God we have morphine."

The *Abigail* was lumbering about like a freight engine in a roundhouse.

330

Mason Deems screamed his orders from the helm, while the others slowly sheeted in the mainsail and spanker, keeping them carefully angled to the wind. The mizzen sail was already gone, torn to shreds by a powerful gust, but the jib and jumbo were still set, giving her the stability she needed.

Rachel came on deck, calling for Mr. Huntoon.

He was directly behind the wheelbox, working the spanker sheet with Starr and Jimmy McHale.

"If you want to talk to him, grab a line and give him a hand," growled Deems.

"We need a wood file, boiled in water, and something to make a splint," she shouted.

Deems gave a laugh, bitter and contemptuous. "We need a quiet sea and a gentle breeze, too. But first we need to come about!"

The *Abigail* was broadside to the wind now, in the most dangerous part of the maneuver, and the rain was hitting her as hard and straight as the spray from a machine gun.

"Grab an end, honey!" shouted Huntoon. "Mr. Deems, he may be a Presbyterian, but he know how to handle a schooner."

"We can use all the help we can get in this wind," added Starr. "Do as he says!"

Rachel picked up the line and began to pull in the same slow rhythm as the three men. The rain was cascading down, and in spite of Deems's order, she was not wearing weather gear. In a few seconds, her hair plastered itself to her face and her blouse soaked to her breasts.

Amidships, Tom and Danny Tracy and Martin Mahoney were hauling the mainsail sheet with Hugh Dawson.

"Pull steady, boys," Dawson was saying, "but not too hard. We don't want to tip this old lady over or break her up."

"Ain't that what you're plannin'?" grunted Danny Tracy. His complexion was as white as the foam on the waves, and a dribble of green bile ran with the rainwater down the front of his oilskin.

"Shut up, son." Martin Mahoney spat a brown gob of tobacco that flew into the air and splatted against the sail.

The great square of canvas was stretched so wet and so tight that it looked almost transparent. Every timber groaned under the strain of it.

"We *may* sink her, son," said Dawson, "but what we're tryin' to do is to save her."

Danny squinted into the rain. "My brother says you and that fuckin' Prod up there at the helm tried to set us afire, and you'll do your damnedest to keep us from Ireland."

"Pull steady, son," growled Dawson, "or you'll be dead before the Royal Navy ever gets the chance to kill you."

Tom Tracy glanced over his shoulder at the black mustache and the black eyes and the black oilskin that made Hugh Dawson look like the villain in a picture-show melodrama. But in the slashing rain, they all wore black oilskins, and they could be nothing but allies.

"Stop lookin' at each other and fetch in there!" screamed Deems over the roar of the wind.

"Fuck him, too," shouted Danny Tracy.

"Shut up, son," grunted Martin.

Because of the shape of her hull, the *Abigail* did not point well into the wind, but she was answering to Deems's grip like an obedient mount.

Tracy felt the bullets of rain starting to hit him in the side of the face instead of the back. That meant the moment was almost upon them. Every hand knew that when the ship turned into the wind and the sails began to slap, they would have just seconds to lower. The faster they dropped the sail, the less likely the damage to crew or ship. And the water-soaked canvas would come down fast.

The sheet connected to the gaff controlled the angle of the sail to the wind, and halyards on both sides of the ship raised and lowered the canvas. The halyard on the starboard side connected to the boom throat, which wrapped around the mast. The port-side halyard connected to the peak of the boom, which carried most of the weight of the sail.

"When she starts to luff," shouted Dawson, "Martin ties the sheet and secures the boom."

"Right." Martin spat.

"Tommy takes the throat halyard. Danny and me take the peak."

"Why you and me?" squawked Danny.

"Shut up," grunted Martin.

"Because you and me is closest to the port side, sonny boy," answered Dawson.

"Pull her in a bit more," screamed Deems. "A bit more."

Now Tracy felt the rain hard against his left cheek. A wave burst over the bow and the spume blew straight down the length of the ship. They were into the wind. The sails went slack and began to flap madly.

"They're luffin'!" screamed Mason Deems. "Drop 'em now!"

Henry Huntoon secured the spanker sheet in an instant. Starr and Jimmy released the halyards, and the sail came screaming down the mast.

Martin Mahoney fumbled to secure the mainmast sheet. Tracy ran to starboard and loosened the main throat halyard. Danny and Dawson jumped to port and released the peak. Mason Deems held her into the wind. But the wind shifted suddenly a few degrees to the north, and the rolling seas knocked the *Abigail* a point toward the south. The half-set mainsail bellied out, and the boom swung hard to port.

Martin Mahoney felt the line rush through his fingers and the boom smashed into his face.

The sea blew up over the starboard side, knocking Tracy to the deck and then pounding after the boom.

Danny Tracy and Hugh Dawson had no chance to react. The boom swung out over their heads. The *Abigail* heeled suddenly. They lost their balance, and the wave knocked them both over the side.

"Danny!" screamed Tom.

"Forget them!" shouted Deems. "Drop the sail!"

The rest of the crew were rushing forward, while Deems tried to turn the bow into the wind again.

Tracy scrambled across the deck to the port rail. Dawson's slicked black sou'wester appeared first in the white foam. Somehow he had managed to keep his grip on the halyard, and he was riding up the side of a wave that had just rolled over the *Abigail*.

The wave lifted him high enough that he was on eye level with Tracy. His face seemed calm. His jaw was set at a familiar angle, as though he had just snapped his pipe between his teeth. Tom Tracy saw no terror, as though Dawson did not fear death or, more likely, did not intend to die.

Then Danny Tracy's head appeared behind Dawson, higher up the slope of the wave. His eyes were wide with fright. He was flailing madly, and his oilskinned body beneath the water made him look like a large black insect trapped in a gray-green stream of spruce gum.

Tracy screamed his brother's name above the wind, but the wave rolled on and carried the boy away from the ship.

Had the schooner been under sail, Danny and Hugh Dawson would both be riding the wake to their deaths by now, but the *Abigail* was wallowing and the mainsail was luffing again.

"Drop the sail!" Deems was screaming. "Drop the sail!"

Henry Huntoon pulled the halyard from the water and wound it several times around a belaying pin. Then he shouted, "Stand clear!" and with a snap of his knife, he cut the line. The canvas collapsed and the gaff came thundering down on top of it.

At the same time, Tom Tracy was tearing off his oilskin and his shoes.

"No, Tommy!" Starr shouted.

"Don't do it, Tommy!" Rachel was rushing forward after Starr, her hand clutching a safety line.

"We're losin' Danny!" Tracy pushed Starr aside and tried to climb onto the rail.

Starr grabbed him by the collar.

Tracy kept struggling. Rachel let go of the line and threw her arms around Tracy and Starr at the same time. "No, Tommy! Padr'ic's right!"

Tracy tried to throw them both off, but he did not have the strength.

While they wrestled, Henry Huntoon dragged Jimmy the Butcher to the rail and together, they began to haul on the line that ran out into the water. Dawson was moving toward the ship, and somehow, in his flailing, Danny had found the tail of the halyard and was riding it as well.

"Hey," shouted Huntoon. "Stop your dancin' around and give us a pull! We got two black seals on the line."

In an instant, three more were hauling on the halyard, and Hugh Dawson was bouncing against the hull. Starr hurriedly made a loop in another line and dropped it down. Dawson grabbed for it, and when he had it, he released the halyard.

But Tom Tracy's eyes were riveted to the black figure six or eight feet behind Dawson. "Hold on, Danny! Hold on!"

The boy seemed to be weakening. A small wave washed over him, and for a moment he disappeared.

"We're losin' him," cried Tom. "Pull harder!"

He yanked the rope, but Danny's body did not move through the water.

"He lost the rope!" cried Henry. "And he ain't kickin'!"

"Kick, Danny!" called Starr.

"C'mon, Danny!" screamed Rachel.

"Kick! Like a trouper, kid!" shouted Jimmy the Butcher, then he dropped the halyard and fell back to a safety line.

Danny sank again. He did not have the strength to reach the ship.

Starr looked down at Dawson, who had grabbed the halyard again and was looking back at Danny.

"Help him, Hugh! Help the kid!" called Starr.

Tracy saw Dawson's eyes turn to him.

"Help him!" cried Tracy.

A wave lifted Dawson and bounced him gently against the hull. He gave Tracy one more look. The gaze was calm, almost serene, thought Tracy, the expression of a man who had won a victory. He looped the lifeline around his arm and put the halyard between his teeth and pushed away from the hull.

Tom Tracy did not feel the driving rain or the pitching ship, he did not hear the screaming wind or the shouts of the others. His eyes and mind were focused completely on the two black heads bobbing toward each other in the raging sea.

A wave swept down on them and they disappeared.

"Tighten the lifeline!" called Huntoon. Everyone pulled, the rope snapped taut, and Dawson's head popped up again. He reached the boy and threw the lifeline around his chest. His movements were slow and labored now. The heavy oilskin and the bitter cold and the pounding of the sea were wearing him quickly. But he still had the strength to yell at the boy and slap at his face and make him keep his head out of the water.

"C'mon, Hughie, my boy," muttered Starr to himself. "C'mon!" he shouted at the top of his lungs.

Dawson turned toward the ship and shot a black arm into the air. "Pull!" he screamed over the wind.

"Pull!" screamed Tracy. "Pull now!" He grabbed the lifeline from Starr's hands and began to haul madly while the others pulled hard on Dawson's halyard. The two black heads shot back toward the ship. Fifteen feet, ten feet, five . . .

"Don't give up, Hughie!" Starr called.

"C'mon, Dawson! Get him aboard and I'll tell you another joke!" added Jimmy McHale, who had retreated now to wrap his arms around the mainmast.

Then the *Abigail* shivered. A huge sullen wave smashed into her bow and swept down the length of her, slamming people to the deck and burying two black heads in seawater.

"Pull!" screamed Tom Tracy, before he was back on his feet.

"Pull!" His hands had been toughened to leather, but he tore so frantically that he covered the rope with his blood.

Danny Tracy appeared again from the water, unconscious. Padraic Starr grabbed the line with Tom Tracy, and together they pulled. The boy came out of the water, slammed up the side of the ship like a fish, and dropped onto the deck.

"Pump out the water," cried Rachel.

Tracy grabbed the boy's arms and began to work them like levers.

Starr grabbed Dawson's halyard. But Henry Huntoon had already stopped pulling. Starr tugged once, twice. The line had gone slack. Huntoon looked at Starr and shook his head.

"Damn," said Starr.

Rachel and Tom were kneeling by Danny, pumping the seawater out of him like a sideshaft engine. All at once, he retched and rolled over.

"Thank Christ," said Tom Tracy.

"Thank Dawson," said Rachel.

27

The great storm thundered across the Atlantic and blew into the Irish coast on Thursday morning. For three days it reminded the people of Connemara that spring was a fragile time. But when the sun appeared again on Palm Sunday, its path across the sky had risen high enough that even the drinkers in Finnerty's dark pub could see the change.

In the fields, the heathers were sprouting, while tulips showed green shoots in the window boxes and dooryards. At the estate on the Ballinakill Peninsula, foaling season had arrived, and on the hillsides, the ewes were dropping their lambs. Although it was still Lent and the priests wore purple in the churches, the sun had brought Easter to the earth.

But springtime meant spring offensives. On the Western Front, waves of British youth were once more hurling themselves against German defenses, while German periscopes were once more cutting wakes through the waters of the British Isles. The tone of the diplomatic notes between Washington and Berlin had grown more bellicose, the Germans claiming the right to sink armed Allied merchant ships without warning, and it seemed that soon they would extend their claim to neutral vessels as well. While the days warmed, coastwatchers reported the return of the U-boats to the shipping lanes, and the current carried wreckage into every Irish inlet and bay.

For Deirdre Hamilton, the increase in U-boat activity had meant the doubling of wireless traffic, and on this Sunday morning, her headset was alive, because thirty miles to the north, in Blacksod Bay, a U-boat had been sighted. Since the beginning of the war, U-boat commanders had been taking refuge among the deserted islands and inlets of the west coast, repairing damage, then slipping away with the night tide. But this German would not escape. He was running on the surface, apparently too damaged to dive, while a destroyer and two trawlers closed in.

One of them, against regulations, was transmitting in the clear, and Deirdre found the commentary more exciting than an Erskine Childers novel. As she followed word for word, she realized that she had at last mastered the strange alphabet. She held the headphones tight and wrote:

"D-E-S-T-R-O-Y-E-R-O-P-E-N-I-N-G-F-I-R-E . . ."

Constable Colin Shea was pumping his bicycle up the Dunslea road, toward the sound of a petrol-driven generator.

He was new to the district, new to the RIC, and as skinny as the carbine strapped to his back. His uniform fitted like a sheet. His policeman's hat, a half-size too big, rested comically on his ears. But young Constable Shea, all of twenty years old, was zealous and eager, and he understood the importance of the cable traffic passing between Dunslea and Dublin Castle. The rebels in the district were planning trouble, and it was up to the RIC to stop them.

He got off his bicycle at Deirdre Hamilton's cottage. He was perspiring from the climb, and the armpits of his green tunic were soaked through. He flicked away a droplet of sweat that gathered in the patch of hair between his eyebrows and mopped the sweat from his hatband.

He wheeled the bicycle around the side of the cottage and peered into the kitchen. Three peat bricks were burning on the hearth, and a kettle steamed above them. However, the constable did not announce himself.

He leaned the bicycle against the cottage, then went around to the shed. An old ram with dirty brown wool studied him for a moment, then went back to scratching himself against a fencepost. Shea unstrapped his carbine and pushed the door. The noise of the generator grew louder, and the smell of petrol stung his nostrils. He stepped around the generator and checked the loft, then he came back outside. His eyes followed the power cable from the generator to the roof of the cottage. And then he saw the antenna.

"D-E-S-T-R-O-Y-E-R-S-T-A-N-D-I-N-G-O-F-F-F-I-R-I-N-G-A-T-U-B-O-A-T . . ."

As she wrote, Deirdre was not certain which side she wanted to win. The Germans were helping the rebels. But her heritage and upbringing still made her proud to be Anglo-Irish, and she almost cheered to write, "U-B-O-A-T-H-I-T-G-U-N-C-R-E-W-D-E-A-D . . ."

In her excitement, Deirdre leaned too hard on her pencil. It snapped. She reached for another and saw the carbine aiming up at her from the trapdoor.

A more experienced officer would not have shouted, "Get your hands up, you bloody traitor."

A less startled rebel would not have turned and fired her .22 before trying to talk her way out.

The bullet hit the floor and tore up a burst of splinters. But the constable did not budge. He kept his elbows on the floor, his face to the sight, and he squeezed the trigger. Nothing.

Deirdre fired again. The floor beside the trap jumped with dust. As the deputy dropped through the door, a split rung snapped on the closet ladder. He lost his balance and lost his grip on the gun. Deirdre leaped across the attic, snatching for the carbine before it disappeared after him down the opening.

His hands flashed back toward the stock, but Deirdre had it. She slammed the trap, and he screamed. Then, for a few moments, there was silence.

"Miss Hamilton, I'd appreciate it if you'd be givin' me back my carbine." The muffled voice was filled with the pain of squashed fingernails and damaged pride.

Deirdre said nothing. Her hands were shaking. Her mouth was dry.

"We know what you're involved in, madam," said the voice, a bit more angrily. "Give up and it will go easier."

Her mind was clearing. She realized now what a foolish mistake she had made. She heard the young constable step back into the kitchen.

"This whole matter might be forgotten if you would be willing to cooperate."

"What matter?" she said.

For several seconds, there was no response. What was he doing? What sort of trap was he preparing? Had he found the envelope, the one with Starr's picture? She had been looking at it that morning.

"Yes . . ." The young man's voice wavered. "Yes, perhaps you're right. Perhaps . . . perhaps it's all been a mistake."

She heard his footsteps backing out of the kitchen. Let him go. Act innocent. Anyone can own a wireless.

And what will you use it for, ma'am? To communicate with my fiancé on his boat. *But he doesn't have a wireless.* He's planning to buy one. *But they're expensive.* Yes, well, I have money. *Do you have bill of sale?* Unh . . . well, Resident Magistrate, I seem to have lost it. . . .

They might not believe her.

She heard the rattling and clattering of the constable's bike. She ran to the window. Let him go and act innocent? She watched him swing out onto the road. Let him go. *No.* The envelope. No!

She *was* foolish, a foolish woman pining over an envelope of mementos. She had left it out again, on her kitchen table. Not only did it contain clippings and a photograph of Starr, but the framed citation that accompanied the Victoria Cross. In the hands of that young constable, it offered proof that Padraic Starr had been at her home.

She did not hesitate. She was a fine wing shot, better with a rifle than a handgun. She pushed up the window, aimed, and pulled the trigger. *Nothing.* She released the safety and fired.

The shot kicked up the dirt to the right of the bicycle. The constable swerved and dropped his legs to the ground to keep himself from going off the road. Another shot whined off the outcropping beyond him, where the road surface ended and the rocks of the cliff protruded from the earth. The drop to the strand was forty feet, and more in some places. He jammed the envelope into his belt and pulled his legs onto the bike.

Deirdre aimed once more and squeezed the trigger, but the bike disappeared around the bend.

Deirdre's motorcycle burst from the shed in a cloud of straw and blue exhaust. The old ram made an angry noise, backed up to charge, then ambled back to the fencepost.

Deirdre tore onto the road and around the bend in a few seconds, but the young constable had taken a quarter-mile lead and was pedaling wildly. He did not stop at the Desmond cottage or the Kellihers'. They were all at Mass, Deirdre knew, and the boy seemed intent on driving himself all the way to Dunslea. Had he been smarter, older, or perhaps less panicked, she thought, he would have stopped and thrown the bicycle at her.

Deirdre leaned over the handlebars. Her hair was snapping out straight behind her, and tears were blowing off her cheeks because she had not taken the time to pull on her goggles. To her right, the hillsides were a blur of green. To her left, the bay flashed and sparkled.

She did not know what she would do once she caught him. She could compose no innocently indignant speech, nor could she imagine herself shooting him in the head at close range. But she had to stop him.

She roared past the Desmond cottage. She closed to within a few hundred feet of the bicycle. As she went past the Kelliher cottage, she cut the gap to fifty.

Donal O'Leary heard the growl of the motorcycle. He lowered his jar and cocked his head like a curious hound at a ferret hole.

He was sitting at his parents' table for the first time in four weeks. Seamus Kilkeirnan, who had coaxed him into coming home, drank with him. After Mass, Donal's parents would be returning with Father Breen. Donal's mother had killed two chickens for Sunday dinner, and she had enlisted the parish sage and the parish priest to bring father and son to the same table. That was the first step in bringing them together again.

Donal looked at Seamus. "Deirdre?"

"She ain't expected."

Donal went to the window as the constable sped around the bend with Deirdre twenty feet behind.

"Holy Jesus!" Donal burst out of the cottage.

Above the roar of the motorcycle Deirdre was shouting, "Stop him! Stop him!"

"Stay back! I'm an officer of the king!" screamed the man in the green uniform.

A moment before they crashed, Donal saw the sprouting mustache and the mask of fear. *A boy!* But he had already committed himself. He hurtled into the bike with the force of a motorcar.

Bike and body flew into the air and hung, like a bird in the half-second after it's shot.

Then they crashed onto the rocks at the edge of the cliff. Legs and handlebars tangled. Spokes snapped. Donal's body rolled. The motorcycle spun into a skid, spraying stones like shotgun pellets.

The frightened constable tried to stand while screaming for Seamus Kilkeirnan to assist him in a citizen's arrest. He got halfway to his feet, pulled a leg from between the wheel and the handlebar, and lost his balance.

As he tottered, his face did not show terror. He did not realize that he was near the edge. He grabbed at the air, almost casually, as though reaching for a hat rack someone had moved. He grabbed again. Then he made a small sound and tipped backward. The bike fell after him, and together they bounced off jagged rocks and outcroppings, coming to rest at the base of a boulder forty feet below.

Donal ran to the edge and looked down. The rear wheel of the bike was spinning lazily. Nothing else was moving.

"Mother of Christ."

"He caught me at the wireless. He knew." Deirdre wiped the dust from her face and started down to retrieve her envelope.

Donal could not move. He had never killed before. He felt sick. A bottle of poteen appeared beneath his nose.

"Take a drink of this," said Seamus. "A man needs a bit of a drink, after seein' a terrible accident like that."

"Accident?"

Seamus gave a little nod, then drank down half the bottle. "Have you a bicycle pump? I've a weak patch I ought to be blowin' out."

That afternoon, Resident Magistrate William Clarke sat in his study overlooking the bay and read the report filed by Inspector Hayes.

Seamus Kilkeirnan claimed that he had been coming up the hill when the constable was coming down, and at the moment when they passed, Seamus suffered a blowout on his bicycle. The constable swerved to avoid Seamus, hit a kettle hole, and tumbled over the edge. He was dead when they reached him.

Donal O'Leary was listed as the only witness. The doctor's report stated that Constable Shea had died of a broken neck. The doctor was somewhat puzzled by the bruised fingernails on the constable's right hand but said that in such falls, many unusual bruises occurred.

"Do you believe this?" asked Clarke.

Hayes's smile shortened. "I've done my best, sir. But the investigation will continue."

"Very good."

Just then, Clarke's grandchildren, a pair of little redheaded boys, tumbled into the study, shouting for Gran'ther to take them riding. At the sight of the inspector, who looked like a soldier in his green uniform, they stopped and fell silent.

Clarke smiled at the boys. "Run along, lads. Busy yourself while Gran'ther talks with Inspector Hayes. We'll go for a gallop after tea."

"Handsome youngsters," said Hayes after they had gone off.

"Here through Easter."

"Perhaps by then, we'll have this matter cleared up."

"I hope so, Inspector." Clarke went over to the table by the window and lifted the port decanter. "Now, about the readiness of your barracks personnel . . ."

"I have six . . . five younger constables, all excellent marksmen and strong cyclists, plus two older gentlemen, nearing pension age, who remain in the barracks, handling the desk and the telegraph key."

Clarke came over and slipped the report from Hayes's hands. "Have them read this, so that they may speculate on the fate of their colleague. Then order your men to release the safeties on their carbines. I will be requesting reinforcements."

"Has your informer given you new information?"

"No, but my suspicions have risen." Clarke flipped through the report. "And remind your men that in the last Fenian rising, RIC constables and their barracks were the prime targets."

"Yes, sir."

"I want you to be ready for anything, and I want the local coastwatchers alerted as well."

"To what?"

"A rubber dinghy rowing in from a U-boat, an unfamiliar trawler pulling up at the dock . . . anything."

The two little redheaded boys ran shouting past the window of the study. Clarke turned and looked out. The boys galloped into the field that rolled down to the bay. One caught the other by the arm and they both went tumbling across the new grass.

Clarke's cheeks flushed suddenly. "Damn this island and damn this race and damn this whole bloody business. When will it end?"

"After Home Rule, I hope."

"Home Rule is a farce if Ulster isn't part of it."

Hayes had lost his smile. He stared straight ahead. "I'm no politician, sir. I'm simply here to keep the peace and uphold the law."

"And you will." Clarke watched the two little boys, and his gaze traveled beyond them, across the bay, to the tiny white cottage where Logan O'Leary lived. "By week's end, I will deliver to you a list of names. They are to be watched, and you are to arrest them all on Saturday night, after the Easter Vigil."

"What charge, sir?"

"Conspiring against the Crown."

"May I ask why you choose to wait until then?"

"Caution . . . reluctance . . ." Clarke shrugged. "Hope."

The framed photograph smashed against the wall above the fireplace. The glass shattered.

"You still love him."

"No, Donal."

He snatched the photograph from the floor and held it above the flaming turf. Then he looked at her.

"Go ahead." She backed into a corner and wrapped her arms around her waist. "Burn it."

He looked down at the photograph. "The great war hero, Victoria Cross and all. And to think he enlisted just to get in some gal's knickers."

"Burn it," she repeated.

"You don't need the picture 'cause you'll be seein' his pretty face before Friday. Is that it?" He came over to her. The smell of the poteen moved ahead of him like a shadow.

"I don't care if I never see him again. That picture could have ruined everything."

WILLIAM MARTIN

"It ruined a lad's life." He put his head down and covered his face with one huge hand.

She slipped the picture from his hand and threw it into the fire. Padraic Starr's face curled, the chemicals in the photograph browned and bubbled, and then he was gone in a small burst of flame.

"There," she said.

He wiped a forearm across his face and snorted back into his throat. He worked something around in his mouth for a moment, then swallowed. "It's a fine damn rebel I'm turnin' out to be. I don't know who to hate and who to love and I'm as grieved to kill a constable as I was when me own brother died."

The firelight flickered and their shadows danced on the cold white walls.

"If more constables had died, your brother and mine wouldn't have had to." She slipped her arms around his wide waist. "Don't lose your stomach for it, Donal, and I won't lose my heart for you."

The wind blew and turf smoke puffed back down the chimney. They watched it billow into the room and roll up to the ceiling.

She admitted to herself that she was as frightened as he was. She thought she knew what she would do when the fighting started. She prayed that she would know what to do when she saw Starr again. But she did not know what she would do without Donal's big, solid body.

She brought her mouth to his and tasted the poteen on his lips. He lifted her up and carried her to her bed.

"Murder was what it was."

Logan O'Leary looked up from his pint.

Since the death of his younger son, he had spent most of his time tending his sheep or sitting in a dark corner at Finnerty's. The sheep needed little watching. He could sit in the field and let his mind wander across the hilltops and down to the sea and back to a time when his sons were small. But when his mind wandered to places where the pain was too deep—to the violent death that one son had faced, to the violence that the other was bringing upon himself, to the terrible thing he had done to save his second son—Logan took himself to Finnerty's and lost his pain in the pint.

"What was murder?" he said.

344

"What happened in front of your cottage yesterday morning."

Logan scratched at his beard, and a few hairs fell loose. One of them dropped into his drink. "Seamus said it was an accident."

William Clarke folded his hands and stared across the table.

It was ten o'clock on a bright Monday morning. Mrs. Finnerty was polishing the pint mugs. An old dog was chewing at the rash on his flank, and his leg kicked in time with his bite.

"Would you care for a pint, RM?" Logan asked.

"Someone will pay for that murder, Logan."

"No murder that I know of." Logan took a drink.

Clarke tapped his riding crop on the table. "Was it Donal killed the constable?"

Logan stopped drinking.

He had drunk too much to lie convincingly. He put both hands on the mug so that they would not shake and lowered it to the table. He fixed his eyes on the head of foam, and after a moment picked out the hair. "It was . . . it was never my son."

They could go on like this all morning, Clarke thought, and he had no wish to torture Logan O'Leary any further. Logan had already given up the name of young Cooney to protect his son in the matter of the wire-cutting. Even if the constable's death *had* been an accident, Logan would not be able to refuse the deal that Clarke was about to offer.

"I'm planning to arrest your son." Clarke stood and put on his riding cap.

"He did nothing."

"He is the local commander of a rebel cell." Clarke leaned on the table and whispered so that Mrs. Finnerty would not be able to hear. "He will be arrested and charged with Constable Shea's murder, unless you deliver to me, by the Easter Vigil, the names of the other cell members, their plans, and the plans of one Padraic Starr."

"I can't do nothing of the sort. I don't know them things. And I ain't seen Paddy Starr since the last snake left Ireland."

"By Saturday night." Clarke stood and left before Logan O'Leary could say any more.

Logan swallowed his Guinness and called for another. He did not believe Seamus Kilkeirnan's story any more than the resident magistrate did. If his son was charged, his son would be convicted and hanged. If he had to make himself an informer, like Jack Tracy, to save his own son, then an informer he would be.

28

On Palm Sunday, they offered a service for Hugh Dawson.

The priest invited Mason Deems to join them. Deems refused unless the Papists used the King James Bible. The priest closed his Douay version and held out his hand to the mate. "I'll take yours, then."

Mason Deems came forward with his Bible. Although he was now commanding the quarterdeck, he seemed to have grown smaller and harder since the storm, like a piece of leather after it has been wetted and left in the sun. He had lost his strongest ally, and he had saved the ship that should have sunk. "If you're praying for a good Presbyterian and a loyal subject of his majesty, I'll join you."

"Me, too," said Henry Huntoon. "Any man who can set a bone like the father, he must have a straight line to the best healer of them all."

And for a few moments, the people of the *Abigail* were drawn together to pray for Dawson and hear the Passion According to St. Matthew.

But for Tom Tracy, prayers alone could not lay Dawson to rest. Night after night, he looked up again from the boiling waves, into Tom Tracy's eyes, and night after night, his calm gaze said, *I will sacrifice myself to save your brother, but you will never forget what I have done.*

To counter Hugh Dawson's heroism, Tom Tracy reached into the most painful place he knew, for the image of another who had sacrificed himself. He saw the hangman's bloody rope burn chafing against Jack Tracy's respectable white collar, and he kept his hatred strong. But his night thoughts, whether he lay awake in his berth or sat in the crosstrees, were no longer clear, except for one: History had not chosen him, nor had God. Like Hugh Dawson and Jack Tracy before him, he had made his own choices.

"Nature did the job I was dreadin'," whispered Padraic Starr.

"Dawson?" answered Tracy. "A brave man."

"There's good on both sides, Tommy. That's always been the hell of this thing." Starr looked up at the sky. "Do you think

Christ knew what he was doin' when he got Himself crucified in springtime?"

It was Holy Thursday, the first warm night of April. The Pleiades rode higher than they had since October. The air seemed to smell of land. And the wind had come around to the southwest, pushing the *Abigail* along like a gentle mother hurrying her child.

"I don't know about Christ, but Dawson knew what he was doin' in that storm."

"It won't be as hard to kill Deems."

"Pratt needs him, Padr'ic. We can't kill him."

"He set the fire, he launched the rockets. It could have been Rachel burned to death as easy as Jenny," said Starr evenly. "What Dawson did don't wipe that out, Tommy. So don't go soft on me now." Starr patted Tracy on the shoulder, then he went up the quarterdeck and disappeared.

Off the port bow, the sky seemed luminous. The moon would soon rise and wash away the delicate web of starlight above the ship. Perhaps, thought Tom Tracy, the sight of it would bring the ancient song to his head and wash away his doubts as well.

"You know, Tommy," Martin Mahoney's voice came out of the shadows, "if you want to stay aboard with the girl, and keep Dann-o out of the trouble too, I'll do the killin' at Ballinakill House."

"He was *my* father, Martin. I'll avenge him."

"Before you was even a twinkle, he was *my* best friend."

"Did he kill Clarke's father?"

Martin worked his tobacco around in his mouth. "We were the Land League in Connemara, tryin' to protect the tenant farmers from gettin' thrown off their land. We wanted to talk, but we had to do a bit of shootin' 'fore anyone bothered to listen."

"Did my father kill Black George Clarke?"

"There was killin', and a few beatin's, but . . . I know for a fact your da had nothin' to do with that shootin'."

"Padr'ic said there was more to you than anyone ever knew. You kept a fine secret until that night at the bridge."

"That's *my* magic." Martin smiled. His lower lip was stained brown from tobacco. "Remember what I said, Tommy. If you want, I'll do your killin' for you."

A small sliver of light appeared at the horizon. For a time, both men watched silently as it cast its silver net across the waves.

"I'll do what has to be done."

"I wouldn't want to see you waste *your* magic . . . for thinkin' and talkin'."

Tom Tracy tugged at his black beard. "It's time to shave . . . before we meet our relatives."

Rachel was in bed. She wore a pink flannel nightgown, and her hair was loose around her shoulders. The oil lamp on the small shelf above her head cast a dim light. The cabin was small, with barely room for the berth, a stool, a washstand, and the suitcase she had had with her when she went to the Tracy apartment on that Sunday morning.

She was reading the Bible, from the Book of Exodus. She had gone through the plagues and the flight from Egypt, and she had read on to the Ten Commandments and Laws Relating to Justice. *Eye for eye, tooth for tooth, hand for hand, foot for foot, burning for burning, stripe for stripe.*

The Christians believed that Christ came with a new law, the law of love. But aboard the *Abigail*, thought Rachel, and down the long corridors of Irish history, it was the voice of an Old Testament God that echoed.

There was a knock, and Starr pushed open the door.

She slipped a finger into the book to keep her place. "What do you want?"

"Reading the Bible?"

"Exodus, for Passover."

" 'The joints of thy thighs are like jewels. . . . Thy throat like the best wine, worthy for thy beloved to drink, and for his lips and teeth to ruminate.' "

"Are you drunk?"

"My favorite quote from the Bible. Solomon's Canticle of Canticles." Starr pulled over the stool and sat by her berth. "The Christian Brothers said it foretold Christ's love for the church . . . Christ nibblin' His church on the neck. Us kids knew it was just old Solomon, as randy as a billygoat."

She sniffed at the air. "Stone cold sober."

He touched the knee beneath the covers. "It's been hard, stayin' away from you these last weeks."

She pulled her leg away. "Don't, Padr'ic."

His hand did not linger. "I've thought more than once about our night at the bridge."

He had come to her at last. In the weeks since they left Boston,

348

she had expected it. At times, she had hoped for it. His soothing words, in the first days of the trip, had given her strength. And now, on the night of the seder, when she was feeling lonely and homesick, he had come to joke and comfort her and perhaps, like her father, take her in his arms and hold her gently . . . as if he knew what she was thinking, what she needed.

"It was a wonderful moment." He smiled behind his red beard. "If I had been less of a gentleman when I slipped my hand into your skirt—"

"You knew exactly what you were doing," she said calmly.

He placed his hand on her knee again. "You think you got me figured. You think I do nothin' but for the risin'."

"Nothing." In Boston, he had used his charms to get what he needed. On the ship, he had done nothing that would anger Tracy or the captain and endanger his mission. But she had forgiven him for all of it because God needed men like Starr. As she read from Exodus, she realized that He had needed them since Moses.

"Well, you're right." Starr smiled like a little boy caught in a lie. "But that don't mean I've no strong feelings for you."

She touched his hand. "I have them for you, too, Padr'ic, in spite of everything."

He turned his hand over and enclosed hers. "I didn't want you to come. Now I'm glad you did."

"But I've changed, Padr'ic."

"What you went through, darlin', it'd change anybody." He brought her hand to his face and opened the palm of it against his beard.

"I haven't said the things you wanted."

He drew her palm across his lips. "The voice of reason you've been."

"And I'll continue to be."

"In Boston, reason told you that the time for rebellion was here." He kissed her open palm. "For the Irish . . . and the Jews."

She drew in a sharp breath. She tried to pull her hand away, but he held it gently. Since that Sunday, she had feared what would happen when a man touched her again. That was the reason she had resisted Tracy's gentle advances. The Bible slipped from her fingers.

"I want you with us when we go ashore." He kissed her palm. "I want your Enfield, and I want your spirit." He kissed again and inhaled deeply, like a man toying with a delicate flower.

"But the bloodshed—"

"I'll protect you, darlin'." He turned her hand over and kissed the back.

"But all the others who'll die—"

"We all die someday." He kissed the backs of each of her fingers, his lips and tongue teasing gently at the sensitive places between. "But most don't get a chance to die for something great."

"I don't want to die." She felt her breath coming faster. "I don't wany any of us to die—"

"We won't."

"—for Ireland or Zionism or—"

He turned her hand over and held the palm to his mouth. "We won't die. We'll live forever."

"Oh, Padr'ic." She twined her fingers through the curls of his beard.

He kissed her palm, then her wrist, the sensitive spot at the crook of her elbow, and then her lips.

In two days, thought Tom Tracy, they would be off the Irish coast. In three days, if his resolve remained strong, he might be dead or hunted among the Twelve Bens.

He looked at the berth above him and listened to his brother's steady breathing and realized how much he wanted Rachel. Since their talk that night, he had not tried to touch her. It was his way of showing his love and his understanding of the terror she had been through. And he feared that because of that day, he might no longer be able to show her any kind of love.

But he wanted her. And there was so little time.

He pulled on his trousers and a clean shirt. He was glad that he had shaved and washed and changed his underwear.

The moon had risen higher, and it threw his shadow ahead of him. He mounted the steps to the quarterdeck and saw the beam of yellow from her portlight. She was awake. He nodded to the priest at the helm and went below.

The door to the captain's cabin was open. Jason Pratt was sleeping soundly after a dose of morphine. Deems's door was closed.

Tracy raised his hand to knock, then he heard whispers, the rustling of sheets, sounds that filled him with envy and anger. Since the fire, Padraic Starr had done nothing to make Tracy jealous. Now he was with her.

Tracy put his hand on the doorlatch, but could not bring himself to turn it. Whatever was happening in that cabin, he did not want to see it. He started to leave, then he pivoted and kicked in the door. The slats shattered beneath his foot, and the door smashed against the bulkhead.

Rachel screamed. Padraic Starr jumped off the berth. Whatever had happened had not gone far. Starr was dressed, and Rachel's nightgown still covered her.

"I told you I'd kill you, Padr'ic, if you touched her."

Starr jumped back and put up his hands. "Is this any way for a good Catholic boy to be actin' on Holy Thursday, with Christ sweatin' blood in the garden at the very moment?"

"Get out, Tommy." Rachel pulled the blankets up around her neck. "Get out, both of you."

Starr looked at her and smiled.

The old Celtic sin-eater, thought Tracy. For a fee, he would come to the home of a dying man. A grand and lavish meal would be set. The sin-eater would fill his stomach and drink his fill, and when he left, the sins of the dying man would be carried away upon his soul.

Starr's eyes seemed to caress Rachel's body. "You didn't say that earlier."

Tracy swung a foot at Starr's face. Starr caught it and pushed, slamming Tracy against the bulkhead. Tracy pulled his foot away and tried to dive at Starr, but a piece of leather snapped past his nose and cracked on the deck.

Mason Deems stood over them. He held the quirt in one hand and the pistol in the other. "Take this outside, or I'll shoot you both." His small face turned to Rachel. "I'll shoot you all three."

Starr picked himself up and saluted. "Aye, aye. We'll fix the door in the morning, sir."

Starr went out, and Deems returned to his cabin.

Tracy looked at Rachel. "You said you weren't ready for anyone."

"Leave me alone, Tommy." She fumbled about under the covers until she found the Bible. She opened it and pretended to read.

"Do you love him?"

"Leave me alone."

Starr was leaning against the stern rail. Bright moonlight bathed the deck. "I guess the mate's good for somethin' after all, Tommy . . . breakin' up fights."

Tracy came up the companionway. "Do you love her?"

The priest offered to leave the helm so that the gentlemen could argue in private.

Tracy repeated his question.

"She's a fine handsome woman, Tommy, with breasts as welcomin' as—"

Before Starr could finish, he was taken by a sharp right hand that neither he nor the priest even saw in the moonlight. For a few moments, he lay motionless on the deck.

"I heard stories about your right hand," said the priest.

Tracy called Starr's name, but Starr did not move. He repeated it, but there was no response. He knelt on the deck and turned Starr over and felt the tip of a knife against his belly. "You've a fine punch, Thomas, but you'll be no match for this, if ever we come to it."

"After all these years," muttered the priest, "I think I'm beginnin' to understand why the church wants celibate priests."

Starr looked up. "Why would that be, your eminence?"

"Can you imagine two priests makin' such fools of themselves over a woman?"

"She loves me, that's for certain," said Starr. "But she loves Tommy, too. She don't know whether she wants the rebel fighter or the righteous politician." He looked up at Tracy. "All I can offer's the rebel. Play both roles, and she's yours."

Tracy dropped Starr on the deck, then went below once more.

The priest said, "I've never heard one rival tell another how to win the lady away."

"The reason, your eminence"—Starr worked his jaw back and forth where Tracy had hit him—"is that it's the rival I'm tryin' to win."

He went back to her. He did not know what he was thinking, or what he would say, but he had to see her again. And he still wanted her.

He tapped on the frame of the door. The lower slats were shattered where his foot had gone through them. "Can I come in?"

"Leave me alone," she said angrily.

"No." He opened what was left of the door.

She pulled the covers up around her neck. "You had no right to break in on us, Tommy."

"After the things you told me the night I came to you, you had no right to let him do that."

352

"He came to persuade me to go ashore." She lowered the covers a bit. "He says he'll need my Enfield and my spirit." She laughed at the word. "My spirit. The rest just . . . happened."

Tracy rubbed the knuckles of his right hand, where he had punched Starr. "I want your Enfield and your spirit, too. I would have said so, if I thought I'd get a reception like that."

"Damn you, Tom Tracy." She threw off the covers and swung her legs out of the bed. She wore a pair of black wool socks that made her look like a vulnerable little girl. "I don't know what just happened with Padr'ic. I never know with him, but I know that I love you. And I don't want to see you die."

She threw herself into his arms. She pulled his face to hers. She pressed her lips against his until it hurt. She pushed her tongue into his mouth again and again, in a frantic expression of love and longing and fear for the future.

He cupped his hands around her bottom and pressed her against his corduroy trousers. The flesh beneath the flannel was soft and enticing, and he could feel the roundness of her belly against his hips. He inhaled deeply and tried to kiss her neck.

But she broke the embrace. There were tears in her eyes. It was not a kiss of passion, after all, but a kiss of anger and frustration. "I'm sorry, Tommy. I'm as confused as you are."

"I'm not confused."

"You were at the beginning, and I thought there was only one answer. Then something terrible made you certain but confused me. Then Dawson saved your brother—"

"Dawson changes nothing," he whispered. "What Dawson did can't right all the old wrongs. That's why we're sailin' to Ireland."

She looked into his eyes. His skin, where it had been unprotected, was red and windburned. "Is that what Padr'ic said?"

He nodded. "Padr'ic says some good things."

"Do you believe it?"

"Dawson was a good man, but I've made my decision, and it's the right one."

She brought her hands to his cheeks. The shaved skin was smooth and white. "I'm glad you took off the beard, Tommy. You look more like yourself. It makes it easier to believe you."

"Then believe me."

"I don't know what I believe anymore. Rebellion's for the future, but there's no future watching a brave man drown, or seeing some sad chorus girl burn to death."

"We'll build the future, Rachel." He pulled her to him. Her breasts felt soft against his chest. He wanted her desperately, in every way. "Stay with me. Tell Padr'ic you're staying with me. When we land, fight with me. And when it's over—"

She put a hand over his mouth to quiet his excitement. He had become all that she had wanted him to be in Boston. But he had become another Starr, not the man she had fallen in love with. "Just hold me, Tommy."

He kissed the palm of her hand and whispered against it, "When it's over, we'll marry and stay in Ireland, or go to Palestine, or back to America—"

She took his hand and drew it to her breast. Whatever he had become, she would stay beside him. "Just don't die, Tommy."

"We won't die." He felt the tender flesh tightening beneath his fingertips. Their lips touched. "We'll live forever."

She felt a chill. "Padr'ic said the same thing."

"That's the magic, darlin'." Tracy blew out the oil lamp. "But I have magic of my own."

His hands dropped to her waist and bunched up the flannel around her hips. She felt a cool draft on her legs, then her thighs. He pushed the nightgown higher, gently nudging her arms till she raised them, and he slipped it over her head. Then he kissed her breasts and her belly and laid her back on the berth. And when his nakedness covered hers, she whispered it again. "Don't die, Tommy."

"We'll live forever."

"Yes." She pulled the blanket up over him and felt the warmth and opened herself to him.

29

*I*t was the kind of Good Friday that Tom Tracy had always preferred, a bright, fresh day to make the deep gloom inside the church seem all the more momentary. Easter was coming. Like the others, however, Tom Tracy would have preferred clouds and dense fog to cover the *Abigail* from British trawlers.

The priest was at the bow and Danny Tracy in the mainmast crosstree, their binoculars trained for British ensigns and smudges of funnel smoke.

It was possible that the people who had sent Hugh Dawson to Boston had ordered the interception of American ships approaching the Galway coast. But Jason Pratt assured his crew that with false papers, a cargo of medical supplies, and the Pratt reputation in England, they would brazen their way through.

While Tracy and Starr taught Rachel the fundamentals of the machine gun, however, the *Abigail* would be a most suspicious-looking vessel. Nevertheless, Starr said that everyone who went ashore had to learn to use it, because the machine gun would decide the fighting. If something happened to him, Starr wanted the others to be able to teach the operation of the gun to the IRB.

Starr and Tracy took a gun from the hold and assembled it between the afterhouse and the spankermast. A vessel approaching from bow or stern would not be able to see it. And it would be visible only faintly, as a silhouette, through the balustrade that ran along the sides of the schooner.

"I guess Rachel's yours," said Starr. "I never could have convinced her to learn about this."

"I think you knew what you were doing last night." Tracy revolved the gun in its carriage and pointed it at Starr. "Making me jealous to make me go after her again."

Jason Pratt, on crutches and morphine, came down the quarterdeck. It was his first appearance since the storm.

Starr jumped up. "Glad to see you about, Captain. If the Brits come aboard, we want our best man to meet 'em."

Pratt looked at the machine gun. "If the Brits see that, we'll meet 'em for certain."

"As long as the lookouts give us some warning," said Tracy, "we'll be able to break it down and stow it before anybody gets close."

"These beauties'll turn the tide, Captain." Starr patted the corrugated water tank around the barrel of the gun. "A thousand rounds a minute, range to a thousand yards. Even Miss Levka has to know how to use it."

"Mornin', Cap," shouted Jimmy the Butcher from the main cargo hatch. He was stretched out taking sunshine and whiskey.

Pratt hobbled to the quarterdeck rail and looked down at him. "Drinking again?"

"My friend the mate's takin' care of me."

Pratt glanced back toward the helm and Mr. Deems. "So he's your friend, now?"

"Naw, but he's keepin' me loose. Yep. Keepin' me loose, keepin' me happy."

"Deems knows that Jimmy McHale, drunk and happy, is more trouble than Jimmy McHale, sober and bitchin'," explained Tracy. "Anything to slow us up."

"Hey, Cap." Jimmy took a swallow of whiskey. "Did you ever hear the one about the one-legged sea captain and the boatload of Irish fools?"

Rachel looked down at the bow churning through the water. "I hope I'm not bothering your privacy, Father."

The priest held binoculars to his eyes. "You are most welcome. Just keep your eyes sharp."

The horizon was clear. The breeze was light from the west. The aroma of Henry Huntoon's salt cod stew mingled with the smell of the donkey engine exhaust, floated up, and hung in the belly of the foresail. The engine had been started to run the generator and provide eletrical power, for they were now within wireless range.

"Something's bothering you?"

"I'm going to learn how to use the machine gun."

"You've resisted till now."

"Tommy convinced me."

"I suspect that Starr was behind it somehow." O'Fearna lowered the binoculars. "He understands how to reach people. Some need to be goaded, some inspired, some need to think they're doing it because they're as guilty as original sin and it's the only way to wash away the stain. Some need to believe they're making the decision of their own free will."

"Sounds like you're describing your own job," said Rachel.

"My former job."

"You're still a priest, I think, after all you've done to comfort people on this ship."

"I've said a few eulogies and cared for the wounded." The priest smiled. "Tomorrow I'll unload guns, and the day after, I'll care for the people they wound and eulogize the ones who get killed. Another reluctant rebel."

"Just like me." Rachel leaned over the starboard side and squinted against the reflection of the sun. "Look, Father."

It protruded from the waves about three hundred yards out. If not for its wake, a small wedge of white water on a calm sea, it would have been all but invisible.

"A periscope?"

"Captain," called the priest softly. "Captain!" he cried. "Off to starboard. A periscope."

Starr and Tom Tracy leaped up. Jason Pratt clumped to the stern and pulled his binoculars from the deck box. All eyes turned to starboard.

"Holy shit!" shouted Danny Tracy from the crosstree. "A submarine."

"Asparagus stick . . . German," said Pratt.

"He won't bother us," said Starr. "We're neutral. And we ain't carryin' any heavy armament."

Pratt glanced at the machine gun. "That's no slingshot. As for neutrality, who knows what the Germans are telling their commanders this week?"

"Do we break the gun down, then?"

"No," answered Pratt. "If he's seen it, breaking it down will seem more suspicious. If he hasn't seen it, let's not attract attention to it, because right now he's looking us over for hidden armaments. He thinks we're a Q-ship."

"What's that?" asked Tom Tracy.

"An innocent-looking schooner that lures the Kraut to the surface, then rolls out the heavy guns and blasts him."

"But the American flag?"

"Q-ships may show neutral colors to draw the U-boat close."

"We gonna fight this guy?" Danny Tracy dropped from the ratlines, rushed to the quarterdeck, and grabbed his Enfield. "I'm ready."

"Put up the gun," said his brother.

"I ain't afraid."

"I am." Starr grabbed the rifle from Danny's hands and snapped it across the deck to Martin Mahoney, who was leaning on the afterhouse roof as casually as a man at a bar.

Martin caught it and dropped it from sight. "We'll have no itchy trigger fingers gettin' us sunk."

Danny went over to the machine gun. "I'm ready if I'm needed."

"Should we drop the sails and talk?" said Tom Tracy.

"Talk," said Deems. "Have a pleasant chat with the Hun."

"If he's cautious," said Pratt, "he'll play by Declaration of London regulations and demand our papers, and we'll be able to do some business with him. If he thinks we're a Q-ship, he may start firing as soon as he surfaces. And there's always the chance he'll give us a torpedo and be done with it."

For a time, the *Abigail* was silent, except for the steady beat of the donkey engine in the forward house and the rush of the wind against the canvas. Nine people were transfixed by the shaft of metal running toward the ship, and the only movement was Jimmy the Butcher's hand carrying his pint to his lips.

Softly, Jimmy began to hum, then to sing. *"Iss diss not ein sub-ma-rine? Ja diss iss ein sub-ma-rine."*

Pratt glanced at Jimmy, then he looked up at the sails, then he began to shout orders.

"Ein de schoene, ein de schoene, ein de schoene, sub-ma-rine."

"Mr. Deems, swing her to port. Let's keep the target as small as possible and try not to seem too eager to stop. We don't want him to think we're tricking him somehow."

"Yes, Captain."

"Iss diss not ein frightened ship? Ja diss iss ein frightened ship."

"Get away from that machine gun."

Martin grabbed Danny by the collar and pulled him to the port side. "He means you."

Jimmy pirouetted about, leaped up onto the hatch cover, and began to do a little dance. *"Sub-ma-rine, frightened ship, frightened ship, sub-ma-rine, ohhh—"*

"Mr. Tracy, raise the centerboard."

"Raise it? But—"

"Now!"

"Aye, aye!"

Jimmy began to flail his arms as though directing a chorus. *"Ein de schoene, ein de schoene, ein de schoene, I'm gon-na shit!"*

"And shut up that drunk!"

Tracy and Starr ran down the deck. Starr grabbed Jimmy by the collar and hauled him off the hatch. "Lend a hand and stop makin' a fool of yourself."

"I'm scared, Paddy. They might kill us."

Tracy loosed the centerboard burton.

Starr grabbed the line with him, then shoved the end of it into Jimmy's shaking hands. "If you're scared, pull."

"No thanks, three men on a rope . . ." Jimmy tried to throw the rope down and walk away.

"Pull!"

Jimmy's squinty left eye was screwed tight with fear. "I thought this centerboard thing kept us steady. What are we pullin' it up for?"

"Don't ask questions," shouted Starr. "Just pull!"

They heaved, laying all their weight onto the rope. The centerboard rumbled below them and rose back into the ship.

The conning tower broke the water first, looking like several large oil drums welded together and trimmed with railings and wires. The squat ugliness of its form seemed well suited to the supreme ugliness of its function. It was not a vessel meant to be admired. It was not even meant to be seen. Before the rest of the U-boat was out of the water, the silhouettes of half a dozen men began to scurry about the tower.

"I'd give every book of the Old Testament for a cannon at this moment," said Mason Deems.

"He's vulnerable for about sixty seconds." Pratt leaned on the shrouds and watched through his binoculars. "Not much time to get a good shot."

The net-cutter appeared at the bow, then the deck gun. The water a hundred feet on either side of the conning tower boiled up, then all at once it settled, turning flat and smooth. Hatches popped open and men seemed to climb straight out of the sea, so close to the surface was the main deck.

"The sixty seconds are just about up, Mr. Deems," muttered Pratt, "and the God of Israel did not send us a cannon."

"This is not the time for blaspheming," said Mason Deems.

"Do we lower now, Captain?" called Starr.

"Not until they tell us to."

Lookouts in blue woolens and boots ran to the bow and the stern. Others took their places on the conning tower. And four sailors began to work the deck gun.

Starr called out the steps as they followed the drill. The stopper was pulled from the muzzle: "Unplug . . ." The door was opened at the back of the gun: "Breech . . ." A shell was rammed in: "Load . . ." The gun swung toward the *Abigail* and tilted: "Aim . . ."

Rachel came down the deck to the mainmast pinrail, where Tracy and Starr were standing. "Friends of yours, Padr'ic?"

"Old and dear, my darlin', old and dear." Starr pulled off his scally cap and waved it at the U-boat.

He was answered, in the space of a second, by a puff of smoke, the sound of an explosion, and a column of water twenty feet forward of the bow.

Starr looked up at the quarterdeck. "Do we lower now, Captain?"

"The German has expressed himself rather plainly."

"I'd rather fight and go down like a man," grunted Deems.

Pratt pivoted toward him. "This time there's no freighter nearby to pick up the survivors. We'll do what the German tells us."

The sails were quickly dropped. The U-boat swung its bow toward the *Abigail*.

"He's closing," said Pratt. "If he thought we were a Q-ship, he would've stood off."

It looked like a long sliver of gray steel slicing through the water. When it was within a hundred yards, the sound of the diesels changed pitch. The engines reversed to backwater.

"That means he ain't gonna sink us?" asked Danny.

"It means he's not opening fire," answered Pratt.

"Yet," said Deems.

Padraic Starr bent down and loosened the knife in his boot.

"That should frighten them," said Rachel.

"A nervous twitch, darlin'. I'm hopin' we can talk our way out." The knife disappeared into his sleeve.

"They've been at sea a long time," said Tom Tracy. "Full beards on every face, even the captain."

"Maybe they'll go away if we offer 'em some hot water and soap." Jimmy the Butcher stood on the cargo hatch.

"Maybe they've used up all their torpedoes." Rachel wrapped her hands around the mainsail shrouds and looked out through one of the squares of rope, like a child peering through a picket fence.

The commander of the U-boat brought his speaking trumpet to his lips. "*Guten Morgen*. If anyone aboard touches the machine gun, we will open fire. Understood?"

Pratt put out his hand, and Deems gave him his trumpet. "Understood."

"Speaks good English," said Tracy.

"Most of them do," answered Starr.

"I thought you said you'd put the gun where it couldn't be seen." Rachel was trying to sound more sarcastic than terrified.

Starr slipped his foot through two of the balusters in the rail. "He couldn't have seen much more than a silhouette between these."

"You are an armed merchant ship in a war zone," shouted the German. He had a blond beard and under his jacket wore a woolen turtleneck that might once have been white.

"We are a *neutral* ship," responded Pratt.

"*Ja,* and the machine gun that you try to hide?"

"Self-defense."

The German shouted. "You have five minutes to abandon."

Starr looked to the quarterdeck. "Tell him the truth."

"The Irishman would deal with German." Mason Deems secured the helm and stood beside Pratt. "Scum to scum."

Pratt brought the speaking trumpet to his lips once more. "We are an *American* ship."

"That is why we are being so polite."

"You can't sink an American ship."

"You carry a machine gun, but American ships need no defense. Your President Wilson has seen to that." The German paused. "Unless, of course, you carry absolute contraband . . . like machine guns. Our Government's *Frye* note of November 29, 1915, is quite clear in this matter."

"Our luck to be stopped by a German lawyer," grunted Tracy.

"We've obeyed your commands," persisted Pratt. "Come aboard and examine our papers."

"After you are in the boats."

"Refuse, Captain." Padriac Starr leaped the steps and ran to the stern. "If we go into the boats, we may never get aboard again."

"Obey him, Captain," whispered Mason Deems. "You may live if you do."

"Don't listen to *him*," shouted Danny Tracy. "He just wants to see us sink."

Martin Mahoney cracked Danny across the back of the head. "Shut up, damn you, and let the captain think."

"Tell him the truth." Starr grabbed Pratt's arm. "Get us through this and Ireland will never forget you."

Pratt looked at Starr, then Deems, then brought the speaking trumpet to his lips. "The laws of visit and search require that you come aboard before we are made to abandon."

The U-boat commander conferred with his lieutenant, then swung his trumpet at Pratt again. "I will not send men aboard an armed ship, even a neutral. I will not be trapped."

"There is no trap." Starr lifted himself to the spankermast rigging so that the German could see him. "We're gunrunners, going to Ireland."

At that, the German raised his binoculars and studied Starr. "I think you are a British navy Q-ship."

"There are no women in the British navy!" Starr answered.

"A man dressed as a woman," came the reply, "to create the trap."

"Nein!" Starr leaped from the rigging.

"Four minutes," was the German's response.

"Nein!" Starr bounded off the quarterdeck and raced forward to the mainmast pinrail. Without warning, he grabbed the shoulders of Rachel's jacket and blouse and tore them open.

She screamed and tried to pull away.

"A woman!" cried Starr. *"Ein fräulein!"* He reached forward and ripped away her undergarments, revealing her breasts. She tried to raise her hands to cover herself, but Starr pinned her arms.

Tom Tracy started to lunge for Starr, then he heard the cheer rise from the deck of the U-boat. He turned and looked across the water.

After a long look through his binoculars, the German said, *"Ja. Fräulein."*

And the strange, guttural laughter of a dozen woman-starved sailors rolled across the water.

"Damn you, let me go!" cried Rachel, her face contorted in anger and embarrassment. "Let me go!"

But Starr's eyes were fixed on the U-boat, and for all her struggling, he held Rachel powerless.

"That's enough, Starr!" Tracy grabbed Starr's arm.

Starr swung a forearm and pushed him away. "It's working, Tommy. Give them a long look."

"Enough, dammit!" Tracy pulled off his peacoat and threw it across Rachel.

Starr released her.

Tracy put his arms around her, and she pulled away. "Don't touch me, either of you."

Tracy turned on Starr. "You son of a bitch. I ought to shoot you."

Starr kept his eyes on the German. "I'll do anything to get out of this, Tommy. Don't get in my way again."

Rachel tried to pull her dress back together. Buttons were popped, straps torn, and her hands were trembling. After a moment, she slumped onto the cargo hatch and pulled the peacoat around herself.

Jimmy the Butcher dropped down beside her and offered her his pint. "You know, honey, with them knockers, you got a good future in burley."

The German commander was still laughing. "So, a woman. In her honor, I will give you *another* five minutes."

Starr ran again to the quarterdeck and snatched the speaking trumpet from Pratt's hands. "We are your *allies!*"

In a soft voice that only Pratt could hear, Mason Deems said, "Are we, Captain?"

"You are armed neutrals," shouted the German.

Starr leaped onto the rail and rapped an arm around a shroud. "We're gunrunners rebellin' against Britain. Your government's sendin' a ship to help us."

At that, the speaking trumpet dropped away from the German's mouth. He looked to one side, then the other. He spoke with his officers. One of them handed him a clipboard and he studied it.

Tom Tracy went over to the cargo hatch and dropped down beside Rachel. "I'm sorry. I'll never let him near you again."

Her head was down, her eyes fixed on the tops of her boots, her arms wrapped tight around her, and her chin pressed against the closed collar of the peacoat.

Tracy put an arm around her shoulder. "Let me take you to your cabin."

She shook her head and pulled away from him.

"You'll feel better, Rachel."

"You let him do it, Tommy. You let him humiliate me."

"The German would have opened fire. You saved the ship."

She gave him a look filled with contempt. Her shoulders shuddered involuntarily. "I don't care about the ship or the machine gun or last night. I just want to live through this."

On the U-boat, the commander raised the trumpet. "What is the name of this German gunrunner?"

"I was not told," answered Starr. "But she flies a neutral flag."

"Where bound?"

363

"Bay of Tralee."

The German scratched at his beard and conferred again with his officers. Then, "Put out your ladder."

"Consorting with the enemy," hissed Mason Deems.

In a few minutes, a German raft was knocking against the hull of the *Abigail*. A young lieutenant and four dirty sailors were climbing the ladder, bringing with them the stink of diesel fumes and unwashed male bodies. They had doughy, white faces and matted, oily beards, and one sailor's eyes were rimmed in yellow crust.

Starr stood at the top of the ladder to greet the Germans and help them up. *"Wie geht's, wie geht's?"* he said to the lieutenant, who hesitated at the rail for signs of danger before stepping onto the deck.

He was young, thought Tracy, early twenties, but there was a hard look about him, the look of the hunter, or the hunted. His gaze swept the deck, falling first on Tracy, then turning to Rachel, who leaned against the mainmast, her hands still wrapped around her waist. The eyes lingered on her an extra second, because women were a rare sight on the Atlantic. Then they traveled to the quarterdeck, took in the captain at the top of the steps, Martin and Danny on the port side, the machine gun. Sudden movement near the forecastle brought the German's hand to his holster. Henry Huntoon and Sean O'Fearna were coming out of the galley, each carrying steaming mugs.

"Fish stew for our German friends," said Starr.

"Nein," barked the lieutenant. He drew the pistol, and the other Germans leveled their Mauser Gewehr 98s. "Bring everyone forward."

"There's no need for guns," Starr protested.

"Everyone forward."

"On this ship, the captain stays on the quarterdeck." Jason Pratt turned imperiously and hobbled back toward the helm.

"He's also got a busted leg, Lieutenant. He can't come down." Starr spoke from the corner of his mouth, as though sharing a secret. "Now let your men have some hot stew while me and the captain tell you what you want to know."

The gray eyes regarded Starr as coldly as the periscope studies the merchantman.

"We'll show you the false manifest, we'll take you below, and you can see the way we're doin' our smugglin'." Starr glanced at the sailor with the crusty eyes. "We'll even give you some medicine for that lad's infection. We'll prove there's no friends of England aboard the *Abigail*."

"If we had not been ordered from the Bay of Tralee, Herr Irish, you would now be in an open boat rowing for the coast." The lieutenant barked several orders in German, then turned and strode toward the quarterdeck with two sailors following him. Two other sailors held carbines leveled on the small group by the mainmast.

Starr looked about, then whispered to Tracy, "Where the hell's Jimmy?"

"He went up onto the quarterdeck."

Starr looked aft. "I don't see him, nor Deems neither."

One of the German sailors stepped closer to them and knitted his brow, as though trying to understand. Starr took a cup of stew from the priest and handed it to him. Then he followed the lieutenant up to the quarterdeck.

The sailor was about eighteen. His beard was merely a few swirls of black around his chin, his blue woolen jacket hung on him like a rag, and there was a scratch across the left lens of his wire-rimmed glasses. With one hand, he held his carbine, mostly on Tracy, and with the other, he brought the cup to his nose and sniffed cautiously.

" 'S good." Henry Huntoon gave him a smile.

The sailor raised the cup to his lip and took a small sip.

"*Ja?*" said the sailor with the infected eyes. He was older and taller and smelled worse than any of his mates, and he had been hovering near Rachel since stepping aboard.

"*Es Schmeckt,*" said the younger sailor. He tilted back his head and poured half the stew into his mouth. The broth dribbled across his cheeks and down his neck. A small piece of salt cod caught in the hair beneath his mouth. He dragged a sleeve across his face and looked at his mate. "*Ja. Der Schwarze kocht gut.*"

"*Und das Fräulein?*" The other sailor grinned at Rachel. "*Kann sie gut ficken?*"

The two sailors laughed.

"Scum," muttered Rachel.

With the barrel of his carbine, the sailor gently nudged the peacoat open and tried to see Rachel's breasts.

Tracy grabbed the barrel and shoved it into the air. "*Nein.*"

The muzzle of the other carbine rammed against his backbone. "*Nein,*" said the younger sailor.

On the quarterdeck, the lieutenant pulled out his pistol and bellowed, *"Hände weg!"*

The two sailors stepped back.

Rachel turned to the quarterdeck. *"Danke schöne, Herr Leutnant."*

The lieutenant and one of the sailors were standing on the starboard side. Pratt had spread the ship's papers on the afterhouse roof, and Starr was explaining them to the German. The other sailor was on the port side with his gun leveled at Danny and Martin.

Where was Jimmy? wondered Tracy. And where was Deems?

Rachel buttoned the peacoat and jammed her hands into her pockets and felt the grip of Tracy's pistol.

Then Tracy noticed a change in the sound of the donkey engine. Someone was drawing power. And he knew where Deems had gone.

At the same time, the sailor with the glasses stepped toward the port side and squinted toward the horizon. But his vision was bad, and worsened by days of semidarkness in the U-boat, followed by a few minutes of bright sunshine above.

"I think he sees smoke," whispered Rachel.

"A ship." Tracy could see four stacks pumping out a thick black cloud. Deems had already done his damage.

"British destroyer," said Henry Huntoon. "Three miles out and comin' fast."

"I think it may be time for a bit of prayer." Sean O'Fearna blessed himself. A drip of perspiration had collected on the tip of his nose.

Tracy glanced toward the U-boat. The lookouts were still scanning the sea in every direction. But the *Abigail* blocked their view across the fifteen degrees of horizon that mattered. They had not yet seen the destroyer.

But the young sailor had. *"Herr Leutnant . . ."*

"You'd better hurry, Lieutenant," called Tracy. "Otherwise we're all in trouble."

While everyone had been watching the Germans come aboard, Jimmy the Butcher had sneaked down to the main cabin and broken into the captain's liquor supply. He had downed half a decanter of vintage port in three gulps, and he had refilled his empty pint bottle from the captain's quart of single-malt Scotch.

Now, with a pleasant fog rolling through the passages in his

366

head, he hurried along the companionway, past Rachel's cabin, then the captain's. Then he stopped.

Mason Deems was hunched over the wireless in the captain's cabin like a bad poker player protecting a royal flush. The code book was open in front of him.

"Hey, you."

Deems looked at Jimmy with eyes gone small and black. He hissed something that Jimmy could not make out. Then he put his finger on the telegraph key and tapped out a message.

"What the hell are you doin'?"

"Catching Germans and Irish at once."

"You're givin' us away! If you can't set us on fire, you give us away to the Brits!" Jimmy lurched into the cabin, and Deems lashed out suddenly with the quirt, like a striking snake.

The leather slashed across Jimmy's cheek.

"Now stand back," Deems hissed.

Jimmy the Butcher brought his hand to his cheek and looked at the blood that came away on his fingers. The fog parted suddenly. "Not this time, you bastard. You can set us on fire and blame me, but not this. Not this!" He pulled out his seaman's knife and threw himself onto Deems's back.

Mason Deems reached for his revolver.

For some men, danger acts like a drug that heightens the senses and slows time. In an instant, Tom Tracy saw the rising unravel, and yet, each event seemed to happen like the next step in a dance.

The young sailor beside him shouted *"Herr Leutnant!"* again. At the quarterdeck, the German lieutenant looked toward the destroyer. Then two pistol shots popped somewhere below. Padraic Starr leaped for the companionway, but the German at the helm delivered the stock of his gun to Starr's belly, slamming him to the deck. The lieutenant pulled his pistol, then shouted something to his commander. On the U-boat, a sailor came from below and handed a message to the commander.

The commander glanced at it, then raised the speaking trumpet and cried, *"Sie rufen die Engländer. Töte sie!"*

"Töte sie!" shouted the lieutenant to his men.

"They've just been ordered to kill us," cried Rachel. "Deems called the British."

The two sailors near the mainmast looked at each other, as though they did not know what to do next.

"Töte sie!" shouted the lieutenant, and he turned his Luger at Starr. As he did, the knife dropped from Starr's sleeve, spun through the air, and dug into the German's chest.

At the port side, a pistol fired, and a German sailor fell at Martin Mahoney's feet. Then, in a swift motion, Martin pulled his pistol from the hole it had blown in his pocket, dropped behind the afterhouse, and fired at the German by the helm.

The German's head snapped back, and he tumbled over the side.

The two young sailors amidships reacted at last, more in terror than vengeance.

The sailor with the crusty eyes turned his carbine on Tracy.

Rachel screamed, "No!" And as instinctively as a mother protecting her child, she pulled Tracy's pistol from the peacoat.

The German swung his gun at her. Tracy knocked it aside, and the bullet tore through a sail.

Henry Huntoon lunged forward and buried his carving knife in the German's back.

At the same time, the sailor with the glasses was turning his gun back and forth, first on Sean O'Fearna, then on Henry Huntoon.

O'Fearna threw his arms around the sailor's neck and screamed, "No, lad!"

Behind the scratched lenses, the sailor's eyes went wide with fright. He drove the butt into O'Fearna's belly. The priest tumbled back, but as the sailor tried to level his Mauser, Tom Tracy snapped his knife from his belt and drove upward. It caught the sailor just below the navel, and the force of Tracy's motion carried it upward, through the belt to the breastbone.

The sailor looked down at the gray tubes of intestine appearing in the bottom of the wound, said, *"Oh, mein Gott,"* and dropped to the deck.

Tom Tracy looked at the blood covering his hand and nearly vomited. But he had no time.

"Feuer!" shouted the German commander.

Starr screamed, "Help me mount the machine—"

The roar of the five-inch gun drowned Starr's words and shook the *Abigail* to her keel. Tracy felt the explosion vibrate through him. And now, he thought, it was over. He recalled the hopelessness of his first alley fight, when he hit the neighborhood bully his best punch and the bully laughed. Tracy grabbed Rachel and threw her to the deck and threw himself on top of her. He told her he loved her and began to pray.

But in their fury, the gun crew had fired too soon. The shot tore through the spanker rigging, ripping away shrouds and ratlines a few feet above Jason Pratt's head.

At the same moment, Starr and Danny Tracy were lifting the machine gun and ammunition pannier to the afterhouse roof.

"You know the drill!" screamed Starr. "Fast!"

He dropped behind the gun and popped open the chamber.

Danny expertly laid the belt of .30 caliber bullets in place.

Starr closed the chamber. He had a few seconds before the German gunners found their mark and ended the *Abigail.*

He pulled the trigger and the gun clattered off a dozen rounds before jamming. He tore open the chamber and pulled out the jammed shells while the German commander screamed at his crew.

"I'll feed!" Danny Tracy knelt beside Starr and held the munition belt by the chamber.

"Ladet die gewhere!" Load!

Starr pulled the trigger. This time, the gun ran like a rod-and-piston. The water in front of the submarine rose into a dozen exploding splashes. The bullets danced up the side of the U-boat, onto the deck, leaving deep dents in the sheet-metal skin.

"Und Zielt!" And aim!

Star tilted the gun a few more degrees.

"Feuer!" Fire! called the commander, but too late.

Starr's bullets rattled off the deck gun and tore into the crew, and four German sailors were ripped to pieces.

The commander shouted frantically through the voice tube. Four more sailors raced from the forward hatch and fell like targets in a shooting gallery.

Then Starr swung the gun at the conning tower and stitched a line of slugs from the deck to the weather screen, killing two lookouts.

The German commander screamed, *"Tauchen! Tauchen!"* into the voice tube, then he dropped down and disappeared.

The water at the bow began to bubble. White froth rose around the deck gun and turned pink with blood. The bodies of the dead and wounded sailors floated off, but Starr continued to fire, concentrating now on the forward section of the conning tower and the two delicate shafts of the periscopes.

Then the water closed over the conning tower. For a few seconds, the gray hull reflected the sun's light back to the surface, then the water turned blue and still.

Tracy looked up. The smoke of the machine gun and the sick-sweet stink of gunpowder rolled down the deck.

Rachel raised her head, and suddenly the machine gun roared once more. She brought her hands to her ears and buried her face against Tracy's chest. Starr was firing into the water at the remnants of the men still floating there.

When the clattering stopped, Sean O'Fearna cried, "Have a little mercy, Starr . . . on all of us."

"That Kraut captain ordered your death," answered Starr. "I want those bodies to sink, because the Brits'll never believe we did that damage with handguns."

The destroyer was closer now, coming hard, its black smoke leaving a long dark shadow on the water.

Jason Pratt, who had stood motionless at the rail through all of the firing, ordered Henry Huntoon to bring out the flags and signal that the U-boat had submerged. Then he told Starr to throw the machine gun over the starboard side.

"We can hide it."

"Not enough time," answered Pratt. "The Brits may not have seen it yet, but they're getting close enough. There's no time to break it down or bury it in the hold. Depending on what Deems told them, we may have a lot of talking to do."

Starr looked out at the destroyer, then looked at the gun.

Jason Pratt slammed a crutch down on the roof beside Starr. "Dammit! Obey my orders."

Starr, Martin, and Danny threw the gun overboard. It splashed in a cloud of steam and sank.

"You saved us, Paddy," said Martin.

"You did pretty good, too, Uncle Martin." Danny was trembling and trying so hard to keep himself oblivious to the dead Germans that he tripped over one.

"Your uncle's a dead shot," said Starr.

Martin responded by spitting a wad of tobacco into the water. Then, all at once, he vomited tobacco and bile down the side of the ship.

"Stop your jawin' and pukin'," hollered Pratt. "Let's raise sail."

Tom Tracy glanced at the boy he had just killed, then went to the starboard side and grabbed the main throat halyard. He looked out toward the water, and his heart rose to his own throat.

It was coming. It leaped from the water two hundred yards away, then dove, then leaped again like a dolphin. The gyro mechanism of the torpedo needed a hundred yards of running before it found its depth and steadied itself. But *it was coming.*

"Captain!" he shouted.

The torpedo was down now and speeding, straight and hard at the hull of the *Abigail*.

Pratt hobbled to the side and grabbed a shroud. "Hold on to something."

The priest blessed himself.

Rachel ran to Tracy's side and looked into the water. "Oh, my God . . ."

"I am heartily sorry," added Tracy.

Starr saw the deadly white wake and screamed, "No, dammit! No!"

The nose of the torpedo was red. Tracy watched it, transfixed, fascinated, terrified. It reached the ship. He closed his eyes.

Nothing happened.

He looked down again. The narrow wake was fizzing up around the hull. But nothing happened.

The torpedo sped under the *Abigail*, passing a few inches below the keel, and raced on harmlessly.

"Mr. Tracy," called Jason Pratt, "the next time I order you to raise the centerboard, don't ask questions. Do it."

"Aye, aye, sir." Tracy's voice cracked, and he felt ice-cold sweat at his armpits.

"He never fired at a shallow-drafter like the *Abigail* before," continued the captain. "With that destroyer bearin' down, he won't waste another one figuring out how much water we draw!"

The patched, weatherbeaten sails of the *Abigail* rose quickly and bellied out. She swung with the breeze and began to run toward the destroyer.

Henry Huntoon was at the bow, flashing his signals with the flags, warning the destroyer that the submarine was firing torpedoes. A sailor on the bridge acknowledged the signals, and the destroyer rushed past the *Abigail*, its four stacks blowing heavy smoke, the British naval ensign fluttering on the mast.

"Send up a cheer," called the captain. "Make it look like you're glad to see them!"

Danny Tracy pulled off his hat and waved. Martin Mahoney managed to applaud. The priest waved both hands high above his head.

371

"I never thought I'd be glad to see that flag," said Tracy.

"Rule Britannia," said Rachel. "And damn all you blood-stained Irishmen." She dropped the pistol and turned toward the quarterdeck.

Padraic Starr found Jimmy propped against a bulkhead in the companionway, the belly of his jacket soaked in blood.

Jimmy took a sip from his pint and said, "I played my best scene with no one watchin'."

Starr knelt beside him and brushed back his hair. "You done good, Jimmy. You were brave."

Mason Deems was lying over the wireless. A pool of blood had spread on the floor at his feet. Starr rolled him over. The handle of Jimmy's knife protruded from his chest, and the pistol was still clutched in his hand.

"The dirty bastard," muttered Starr.

"Shootin' me in the gut."

"He put one into the wireless, too."

Starr picked up the pad of paper beside the wireless. The message read: "53 38 N 13 58 W SCHOONER ABIGAIL UNDER U-BOAT ATTACK STOP IRISH GUNRUNNERS ABOARD STOP"

Beneath the words were the dots and dashes of the international alphabet. It seemed that Deems had coded and sent the first sentence to bring the British running, and he was coding the second sentence when Jimmy found him.

Starr took a deep breath, then slipped Jimmy's pint from his hand and took a swallow. "You done good, buck-o."

30

On that same Good Friday morning, in the Bay of Tralee, another German U-boat broke the surface.

Three men pushed a rubber dinghy away from the U-19 and paddled it toward shore. When they drew near the wide, white, deserted beach known as Banna Strand, the dinghy tipped and tumbled them into the surf.

They dragged themselves onto the sand and rested. Two of

them were young and strong and soon ready to push on. But the third was in his fifties, exhausted by his plunge into the cold waters and his years of diplomatic effort and exile.

His name was Sir Roger Casement. He had been in Germany trying to raise money and guns and organize Irish prisoners of war into a brigade to fight Britain. The British rulers of Ireland considered him a traitor. The rebels of Ireland considered him a symbol of their resistance in the wider world, a knighted Protestant fighting for Irish independence, and they had expected him to remain as their representative in Germany.

However, Roger Casement believed that Germany had failed the Irish. "They want to get rid of the whole thing," he wrote, "at the cheapest cost to themselves—a tramp steamer, twenty thousand old rifles, four million cartridges, and ten machine guns. We go to our dooms—and the German government washes its hands of all responsibility."

Ireland's European champion, tired and sick, had come home to stop the rising or die as part of it.

While the others went on to Tralee, Casement hid himself near the ruins of an ancient fort. He listened to a skylark and smelled the Irish primroses and was discovered by an Irish constable. He claimed he was an English author out for a stroll, but the constable looked at his soaked, smelly clothes and the small boat still rolling in the surf and arrested Roger Casement.

On that same Good Friday morning, in another part of Tralee Bay, the British auxiliary cruiser *Bluebell* stopped a freighter named the *Aud* and ordered her to follow to Queenstown. Although she flew Norwegian colors, her crew were German, and in her hold she carried the weapons of which Casement had written.

The *Aud* had left Germany on April 9, slipped through the British blockade of the North Sea, and worked her way south for a rendezvous in Tralee Bay. Her first meeting was to have been with the U-boat carrying Casement. Then she was to have met with Irish pilot boats that would carry both Casement and the guns to shore.

However, plans relayed from Dublin to New York to Washington and then converted into German diplomatic code and sent back to Berlin could often lose detail in the translation. The *Aud* and the U-boat never came into contact. The captain of the pilot boat saw the freighter in the bay, but was told not to expect the guns until Saturday, when the gunrunner would show two green lights or make wireless contact. The *Aud* carried no wireless and showed no lights, and the captain of the pilot boat went home to bed.

Admiral Sir Lewis Bayly, acting on the information from those "reliable sources" of March 23, had tightened the Royal Navy net around Ireland. Destroyers and auxiliary vessels covered the coast from Galway Bay to the Dingle Peninsula. And a freighter cruising off Tralee for nearly two days could not escape attention.

On the morning of Holy Saturday, as Sir Roger Casement was arriving in Dublin, the *Aud* was steaming under escort into Queenstown Harbor. When she reached the main channel, her engines suddenly stopped. The German ensign fluttered to the top of her mast. The crew took to the lifeboat. Then, while Admiral Bayly watched from shore and the escorts circled like sheepdogs around a rampaging ram, the old freighter drifted to starboard and blew up.

The cargo that settled onto the bottom of the channel included twenty thousand 1902-model Russian rifles, captured at the Battle of Tannenberg and practically obsolete. Roger Casement had been right about the German assistance.

The capture of Roger Casement and the sinking of the *Aud* were, for the men at Dublin Castle, a double shot of Scotch after a week of cold water.

On Monday, Major General Friend had shown Lambert-Jones a letter from Brigadier General Stafford, in charge of the defense of southwest Ireland:

> *Dear Sir,*
>
> *I am writing to inform you of my suspicion that a shipment of arms is to be landed on this coast as preparation for a rising on Saturday.*
>
> *Several informers have given us intelligence to this effect. We have also noticed increased autocar traffic in certain remote coastal areas such as Fenit, which means they may be gathering to distribute contraband. And there is a general mood of unease throughout the district, where, as you know, we have numerous pockets of disaffection.*
>
> *May these observations assist you in the overall defense of Ireland.*
>
> *With Respect,*
>
> *Brig. Gen. W. F. H. Stafford*

374

"Stafford's quite perceptive, if you ask me, sir."

"And this gives away nothing about our code-breakers, if such people exist." The general rolled his eyes at their little secret. "Come along while I show this to Nathan."

The undersecretary's office overlooked the small triumphal arch at the Castle entrance. A small arch, thought Lambert-Jones, for England's small triumphs in Ireland.

Sir Matthew Nathan read the note quickly, then held it in front of him and tapped at it with his pencil. "The general sounds convinced."

"I hold Stafford's opinions in high regard, Undersecretary," answered Friend.

"It's more specific than most recent reports."

"It is more than rumor and speculation, Sir Undersecretary," said Lambert-Jones.

"We have our own informers right here in Dublin, and they tell us that the Volunteers are fragmented and totally without plans for rising."

"Then you intend to have no response?" General Friend snapped the pencil he had been toying with.

"Castle policy is firm: 'minimum action, maximum inaction.' I want nothing short of conscription to bring out the rebels. Conscription, we know, will do it."

"At the very least," offered Lambert-Jones, "the county inspectors in the south and west should be alerted."

Nathan stroked his mustache and said, "All right. We'll also alert the chief of the Dublin Metropolitan Police. It can't hurt to be ready, I suppose."

Friend took another pencil out of the holder on Nathan's desk and toyed with it. "I would like permission to disarm the Irish Volunteers."

Nathan shook his head. "I can't allow it."

"It's the only guarantee of peace."

"It guarantees a pitched battle in the street."

"If we increase the military garrisons, as Lord French suggested last week, a pitched battle will have the hoped-for results."

Nathan stood. "The job of every politician in this castle, from the viceroy to the undersecretary, is to *avoid* a pitched battle, General."

After a moment, Friend slipped Nathan's pencil into his pocket and quietly requested permission to draw up contingency plans for arresting the leaders and disarming the Volunteers. To that the politician agreed. Had he known the full extent of the military's intelligence, thought Lambert-Jones, he might have done nothing differently.

As Lambert-Jones left the office, Nathan looked at him. "Our friend Clarke believes that the death of that constable in Dunslea has something to do with all this. He's even requested reinforcements in his district."

Lambert-Jones tugged at his tunic. "I consider the resident magistrate at Dunslea to be most astute, sir."

On the Wednesday of Holy Week, an informer reported that there was to be no arms shipment. But the atmosphere about the Castle did not improve. In his walks through Dublin, Lambert-Jones still smelled rebellion, and he did not believe the government was prepared. Then came the good news about Casement and the German gunrunner.

The crisis was over. The rising, if indeed there was to have been one, could not take place, and General Friend left for holiday in London.

As he walked to lunch on Saturday, Lambert-Jones met Sir Matthew Nathan in the courtyard. The day was gloomy and overcast, but the undersecretary seemed in excellent spirits.

"Breathing a bit easier, are we, Ian?"

"We still have unanswered questions."

"The Volunteers can have their mobilization and march tomorrow," said Nathan. "You may be sure it will not be a march conducted in high spirits."

"I hope not, sir,"

"That lunatic Casement couldn't bear the disgrace he suffered in Germany, and so he had to make this ridiculous effort."

"I see it somewhat differently, your honor." Lambert-Jones raised his chin slightly. Whenever he spoke with politicians, he felt his way carefully, like a night raider crawling through the barbed wire. "This incident suggests that the rebel leaders are in contact with our German enemies. They should be interned on that basis alone."

Nathan patted the young lieutenant on the shoulder. "Our friend Clarke said he invited you to Ballinakill House for the weekend. Take him up on it, why don't you? Get yourself out of the city. The Irish Volunteers will be here when you get back,

376

still marching up and down the quay with their bird guns and pieces of wood."

When Lambert-Jones returned to his office, a telegram was on his desk:

DISTRICT QUIET SINCE SUNDAY STOP NO SIGN OF STARR OR SUSPICIOUS ACTIVITY STOP HAVE PLANNED ARRESTS FOR THIS EVENING STOP STILL EXPECTING YOU AND MISS CAR-RUTHERS FOR PLEASANT OR AT THE LEAST INTERESTING DAY TOMORROW STOP SIGNED CLARKE

Lambert-Jones wrote out a response:

MISS CARRUTHERS AND I WILL ARRIVE CLIFDEN STATION HALF-SIX TRAIN THIS EVENING STOP SIGNED LJ

31

It was the night of the Easter Vigil. Soon they would be in the Bay of Dunslea.

Padraic Starr sharpened a straightedge and shaved off his beard. He cut himself on the chin and at the hinge of his jaw. In spite of the knicks, his face was smooth and white and more youthful, it seemed, than before the voyage began. Perhaps it was the magic. He put on clean underwear and socks, then he dressed in a pair of flannel trousers and a white wool sweater that he had saved for this night.

The deck, so recently covered with blood, was clean and quiet, washed white by the starlight. The *Abigail* was running before the wind, and the last clouds were blowing off toward the east. It would be a fine morning for the Resurrection.

He went first to Rachel's cabin and knocked. She told him to go away. She had not come out since the Germans were driven off.

"I'd like to apologize for yesterday."

"Accepted. Now please go away."

All of his care and quiet seduction had failed. When the Germans appeared, he had done what was necessary to save the ship, but he knew that this time she would not forgive the rebel his rebellion.

He went across the companionway to the mate's cabin. Jimmy the Butcher lay on the berth and Sean O'Fearna kept the deathwatch. Although the port was open, the room had the sick smell of used breath.

Jimmy opened his eyes. "Hey, Paddy, they won't say old Jimmy the Butcher's a chickenshit no more, will they?"

"You saved the risin'."

The lines creased around Jimmy's mouth and his eye crinkled. "That little shit was callin' the Brits."

The British destroyer had steamed off in pursuit of the U-boat, but a trawler had been alerted to offer assistance to the *Abigail*. Late Friday afternoon, the trawler had bumped alongside and the commander had boarded.

After examining Pratt's papers and making a quick check of the hold, he had taken three glasses of port and pushed off, saying, "We're on the watch for bloody gunrunners. Much rather be keepin' Gerry off the backs of Yanks haulin' medicine for our boys."

Now, Starr took his Victoria Cross from his pocket. "Without you, Jimmy, we'd have no risin' at all." He pinned the medal to the pillow beside Jimmy's head. "A hero is what you are."

"Thanks, Paddy." Jimmy's eyes filled with tears. "Hey, Father, I been in and out so many times, I can't quite remember— did you give me the last rites yet?"

"I prayed for you, Jimmy."

"C'mon, Father, don't kid a kidder. The last rites. Extreme Unction. The sacrament of the dyin'."

"I'm not the priest I used to be, Jimmy. It may not be the kind of anointin'—"

"You may not think you're much of a priest," said Starr, "and we may not be much of a parish. But we're all we've got. So put on the collar and the purple stole, and I'll pray with you. And gettin' me to do *that* is the work of a master Catholic."

And so, for the first time in six weeks, Sean O'Fearna bestowed one of the sacraments. When he was done, he felt like a priest once more. Starr blessed himself and blew out his candle. Jimmy gave the priest a wink and closed his eyes.

"For all his drunkenness and all the times that his procuring helped men to commit adultery, I have just guaranteed that Jimmy will see the face of God."

"You've done him a grand service then," said Starr.

"It's a fate I wish I could be certain of, but"—O'Fearna smoothed the stole—"God's mercy is great."

"It must be, if he could be puttin' up with *us* since the Garden of Eden."

Jimmy's eyes popped open and he grabbed the priest by the stole. "One day, Mike forgets his lunch, see—"

But Jimmy never told the joke. After he was gone, Starr closed his eyes and led the priest back to the fresh, clean air of the quarterdeck.

"The Butcher Man with us?" Henry Huntoon was sitting on the afterhouse roof, smoking his pipe.

"Jokin' his way into heaven right now," said Starr. "Old St. Pete's laughin' so hard, he's forgettin' that Jimmy could use about a thousand years in purgatory."

The priest looked up at the sails. "Fair breeze this evenin'."

"Clouds blowing off," Jason Pratt sat in a deck chair beside the helm, his broken leg stretched out straight. "They should be gone by the time the moon rises."

"Ain't there a song?" Danny Tracy was at the helm.

"Indeed there is." Starr glanced at the priest.

"A noble song about bold men fighting for the redemption of Ireland." O'Fearna repeated those words, seven weeks after Starr's confession, with new understanding of their irony and their truth.

"And, Captain, you're one of the boldest." Starr took Pratt's hand. "We'll never forget."

The lamp in the forecastle was slung low, throwing deep shadows onto the faces at the table. A sailcloth was spread in front of them, and on it a map of Dunslea had been drawn.

Padraic Starr lit a cigarette and looked at his small army. He knew what he could expect of Danny and the priest, and he knew he could count on Martin Mahoney until his last breath. But after killing the German sailor, Tom Tracy had once more grown silent and brooding, and Starr feared that Rachel would be able to sway him from his task.

"Now, then, lads," Starr began, "we've only a few hours, so let's go over it once more. After we've landed the guns and gath-

379

ered the boys, we'll have three goals, the three *B*'s." He jabbed his finger at the map. "Bridge, barracks, and Ballinakill House."

"The head of the snake," Martin spat into his can.

"How do we land the guns without a wireless?" Tracy sipped his tea.

"We show two green lights to bring O'Leary and the others in their fishin' boats."

"Donal O'Leary . . ." Tracy lowered his mug. "Mixed up in the same kind of foolishness his brother was."

Starr glared across the table. "And never's the time he speaks the Tracy name without spittin'. But tomorrow, I'm expectin' you to show him what it means to be a Tracy."

"We'll *both* show him." Danny Tracy puffed his cigarette. He had not shaved that evening because Starr said the beard made him look older.

"You aren't goin', " said Tom.

"In a pig's ass," said Danny.

"You don't even know what it's about." A woman's voice echoed from the deck, and Rachel stepped into the forecastle. This time, she had recovered quickly from the humiliation and horror. She wore a dark skirt, Tracy's blue peacoat, and the hard edge that she had been honing in her cabin all day.

Danny sat up straight. "I know what I'm doin'. I'm a *man* now. You all seen that when the Germans come aboard."

"Don't pay her no mind, lad." Padraic Starr pulled the cigarette from his mouth and snuffed it out in the palm of his hand. "You done fine."

"There's no one thing that goes to makin' up a man," said the priest. "Don't be thinkin' that all it takes is feedin' a machine gun."

"Or killing a resident magistrate," said Rachel.

"He's got a name to clear," Padraic Starr slammed his hand with such force on the table that a tea mug spilled onto the deck. He had killed Germans, he had cajoled the captain and the mate, he had joked, he had threatened, but he had never before showed his anger to any of them.

But Rachel was not cowed. She went over to Tracy and looked into his eyes. "He's dragging us all into hell."

"Hell or redemption," said Starr.

The priest gave a sardonic laugh.

Rachel turned to Starr. The ship was riding into a swell and the lantern was swinging, so that the shadow danced on her face like a signal of alarm. "That's what you always tell yourselves when the wars start. But you saw the insanity of it yesterday. You fought the Germans that are helping you, and it was the British that saved you. And Tommy had to kill a boy not much older than his brother. This is madness."

"A simple thing to call someone else's fight madness," said Starr.

"I'm fighting for all of you." Rachel slammed her hand on the table, as angrily as Starr. "There's still time."

Starr leaned across the table. "The fight starts tomorrow, darlin'. I don't think Jack Tracy'd be wantin' us to miss it."

Tom Tracy said nothing. He felt the motion of the ship and watched the beam of light swinging from one face to the other. And he listened.

"If you're dead, Tommy, you can't make a difference to anyone. And when you're dead, they'll forget you."

"Ireland has a long memory." Starr leaned back, so the light could not reach his face. "They'll remember Tommy, just like they remember his old da in Dunslea, in Galway . . . even Dublin."

"Dublin?" said Daniel softly.

"Bailey's Pub, to the exact, where I stopped one fine day last May, with the Victoria Cross 'round my neck and the cheers of Dublin ringin' in my ears, and every man in the place ready to stand me to a pint. Most of them thought I was a patriot. A few thought I was a damn fool, but a brave one just the same.

"None of them knew I enlisted for no better reason than to please a Protestant girl." Starr brought his hand to his cheekbone and picked a small piece of paper off a shaving cut. "And none of them knew that I'd made up my mind to desert.

"They crowded around me and bought me whiskeys and porters, and somebody pulled out the paper with the stories of all the Irish V.C. winners and somebody said, 'So you're from Dunslea. I know Dunslea.' 'Oh, yeah,' said another. 'Do you recall Jack Tracy?' "

Starr leaned forward, into the light, and looked at Danny. "Irish memories are long, boy.

"Then somebody else shouted, 'Jack Tracy, *that* damned murderin' informer?' 'No informer at all, but a martyr, and a saint for certain,' says somebody else. And before I know it, there's men tearin' up a Dublin pub over the memory of your own father. It was then I decided to do what Jack Tracy asked of me in his death cell." He paused and looked at each face. "So there'd be no disagreement about the best man I ever knew."

"Did he tell you to do this to his sons?"

"If I could cleanse Jack Tracy's name, I would, but only a Tracy can wipe it clean the way it should be."

The lamp squeaked as it swung. The timbers of the *Abigail* creaked. Starr and Tracy studied each other as though their faces would answer some unanswerable question. Martin cracked his knuckles. Danny picked at his beard. The priest loosened his collar.

At last, Rachel whispered, "You've goaded us. You've toyed with us. You've"—she pulled her peacoat around herself—"humiliated us. And you dangle the name of Jack Tracy like a piece of meat in front of his sons. Why?"

"Because I loved him."

"No more than the rest of us," said Tom

Starr looked at each face individually. "But he loved me too much. My soul won't ever be clean till I clear his name, till I pay him back . . ."

————— 1 9 0 0 —————

The wagon jerked to a stop at the place where the Clifden road met the car path from Cleggan. The mist had rolled in, obscuring the moon and hanging so low that it covered the tops of the telegraph poles.

"What's wrong?" asked the boy.

"A rider, comin' out of the hills," said Liam O'Leary. "Stay down."

The boy pulled the straw over his head and listened.

"Can you tell who it is?" Jamie Hamilton's voice caught in the back of his throat.

"Tracy. It's Jack Tracy . . . the fuck."

The boy heard hands slap against the stock of the shotgun. He popped his head up from the straw. "You ain't plannin' to shoot Jack Tracy, are you?"

Liam O'Leary pushed the boy's head. "Stay down, damn you."

The boy spit dry straw and prayed that Jack Tracy would not find him.

"Whoa up there, lads," Jack Tracy's voice rumbled across the road.

"Who is it?" growled Liam.

"You know damn right well who it is."

The boy could hear Tracy's horse breathing hard. He could almost smell the sweat.

"You and us, we're done talkin'," said Liam O'Leary.

"I'm here to stop you."

"We asked your help, and you refused," said Jamie Hamilton.

The boy raised his head from the straw. He could see Jack Tracy, on his horse, just beyond the head of O'Leary's donkey, in dead line with O'Leary's gun.

The boy slipped down and searched about for the small wooden box that held the three pistols.

"Snap the reins, Jamie," said O'Leary. "Ride over him."

The boy could not find the box in the straw. He did not know what he was going to do, but he could not let them shoot Jack Tracy. The cart jerked forward by a foot or two and stopped. The boy looked up. Tracy held the donkey by the bridle and laid his shotgun over the pommel of his saddle.

"You're ridin' to your deaths, boys."

"We've a plan, Jack Tracy," said Jamie Hamilton.

Tracy laughed, a strange sound in this lonely spot.

Jamie said, "Get out of our way, Jack Tracy. We've a night train to catch in Clifden."

"Out of our way or we'll blast you where you sit," said O'Leary.

"You're ridin' into a trap, lads." Jack Tracy hesitated. "And it was me that set it."

A nighthawk screeched. A dog barked. The boy could not tell the direction of the sound because the mist was heavy on the upland, and the straw poked in his ears.

"They know that someone's plannin' to kill the queen in Muckross House. You'll never get near."

"You're lyin', Jack Tracy," said Liam O'Leary. "You're a Fenian."

"I been a Fenian. I been a Land Leaguer. Now I'm a Parnellite."

"Once a Fenian, always a Fenian, and Fenians don't inform."

The boy could hear the rage rising in Liam O'Leary's voice.

"They don't know who you are, lads," Jack Tracy said, sounding more reasonable, "but they know what you're about.

So it's time to give up your plan and go home. There'll be none the wiser."

"You informed on us!" The hammer cocked into place on O'Leary's shotgun. "You informed! You bloody bastard!"

"Uncle Jack, watch out!" The boy burst from the straw and grabbed at O'Leary's arms, but the gun went off.

A spray of birdshot tore away most of the donkey's head and splattered into Jack Tracy and his horse. As Tracy went down, both his triggers released. The boy felt the rush of air and the force of the buckshot, but two large bodies protected him from the blast, and the shotgun was angled upward, over his head.

As the shots echoed along the low run of hills, there came a sound of falling. The donkey collapsed in its traces. The horse hit the ground and pinned Jack Tracy beneath it. Jamie Hamilton tumbled backward and dropped off the cart. And the enormous body of Liam O'Leary landed on top of the boy in the straw.

"Liam?" said the boy softly. "Liam?" He reached up and put his hand on Liam's chest, then he touched the face. It was warm and wet and felt like thick stew. He pulled back the hand and wiped it on the straw.

"Paddy?" came the voice.

"Uncle Jack! Uncle Jack!" The boy jumped out of the cart and stumbled over the body of James Hamilton. Even in the dark, he could see the darker gouts bubbling from the side of Hamilton's head, and the left hand, raised to fend off the blow, was fingerless.

"Paddy! Paddy!"

The boy ran to the front of the wagon and dropped to his knees. Somewhere up the road, another dog had begun to bark.

Jack Tracy lay on his side with his dead horse on top of him. His left leg was covered with little buds of blood that were blossoming quickly on his gray trousers. Blood was oozing from several holes in his cheek, and the ground where the boy knelt was covered with the blood and brains of the animals that took the force of O'Leary's shot.

"Uncle Jack!"

"Did I hit the others? Are they dead?"

"Are you all right?"

"Are they dead?"

"I . . . I think so."

"Damn."

"Are you all right, Uncle Jack?"

"I'd be a lot better if I didn't kill them boys. If you didn't grab that gun, I'd be a lot worse."

"Can you get up?"

"I don't know. I think my right leg's broke."

"Let's try to get you up." The boy slid his hands under the horse's neck. "We'll count three, then you try to push him off."

The boy could barely raise the horse's neck, and Jack Tracy cried in pain when he tried to move.

"Broke, dammit." He slammed his hand down on the horse's flank. "Broken leg, dead horse, two dead fools, and one live one."

Tracy glared up at his nephew. "Why on earth did you do this without talkin' to me first? What got into you, lad?"

"I . . . I hate the Brits as much as any man, Uncle Jack, and this seemed like a good way to show it."

Jack Tracy spit blood onto the ground at Starr's feet.

"We'll never have a chance to get Victoria again."

"Thank the good Christ Himself."

Another dog began to bark, somewhere to the west. Paddy Starr looked down the road. In the misty distance, he could see the lights of Cleggan, and someplace closer, a pair of kerosene lamps were bouncing up the road.

"RIC night patrol, Uncle Jack."

Tracy strained his neck to see the road. "Damn."

"We have to get you up. We have to get out of here."

They tried again to lift the dead horse, but it was too heavy and the pain was too intense. Jack Tracy screamed and brought a hand to his mouth to muffle the sound.

The lights were closer now, and another dog was barking, just a few hundred yards away.

"They're comin' fast," said Jack Tracy. "They must've heard the firin'."

Paddy Starr crouched down and slid his hands under the horse's neck. "We've got to get you up."

Then his uncle's left hand was at his collar, pulling him down to the bloody face. "Get yourself out of here, lad. Hide up in the hills till we're gone, then go home, straight home, and never . . . never again do something this stupid!" With the last word, the blood on his lips sprayed into Paddy Starr's face.

"I can't leave you."

"I'll talk my way out of it, son. Now go."

Paddy Starr stood and stepped back. The kerosene lanterns

were closer now, and the rhythmic sound of two pumping bikes and two panting riders was rolling on ahead of them. Paddy Starr felt angry, disgusted, and sick at his stomach. There was blood everywhere, all over the road, all over his friends, all over himself. And what he had planned to do was not stupid. It was the act of a patriot. It was something Jack Tracy himself would have done in his younger days. He wanted tell his uncle that. But he was running away. His act of cunning and bravery, so carefully planned, was turning into the flight of a coward. But he was no coward, and there was no man in the world whose admiration he wanted more than Jack Tracy's.

The lights were coming closer. He would stay and meet them beside his uncle. He crouched down. Jack Tracy smacked him across the back of the head.

"I'm staying."

"Do you want to hang? You can't be that much of a damn fool. Get up and run!"

"No."

"You'll not be doin' anyone any good here." Tracy wiped the blood from his cheek. "But if you run away, you might get a chance to do us some good someday."

Paddy Starr stood again and stepped back.

"Run, lad," hissed Jack Tracy through the blood. "Run."

32

Down that same deserted road a rider galloped on the night before Easter. The hooves of his horse pounded into the damp earth, and the moon, just risen above the low run of hills, threw his shadow ahead of him like a spirit.

The capture of Roger Casement and the sinking of the *Aud* had quieted Dublin Castle. But these events had brought crisis to the Irish Volunteers. Like a set of Russian dolls, each one large enough to contain the next, the Irish Volunteers enclosed the Irish Republican Brotherhood, which itself enclosed the secret Military Council led by Padraic Pearse. It was within the Military Council that the rising had been planned.

Eoin MacNeill, the man who led the thirteen thousand Irish Volunteers that drilled on Sunday mornings, had learned that week of the rising. Initially, he had opposed it, then later reversed himself. But after learning that Casement was under guard in Tralee and the German arms were at the bottom of the Queenstown channel, he took an ad in the Dublin Sunday *Independent:* "Owing to the very critical situation, all orders given to the Irish Volunteers for tomorrow, Easter Sunday, are hereby rescinded."

Then he summoned messengers to his home.

One of them, who had traveled on the Midland Great Western Railway to Clifden, was now tethering his horse in front of St. Brendan's, among the jaunting cars, carts, and autocars of the Dunslea parish. It was the night of the Easter Vigil, and the rear doors were swung open because the crowd had overflowed the church.

The messenger excused his way through the vestibule, touched his fingers to the holy water font, and blessed himself. The air was heavy with the smells of incense, candle wax, and the unwashed bodies of men who had come straight from the fields or fishing boats.

Christ was in the grave. He was not with them. His tabernacle was open and empty. The crucifix was shrouded in purple cloth. But all across the nave, candles glimmered in the hands of the faithful, soft and beautiful symbols of hope.

"You look to be a stranger," whispered Seamus Kilkeirnan. "Would you want a candle?"

"I'm lookin' for Donal O'Leary."

Seamus lowered his candle, and his face dropped into shadow. "Who is it that's doin' the lookin'?"

"Flynn. Irish Volunteers, if it's any business of yours."

Seamus took a candle from the box behind him, lit it with his own, and handed it to Flynn. "You'll find him sixth row down on the left. Sittin' with his parents and his Protestant lady friend."

In the candlelight, Donal O'Leary's hand touched Deirdre's. She turned her palm into his, and his hand closed around it.

A small gesture. In a Catholic church, seated between Donal and his parents, it seemed to Deirdre a small sacrilege. But there was little time left. Beneath his calluses, she felt the perspiration. He was frightened, she knew. He had good reason.

387

Hope was fading. Starr had not arrived nor sent word. And Easter rose with the sun. They would attack the barracks without Starr's weapons or his spirit. Donal would lead twenty poorly armed men against a half-dozen trained constables secure in their barracks.

Kathleen Mary O'Toole O'Leary glanced at her husband. She had seen her son's hand touch the young woman's, and she was smiling, the way she did when one of the ewes dropped a lamb, when life promised to go on, as it would even with a Protestant daughter-in-law.

Logan did not smile back. His throat was as dry as ash. He would have given half his flock for a pint. But Finnerty's was closed. He would have given half his soul to be in another county, or his grave, but he was here, and the list was in his pocket.

From the corner of his eye, he watched the fingers twine together. The last name he had written on the list belonged to the woman holding his son's hand. There were ten names on the list and a description of the plans for Easter Sunday. Most of the information Logan had gotten from Seamus Kilkeirnan after he had gotten Seamus drunk. And when the drinking was done, he had added Seamus's name to the list, as well. But he could not bring himself to deliver it.

Now, Donal was climbing over him and going outside with a stranger who had just slipped down the aisle. Logan watched them for a moment, then Deirdre got up and went after them.

The message was on a note card:

> *Woodtown Park*
> *Rathfarnham*
> *Co. Dublin*
> *22 April 1916*

Volunteers completely deceived. All orders for tomorrow Sunday are entirely cancelled.

> *Eoin MacNeill*

"Written a few hours ago, by MacNeill himself." The messenger had his reins in his hand, ready to ride.

"Do these orders agree with Pearse? It's one thing we've been hearin', then the other, all week."

"This is the final word," answered the messenger. "I'd love to be stayin' for the vigil, but I've other stops to make. How long to Westport by horseback?"

Donal smiled. He almost laughed. He clapped the messenger on the shoulder and told him that if he waited until the end of the service, he could have himself a cup of tea and Donal would find someone to drive him.

"I'll take a snort of somethin' stronger than tea, if it's about." The messenger's eyes shifted to the woman who had just come out of the church.

Donal introduced his future wife and handed her the card, then he led the messenger toward the quart of Jameson's he kept on his boat.

A voice growled out of the darkness and startled Deirdre. "Thank Christ."

Deirdre looked up.

Logan was beside her. "I knew your bunch was up to somethin', darlin'. I hated to think what was goin' to happen."

"Did you never learn it's impolite to read private business over people's shoulders?"

"Will you be obeyin' this order?"

Deirdre said nothing.

Logan rubbed a hand across his beard. "Darlin', Seamus told me everythin', and I been worried to death. Will you be obeyin' this?"

"We'll be obeyin' it indeed." Donal came back through the shadows of animals and carts. He smelled as though he had taken a long swallow of Jameson's himself. "If it's any business of yours."

"When my son and the woman he loves are facin' a bloody fate, it's business of mine." Impulsively, Logan gave Deirdre a kiss on the cheek. It was the first time he had ever touched her. Then he pumped Donal's hand and clapped him on the back, and as the tears rose in his eyes, he turned quickly and went back into the church.

Donal and Deirdre remained outside, in the small square. A horse pawed at the ground. The moon was rising higher, casting silver light on the bay beyond them.

"I feel like they just lifted the rock of Cashel from off my chest," whispered Donal.

"It's a reprieve, Donal. The fight'll come someday."

He wrapped his arms around her. "Not tomorrow, darlin'. You and I will marry."

She looked into his eyes. "But what if Padr'ic comes with the guns?"

The old jealousy rode across his face like a shadow on the moon. "I hate to say it, but I don't think he *is* comin'. The Tracys turned him in, or the Brits got him in Boston, or they got him at sea, or he took his money and found himself a gal and started a new life in America. If he was comin', he'd be here by now."

She knew he was right. She tried very hard to keep the tears from brimming in her eyes, and when they did, she pulled his big solid body to hers and held him tight. "We'll marry, Donal, and maybe the fight'll never come."

"Where the hell have you been?"

"I've good news for your honor."

A turf fire sputtered in the library. Logan stood on a handsome carpet, surrounded by oak paneling, leather furniture, leather-bound books, and pictures of the hunt.

The resident magistrate, dressed in evening clothes, folded his arms and sat on the edge of his desk. "We missed Easter Vigil services in Clifden because we were waiting for you."

"Beggin' pardon, your honor, but it sounds like you're havin' a fine service right in your own parlor." Logan glanced through the office door and across the foyer.

One of the Clarke's daughters and another young woman were singing while Mrs. Clarke played "Nearer My God to Thee." A man's voice had also been singing, but now the man was crossing the foyer. At the sight of the red tunic and the medals, Logan O'Leary lost his smile.

"Lieutenant Lambert-Jones," explained Clarke. "A guest for the weekend."

Logan eyed him warily, then raised a hand and pulled at his forelock.

"This must be your . . ." Lambert-Jones avoided saying *informer*. "The gentleman you were telling me about."

"I've been waiting for a list of names, but Logan tells me he has good news instead."

"That's what I said, your honor, and that's what I have." Logan wet his lips and widened his grin. His eye had fallen on the decanter of port.

"If the news is good, Logan, we'll all drink a toast," said Clarke.

Logan looked again at the red tunic.

390

"The lieutenant's from Dublin Castle itself," Clarke explained. "Speak freely."

"Well, then, your honors, I'll tell you that there's not to be a rising. There's no trouble planned for tomorrow or any time soon, that I know of." Logan looked from one face to the other, expecting smiles or expressions of relief, or perhaps his drink.

"Where did you hear this information?" asked Clarke.

"A rider brought a message to the vigil service."

"To whom?"

"Now, sir, you wouldn't want me to be tellin' that." Logan cleared his throat. "But I'll tell what it said." And he recited the note, word for word.

Clarke looked at Lambert-Jones. "Do you believe it?"

"If what we heard in Dublin is true, then the rising is off for certain." Lambert-Jones cocked his head and studied the shepherd.

Logan looked down at the carpet.

In the other room, the ladies were now singing "Come Thou Almighty King."

"What do your people say about Padraic Starr?" asked Lambert-Jones.

"That he ain't comin'."

Lambert-Jones studied O'Leary's face and searched for some trace of the lie. Beneath the beard and the pockmarks and the whiskey veins, he saw only fear. "You're certain of this? Who's your source?"

Seamus Kilkeirnan had told Logan that the Volunteers had given up on Starr. Seamus had heard it as speculation from Donal, but he had stated it as certain as the faith.

"I can't say, your honor, but it's what I know."

William Clarke went over to the decanter and poured three glasses of port. "If it's true, it's a double dose of good news, calling for a double dose of port. No rising, and no Starr."

Logan drank before the others had their glasses. With the wine improving his confidence, he said, "Now that we've such good news, we can be forgettin' about that list, can't we?"

"We have an action planned for this evening," said Clarke, "to stop a rising before it happens."

Logan finished his drink and held his glass for more.

"This is vintage," said Clarke.

"That it is, your honor, that it is, and a fine way to slake a thirst."

391

Lambert-Jones sipped his port and smiled as Clarke filled the glass a second time. Meeting the countryfolk could be an education, he thought.

Logan swallowed half the glass in a single gulp, then licked his lips and furrowed his brow. "Excuse me for sayin' so, your honors, but if the risin' ain't about to happen, you'd be doin' better to let it alone."

"With an attitude like that, you could find work in Dublin Castle," said Lambert-Jones.

"There's merit to what he says," answered Clarke.

"Thank you, your honor." Logan raised his glass in a small toast and smiled. The wine was staining his teeth red. In their presence, he was beginning to feel like one of the town's important men, doing what he could to keep the peace.

A lorry rumbled up the drive and stopped in front of the house. The butler ushered Chief Inspector Hayes into the study. Hayes brought news: A stranger had come into the church, and Donal O'Leary, Deirdre Hamilton, and Logan O'Leary had followed him out.

Logan felt the lieutenant's eyes on him, like the tips of two bullets.

"Your son?" said Lambert-Jones.

"We all know me boy's in the Volunteers. That's why in the hell I'm here, and why I know so much." Logan looked from face to face, feeling suddenly like a drunk trapped by three thugs in an alley.

"We also know," said Clarke gently, "that Donal would have led the rising."

"But there ain't to *be* a rising, so there's no need for the list. You've said that yourself."

Clarke went over to the fireplace and poked at the turf. "A plan that dies of its own does not need us to breathe life back into it."

"You know the mood of your district better than I, Resident Magistrate," said Lambert-Jones.

"But what about Constable Shea?" Chief Inspector Hayes was smiling, as always.

"Quite so." Clarke poured a glass of port for the inspector. "In times like these, we can wink at a great deal, wire-cutting, amateur conspiring, but not murder."

He brought the decanter to Logan and filled his glass again.

"Give us Constable Shea's murderer, right now, and we will dispense with the list."

Logan looked down at the red wine filling his glass and then into the eyes of the resident magistrate.

Clarke smiled at him, although the others could not see it. "The name of Shea's murderer, Logan, or I shall be forced to arrest your son."

Logan sipped the port, then he drained the glass in one gulp and gave the name that seemed the most logical. "It was Seamus Kilkeirnan killed the constable. Seamus pushed him over the edge."

"Inspector, arrest Seamus Kilkeirnan."

"Yes, your honor. Anyone else?"

"We'll leave everyone else to enjoy their lamb joints and meditate on the Resurrection."

33

*I*n the beginning, God created heaven and earth.' "

The moon was now risen full. The tiny ship slipped silently along, a black silhouette against the luminous sky and silver-limned sea.

" 'And the earth was void and empty, and darkness was upon the face of the deep; and the spirit of God moved over the waters.' "

The coast of Ireland lay within view, a dark mass swept at long, lonely intervals by lighthouse beams.

" 'And God said: Be light made. And light was made.' "

A small flame appeared beneath one of the wide, arching sails. Another sprang out of it, and then a third.

" 'And God saw the light that it was good.' "

The hot wax dripped onto Rachel Levka's hand as Henry Huntoon touched his candle to hers. Then she touched her flame to Tracy's, and Tracy touched his to Starr's, and Rachel climbed to the quarterdeck to light the candle that Jason Pratt held.

Sean O'Fearna stood on the aft hatch, the book open in front of him, but the words were etched in his memory, words central to no single faith, but to all of life. " 'And he divided the light from the darkness.' "

The flame in Rachel's hand moved aft to the helm. Flames flickered to life in the hands of Martin Mahoney and Daniel Tracy. And Rachel's flame came forward again.

The priest closed the book and touched a candle to Starr's, and the circle was complete. "While we wait for the Messiah, whether he rises for us tomorrow or"—O'Fearna glanced at Rachel and gave her a small smile—"comes to us in the far future, we can all find truth in these words."

"Amen," said Henry Huntoon.

Rachel slipped her hand into Tracy's. He looked at her and tried to smile, but the candle created on his face a strange pattern of light and shadow.

He was thinking of his father. Jack Tracy had tried to divide the light from the darkness in his own life. He had made himself a blood sacrifice for Ireland. Now, one of his disciples, as flawed and foolish as the first apostles, had called them all back to sacrifice themselves for his beliefs. And who would benefit? he wondered. Would they? Or Ireland? Or the disciple himself?

Tracy looked up at the sails and the sky and the moon rising higher. Blessed is the shepherd who lays down his life for his flock. But why did he let himself walk the gallows when another could have gone in his place? Why did he leave his wife with three children and die for Padraic Starr? Because he believed that his death would matter, that people would remember a man who died trying to stop the bloodshed. And because a man in Dunslea had condemned him in an act of vengeance.

And why did Starr tell them the truth? To calm his own conscience after all he had brought them through? Tracy wished that Starr had not told them, for the truth turned a grand act of rebellion and revenge into a personal quest for forgiveness, the Celtic sin-eater atoning for his transgressions.

"On this night," said the priest, "we know that there is light and darkness, hope and desolation, good and evil, in each of us."

Tracy felt Rachel squeeze his hand.

"And even when the light is as feeble as these few candles against the firmament, when the thread of hope is as slender as it was on the night of the first Easter Vigil, we must believe that God gives us the strength to endure and the wisdom to find the right path."

Would Tom Tracy sacrifice himself? Would he stop the bloodshed? Would he exact his own vengeance? Would God give him strength and wisdom? After three thousand miles, he no longer knew.

The sails of the *Abigail,* from a distance, curved as gracefully as the wings of a great seabird riding the wind toward home. The horizon behind her was a hard, straight line. And now, another line was appearing in the sea and speeding straight for her hull.

It moved through the water at forty knots. It came from more than a mile away. It carried eighteen pounds of trinitrotoluene in its nose. A tank of compressed air drove an engine that spun a shaft that turned two propellors at its stern. After it had traveled a short distance, a small lock spun itself off a threaded shaft, exposing its detonator. It had been fired by the U-boat commander who had endured the killing of half his crew and a day's pursuit by a destroyer, and he had resolved to avenge himself on the three-masted British Q-ship that lured him into the trap.

Henry Huntoon saw the white wake first. It glowed like phosphorus in the moonlight.

"Torpedo!"

Jason Pratt lifted himself from his chair and looked.

There was no time to study its path. No time to calculate its depth. No time for the people aboard to brace themselves or embrace each other or murmur a prayer. Barely time to scream, "Hard aport!"

And no time for the square-hulled *Abigail* to respond.

The bright night brightened with a flash that froze eight people for an instant in orange light.

Padraic Starr was tipping back over the rail. Sean O'Fearna was flying into the air. Tom Tracy and Rachel Levka were turning to each other. Jason Pratt was crumpling on a useless leg. Danny Tracy was spinning with the wheel. Martin Mahoney was grabbing the lifeboat davit. And Henry Huntoon was disappearing in the flame.

The concussion crushed the boards and splintered the deck and snapped the eighty-foot mainmast like a stick of candy. Tom Tracy felt the air sucked out of his lungs. Rachel Levka had the coat torn from her back.

In the instant after the flash, a great column of water climbed half as high as the mainmast and stood suspended for a second above the ship. The deafening roar of the explosion rose with it, then the water collapsed, crashing like a pile of rocks onto the deck.

The splintered wood supporting the mainmast gave way. The deadeyes popped. The shrouds tore out of their backstays. And the eighty-foot fir tree fell.

With it came line and rigging, boom and gaff, and the enormous square of canvas. Tom Tracy tried to roll away, but the sail settled over him like a tent.

He heard Rachel screaming somewhere in the darkness nearby, and the priest making a terrible, almost irrational sound, as though some intense pain had turned him into something subhuman.

And now, as he struggled to clear his head and fight his way out from under the canvas, Tracy felt Rachel's body sliding into him. He grabbed her leg and held on, but he was sliding away from her, because the deck was tilting and the water was rushing in and the *Abigail* was going over.

The torpedo had torn a thirty-foot hole in the hull. The cargo of guns and bullets and medicine was hemorrhaging into the sea. And as the old schooner turned on her beam ends, her human cargo was going as well.

Rachel screamed.

Tom Tracy lost his grip on her leg and tumbled toward the rail, but the rail was gone, torn out by the blast, and Tracy plunged into the bitter black water.

Beneath the surface, fighting shock and feeling his lungs scream for air, he felt a body slam into him. Rachel. *Rachel.*

He popped to the surface. The blackness grew a shade brighter, but he could see nothing, not even the moon. Somewhere above him, the priest was still shrieking. Somewhere off to the left, a weak, pain-fractured voice was calling. But Tracy could no longer tell where the ship was or where he was, and the icy water was lapping at his chin and soaking his clothes and dragging him down once more.

Then something splashed out of the water beside him. It coughed and cried his name, and its mouth filled with water. Rachel. *Rachel*

He grabbed her by the hair and pulled her to the surface. She coughed again. She retched. And in the darkness, he could see the wide whites of her eyes.

"Tommy! Where are we? Tommy!"

Tracy pulled off his heavy wool sweater, and with his knife he slashed off the remnants of her peacoat. "Don't sink! Stay afloat!"

"Where are we?"

"We're under the sail."

"No!" And she began to swim away.

"Stop!"

"No! Let me out, let me out!" The old fear, the terrible panic, was settling on her again. She was trapped beneath another body, beneath another mother. "Let me out!"

He grabbed her by the hair and yanked hard. "Stop, dammit! We don't know where we are. Stop."

She swung back to him, and the steam from her breath blew warm against his face.

"I don't know which way to swim," he said.

The sounds of the dying ship seemed to fill the strange dark tent. The boards were groaning and creaking under crushing new pressures. The cargo and equipment were shifting, breaking loose, tumbling and crashing down the deck. The shrouds and rigging were snapping with the sounds of giant bowstrings drawn too taut.

And now, suddenly, Tracy felt the canvas forcing itself down on his head. The mast had snapped off, and it should have floated free, but it had fouled in its own line and was sinking with the ship, sinking with them beneath it.

"The knife!" screamed Rachel. "Use the knife!"

Tracy still held it in freezing fingers. He drove it straight up, into the belly of the canvas, and ripped with all his strength.

"Hurry, Tommy!"

A shaft of moonlight, as bright to them as the morning sun, dropped through the rent in the sail. Tracy poked his head through it, and his heart sickened. Laid out on her side, the *Abigail* looked enormous, like a living being in her final agony. The deck stood straight out of the water, and the polished brass cap of the binnacle glinted in the moonlight.

And something on the vertical deck was moving. Sean O'-Fearna was hanging, upside down, by a halyard that somehow had wrapped itself around his leg. He was shaking his head and flailing at the air and grabbing at his ears, but the rope held him tight.

"Father!" screamed Tracy.

The priest did not hear him. He could not hear. His eardrums had been shattered.

Tracy reached through the hole in the canvas and pulled Rachel up and out. The plunge of the *Abigail* had slowed for a moment as the spanker and the foresail provided buoyancy, but Tracy could hear the sails starting to rip under the weight of the sinking ship. The *Abigail* was going, and there was nothing that Tracy could do.

He pushed Rachel away from the ship, and the sail that a moment ago had threatened to drown them now became their raft. They ran up the length of it, knee deep, then waist deep, then chest deep in water, and when they reached the boom, they pushed off and swam away from the hull.

The *Abigail* groaned like a great old tree splitting in the wind. The bow rose slightly, the stern settled deeper. Then she seemed to hesitate, holding on to the last moments of life, giving her only passenger a few final seconds to make his peace.

The figure hanging on the deck stopped struggling. He blessed himself, then he stretched out his arms to the water rising mercifully toward him.

Tracy shouted, "Swim, Rachel, swim away!"

But Rachel did not move. She looked at the *Abigail* with the sickened fascination of someone watching her home burn to the ground.

The old schooner tipped slightly, as though she might turn turtle, and then, all at once, she went. She did not lift high into the sky before plummeting. Instead, she stayed on her beam ends, and with the priest folding his arms in repose, she went silent and dignified by the stern.

Huge bubbles rushed to the surface from her shattered hull. The debris floating above her was tossed about crazily. The water turned white and frothed. Waves rolled out in every direction from the sinking shoal of wood. Then the water settled to smooth blackness. The night was silent, and they were alone on the ocean.

And they were freezing to death.

The mainmast had finally floated free, and it was drifting toward them.

"C'mon," said Tracy. "We'll use the sail for a raft."

But she did not respond. Her eyes were glassed over, and she was barely staying afloat.

They had been in the water for at least five minutes. He knew that they could not survive longer than ten. But he would not let them give up.

"C'mon."

Then he heard someone call his name. It was Martin's voice. Then he heard the clanking of oarlocks, and off to his left the white hull of the yawlboat reflected the moonlight.

"Hey, Tommy!" It was Danny.

"By the mainmast!"

The moment that Huntoon shouted the warning, Martin Mahoney had calmly released the yawlboat davits. While the column of water was rising above the *Abigail,* the yawlboat was slapping onto the surface, tipping, then righting itself, and Martin and Danny were lowering on the davit ropes.

Jason Pratt's yawlboat was better stocked than many of the cargo schooners that sailed the Maine coast. Wool blankets, salt cod and ship's biscuit, and a fair supply of brandy were kept in a small forward compartment, along with charts and navigational tools.

Tracy and Rachel were soon stripped of their wet clothes, modesty be damned, wrapped snugly in several layers of wool, and served metal mugs of brandy by Martin Mahoney. Meanwhile, Daniel called the others, but there were no answers.

Then, as her body warmed and her mind began to thaw, Rachel saw something white reflecting the moonlight. "That's a face," she said softly. "Over there. It's Padr'ic."

If Starr had not shaved, they would never have seen him.

"Padr'ic!" called Danny. "Padr'ic, hang on! We're comin'!"

Starr slipped off the wreckage he had been clinging to.

"Padr'ic!" cried Tom Tracy.

Starr began to swim off into the darkness.

"His mind's freezin' up," said Martin. "Pull harder!"

"Padr'ic!" cried Danny.

But Starr kept swimming.

"Padr'ic, wait for us!" called Rachel.

At the sound of her voice, he rolled over onto his back. Then he called her name. "Are you all right?" he said weakly.

"Cold, Padr'ic, cold but better."

He grunted and tried to swim away again.

Danny held out an oar. "Grab it, Padr'ic!"

Starr put his face in the black water and swung his arms feebly. Danny put the oar directly in front of him.

Starr half rose from the water and knocked it away. "Leave me alone! It's over. Let me go!"

"Bejesus, we won't be doin' that," said Martin. "We didn't

come three thousand miles to let you throw in the towel, you son of a bitch." Martin leaned over the side of the boat and grabbed at Starr's collar.

Starr avoided it and kept swimming toward the darkness. "I failed. I failed all of you. I failed Jack Tracy. Go the hell back to America."

"We're in Ireland," shouted Tom. "We're joining the rising."

"Without guns?"

"We've got guns!" cried Danny. "A dozen Enfields."

And Starr rolled over in the water once more.

"And a thousand rounds. I loaded them last night," Danny said. "If you didn't let me come with you, I was plannin' to steal the boat and come ashore myself."

"There now," said Martin. "How can you be givin' up with spirit like that?"

Tom saw the guns at the stern, then he looked at Rachel. She was shivering.

"Now get in, damn you," growled Martin, "and stop feelin' sorry for yourself. Jack Tracy let himself hang for you, and never's the time you heard him cryin'!"

Padraic Starr grabbed Danny's oar.

34

*D*eirdre awoke when the sky first brightened. She rolled over and felt Donal beside her. On other mornings, he had sneaked back to his boat at dawn, before the gossips were out of bed. But today, the gossips would be going off to sunrise services, so she let him sleep.

He had shared her bed for a week, and this last night had been the first that he did not toss about or cry out or wake soaked in sweat. She had slept well herself, because without the rising to worry him, Donal had been able to satisfy her desires as well as his own. He was a good man. She could be happy with him, no matter what.

She drew a kettle of water from the cistern and threw a turf brick into the stove. When the turf started to smoke, she went outside.

She had not decided which lamb she would sacrifice for Easter dinner. Until the night before, she had not expected that there would *be* an Easter dinner. She watched the sheep nibbling peacefully along the edges of their own shadows, oblivious to the tower of Dun Slea or the dark blue sea beyond.

It was the kind of morning she always imagined when she thought of Mary Magdalene on her way to the tomb. The warm light and chilled air of the April dawn filled her with hope. She told herself that the marriage of a Protestant woman and a Catholic man could bring more good to Ireland than all the rifles that Padraic Starr had ever promised.

She went into the privy, hiked up her nightgown, and dropped onto the cold seat. And through the small window, she saw him.

He was on the battlement of Dun Slea, looking through a pair of binoculars. Then he was gone. She blinked her eyes. She told herself it was an apparition. Then the red hair appeared again. He was squinting into the bright, slanting rays of the sun.

He had come back. He was with them.

She ran to the barn and bridled her gray pony.

The sound of pounding hooves woke Donal O'Leary and drew him to the window. Deirdre's pink nightgown was fluttering out behind her as she rode off. Donal pulled on his pants and grabbed his pistol and went after her.

"Rider comin'." Danny Tracy was looking down the road, while his brother and Padraic Starr studied Ballinakill House through the binoculars. "A woman in a nightgown. A guy chasin' her on a bike."

Starr came across from the east side and looked down. Then he drank a long swallow from the brandy bottle he held by the neck.

The night before, after wrapping Starr in blankets and hanging the soaking clothes on a makeshift line, Martin and Danny had raised sail and pointed the yawlboat east, on the heading that Jason Pratt had set for the *Abigail*. With the approach of dawn, the silhouette of Dun Slea had appeared against the gray sky like a black beacon.

They had anchored the yawlboat in shallow water, near an outcropping of rocks that shielded the white hull from view.

Starr, Tracy, and Rachel had put on their clothes, which were half-dry, with icy wet seams and pockets. Then Starr had led them across the strand, to the place in the rocks where, if they turned sideways, crouched, and pushed, they would be admitted into a dark, foul-smelling cave. From there, he had led them through a maze-like passage, to a staircase, to a stone that still rolled smoothly after seven centuries, and eventually to the battlement atop Dun Slea.

It was not the way Tom Tracy had expected to arrive in Ireland. Looking down the bay from the ancient fort, he felt none of the emotions he had expected. He was numb to his old anger or the patriotic fire of a man who had returned to his birthplace to begin a rebellion. He was cold, exhausted, and the brandy burned in his stomach.

And the torpedoing of the *Abigail* had turned the great irony in upon itself once more. In a world gone crazy, even allies destroyed one another.

He raised his binoculars and pointed them across the bay toward Ballinakill House. He revolved his finger and pulled the front door into focus, like a dream. He was looking for something to remind him of his hate. Instead, he saw a young woman. She was wearing a nightgown and robe and holding a basket under her arm. He remembered her from that day long ago. In her innocence, she had invited him for tea before her father slammed the door.

Deirdre Hamilton ignored Donal's shouts. She rode to the point, up the path, past the ruins of the chapel and the cemetery, to the base of the cylindrical stone tower that perched on the cliff like the last petrified tree in Ireland.

She ran into the port and up the stairs in her bare feet. She called his name. She burst into the sunlight.

He had come back. He was standing on the other side of the battlement. She ran toward him. She threw her arms around his neck and kissed him. But she felt none of the passion or confidence she had remembered, and she tasted liquor. She stepped back and looked around with sudden embarrassment.

There were four others on the battlement. The big one glanced at her briefly, then turned and brought his binoculars to his face. He looked like Jack Tracy. The boy holding a rifle looked like another Tracy. The older man calmly chewed his tobacco. And over by the rifles, a young woman sat with her knees pulled up to her chest. She was shivering, but her eyes were on Deirdre, and the intensity of her gaze made Deirdre fold her arms across the outline of her breasts.

Finally, Starr reached out and put his hands on her shoulders. "We made it, Dee." His voice was filled with the sound of defeat washed over by brandy.

"We thought you were dead," Deirdre said to Starr.

"Damn near." He pulled her to him and held her tight, the way a brother would hold his sister after a parent had died. "But, such as we are, we've come to join the risin'."

"There's not to be a risin'." Donal O'Leary's harsh voice rose from the stairhole ahead of him.

At the sound, Deirdre pulled away from Starr and stepped back.

"The risin's been called off." Donal appeared in the sunlight, his beefy face red from his ride, the sweat soaking through his beard.

"No risin'?" Starr turned to Deirdre and let out a bitter laugh.

Deirdre shook her head. "No risin'."

"Shit," said Danny Tracy.

Martin Mahoney spat a gob of tobacco. "I told you about that cursin'."

Starr laughed again. "No risin'. That's a good one. They're jokin' us, Tommy."

Tracy lowered his binoculars for a moment, but said nothing.

"We're glad you're alive." Donal handed Starr the note. "But there's no risin'."

Starr read it. "*Volunteers deceived?* What does this mean?"

"The final word," said Donal.

"Volunteers deceived? Who deceived them?"

Donal took off his coat and dropped it over Deirdre's shoulders. "I don't know."

Starr stalked over to the battlement. Rachel was sitting by the rifles. "Volunteers deceived. Gunrunners made damn fools of. Isn't that what you've been hopin' for, darlin'?"

"Get away from her, Padr'ic," said Tom quietly.

"Volunteers deceived, Tommy." Starr tipped his head back and drank from the brandy bottle. "That's what we've come back to."

"We've come to join a fight, but if nobody wants to join us . . ." Tracy was not relieved by the news, nor was he surprised. The history always seemed to end this way, in futility, until the fighting began again. Through the binoculars, he watched the young woman in front of Ballinakill House. She was taking Easter eggs from the basket and hiding them in the bushes and around the lawn.

Donal studied Tracy, then looked at Starr. "Is this Yank who I think he is?"

It was to have been one of Starr's small moments of triumph, but like the others, it was taken from him. Before he could speak, Danny Tracy stepped in front of Donal and said, with the pride of someone who had fought the Atlantic to get there, "That's Tom Tracy, and I'm Danny. We're Jack Tracy's sons."

"Well said, lad." Starr drained off the last of the brandy.

Donal O'Leary looked from one brother to the other. "Jack Tracy, that damned—"

Starr brought his finger to his lips. "Be careful what you say, Donal. The big one's got a good right and the little one's got an Enfield."

Donal pulled himself up straight and puffed out his chest. He was bigger than any man there, but he looked slightly ridiculous in suspenders and undershirt. He stepped onto the stone platform that ran around the inside of the battlement. "The last time I saw you, Tom Tracy, I beat the bejesus out of you."

"*I* beat the bejesus out of *you*," answered Tracy.

Donal scratched at his beard, then his mouth curled in the beginning of a smile. "If you did, it was the last time it happened. I've cursed you more than once since then . . . you and your whole damn family."

"You were wrong," said Tom Tracy calmly.

After a moment, Donal offered his hand. "I never thought you'd come back for this. I figured you for gutless."

Tracy took Donal's hand and looked at the rough, weathered face. He was not searching for respect, but he saw it.

"We come back to clear our da's name," said Danny.

Tom looked at his brother. "It needs no clearing, Dan. And it never did."

"Then we come to join the fight." The boy looked Donal in the eye. "If there's one startin'."

"There might be if we saw more guns," said Donal. "What happened to the guns?"

"Volunteers deceived. Ship sunk. Guns and good men at the bottom of the Atlantic." Starr smashed the bottle on the stone

404

floor. Glass flew into the air and sparkled in the morning light. "That's what happened to the guns. We bungled it."

"We tried." Tracy raised his binoculars and looked across the bay again.

"What are you lookin' at?" demanded Starr.

"An old man and his daughter." Tracy could summon no anger for Donal O'Leary, and no hatred for what he saw through the binoculars. William Clarke had come out, wearing a bathrobe and slippers. He was taking eggs from his daughter's basket, hiding them around the front door, and laughing happily.

Starr snatched the binoculars and looked.

"Colored eggs," said Tracy.

"I can think of folks hereabouts who'll scrape to find a *brown* egg this fine Easter morning," answered Starr.

"That's for sure," said Donal.

"We come to kill him, Tommy, for killin' your da." Starr looked through the binoculars again, as though the sight of William Clarke gave him strength . . . or fresh anger.

"And we come to start the risin'," said Danny.

Starr lowered the glasses and grinned at Danny. The old Celtic sin-eater returned. "I like your spirit, boy."

"And we like yours, Padr'ic." Deirdre ignored the broken glass and went over to him.

"If there's no risin', what are you plannin'?" said Donal, trying to turn Starr's attention from Deirdre.

But Starr ignored him and stepped off the platform.

Deirdre put her arms on Starr's shoulders and looked into his eyes. "Guns or no, rising or not, it's a miracle you've come back to us. Let's celebrate that."

Rachel Levka watched Starr embrace the Irish woman. He had the magic, Martin Mahoney had said, and now, Rachel saw it again. The defeat and depression were leaving his face. He was becoming once more the confident rebel who had wrapped his arms around Rachel six weeks before. And for an irrational moment, she felt jealous. Perhaps that was what he wanted. Perhaps it was another small play in his struggle for Tracy. But Rachel had learned. Starr's story had taken the magic out of him. It was Jack Tracy who had the magic. It was Jack Tracy's dreams and bravery and tormented soul that had brought them back on the day of the Resurrection.

Starr held Deirdre tightly, while Donal O'Leary's face reddened. "We've twelve guns and a thousand rounds of ammunition, my darlin', and I'd rather make a new miracle than celebrate an old one."

Deirdre's eyes shifted nervously to Donal, then she stepped back and took Starr's hands in hers. "Come to my cottage. I'll make tea, and we'll decide what to do." She looked around. "All of you come."

"Am I invited?" growled Donal.

As though answering to the challenge in Donal's voice, Starr drew Deirdre to him once more. She did not resist. Donal stepped off the battlement. The moment that Deirdre and Donal feared had arrived, in the bright sunshine, in front of four strangers. Deirdre raised her face to Starr. Donal raised his fist. But Starr merely kissed her on the cheek, as brief and modest as a parish priest. Then he turned her toward Donal. "Go to your man. Stand by him."

Donal grabbed for her like a father snatching his child from the path of a lorry. On his face a father's emotions seemed to clash, the joy at saving his child from danger, the anger that she had placed herself before it to begin with.

Starr looked at Tracy. "And if you think you must, you go to your *woman*."

"He'll do what he wants." Rachel stood.

Starr picked up two rifles. "That he will." He flipped a rifle to Tracy. "As for me, I'm startin' a fight."

Martin Mahoney spit a stream of tobacco over the battlement.

Danny Tracy pulled back his rifle bolt and slammed home a round. "I'm ready."

"Good lad."

"They've called it off, Pad'ric," said Donal.

Starr rammed the second rifle into Donal's hands. "We've five good men and at least one good woman standin' right here. Plus plenty more in the brigade."

"Mostly unarmed," said Donal.

Starr pointed at the guns. "Twelve rifles."

Donal looked at the rifle in his hand. "It's a fine-lookin' weapon, but we can't be winnin' a risin' with a dozen Enfields and a thousand rounds."

"That's why you begin a risin' by strikin' at the barracks." He turned to Deirdre. "Ain't that right, Dee?"

She nodded. "That's the way it's always been."

"Are you with me, darlin'?"

Deirdre picked up a rifle and stood beside Donal. "We're both with you."

Donal put his arm around her.

And Rachel understood a bit more. This hulking fisherman was frightened, like any man facing death. But if he faltered, Starr could take his woman. Rachel looked at Tracy and hoped that now, such simple threats had lost their meaning for him. In the little time left, she had to make Tom Tracy hear his father's voice . . . and her own.

"All right, then." Starr slapped Deirdre on the shoulder, like a comrade. "You take your motorbike and head 'round the point. Collect what boys you can, and meet us back here in two hours. Brigade Commandant O'Leary and me, we'll arm 'em and give 'em the plan."

Rachel slipped the binoculars from off Tracy's shoulder and looked across the bay. "Little boys," she said, almost to herself.

Starr continued to snap out his orders. "While Deirdre's collectin' the lads, the five of us'll make a little visit to Ballinakill House."

Tracy brought the rifle to his face and pointed it across the bay, testing its aim.

Starr watched him. "We'll take the yawlboat across, Tommy, avoid the center of town entirely."

Tracy lowered the rifle and studied it and tested its heft in his hands, as though he had every intention of using it. But he said nothing.

"Little boys," said Rachel again, more loudly. Then she gently took the rifle from Tracy's hands and gave him the binoculars.

He brought them to his eyes. Clarke and his daughter had gone back into the house, and two little redheaded boys in pajamas were scurrying about in front of the house, hunting for Easter eggs. A cold breeze blew up from the sea. Tom Tracy shivered.

"Did your father send you here to kill little boys?" Rachel spoke loudly enough that Starr heard her.

He came over and snatched the glasses and looked at Ballinakill House.

"The next generation, Padr'ic," said Rachel.

"They won't be harmed," answered Starr. "I'm not a man to kill kids. That ain't what this is about."

"They'll remember the rebels who dragged off their grandpa," she said evenly. "They'll hate forever, just the way that magistrate hates, or Tommy hates, or I hate the cossacks."

Starr looked around at the others. He thought about it for a moment. "Then they won't see it happen. We'll take him on the bridge, when he drives to church."

"If the rising's been stopped," said Rachel, "there may be a reason. They may be talking in Dublin or London. Find out if they're talking first."

"In my life, darlin', Ireland's been talked out of a lot," said Martin Mahoney.

"The voice of wisdom." Starr picked up his rifle again and adjusted the strap. "Men all over Ireland were ready for the risin' two days ago. Once word spreads that we've started the fight, they'll pick up their pikes and bird guns and join us. The time for talking is over."

Tom Tracy took his rifle from Rachel and strapped it over his shoulder. Rachel turned away and brought the binoculars to her eyes to hide her tears.

"Jack Tracy'd be proud, Tommy." Starr clapped him on the arm.

"The time for talking never ends," he answered softly.

Starr pretended he did not hear Tracy and turned to Deirdre. "When are Anglican services in Clifden?"

"Ten o'clock. Clarke usually drives out around nine."

"Good. There won't be many about between the Masses at St. Brendan's. We'll have plenty of time to collect our men." Starr looked up at the sun. "It must be about seven o'clock."

"Seven?" said Donal. "Mother of Jesus." He ran to the battlement and looked down the road. "Right on time."

"RIC?" said Starr.

"Two of them, and they'll be after lookin' around when they see the horse and the bike."

"Then we'd best be convincin'," said Deirdre.

"Your horse, Donal?" Constable John Ryan was fifty, one of the oldest constables and best drinkers in the district. Guinness had expanded his girth and stretched his jacket so that the white undershirt showed between the lower buttons.

"My horse, John."

"Who rode the bicycle?" demanded the other constable. He was younger and more suspicious, and Donal did not recognize him.

"Well, it . . . ." Donal looked down at the ground and scratched his foot in the dirt. "It must belong to the coastwatcher."

Ryan said, "That ain't possible."

"Why?"

"Seamus Kilkeirnan takes the early shift on Sundays, and we arrested him last night."

"You arrested Seamus? What for?"

"None of your damn business." The young constable un-shouldered his carbine and walked to the edge of the cliff.

"He was taken for killing Constable Shea." Ryan stepped around Donal and looked into the dark interior of the tower. "Somebody here with you, Donal?"

Deirdre smiled out of the shadows and brought her hand to her lips. "Don't tell your friend."

John Ryan looked her up and down, then winked and whispered, "Good luck to you, darlin', and to hell with them that pass judgment."

She blew him a small kiss.

"Ryan!' cried the other constable.

Ryan dropped the carbine from his shoulder.

"There's a boat below. Watch your—"

Deirdre Hamilton pulled a pistol from the pocket of Donal's coat and pressed it against the back of Ryan's head. "Don't move."

Constable Ryan dropped his carbine. "And a fine spring day to you, too."

Then Starr sprang from the shadows.

"You!" cried the constable. "They said you was dead."

"I am, John. I'm a ghost."

"Mother of Jesus!" The constable blessed himself.

Starr leaped past Ryan, his knife flashing into the sunlight. But the second constable lay on the ground, unconscious.

"I think I busted his jaw," said Donal. "I heard it crack when I hit him."

Starr crouched down and looked at the face. He touched the lower jaw. Only one side of it moved."Busted. You recognize this one?"

Donal shook his head. "He's new. He must be the replacement for Shea."

"The one Seamus killed?"

"Seamus killed no one."

"Who did?" whispered Starr angrily.

"I did," whispered Donal. "I had no choice."

"Has Seamus been keepin' his mouth shut?"

Donal nodded. "As far as I know, but he'll talk if they press him, or give him enough poteen."

Tracy appeared in the doorway.

Constable Ryan looked hard at him. "First I see a ghost, then, if I ain't mistaken, a Tracy."

"Hello, John." Tom Tracy offered his hand to a man he had known from boyhood.

Ryan lowered his right hand and shook with Tracy.

"Now, hands up again," said Tracy gently.

Starr came down the curving wall to the entrance. "You remember Constable Ryan well enough. Would you remember an old geezer named Seamus Kilkeirnan?"

Tracy almost smiled. "He's not an easy one to forget."

"Well, he's in jail for something he didn't do. We're going to have to get him out."

35

The taste of strong tea and the smell of burning turf came back to Tom Tracy as though he had never left. He was at home, in a small, peaceful cottage on the Bay of Dunslea. But he felt sick. After six weeks at sea, he felt the room around him rising and falling, like a ship at anchor in a quiet bay, but his sickness came from something deeper.

On the table in front of him, beside his teacup, was the Colt revolver he had first touched in Starr's duffel bag, six weeks before.

Rachel rubbed her hands over the turf and held out her skirt to dry it. She said his name.

He looked up.

"Would Jack Tracy be proud?"

He looked again at the gun.

Deirdre came in, pulling on her gloves. She looked at Rachel. "Stay here and warm up. But I can't tell you where you should be when the fighting starts."

"Are you frightened?" Rachel asked her.

Deirdre picked up her goggles and put them on the top of her head. "No. This is what we've waited for." She sipped her tea and swallowed twice to get it down.

The back door opened, and the volatile smell of petrol floated in. Out by the shed, Donal O'Leary was filling glass jars and bottles from a jerry can. Martin Mahoney held the funnel, and Danny stuffed a rag into each bottle after it was filled.

Padraic Starr followed the smell into the room. Like Donal, he now wore the green uniform and black crossbelt of the Royal Irish Constabulary. "It's time, Tommy."

Rachel turned and held her hands out to the fire again.

"I'm not going."

She brought her hands together and folded them tightly, as if in prayer.

"You've come this far, Tommy," said Starr.

"The other day, I saw how hard it is to stop the fighting, once it starts, and how brutal we can be." He picked up the pistol. "The Jack Tracy who saved your life on the Clifden road wouldn't want his sons to die for revenge, or throw themselves into a fight they can't win."

"Put it down, Tommy," said Starr.

"None of us are going." Tracy pointed the pistol. "Not until we know what's happening in the rest of Ireland."

Starr turned to Rachel. The high-necked green tunic made him look like a soldier. "I guess you've won, darlin'."

"I've won nothing." She looked into the fire. "It's his decision."

Starr went over to her and put his hand under her chin. Her hair was frizzed from the dampness, and white streaks of sea salt were caked in the part. Her dark eyes had been made darker by deep circles of exhaustion.

"Like Brandeis and the old rabbi said, this world's a complicated place. There's a time to try to unravel the knots with talk, and a time to cut clean through them. When I first met you, you believed that. That was why I was willin' to play your lover."

Tracy lowered his pistol.

"Now, Padr'ic," said Deirdre, picking up her revolver, "a gentleman's not so free with his talk."

Starr grinned at Tracy. "It started that long ago, in an alley by the Northern Avenue Bridge."

Rachel pushed Starr's hand from her chin.

Tracy looked at Rachel. They both knew what Starr was trying to do. For six weeks, he had been doing it.

Tracy raised the pistol again. "We've had enough of this, Padr'ic."

Starr's face, always on the edge of a smile or grin, suddenly grew serious. He removed his constable's hat and wiped the perspiration from the headband. Then, without looking up, he said very softly, "I guess you're right. I'm sorry. But I thought by now, you all understood what I have to do."

"I understand, darlin'," said Deirdre.

"But Tommy don't." Starr looked at the muzzle of Tracy's pistol. "I hoped the story of what your da did for me would make the difference."

"It did." Tracy aimed the pistol at Starr's chest. "If Jack Tracy was with us, he'd say to wait and see if the talking could do it before the fighting. Politics before rebellion."

"A noble sentiment." Starr put on his hat and straightened himself. "But a bit naive."

"Stop, Padr'ic."

Starr went toward the door. "Cower if you want, but your da saved me from the gallows, Tommy. He saved me for this day."

"He saved you because he was a good man. Now stop."

Starr pushed open the door.

Tracy straightened his arm, and Deirdre Hamilton snapped her pistol over the back of his head. Tracy's face hit the table and he collapsed unconscious.

"Damn you," cried Rachel. "He was aiming high."

"I couldn't tell, dear," answered Deirdre. "I'm sorry."

Starr took Tracy's pistol and slipped it into his belt. "After all this distance, he ends up like a drunk on the floor."

"Better than dead." Rachel knelt and cradled his head in her arms.

Starr strode out the door. Chickens scattered in the yard. "Tom ain't comin'."

"I ain't seen a Tracy do more than talk yet," grunted Donal.

Martin spat brown tobacco at Donal's feet. "I'm the Tracy brother-in-law, and I'm plannin' to kill Clarke. So leave your opinions to yourself."

Danny Tracy wetted his dry lips and picked up his rifle. "This Tracy ain't just talkin'."

"Good lad." From his belt Starr pulled his own scally cap.

"I've got me an RIC visored hat, now, Dann-o. This here's a bit wet, but it might look good on you."

Danny took the tweed hat with the reverence of an acolyte touching a relic.

"Put it on," said Starr. "You've earned it."

The boy threw his own hat in the dust and perched Starr's at an angle, just as Starr had always worn it.

"It looks grand," said Starr. "Grand."

Rachel came to the doorway and watched, but she knew there was nothing she could do against Starr now.

Danny Tracy smiled proudly.

"He has the magic," whispered Deirdre in Rachel's ear.

Off on the hillside, the sheep were lowing, a mindless yet mournful sound.

Deirdre took her motorcycle and headed around the point to collect the men of the brigade. Starr and Donal strapped RIC carbines to their backs and climbed onto the bicycles. Daniel and Martin Mahoney boarded the donkey cart. And they were ready.

As he went by her, Starr looked at Rachel and said, very softly, "Tommy should remember a few good hollows where you can hide from the fightin'." Then he rolled on.

Martin pulled out a brown chunk of tobacco and broke it in two. "My last one." He put a piece in his mouth and the other back in his pocket.

"Oh, Martin," Rachel cried. "Be careful."

"I'll watch over the lad. Nobody knows better than me what's goin' through his head." He reached down and touched Rachel's face.

She held tight to his hand for a moment, then he called to the donkey.

"Mother of Jesus," said Kathleen Mary O'Toole O'Leary. "Donal's gone and joined the RIC."

"What on earth are you blatherin' about?" Logan looked out the window. "Mother of . . ."

Logan was wearing his only white shirt and his only cravat in honor of the Risen Savior, who had seen fit to save Logan's only son. That Seamus Kilkeirnan had taken Donal's place was something Logan planned to pray over at Mass.

"What kind of Easter getup is this?" Logan came to the door of the cottage. "Where did you get these . . . You. *You!*"

Padraic Starr saluted. "Top of the mornin', squire."

Donal O'Leary pushed past his father and went into the cottage.

"What have you done now, Donal?" cried his mother.

"Nothin', yet." He came out of his bedroom a moment later holding a pair of wirecutters and something wrapped in a greasy rag. He threw the rag onto the fire, and the flames jumped. He jammed the wirecutters and pistol into his pocket.

"A gun! Donal, I don't like guns."

"Neither do I." Donal removed the oil lamps from either side of the hearth. They had wicks to light and would shatter when thrown.

"What on earth are you doin'?"

"You're a saint, darlin', for livin' with that man so long. And I love you." Donal kissed his mother on the forehead.

Outside, Logan O'Leary was staring at Starr. "I thought you was dead. I even prayed for it."

"I ain't surprised the prayer was ignored." Starr grinned. "You never was much of a Catholic, even when you put on a tie for Easter."

Until the death of his younger son, Logan O'Leary had never known despair. Until the messenger from Dublin brought good news, he had never known the joy that came with relief from anguish. But he had always been on excellent terms with anger. He tried now to summon it. He tried to pull himself out of his slouch and hurl himself against this smiling rebel. But his anger would not come. It could not stand against the new despair sweeping over him.

Donal came out of the cottage with his mother at his heels.

"Logan, they're after doin' somethin' dangerous," she said.

"We're after springin' Seamus." Donal looked hard at his father. "*Somebody* informed on him, and now he's in jail."

"Who'd do a filthy thing like that?" Logan managed to get the words out before his throat closed around them. He was not a complex man, nor was he given to contemplating the ironies of life. But in trying to save his son, he had given his son reason to throw his life against the RIC.

"Whoever done it," said Kathleen, "let him undo it. You and your friends stay here. We'll get Deirdre, and we'll have a nice joint after Mass."

"That sounds grand," said the man in the donkey cart.

Kathleen and her husband looked up. It was not a moment for

414

recognitions or reunions, but she stepped closer to the cart, squinted in the sun. "Martin? Martin Mahoney?"

Martin pushed his tobacco into his cheek so that he could smile.

"You run off to America," she said. "You run off without ever sayin' goodbye."

Logan looked at his wife. Although the mist was thirty years thick, she played with her apron pockets like a nervous young girl.

"A long time," said Martin, "but I brung back my nephew, Jack Tracy's boy."

Logan came around the cart and looked up at Daniel Tracy. "Are you in this mess, too?"

Danny held up the rifle. "I'm here for my da."

Logan put his hand on the boy's leg. "I knew your da. He lived right here in this house."

"Many's the happy night I had by this hearth." Martin looked at the tiny white cottage. "It's a terrible pity I can't see it in a better way now."

"You can," said Kathleen. "Come in and have my lamb."

"I'm afraid not, missus." Padraic Starr picked up his bicycle.

Logan squeezed Danny Tracy's leg. "There was a time, lad, I hated your father."

"With good reason." Donal mounted his bicycle. "He killed your brother."

Logan did not look at his son. His eyes were fixed to the boy's. "It took me a long time, but son, I figured out that your da was a fine man, doin' what he had to."

"Let's go." Starr pushed off on his bicycle.

"Keep the lamb hot," said Donal to his mother.

Martin gave a small wave to Kathleen O'Leary, then snapped at the reins. The cart lurched ahead. And Kathleen brought a hand to her mouth.

Logan started to walk along beside the cart, still holding tight to the boy's leg. "A good man, do you hear me? He'd think it damn stupid of his son to be throwin' away his life in Dunslea . . . for nothin'." And then he shouted it down the road, at the backs of the two green uniforms. "For nothin'! They ain't got any evidence against Seamus. He'll be sprung before he grows a good thirst."

But the riders did not turn, and the cart began to move faster. Logan looked into the young face. The scraggly black beard covered the pimples, but it did not conceal the fear in the boy's eyes.

415

"For nothin'," he whispered through clenched teeth.

Martin snapped the reins again, and the donkey pulled away.

"For nothin'," shouted Logan after them. "For nothin'," he said to his wife.

Martin Mahoney looked at his nephew. "He may be right. You're free to jump off this cart right now, if you think so."

"Do you think so?"

Martin spat. "There was a time I burned as hot as Starr. I guess my fire never went out."

"Will we die?"

Martin threw an arm around the boy's shoulders. "You won't. *I'll* see to that."

"For nothin'," said Logan softly.

He and his wife watched them until they had disappeared around the bend. Then Kathleen Mary O'Toole O'Leary slowly blessed herself and went into the house. Logan remained in the middle of the road, contemplating the cliff where the young constable had died a week before and wondering if the fall would kill him quickly.

The door of Tim Cooney's cottage cracked open and the smell of fresh bread slipped out.

"It's Donal. We've a job."

Cooney stepped out and closed the door. He was buttoning a celluloid collar to his best white shirt. "The rising, is it?"

Donal nodded. "That and Seamus. They took him last night. With a bit of proddin', he'll talk till Guinness runs out of malt."

"Guns?" he asked Starr, as though he had been chatting in the pub the night before.

"A dozen, hidden up at the dun."

"A dozen?"

"Atlantic took the rest. Do you have your Mauser?"

"If you've a plan."

"Cut all the wires into the town. Take Clarke when he crosses the bridge on his way to church. Use Clarke's wife to negotiate for Seamus and force Hayes to disarm his unit."

"And if Hayes refuses?"

"Deirdre's gone to get help. We'll have the brigade by ten o'clock, each with an Enfield."

"Fourteen of us against eight constables?"

"Sixteen of us." Danny Tracy held up his rifle.

"Who's that?" asked Cooney.

"Jack Tracy's lad," answered Starr. "Come back from America."

Cooney did not look a second time. "Sixteen of us, out in the open. Our faces known to everyone."

Starr stepped back into the road and looked down at the town. It was early, and the shadows of the Twelve Bens still lowered over Dunslea. Only the steeple of St. Brendan's caught the sunlight.

"We'll pull back into the hills," Starr said, "like we planned. Unless you lads forgot to stock the hideouts."

Donal shook his head. "There's three holes full of poteen and potatoes and dry turf."

Starr smiled. "There, now, Tim, what Irishman could ask for more?"

Cooney looked up toward the mountains. "There's sage grouse, too, and salmon in the streams." He went back into his cottage.

In the moment when the door was open, Starr glimpsed Cooney's two little boys and his handsome wife. She was standing by the stove, her hands folded in front of her. Starr had never known such a life, and he was glad now that he could not know the pain of giving it up. The door closed discreetly.

When he came out, Tim Cooney was dressed in brown scally cap and work clothes. His Mauser was strapped over his shoulder. His wife closed the door behind him without a word. A curtain was pushed back, and two small faces appeared at the sill.

Starr saw them. He tried to smile, but he could not. Then the wife's face came to the window. Starr put his head down and followed Cooney to the back of the donkey cart.

"You know, Timothy, there's them that won't hold it against you if you stay here with your boys."

"Them boys might hold it against me."

"You're a brave man, Tim Cooney."

"I've reason to be brave."

"I can't let you loose," Rachel Levka said. "I don't have the key. Starr took it."

"Then you'd better go for help," answered Ryan. "Constable Flanagan here, he's got himself a busted jaw. He's sufferin' somethin' terrible."

Ryan's left wrist was cuffed to Flanagan's left ankle, his left ankle to Flanagan's left wrist. They were both in union suits now covered in dirt and straw.

"You have to let us out, darlin', or else you'll be in trouble as big as your friends."

Rachel was frightened and confused. They had left her alone with Tom Tracy unconscious and two constables who began to cry for help as soon as they realized she would not shoot them.

She told herself to think calmly and clearly. She sat back on her haunches and looked at the two constables. Shafts of sunshine slipped through the chinks in the boards, creating curtains of dusty light, and the loft was warming quickly.

"Rachel," came a voice from below.

She jumped and reached for the pistol in her pocket.

"Well, Tommy Tracy, you've got yourself a skittish young rabbit here," said Ryan.

Tracy climbed into the loft and rubbed the back of his head. "I've got a damn big egg back here, too."

Ryan laughed. "Why in the hell didn't you stay in America, then? Bump your head there, so they tell me, you can go to an icebox and chip a piece off the block and take care of the lump in no time at all."

Tracy slipped down onto the floor beside the constable. "How's your partner doin'?"

"Not too good. Hey, Flanagan!"

Flanagan tried to respond, but all he produced was a cry of pain.

"Not too good." Ryan smiled at Tracy. "What in hell are you doin' here, Tommy?"

Tracy rubbed the back of his head and looked at Rachel. "I'm not quite sure."

Ryan shook his head. "I figured by now, you'd've made somethin' of yourself in America."

"He did make something of himself in America," said Rachel softly. "He was a politician."

The constable smiled. "A politician, is it? That's what your da always wanted to be, but he always ended up the other."

"I guess that's what happened to me." Tracy sneezed in the dusty loft.

"God bless. And your da got a bum deal. Nobody knows that better than me." Ryan raised his head from the floor and tried to see his partner. "Hey, Flanagan! . . . Is he out?"

Tracy nodded.

"I liked your da, Tommy, even if it was me found the box of pistols that done him in. So let me give you this bit of warnin'." He gestured for Tracy to come closer.

Tracy bought an ear to the constable's lips.

"Your friends is in more trouble than they know."

Tracy raised his head a moment and looked at Rachel, who had drawn closer.

"If they think they're goin' up against the usual eight constables, they'll be gettin' a surprise they won't damn soon forget."

"Why?"

"Because a half-dozen more been brought in on the sly over the last few nights. We got 'em sleepin' on the floors, we do."

"Thanks, John," said Tracy.

"And one other thing—we got a wireless in the barracks now. Even if they cut the telegraph cable, we'll have backup from Clifden in half an hour."

Tracy rubbed the back of his head.

"Now then, can you see your way to lettin' me out of these things?"

"If I could, I wouldn't." Tracy patted him on the shoulder. "I can't think of a safer place for a constable to be this fine Easter morning."

Tom Tracy looked across the bay toward Ballinakill House. Every slate on the roof seemed to stand out in the brilliant sunshine.

Rachel came out of the cottage with the binoculars.

"I have to save them," he said, "and keep them from starting a fight if there's a chance that people have decided to talk in Dublin."

"They won't go against the barracks until they've kidnapped the magistrate, will they?"

"That would be stupid." Tracy took the binoculars and brought them to his eyes. "Besides, Clarke's getting ready to leave."

A servant was bringing the long yellow roadster around to the front, and the family was coming out of the house. Tracy recognized Clarke and his wife, the two little boys, and Clarke's daughter. Clarke's suit was gray, finely tailored, and he wore a red rose from the Ballinakill hothouse in his lapel. Now he looked like a magistrate, and Tracy felt his old hatred. The ladies wore wide-brimmed hats and light topcoats in springtime pastel. The little boys were in matching sailor suits and short pants. Then another young woman appeared, as beautifully dressed as the Clarkes. And all of them were dazzled by the bright red tunic of the British soldier who came out last.

"We'll take the Rolls," said Clarke. Ian, you and your lady fair should have the pleasure of riding in my De Dion Bouton."

"My husband must like you, Lieutenant," said Mrs. Clarke. "He rarely allows anyone to drive the De Dion Bouton."

The butler brought the little two-seater around.

Lambert-Jones took a few instructions and helped Miss Carruthers into the car.

"Do you know the way, Ian, in case we run a bit ahead?"

"William drives much too quickly for his own good," said Mrs. Clarke.

"I'll watch your dust."

After the butler turned the top back, the Rolls-Royce glided down the drive. The two little boys, whose father was in the Royal Navy, turned and waved their white sailor hats at the British soldier and his lady.

As the roadster went through the great stone gates at the end of the drive, it looked as though the boys were waving flags of peace.

Lambert-Jones climbed into the two-seater and put his hand on the gearshift.

Miss Carruthers put her hand on top of his. "Thanks ever so, Ian, for bringing me out here this weekend."

"My pleasure, darling." He started the engine and waited for it to warm.

"Perhaps we can provide a bit more for your pleasure this evening," she said.

He did not allow the expression on his face to change. "How so, my dear?"

"My chambers are quite far down the hall, and quite unchaperoned." She ran her middle finger across the back of his hand, to the tip of his middle finger.

"You have defined the strategy, my dear. I will develop the tactics. I think the possibilities for success are quite high."

She kept her hand on his as he threw the shift and the small French car kicked ahead.

The sky was deep blue and the bay sparkled in the sunlight.

He could not believe that Easter had dawned so peaceful and promising.

"They're on the move," said Tracy. "Two cars."

Rachel wheeled a second bicycle out of the shed and around to the front of the cottage. "How long will it take them to get to town?"

Tracy was following the long yellow autocar with his binoculars. "I can't remember. Ten minutes . . . not much more."

The car disappeared into a stand of trees, flashed into the sunlight again, then slipped behind a fold in the hillside.

"Can we beat them on bicycles?" asked Rachel.

"The road on this side is straighter, and it's all downhill."

"If Padr'ic knows it's suicide, maybe he won't go through with it."

"It's not Padr'ic I'm worried about." He picked up the bicycle that Donal had left behind.

"I want to come with you. Maybe . . ."

He swung a leg over the bike and tested the bell.

She ran a hand through her salt-matted hair. "Maybe I can help."

He rang the bell again. A goat came trundling from somewhere, drawn by the sound. Tracy looked at the goat's eyes.

"Dammit, Tommy, look at me, not the goat!"

He turned to her. "I'm thinking of Padr'ic, and that first Sunday. I tried to throw him out of my house, but it didn't take."

She straightened her hair again and buttoned the top of the gray sweater. "What he said about that alley, it was only half truth, Tommy."

"No explanations." He leaned over his bike, put his hand under her chin, and kissed her. "Stay with me if you can."

Tracy pushed off, and Rachel followed on Deirdre's bicycle.

The goat stood in the middle of the road, watching after them, its tail twitching stupidly.

36

But for the squawking of the gulls around the quay, Dunslea sat quiet. The eleven-o'clock Mass was two hours away. The sunrise worshipers had gone back to bed or breakfast. The air was heavy with the aromas of burning turf and bacon.

Padraic Starr and Donal O'Leary pumped their bikes past the row of buildings on the south side of the bridge and stopped in the small square before the church. They laid the bicycles against the low stone wall between the square and the road. A line of trees ran along the riverbank and protected them from view of the barracks. Twenty yards to their left, the sunlight had finally fallen across the bridge. But the trees cast deep, chilly shadows.

Donal O'Leary shivered. He pressed his arms against the sides of his tunic to soak up the cold perspiration on his flanks.

"Relax, Donal, my boy. And listen to the lovely sound that the river makes when it kisses the sea." Starr cocked his head.

There was nothing more peaceful than the sound of a gentle-runnin' river, Jack Tracy had always said. And nothing more deceptive, Padraic Starr thought now.

The cart rattled into the square and stopped at the front steps of the church. Danny Tracy jumped down and ran toward the wall.

Starr waved the boy back. "Into the church. Now."

Martin grabbed Danny by the collar and pushed him up the steps. "Inside, for a bit of prayer, before the fightin'."

"He seems a brave lad," said Donal.

"He is, and as frightened as the rest of us." Starr listened to the river a moment longer, to the sound that Jack Tracy had wanted his children to hear every day of their lives. If he had betrayed Jack Tracy in order to repay him, Starr was sorry. He said a small prayer of his own . . . not to God, but to the spirit of Jack Tracy, whose body lay perhaps a hundred feet away, in the graveyard by the square.

Cooney came to the wall and crouched down beside them. "Telegraph lines." He pointed to the wire that stretched from the RIC barracks on the north side of town, across the bridge, to a pole at the end of the stone wall.

Starr took the wirecutters from Donal. "Give a whistle if we get visitors."

The yellow Rolls-Royce appeared briefly. The chrome on the bumpers and sidelights glinted in the sun, and then it was gone.

Tracy was losing, but he could go no faster.

When he was a boy, this ride had been a giddy, exhilarating, four-mile hurtle from the ruins of the ancient fort to the square in front of the church. In those days, he had known every twist and hazard, every kettle hole and misplaced rock. At first, he had been terrified by the cliff and the ocean to his left, but his father had reminded him that the road could hurt him only if his fear made it stronger than it was. When he had mastered the road, his father said he was on his way to becoming a man.

The smaller car appeared briefly on the opposite side of the bay, then disappeared again into the landscape.

If he did not fall, there might still be time. He looked over his shoulder. Rachel was a hundred yards behind him, and keeping pace.

Then Tracy came to a turn as familiar as the frown on his mother's face. He smelled the aroma of the turf smoke once more. He saw the bay as he had seen it every morning for the first ten years of his life. The little cottage appeared, whitewashed and thatched and tucked neatly into the side of the hill.

A woman came to the door and looked out. She could have been his mother. But the man looking down at the rocks on the side of the road was never his father. It was Logan O'Leary, already mourning his son.

Tracy shouted, "Gangway!"

Logan looked up. His eyes widened, as though he were seeing a ghost.

The bike careened past.

"Jack!" he shouted. "Jack Tracy!" He ran into the middle of the road and called after the big Black Irishman hunched over the handlebars.

Rachel shouted, "Watch out! Get out of the road!"

Logan turned. Another rider was shooting straight at him. He waved his arms and cried for her to stop. She swerved to the right and hit a rock.

She threw out her feet to keep from going over. Her heels dug in the oiled surface. A huge pair of hands grabbed her handlebars.

"Was that him? Was it? Or am I seein' things?"

"Who?"

"Jack Tracy. Jack Tracy's been dead sixteen years, but I'd swear on a sack of barley that he just went by."

Rachel pushed him away. He seemed like a crazy man, with bulging eyes and red whiskey veins throbbing in his nose.

"Was it Jack Tracy?" the man screamed.

Rachel started to roll down the hill. "It was Tom Tracy. Jack Tracy's son."

"What?"

But Rachel was already speeding away.

Kathleen came outside. "Logan, who was that?"

Logan stood in the middle of the road, hunched and desolate. "It looked like Jack Tracy, goin' off to save another damn-fool O'Leary."

The sunrise service had been more crowded that Father John Breen had expected. Perhaps his eloquence was drawing them from other parishes, he thought with a small laugh . . . either that or he was bringing sinners back to the fold. He opened the side door of the church and stepped into the sacristy.

So many had taken Communion that he needed to refill the ciborium before the next Mass. He slipped the box of unconsecrated wafers from the cabinet and shuffled onto the altar. His mind was on the small things of the day, the painful bunions on his insteps, the aroma of soda bread baking in the rectory, the beauty of the hothouse lily that Magistrate Clarke had sent, and him not even a Catholic.

"Good morning, Father."

The priest looked out into the nave. An older man and a boy were sitting halfway down the right side of the church. "Good morning. Strangers, are you?"

"Yes, Father."

"From a long way?" The priest took the ciborium from the tabernacle and filled it with wafers. Over his cassock he wore an old sweater, the color of pea soup, and with each movement of his arms, the holes in the elbows seemed to stretch wider.

"A long way now," answered the older man, "but once from Dunslea."

The priest turned and looked at the man again. "Would I be knowin' you, then?"

The man shook his head. "I think not, Father. I left here before your time."

"Well, the Mass ain't for two hours, but you're welcome to sit and pray, or perhaps you'd like a cup of—" The priest put the box of wafers on the altar and came down to the communion rail. "What is it that I see at the back of the church, beneath the holy water?"

"Enfield rifles, Father," said the younger one with the scraggly black beard.

The old priest threw back his shoulders and shouted, "Rifles, is it? In my church?"

"We're sorry, Father," said the younger one, "but—"

"And a Yank. You're a Yank, and you've the audacity about you to say you've brought two Enfield rifles into my church on Easter Sunday, but you're sorry? Who in the name of St. Peter do you think you are?"

"Are you Father Breen?" asked the older one.

"Don't answer me a question with a question, mister. Answer my question. Who are you and what are you doin' in my church?"

The older one genuflected in the aisle, then came forward. "If you're Father Breen, you'll remember this lad's father. You were summoned to the barracks to hear his confession a long time ago."

The priest looked at Martin, then looked hard at the boy, then opened the communion rail and went down the aisle. "Holy Mother of Jesus," he whispered softly. "Jack Tracy if ever I seen him."

The boy licked his lips and said, "We've come to clear his name."

"Clear his name? Of what need is there to clear the name of as good a man as ever took breath?"

Just then, the door swung open. Tim Cooney and a constable came in. Both were carrying rifles. Cooney put his down with the others, dipped his hand in the holy water, and blessed himself.

"This is a house of God, Tim Cooney, and . . . You. *You!*"

Padraic Starr made the Sign of the Cross. "Bless us, Father, for we all have sinned." He unstrapped his carbine and put it under the holy water font. "For bringin' weapons of destruction into the house of God. We're heartily sorry."

Father John Breen shuffled a few more steps down the aisle.

"I've prayed for you, Padr'ic. I've done what I could to protect you these last weeks. But most of all, I've prayed that you'd never come back."

"Well, Father, God must have other plans."

"Has He spoken with you, then?"

"He told me it was time for the risin'," said Starr with complete seriousness.

"On Easter?"

"What better day?"

The priest took a deep breath. It was colder in the stone church than it was outside, and the vapor from his breath floated into the air.

"Will the clergy of Ireland support us?"

"I can't say for them." The priest looked at the boy, who was nervously wringing his scally cap in his hands. "But it seems that the spirit of Jack Tracy is with you, and that counts for somethin' to this old priest."

"See that, Danny?" Starr said. "You're bringin' your da's name back to life."

The priest looked at the boy. "No man knew better than Jack Tracy what's been happenin' here for the last few centuries, son. No man better knew how complicated it all is."

"He also believed there might come a time to wipe clean the slate," said Starr.

"You can't wipe clean a slate etched by time, Padr'ic." The priest stood up straight and buttoned his sweater. "Now, then, I'll give you sanctuary, if that's why you're here. I'll do your talkin' for you if you want." He slipped his fingers into the black crossbelt of Starr's green uniform. "But if you've started killin' constables—"

The rear door of the church opened, and Donal O'Leary looked in. "They're comin'."

Starr turned and headed out of the church. "We've killed nobody, Father, yet."

Tom Tracy swept around the last turn and saw the town.

The joined rowhouses were still painted in pastels set off by stonework and whitewash, soft colors to complement the intense greens and hard grays of Connemara. Turf smoke curled from almost every chimney. The slate roofs glistened and ran trickling with morning mist. The trees shielded the small cemetery beside the church, where his father had turned to earth. The gulls circled above the fishing boats. And the river reached the bay in a gentle roughness of waves and white splashes, as it had for a thousand years.

In America, things changed by the month. In Ireland, nothing changed . . . ever.

The yellow Rolls-Royce roadster was gliding into the north side of town. Tracy flashed past the old Cooney cottage and saw two little boys peering out a window. The last time he looked, Rachel had been two hundred yards or more behind him, a small cautious speck pedaling down the hill. And now, in the town below, he saw two men in green uniforms pedaling toward the bridge.

Then he hit a bump in the road. Bike and rider flew into the air. The bike landed on both wheels, and the rider landed with a jolt on the pointed seat. The rider held the road, but the second bump came too soon. This time the rider landed first, gashing his knee and cracking his forehead on the hard-packed dirt.

The bike crashed after him in a twisted jumble. He rolled over and sat up and saw the car moving toward the bridge below him. He slammed his hands against the ground.

William Clarke loved his roadster almost as much as he did his horses. He relished the elegant comfort of the leather seats, the immediate response of the steering, the smooth, subtle power of the twelve-cylinder engine. Even here, on the rough roads of Connemara, the craftsmanship of Rolls-Royce proved true.

He drove slowly past the barracks and along the row of joined housefronts. Except for the chatter of two little boys in the back seat of Clarke's car, the town was quiet.

"Gran'ther." The older boy poked his head over the front seat. "Gran'ther."

"You needn't shout, William."

"Gran'ther, the lieutenant isn't behind us." The voice was filled with the sense of alarm that every little boy could muster when a small crisis loomed. "Shouldn't we turn back and find him?"

"Don't worry, son," said Clarke. "I'm sure he's taking his time to enjoy the scenery."

"Remember, William," said the boy's mother, "back in dreary old Dublin, they don't have such beautiful sights as we see every day."

"Indeed not," said Clarke. He moved left as he turned up onto the bridge, making room for the two constables pedaling in the other direction.

"And I would wager," said Mrs. Clarke, "that they don't have the kind of fine constabulary we have here, either."

"Top of the mornin' to you, squire and missus, and to all the whole family." The constable gave a crisp salute as he went by.

"And to you as well," said Clarke. A redheaded constable, he thought idly. Unfamiliar. One of the reinforcements. But now, what was this on the second bicycle? What was *Donal O'Leary* doing dressed as a constable?

Red hair and *Constable* O'Leary. Clarke's mind made the connections an instant too late. He slammed his foot on the brake as O'Leary's bike swerved in front of him. The car jerked to a stop, and the two little boys tumbled forward.

Above the sound of the gentle-runnin' river came the leather-and-metal clatter of arms. O'Leary unslung his carbine. Tim Cooney rose from behind the wall of the quay and cocked his rifle. Another man, older and unfamiliar, stood near the wall across the road and aimed his gun. And the constable behind the car dropped his bicycle and snapped his carbine to his hip.

Clarke's daughter threw her little boys onto the floor of the car and threw herself on top of them.

Mrs. Clarke screamed and tried to open the door.

"Quiet!" snapped the one at the rear. He jumped over the bumper and into the backseat.

The young boy screamed. The older boy looked out from under his mother.

"You!" said Clarke. "You bastard!"

Starr pressed the muzzle of the carbine against Clarke's head.

Adelle Clarke tried to knock the gun away. Starr grabbed her hand and wrenched it back. "Sit still or I'll break your arm."

Clarke turned and tried to rise. Donal O'Leary jumped onto the running board and shoved him back into his seat.

"You haven't a chance, you bloody cowards!" cried Clarke. "Not a chance!"

The sound of another engine rumbled down the road and into the town. The gears clattered like a handful of bolts dropped into an empty bucket, because the driver had to stop suddenly and was shifting clumsily.

Starr saw the red coat behind the wheel. He called to Cooney, "Take out the car, Tim."

428

"No!" Mrs. Clarke tried to stand again. "They're our guests."

Starr pushed her back into her seat. "Just the car, missus. Just the car."

Tim Cooney dropped to a knee and aimed at the target, perhaps fifty yards away, and squeezed off four shots.

The gulls screeched into the air. The children screamed. Their mother tried to cover their ears. And Padraic Starr tried not to look at them.

The first bullet hit a front tire, and the car sagged forward. The young woman in the passenger seat screamed. The soldier threw his body over her. The next two shots hit the grille, and the fourth struck a rear tire.

The soldier jumped up and pulled the lady from the car and ran back toward the barracks, no more than twenty feet from where the car had stopped. But his right leg was as stiff as the stock of a gun.

He limped. Then the medal from Neuve-Chapelle flashed on his chest. Starr brought his lips to Clarke's ear. "What in hell is *he* doing here?"

"He was invited," answered Clarke, "for a pleasant weekend."

Three constables were rushing out the barracks gate. The soldier pushed his young lady to safety behind the wall. Then he turned and looked down at the bridge.

Padraic Starr stood slowly and looked straight at the soldier. Then he took off his hat and spun it into the river, so that Ian Lambert-Jones could see the red hair and know that it was Starr, back from America to start the rising.

Tom Tracy's bicycle was ruined. He was running down the road, blood streaming down his leg and the side of his face. He stopped when he saw the first muzzle flash. By the time the sound of the shot reached him, the muzzle had flashed three times more.

"Tommy! Tommy, what happened?" Rachel rode up behind him.

"We lost the race."

With the two green uniforms clinging to it, Clarke's long yellow car sped off the bridge and disappeared behind the church.

Rachel threw her arms around Tracy's neck. "I saw the broken bike—I thought you went over the cliff."

"I'm all right."

She tenderly wiped the blood from the scrape on his forehead.

But he was looking down at the church. The front door was opening, Starr was calling, and the slender figure of Danny Tracy was jumping up from behind a wall and running toward the church.

"Jesus," said Tom.

"Padr'ic will never kill Clarke in the church," Rachel said. "He'll never ask Danny to do it."

"But it's started." He picked up her bicycle and climbed on, but the front tire had gone flat. "Now I know why you were so far behind." He threw it down. "I'll run."

She grabbed his arm. "Don't get killed, Tommy. Please."

He drew her to him and kissed her. He felt her warmth and closed his eyes and thought, for just a moment, of the first time they'd kissed in the oval at Union Park Street. "I love you, Rachel."

She wrapped her arms around him, and he buried his face in her matted, salty hair.

"We can still warn them," he said. "We can still save a few lives. We might even be able to talk them out."

The echoes of the gunfire reached the home of Logan O'Leary. He was sitting on the cliff, looking down at the rocks, and his wife was sitting beside him. He raised his head and counted the echoes.

"Four shots," he said.

Kathleen Mary O'Toole O'Leary blessed herself.

Logan stood and went toward the house.

"Where are you goin', Logan?"

"If Jack Tracy can throw himself away a second time to save an O'Leary, I guess I can do it once."

A moment later, he came around the house leading his mule on a tether. His birdgun was strapped to his shoulder, and he wore a cartridge pouch at his hip.

37

The hand touched the telegraph key, but on the first strike, there was no spark. The operator turned to a deputy. "Start the generator."

"Line cut?" Brian Hayes hurried down from his family quarters, strapping his crossbelt and buttoning the neck of his tunic.

"Yes, sir," said the operator.

"Use the wireless. Request immediate help from Clifden barracks."

"I'd like to offer my assistance, Chief Inspector." Lambert-Jones stepped into the small communications room and saluted.

Hayes glanced at the red coat. "I'll take all the advice I can get."

"Thank you, sir." Lambert-Jones tried to keep the professional calm in his voice. Starr had come back like an answer to his prayers. His chance had arrived, and he would not fail for panic or carelessness. "Request Clifden to alert the military garrison at Galway. This may be the beginning of a general rising."

Hayes ordered the message. Then he led Lambert-Jones through the barracks. The floors rumbled with the steps of a dozen men rushing from their rooms. Some looked terrified, others seemed excited, and a few were half asleep. As each man went into the mess room, he snapped a carbine from the gun rack and the sergeant checked off his name.

"We're prepared to surround the church, Chief Inspector," said the sergeant.

"The church is a sanctuary, Sergeant."

"That it is, sir. That it is."

"Perhaps you should keep the men out of sight until further orders," offered Lambert-Jones. "We don't want them to think we have any more than the normal force here."

Hayes nodded and gave the order to his sergeant. Then the officers went outside to study the church.

Jane Carruthers was standing in the bright sunlight by the gate. Her dress was torn, her hair unkempt, and her yellow hat lay in the middle of the road, beside Clarke's De Dion Bouton. Now that she was safe inside the barracks walls, the shooting had become a grand adventure.

431

"Are you sure you wouldn't want to go inside for tea, dear?" said Lambert-Jones.

"Absolutely."

"Or get out of the bright sun to protect your skin?"

"Don't try to get rid of me, Ian. When my friends say 'What did you do in boring old Connemara?' I'll have an answer for sure."

Hayes smiled, and Lambert-Jones gave him a look.

"Oh, Ian," Jane cried, "the church door is opening."

Two little sailors ran out of the church, followed closely by their mother and grandmother in fluttering Easter finery. They hurried across the square, like a family slipping early from Mass. However, they did not direct their nervous glances back toward the church, where, on an ordinary Sunday, the devout gossips might already be whispering about them. Instead they were looking at two men with rifles who watched them from behind walls.

The four scurried across the bridge, with three constables covering them. As they came up the road, Jane Carruthers and Lambert-Jones ran out, swept up the little boys, and hurried back to safety. Lambert-Jones handed the younger boy to Clarke's daughter and told Miss Carruthers to take them all upstairs to the quarters of the Hayes family.

"Aye, aye." Miss Carruthers saluted.

"Are you all right?" Hayes asked Clarke's wife.

She straightened her hat and her posture. "I'm quite fine, gentlemen." She pulled a folded piece of paper from her purse and hesitated, uncertain of which direction to offer it.

Lambert-Jones clapped his hands behind his back.

Hayes opened the note and read it. " 'Hand over Seamus Kilkeirnan. Then all six constables and Lambert-Jones, too, come down the road, single file, hands up, unarmed. Then RM will be released.' Signed by Donal O'Leary, Brigade Commandant, Irish Volunteers, and Padraic Starr, Military Council, Irish Republican Brotherhood."

"Rather extreme," said Mrs. Clarke.

"Ridiculous," answered Hayes.

"Are we to assume that a rising has begun?"

"If it has, madam," said Lambert-Jones, "you could not be in better hands." Then he led her to the stairs on the side of the barracks. When she reached the top, she turned and looked down toward the church.

"No fear, madam," said the lieutenant. "They don't know what they're up against."

She gave him a weak smile and went inside.

"I trust your wife will keep the ladies out of our way for the next hour or so," said Lambert-Jones to Hayes.

Hayes glanced at the top windows. Two little girls had pushed aside the curtains and pressed their foreheads to the glass. Hayes gave them a little wave. "She has been prepared for this, Lieutenant. And so have my children."

Lambert-Jones went back to the gate and looked down at the church. "How many constables have you under your command, Inspector?"

"Fourteen. Twelve in the barracks, two on patrol—"

"Without their uniforms."

"At the very least." Hayes looked at Lambert-Jones's chest. "You're wearing the medals. Any suggestions?"

Lambert-Jones smiled. "We should give them exactly what they're asking for. And once they have it, we'll give them a bit more."

It was still cold in the church. In some years, the sun did not warm the stone walls until June.

"You've violated the sanctuary, Padr'ic." Father John Breen stood at the communion rail, and his voice echoed to the back, where Starr and Cooney were peering out the little windows in the door. "Bringin' guns and hostages into here is a sin. And I apologize to the resident magistrate that I ever thought well of you."

"You never thought well of me, Father. But you were kinder than most."

"I accept your apology." William Clarke stretched his neck to adjust the rope. Above his butterfly collar and blue polka-dot cravat, he now wore a noose fashioned from the church bell rope, and his hands were bound in front of him.

Danny Tracy clutched the end of noose rope the way a man holds a leash when he doesn't trust the dog.

But Clarke spoke calmly. "The question, Father, is whether *God* will accept the apologies of anyone else in this room."

"You might get a firsthand answer to that before the day is out," said Starr.

"If it happens, I won't be the only one." Clarke looked at the boy. "Don't you think you deserve a bit longer life, son?"

433

Danny wrapped the rope more tightly around his hand.

Starr came down the aisle to the bench where Clarke was sitting. "That's something we all thought when his old da was strung up sixteen years ago."

Clarke looked at the boy again. "How old are you?"

"Sixteen," said Danny.

"And an American?"

Danny nodded.

"Jack Tracy's son?"

Clarke was not surpised. Not even the appearance of Padraic Starr in the uniform of the Royal Irish Constabulary had truly surprised him. He had been startled and angered, however, because after the reports from Dublin and Logan O'Leary, he had let down his guard. And this was the result.

The boy pulled himself up straight. "You killed my father."

"The evidence convicted him, son, whatever you may have heard."

Seamus Kilkeirnan stood when the British officer stepped into the jail. "Top of the mornin', General."

Lambert-Jones studied the little man for a moment, hoping that a cold stare might be unsettling.

"Did I hear shootin' a while back?"

Lambert-Jones opened the cell door. "You're free to go."

"Am I now? Am I that? The king himself decided that Seamus Kilkeirnan's not the kind to go around killin' constables, is that it?"

"You are part of a prisoner exchange."

"Who is it bein' exchanged for me?"

"The resident magistrate."

"The RM?" Seamus scratched his head. "*He* killed the constable?"

Lambert-Jones grabbed Seamus by his dirty lapel. "Don't act the dumb fox with me. Your friends are getting you out, but remember that as you cross the bridge, a constable who is the best marksman in the district will be aiming directly at your head."

Seamus pulled on his hat.

"If you say *anything*, at *any* time, or begin to run, he has orders to fire, at his own discretion."

"His discretion, my head." Seamus Kilkeirnan stepped back into the cell and closed the door. "If it's all the same to you, General, I'll be stayin' here where it's safe."

"No, you won't." Lambert-Jones pulled open the cell door.

"I didn't kill no one, and I ain't much of a rebel, so's, whatever's goin' on out there"—Seamus dropped onto the cot and folded his arms and his legs—"you'll include me in the d'ruthers."

"Very well, then. Take off your clothes."

Seamus jumped up. "Now just a minute."

Lambert-Jones pulled his revolver and pointed it through the bars.

"Well, since you put it that way, General, I'll give you everything, right down to me union suit."

Lambert-Jones wrinkled his nostrils. "That won't be necessary."

"Padr'ic, Padr'ic . . ." Donal burst in at the back of the church. "Get Clarke ready. Hayes just shouted down that they're comin' out in five minutes. We won. As simple as that."

"As simple as that," muttered Starr.

Danny Tracy yanked on the rope. "Did you hear that? We won."

"You've won nothing," said Clarke. "You'll all hang."

"As simple as that," repeated Starr. "Too damn simple." Starr rounded on Clarke. "What's the trick?"

"What do you mean?"

"The trick! The lads in them green uniforms are all Irish and mostly Catholic, but they're sworn straight to King George himself. They wouldn't throw down their guns without a fight, not unless there's a trick."

"Don't you want them to give up?" Father Breen came down off the altar. "It's better than bloodshed, isn't it?"

"I'll have armed men comin' down the road within the hour. That's when I expect them to surrender. When they see the size of what's against them."

"There'll be hundreds comin' to Mass in an hour and a half," said the priest. "You can't be havin' a fight then."

"By then we'll have the barracks."

"It will never work. Violence never has." Clarke looked at Danny. "Your father would have told you that."

"What's the trick? What's my old commander doin' here? Your horse didn't stumble over him at the Dublin showgrounds."

"As a matter of fact"—Clarke looked around—"he did."

* * *

435

"Get off the street! Get off the street and into shelter!"

"Tommy, he's yelling at us."

"Ignore him."

A constable fired his carbine into the air.

Rachel screamed and stumbled on her skirt and fell forward. "Dammit, Tommy, they're shooting at us."

"A warning."

She rolled over and sat down. The perspiration collected on the tip of her nose and dripped onto her skirt. "I can't go on."

They were in front of Finnerty's. The church was a hundred yards away.

"Come on, Rachel." He knelt to help her, and his body wanted to drop down beside her. His lungs were burning. His knee was throbbing. His sock was soaked in blood.

"Get off the street and into shelter," shouted the constable through his speaking trumpet.

Tracy raised his hand and waved in acknowledgment. Then he tried to help Rachel to stand. "I'll have to leave you here. There isn't much time."

From the barracks, an old man appeared. He wore a dirty suit jacket and a scally cap pulled low over his ears. *Seamus.* Then four constables walked out in single file with their hands up.

"They're starting some sort of exchange," said Tracy.

She forced herself to stand. He took her hand, and they ran.

"They're only sendin' four," said Starr. "I ordered six. Plus officers."

"And the constables who lent you their uniforms." Clarke was standing on the step of the church, so that he could be seen at the barracks. Martin and Cooney were out by the wall. The others were in the vestibule, behind Clarke.

"Shut up, Resident Magistrate," said Starr calmly.

"Say, Padr'ic," said Donal. "Seamus is walkin' damn funny for the Seamus I know."

Tom Tracy rushed in the sacristy door. "Padr'ic!"

Starr whirled and aimed his carbine toward the altar.

Tracy threw up his hands. "They've set a trap for you, Padr'ic. There's twelve of them up there."

"Twelve?" Starr lowered the gun. "Who told you?"

Tracy came down the center aisle with Rachel close behind him. "We got it out of the old constable, Ryan."

Starr turned and grabbed the rope from Danny and pulled

viciously. William Clarke flew back through the door as though someone had shot him. He landed on his back and cracked his head on the slate floor of the foyer.

"You said no tricks." Starr pointed the carbine at Clarke's head. "The lieutenant's just another horsey-boy, is he?"

Tom Tracy tried to push the gun aside. "Stop it, Padr'ic."

"He's a dead man." Starr slammed in a round, then told Donal to close the doors.

"What about the others?" asked Donal.

"Tell them to open fire."

"Don't do it," said Tracy.

Starr turned on Donal with the carbine. "I said open fire. Kill them all before they get the chance to kill us." He was enraged. He went to the door and aimed his weapon.

The constables approaching the other side of the bridge stopped, then they ran. Starr fired a shot. It rang so loud in the little foyer that a trickle of plaster floated down from the ceiling.

Before Starr could fire again, Tracy grabbed him by the shoulders and pulled him back. Starr slammed the butt of the carbine into Tracy's stomach and knocked him backward. Then he whirled and pointed the gun straight at Clarke's chest.

"Don't do it," cried Donal.

Starr pulled the bolt and ejected a shell.

Rachel jumped in front of Clarke's body. "Don't shoot him."

"He's just like every other Brit, always ready to talk politics and peace and make you think you're part of the process, but always ready with the tricks."

William Clarke rolled onto his stomach and used his legs to push himself across the floor, away from Starr.

Father Breen stepped out of the shadows and put his hand over the muzzle of the carbine. "Kill a man in church, Padr'ic, and you'll burn for eternity. Besides, in a fight like this, it's the calm ones who prevail."

Starr studied the priest a moment, then lowered the gun.

Rachel released her breath. She wiped the palms of her hands on her skirt and helped Clarke to his feet.

"Thank you, my dear. You've saved my life, for the moment." Clarke stretched his neck to adjust the noose. The skin above his collar was rubbed red and raw.

"You're a dead man before this day is out," whispered Starr.

"Save your . . ." Tom Tracy was sitting on the floor. The rifle butt had knocked the air out of his lungs. "Save your hatred,

437

Padr'ic. You may need it. They have a wireless in the barracks, too."

"Wireless?" Starr's face turned the color of his uniform.

"That means they've already called for help," said the priest.

"Mother of Jesus," said Donal.

Danny Tracy looked from Starr to his brother.

"That cuts off our escape into the hills," said Starr.

"And you'll have two lorries of RIC comin' straight down the road on this side of the river in twenty minutes," added the priest. "I suggest you allow me to negotiate for you while you remain in the sanctuary."

"It's no longer a sanctuary," said Clarke. "They've discharged weapons from the church door."

"All the more reason to negotiate." Rachel went over to Starr. She put her hand tenderly on his shoulder. "Tommy and I came to warn you and try to get you out before there's any bloodshed."

"If you haven't killed anyone," said Clarke, "we can still negotiate."

Rachel looked at Clarke. He seemed a moderate and reasonable man. She nodded in agreement. "There. You see, Padr'ic—"

"He wants to negotiate the noose from his neck to mine."

"That isn't true," said Clarke.

"We'll do our talking from Dun Slea. Once we've joined with the others, we'll have some strength. Then we'll find a use for the resident magistrate."

"How much strength do you have?" said the priest.

"A great deal, apparently," said Clarke dryly. "Haven't you been inspired by the support of the townspeople?"

Padraic Starr pulled the Colt revolver from his belt and handed it to Tom Tracy. "He's makin' me mad, Tommy. Keep him covered so I don't kill him . . . yet."

Clarke studied Tom Tracy. "Another son returned from distant shores?"

"Damn right," said Starr. "With more reason to kill you than I have."

And for Tom Tracy, the moment arrived. The power of the gun surged through his hand, as it had that first morning when he reached into Starr's bag. The gun seemed to raise his arm by itself, straighten it, and aim. For a month, he had rehearsed this moment, right up to the instant when he squeezed the trigger and obliterated the face of William Clarke. But for as long, he had known that it would be futile.

438

"Tommy," said Rachel softly. "Tommy, this isn't why we're here. We're the peacemakers."

"Blessed are the peacemakers," whispered the priest.

"Save the scripture," muttered Starr.

"Your father was hung on the evidence," said Clarke. "Someone killed *my* father in cold blood."

Tracy felt the gun breathe in his hand.

Rachel saw no tension or uncertainty on his face. He seemed completely composed, almost as though he were allowing the gun itself to make the decision.

"Shoot if you want, Tommy," said Starr. "When the boys join us, we'll still be able to take the district, whether we have a hostage or not."

Tracy looked at his brother. Danny Tracy's face had gone white. The boy took several steps back and dropped the rope.

"This is it, Dan. Do you want this gun to go off?"

Danny drew his top teeth over the tuft of hair at his lower lip.

"Do you want his brains splattered all over your face?" said Rachel. "Will that make you feel better that you never had a father?"

Danny shook his head.

Tom Tracy's eyes shifted to Clarke's face. It would be easy, he thought, to let the gun have its way.

"Go ahead, Tom. He's standin' there now, thinkin' of every damn crime he can charge us with. Shoot him so he cuts it out."

"I'm thinking of my grandchildren," said Clarke calmly.

Tracy saw the red rope burn chafe against William Clarke's respectable white collar. He thought of his father in the casket. He remembered the last time he had talked with his father. The gun lost its power, and his arm dropped. He looked around. "If we're pulling back to the old fort, let's go."

The priest blessed himself slowly, and Rachel sagged back against a bench.

"Later, then." Starr pulled a box of matches from Clarke's jacket pocket. He jammed a match into his teeth and chewed. "Take him to his car and start the engine."

Then Starr turned to the priest. "Goodbye, Father."

The priest took his hand and shook it. "I don't know whether to say God damn you or God go with you."

"Neither does anybody else."

* * *

Ian Lambert-Jones and Chief Inspector Brian Hayes were standing by the barracks gate. Lambert-Jones held binoculars to his eyes.

The front doors of the church swung open. Two green uniforms raced out. One ran straight to the wall. The other went to the donkey cart and pulled a crate out of the back.

"What are they doing?" Hayes asked.

"They've made petrol bombs."

In the north row of houses, someone's head poked out a window, and Hayes barked. The head pulled back like a frightened cuckoo bird, and the window slammed. Then Hayes brought the megaphone to his lips. "Brigade Commandant!"

Lambert-Jones made a disgusted grunt. Each time the constable spoke of rank, he glorified these rebels into true soldiers. But then, one of them was.

"Brigade Commandant O'Leary! What is the problem?"

"You only sent out four when it was six we were askin' for."

Then Starr and Tim Cooney jumped up and ran across the square to the quay, to the protection of another low wall. Starr shouted, "Don't try to follow us, or Clarke will die!"

He pulled something from his teeth and scratched it on the wall. A flame appeared in his hand. He touched the flame to the neck of a bottle, then flung the bottle at the bridge.

Glass shattered. A stain of petrol darkened across the dry boards and erupted into flame.

Tim Cooney rose and tossed another burning bottle. A second sheet of orange fluttered to life on the bridge.

Lambert-Jones turned to Hayes. "Bring out the lorry. Right now."

"But he warned us!" said Hayes.

"Load the lorry and attack now! Surprise them and you might save the magistrate!"

Hayes hurried into the yard and screamed the order. A dozen constables piled into the back of the lorry, while Hayes pulled open the passenger door and looked at Lambert-Jones. "After you, Lieutenant."

Lambert-Jones put a foot on the running board. "I'll ride here."

"That's a fine way to burn your ass."

"I want Starr to see me clearly."

Hayes looked up at the windows of his quarters. Orange flames were dancing in the reflection on the glass, and four little faces were turned toward the burning bridge. He gave a wave, but none of the children saw it. He slid into the passenger seat and slammed the door.

Lambert-Jones put both feet on the running board and hooked his arm around the mirror. Then he unsnapped his holster and pulled out his revolver. "At your order, Chief Inspector."

Hayes gave the driver a nod, and the lorry lurched forward.

The bridge was burning from one end to the other. Black smoke was riding the currents of heat high into the sky, then flattening out above the bay like an angry cloud.

Donal O'Leary and Martin Mahoney had retreated to the car. Donal had taken the wheel from Danny. Martin was at the corner of the church, looking back toward the bridge.

The lorry burst through the barracks gates.

"They're coming!" cried Starr. He flung his last petrol bomb at the bridge, and it disappeared into the flames. Then he grabbed Cooney by the collar. "Let's go!" They ran across the square.

Like some aroused beast, the lorry was picking up speed as it thundered down the road.

"They're coming!" shouted Starr again. "Kill him! Kill Clarke!"

Martin leaped onto the rear bumper of the car. "Back it up."

Donal O'Leary threw the shift into reverse, and the gears crunched. The long yellow roadster shot into the middle of the road, so that everyone could now see the lorry speeding toward the flaming bridge.

"Kill him!" Starr was screaming. "Now!"

Tom Tracy held the gun to Clarke's head.

"Don't do it, Tommy!" said Rachel.

"I told them we'd kill him, and they're still comin'. Do it. Now!" Starr's fury came screaming ahead of him. "Do it!" He reached the car and jumped onto the running board. "Now!"

"No!" answered Tracy. "He's more valuable alive."

Starr grabbed for the revolver in Tracy's hands. Martin Mahoney swung the stock of his rifle into the back of Starr's head, knocking him unconscious into Rachel's lap.

"Let's go!" shouted Tracy.

Donal turned and shouted, "Tim! Hurry up!"

Tim Cooney was fifteen feet from the car, on one knee in the middle of the road. "Two shakes, Donal." He raised his Mauser.

Tracy watched the lorry shooting toward the bridge. It was the dun color of river bottom, except for the red coat clinging to the mirror. The British lieutenant pulled himself against the door so that he would not be burned. He was as brave as Starr, thought Tracy.

Tim Cooney cocked his head over the sight.

The lorry reached the bridge and disappeared. The fiery cloud billowed out around it. Then the beast exploded from the flames, onto the road, and came straight for them.

But Tim Cooney calmly fired at the windshield. A star of glass exploded on the driver's side. The lorry swerved suddenly and crashed into the wall of the quay.

Lambert-Jones dove from the running board while the constables poured out of the back.

Cooney stitched a line of bullets across the grille and flattened both front tires. "Now," he said calmly, "we can leave."

Lambert-Jones shouted, "Open fire!"

A dozen shots cracked and echoed from the men around the truck. There were little explosions of dirt. Three bullets hit the back of the Rolls. One caught Martin Mahoney in the leg. And another hit Tim Cooney in the back of the head. His rifle flew into the air, and he slammed forward onto his face.

"Oh, no," said Rachel.

Tom Tracy pulled at the rope around Clarke's neck. "Stand up!"

"I'll be cut to pieces!"

"Stand up!" Tracy stood in the back of the car and pulled Clarke up in front of him. Then he pushed the revolver against Clarke's temple.

Lambert-Jones raised his hands. "Hold your fire."

"Let's go!" shouted Tracy.

The car sped up the hill and out of the town, with Rachel gripping Starr's belt so that his body would not tumble out.

38

W e should have given ourselves up," said Rachel.

"And spend ten years in Kilmainham Jail?"

"Not necessarily," said Clarke.

"Twenty, if you have anything to do with it." Starr was standing on the running board, massaging the bump on his head.

"None, if *I* have anything to do with it." Tom Tracy sat beside Clarke in a jump seat.

Clarke twisted his head and pulled at the noose around his neck.

Tom Tracy wrapped his hand around the end of the rope. The fighting had begun. It would be impossible to stop until it had been resolved. As the autocar pounded over the ruts, past the south row and the little cottages and the faces of the two little boys peering from Tim Cooney's cottage, Tracy wondered if now, there was nothing to do but see the battle through to its end.

Danny Tracy wetted his lips and began to speak, but no words came out. He had wrapped his hands around the stock of his Enfield to keep them from shaking. He had said nothing since the fighting began.

"Something on your mind, Master Tracy?" said Clarke.

Danny looked across at the resident magistrate. "What we're doin', it's for Ireland. It ain't like we're stealin' or nothing'."

"Don't be pleadin' with him, Dan, " said Tom Tracy.

"Yeah. He knows why we're here." Martin Mahoney slipped off his belt and tightened it around his leg. The bullet had severed a blood vessel, and he was bleeding onto the leather upholstery.

Clarke squinted in the sunlight, screwing his left eye at Martin. "You've appeared before me at petty sessions, have you?"

Martin shook his head and spat onto the floor.

"Spittin' in the magistrate's car," said Starr. "One more crime you'll be charged with if we lose. But then, we'll not be losin', I think."

Up ahead, a man on a mule was waving his arms.

Donal stopped the Rolls.

Logan slipped off the mule's bare back. "I was comin' to help—" Logan saw Clarke sitting on the jump seat. "I was comin' to try to save you, Donal."

"Comin' like a whirlwind, too." Starr jumped from the running board and looked back toward the town.

The bridge had burned through. People were rushing from their houses and forming bucket brigades, but the flaming planks and beams were collapsing into the river and sending up hissing clouds of steam.

"You started it good and proper this time, Paddy Starr," said Logan O'Leary.

"I plan to finish it, too."

Logan looked over Starr's shoulder at the burning bridge. He looked at his son, who was staring straight up the road. He looked at the noose around William Clarke's neck, and his eyes followed the rope to Tom Tracy's hands.

"I thought you come to save these people, like your da wanted."

"My da wanted Irish freedom." Of that and only that was Tom Tracy certain.

"And don't we all." Starr jumped back onto the running board. "The Clifden unit just pulled into the square. Let's be movin' on."

"Wait!" shouted Logan. He grabbed the mirror on the driver's side. "If I can't stop you, I'll fight beside you. I've brung me gun." He held it up and shook it at his son. "I'm ready."

"There's no room for informers in this car," said Donal bitterly. Then he stepped on the accelerator and the Rolls shot up the road.

Tom Tracy looked back at the tormented, whiskey-red face, at another father trying to save another son, another father called informer, another ready to die. It never ended, he thought.

"Donal, wait!" cried Logan. "Wait!"

The car swung around the bend, and Logan O'Leary was gone.

"Brigade Commandant O'Leary," said Clarke over his shoulder.

Donal grunted.

"I know for a fact that your father did not inform on Seamus Kilkeirnan or anyone else."

"You're lyin'."

Rachel looked at Donal. "He's your father. If he informed, maybe he did it to save you."

"Indeed. The son is the hope of the future." William Clarke looked up at Tom Tracy. "Not the prisoner of the past."

444

"You came to that knowledge a bit late, didn't you, Resident Magistrate?" answered Tracy.

Clarke looked down at the hands bound in front of him. "You demonstrated it to me in the church. In your way, you're a brave man."

At that, Danny Tracy raised his head.

Clarke smiled at the boy. "Sometimes, son, there is greater courage in not killing."

"Greater brains, too," grunted Starr. The car hit a bump, and he had to grab Rachel's arm to keep from bouncing off. "Tommy knows you're more valuable alive than dead."

Tracy wrapped his hand around the noose rope once more. The fibers of hemp cut into his hand like small splinters. Starr was right. But so was Clarke. That, as always, was the hell of it.

Father John Breen watched the lorry rumble up the Dun Slea road with fourteen armed constables riding in the rear, and Hayes and Lambert-Jones on the running boards. He shook his head and said a prayer and hung a sign on the church door: *Due to public emergency, Easter Mass will be delayed.*

He was wearing his purple stole and carrying his holy oils. He had given the last rites to Tim Cooney and the dead constable, and he expected he would bestow the sacrament several times more before the day was done. He mounted Old Flavius and kicked his flanks up the Dunslea road.

After a time, he came to the home of Tim Cooney.

The door cracked open and a woman's voice called to him. He dismounted and went to the door. From the windows, two little boys were watching.

"I heard the shooting, Father," said Cooney's wife. "I seen them go by in the yellow car, but my Tim Cooney wasn't with them."

The woman's face was mostly in shadow. But the old priest could see the moist whites of her eyes, wide and painfully expectant. God had never made this terrible task easy for him.

"Your husband stands before God. He'll be judged a good man."

He heard a small, sharp intake of breath, then the woman said, "I'd invite you to tea, but . . . but . . ."

"At church, then, later," he said gently.

And the door closed.

He looked down at the two little boys. One smiled. What would he remember of this day?

A short distance more, and he came to a great hulk of a man sitting by the roadside, crying like a child. He dismounted again. "Logan! Logan O'Leary!"

"The RIC just went by, on the way to kill my boy." He pointed to the line of fluid running up the road. "And my boy drivin' a car with a shot fuel tank."

The priest touched the fluid and smelled. "Petrol. They won't be gettin' far. Maybe we can do a bit to save them."

"I can't, Father." Logan buried his face in his hands.

"Come along, Logan. Despair's as bad a sin as lust!"

Logan looked up. The drool and spit formed into strands between his hands and face. "I'm sorry, Father. I should never have told that damn Clarke a thing. A thing!"

"Don't be thinkin' that, Logan. It would've happened, now or later."

"But maybe not here."

The priest stood and kicked Logan in the flank. "Come along. There may still be something we can do."

The Rolls-Royce began to sputter as it passed Deirdre Hamilton's house.

"Nearly out of petrol," said Donal.

"The tank was filled yesterday," said Clarke.

"It doesn't matter." Starr looked up ahead. "We're almost there. We'll join up with our people and make a fight of it."

The car came over a low rise, and there, on the promontory, commanding views of ocean, bay, and road, was Dun Slea, as deserted as it had been for the last two centuries.

Before the car stopped, Starr was off the running board and racing up the path to the ruins. "Hello! Deirdre! Hello! Irish Volunteers!"

The echo of his words off the rocks made the only answer.

When he was close enough to the tower to see that Deirdre and the Irish Volunteers were not there, he stopped running. Then he stopped shouting. His echo rolled away, and he dropped to his knees. His green uniform seemed to disappear into the tall green grass around him. A gull circled above.

"No one," said Rachel. "No one to fight with him, at last."

"So much for the rising," said Clarke.

"Don't be so certain, Resident Magistrate," said Tom Tracy, unwilling to allow Clarke any comfort in Starr's defeat. "They canceled the rising last night. It might take time to get it started again."

"Well, *I* ain't here for my health." Donal jumped out of the roadster. "And damn soon, there'll be others."

Martin wobbled to his feet and put a hand on Danny Tracy's shoulder. "Help me up the hill, lad."

Rachel looked at Tracy. In the church, she had thought that the crisis had ended. Now she feared that somehow, Starr would find it in himself to rally them again, rally them all to their death. "What are we going to do?"

"That's up to the resident magistrate."

"You hold the gun, Mr. Tracy. That gives you the power."

"There may be other ways," said Rachel.

"Not today," answered Clarke.

Tracy pulled Clarke out and slammed the door. It banged like a rifle shot.

At the sound, Padraic Starr jumped up. He looked back at the car, then up at the smoke settling above the bay, then he ran into the open port on the tower, as though taken by an idea that would turn the day. When he came out, he cradled three rifles in his arms. He dropped them among the rocks that once had been the outer wall of the chapel. A moment later he came staggering out with a fifty-pound box of ammunition.

When the others reached him, he had laid the rifles out in a wide perimeter, from the cemetery on the east to the ancient chapel wall on the west.

He flipped Donal a rifle. "We can't run no farther. So we'll make a stand right here, on the stones of Bloody Sean Slea."

Donal looked off toward the hills on the far side of the road. "They must be comin'."

"And we'll be here when they get here."

"You can't hold off fourteen constables for long." Tracy came up the hill with Clarke in tow. "We can still use Clarke to negotiate."

"Our column'll be here any minute," said Starr.

"An unarmed column ain't much good," said Donal.

Starr looked from Donal to Tracy. His face was covered in grime and sweat, but beneath it an expression of calm resolve had replaced the fury. "Run if you like, lads. I'll be happy to take the glory."

"I never said I was runnin'," answered Donal.

Martin Mahoney came up the hill, supported on one side by Danny and on the other by Rachel. "I ain't runnin' anywhere. I can't, and I ain't." His left leg was soaked with blood, and his florid color was beginning to fade. "Pick me up a rifle, boy."

Danny handed him a gun.

"I'll buy the time. The rest of you's run."

"Thanks, old man." Starr looped an Enfield over his shoulder. "But I'll not be desertin'. If you've a mind to fight, get yourself up in the tower. Down here it'll be hit and run, stall and retreat."

"We can hold 'em off for a day if we have to." Martin threw his arm around Danny's shoulder, and they went up the path to the tower.

"It's hopeless," said Clarke.

"You may be right, squire." Starr looked at the four faces around him, then he gazed off across the green hillsides to the south. "We may get no relief at all. And even if we get it, we might not win the day anyway."

"So why throw the lives of all these people away, along with your own?" Clarke pulled himself up straight and stretched his neck to loosen the pull of the rope.

Clarke had courage, thought Tom Tracy. And he had not lost his wit. But his argument had no strength against Padraic Starr, because, somewhere on the ride from town to the ancient tower, or in those defeated moments in the grass, the fight had taken on a new dimension in Starr's mind.

Tracy watched him walk to the edge of the cemetery. Three Celtic crosses rose among the headstones, so that the field looked like Golgotha. For a time, Starr seemed to contemplate the crosses, as though deciding his own fate. Then he turned. "It's time for the blood sacrifice, just like Pearse said."

"Madness," answered Clarke.

"If we can't fight among the Twelve Bens, we'll do it in the minds of the people. Christ spilled His blood and started the faith. We'll spill ours and start the risin'."

"Christ spilled His and started *two* faiths," answered Rachel. "And this is where they've ended up."

Starr looked at her and smiled as though he were passing her on the street. Then he unshouldered his Enfield and pointed it straight at her head. No one moved. "In another time or place, my Hebrew darlin', I'd feel that God gave me the right to blow off your pretty head for blasphemin' the Risen Savior." He lowered the gun and grinned. "But you're right. A fine damn mess. Ain't it, Resident Magistrate?"

"Insoluble," answered Clarke.

"Until washed clean with blood."

Then they heard the sound of the lorry rumbling up the road.

Starr put up the gun and slung two more rifles over his shoulders. "All right. Martin has the tower. The rest of you's, I free you all. You've taken a part and started the fight. Now get on the yawlboat and get the hell home and spread the word."

"How, may I ask, are they to do that?" said Clarke.

Starr looked at Tracy and smiled. "I leave that in the hands of the smart talker."

Donal slid the bolt on the rifle. "I'm no talker. I'm stayin'."

"Good lad. The rest of you's, good luck and a long life."

Rachel Levka slipped a hand into the crook of Tracy's arm and looked at Starr. "If we get away, we'll tell the truth."

"Whose?" said Clarke.

Starr grinned at him. "A fair question. Your truth, or Jack Tracy's?"

"Who once told me never to run away from a fight," said Tom.

"And also told you to stand up in Congress and speak for Irish freedom," said Starr. "I'm tellin' you, now I see he was right, all along."

Rachel pulled Tracy closer to herself.

"Things happen for a reason, Tommy," said Starr. "Jack Tracy saved me for this fight. And back at the church, you saved Clarke because he's your ticket out of here. Take it, and when we meet him again, we can both tell Jack Tracy we done his biddin'."

The RIC were drawing closer. The lorry backfired, and a flock of blackbirds rose from the field.

Starr grabbed Tracy's hand, but he did not shake it. Instead, he slammed one of his rifles into the palm. "When a man's goin' into the unknown, the least you can do is give him a pint o' porter or a well-made gun."

Tracy looked down at the rifle and thought of the blood they had spilled to get it there. "An old Irish proverb?"

"I just made it up."

"Then I should be givin' *you* a gun or a good drink."

Starr grinned. "This old Celtic sin-eater *knows* where he's goin'."

"God be with you, you bastard."

"Politics, not rebellion, isn't that what you said, Tommy?"

"Somebody's always sayin' it."

"While I'm doin' my rebellin' down here, see if you can do a little politickin' with the RM in the tower. I'll start the faith, and you play the apostle."

Then Starr snatched Rachel around the waist and pulled her to him and kissed her full on the lips. "That's for all the pain I caused you, darlin'," he whispered. "And for all the things I said about you that I didn't mean."

She wiped away the tears that rolled from the corners of her eyes.

"I've given you reason enough to cry these last weeks, but at least I brung you two together."

She wrapped an arm around his neck and pulled his face to hers and scraped her cheek on his morning stubble. Then he gave her a sharp whack on the bottom. "Go, damn you, and I'll buy what time I can."

She looked into the blue eyes and whispered, "Thank you, Padr'ic." Then she hiked up her skirt, took the hand that Tom Tracy offered, and went toward the tower.

Starr shouted after them, "If not for this fight, Tommy, I'd've fought you for *her*. Take good care of what you've won."

"Forever."

A moment after they disappeared into the tower, the RIC lorry bounced to the bottom of the path.

Starr picked up another rifle. "Well, Donal, me boy, this is it. Let's entertain 'em till Deirdre arrives."

Donal looked off toward the hills. "Maybe she'll be here, maybe not. But it's for sure that if I run, she'll marry you instead of me."

Starr grinned. "When it's over, marry her quick and birth us some kids who can see both sides of a stupid argument."

They watched the constables fanning out, hiding behind boulders and old walls and hillocks. "They'll make a semicircle and try to close in on us. We'll start wide, then pull back as we can. If anyone gets behind you, count on old Martin." He pointed to a place that provided Donal O'Leary with good cover.

"Good luck, Padr'ic." Donal ran toward one of the monumental crosses in the middle of the graveyard. Starr went in the opposite direction, to an old wall about a hundred yards away from the tower.

450

"Starr!" screamed Lambert-Jones. "You're surrounded, with no escape."

Starr did not answer. He checked each rifle and made sure that the magazines were full.

"We're holding our fire, Starr, until you respond."

Starr raised his head. "You'll continue to hold your fire, too, for we've got us one resident magistrate who's a dead man when you start shootin'."

Brian Hayes looked at Lieutenant Ian Lambert-Jones. "What do we do?"

Lambert-Jones had learned his lesson. He had studied the terrain before the fighting started. He looked at the constables deployed around the ruins, and then at the hillsides rising behind them. If they were attacked from behind, even by farmers using birdguns, they would be cut to pieces.

"Do we know how many are in the keep?"

"Two, three, maybe four. The fire and smoke at the bridge were too thick."

"I say that we attack. Now."

"But they'll kill the magistrate."

"They said so at the bridge, but once you've killed a hostage, he loses his value to anyone."

"But—"

"Starr came here because he expects to meet reinforcements. If you want your men pinned down, hold your fire and play Starr's game." He raised his binoculars and tried to count the heads on the top of the tower.

Hayes pulled at his gloves and looked at the terrain and the men taking their positions.

"The RM knew the possibilities last night, when he canceled the arrests," said Lambert-Jones. "He would want you to stop this."

Hayes pulled at his gloves again and ordered his men to open fire. The carbines began to pop and echo from the rocks all around the old tower.

Padraic Starr picked up a rifle and aimed it at the lorry, where Lambert-Jones and Hayes were crouched. The Enfield was a solid weapon that sighted out to a thousand yards, much more accurate than the Mannlicher carbines carried by the Royal Irish Constabulary.

He ignored the ricochets and bursts on the wall around him and squeezed off two shots. The first hit the bonnet of the lorry. Hayes and Lambert-Jones ducked. But Hayes did not drop quickly enough, and the second shot killed him.

The sun beat down on the top of the battlement.

Martin Mahoney poked his head into an embrasure and fired. Immediately, the wall around him danced with small explosions of stone and lead. He ignored them and fired off a whole magazine, spraying the bullets in every directions across the ruins. Then he handed the rifle to Danny, who gave him another.

On the other side of the battlement, Tom Tracy removed the noose from William Clarke's neck, while Rachel cut the bonds at his wrists.

Clarke rubbed the raw flesh. "Starr called you a smart talker. I'm afraid you'll have to be, Mr. Tracy."

"This is my proposal—" Several shots hit the battlement to his right, and Tracy dropped down. "My brother, Rachel, my uncle, and I leave through the secret tunnels beneath the tower. We get back into the yawlboat and sail to Galway—"

A bullet somehow richocheted off the inside of one of the embrasures and bounced off the floor, narrowly missing Rachel.

"Be careful, dear," said Clarke.

She did not move. There was no sense in moving, she thought, if the bullets were flying so wildly.

"When this is over," continued Tracy calmly, "you tell the constable that we jumped off the car and disappeared into the countryside someplace between here and the town."

Clarke listened and nodded thoughtfully.

"When we land in Galway, we give the false names we swore in Boston, so that we can ship back to America. And you do what you can to keep the authorities from investigating us."

Martin Mahoney pulled his last chaw of tobacco from his pocket and jammed it into his mouth. Then, without a word, he took another rifle from Danny and poured fire down at the constables.

Clarke looked hard at Tracy and said, "Why should I do any of that?"

"Because we haven't killed you." In negotiation, Tom Tracy had learned from James Michael Curley that before discussing the finer points, restate the obvious if it strengthened your position.

A run of bullets danced across the top of the wall, and Clarke ducked instinctively. "Dear boy, not committing a crime does not entitle one to special treatment."

Tracy pulled the Colt revolver from his belt, but he did not raise it.

"I believe in the rule of law," said Clarke.

"The same law that's kept this country in poverty, under Britain's thumb for three hundred years? Cromwell's law?"

"That and the law of Parliament in 1914. Home Rule. I am sworn to the law." Clarke looked down at the gun in Tracy's hand. "Your father was duly prosecuted. And you all shall be as well. You've entered the country illegally, you've been involved in arms importation, subversion, and kidnapping. Spare my life and I shall recommend whatever leniency I can. But you shall not sail away."

Danny Tracy called to his brother. "There's men comin', Tommy."

Tracy went to an embrasure, and immediately a spray of bullets swept over his head. He dropped down, then cautiously raised his head and brought his binoculars to his eyes. There were six, five men and a woman, running over rocky hillsides too dangerous for a horse or a mule. One of them was carrying a rifle, the rest had pikes and shovels.

Help was coming, but too little. Below him, Starr and Donal O'Leary were still firing steadily, although both had pulled back from their original positions and puffs of smoke were rising from the rocks and ruins all around them. The semicircle was closing.

Tracy turned and pulled out his pistol again. Now was the time to bluff. "Twelve men, reinforcements, on the way."

He came over to Clarke and put the revolver to his head.

"Tommy—" said Rachel.

"I'll have no chance to play the apostle in jail. I might as well join the fight. Five of us on this side, a dozen more on their way, and your constables in a crossfire. We might even win."

"You might still lose."

"But you'll be dead."

"And if I let you leave, what keeps me from sending them after you the minute the fight is over?"

"Trust," said Rachel.

Tracy lowered the gun.

"Trust," repeated Clarke, "a noble concept, Miss—"

As Rachel said her name, another shot ricocheted through an embrasure and off the stone floor

"Donal's hit," cried Danny, and he jumped up. Immediately, shots whistled and whined around him. He dropped down again.

"Is trust possible?" asked Clarke.

"As an old friend said last night, there's light and dark in all of us." Rachel removed the gun from Tracy's hands. "We just have to hope we find the light."

William Clarke looked at Tracy. "I chance my arm if you chance yours. Is that what you're asking?"

Tracy nodded. "You think my father killed yours. I think you loaded a legal gun and shot mine. Maybe we're both wrong."

"Trust," repeated Rachel, and she held out the pistol to Clarke.

"Not *that* much trust." Tracy snatched the handle and shoved the gun back into his belt. "If *you* can't trust that much, either, let these three go and put me on trial."

Clarke shook his head. "I'm sorry. I can't do it. I'll offer you all the leniency I can argue after, but not clemency for anyone."

Tom Tracy wiped the sweat from his forehead.

"Donal's down!" cried Danny.

"More bullets!" called Martin Mahoney.

Danny picked up a loaded Enfield and ran over to him. "Donal's down!"

"I know." Martin spat tobacco and raised his head again and fired off another magazine.

Danny squinted in the bright sunlight, and when the smoke had blown off, he shouted, "You got one!"

"I did?" Martin dropped back and dropped the rifle. "Are you sure?"

"What's wrong?" cried Danny. "You got one."

"I wasn't tryin' to hit him." Martin shook his head. "Just some Catholic farm boy lookin' for a pension. Damn."

Danny grabbed the rifle and took Martin's place.

"Are you all right, Martin?" Tracy crawled over to him.

Martin nodded, then he shook his head. What color was left in his face drained from it. "I was tryin' to miss." And he vomited codfish, green bile, and tobacco onto the stone floor beside him.

Danny Tracy looked down at the mess and curled his nose, then moved to the next embrasure.

454

Martin's eyes were going glassy. "You lads better keep up the fire, or we'll be surrounded before you can say Jack Johnson."

Danny Tracy fired wildly at the puffs of smoke rising like small signals all around the tower.

Tom Tracy poked his head into an embrasure and saw Donal O'Leary pulling back to a place close by the tower. The middle of his green tunic was soaked through with blood. He had to be badly wounded. And now Starr was running low over broken walls and fallen pillars, closing his own circle of defense. He had been hit in the shoulder, and his left arm was hanging limp. He reached a small mound where the ground had grown over a pile of rocks. He dropped and fired. But the position was not safe. The constables still had him flanked.

Tracy heard his brother fire several rounds at muzzle flashes off to his right. Then he saw Starr rise from behind a rock. As soon as Starr began to run, the carbines popped and wisps of smoke fluttered into the air.

Tom Tracy took an Enfield and leveled it, ignoring the ricochets around him, and fired a half-dozen shots to protect his cousin.

Starr reached cover about fifteen yards from the port, but before he could drop, a bullet slammed through the middle of him.

"Padr'ic's hit!" screamed Danny. He picked up another rifle and ran for the stairs.

"Danny, stop!" Tom Tracy grabbed his brother's arm.

Danny pushed him away and dropped into the darkness.

Rachel screamed for Tom to stop. She could not lose them all. But he stumbled down the stairs after his brother. She started after them, and Martin screamed, "Stop! Them boys'll be dead for sure if you don't hand me another rifle so's I can give 'em some cover."

Just then, the wind changed. The muzzle smoke blew off to the south, and for a moment, William Clarke smelled something else, terribly, painfully familiar. An emotion came back to him, from where, he did not know, but it was strong enough that his stomach turned.

Clarke crouched down and went over to the other side of the wall, where Martin Mahoney held his position. The smell grew stronger, the emotion stronger. It was grief, then it was anger. Then he knew. *He knew.*

The answer to it all, to his own hatred, to Tom Tracy's, to it all, in a pile of vomit. The sickening sweet stink of it, mingled with the earthy smell of tobacco. It was the tobacco that told him, the tobacco that had made the smell stay in his head for decades. This same man had spit up this same stench after killing William Clarke's father thirty years before.

Below them, Danny Tracy burst out of the tower, and the constables began to fire at him.

Clarke peered over the wall and saw what was happening. Then he saw Jack Tracy's face, jagged with birdshot. Suddenly he knew he had to save them if he could.

He turned to Rachel as she crawled over with two rifles. He grabbed her by the arm. "Go! Get out of here. The three of you. Get down to the boat as fast as you can, because they won't be held off much longer."

"Why are you doing this?"

"I've decided to chance my arm. I'm giving Jack Tracy the lives of his two sons. And you . . . you're an innocent."

Martin finished firing one rifle and called for the other.

"What about Martin?" said Rachel.

"He stays," said Clarke firmly. "You go."

"Why?"

"Go!" shouted Martin. "I can't make it. But I'll be coverin' you for as long as I can. For as long as there's blood."

Rachel gave Martin a kiss on his dusty, sweat-covered cheek. She looked at Clarke. He smiled at her and reached out his hand. "You saved my life back in the church. Thank you." He brought her hand to his lips and kissed it.

Another skein of bullets splattered against the granite wall and ricocheted through the embrasures. There was little time. She turned and ran to the stairs and dropped into the darkness.

Martin Mahoney and William Clarke looked at each other. They both knew.

Martin said, "I been sorry every day of my life. First that we didn't win what we went after in them days, then for killin' your da, but most of all for Jack Tracy."

"I'll be sorry for Jack Tracy every day from now on." Clarke looked out. "They're closing in, and Starr isn't firing. You'd better try to hold them off another five minutes or so, but don't hit anyone."

"Hand me another rifle, then, squire."

* * *

Danny Tracy flew through the fusillade and dropped beside his cousin.

Starr had been hit three times. His left arm was near useless, there was a trickle of blood at the corner of his mouth, and a red stain was widening in the middle of his back.

"What are you doin' here?"

Danny sniffled and wiped his nose. "I'm here to fight beside you. I ain't no coward, Padr'ic."

"Get out of here, boy."

"I ain't no coward. Not like my brother."

With his good hand, Starr slapped Danny. "Don't you be sayin' that about Tom Tracy."

Danny brought his hand to his face. The imprint of Starr's fingers reddened into the cheek.

"He's got more balls than me an' Donal put together. And if I know him, he's talked you all back to Boston by now." Starr closed his eyes a moment as a wave of pain seemed to flow through him, replacing the blood that was pouring from his wounds. "Take advantage of a smart brother, and go."

A constable appeared off to the right, running from one broken wall to another, trying to gain the flank. Starr cradled the rifle in his left elbow and fired. The gun kicked wildly because he lacked the strength to hold it. But the sound of it was enough to send the constable diving.

"Where the hell's Donal? That one should have been his."

"He's someplace over by the old graveyard," said Danny.

That brought a strange smile to Starr's face. "A good place for him, I guess." Then a frown hardened in the blood. "But not for you."

"I'm staying." Danny raised his head and fired several wild rounds toward the lorry.

"Do you want to hang? You can't be that much of a damn fool. Get up and run!"

"No." He fired several more rounds off to the left, where the constables were crouched low and running.

"You'll not be doin' anyone any good here, but if you run away, you might get a chance to do us some good someday."

Danny Tracy leaned back on his heels, and carbines began to crackle from three sides. He ducked down again and pulled off the scally cap and stuffed it into his pocket.

"You done a share, Dan. You cleared the family name. They'll always remember that it was a Tracy helped start the risin'. That's what I wanted for your da. Now run, lad," growled Starr through the blood. "Run."

Tom Tracy was on his belly. He had crawled out of the tower and was dragging himself slowly toward the spot where his brother and Starr were hidden.

Rachel hurried down the staircase that wound around the inside of the tower. She went through one floor, then another, and every time a carbine popped outside, she imagined Tom falling dead, and it drove her on. She could save them if she reached them in time.

As she rushed past one of the archer's windows overlooking the ruins, she saw Danny burst from behind a rock and run toward the tower. Puffs of smoke rose everywhere.

She cried, "Please don't die, either of you," and she stumbled down through the ancient darkness.

When Tom Tracy saw his brother jump up and start to run, he rolled back and reached the port just as Rachel arrived at the bottom of the stairs.

"Tommy! Tommy!" she cried.

"Stay down!" he shouted.

The bullets seemed to be following Danny Tracy. Tom heard them zinging through the port and bouncing off the round walls like marbles in a bucket.

"Tommy!" cried Rachel.

"Get down!" he commanded, and she dropped behind a pile of rubble in the middle of the floor.

Then Tracy looked out at his brother. "Come on, kid. You can make it!"

As Danny approached the safety of the tower, the firing intensified. The noise became deafening. He stumbled and fell. He got up and ran. A shot exploded at his foot, then another. They had him in their sights. But he dove into the darkness, rolled to his left, and into his brother's arms.

"Are you all right, Dan?"

The boy gulped down several breaths. "Yeah."

When the target disappeared, the firing receded quickly.

Rachel raised her head. "Tommy, Clarke says we can go. We should go now!"

"Why?" Tracy's voice echoed strangely between the gunshots.

"He said it was time to chance his arm."

"And Martin?"

She shook her head.

The gunfire outside had diminished to isolated splatters, like the last loud raindrops that pop on the pavement as the thunderstorm ends.

Tracy looked out to the place where Starr was hidden. A plume of smoke rose from his position. He was still firing.

"Padr'ic told us to go, too," said Danny.

"All right, then." Tracy pushed his brother toward the dungeon entrance behind them. Then he reached out his hand to Rachel and smiled. "Let's go home."

She stood from behind the pile of rubble on her side of the tower. She was smiling. She ran toward him.

"Stay low" was the last thing he said to her.

The firing increased suddenly, and he never understood why. Several constables saw his hand in the opening of the port and used it as a target.

A spot of black appeared at her left temple. Her eyes opened wide. The impact of the shot lifted her into the air.

"Oh, God!" Tracy brought his hand to his head.

And she slammed onto the rocks that Bloody Sean Slea had laid nine centuries before.

"Rachel!" cried Tracy.

She was not dead. He had not seen it. She had stumbled on her skirt. She had tripped on a stone. She was going home where she belonged. Her ran to her and put his hands under her arms to lift her.

"Hey, Tommy!" Danny reappeared from below. "Oh, shit!"

Tracy knelt down and brought his hands to her face and felt her blood.

"Oh, God," cried Tom Tracy. "Oh God."

"C'mon, Tommy."

"No!" In the dark, damp tower, the bullets rattled and danced, and Tom Tracy felt that his own life had ended.

"C'mon!"

"No!" He wouldn't leave her. She had never left him, no matter how difficult he had been, how indecisive in Boston, how single-minded on the ship. She had always been there. He would not leave her now, when she needed him.

Another fusillade tore through the doorway. Danny dropped to his stomach as the bullets ricocheted around them. Tom Tracy did not move.

"Tommy." Danny's voice trembled. "She's dead, and Padr'ic's out there dyin' for us. Let's go!"

He shook his head and held her to his chest and rocked back and forth.

"Well, dammit!" Danny tried to make himself angry and snap his brother from his shock. "I leave you here, bawlin' like a baby, and it's right where they'll find you. I'm goin', like Padr'ic told me. I'm goin' where I can do some good."

Tom held her and rocked and moaned in agony.

"Where we can do some good, Tommy." Danny grabbed his brother by the shoulder and shook him. "Some good."

Tom stopped rocking. His brother's frantic words struck something that snapped the shock, at least for a moment. He raised Rachel's face to his and kissed her lips. They were still warm and moist, filled with the life that, for a moment, they thought they might find. He held her face to his, and his tears washed into her blood.

Another spray of shots blew through the port.

"C'mon, Tommy. We gotta go."

He kissed her once more. He laid her gently on the stone floor. And Tom Tracy followed his brother down the stairs to the dungeon, away from the sound of the gunfire and the body of the woman he loved, past the stone that still rolled smoothly after seven centuries, down another dark stairwell, and another, through a long tunnel, to a cave that smelled of low tide, and across the clean sand to the yawlboat. The rifles were still firing above them, but Tom Tracy no longer heard them. And later he remembered nothing of his escape.

The firing had stopped. The fight was over.

Ian Lambert-Jones was running up the path, followed closely by Father Breen and Logan O'Leary.

Lambert-Jones found Starr near the entrance to the tower, where he had fallen in his final retreat. He raised his revolver and with his boot pushed Starr onto his back.

Starr's eyes flickered open. "How's the leg, General?"

"It still hurts."

"Better your leg than your head." Starr's face was caked with sweat and dirt and dried blood, except at the corner of his mouth, where the blood was still wet. Starr moved his tongue around his lips, and the blood trickled out.

Lambert-Jones knelt next to him. "What about the rising?"

"Did we win?"

"No," said Lambert-Jones. "Who planned it?"

Starr's lips formed the word *Me*.

And Ian Lambert-Jones felt the point of Starr's knife against his scrotum. The British lieutenant pointed his revolver at Starr's head.

"Fire if you'd like, but I'll take your balls with me." Starr pressed harder. "Think of all the little Brits I'd keep . . . keep from muckin' up the world."

A drop of perspiration rolled from the tip of Lambert-Jones's nose and splattered onto Starr's cheek.

Starr forced a smile. "Nervous, General?"

"Take the knife away, Starr, and I'll summon the doctor."

"No . . . I'm enjoyin' this. It'll be my last pleasure. Like a . . . like a final meal."

"It'll do no good."

Starr pressed harder and cut into the fabric. Lambert-Jones tried to pull back, but the knife followed him.

"Promise me somethin', Lieutenant, and you can keep your balls."

"What?"

"Tell your little ones that it was an Irishman saved their daddy's life . . . an Irish patriot . . . and—"

Lambert-Jones tried to move away, and Starr pressed the knife harder.

"Tell them that they felt his knife before they was ever born. Let them think on the good and the bad and make up their minds."

"I'll tell them."

"I'll trust you." Starr lowered the knife.

Father Breen came across from the place where Donal O'Leary had fallen and knelt beside Starr. "Excuse us for a minute, Lieutenant."

Lambert-Jones stood, but his leather calf-boots remained by Starr's head.

Father Breen gave the soldier an angry glance, but there was no time for arguing. "Now then, Padr'ic. Confess your sins."

"I'm a sinner," said Starr softly. "And so are you."

Breen smiled. "I guess that'll do. Now make a good Act of Contrition."

"I said I was a sinner. I never said I was sorry."

"Say it, Padr'ic, for the good of your soul."

Lambert-Jones was growing impatient. He knelt again beside the body. "Is the rising going to happen anywhere else in the district?"

Starr shook his head.

"This is the extent of it?"

Starr's fading vision caught something on the hillside just over Lambert-Jones's left shoulder. He thought he saw the silhouettes looking down at him. They had come after all. They had no guns, nor any plan, but when the shooting started, they had come to join the fight. They had been too late, but perhaps, next time . . .

He looked at the red tunic and the medal from Neuve-Chapelle. "Just remember my message for your little ones."

"Get out of here now," said the priest, "so that I can try to save his soul before he dies."

Lambert-Jones did not move. He was mesmerized by the strange look of satisfaction in Starr's eyes.

"All right then, Padr'ic," said Father Breen. "It may be hard in front of a Brit, but can you not say you're sorry?"

Starr tried to shrug. "There's things I done I'm sorry for, and things I done . . . I wish I done more. That's what I . . ."

The priest leaned forward and whispered into Starr's ear, as though one spirit could breathe prayer into another as it left on its journey. "Oh my God, I am heartily sorry for having offended thee . . ."

Lambert-Jones walked into the tower. He saw the girl dead on the floor, a reddish puddle congealing around her head. He went over to the stairs and went up, through the dark, cool air, past the little slivers of light slanting through the archer's windows, to the glare at the top.

He hesitated a moment before stepping into the sun.

"Hello, Ian," said the familiar voice.

He put up his gun. "There have been times this morning when I never thought I would see you alive again."

Clarke grunted and said, "Whose idea was it to open fire?"

"Mine, sir. Purely tactical."

"Rather lucky for me that this gentleman was not the hot-headed sort." A fly landed on the wound that had bled Martin Mahoney to death. Clarke waved it away.

"Casualties?"

"Several wounded. Two dead. The lorry driver in the town and, I'm afraid, Inspector Hayes."

Clarke shook his head.

"Where are the others?" asked Lambert-Jones.

"Two of them turned coward halfway up the road. They leaped out of the car and ran off. I don't expect we'll be seeing them again." Clarke pulled off his cravat and removed his collar. The skin on his neck was beginning to ooze clear fluid.

"What about the boy who ran out to Starr?"

"That was no boy. It was this man."

"So it was the dead woman who was firing from the top?"

"Dead woman?" Clarke's heart sank.

"Took it in the head."

"Oh, yes, indeed. She wasn't a bad shot." He shook his head. The blood of innocents, he thought.

The sun was high now. It was baking into the battlement. Clarke looked out at the Atlantic and saw the white-hulled yawl-boat, a quarter mile off, heading south.

"I wonder who's on that," said Lambert-Jones idly.

"Somebody quite happy he was not here this morning, I'm sure."

A gentle breeze blew down the bay. It carried from some other town the sound of a church bell chiming for Easter.

And then an angry voice cried up from below, "God damn you, William Clarke. God damn you and the Brits and the whole goddamn RIC."

Clarke recognized the voice and felt the pain of a father losing another son. He could not listen. He turned and walked away.

Lambert-Jones looked through one of the embrasures and saw Logan O'Leary, at the base of an ancient Celtic cross, cradling his boy in his arms.

"I did everything you wanted," cried Logan. "I informed, I told lies, I did it all to save me boy, and you killed him still. You killed him, you bloody bastards! And you'll pay, all of you. You'll pay one of these days. I promise!"

Lambert-Jones turned away as Logan's voice became a running stream of hatred, grief, and threat.

Clarke cocked his head toward the sound. "That's how it always ends, with the seeds of another beginning."

"Before he died, Starr said that this was isolated. There's no general rising. He was the only one."

"Do you believe it?"

"I hope it."

Clarke's eyes were on a distant hillside. Six silhouettes had been there a moment ago, but all save one had disappeared again into the green. The lone silhouette, female, sank slowly down to the grass and hunched over. Deirdre, too, thought Clarke in amazement, a Protestant.

"We've had many chances to chance our arm, Lieutenant, but too many times, for fear of losing our arm, we've ended up shooting ourselves or our children in the head."

Clarke took off his jacket in the gathering heat. "There may be one Starr, but there are many others like him." And many, he hoped, like Starr's cousin.

Then Lambert-Jones wrinkled his nostrils. "Do I smell vomit?"

"That's the past, Lieutenant."

39

The breeze blew fresh that Easter afternoon, and the yawlboat ran fast to the south. Tom Tracy remembered little of the journey, except for the terrible coldness of the left hand that he trailed in the water until the ocean had cleansed it of her blood.

The British trawler that had stopped them on Good Friday picked them up off Inishmore, the largest of the Aran Islands, and brought them to Galway city.

Daniel Tracy told the story of the torpedo attack, and the shocked, haunted face of his older brother told it again without words. The trawler captain and the customs men in Galway believed it because they knew the look of the torpedo survivor. They had seen it often since the beginning of the war.

The brothers were taken to the seamen's shelter while the false names that they gave were checked against the false crew list filed at the United States Shipping Office in Boston.

The following morning, the Galway newspaper reported a "serious but localized disturbance in the village of Dunslea, resulting in the death of four rebels and two constables." But by that afternoon, the fighting in Dunslea had become like the dumb show before the play.

On Easter Monday, the Irish Republican Brotherhood, led by Padraic Pearse, decided that it was time for the blood sacrifice, regardless of Casement's capture, the sinking of the *Aud,* or their own disorganization. They marched down O'Connell Street, stopped in front of the General Post Office, and charged. They broke down the door and took possession of the building. Then Padraic Pearse emerged to read the declaration of independence he had written for Ireland.

Another detachment of rebels attacked Dublin Castle itself. From his window, Sir Matthew Nathan watched them shoot down the guard at the gate and then fall back, believing the Castle to be better protected than in fact it was.

In County Galway, rebels attacked the RIC barracks at Clarenbridge. Negotiating through the parish priest, they tried to force surrender, but the police held out. They then marched to Oranmore, took possession of the village, cut the telegraph lines, tore up the railway, attempted to blow up the bridge leading to Galway, and attacked the barracks. They retreated in the face of police and military reinforcements, and eventually joined another body of rebels at Athenry.

Ian Lambert-Jones hurried back to Dublin that morning with his report on the Dunslea disturbances, which were quickly forgotten in the Dublin fighting. On Tuesday morning, as he climbed to the top of the quayside building to observe the Post Office, he was shot in the chest and died instantly.

By the end of the week, most of the handsome buildings in Upper O'Connell Street were in ruins. British troops ringed the city, artillery batteries were dug in on the Trinity College campus, and gunboats in the River Liffey lobbed shells at the General Post Office. On Friday, after suffering heavy losses, with no hope of victory, the rebels surrendered. They were marched down O'Connell Street, across the bridge, to the Richmond police barracks. And all along the route, the people of Dublin cursed them and spat upon them and hurled stones at them for the destruction they had caused.

Resident magistrates in the south and west swore deputy constables by the hundreds from among the local populace, and the flame of the rising flickered.

The rebels of Galway, and others like them all over Ireland, were convinced to disperse by local priests, then one by one they were apprehended and sent to Dublin.

By the Sunday after Easter, Ireland was again quiet, except for the quiet fury of those who believed that the rebels had destroyed all that Ireland had gained in Parliament.

That morning, Danny Tracy sent a telegram to his mother.

TOMMY AND ME SAFE STOP SHIPPING ON SCHOONER FOR
NEW YORK STOP HOME SOON STOP LOVE DANNY

They took their places as able-bodied seamen aboard the *Nancy Lee,* a four-masted schooner running back to New York with a light cargo of Belleek china and Irish whiskey.

Danny Tracy, known as Joe Dunne, was well liked by the crew, but they avoided his brother, who seemed a man of black mood and brooding temper, with a quick right fist that he used only once and did not need to use again.

At night, Tom Tracy climbed to the crosstrees and looked west and thought about the sacrifice of Padraic Starr, who had given his blood for Ireland, and the blood of others as well. And he thought about the promise of Nigel Stewart, on that terrible Sunday morning, that blood brings blood. And he thought about Rachel.

And he cried.

He felt the rhythmic motion of the ship. He looked into the blackness, into the endless depths and heights. And he found nothing that gave him comfort.

When the Dunne brothers arrived in New York, they were met by federal agents who questioned them about the sinking of the *Abigail,* which had become, as Tracy expected, an international incident. On the night of the sinking, the German commander had wired a message to Imperial headquarters: HAVE SUNK BRITISH Q-SHIP FLYING AMERICAN FLAG. The commander never made an official report, because the next morning, the U-boat struck a mine and was lost with all hands. And so, the story belonged to the Dunne brothers. In great detail, they described the mate's attempt to summon the British during a legal visit and search, and the fury of the German commander when the sailors killed his boarding party in self-defense. The incident was judged sufficiently complex that the United States accepted the apology of the German government, while the Dunne brothers disappeared.

During their five weeks at sea, much happened in Ireland. The British ignored the Irish Parliamentarians who urged moderation in the treating of the rebel prisoners. The British, after all, were fighting for their survival against the Hun. They would not treat with treason in their own backyard. One by one, starting with Padraic Pearse, the rebel leaders were put against a wall, blindfolded, and shot. Their bodies were thrown into quicklime, their last words suppressed, and in the minds of the Irish people, they became martyrs.

After that, the British relented, for they had turned not only the Irish against them, but Irish-Americans as well. And in the bloody spring of 1916, the British needed all the American friends they could find. They imprisoned the remainder of the rebels, then released them a year later, as a gesture of goodwill before extending military conscription to Ireland.

Among them was the young man who had commanded the garrison at Boland's Mill during the Easter fighting. He was the highest-ranking rebel to have survived. In 1919, he went to America. His name was Eamon De Valera. . . .

"A marvelous thing, just marvelous," said James Michael Curley. "Not three years after the rising, and you're the president of the Irish Republic."

De Valera gave Curley a watery smile. He was a tall and slender man, with a precise manner of speech and habit that did not invite good-fellowship, but his bravery and resolute stubbornness had inspired Ireland. "I am only the president of the Sinn Fein party, your honor—"

Curley raised his hand. "No 'your honors' necessary. I'm out of office at the moment, beaten by an alliance of Irish ward bosses and Protestant businessmen, ordinarily natural enemies on the order of the mongoose and the cobra."

"The waters of American politics are swift," said De Valera.

"And treacherous," said Tom Tracy. He sat on the edge of his desk, calmly swung his leg, and studied the former mathematics teacher who now spoke for Ireland.

"Like the waters between Scylla and Charybdis," added Curley. "We were taking the power from the ward bosses and raising the taxes on the businessmen. And all for good purpose. But they ganged up on us."

De Valera removed his spectacles and carefully polished them. "I suspect that you will be back."

Curley simply smiled. Out in the main hall of the Tammany Club, the band was playing "The Rising of the Moon."

"It is your great good fortune that you can worry about political alliances and their effect upon your elections, because you know that the winner will take his seat in a constituted government." De Valera put on his spectacles. "We of Sinn Fein, duly elected by the Irish people, are still fighting for recognition . . . and the very survival of a new republic."

Curley rose from behind his desk and hooked his thumbs into his vest. "I want you to know, Mr. President, that the Tammany Club will do anything and everything in its power to help you get this Irish Republic off the ground. Isn't that right, Tommy?"

"Absolutely." Tracy tightened his red silk tie and tugged on his cuffs.

De Valera gave Tracy, or more specifically his expensive suit, a brief and unimpressed glance. "My journey to America has a threefold purpose. I'm here to raise money for the newly elected Irish Parliament—"

"Dail Eireann," said Tracy, using the Gaelic name.

De Valera's face brightened. "Very good."

"Tommy grew up in Ireland," said Curley. "But he hasn't been back since—"

"Nineteen hundred," offered Tracy.

"You must come back, once we're a republic."

Tracy felt De Valera's eyes examining him as they would a student reciting his multiplication tables. De Valera seemed to Tracy the perfect combination of rebel and politician. There was iron in the calm demeanor and precise speech, and iron would last longer than the fires that had burned so bright and hot in Padraic Starr.

Tracy casually continued to swing his leg. "To deserve a trip to the Irish Republic, I should help you to win it."

"You may help me in America." The corners of De Valera's mouth turned down in a sober smile. "Along with raising money, I hope to convince one of your major parties to recognize the Irish Republic in its national platform. And I am going to speak against Article 10 of the League of Nations Covenant, which is clearly anti-Irish."

Curley looked at Tracy. "A man who fought on Easter, and a politician as well. He makes us proud of our profession."

"Also an escapee from Lincoln Jail who stowed away to leave Ireland," said De Valera. "In America, I can play the politician, but I fear that in Ireland, we still face a fight, unless we receive the full support of you in America."

"All the more reason for us to help you." Curley pointed to the painting above his desk, in which the founders of America signed the Declaration of Independence. "They had to fight, too."

"The world was much simpler then," said Tom Tracy. "They could see the simple truth of things."

The door to the office swung open and Standish Willcox looked in. "Time, your honor."

In the hall, the band began to play "Tammany." Curley paced around the room, took several deep breaths, and his barrel chest expanded. "Now, Mr. President, let's go tell the people about Ireland."

Curley kept Tom Tracy on Tammany salary, but gave him to De Valera, and for the next year and a half, Tom Tracy traveled America on what amounted to a victory tour for the president of Sinn Fein, although no victory had been won. In every city, Tracy used his knowledge, learned something new, and did whatever he was asked. He set up interviews, arranged banquets, handled details, and when De Valera was exhausted, protected him from the press.

When De Valera ran afoul of Irish-American politicians, who felt that he was stealing their space on the front pages and their power as advocates for Ireland, Tracy offered advice and sought the help of Curley. When De Valera organized the American Association for the Recognition of the Irish Republic, Tracy went to Washington and became the secretary. When Congress, ratifying the treaty that ended World War I, included a statement supporting Irish "self-determination," Tracy poured the champagne.

The Democrats and Republicans did not recognize Dail Eireann, however, and Congress did not go further in its support of an Irish Republic. But in some ways, De Valera's visit was a success. He raised millions in bonds, and Article 10 was struck from the League of Nations Covenant.

And Tom Tracy was rescued at last from his grief. His year and a half with De Valera justified for him all that had gone before. He played Starr's peaceful apostle. He fulfilled his father's dreams. And he knew that Rachel would have approved.

When De Valera sailed back in the summer of 1920, back to

the fighting between flying columns of Irish Republican Brotherhood and the British Black and Tans, Tom Tracy was in New York to say goodbye.

"You will be welcome, Tom, should you ever decide to come back." De Valera gave him that familiar sober smile, "If you wait long enough, you'll be able to stay in the president's quarters . . . in Dublin Castle."

Tracy took De Valera's hand. "It's then that I'll be coming."

Tracy watched the horizon until long after De Valera's ship had swept past the Statue of Liberty and disappeared. He watched, and he thought of the people who had died.

As far as the world knew, Rachel Levka had sailed as a passenger on the *Abigail*. She had been following Rabbi Mossinsohn to London but had met a torpedo instead. Padraic Starr had died unknown and unmourned. Martin Mahoney had simply disappeared, in that mysterious way that quiet old bachelors sometimes do. But all of them, in Tom Tracy's mind, had been heroic. Whenever Tom talked with his brother, Danny called them heroic as well, and he promised that if the fighting got bad enough, he would give up his new work as a bricklayer and go back to Ireland.

"They were brave," Tom would say, "but when people talk about heroes and heroines, I remember the look on Avram Levka's face when I told him his daughter died a heroine for Ireland."

He stared at the horizon and the great statue and wiped a tear from his eye. . . .

The horizon never changed. It was always hard and straight and a shade darker than the blue sky above it. And the village of Dunslea seemed hardly to have changed in fifty years.

Electrical lines and telephone wire ran along the poles that Donal O'Leary had climbed so often in '16. There were more automobiles, but none so large or beautiful as William Clarke's Rolls-Royce. The primary means of travel was still the bicycle pedal or the hoof. There were fewer people, for the hard west country demanded much and offered little. Opportunities were greater in the cities and, of course, in America. It was still said, without exaggeration, that Ireland's main exports were Guinness . . . and men.

The RIC barracks was now a struggling agricultural school

set up by the government to encourage people to stay on their farms. The O'Leary cottage, like so many others, had been deserted and had fallen to ruins. Ballinakill House had been sold to the Catholic Church in 1924 and was now known as Ballinakill Abbey.

The children of two widows, one named Cooney, the other Hayes, had grown and moved away and been forgotten. But an old woman still lived in a cottage on the Dunslea road. On weekend afternoons, she climbed to her loft and took the sailcloth covering from off the wireless and listened to the meaningless dots and dashes dancing between ship and shore. When she felt lonely or depressed, she pulled out an ancient envelope, filled with photographs and tattered clippings, and read about the day when the two men she loved died together for Ireland.

Finnerty's was still in the south row. It sported a new electrical sign—blue and red borders setting off a black frothy pint of Guinness. And in the window hung a banner that had appeared in many pubs during that anniversary year: *To the Men of Sixteen: Pearse, Plunkett, Connolly* . . .

The year after De Valera went back to Ireland, the British tired of the brutal fighting and negotiated a treaty. The rebels were given control of the south, while Ulster remained with Britain, as the Protestant Unionists had wanted from the day Home Rule passed. Little had been won by the fighting that could not have been had without it. So Catholics of the south, pro-treaty and anti-, turned against one another and fought a bloody civil war for another year.

Now, fifty years later, the south was a peaceful if not prosperous republic. The north was a quiet if not peaceful province of Britain.

The joined rowhouses of Dunslea were still painted in pastels set off by stonework and whitewash. Turf smoke still curled from every chimney. Trees, grown taller now, still shielded the cemetery by the church. Gulls circled ceaselessly above the bay. And the river met the sea in a gentle roughness of waves and white splashes, as it had for a thousand years. The metal bridge, however, was a mere fifty years old.

They parked on the quay, and before they climbed out of the car, they looked down the bay toward the hard blue horizon.

"It's beautiful."

"It looks just as it did that day."

"Shall we make a visit, Tom?"

He reached over and patted his wife's hand. "That's why we're here, Ursula."

In the fiftieth year, Tom Tracy had accepted De Valera's invitation. He and Ursula, his two sons, Patrick and Hugh, and their wives and young families had stayed at the State Apartments in Dublin Castle as guests of the venerable president. They had dined with De Valera and attended several fiftieth-anniversary receptions. Then, while their sons went on to London, Tom Tracy and Ursula had headed west in a rented Ford.

It had been a good life, thought Tom, as he drove toward the Twelve Bens. Ursula O'Day and their boys had been the best part of it. Without them, his life would have been nothing. And, in his own mind, he had done all that his father had asked. He had helped Ireland often throughout her history. He had been elected to the Boston City Council and the Massachusetts Legislature, and whenever Curley was elected to City Hall or the State House, Tracy had joined the administration.

In 1942, Curley had gone to Congress from the Eleventh District. In 1945, he had been elected mayor of Boston for the fourth time. Tracy had decided to run for Curley's congressional seat, and when he was trounced by Joe Kennedy's war-hero son, he had realized that his time was passing.

He had joked often that he was one of the most honest—and poorest—politicians in Boston, and he had decided, at fifty-six, to put his skills to work in the private sector, with Daniel Tracy & Co., General Contracting. His political connections and his influence with Monsignor John Tracy had helped the company to win several major contracts in an era when the Catholic Church was building hospitals and schools in every section of Boston. In the process, Tom Tracy had built a financial foundation for his family.

Now, in his final years, his heart failing, his brothers gone, his painful memories buried beneath the scar tissue of a successful life, he had decided to make the pilgrimage to the place of his birth.

The townspeople of Dunslea nodded and pulled at their caps when they saw the handsome woman and the gentleman in the finely tailored seersucker suit.

Tom Tracy and Ursula walked along the stone wall at the edge of the square, past the steps of the church, and into the small graveyard.

It was midsummer. It had been raining. The overgrown grass was wet, and soon their shoes and his trousers were soaked through.

"Here's my father," said Tom.

They blessed themselves and knelt before a small headstone and prayed.

Then Tom saw the name Hayes on a fine large Celtic cross. "Royal Irish Constabulary. Killed in the line of duty. April 23, 1916. May God Have Mercy on His Soul."

"Over this way," said Tom softly. He leaned on his father's headstone and pushed himself to his feet and went toward the corner beyond the Hayes monument. It was there that he expected he would find the others.

He saw Tim Cooney first, a neat little monument, and he remembered the cool courage.

He stumbled on a little brick border around another plot, and his wife caught him by the elbow. But he was hurrying, and he stumbled again.

He went past another headstone that had no name, but just the words "He Repaid a Debt on the Easter That He Died." That would be Martin Mahoney, thought Tracy. But what was the debt? What did he hold over Clarke that day?

Then he saw a small white cross in a distant corner. "Padraic Starr. Born in Dunslea, 1884, died in Dunslea, 1916, Requiescat in Pace."

He went past Starr quickly.

"Tom!" called Ursula. "Isn't this him?"

"Over here." His heart was pounding hard. He took out a nitroglycerine tablet and put it under his tongue.

"Are you all right?"

"A precaution. I'm fine. I see her."

"She wouldn't be here. This is a Catholic cemetery."

The old man turned the path and stopped by a modest headstone. He pulled out his handkerchief and blew his nose.

"Tom," said his wife gently, "the name on that is Rachel *Leary*."

"It's her."

The headstone read: "Rachel Leary, born ca. 1892, died April 23, 1916." Beneath that was a single word: "Trust."

"Clarke asked her name that day, but with the gunfire and all . . ." His voice trembled. He took off his glasses and wiped his eyes.

"Do you want another pill?"

He shook his head. Then he blessed himself and knelt. Ursula joined him. But Tom did not pray long. He had prayed for her every day of his life, and he had prayed for the others, too, for all who had died that day, for all who had died on both sides in the bloody months and years that followed.

When they were done, Ursula said, "A Jewish woman buried in consecrated ground . . . I don't think Jesus will mind."

Tom looked at her. It was a silly, canon-law thing to say, and for a moment he was angry. But Ursula was the only person who knew the story, and never once had she spoken in jealousy of the first woman he had loved.

"No, I don't guess He will. Nor Jehovah, neither."

After a time, Ursula suggested that they drive to Dun Slea and explore the ruins.

He shook his head. "You go. Drive straight up this road, and you can't miss it. A big stone . . . thing." He had to take out his handkerchief again.

Ursula put her hand on Tom's arm. "Are you sure you're all right?"

"Yes, yes," he said irritably. "Go on. I'll meet you beneath the Guinness sign in an hour."

She patted his arm. She had learned early in their life together that there were times when Tom Tracy wanted nothing but to be alone with his memories and his black moods. And after he had sat with them for a time, they would fade like a child's bad dream. "In an hour, then."

"Remember to drive on the left. And don't hit any sheep."

She gave a wave over her shoulder.

After she had puttered off, Tom Tracy went back to the corner cemetery and lowered himself to the tall grass and sat with Rachel and the others. For some reason, his left hand felt icy cold. He slipped it into his pocket and listened to the sound of the gentle-runnin' river.